ALSO BY KATHRYN HARVEY

Butterfly

STARS

STARS

A NOVEL

KATHRYN HARVEY

VILLARD BOOKS ★ NEW YORK ★ 1992

All rights reserved under International and Pan-American Copyright Conventions.
Published in the United States by Random House, Inc., New York, and
simultaneously in Canada by Random House of Canada Limited, Toronto.

Villard Books is a registered trademark of Random House, Inc.

Library of Congress Cataloging-in-Publication Data

Harvey, Kathryn.
  Stars: a novel/Kathryn Harvey.—1st ed.
    p. cm.
  ISBN 0-394-58798-7
  I. Title.
  PS3558.A7185S7 1992
  813'.54—dc20   91-50063

Manufactured in the United States of America
98765432
First Edition

Book design by Debbie Glasserman

For Harvey Klinger, the best agent in the world.
And a real sweetie-pie.

Acknowledgments

Special thanks go to some special people: Kate Medina and Jonathan Karp at Random House; at Avon Books, Carolyn Reidy. For support above and beyond the call of duty, thanks to Ginny Pope, and, as always, to my husband, George.

P.S. Secret message to niece Amy: Chapter 32 is just for you!

Too low they build, who build beneath the stars.

EDWARD YOUNG (1683–1765)

STARS

From the *Los Angeles Herald,* July 4, 1932:

> Palm Springs, California—Early this morning famous movie direc-
> tor Dexter Bryant Ramsey was found dead at Star's Haven, the Mount
> San Jacinto home of glamorous film star Marion Star. Discovered by a
> servant just before dawn, in what has become known as the Obscene
> Bathroom, the body of the slain Ramsey was naked, with a single
> bullet through the head. Police have launched a massive search for
> Miss Star, who, according to witnesses at the scene, vanished mysteri-
> ously during the night. While a motive for the murder has not yet
> been established, speculation is that Marion Star, who is known for
> her flamboyant life-style and sexual excesses, may have carried out a
> brutal act of revenge . . .

From the "Unique Offerings" section of the *Palm Springs Realtor,* 1984:

> Located near summit of Mount San Jacinto: forty-two room mansion,
> plus outbuildings, on 92-acre property known as Star's Haven, built
> 1927, electricity added 1930, unoccupied since 1932. Access: fire road
> from Highway 111, one mile past the Windy Creek turnoff. Sell or
> trade, best offer.

Excerpted from Sue Cook's column in *Palm Springs Life* magazine, 1988:

> Who is the anonymous buyer, at last, of the mystery-shrouded Star's
> Haven, which has stood empty in its mountain solitude for nearly sixty
> years, site of the sensational Dexter Bryant Ramsey murder, which is still
> unsolved after all these years? What are his or her plans for the sup-
> posedly haunted mansion? What is contained in the steady stream of

unmarked trucks and vans that are making the long drive up the fire road to the top? And is it true that the work going on around the clock at the base of the mountain is preparation for a tramway that will climb six thousand feet to the property? One can only speculate . . ."

The invitations to the Christmas ball at Star's on Mount San Jacinto went out weeks ago. They were printed with the resort logo: an elegant silver star against a dark blue background, and the resort's slogan underneath: "Star's—Explore the Fantasy . . ."

Black tie only.

DAY ONE

··★

"I have a surprise for you," he said, and she moaned softly as she felt him enter her one more time. They had been making love for what seemed like hours; he had remarkable staying power, and he had been very inventive. And now he had a surprise for her?

"What is it?" she said breathlessly, stirring beneath him on satin sheets damp from their afternoon of passion.

When he rolled away from her onto his side, she gave him a questioning look. She had thought they were going to start again. "Keep your eyes closed," he whispered, and when he caressed the inside of her thigh, she was startled by the sudden electricity of his touch. It amazed her that, after all this time, she was still sexually aroused. Was there no limit to her appetite? Not with Sanford, she thought, laughing softly, deep in her throat. Not with the greatest lover in the world. "What's my surprise?" she said.

"A going-away present, so that you will remember me while you're gone. I wrapped it specially," he said softly, his lips brushing her ear as his hand moved in teasing circles inside her thigh. "In the most beautiful package I could find, just for you, my beautiful movie star."

She felt a quick pang. She wished he wouldn't call her that. "Where?" she said. "Where is it?"

When he touched her and said, "Here," her eyes flew open. In the mirrored ceiling above the bed she saw herself, sprawled on the peach satin sheets, and him stretched out beside her, one hand propping up his head, the other between her legs. She saw his muscular arms, the dark hair on his chest and back, and the erection . . . His recuperative strength was as astonishing as his staying power.

Her gaze moved to the hidden hand. What was he doing?

She gasped. She felt—

He smiled, watching her startled expression as he slowly drew the necklace out.

"When did you—" she began as the pearls slowly appeared, one by one. She hadn't felt the necklace go in, but now, as it emerged with agonizing slowness, she thought she could feel each hard, round pearl pressing into her as if they were fingertips, exploring. When it was all the way out, she looked at him, into amused gray eyes that she had once thought dangerous, and she marveled again at the way he kept the magic in their lovemaking alive after all these years.

She reached for the necklace, but he said, "Wait," and swirled it around first in the crystal goblet of champagne that stood on the peach carpet beside the bed. Then he draped the string of fat, soft-looking pearls across her throat, saying, "For my movie star. My beautiful movie star."

He bent to kiss her, and she put her arms around him, drawing him hard against her, feeling the heat of his body against her bare skin. They kissed deeply, and she tried not to cry, tried not to think of the treachery she was planning. She loved him so much, just so very much, that he must never find out what she was about to do.

As the white stretch limousine sped along the desert highway toward the wintry dusk, Carole Page reached for the bottle of champagne nestled in the silver ice bucket and refilled her glass. She saw that her hands shook, and she wondered if her two fellow passengers had also noticed. Carole didn't know the women she was traveling with. They had murmured polite but brief hellos to one another when the Star's limousine had picked them up at the Beverly Hills Hotel two and a half hours ago. During the long drive from Los Angeles into the desert, not another word had been spoken.

But there was a lot of thinking going on. And weighing heavily upon the mind of Carole Page, a movie star who had recently crossed the terrifying Forty milestone, was sex—not pleasure-sex, such as she had experienced a few hours ago with Sanford, when he had surprised her with the pearl necklace, but business-sex. She looked at her gold Cartier watch, a gift from her husband when she had finished her third picture, and realized that she would be arriving at her destination very soon. Only a short time remained in which she could still change her mind and turn back.

But that was why she was in the Star's limousine, she reminded herself as she sipped the icy champagne, wincing because her lips still hurt from the collagen injections. She hadn't taken her own car because she couldn't risk getting scared and backing out at the last minute, turning around and going home. In the Star's limousine, she was committed. When Sanford had asked why she wasn't taking their own Rolls-Royce and driver into the desert, she had fumbled through some excuse about the possibility of his needing the car while she was gone; besides, once she was up the mountain and checked in at Star's, she wouldn't be needing the car again. She had searched his face to see if he bought it; he had. That was right after she had sneaked the condoms out of the bathroom and into her purse and Sanford had nearly caught her at it. He certainly would have enquired why she needed *those*, when she claimed she was going to Star's for a much-needed rest by herself after finishing her latest, exhausting film.

She realized she needn't have worried. It would never occur to Sanford to be suspicious about anything his wife did. Trust was one of the mainstays of their enduring marriage. As was sex. Carole had never known a lover like Sanford. She felt the pearls resting between her breasts and marveled again at the inventive way he had given them to her. They had made love one more time after that, and then Carole had gotten ready for the long drive to Star's.

Wondering vaguely about the two silent women who were riding with her, wondering who they were, why they were going to Star's, and if they thought she was drinking too much (after all, the Dom Pérignon had been provided for the three of them and so far she was the only one helping herself), Carole turned her gaze to the smoked-glass window and looked out at the passing scene. The late-afternoon desert looked eerie, she thought, almost menacing; the shadows that were pooling between sand dunes and cacti seemed too deep, too dark, as if dangers were hidden there. And the old highway they had turned onto from the freeway was strangely empty. When Carole realized they hadn't passed another car in some time, she was suddenly gripped by panic. What did their driver look like? She couldn't remember, just a vaguely handsome young man in a black uniform with shiny silver buttons. And the Star's logo embroidered in silver over his left breast. But who *was* he? Had he said his name when he had helped her into the car? When he had pointed out the champagne, the crystal decanters of scotch, gin, and vodka in the bar compartment, the gold foil box of Godiva chocolates, had she bothered to really look at him and see who he was?

Carole snapped her gaze back from the spooky, lonely desert and stared at the solid partition that separated the front seat from the passenger compartment. Fighting the impulse to press the button that would lower the divider and give her a view of the chauffeur and the highway up ahead, she sipped her champagne again and wondered again if she was drinking too much. But she needed it for courage, she told herself, to go through with her plan.

How was it possible, she wondered, for three people, even if they were strangers, to ride in the same car for such a long time without speaking?

But then again, what would she say to them? "You see, ladies, I'm not really going to Star's for a rest now that I've finished my latest picture, even though that's what my press agent is telling everyone. I'm going there to seduce an unsuspecting man, a man I hardly know. And I'm doing it to save my marriage."

No, she couldn't say that. Instead, she drained her champagne glass, reached for the bottle, and blurted, "I don't normally drink like this, but I'm just so nervous."

The other two looked at Carole as if she had just materialized in their presence.

The one sitting opposite, a woman in her fifties who wore tortoiseshell glasses and an old-fashioned page boy, blinked at her and said, "Nervous?"

"Yes," Carole said, sweeping a strand of ash-blond hair from her face and waving toward the snow-covered mountains that seemed to be creeping closer and closer to the car. "I'm terrified of tramways."

"Tramways! What tramway?"

Carole gave her a puzzled look. "Why, the one that takes us up to Star's. The resort is up there," she said, pointing to the formidable snowy peaks that had been so distant during the drive but that were suddenly there, almost next to them, looming and threatening. "On top of Mount San Jacinto. There's no other way to get to Star's than by tramway."

The other woman looked out the window, craning her neck to see the top of the mountain. "Yes, I know Star's is up there," she said. "But I thought there would be a road." She paused, studying the snow-covered mountain. "My God, it looks like the Alps! I'm not prepared for snow," she said plaintively. She picked up the attaché case that had been between her feet and drew it against her, as if for protection.

Taking in the woman's light linen pants, rayon blouse, and open-toed shoes, Carole thought of the small overnight case that had gone into the limousine's trunk—the woman's only luggage. Back at the Beverly Hills Hotel, the chauffeur had had to use some skill to get all of Carole's matched eelskin pieces into the trunk; after all, she was going to be at Star's for several days. He had also had to wrangle with the baggage of the third passenger, the woman who sat next to Carole and who so far had not spoken. She, too, had brought along a surprising number of suitcases, except that hers were all unmatched and included a set of skis and a large nylon duffel bag, which had been stacked on the front seat next to the driver. All she had brought into the car with her was a small black bag that resembled a medical kit. Carole had glimpsed a name stamped in the leather in gold: J. Isaacs, M.D.

As she refilled her glass and tried not to gulp it all down at once, wishing that the champagne would at least numb the pain in her pumped-up lips,

Carole took another look at the woman facing her and realized now that she was somehow familiar. It came to her after a moment: she was an actors' agent named Frieda Goldman, with whom Carole had brushed elbows during an after-Oscar party last April. Ms. Goldman must have represented one of the nominees to have gotten into such an exclusive bash, and Carole wondered who it had been. When she saw the way Frieda hugged the attaché case and looked anxiously out the window, checking her watch every few minutes, Carole decided that she must be going to Star's to work a deal. A *hot* deal. In fact, Carole realized as she caught the smile playing around Frieda's lips, the woman looked as if she were bursting with good news. Carole wondered for a moment what it was; then, retreating into the luxurious embrace of her silver fox coat, she steered her thoughts back to the subject of sex and the complex problem of how she was going to get into Larry Wolfe's bed.

The car turned off the old highway and followed a rutted road that wound toward the foothills, gradually climbing up from the desert floor. As the limousine slowed down and rolled to a stop, the three passengers looked out and saw a guardhouse and a gate barring the road. This was the first of three checkpoints designed to keep sightseers, unwelcome guests, and paparazzi away. There was nothing else here, just the lonely road that didn't look as if it had been traveled in years, flat tracts of scrub that rose in gentle drifts against the foothills, and a uniformed guard who engaged the chauffeur in a brief conversation while the desert wind fluttered the papers on his clipboard.

When the car was moving again and Carole saw a sign at the side of the road that read TRAMWAY BOARDING AREA—2 MILES, she realized with dismay that in just a few minutes there would be no turning back. She reached for the champagne.

Snow! Frieda Goldman thought as she looked at her watch for the zillionth time since leaving L.A. She should have expected it, since this place was on top of a mountain, and this *was* December. Oh well, Frieda thought, barely able to contain her excitement, I can cope with anything, even snow, if it means nailing the biggest deal in Hollywood.

And for the past few hectic, furious days, Frieda had had to cope with a lot. She couldn't believe how complicated things had gotten. First, Bunny mysteriously extending her stay at Star's when she was only supposed to have been there for a couple of weeks—four months ago! Then, her inexplicable refusal to talk to Frieda on the phone, and now this dramatic cavalry charge up a snow-covered mountain. It hadn't been easy getting a room at Star's; the place was booked up months in advance. Only a last-minute cancellation had saved Frieda. She had telephoned Syd Stern, the director, and promised him that she would have Bunny signed, sealed, and delivered to him by tomorrow.

When Frieda had hastily packed that morning, she had thought of Palm Springs, which was at the foot of the mountain, an oasis of desert warmth, palm trees, and sunshine. She had thrown some toiletries, her few cosmetics, a spare blouse, and a change of underwear into her over-night case and grabbed a taxi to Beverly Hills. But now, as she gazed uncertainly at the mountain that seemed to grow right before her eyes, she pictured snowdrifts, frost, and icicles.

Frieda was anxious to see the resort that had industry tongues wagging. Star's was kept wrapped in secrecy, like a giant Christmas package in gold foil and silver ribbons. You never read about the place in magazines or newspapers; its rare advertisements disclosed nothing; and travel agents couldn't provide brochures. You heard about it through the movie col-ony's grapevine, those who had been to Star's possessing bragging rights over those who had not. Frieda recalled what one of her clients had told her about Star's, about a "diversion" that was offered—some sort of discreet escort service, for both men and women. Ostensibly the escort was a dinner companion or a dance partner, but the service could extend to the bedroom, if that was your wish. It reminded Frieda of her last trip to New York, when she had been sitting alone in the bar of her hotel and a smooth young man in a bellman's uniform had quietly approached her. "You visiting Manhattan alone?" he had asked politely. "You a guest here at the hotel? I tell you what, you need anything, day or night, you dial housekeeping and you ask for Ramon. I get it for you." He had leaned forward and, with a conspiratorial wink, added, *"Anything."*

Frieda had been appalled then, as she was now, at the thought of having sex with a total stranger. She hadn't been with a man since Jake died, sixteen years ago; it was a long time to be celibate, but Frieda believed that sex had to stem from love, especially for a woman of fifty-three with two grown children and five grandchildren. As she wondered what the Star's "escorts" were like, she thought of the chauffeur who sat on the other side of the solid partition and the way he had smiled at her back at the hotel when he had taken her overnight case. A flash of white teeth, dimples high on the cheeks, a square *GQ* jaw, and long, long black hair. Did he do "escort" work, she wondered, when he wasn't driving the Star's limousine?

Frieda pushed the thought from her mind. She wasn't going up that iceberg to get laid, she reminded herself, she was going up there to find Bunny. And soon. The deal wasn't going to wait; she had to get Bunny's signature on these papers within the next twenty-four hours, as she had promised Syd Stern. As the car whispered through the desert sunset, putting miles between its passengers and civilization, Frieda wondered again what had happened to Bunny. The poor girl seemed to have holed herself up in that mountain hideaway, as if the wounds of losing the Oscar in April had not yet healed. Was that why Bunny wasn't taking her calls? Whatever funk the kid was in, she was going to be snapped out of it soon, in a big way. Frieda could hardly stand it, she was so excited. Why didn't the limousine go faster? Just wait until Bunny heard the news—wait until the *world* heard the news!

The sound of glass clinking brought Frieda back to look at Carole Page, who was just about to drain the bottle of Dom Pérignon that had been intended for the three of them. Frieda didn't mind not having any; she had declined it, in fact, because she was saving her celebrating for when she showed Bunny what was in her attaché case. Frieda had brought along a bottle of Mandarine Napoleon, Bunny's favorite liqueur, just for the special moment. They would pour it over ice and toast each other, the world, and beautiful, beautiful life.

As the empty champagne bottle went back into the ice bucket, something made Frieda think that Carole Page wasn't drinking out of nervousness over a tram ride, but because of deeper, more disturbing causes. Frieda had heard rumors around the industry that Carole's latest movie was a bomb, her fourth in a row, signaling a career in trouble. Frieda tried to be discreet in her scrutiny of the beautiful actress, but she couldn't miss the familiar haunted look around Carole's eyes. One saw it everywhere in Hollywood: the look of a woman swept up in the grip of the aging process and terrified of it. Carole Page had been spectacular in her twenties and early thirties, filling a movie screen with a sparkle and dazzle that was uniquely her own. But then, inch by inch, it seemed the sparkle had begun to tarnish, the dazzle to fade, until now a pale shadow of fear hovered in those sapphire eyes. Frieda had seen it time and again in her years as an agent; it was an affliction as old as the movie industry itself. Beautiful women were not allowed to age.

Feeling a sneeze coming on, she reached into her alligator handbag for a tissue. Not quite catching the sneeze before it escaped, so that she muffled a small *quack* with her Kleenex, Frieda smiled apologetically at the woman sitting next to Carole, who had briefly looked over at her. That she was a doctor was apparent from the medical bag and the name stamped in the leather. And she looked doctorish, Frieda thought, with no makeup, mahogany hair braided into a thick coil at the back of her head, and strong and capable hands with neatly trimmed fingernails. Frieda guessed that the doctor was in her late thirties, with no wedding band in evidence, and she wondered what was bringing *her* up to the snowbound resort.

The car stopped at a second gate, where another guard checked the passengers against his list on the clipboard, and then it continued along a road that grew narrow and steep as it wound into the foothills. Suddenly, the sunlight was gone and night swept across the desert. High granite walls closed in on the limousine as it cut through a canyon floor littered with huge boulders and prehistoric rock formations. Long shadows spilled from rugged ravines and gullies, the scrub gave way to stunted pine trees, and the air grew icy, even though there was no snow at this level. Frieda could imagine what the resort was going to be like: appallingly rustic with unbearable movie snobs paying out tons of money to "rough it." But she warmed herself with the thought of the 15 percent of the multi-million-dollar deal she was going to get, as soon as Bunny signed the papers.

"This must be it," Carole said as the limousine drew to a halt in front of a small, plain building that had no windows, no signs indicating what it was—just an ordinary, unassuming door. There was a tiny parking lot next to it, filled with Jaguars, BMWs, a classic Corvette, and two bright-red Ferraris. And a uniformed guard patrolling it. Just beyond the flat roof of the small building the first of the cable towers could be seen, along with the corner of the shed that housed the massive tramway machinery.

When the chauffeur opened the passenger door, letting in a gust of arctic air, Carole briefly held back, thinking that this was her last chance to abandon her insane plan and turn around and go home to Sanford. But, reminding herself that what she was going to do she was actually doing for him, she slipped her hand into the driver's gloved hand, returned his smile with one that she hoped was equally charming, and walked toward the plain door. Frieda Goldman came out next, clutching the attaché case and feeling the alpine air sweep down the mountain and slice through her summery clothes. The driver flashed her a sexy smile, and she noticed how strong his grip was. She hurried after Carole, praying that the building was heated. The third woman came out last, drawing her down-filled jacket over her chest with one hand, carrying the medical bag in the other. She didn't accept the driver's hand; she didn't receive or return his smile, because her eyes were fixed on the mountain that rose before her in formidable majesty and promise. She followed Carole and Frieda through the unassuming door and was at once met by a clearer, more breathtaking view of the mountain, seen through the glass wall on the other side of the room. She also received a shock. This little building was the tramway boarding lounge, and it bore no resemblance to the inhospitable wilderness surrounding it.

Dr. Judith Isaacs had once flown on the Concorde to London for a medical convention, and the British Airways boarding lounge in New York reminded her of this one—filled with people milling around a bountifully spread buffet and a fully stocked bar. But the Concorde lounge was done in a muted traveler's gray, while the waiting area for the Star's tram had been done in trendy desert romantic—white linen sofas, knobby pillows, Indian rugs, pre-Columbian sculpture, and palms and cacti in massive southwestern pots.

Judith quickly scanned the crowd for children, but she saw none. She had been promised that there would be no children at Star's. She relaxed an inch.

"Seventy percent of your patients at Star's will be there for plastic surgery," she had been told during her employment interview, and as she looked around at the other guests who were quietly waiting for the tram, sitting with their sable coats and lynx jackets, their ski poles and golf bags, wearing faces that were famous or looked as if they should be, she wondered what these beautiful, perfect people could possibly do surgically to improve themselves. Maybe a few of them would end up as her patients, she thought; maybe Carole Page, who had been so nervous in the car, drinking all the champagne and touching her lips every so often, would wind up in Judith's examination room. Judith surmised that the actress had had her lips augmented—the whitish, unnatural outline of the lips and the slightly flattened indentation in the upper lip were telltale signs of collagen injections. Judith also wondered if Carole had come to Star's for further cosmetic surgery, although what else that slender, large-breasted body could possibly need she couldn't guess. But it didn't matter to Judith. Whatever ailments these rich and famous people brought to her—face-lifts or tennis elbows, nose jobs or ski injuries—it wouldn't be like practicing real medicine. Dr. Isaacs had sworn never to practice real medicine again.

She went to the cold glass wall and looked up at the snowy mountain that stood in the gloom of desert twilight. The actual peak of San Jacinto was hidden behind swirling mists, so the resort couldn't be seen, imbuing it with further mystery and heightening her anticipation at working at a place she had never seen. The jagged slopes and roughly hewn ravines were painted in strange, almost unnatural colors, intensely sharp and deep, with the surrounding Santa Rosa Range glowing a golden russet where bottomless purple shadows filled canyons and arroyos. It reminded Judith of the Maxfield Parrish painting that hung in her master bedroom. That *had* hung in her master bedroom.

She watched movements in the reflection of the lounge behind her, some of the couples sitting close together, murmuring over drinks, other guests sitting alone, fingers drumming nervously, their eyes casting furtive but knowing glances. Judith wondered how many illicit rendezvous were being put into motion tonight, like the dark-haired actress by the bar, known for her bitchy role in a nighttime soap opera—she kept glancing over her shoulder at a sandy-haired jock sitting in the corner, who was clearly pretending to read a copy of *Hollywood Reporter* while he returned those quick, veiled looks. Romance was in the air, Judith thought; perhaps more accurately, sex was in the air. The occasional laughter seemed to ring with it; the champagne glittered with it. When she saw the chauffeur on the far side of the lounge bringing her luggage in, so tall and young and broad shouldered, she realized that he, too, seemed made for sex.

Then in the window's reflection she saw Carole Page come away from the bar with a sparkling glass of wine, and Judith thought how perfectly the actress fit in with this beautiful crowd, slender and stunning with thick ash-blond hair cascading over the wide shoulders of her silver fox coat. Carole cast an anxious glance around as she crossed the lounge, and then she came to stand next to Judith at the window. They stared in silence at the fragile-looking tramway cable that looped away from the foothill station, rose up between craggy pine-covered bluffs, and disappeared into the clouds at the top. After a moment Carole said, out of the blue, "They say it's haunted," as though she and Judith had been having a conversation.

"I beg your pardon?"

"The mansion up at Star's," Carole said. "It used to be owned by that silent movie queen who disappeared mysteriously back in the thirties. It was called Star's Haven, and there was a sensational murder there, some movie director who was a sexual deviate. They call it the Obscene Bathroom Murder. Marion Star was the main suspect, and she vanished. They never found out who killed him."

Judith stared at Carole for a moment, then looked back at the mountain that was rapidly being swallowed up by the night. She thought of the employment interview she had had with the resort's general manager a few weeks ago, and how there had been no mention of the owner of Star's or the identity of Judith's real employer. And she realized now how strange it was to be going to work for someone she had never met, whose name she didn't even know. So she said to Carole, "Do you know who owns it?"

"No, and I don't know anyone who does. I have friends who've stayed here, but no one's ever met the owner. There's a rumor that he or she has a sordid past, but I don't know."

They fell silent again as they watched the toylike tram car make its way slowly down the mountain. It didn't look large enough to hold all these people, and the cables didn't look strong enough. Carole was thinking that maybe she *was* afraid of tramways after all and took a healthy drink of the champagne. Judith thought that the cable needed only be strong enough to take her up the mountain, because once she was up there she was never going to come down again.

At the buffet, Frieda Goldman inspected the bountiful offering and decided upon a giant mushroom stuffed with crab. As she nibbled on it, wondering how many calories it contained, she looked around the lounge, which had come as a surprise. She recognized many who were here; mostly they were movie people, and they all seemed electrified. The air was charged with excitement and anticipation, and when she saw the rich flash of diamonds and gold, her vision of the mountain resort underwent some fine-tuning. It might have snow and frost, but it would be luxuriously elegant; only the best. She was beginning to suspect that that was why Bunny had stayed so long—she was having too much fun. Possibly, Frieda speculated as she caught sight of the sinfully handsome chauffeur again, the homely little Kowalski girl from Scranton had found love and romance at last.

Frieda crossed the lounge to where Carole Page and the doctor were standing, and she murmured, "Good lord," her eyes growing wide behind the tortoiseshell glasses. "It's the North Pole already." She shook her head and her iron gray hair stayed in its perfect page boy.

"I've heard that Star's is like a smaller version of Hearst Castle," Carole said in a quiet voice, as if afraid of disturbing the mountain. "It's full of incredible movie history. A lot of people go up there to see where the murder took place. But I came here for a rest." Which wasn't true. Carole was here because Larry Wolfe was coming to write Marion Star's story. Carole hoped to seduce him, get what she wanted, and be down the mountain as fast as she could.

Judith said, "There's going to be a Christmas ball next Saturday night, and I understand it's very difficult to get an invitation. But as guests, of course you'll both be invited."

"I won't be here for the ball," Frieda said, hugging her excitement to herself. "I'll be gone before then."

"So will I," Carole echoed hopefully.

They were both wrong.

....★

Philippa had just dictated "Praise your successes" into her tape recorder when she looked up and saw, through the large window over her desk, a young man walk up from the beach toward the terrace of her house. He was shirtless, his lean, muscular arms and chest glowing in the Australian sun. Barefooted and hatless, all he wore was a pair of tight jeans. As he climbed the steps of the terrace, Philippa saw strong thighs, a sexy rear end, and a promising bulge that strained against his zipper.

She stared at him, her hand still holding the microphone, the tape still running.

He continued to come brazenly onto the terrace. Behind him, sunlight danced like stars on the spiky water of the Swan River, where boats of all types tacked through the broad channel, their white sails full and majestic. Through her open window, Philippa could hear the laughter and shouts of vacationers on nearby beaches, the drone of outboard motors, the cries of sea gulls. In a flash of red, black, and white, Santa Claus suddenly flew by on water skis, his white beard blowing back in the wind as he waved to those on shore, reminding everyone that it was December, the peak of summer, and Christmas was just two weeks away.

Philippa watched the young man walk to the end of her Italianate swimming pool and come to a stop amid the tall Doric columns that encircled the shimmering green water. His stance was casual and careless as he stood in the sunshine, long blond hair whipping about his bare shoulders, an air of expectancy about him. Philippa was mesmerized, the microphone forgotten in her hand.

And then, with a complete lack of concern, the young man reached down and unzipped his jeans. Down they came, revealing more blond hair, more golden skin without a patch of whiteness anywhere, as if he were a young god who had just been born out of the sunlight. He looked like a typical Australian surfie, of whom Philippa had seen so many on the beaches at Sydney and Melbourne. Here, in Perth, on the coast of Western Australia, his likes would be found on pearling boats or windsurfers, one of those reckless, arrogant young Aussies who scoffed at mortality and believed in their own eternal youth.

Philippa noted how unself-conscious he was, not caring that someone might be watching, as he raised his arms over his head and stretched languidly. When Philippa saw his erection, she drew in a sharp breath.

Switching off the tape recorder, she got up from her desk, walked through the house to the living room that stood open to the terrace, and listened for sounds in the kitchen. Had the cook seen the young man?

While Philippa remained there, watching him, he paused to look around and then dived into the lime green water, cutting it with barely a splash.

A speedboat suddenly shot by on the river, leaving a foaming wake of spume and spray, the boatload of partiers shouting, "Hello there!" and "G'day!" before they disappeared from view.

Philippa's villa was on the northern bank of the Swan River, on a street called Jutland Parade in the posh suburb of Dalkeith in Perth, Western Australia, considered to be the country's most expensive district. It had been nicknamed Millionaires' Row, for good reason, and tour buses drove by regularly. Locals called it the Great Wall tour, because all sightseers saw were high walls surrounding hidden estates. The millionaires behind their high walls communicated with the outside world through intercoms at their locked electronic gates, and whenever they ventured forth from their protected estates, they went in cars with smoked-glass windows. Or the other way, over the water in sloops, ketches, and motor yachts.

At low tide one could walk all the way to Point Resolution, where tall eucalypts gave way to bamboo thickets, wild fig trees, and castor oil plants. From there, one had a breathtaking view of the various Fremantle marinas where the sailboats of the rich bobbed in the wind. Beyond lay the blue water of the Indian Ocean, with its choppy waters and the murderous wind that sailors called the Fremantle Doctor.

Listening again for sounds of her servants, but hearing nothing in the quiet, subdued house, she ventured out into the blinding sunlight of the terrace.

Because of the heat, Philippa had been working in shorts, a blouse tied in a knot over her midriff, and no bra. She had been working in her study, where she was writing her new book, *The 99-Point Starlite Weight Loss and Beauty Plan.* It was a follow-up to her previous book, *The Starlite One-Hour Diet,* which had topped the best-seller lists for over a year. The 99-Point Plan wasn't in fact new; it was a summation of the entire Starlite program, the summation, in fact, of Philippa's life work. "Praise your successes," which she had just dictated into her recorder, was point forty-three in the plan.

She walked to the edge of the pool and watched in fascination as the youthful, golden body swam back and forth beneath the water's lime green surface. When he came up for air, flipping his blond hair out of his face, he didn't seem to notice Philippa, but plunged back under and swam toward the other end of the pool.

As Philippa watched him do a few more laps, she realized how aroused she was. She glanced back toward the house to see if anyone was watching. Wrapped in the baking summer heat, feeling strangely detached and other worldly, she stepped down onto the first step, barely aware of the water that was cold and warm at the same time as it lapped over her ankles.

The hot sun beat down on her as she descended another step, impelled not so much by conscious effort as by something deeper, more instinctive. The white walls surrounding the terrace seemed to pulsate with sunlight, the palms and ferns sitting in giant pots were almost too green, their waxy fronds shimmering like emeralds. Philippa's villa was of Aegean design, having been built by an Australian beer mogul who had once visited Greece and fallen in love with the stark white masonry of the Greek islands. The house was Philippa's temporary hideaway from the world; she had inherited it a year ago and had come here to nurse her secret pain. A pain that was with her always, even now as she felt the sparkling water swirl around her thighs and soak the edge of her shorts.

Philippa Roberts headed a financial empire that earned millions each year in profits; she owned a yacht and a private jet and a priceless collection of rare Western Australian Aboriginal artifacts. She could buy anything she desired, travel to any place in the world she wanted. But when the probate court finally granted her title to the villa, she had taken one look at it and thought, I will write my book here. She had rarely set foot outside the villa in ten months, except to walk down to Point Resolution at the same hour every day, to keep her private vigil.

She left the bottom step and stood in water up to her waist in the shallow end. The young swimmer reached the far end of the pool and burst out of the water in a spray of gold and silver drops. He was about to plunge back in when he saw her; he froze, rivulets streaming down his body, his chest heaving. He stared at Philippa for a moment, then he swam toward her, his head above the water, his eyes on her.

He swam right to her, and when he stood up, he was so close that Philippa could see water glistening on his blond eyebrows and lashes. Strangely, his breathing seemed easier now. Without saying anything, he put his hands together, scooped up some water, and dribbled it over

Philippa's blouse. The sudden wetness shocked her; it also excited her. He continued to pour water onto her until her blouse was soaked and her nipples could be seen through the transparent fabric.

Then he reached down to the knot over her midriff and slowly untied it. Then, undoing the buttons, he gently slipped the blouse off her shoulders and let it fall onto the water, where it floated away on the pool's subtle tide. Philippa shivered despite the summer heat, and when he put his hands on her breasts, she felt a shock go through her. It shot through her chest, down through her heart, and touched a point deep inside her, where she carried her pain. The pain responded briefly—a sharp, sweet stab. And then, to her amazement, the pain began to abate, as if his hands on her bare skin were a balm.

The scene seemed to unfold in slow motion as she stood there unmoving, bewitched, his hands gently caressing her breasts. Then he ducked under the water and began to pull her shorts down. When they were off, he moved her legs apart and swam between them, brushing her inner thighs with his long silken hair. He surfaced behind her, reaching around and cupping her breasts; his tongue went to work on her neck, while she felt his erection pushing against her buttocks.

Philippa felt as if she were on fire, even in the water. His hand slid down, over her belly, her navel, down under the water to explore. She leaned back against him as his finger slipped inside, and she felt the pain begin to melt away. She turned impulsively and sought his mouth with hers.

As they fell back into the water, kissing, their passion becoming more urgent, a chime sounded inside the house, the signal that a car was coming through the electronic gate. But neither of them heard it.

Out on the red-brick drive, the taxi rolled to a stop just as Nyree, Philippa's half-caste Aboriginal housekeeper, came hurrying down the steps.

"Miss Charmer!" she said when the passenger got out.

"Hello, Nyree," Charmie said as she stepped onto the hot red bricks and squinted in the blinding sunlight, which seemed to her crisper and more transparent than the sunlight of California. Nyree was a descendant of a Pilbara tribe; she was tall, with silky brown hair drawn back in a tight knot, deeply set red-brown eyes, and a wide mouth that was quick to smile, despite the air of snobbishness that she seemed to affect. No one knew exactly how old she was, but most people guessed somewhere between fifty and sixty, and she carried herself with a dignity that some considered uppity. She had been with Philippa for nine months and was intensely protective of her employer. The uniform she wore was Nyree's idea; she had insisted upon it.

"Miss Charmer!" she said again.

"What's wrong, Nyree? You seem surprised to see me. Didn't Philippa tell you I was coming?"

The household had indeed been informed of Charmie's sudden visit, with the staff being alerted that, since Miss Charmer always spent Christmas with her family in America, this was an unusual visit and that therefore special considerations might have to be made. They had no idea how long she would be staying or what she and Miss Roberts would be doing while she was here. There might be a small Christmas party, Philippa had told the housekeeper, or an excursion on the river, possibly a shopping expedition to nearby Perth.

"Yes," Nyree said hesitantly. "But we thought you would be getting in later. You're early."

Charmie smiled. "We had a strong tail wind."

"You should have called, I would have sent the car to meet you."

"Taxis do me just fine." When Charmie started toward the house, Nyree signaled to the houseboy to pick up Charmie's suitcase and said, "Is there anything I can get for you, Miss Charmer?"

"There sure is! A gin and tonic, please, Nyree. Tall, and easy on the tonic. Where's Philippa, in her study?"

Nyree stepped quickly in front of her. "I'll tell Miss Roberts you're here."

"Don't bother, I'll surprise her," Charmie said, perplexed by the woman's uncharacteristic skittishness. She went up the steps, delivering herself into the cool interior of the Aegean-style house. As she passed through the foyer, where a Lucite wall displayed Aboriginal bark paintings, she wondered why Nyree had seemed so flustered. Charmie knew she had been expected; she had spoken to Philippa on the phone before she had left L.A.

She was the chairman of the executive committee of Starlite Industries, of which Philippa was founder and CEO, and she was here on business. Since Philippa had decided to exile herself temporarily in this southern corner of the globe, Charmie had taken over the day-to-day operation of the corporation at the Los Angeles headquarters, reporting to Philippa by phone. She had come to Western Australia three times in the past ten months, partly for pleasure, to visit her best friend, but this trip was not for pleasure. Charmie had not said anything about it over the phone to Philippa, but she was bringing disturbing news.

Charmie heard the splashing in the pool before she reached the terrace. She thought she might quickly change into her swimsuit and surprise Philippa by joining her in the pool, when she saw two heads of wet hair in the sunlight, Philippa's auburn curls looking redder than usual, and the other a golden blond—

Charmie stopped and stared.

Philippa was on her back with her eyes closed and her arms stretched out as she held on to the side of the pool, while the young man floated on top of her, his body creating waves as he moved back and forth. When he saw something out of the corner of his eye, he looked up and, seeing Charmie standing there, he suddenly stopped and murmured, "Uh oh."

"Don't stop," Philippa said, but when she saw the look on his face as he drew away from her, she turned around and gave her friend a startled look. "Charmie!" she said. "You're early!"

"Hi, Philippa," Charmie said with a smile as she strolled out onto the terrace and leaned against one of the Doric columns. Then she looked at the young man, who was standing up in the waist-deep water and smiling at her, unabashed at his nakedness. "Hello, Ricky," she said.

"Hello, Miss Charmer. Nice to see you again."

"Well," Philippa said with a sigh, "I suppose that's that!"

Charmie said, "I can go back inside if you want," but Philippa laughed and said, "No, it's all right. Hand me that robe, will you?" She pointed to the thick terry cloth bathrobe that had been placed beside the pool earlier, in anticipation of her "swim" with Ricky. Turning to the young man, she said, "I won't be needing you for a while. My morning's notes are still in the tape recorder. Transcribe them, please, and then you can take care of the correspondence."

"Right-o, Miss Roberts!" he said, and in one swift movement the unself-conscious young man hoisted himself out of the pool, treated Charmie to a brief flash of his rear end, and then disappeared through the columns and into the house.

"Well!" Charmie said as she watched Philippa wrap herself into the robe, envying her friend's slender figure. Only one year older than Philippa, but heavier, Charmie had long since given up the diet battle. The two friends had come a long way since their days at the Tarzana Obesity Clinic. Philippa had weighed 210 pounds then.

"How long has *this* been going on?" Charmie asked.

"About a month," Philippa said. "It happened by accident. I certainly had no intention of getting involved with my secretary." She turned and faced her friend. "Ricky helps take away the pain, Charmie."

"Whatever works," Charmie said, and then she was silent for a moment, gazing at the rippling water in the pool, a wistful look on her face. Then she said, "What would Esther think?" referring to Philippa's daughter, who was attending college in California. Ricky was only a few years older than Esther.

"I don't think she'd like it," Philippa said as they walked to the shaded part of the terrace. When Philippa had told her daughter that she had a male secretary, Esther had said that was "cool." But as far as having sex with him . . .

"How was your flight?" Philippa asked as they sank into softly cushioned garden chairs beneath a striped awning. The white wrought-iron table had already been set with a chilled bottle of wine, a bowl of Tasmanian apples, mangoes, and kiwifruit, and a wedge of Brie and crackers. All of which Nyree had thoughtfully set out for her employer when she had seen what was happening in the pool.

"It seemed to take forever!" Charmie said, eyeing the food with some skepticism. During her visits to Australia, she had developed a taste for local food, none of which was in evidence here. "Why does Australia have to be so far away! And how is the book coming?"

"So far so good," Philippa said as she reached over to a box embedded in the thick white wall and pushed a button. When she heard a masculine voice say, "Yes, Miss Roberts?" she said, "Ricky, please bring me yesterday's pages."

"Are you in love with him?" Charmie asked quietly.

"With Ricky?" Philippa said. "No. But I think he is with me, or perhaps with the *idea* of me. It will pass—these infatuations always do."

"I take it then that Esther isn't coming down to join you for Christmas?"

"My daughter is in love! And this time I think it's for real." Esther was studying biochemistry with the intention of going into research; she had recently informed her mother that she was having a "real" relationship with another biochem major. "Esther asked me if it was all right if she stayed in California for the holidays. I told her I didn't mind." She looked at her friend. "But speaking of which, why aren't you in Ohio with Nathan and the kids?"

Charmie placed the leather portfolio she had brought with her on the table. "Philippa, we need to talk," she said, suddenly serious.

Philippa looked at the woman who had been her closest friend for years. Charmie was a self-described unrepentant sensualist who embraced life with every one of her five senses. The flamboyant caftan she was wearing, swirling around her generous figure in outrageous flamingo pink and aquamarine rayon, was typical of her wardrobe, which consisted mainly of rayon and silk outfits that draped, floated, or swam around her body. Her hair, a dark steamy blond that was almost the color of butterscotch, was worn on top of her head in a careless cloud tied up in a matching pink and green rayon scarf. Large, blocky jewelry finished the picture: a strand of plastic beads the size of golf balls around her neck, huge plastic bangles clacking on both wrists.

"Is it bad news?" Philippa asked quietly.

"It isn't good," Charmie said, and she noted the immediate response in her friend's eyes, a mental squaring of the shoulders that Charmie had witnessed a number of times over the years, whenever challenges had risen up before Philippa. Charmie hoped that her friend would be able to face this new crisis with the same resolve with which she had faced all the others. Philippa was a woman who had fought to believe in herself, just as she had taught others to fight to believe in themselves instead of measuring themselves according to other people's opinions. "Ignore what anyone else thinks," Philippa had once said, standing at a hospital bedside, while Charmie had struggled to stay alive. "Forget everyone else and stand up for yourself and go your own way." Charmie's life had turned around after that moment, and she hadn't looked back since.

Nyree appeared with a tray of drinks, a tall, frosty gin for Charmie, iced tea for Philippa. She gave her employer an inquiring glance, looked over at the pool, and then disappeared back into the house.

"Whatever your bad news is, Charmie," Philippa said after tasting the tea and appreciating its invigorating snap, "I'm glad you're here. I think I have some *good* news. Ivan Hendricks called two days ago. He has news for me, and he's coming to report in person."

"Ivan!" Charmie said, brightening suddenly, as the memory of an explosive sexual encounter she once had with the private investigator flashed into her mind. "What's it about?"

"He says he thinks he's found my sister."

When Charmie gave her a guarded look, Philippa quickly added, "I know, he's said that before. But this time he sounded quite certain. He says he has hard evidence to show me. Oh, I know I shouldn't get my hopes up, but I can't help it." For years, Philippa had been searching for her sister, a twin from whom she had been separated at birth.

"When will he be here?"

"Soon. He said he was coming in on the morning Qantas flight."

A tall shadow fell over them and they looked up to see Ricky standing in the sunlight, his wet golden hair combed back into a neat ponytail. The jeans had been replaced by crisp white Bermuda shorts, and he wore a starched safari shirt, open at the neck. He smiled broadly as he handed Philippa a sheaf of papers, and said, "Yesterday's pages, Miss Roberts."

"Thank you," she said, taking them. Charmie watched him walk back into the house. "My, my," Charmie murmured, still amazed at what she had seen in the pool.

"Here you are, my latest notes," Philippa said, handing the pages to Charmie. "Tell me what you think."

Charmie read the points out loud. "Point Thirty-six: *Soft* butter spreads more thinly. Thirty-seven: AbdomIN." She looked at Philippa. "I like that one. It's new, isn't it?"

"I thought it up last week."

Charmie resumed reading: "Point Thirty-eight: A pint of fluid weighs a pound. Point Thirty-nine: Don't eat over the sink." She looked at Philippa again and their eyes locked for a second, both remembering the days when Charmie would make a panful of spaghetti carbonara and stand over the sink and eat it, straight out of the skillet, and then hastily do the dishes before her husband came home.

Charmie sighed and handed the pages back to Philippa. Old habits, conquered long ago. "I like it," she said. "Do you have all ninety-nine?"

"Not yet, I'm shy about ten."

"How about 'Sex burns calories'?"

Philippa laughed. The book had, in fact, been Charmie's idea. Four years had passed since the last Starlite best-seller, and writing a new book had seemed to Charmie good therapy for Philippa, who was still trying to deal with a tragic and untimely death.

"So," Philippa said. "Why are you here?"

"For two reasons, actually. Here's the first," Charmie said as she laid an item from *The Wall Street Journal* before Philippa. "This company has been quietly buying up Starlite stock."

After Philippa read the article, she gave Charmie a puzzled look. "They've bought nearly three percent of our stock. What do you suppose it means?"

"We have no idea. I did some looking into this Miranda International, which is based in Rio, and they're mainly involved with importing rubber and tropical nuts."

"Have you contacted them?"

"Alan was on it when I left," she said, referring to the chief financial officer of Starlite, also a member of the executive committee.

"Do you suspect they're planning a takeover?"

Charmie shrugged. "It's a mystery to us. But we'll have to hurry and put a stop to it. Alan is going to request that they sign a standstill agreement. Keep your fingers crossed that they do."

As she reread the article, Philippa's bafflement deepened. Who or what was Miranda International, and why had they suddenly shown such aggressive interest in her company? "A takeover wouldn't make sense, Charmie. We don't have a lot of cash on our balance sheet, which would make us desirable. And Starlite has never been regarded as a good short-term investment. What on earth do these people have in mind?"

Charmie felt more concern than she showed. Heavy buying posed a real threat to Starlite; she and Philippa could lose the company. She was praying Alan Scadudo would get Miranda to sign a friendly standstill agreement.

"That's what I asked myself," she said, reaching into the folio again and bringing out another set of papers. "All of a sudden there's a lot of active trading involving a company that has had very little activity recently on the New York Stock Exchange. And people want to know why. You should have seen the switchboard light up when this article came out. Everyone wants to know if Starlite is planning on coming out with a dynamite new product, or if we've brought in some high-powered executive, or if maybe there's a larger company that wants to take us over. Everyone is asking what inside information does Miranda International have that suddenly makes Starlite so desirable? And Philippa, there isn't anything. There's no reason at all why another company should suddenly go after us. So I did some research to see what it was that Miranda could possibly be interested in."

"And what did you find?"

"Plenty, and all of it mighty peculiar. First of all, I went through our books and found out that, for some reason, Starlite's financial reserves are way down. So I went through accounts payable and receivable. At first, I didn't come across anything unusual. But then I found this." She handed Philippa a computer printout.

"As you can see," she explained while Philippa read the sheet, "this is a list of our vendors, everyone who supplies Starlite. Now here you see Specialty Foods, from whom we buy products for our frozen food line. If you recall, we switched to them last year when we dropped our account with Canaan Corp."

"I remember," Philippa said.

"But look here." Charmie pointed to an item on the list, her plastic wrist bangles grazing the page.

Philippa read it. "Canaan is still on the books. Why?"

"Look again. It's not Canaan, it's *Caanan*. The spelling is different."

Philippa looked at Charmie. "A typo?"

"That was what I thought until I went back through the payouts for the past year and discovered that we've been paying regularly to this Caanan Corporation. I called our plant in San Francisco, and they said they've only received supplies from Specialty Foods. Nothing from Canaan in over a year. So then I went back through the invoices, and I found this." She handed Philippa a standard invoice sheet, with a logo and the name "Caanan Corporation" at the top in red print.

"If you look closely," Charmie said, "this looks very much like an invoice from Canaan Corporation, but there's that misspelling. And look, the logo is slightly different."

"What about this address?"

"It doesn't exist. And this phone number is out of order."

"A bogus company? How much have we paid out to them?"

"Nearly a million dollars."

"My God."

"Do you know what I think, Philippa? That after we terminated our account with Canaan, someone got into the main computer bank, doctored the Canaan name so that at casual glance it still looked the same, had some invoices printed up, and then had checks sent out."

"But why wouldn't accounts payable catch it? They know we stopped dealing with Canaan over a year ago."

"Philippa, do you know how many people we have working in that department? An accounts clerk with a daily printout load looks at this invoice, runs it through the computer, sees that Caanan is one of our regular accounts, and cuts the check. She probably doesn't even know we changed over to Specialty Foods."

As Philippa looked at the papers spread before her, the enormity of it began to sink in. "This could only mean that someone *inside* Starlite is embezzling."

"And what's worse," Charmie said, "if it hadn't been for this Miranda thing I never would have caught it. Whoever it is could have kept it up indefinitely, or at least until we ran a major audit, by which time he or she would have gotten away with an even bigger bundle."

Philippa looked at Charmie. "But who could it be, Charmie? Surely it couldn't possibly be one of us."

By "one of us," Philippa meant one of a small group of friends who went back many years to the very early days of Starlite, when Philippa had run the business from her living room.

"I was wondering if the two could be related," Charmie said. "Could someone inside Starlite be embezzling funds and then turning around and buying up shares? Because then it would mean that someone inside Starlite is planning a takeover."

"Charmie," Philippa said as a new thought struck her. "Who at Starlite knows you're here?"

"No one. I didn't think it was a good idea to alert the culprit, if there is one. They all think I'm in Ohio with Nathan and the children. Nathan has instructions to call me here if I receive any calls at his place."

"But Alan knows you came to see me."

"No. I didn't think it wise to tell him. Or Hannah."

"Do you suspect Alan?" Philippa said in alarm. Alan had been with the company since the beginning; he was one of the founding members.

"No, I don't suspect Alan. But I thought it prudent to practice extreme caution for the moment, until we know for sure what's going on. The two items might not be related at all. Or they might be. But whatever is going on, it's damned serious and we have to be careful."

"Yes, of course," Philippa said, but she felt suddenly cold inside the thick bathrobe.

Nyree appeared from the living room just then to announce the arrival
of Ivan Hendricks, the private investigator.

"Thank you, Nyree. Have him wait in the living room, please, while
I go and dress. Pray that it's good news, Charmie," Philippa said as she
stood. "I could use some right now."

She joined them a few moments later, after she had changed into slacks
and a blouse and dried her hair. Charmie and Ivan were seated in the
spacious, high-ceilinged living room, where white plaster walls and a black
slate floor showcased antiques from Australia's pioneer days.

Ivan Hendricks rose when Philippa came in. He was in amazing shape
for a man in his fifties; Philippa often thought the compact body and short
crew cut made him look like a retired marine drill sergeant. She had
known him for twenty-five years, and he knew all of her secrets, including
the ones Charmie didn't know.

"What do you have for me, Ivan?" she asked after they embraced and
sat down.

"A bombshell this time, Miss Roberts. You're not going to believe it."

Nyree came in and placed a tray on the coffee table containing a crystal
decanter of twelve-year-old scotch, a plate of deviled eggs, which Ivan was
partial to, plus two iced teas and freshly cut-up vegetables. Charmie eyed
the offering, then said to Nyree, "Haven't you got anything better than
this?"

Knowing Miss Charmer's tastes, Nyree said with a wink, "The meat
pie's just heating up, and I baked a fresh lamington this morning because
I knew you were coming."

As Ivan helped himself to the scotch and a deviled egg, he glanced
across the coffee table at Charmie and smiled. He had always appreciated
the gusto she had for living. She was a voluptuous woman with a voluptuous appetite. A woman like her, he suspected, must be a feast in bed. He
too was recalling the one stunning moment in which he and Charmie had
come together.

"God, but it's hot down here," he said as he removed his rumpled
jacket, a Qantas boarding pass sticking out of the pocket. "It's sixty-eight
degrees in Palm Springs, with snow on the mountains, Christmas lights
in the streets, and greed in the air. I was sorely tempted to stay there."

He set his briefcase down and pulled out a folder. "It was a stroke of
luck, really," he said as he removed some papers. "Nothing due to my keen
investigative powers, I'm afraid. I was working on another case when I
came across this."

Philippa knew that Ivan Hendricks had other clients; it had been a long
time since he had worked solely for her, years ago, when the prospect of
finding members of her family had seemed just around the corner.

He first handed her a newspaper clipping. "From the classified section of the *Los Angeles Times,*" he said.

Philippa read it. "Anyone knowing the whereabouts of, or information leading to, Christine Singleton, born 1938, Hollywood, California, please contact Beverly Burgess at Star's, Palm Springs. Urgent family business."

Christine Singleton! Philippa hadn't thought of that name in years. She looked at Ivan. "Star's. I've heard of it. It's a resort in the mountains overlooking Palm Springs."

"Look at this." Ivan produced a page that had been removed from an expensive glossy magazine. It was a full-page ad that consisted of a splash of silver stars against a midnight blue background. In the lower half of the ad, bold silver letters read "STAR'S." And underneath, *"Explore the Fantasy . . ."*

"Let me tell you," Ivan said, "I had a heck of a time getting to this place. For one thing, you can't get there except by tramway, and you can't get onto the tramway unless you have a room reservation or a dinner or lunch reservation. I managed to go up for lunch, and was the place busy! There's a big Christmas shindig being planned for a few days from now, and it seems that everyone who's anyone wants to attend."

"What was the place like?" Philippa asked. "I've heard it's quite amazing."

"Wall to wall movie stars, enough to fill a hundred *National Enquirers,* at least that's what it felt like. Very ritzy. Way out of my league, but right in yours, Miss Roberts. Anyway, I didn't try to contact this Beverly Burgess myself, as you've requested." Hendricks had standing orders not to approach any leads personally. Once, nine years ago, he thought he had found Philippa's real mother, but he had scared the woman off before Philippa could talk to her, and they had never found her again.

"I did some looking around," he said, "and managed to get this press photo of Beverly Burgess. It's not very clear—she obviously didn't want her picture taken."

Charmie stood behind Philippa and looked at the blurry photograph. "I suppose there's some resemblance," she said. "She *could* be your sister, Philippa. Were you fraternal or identical twins?"

"I don't know. Why?"

"Because if you were identical twins, then this woman isn't your sister. But fraternal twins, well, then it's possible."

Despite the fact that this was far more than she had expected Ivan to produce, Philippa forced herself to remain cautious. She had been disappointed too many times. "This still isn't evidence that she is my sister."

"Who else would be looking for you?" Charmie said. "I mean, who else would be looking for Christine Singleton? And what about the year of

birth? You were born in Hollywood in 1938. How many Christine Singletons were born in Hollywood in that year?"

"But remember, Charmie, Christine Singleton wasn't my name when
I was born. That name was given to me by my adoptive parents. This
person might just be someone from my distant past." Someone from San
Francisco, Philippa thought darkly. Or worse, from San Quentin. And
unpleasant, long-suppressed memories suddenly came back.

"But look at the face, Philippa," Charmie said. "I think there *is* a
resemblance. Let's say your sister has been looking for you, just as you've
been looking for her, and she found out that you'd been adopted by the
Singletons."

Philippa's heart began to race. Was it possible? It was difficult to tell
for sure, but the woman in the photograph appeared to be tall and slender,
like Philippa, and there was a haunting similarity in the way she stood,
the set of her shoulders, the way she held her head. The jawline, too, and
maybe the nose. *Was* this woman her twin sister?

"What were you able to find out about her, Ivan?" she asked.

"Well, Miss Roberts, I ran into a rather intriguing mystery there. A
woman like this, who can afford to buy property worth millions and *then*
develop it into a swank playground for the rich, I figure she's got to have
a high profile. Except that she doesn't. I asked around Palm Springs, but
no one seems to know anything about Beverly Burgess. Any dealings the
resort has with the public are done through the general manager, a Swiss
named Simon Jung. Burgess apparently showed up two and a half years
ago, bought this old silent movie star's place up in the mountains, and
converted it into an exclusive resort. I did talk to the woman who writes
a society column for *Palm Springs Life* magazine, and she said she met
Beverly once. Guessed she was in her late forties."

Ivan Hendricks loosened the tie that he had put on during the drive
from the airport. This was the hard part, stopping himself from telling
more. He wished now, as he often did, that the could tell her the truth—
what he really knew. But he had made a promise to someone never to tell,
and Ivan Hendricks always kept his word.

Philippa said, "Excuse me for a moment, please," and left the room.
She went into her study, her private retreat. Aside from an enormous desk
cluttered with papers, books, a telephone, and an Apple computer with
modem and two printers, there were the personal effects she had brought
with her from Los Angeles when she had decided to stay here and write
her book: framed certificates on the walls, letters of commendation,
awards and prizes, and photographs of Philippa with important people
from all over the world. Her entire lifetime, her whole universe, was
compressed within these four walls. Her secretary didn't work in this

room; Ricky had a small office attached to his apartment over the six-car garage, and she paged him now on the intercom. When he answered, she said, "Ricky, will you join us in the living room, please?"

As she turned away, her attention was caught by two photographs on her desk. The first was in a clear plastic frame, a smiling teenager in a jogging outfit—Esther, her daughter, when she was sixteen. The second stood in an antique pewter frame, the picture of a handsome man sitting at the helm of a seventeen-meter racing yacht, with the sun and wind in his face, the spark of victory in his eyes. The photo had been taken the day he had been preparing to compete in the Sydney to Hobart race. It was also the day she had decided to tell him that she would marry him, when she had flown down to Australia to surprise him. But instead she had arrived in time to see the *Philippa* go down not far from here, just off Point Resolution, the site now of her daily private vigils. This villa had been his, newly purchased at the time of his death, and although he had stipulated in his will that it was to go to Philippa, his family had contested it, tying the property up in probate for a long time until at last, one year ago, the court had decided in her favor and Philippa had come down to Perth to claim her painful inheritance.

As she gazed at the attractive tanned face, she thought again how impossible it was to accept the fact that he was dead. Surely he was going to come back someday; surely he was going to wake up one morning, wherever he was—in a hospital or on a remote island—suddenly remember who he was, and come back to her. That was why she walked out to Point Resolution every day and scanned the bay.

"Dare I raise my hopes again, my love?" she said to him now, talking to his photograph, as she often did. "This woman named Beverly Burgess—*could* she be my sister? She owns a resort called Star's. I own Starlite Industries. I've heard of such phenomena occurring in the lives of twins, even ones who have been separated at birth, remarkable coincidences happening in their lives. Could Star's and Starlite be a sign that she really is my twin?"

And wouldn't it be wonderful if Esther and I had more of a family than just each other?

She returned to the living room and said, "We can't waste another minute. I'm going back with you, Charmie. I have to find out if there's a threat to Starlite and who's behind it, if it is one of our friends. And then I'm going to see this woman at Star's. If there's even the slimmest possibility that she's my sister, I have to pursue it. And if she *is* my sister, then the empty spaces in my past will be filled. I'll know who I really am and where I came from at last."

She turned to Ricky, who was waiting, steno pad and pen ready. "Call the airport, see if Captain Farrow is still there, and find out when the jet can be ready to go again. Arrange for a replacement crew to fly us back to the U.S. right away. Arrange for a limousine at the other end, and reserve a suite at the Century Plaza Hotel. Fax Star's in Palm Springs, see if you can get us accommodations. If not, try the Marriott Desert Springs or the Ritz-Carlton, whichever has rooms available. And Ricky, above all, don't let anyone at the Starlite offices know that I'm coming." I need the element of surprise on my side, she thought. I want to observe their reactions when they see me walk through the door.

Finally she turned to Hendricks. "Ivan, go back to Palm Springs and find out whatever you can on this Beverly Burgess. Dig into her background, see what you can come up with. Where did she come from? How can she afford an operation like Star's? Get a room at Star's if you have to; Ricky will arrange an expense account for you. You can report to me when I get to Palm Springs. Oh, and one more thing. Can you have one of your investigators look into a company for me? It's called Caanan Corporation, and I have a strong suspicion that it's a front for receiving embezzled funds."

Finally she turned to Charmie and said, "Come and help me pack. We'll leave at once. Whoever is trying to take my company away from me is in for a big surprise!"

Philippa picked up the photograph Ivan had brought from Palm Springs and looked at it for a long moment. Are you my sister? she asked silently. Do you hold the key to my identity? Will you be able to tell me at long last who I really am?

"Beverly Burgess," Philippa murmured. "Who *are* you?"

⋯⋯⋯⋯⋯⋯⋯⋯⋯⋯⋯⋯⋯⋯⋯⋯⋯⋯⋯⋯⋯⋯⋯⋯⋯★

He knows my secret, Beverly Burgess thought as she looked out at the snowy night. He knows my secret, and he'll use it to destroy me.

She was standing in the highest tower of the mansion known as the Castle, and she sometimes thought ruefully of the parallels between her situation and the fairy-tale story of the princess with a curse on her, forbidden to be seen, or to see anyone, locked away as if lamenting the loss of a lover and living out her days spinning ropes of gold out of strands of her hair.

Except that Beverly's hair wasn't gold any more, or even blond, as it had been. It was brunette now, worn in a stylish Liz Taylor shag instead of the French twist that had been Beverly's trademark for so many years. And she wasn't really a princess, there was no lost lover, and the high tower was in fact her office. The Castle was the main building of Star's, the resort she had owned for the past two and a half years.

Her hair wasn't the only thing that had changed; she had a new name as well. Many years ago, to hide her identity, she had changed her name from Rachel Dwyer to Beverly Highland, naming herself after two streets in Hollywood. And then, three and a half years ago, Beverly Highland had "died." Now she was Beverly Burgess; she had borrowed her mother's maiden name, but kept the Beverly.

The hair and name changes had been made to protect her identity once more, but while the first disguise had fooled people for many years, she suddenly had reason to fear that she might not have been successful this time.

He knows who I am, she thought again as she turned away from the window and looked at the book that lay on her desk. It was called *Butterfly Exposed,* and the man she was afraid of was its author, the tabloid journalist Otis Quinn, who had claimed during a recent television interview that Beverly Highland was still alive.

How could he possibly know? She had been so careful! The staged death—the car going over the cliff and plunging into the ocean—the funeral and burial at Forest Lawn. Beverly had left no traces of that former life, when she had lived for the destruction of one man in revenge for what he had done to her.

Beverly had come out of hiding three years ago, after a brief sojourn on a Pacific island with a young lover named Jamie, where she had spent a few months living totally for herself, indulging in every pleasure from food to sex. But when Beverly had grown tired of that existence she had decided to see the world. Carefully constructing a new identity and a new look for herself, she had traveled to exotic places, and she had felt the old hunger return—the desire to create a place where people could find happiness among beauty and luxury. That was what Butterfly, the establishment she had created above an exclusive men's clothing store on Rodeo Drive, had been—a place where women could seek sexual fulfillment in complete safety and anonymity, and in elegant surroundings. When Beverly had discovered that she yearned to do that again, to offer pleasure to people, she had searched for just the right place, and she had found it at Star's Haven, high up the slopes of Mount San Jacinto.

The heart of Star's Haven was a huge gray stone estate house, built like a castle, with turrets and towers and battlements, and even a drawbridge—a romantic setting plucked right out of medieval England. Built by the silent-movie queen Marion Star, it was a replica of the set used in one of her movies, *Robin Hood*. It had stood boarded up for many years after her death, but had come onto the market a few years ago. Now the forty-two-room mansion was called the Castle, and here Beverly had her executive offices. The resort's main restaurants, ballroom, cocktail lounges, boutiques, and private clinic were also located here, as well as luxury suites for the guests, including four tower apartments that were accessible only by private key-operated elevators. Everything had been going well; the resort was a big success, Beverly had kept her old identity a secret, her past completely unknown. And then this Otis Quinn had decided to exploit the story of Danny Mackay and Beverly Highland and conduct his so-called investigation.

She stared at the book. Although the word *butterfly* was in the title, Beverly regarded it as if it were a deadly spider. The pages were filled mostly with speculation. Quinn hadn't really been able to prove anything; he hadn't found any hard evidence linking Beverly to the brothel on Rodeo Drive. He claimed to have interviewed women who had patronized the rooms above Fanelli's, having sexual liaisons with the men who worked

at the place—"companions" they had been called—who had performed
a variety of sexual acts for money. But Quinn hadn't named any of the
women he had supposedly interviewed, claiming that they all insisted that
their identities be kept a secret, and so Beverly believed he had made the
stories up. Nonetheless, the book was sensational enough to keep it on the
best-seller lists for months. Everywhere Beverly turned, it seemed, the
black and white cover with its pink butterfly was there to mock her. And
bring back memories from years ago . . .

Young Rachel Dwyer, ten years old, finding a photograph of her mother
with two babies in her arms. "Who was the other baby, Mama?" she had
asked, and Naomi Dwyer had said, "Your twin sister. She died shortly
after you were born."

And then Rachel, fourteen years old, all alone while a fierce New
Mexico storm battered the old trailer the Dwyers lived in. Her father
coming home drunk, attacking her, inflicting a pain on her body that she
hadn't thought possible, and shouting, "We got rid of the wrong one!"

Later that night, Rachel getting ready to run away, asking her mother
what her father had meant by "the wrong one," and her mother explaining: "Honey, when I was in the hospital to have you and your sister, we
were broke. We didn't have a dime. There was a depression on, and there
we were with twin babies and no money to pay the hospital bills. So when
a man came to the hospital and said he knew of a nice couple who would
pay us a thousand dollars for one of our babies . . ."

Beverly closed her eyes against the memory. She turned away and
looked out the window again at the dark December night. She could make
out the lights in the valley below, the sparkling spread of Palm Springs—
fabled playground of the super rich, home to three former U.S. presidents,
where it was said there were more golf courses than anywhere else in the
world and more plastic surgeons per capita than any other city. A place
where streets were named Bob Hope Drive and Frank Sinatra Drive; a
desert oasis affectionately known as the Backyard of Beverly Hills.

And Beverly Burgess—once Beverly Highland, once Rachel Dwyer—
was eight thousand feet above above it all.

Beside the window, which was narrow and deeply recessed like the
window of a medieval castle, photographs hung on the wall. There was
one small one, in a silver frame, black and white but yellowing with age.
It had been taken in 1938 and it showed a young woman in a hospital
bed with a baby cradled in each arm. One of those babies was Beverly.
The other was the twin sister her parents had sold, who had been given
the name Christine Singleton, and whom Beverly, after many years of
searching, had ultimately not been able to find.

She couldn't help herself; she was drawn back to the hateful book on
her desk.

Beverly had been shocked when she had first seen *Butterfly Exposed* in a bookstore. She had thought it a coincidence that the book should be named for the operation she had established above Fanelli's. And then she had thumbed through it and, in shock, purchased it. One night's reading had brought back all the old nightmares: Danny Mackay befriending a frightened fourteen-year-old runaway, gaining her trust, telling her he loved her, and then installing her in a cheap whorehouse in San Antonio. And Rachel, terrified and homesick, unable to service Hazel's customers, wishing that Danny would take her away from it all, and Danny coming back and sweet-talking her into performing sex with strange men. "Just lay back, darlin'," he had said, "and imagine it's me who's doin' it to you."

And then, when she was sixteen and she thought they were going to get married, Danny taking her to a back-alley abortionist and forcing her to kill her baby. She had begged and pleaded with him, and afterward he had kicked her out of his car, telling her she was ugly, and that he had never loved her, and that she was to remember his name, because he was a man who was going places. Danny Mackay, he had said. Remember that name.

And remembered it she had, almost to the exclusion of all else. The rest of Beverly's life had been a quest for the perfect revenge against Danny Mackay, and when it had finally come, three and a half years ago, she had thought that their secret, twisted story had come to an end at last.

But now there was this journalist, making up lies and outrageous speculations about the relationship between the wealthy socialite Beverly Highland and the Reverend Danny Mackay, who had controlled a multi-billion-dollar TV ministry and who had been one step away from the Oval Office. Everyone in the country, Beverly knew, was either reading *Butterfly Exposed* or talking about it. And she had heard that a TV miniseries was in the making.

But something even worse than that had happened.

Otis Quinn had declared during a TV interview that he believed Beverly Highland, who was supposed to have died in a car accident the night she had destroyed Danny Mackay, the woman who was in fact responsible for Mackay's death by suicide in the L.A. County Jail, was still alive. And he claimed to have found her.

And now, Otis Quinn was coming to Star's.

Beverly was brought out of her thoughts by a discreet knock at the door. She looked at her watch. It would be Simon Jung, her general manager, making his daily report.

"Come in," she said.

Simon Jung, Swiss born and educated, was a smoothly handsome man in his late fifties, impeccably trim and tailored, whom Beverly had met in Rio de Janeiro at the swank Amanha Restaurant. Simon had an impressive background of over thirty years of hotel management experience, having worked in only the finest establishments around the world. There was nothing he didn't know, it seemed to Beverly, about human nature and pleasing guests, and he was the one person in all the world she felt she could trust.

But even Simon didn't know about her past, that she was the Beverly Highland whom Otis Quinn had written about in *Butterfly Exposed.*

"Good evening, Beverly," he said as he closed the door quietly behind himself.

As always, the sight of Simon in the Armani or Pierre Cardin suit that had been made just for him caused an unwanted reaction deep inside her. Beverly had sworn off men long ago—except for her brief interval with young Jamie. In her travels, when she had stayed at such exclusive places as the Mount Kenya Safari Club in East Africa, Raffles in Singapore, the Hôtel du Cap on the Riviera, and she had met such handsome and impeccable men as Simon, she had been immune. They didn't move her.

But somehow, during her two and a half years of working with Simon in a strictly professional relationship, making Star's a place for the best people to come to, Beverly had found her defenses starting to crumble. And she had discovered an odd new sensation come over her every time she saw Simon. It was vaguely reminiscent of something she had known once, long ago, like the scent of a rare flower or a song once heard. Simon Jung reminded her of something, but she couldn't figure out just what.

"Our latest guests have arrived," he said as he deposited the list on her desk. "You will be familiar with some of the names," he added, speaking with the faintest Lucerne accent. "There is Carole Page, the film actress, who has just finished making a movie and is here for a rest. She was escorted to one of the bungalows and was assured of complete privacy. There is a Hollywood agent named Frieda Goldman, who is here for only one night. Dr. Judith Isaacs, our new resident physician, arrived also. She has gone to inspect the clinic and meet her patients. She said she is pleased to accept your invitation to dine with you later this evening."

Simon went on about the others who had come up on the evening tram: a well-known movie director, a studio executive, two producers, another famous actress, a wealthy realtor and his wife, an oilman from Texas and his female companion, a gemologist from Tiffany, and various others who were distinguished in one way or another. He added, "Mr. Larry Wolfe is due to arrive with his secretary on the next tram. They have requested one of the bungalows. Mr. Wolfe is an avid swimmer and prefers a private pool."

Larry Wolfe, the Academy Award–winning screenwriter, was coming to Star's to write a movie about Marion Star, the mysterious woman who had built this place back in the twenties and then vanished. Beverly had found a diary written by Miss Star and had put it up for auction, and it had gone ultimately to Larry Wolfe, who was not only going to write the screenplay but co-produce the film as well.

Beverly listened as Simon gave his report, and when he was finished, she said, "When is Otis Quinn due to arrive?"

Simon's eyes flickered to the book on her desk. He had not read *Butterfly Exposed,* and he had been surprised to come upon Beverly reading it one day. He knew that the book disturbed her, as did the imminent arrival of its author.

"His reservation is for four days from now. We've booked him into one of the cabins. Do you have any special instructions regarding Mr. Quinn?"

Beverly glanced at the book on her desk. She had read it so many times she had practically memorized it. Quinn had gotten the police to open up the rooms above Fanelli's and let him look around.

"They were like hotel rooms," he had written, *"closed doors off a long corridor. Each room was decorated with a different theme. One was made into a western-style saloon, complete with sawdust on the floor, where women paid to have sex with men dressed up as cowboys. Another room was outfitted to look like a cheap motel room, and there was a four-poster bed . . ."*

"No," she said to Simon Jung. "No special instructions for Mr. Quinn."

Simon continued his report, going through his notes with smooth, perfectly manicured hands, a gold ring glinting in a flash of blue lapis, the insignia of a military academy in Zurich. "Prince Habib el Mahdy has requested a trilingual secretary. And here is a list of the guests who have reserved for the Christmas ball. President and Mrs. Reagan send their regrets."

He then went on to inform Beverly that housekeeping had reported a shortage of bathrobes again. "Many of the guests are taking them when they leave," he said. "Accounting has requested again that we charge for them."

When Beverly had decided to create a special resort of her own, she had traveled around the world, staying in the most exclusive places, such as the Regent Hotel in Hong Kong, the Bel-Air in Los Angeles, and the Pierre in New York, studying them, selecting the finest qualities from each, and incorporating them into her new hotel. There were designer toiletries in the bathrooms, fresh flowers daily in every room, baskets of fruit and cheese for each guest upon arrival. And, of course, the complimentary bathrobes. Beverly had been surprised to discover that some of the most luxurious establishments posted notices in the rooms explaining that the bathrobes were for the use of the guests during their stay, that the robes could be purchased in the gift shop should a guest desire to keep one. If a robe was taken, however, it would be charged to the guest's account. There were no such notices in the guest rooms at Star's.

"Have housekeeping order as many as they need," she said to Simon. "Any that are taken will not be charged for."

It was an issue upon which Simon disagreed with Beverly, but he knew it was pointless to argue. He had discovered that Miss Burgess was not in the hotel business strictly for profit; her livelihood did not depend upon revenue from the hotel. Although he had no idea where her personal wealth had come from, he did know that while in Brazil she had made some investments in emerald mines and coffee plantations.

He placed the report on her desk, paused a moment, then came around the desk and stood next to her. "They are decorating the Christmas tree in the Grand Ballroom," he said. "All the guests are helping. And the chef has prepared the most delicious marinated quail with wild mushrooms. Why don't you join us, Beverly?"

She looked into his gentle gray eyes and realized that she wanted to be part of it all. But one of the prices she had had to pay for destroying Danny Mackay was her freedom. Even though she had changed her hair color and style, she still couldn't risk being recognized. Especially now, with *Butterfly Exposed* being such a big seller and filled with photos of Beverly Highland.

"Thank you, Simon," she said. "But I have work to do."

"Always work, Beverly," he said. "I have known you for over two years, and I have never seen you do anything but work. It's not good," he added softly.

His nearness, the sense of his strength reaching out to her, made Beverly think of the elusive something that Simon Jung always seemed to remind her of—the half-remembered melody, a perfume from long ago. And now, suddenly, for the first time, she realized what it was. Simon Jung reminded her of love.

"Please," she said with a smile. "Go downstairs, enjoy the company, make sure everyone has a good time."

He started to say something, then turned and headed for the door. "By the way," he said, "Ricardo Cadiz telephoned a while ago. He's had to cancel his reservation. An emergency came up, he said."

Ricardo Cadiz was the Argentine novelist who had recently won the Nobel Prize for literature. Beverly had been looking forward to meeting him. "The bungalow will go empty then?" she said. Cadiz had reserved it for two weeks.

"Fortunately we received a fax a while ago from Australia, someone wishing to stay with us as soon as possible."

"Australia?"

"A Miss Philippa Roberts."

Beverly searched her memory. "That name sounds familiar."

"She owns Starlite Industries. She and her party will be arriving in four days. They said that they will be pleased to have the bungalow."

After Simon left, Beverly walked around her office. A model of the resort stood in the center of the room, measuring six feet by five and resting on a large mahogany table. The artist who had rendered the model had put special care into making it as near an exact replica of the real resort as he could, right down to the alpine terrain, the gullies and gorges that cut into the mountain, the miniature pine trees, and even a few bighorn sheep to indicate where the Star's property abutted the border of Mount San Jacinto Wilderness State Park, where the endangered sheep were protected.

Scattered over the many acres were additional guests residences: three large bungalows, each with two bedrooms, full kitchen, and private swimming pool protected by a wall; then the cottages with hot tubs and private gardens; and farther out, the cabins with wood-burning fireplaces and clearings shielded by pine trees. Little winding paths crisscrossed the grounds for guests to follow by golf cart or on foot; green lawns were carefully plotted out, with fountains and private places with stone benches. There were two large swimming pools, tennis courts, a nine-hole golf course laid out in such a way that a total of twenty-seven holes could be played, a driving range, and a ski lift to four runs of varying degrees of difficulty. The health club complex was outfitted with separate men's and women's gyms, saunas, lap pools, indoor running tracks, and the exclusive members-only Starlite salon.

And finally there was the Castle, overlooking Coachella Valley, from where, on clear days, one could see all the way across the desert into Arizona.

Although people came to Star's for the seclusion, the luxury of the place (many arrived with scripts to read and study, contracts to pore over, secret liaisons to enjoy), many also came for the beauty and the history. There wasn't a room in Star's, a wall, a piece of furniture, that did not vibrate with the legends of filmdom's colorful past. People wanted to see where Dexter Bryant Ramsey had been murdered; they wanted to see the two-thousand-square-foot closet where Marion Star had kept her thousands of gowns and costumes; they came to ooh and aah over the stairway bannister down which a drunken John Barrymore was supposed to have come sliding one night. Even Beverly's office housed an interesting bit of history—a polished medieval suit of armor. The story went that in 1932, when Marion was holding one of her parties and a game of hide-and-seek was in progress, a young Gary Cooper had decided to hide in that suit of armor but had gotten stuck inside and hadn't been found for hours.

Whether such tales were truth or legend, it didn't matter; it was the *idea* of Star's that drew many people here.

When she heard someone pass by in the hallway, humming a Christmas carol, Beverly was suddenly reminded of her aloneness. She had no husband, no children, no family. Just a lifetime of painful memories. Had it been worth it, she wondered, all those sacrifices, just to seek revenge on Danny Mackay? If only she could find her twin sister, then perhaps it might have all been worth it. She wouldn't be so lonely then, knowing that at least she had family somewhere.

She had tried to find her sister, hiring a private investigator who had spent years following false trails. After determining that her sister had been adopted by a family named Singleton and raised as Christine, the investigator had lost her trail. The trail had ended there, and Beverly had never found her. And so the final, hard truth was that, despite her immense wealth, Beverly Burgess felt very much alone.

She went to the silver tea service that had been brought up earlier and poured herself a cup of Earl Grey, adding a touch of honey. There was a plate of Italian cookies with the service, Amaretti di Saronno, one of Beverly's weaknesses. The Star's dessert chef was a master at whipping the sugar, egg whites, and apricot kernels into perfect, crisp, light-as-air biscuits, and Beverly, who assiduously watched her weight, allowed herself to indulge in them now and then.

As she bit into one of the astonishingly sweet cookies and followed it with a sip of the exotic-flavored tea, her thoughts went back to the book on her desk.

Why was Otis Quinn coming here? Did he know she was Beverly Highland? Had he some proof? Did he plan to expose her? Or was he coming for some other reason altogether, so that she should be careful not to do anything to put him on the scent? Star's attracted lots of people who were titillating; perhaps he was after another story now that his book about Butterfly had been published. Paparazzi were always trying to sneak in, to snap pictures of a princess, a drug-troubled playboy, an adulterous movie star. But Beverly's tight security system was constantly on the alert to protect her guests; it had even worked well the time Robin Leach had come to do a spot for "Lifestyles of the Rich and Famous." Beverly had permitted no pictures to be taken of guests, only the resort grounds and the fabled Castle where the sensational murder had taken place.

Perhaps that was all Quinn wanted. Maybe he would just come to see the bathroom where the murder took place, or the infamous bedroom where Marion Star had supposedly entertained the entire USC football team one weekend. Perhaps it was the haunting legend that was bringing him here; ghosts made good copy. Or maybe he just wanted a glimpse inside the retreat of the super rich and super famous, to see how they lived and played. Possibly his visit here had nothing to do with *Butterfly Exposed* or his claim that Beverly Highland was still alive.

As Beverly watched the snow fall and obliterate the lights of Palm Springs far below, she felt her old courage and fighting spirit rise up. No matter how determined Quinn might be to uncover people's secrets, she was more determined to protect them. She was prepared to fight him at all costs. No one was going to do an exposé at, or about, Star's.

And she wasn't afraid of Otis Quinn. She wasn't afraid of any man. Once, long ago, there had been a man whom she had feared. But he was dead. Danny Mackay was dead; she was safe. And she need never be afraid of him, of any man, ever again.

4

......................................★

Danny Mackay was dead.

Dead, dead, dead.

And that was exactly how Danny liked it. He had even come around to thinking that being dead was better than being alive.

"I tell you, Bon," he said to his old friend, Bonner Purvis, who was sitting by the window looking out at the Malibu night, "there's a lot more advantages to being dead than I expected. For instance, I can commit any crimes I want, as many as I want, and no one would consider me as a suspect."

Danny stood before the mirror with no shirt on, studying himself, turning this way and that, flexing his muscles. Months of intensive training had gotten him back into shape—better shape even, he thought, than before he had died. Heck, he looked like a man half his age.

Of course it hadn't been easy, reclaiming his former strength. When he had regained consciousness in that old clapboard house in San Antonio over three years ago, he had been told that he had been in a coma for four months. There had been some kind of brain damage, Bonner had explained. Something had gone wrong with his faked suicide in his cell in the Los Angeles County Jail; Danny really *had* died, or almost. So when he finally woke up, to find Bonner anxiously staring down at him, Danny had found himself trapped in a prison of atrophied muscles and wasted flesh. The road back to health had been long and difficult. Many times Danny had almost wanted to give up, when his speech failed him, or his sight blurred, or any number of symptoms randomly struck, reminding him of the injury that had been done to his cerebral arteries.

But finally Danny had had help. A book called *Butterfly Exposed* had come on the scene, and as soon as he read it, a surge of fierce, new determination had flooded his weakened body.

"You know, Bon," Danny said to his friend, "that Quinn guy isn't so dumb. Listen to this." He picked up the dog-eared book and opened to a page he had almost memorized. " *'It is this journalist's theory that Danny Mackay and Beverly Highland had in fact known each other secretly for many years, that their histories had gone back far enough to a point where they were either friends, business partners, or possibly even lovers, and that it was something in that mutually shared distant past that had caused Beverly Highland to lay out a complex and brilliant plan of revenge against the unwitting Mackay.' "*

Danny laughed and tossed the book aside. "Quinn reckons I done her wrong, as the song goes. He's a regular rocket scientist, that one."

He walked away from the mirror and went into the next room to look out a smaller window. Pushing the curtain aside, he surveyed the house next door. There were no lights on inside, no car in the driveway. Otis Quinn had not yet come home.

"Boy hidey, Bonner," Danny said, lapsing into the West Texas speech of his youth, as he always did when he felt good, "it's funny how fate works, ain't it?" He picked up an electric blue silk shirt off the bed and slowly put it on, savoring the feel of the material against his skin. There had been a moment three and a half years ago when for a split second Danny had thought he was never going to feel anything ever again. "I mean," he said as he did up the pearl buttons, "there I was, planning my own fake death and thinking all the while that the bitch had been killed when her car went over the cliff, and now, over three years later, I discover that she faked her death, too! I should have expected it. I wouldn't put it past the bitch to pull a stunt like that. We both had the same idea."

His face suddenly darkened. "Except that her faked death didn't damn near kill her as mine almost did."

He laughed again and ran his hands over the silk. The shirt had cost two hundred dollars; Danny had had it custom-made.

"I tell you, Bon, when I saw that Quinn guy on TV, saying as how he thought Beverly Highland was still alive, and that he had proof . . ." He looped an alligator belt through his pants—no fruity Wall Street suspenders for Danny, no matter how trendy they were. "Well, you were there, Bon. You saw how wild it made me. To think that she's still alive! Of course she is! Once Quinn said it and I got to thinking about it, I realized what a fool I'd been, just like the rest of the world, thinking she had really gone into the drink in that flashy car of hers."

He went back to the mirror and paused, his look turning hard. He was thinking of how Beverly must have celebrated when she heard about his suicide in jail, how she probably popped a few champagne corks while she watched his Houston funeral on TV. The bitch no doubt gloated; she was probably still gloating to this day. But that was going to end. Just as soon as Danny found her.

He looked at his watch—a good Swiss make, but not the fifteen-thousand-dollar Rolex he had his eye on. Danny had been doing some shopping since he arrived in southern California, but he had a lot more to do. Clothes made the man, he always said.

Quinn had said on the TV show that he was currently renting a beach house in Malibu, just past the Sunset turnoff, so it hadn't been difficult for Danny and Bonner to find him. And once they had established which house belonged to the journalist, they had simply taken up residence next door. Now Danny was waiting for Otis to come home. They were going to have a little talk.

And then Danny would know where Beverly Highland was—and he could pay her back for what she had done to him.

One side of his mouth lifted in a smile. When Danny saw how sexy that smile made him look, he had to admit that, after months of being in a coma and more months of rehabilitation in which he frequently blacked out and couldn't remember who he was, after all he had been through in the past three and a half years, he still had the old Danny Mackay magic.

Sure, he was a little older now, and there was gray in the thick reddish-brown hair, but those languorous green eyes and sexy-sly smile still carried an electric charge. He had seen its effect when he had gone shopping for clothes in Houston's famous Galleria. The salesgirls had fallen in love with him; salesmen had shown respect. It had also given Danny a rush to mingle with the River Oaks millionaires—people who had once paid plenty to be on his bandwagon—and go unrecognized. Yes sir, Danny still had the same charisma that he had sent pulsating over the TV airwaves, throbbing into every lonely Christian's living room as he had belted out his sermon on the "Good News Hour." And on a reverse tsunami wave, dollars had come rolling into Danny's Good News Ministries headquarters faster than his large staff could count it, wrap it, and bank it.

But not all of that money had gone into the ministry's accounts; Danny had rerouted some of those blessed greenbacks into special numbered accounts that only he and Bonner Purvis knew about. It was that secret stash that had saved him from a trial and from serving the rest of his life in prison. And now it was his to spend.

So he had health, wealth, and soon he was going to have power. Because he was a dead man, he was invisible. And ghosts could get away with anything.

The thought of it was a real turn-on. A real *hard-on.* He had once been willing to settle for the presidency of the United States; now he could have the whole world.

"The whole fuckin' world, man," he murmured to his reflection.

And his power was going to start with what he was going to do with Beverly when he found her.

The glare of headlights suddenly swept across the opposite wall. Danny went to the window and peered out again. A small blue Japanese car had just pulled into the driveway next door. Otis Quinn was home.

This is it, Danny thought, turning away and hurrying back into the other room. As he did, he tripped on something, and he had to catch himself on the door frame. He looked down; he had tripped on an arm. It was cold and lifeless now; he and Bonner had killed her a few hours ago, when they had broken into her house. It couldn't be helped; they needed to be close to Quinn.

Danny reached down and picked her up. She was naked.

He placed her gently on the bed and arranged her comfortably. He paused to look at her face and realized that she was pretty. What a shame. And he didn't even know her name.

Going back into the other bedroom, he reached for his jacket, slipped it on, and said, "Otis's home, Bon. I'm going over to pay a friendly visit."

Bonner didn't answer; he too was dead.

Danny regarded his friend's white face for a moment, the sightless eyes still staring out at the night. Danny and Bonner had been together for over thirty years, ever since their wild youth back in San Antonio, when they'd been a couple of hot young studs preaching the gospel in tents and servicing horny farm wives. Danny had known all along that sooner or later he was going to have to get rid of his best friend, because he knew too much. Bonner had taken care of everything after the faked suicide; getting Danny's "body" back to Texas, hiding him away, finding some poor bastard to take Danny's place in the coffin, and then nursing Danny back to health. But Bonner had access to Danny's fortune, and he was the only person who knew that Danny Mackay was still alive. Now, not even Bonner knew. And Danny had all that money to himself.

He flicked out the lights, said, "Adios, amigo," and left.

Otis Quinn rubbed the spot below his sternum where it felt as if he had swallowed a live coal. His ulcer was acting up again—ever since he had discovered that the woman whom he had thought was Beverly Highland turned out not to be her after all.

He flicked on the lights of his rented beach house, turned on the stereo, poured himself a beer, and went to the sliding-glass doors that opened onto a weathered sundeck. Standing at the rail, he watched the waves as they pounded the shore. It was a chilly December night; the beach was deserted. As he drank his beer, he looked to his left and was surprised to see no lights on in his neighbor's house.

He didn't really know her. She was one of those golden babe types who didn't appear to work for a living, yet she drove a Mercedes convertible and was always throwing wild parties. Otis had exchanged an occasional "Hi" with her, but she hadn't shown any interest in him. It had occurred to him during the few weeks he had been in this house to go over there and tell her who he was. He didn't doubt that she had read *Butterfly Exposed,* or that at least she had seen him on TV. *Then* she would be impressed, he was sure of that.

Otis could never understand what his problem was with women. He didn't consider himself to be bad looking; well, he was no Mel Gibson, but he was no dog either. He was fit for a guy pushing fifty; he worked out every day to keep himself trim. He still had all of his hair, and he had cultivated an intellectual's beard that he thought nicely complemented the Barry Goldwater glasses. So why was he always striking out?

Otis's stomach rumbled and a great belch erupted from his mouth. Rubbing the burning spot again, he went back inside and decided to fix himself something to eat before settling down to work.

As he slathered Dijon mustard on three slices of extra-sour rye bread, while cold pastrami was heating up in the microwave, he thought of the great break that *Butterfly Exposed* had been for him. Of course, most of what he had written was bullshit, but that was what people wanted. They ate it up. After years of churning out dreck for the supermarket tabloids, Otis had finally hit the big time. And he intended to stay in that big time—by finding Beverly Highland.

When the microwave buzzed, he heaped steaming pastrami onto a slice of rye, topped it with the second slice of bread, heaped the rest of the pastrami onto that, and topped it off with the third slice of rye. Then he went to his desk, set the sloppy sandwich beside his typewriter, and picked up the microphone of his tape recorder. He began to dictate.

"After doing some investigating into the background of my prime candidate . . ." He swiveled in his chair and looked at a newspaper photo lying on the cluttered coffee table. He had written underneath it *"Is this Beverly Highland?"* "I have discovered that she is not Beverly Highland after all. In fact, she was not even in Los Angeles during the time Beverly Highland launched her campaign of revenge against Danny Mackay."

Otis paused, took a healthy bite of his sandwich, chewed thoughtfully, swallowed, and continued: "But luckily, this woman wasn't my only lead. And after thoroughly checking out the others and dismissing them for various reasons, I have narrowed the list down to one name, and I am convinced that she is Beverly Highland. Her name is Beverly Burgess, and she runs the Star's resort in Palm Springs. I did some looking around Palm

Springs and the Coachella Valley, and all I learned was that Miss Burgess had shown up from out of nowhere two and a half years ago with enough money to purchase the abandoned Star's Haven in the saddle of Mount San Jacinto. I'm going to take a closer look at Miss Burgess. I have a reservation at Star's at the end of the week—"

The doorbell rang. Otis clicked off the machine, wiped his mouth on his sleeve, and went to the door.

He looked through the peephole but couldn't see much except the silhouette of a man against the busy traffic of the Pacific Coast Highway speeding by in the background.

"Yeah?" Quinn said through the door. "What do you want?"

"Mr. Otis Quinn? I need to have a word with you. It's very important."

Otis thought a moment. He had a lot of work to do—he had to get his file together on Beverly Burgess and plan his strategy for exposing her. But Otis was a freelance journalist, and he usually got his story ideas for the *Globe* and the *National Enquirer* from tips, which usually came at odd hours, unexpectedly, and very often anonymously.

"Okay," he said, opening the door.

"Hi," said his visitor with a charming smile.

Otis frowned. The man's face was familiar.

"I hope I'm not disturbing you," Danny said in his smoothest, most polite Texas-genteel accent.

Suddenly recognizing who it was, Otis said, "My God," and fell back a step.

Danny grinned. "Close," he said, holding out his hand. "Danny Mackay."

But Otis didn't take Danny's hand. He just stood, staring.

"Mind if I come in?" Danny said. "If this isn't a good time for you, Mr. Quinn, why you just say so. I know what a busy man you must be."

Danny looked at him expectantly, but Otis kept standing there, his jaw hanging down. So Danny came inside, closed the door behind himself, and walked into the living room. "Nice place you got here, Mr. Quinn," he said. "Great view of the ocean. I always said how you could tell God made the oceans first, because they're majestic and humbling, like Himself."

He turned and smiled at the dumbfounded Quinn. "I was wondering if I could have a word with you," he said, ending his sentence Texas style—upward, like a question. Danny knew that it was a way of speaking that generally endeared him to people. They felt comfortable with country.

Quinn started to speak, coughed, regained his composure, then said, "My God, you really are Danny Mackay! And you're alive!"

Danny tipped his head, smiled, and said, "Last time I looked, I was."

"Oh my God . . ."

"You sound like a religious man, Mr. Quinn," Danny said with a grin.

"Oh!" Otis said. "I'm sorry—my God—I mean, come in. No, you're already in. Sit down Mr. Mackay . . . Reverend Mackay . . . Danny . . .

Danny laughed and walked slowly around the room, taking in the scattered books, correspondence, news clippings, empty potato-chip bags, until his eye fell upon a newspaper photo. It was the picture of a woman and underneath it, in red ink, someone had written "Is this Beverly Highland?"

He turned and smiled at Quinn, who was rubbing his stomach. "I reckon I've given you a shock, Mr. Quinn. You thought I was dead, didn't you."

"Well," Otis said, starting to recover, "everyone thought you were, *thinks* you were, thinks you *are!* You sure shocked *me*, Mr. Mackay. For a minute there, I thought I was looking at a ghost!"

"Well, in a way, my friend, I guess you are. But it's a long story, and I don't have time for it now. However, I'll be glad to tell you all about it at some later date."

Otis's eyes widened, and Danny could imagine the cogs and wheels spinning in the man's brain. Danny Mackay—alive! An exclusive interview! Story sold to the top bidder! It would be worth thousands. *Hundreds* of thousands.

"I read your book," Danny said. "It was very interesting. You know, I never saw those rooms above that men's clothing store. Is it true what the newspapers said?"

"Uh, yes," Otis said, suddenly nervous. "My big break came when I met a girl who had worked there. I got her drunk and she told me about the special rooms. Then I got a friend of mine in the LAPD to let me have a look around."

"What did you find?"

"Nothing much, really. I had to use my imagination."

"But was it a whorehouse?"

"Oh yes, there's no doubt about that. But I couldn't believe that a man like you, I mean, that you had any involvement in it, Mr. Mackay." Otis was clearing a chair for his visitor. "Can I get you something, Reverend? Beer? Coffee?" Jesus, Otis thought, feeling the pastrami and rye turning into a Roman candle inside his stomach. Danny Mackay. Here! Talking to *me*. Oh Jesus.

"Otis, you look like a man I can confide in," Danny said, ignoring the chair. "A man I can trust."

"Oh you can, Mr. Mackay, you can!"

"Well, Otis—may I call you Otis? I saw you on TV a couple of weeks ago, and I couldn't believe what you said about Miss Highland still being alive. Is it true? I mean, do you really have proof?"

Otis felt sweat trickle down between his shoulder blades. "W-well, I kind of have proof. I mean, I think I've found her. I mean, well . . ." Jesus, he thought again, trying not to squirm beneath Danny's magnetic gaze. Otis had never met the Reverend in person, but he had heard about the uncanny power Mackay seemed to have over people, simply by looking at them. Otis tried to think. It was one thing to bullshit the public, but he knew he had to be straight with Danny. "No, I don't have actual proof, just a hunch."

Danny smiled. "A newsman's hunch? Kind of like the one that got Woodward and Bernstein the Pulitzer Prize?"

Otis's eyes widened. He liked this—Danny Mackay was obviously taking him seriously. "Yes," he said quickly, feeling self-confidence return. "It's just like that. Boy, I tell you, Mr.—Reverend, it's not easy being a good journalist. So many hacks around these days, you know? I had this hunch that Beverly Highland was still alive, so I started doing some looking. Now, I came up with several leads, and I tracked them down one by one until I think I've found the real one."

Danny reached down and picked up the newspaper photograph. He studied it for a moment, then said, "Is *this* Beverly Highland?"

Otis looked at the picture. No, she wasn't Beverly. She was the rejected one, the woman whose identity he had recently verified. "Let me explain," Otis said. "That woman is the same age as Beverly and lives a rather reclusive existence. She is immensely rich and bears a *resemblance* to Beverly. I assumed that since Beverly was so rich and involved in so many enterprises, she had invented this identity for purposes of tax evasion. Then I did some further research into this woman's background and—"

Otis turned away from Danny to reach for the file on Beverly Burgess, the woman he was now convinced was Highland. He never saw the knife. All he felt was a sudden, sharp burn across his neck, as though his ulcer had exploded and sent heat up his throat, and then there was a warm wetness on his collar.

He gave Danny a brief, perplexed look, and then he slumped to the floor.

Danny stepped over the dead man and went to the desk where he picked up the other half of Otis's sandwich. A bit too much mustard, he thought as he took a bite and chewed, but it was good enough. He couldn't take his eyes off the newspaper photo in his hand, under which Quinn had scribbled "Is this Beverly Highland?"

Suddenly he was sent back three and a half years to a suite at the

Century Plaza Hotel. The outer room was crowded with Danny's presidential campaign staff, and the phone was ringing incessantly. In the inner room, he sat with Bonner, Beverly, and her bodyguard, and Beverly was saying to Danny, "If you want me to save you, Danny, you have to beg me. I want to see you beg, the way I once begged you. One word from me, Danny, and you'll either be the next president of the United States or the world will turn its back on you and you'll spend the rest of your life in prison."

Considering the alternatives, he had had no choice. He had gotten down on his knees, with tears streaming down his face, and he had begged her.

And then she had flung him to the wolves.

He studied the face in the news photo, and while it didn't look exactly like Beverly—the face wasn't quite the same, and the blond French twist had been replaced by dark shoulder-length hair—it *could* be Beverly. Makeup altered a person's face, and she could have had plastic surgery, as she had done once before, years ago.

The longer Danny stared at the picture, the more convinced he became that she was Beverly. He wanted to believe it; he *needed* to believe it.

He read the name in the caption beneath the photo: Philippa Roberts.

Danny smiled. "Philippa Roberts," it said, "currently living in Perth, Western Australia."

So he had found the bitch. And now he was going to go after her and make her pay.

5

....★

Perth, Western Australia

When twenty-seven-year-old Ricky Pemberton had come out from Tasmania five years ago, having given up the excitement of living on an apple farm to go in search of adventure along Australia's west coast, he had not dreamed he would end up as a secretary, to a woman at that. But, as he waited for the faxed communication from Star's confirming their reserved bungalow, he looked through the window of his employer's office, where he saw the shimmering swimming pool and Doric columns standing against the sparkling backdrop of the Swan River, and he decided that he couldn't imagine a better life than working for Philippa Roberts.

And to think that he had landed the job because of a five-dollar pub wager.

It sometimes amazed Ricky to look back on those days—was it only a year ago?—when he had filled his time crewing on boats and hanging about the beach, waiting for the odd job to come along, when his entire wardrobe had consisted of jeans and an old Akubra hat that he'd bought from an Aborigine for the price of a pint. He hadn't bothered with shirts and shoes then; he'd driven a Subaru Brat with a bumper sticker that said OCEAN RACERS GET BLOWN OFF SHORE, and he hadn't known from week to week where the rent money was coming from. But he'd been happy, in a transient, looking-for-an-opportunity sort of way. He didn't want to be a beach bum forever, but he also wasn't possessed of the kind of ambition that drove other young men to go to college and make sacrifices. Ricky, like most of his friends, wanted the good life, the easy way. Many of them found it by working on the millionaire's estates that fronted the Swan River; they worked as bodyguards, boat crew, gardeners, houseboys, even dog walkers. The pay was usually good and the work generally easy.

And that was how the subject of the reclusive American, Philippa Roberts, had come up one evening among Ricky and his friends.

Although Philippa Roberts wasn't the only antisocial person living along the beach from Perth to Fremantle, she was one of the most talked about. For one thing, she had shown up suddenly two months ago, taking up residence in a villa that had stood empty for some time. For another, she headed a company that was so well known that even Ricky was familiar with it, his own mother having been a member of Starlite for as long as he could remember. And so it happened that one evening, after a hard day crewing for tourists, Ricky and his mates had been unwinding over a few beers at their favorite pub, and the name of Philippa Roberts had come up. More specifically, how to get past that high wall of hers and land a cushy job.

Ricky had seen her many times, whenever he happened to be crewing a boat or windsurfing near Point Resolution. She would appear every day at the same time and stand out on the point with her face to the wind, looking out to sea. She would stay for an hour and then walk back down the beach to the Greek-style villa where she lived alone. He had figured she must love boats and sailing. And that was when he had come up with his idea.

"I reckon *I* could do it," he had said.

"It's been tried," said his friend Freddo who, like Ricky, was tan and muscular and blond and believed that the future was only something that happened to other people. "Jacko over there walked right through her gate once, when it was open to let a furniture van in. He knocked on her door and told her he wanted a job. The chauffeur and a houseboy escorted him back through the gates."

But Ricky wasn't thinking of gates, and the wager was made. The wad of fivers was placed in Freddo's care, and Ricky set about to win it.

His plan involved the forty-foot Swan that was tied up at Philippa's private dock, an exquisite racing yacht that was left to sit out there, day after day, bobbing and swinging on the river's current, never taken out, signs of neglect showing in cracked wood and tarnished metal. Ricky chose a day when the wind coming in off the Indian Ocean wasn't too strong; he was counting on Miss Roberts taking lunch on that columned terrace behind her house. Going out on a dinghy with his equipment, he had gotten to work on the yacht, scrubbing the bird shit off the decks. Then, slipping into a wet suit and scuba gear, he went underneath to scrape the slime off the hull. He resurfaced every so often to see if she had come out, and finally his diligence was rewarded. He came up, and there she was, standing on the dock looking down at him.

As he hauled himself out of the water and shrugged out of his gear, he started to give her his prepared opening—"Looks like you need a caretaker for this boat, ma'am." But she spoke first.

"Boats frighten me," she said in a distant voice. "The ocean frightens me."

Ricky stared at her. Close up, he discovered she wasn't bad looking. He had heard that she was maybe in her late forties, and to Ricky, who was twenty-six, that sounded ancient. But he found a face barely lined, a body in halter and shorts that was well taken care of, all topped off with rich auburn hair that waved around her face in the breeze. Ricky had been prepared for a tough, aggressive woman who was all hard edges with no soft center. He had not expected vulnerability.

For a moment he was speechless, just standing there in his wet suit, dripping on the dock. Then he said, "Why? Why do boats frighten you?"

"Because someone I loved died on a boat, just over there. It sank, and he went down with it."

Ricky looked over to where she was pointing, and he couldn't recall any boats that had gone down there recently, not since—

"Are you talking about the *Philippa?*" he said. "God, I had a mate on the *Philippa!* A school chum of mine. We came out to Western Oz from Tasmania together. The *Philippa* was getting ready for the Sydney to Hobart race, and a speedboat struck her. I was standing over there," he pointed to the distant shore, "when she went down."

He felt Philippa's scrutiny from behind large sunglasses. A sea gull swooped down and perched briefly on the high white wall behind her, and then it was off again.

"When I inherited this house," she said, "this yacht came with it. But I don't want it. I suppose I should have sold it, and now it needs repair, doesn't it?"

"It needs work all right. Because it's been moored in one spot for so long, it hasn't weathered evenly. All the wood needs to be revarnished, the main halyard is frayed, I noticed some loose cleats, and you've got to do something about all these bird droppings."

"Can you do it?" she asked.

"It's nothing I can't handle," Ricky said. "She can be in perfect shape in no time. We might have to have her hauled—"

"Then do it, please. And find a yacht broker, send him to my house. I'll pay you a finder's fee, as well as whatever you charge for the repairs. The quicker this boat is gone, the better."

And that had been the start of it. After that, Philippa had found other jobs for him to do, errands to run, and when she had found out that he had had some computer training during his one year at college, she had hired him as her secretary. Ricky decided that his happiness would be perfect now, as the Star's reply began to come over the fax, if it weren't for two guilty secrets that dogged him, both of which he prayed Philippa would never find out: first, that he hadn't had a mate on board the *Philippa,* and second, that he had fallen in love with her.

The sexual aspect of their relationship had happened by accident, barely a month ago, when they had watched the Melbourne Cup race on television together. Philippa had been rooting for a horse she had chosen simply for its name, as she claimed to know nothing about horses or horse racing. When that horse had won, she had jumped up and impulsively hugged Ricky. The hug had lasted a heartbeat longer than necessary; the next moment they were kissing. Neither of them had intended for it to happen, and both had felt awkward about it afterward. But what amazed Ricky most of all was that he was in love with a woman whom he really knew very little about, even after nine months in her employ. He had been surprised when the detective came to the house a few hours ago with news of Philippa's sister. And he had been further surprised to learn that Philippa had once been named Christine. There were more mysteries to his boss than he had been aware of. The horse that had won the cherished Melbourne Cup, for example. Ricky hadn't a clue as to the significance of its name. Why should Philippa have chosen the horse just because it was named Beautiful Dolly?

San Francisco, California, 1950

"That's it, Dolly! Eat up! There's a good girl!"

Twelve-year-old Christine sat at the long mahogany dining table and devoured the spicy pork chops with relish, while her father worked in the kitchen and spoke to her through the open door. She had to laugh when she looked at him: he was wearing a tuxedo, without the jacket, and he had put on a frilly apron to protect his clothes. He had a frying pan in one hand and a spatula in the other, and he danced around the kitchen as he cooked, glancing through the open door every now and then to be sure his daughter was amused.

"Really, Johnny," said a young blond woman who lounged in a leather chair beside the fireplace, flipping through *Life* magazine. "You're feeding the girl entirely too much. She's getting fat."

"Nonsense!" he said, coming in with a steaming bowl of mashed potatoes. "Dolly's a growing girl! My mother fed me like this and it didn't do me any harm!"

"It's different for a man," the blonde said as she inspected her long red fingernails. Christine didn't care for Johnny's latest girlfriend. She didn't act like a guest at all when she came over, turning on the TV set to watch

Milton Berle while Christine was trying to read, or putting one of Christine's records on the phonograph without asking if she could.

"You tell me, Dolly," Johnny Singleton said as he set down the potatoes and did a pirouette for his daughter. "Has my cooking ruined my figure?"

Christine laughed. Her father was so trim and agile. He was perfect, in fact. She thought he looked just like Richard Conte, the actor, except taller. Johnny Singleton was slick, fast talking, sexy, and generous. He wore double-breasted tailored suits and wide-brimmed fedoras like Chester Morris as Boston Blackie. Christine could see her daddy romancing Lana Turner or Lauren Bacall; she imagined him exchanging clever words with Alan Ladd and George Raft. In fact, when Johnny had taken her to see *Call Northside 777*, she had thought for sure that people in the theater would ask him for his autograph, his resemblance to Richard Conte was that strong. And, like the movie star, Johnny Singleton always surrounded himself with pretty women.

It was to help him get over Mom's death, Christine told herself.

"What's wrong, Dolly?" he asked suddenly.

Christine looked down at her plate and saw a pork chop lying there neglected. When she saw the concern on his face, she picked up the chop with her hands and chomped into it. Johnny's face lit up. "There," he said, "nothing like a papa's cooking to make a little girl happy."

The blonde said something like "Hmph" and Johnny disappeared back into the kitchen.

Of course, Christine knew that her father wasn't a movie star. He was a businessman, although exactly what the business was she wasn't sure. Whenever she asked him, he would just laugh and tell her not to worry. They were rich, he said, and that was all that mattered. But there were times when Christine wanted to tell him that she'd rather not be rich if it meant he would stay at home, like Martha Camp's father, who had an office down on Montgomery Street. Johnny's business took him away for weeks at a time, and Christine got achingly lonely for him.

Johnny poked his head through the door and said, "How do you like those potatoes, Dolly? My own recipe. Just made it up tonight."

She looked at the steaming bowl. She didn't want to eat any. She was full. But she didn't want to disappoint him. Hungry more for his smile than for the food, she spooned the potatoes onto her plate and began to eat.

The blonde sighed and pushed herself out of the chair and went into the kitchen. A minor argument arose, which Christine caught only in snatches: ". . . too much." "She lost her mother, for Chrissake." ". . . let her get fat." "It's baby fat, Linda! It'll all dissolve away when she grows up." "Maybe her mother was overweight. Did you ever see her?" "Shut up about that!" And the kitchen door suddenly swung shut.

Christine looked down at herself. She couldn't remember a time when she hadn't been chubby, or what some people called pleasingly plump. But lately she seemed to be putting on weight in the wrong places—her breasts were starting to strain against her blouse, and her thighs were thickening. Christine was beginning to notice similar changes in other girls her age, except that on them the new bulges looked nice. On her they somehow looked like fat.

She was puzzled by what the blonde had just said, because everyone knew that Christine's mother had been slender. There was a photograph of her on the fireplace mantel.

"How's my little doll?" Johnny said now, coming out of the kitchen. He had removed the apron and put on his tuxedo jacket. Christine thought he was the handsomest man she had ever seen. He got down on one knee and looked at her. Christine saw intense love and adoration in those dark brown eyes, and she sent the same love flying straight back to him. Johnny picked up her napkin and wiped her chin. "I'm sorry I have to go out again tonight, Dolly. But you've had a good dinner, haven't you?"

"Yes, Daddy," she said, suddenly resenting the blonde who hovered in the doorway.

"And there's a surprise in the fridge for you. Caramel cheesecake from the deli."

Christine tried to hide her dismay; she hated desserts, she hated anything sweet. It was the one thing she couldn't eat to please her father. Whenever he had a dessert for her, she always saved it for later and then dumped it down the sink when he wasn't around. It was her one small deceit.

That, and the secret thing she did whenever he was away.

"Where are you going tonight, Daddy?" she asked, inhaling the fragrance of his cologne. Most men didn't wear cologne; it wasn't considered manly. But her daddy wore it, and he was the manliest man she knew.

"The Tango Club on Polk Street. I need a little fun, Dolly. I've been working so hard that I've got to relax, have a little fun."

She knew he must have been working hard because he had only come home that morning from a three-week absence, and he had looked jumpy and agitated. "Can't you have fun here with me?" she asked.

He laughed and drew her into his arms. "That's my Dolly! Yeah, we'll have fun, you and me. But we'll save it for tomorrow. I'll take you all over the city. We'll go down to Fisherman's Wharf and have steamed shrimp and lobster. And I'll take you to Golden Gate Park for a hot dog. And then we can go to the movies—anything you want to see! And all the popcorn you can eat." He drew back from her, his eyes shining with joy. "How's that, my little doll?" he said softly.

"Oh, that would be wonderful, Daddy!" she said, getting excited just thinking about it.

Johnny reached up and stroked her hair. Christine saw his eyes grow damp. "You're my little doll," he said tenderly. "I'll never forget the day you were born, when you were placed in my arms, and I almost burst into tears. I'd always wanted a little girl. Boys, you can keep them. But little girls—they're special to daddies. And you're my little doll. Ever since your poor mama died, it's been up to me to take care of you and make sure you're happy. Are you happy, Dolly? How do you like your new teacher?"

"She's all right," she said, wishing that she could go to a regular school with other kids. But Johnny insisted upon private tutors for his daughter. Christine had never been to a school in her life; for as long as she could remember, there had been governesses and tutors and bodyguards. And whenever she went anywhere, it was always in the black limousine with the bulletproof windows and one of the bodyguards driving. Daddy said it was for her protection, because they were so rich. Some people resented other people being rich, so they occasionally did mean things to them.

But Christine felt trapped sometimes, especially lately, since she had turned twelve and she had discovered a strange restlessness start to grow within her. To be confined all day to the penthouse on Nob Hill, in the company of a housekeeper, a teacher, and bodyguards who played cards all day—there were times when it was more than Christine could bear. Which was why she had invented her deception—the secret thing that she did. She knew there would be hell to pay if it was ever found out, because she knew her father wouldn't approve. While Johnny was generous about some things, like giving her food and toys and, lately, all the records she wanted, in other ways he was very, very strict.

"I tell you what, Dolly," Johnny said now. "How would you like some new clothes? I know that's one thing that makes women happy. What do you say we spend the day shopping tomorrow?"

Christine was horrified. Shopping meant going to Charlene's Chubbies on Powell Street, where only fat girls went. She hated not being able to go into the big department stores and buy something off the rack, like other girls did. Like snotty Martha Camp in the apartment next door, who thought she was something special because she was thirteen and thin and almost had a boyfriend. Martha always made fun of Christine's clothes, which consisted mainly of blouses over pleated skirts, or middy dresses with drop waists. Saddle shoes and bobby socks just didn't look right with clothes like that. Going to Charlene's Chubbies made Christine feel like a freak. The message was You're not normal, you're not like other girls.

But how could she tell her father this? His gift to her was food; her gift to him was to eat it. That was the way it had been for as long as she could remember.

One of her earliest memories was shortly after her mother died, when Christine couldn't stop crying. Johnny made her his special macaroni and cheese; Christine had quieted down. Eventually, food had become their love bond.

"Hey, Dolly," Johnny said. "I gotta go now. You do your homework, and tomorrow we'll go out. How's that?"

She pushed away from the table and stood up. It surprised her to discover that her head reached Johnny's shoulders. Surely she hadn't been this tall when he had left three weeks ago. She was thrown into a panic, and she silently begged God not to make her tall as well as fat. She felt large and grotesque enough as it was.

While Johnny called one of the bodyguards into the apartment for a murmured exchange, Christine went over to the record player and thumbed through her latest albums—Perry Como and Frankie Laine. She glanced back at the blonde, who was standing before the mirror over the fireplace and applying fresh lipstick. She was wearing an off-the-shoulder evening gown, which meant she was wearing one of the new strapless bras Christine had seen in *Vogue,* and which she knew she would never be able to wear. The blonde was very thin, like a model, and apparently Johnny liked her that way, which baffled Christine because he seemed to want *her* fat.

And then the blonde did something that puzzled Christine. She reached into her rhinestone evening bag and brought out a bottle of pills. Then, walking over to the fully stocked bar, she poured gin into a crystal glass, put a pill into her mouth, and swallowed. Christine had seen her do that before, and she wondered if Johnny's girlfriend suffered from headaches or something.

Christine glanced over at her father, who was standing in the large foyer of the penthouse, his reflection shining in the floor of gold-veined black marble. He was talking to a man Christine didn't like. There was something vaguely disturbing about him, like the way he was always trying to draw her into a conversation, asking her questions, like did she have a boyfriend, who was her favorite male movie actor? And it made her uncomfortable the way she sometimes caught him staring at her chest. He had strange, flat eyes and pale white hair cut so short that he looked almost bald. There was a scar on his face and she wondered how he got it. His name was Hans, and he had been her bodyguard for the past six months.

Finally Johnny drew Christine into a tight embrace, repeating the promise of a special day tomorrow, and she held on to him as if she would never let him go. She glared over his shoulder at the blonde in the doorway, but the woman wasn't looking. And in an instant Christine felt something she hadn't felt before: jealousy, fury, and possessiveness.

And she knew she was going to do her secret thing tonight. She couldn't help it.

Doing it, however, meant getting out of the apartment.

But that wasn't actually so hard to do. The bodyguards weren't there to keep her in but to keep intruders out, and so they weren't watching for anyone leaving. All she had to do was wait for Will, the one who sat in the kitchen guarding the back door, to get up and visit the bathroom. The bodyguards never knew she was gone because they thought she was in her room, and they never checked on her. Getting back in was a little more difficult: when the elevator reached the penthouse floor, Christine would call from the elevator telephone, and Hans would go into the apartment to answer it. Christine would sneak in while he wasn't looking, and he would think it had been a wrong number.

So now she was in her room getting ready, watched over by magazine photographs plastered over her walls. Beneath the impersonal gazes of Veronica Lake, Rita Hayworth, and eighteen-year-old Elizabeth Taylor, Christine put barrettes into her thick auburn hair to keep it from getting frizzed up in the fog. She had money in her purse and a coat over her dress. As she struggled into her shoes, she wished she could follow the latest fad and wear a loafer on one foot, an oxford on the other, with mismatched socks. But on her she knew the combination would look ludicrous instead of daring.

She waited until she finally heard Will walking across the marble floor to the guest bathroom, then she made a dash across the spacious apartment, the glittery lights of San Francisco Bay flitting by in the corner of her eye. When she was through the back door she paused and caught her breath. There were only two other apartments on this floor, the one occupied by Martha Camp and her family, the other occupied by a retired senator and his two poodle dogs. When she was sure she hadn't been seen, she hurried to the private elevator, pushed the button, and slipped inside. Her heart was pounding. If her father ever found out . . .

A week later they were on the Tiburon ferry, crossing the choppy, gray bay, and they stood on the foredeck of the boat, cold and shivering, but laughing. Christine clung to her father and never wanted to let go; she loved the feel of him, the strong, solid man feel. When she hugged him like this, it gave her the sense of self-worth and self-esteem that she so badly lacked whenever he was gone. Every time Johnny returned, Christine could feel the marrow creep back into her bones; she became real again, existing and deserving to exist.

"There you go, Dolly!" he said, pointing toward the shore. "Tiburon," he said, and she thought he made it sound so romantic and adventurous, like Shangri-la and El Dorado, not just a part of San Francisco Bay.

They had brought blankets, a picnic basket, and a Scrabble game, all of which were being carried by the bodyguards, Hans and Will, who kept an eye on their boss from a discreet distance. After the ferry docked, Johnny and his daughter walked along the main road until they came to a country lane, and they headed down it, shaded by a canopy of trees. The air was young and biting, seasoned with salt from the sea and ringing with the cry of sea gulls. They searched for a place to have their picnic; Johnny wouldn't settle for just any place, it had to be special.

Finally he found a clearing on a rise where the grass was just right, the flowers perfect, the wind not too strong, the sun soft and warm. He spread the blanket and had Christine sit down, like a princess, while he opened the basket and set out plates and napkins, knives and forks, and two crystal goblets. He did everything with a flourish, calling her "madam" and making her laugh. There was enough food for a crowd of people, but they ate it all: cold fried chicken, dill pickles, and hard-boiled eggs accompanied by pumpernickel with cream cheese and two large bottles of milk, which Johnny poured into the goblets.

While they ate Johnny asked Christine about her schoolwork. Did she like her teacher? What were her favorite subjects? And Christine asked him about his latest business trip but, as usual, Johnny was disarmingly evasive. Then they washed their hands on the soapy cloths Mrs. Longchamps had put in a jar, and they settled into a friendly, competitive game of Scrabble.

When they grew tired of the game, they meandered into the conversation they nearly always had in special moments like this. "Tell me again about Mommy," Christine said, and a change came over Johnny. The flash left him, the fast talk vanished; he grew tender and sentimental. "She was the most beautiful woman in the world, Dolly," he said, lying on his back and studying the clouds as if Sarah Singleton's face floated up there among them. "She was always rather fragile, like a porcelain figurine, and there were times when I was afraid to touch her. I never knew what she saw in a guy like me. When we first met, I had rough edges. When I spoke, Brooklyn came tumbling out. I said things like 'ain't' and 'nothin'.' And I thought acting tough was the smartest thing a guy could do."

He lifted himself up on one elbow and looked at Christine. "Your mother was a genuine lady, Dolly. She was all class, and she made me into a gentleman. She corrected my speech and picked out my clothes and took me to the opera. And everywhere we went people stared at us, they were so impressed."

"You still miss her, don't you, Daddy?"

He put a hand on Christine's cheek and said, "Dolly, that's the understatement of the century. When your mother died, when the cancer took her, part of me died, too. I pray to God that I go to heaven someday, because I want to spend eternity with your mother."

Christine was suddenly overwhelmed with feelings of love—for her father, for the mother who had made him so happy. Christine wanted him to talk about her like that someday. "Do I look like her, Daddy?" she asked, because in the few photographs they had of Sarah Singleton, the resemblance between mother and daughter wasn't evident.

Johnny sat all the way up and ran his hands over his slick hair. "You're like her in spirit and heart, Dolly, and that's what counts the most."

They decided to go for a walk then, and Christine saw an opportunity to bring up the subject of his business again. "What exactly do you do, Daddy?" She was anxious to know because Martha Camp said that her father had called Johnny a crook, a gangster, and she needed to tell Martha that her father was a liar.

But Johnny only said, "Don't let other people's opinions of us bother you, Dolly. It's how we feel about ourselves that counts. Respect yourself and others will, too."

She thought about other things Martha Camp had said, about Johnny being a draft dodger and not going to war like everyone else. But Christine knew her daddy had volunteered to enlist, but that he had been rejected because of a punctured eardrum—just like Frank Sinatra. And Christine also knew that Johnny had secretly tried to help a Japanese-American family relocate in another state, but she had to keep it a secret because what he had done was considered unpatriotic.

"We don't want to waste our time talking about me, Dolly," Johnny said as he helped Christine over a muddy stream. "Let's talk about my favorite subject—you! Tell me, what do you want to be when you grow up?"

That was not an easy question to answer, because Christine's choice of destinies seemed to change each week, depending on which magazine she was reading at the time or what movie she had just seen. At the moment, she wanted to be like Myrna Loy in *The Best Years of Our Lives* and take care of Fredric March. So she said, "I want to get married, Daddy. I want to have a husband and children and live in a lovely house."

"Baby Doll," he said, "you can be anything you set your heart on. You don't have to settle for marriage just because all the other girls do. You can reach higher than that if you want. See that bird up there, going from treetop to treetop? He isn't satisfied with just sitting on a perch and being taken care of. He's free. He's soaring. Look at him!"

She squinted up at the sky, and when she saw the bird spread its wings and glide on the currents, she thought, Daddy's just like that. And she felt her own heart soar. And in the next instant she knew what she wanted to do when she grew up. "I want to go into business with you," she said.

He laughed and hugged her, and she frowned. "But . . . how do you make money, why are we rich?"

"I make wise investments, Dolly. That's all there is to it. I just know where to put my money. Do you know what makes a good investment, Dolly? You find out what people want and you put your money into that."

"But how do you know what people want?"

"By asking yourself what you want. Tell me, what would you like most in the world, if you had one wish?"

She thought for a moment, then said, "A pill that would make me thin."

"Ho, Dolly! If I could come up with that I'd be the richest man in the world! But what's a young girl like you worrying about her weight for? When you grow up, you'll be thin, you'll see."

Christine could hardly wait for that, to be grown up and thin. Then Martha Camp and her friends couldn't tease her anymore, like the time Christine was in the lobby of her apartment building when Martha and some other girls came in, and when the elevator doors opened and Christine stepped in, the others jumped back, saying that the elevator was going to crash with so much weight in it. As the doors slid closed she had heard their laughter.

When Johnny saw her glum expression, he stopped on the wooded path and said, "You can be anything in the world that you want to be, Dolly. You might have to fight for it, but if it's your dream, then it's worth it. I haven't always been rich; I grew up in a poor neighborhood that was rough, and fighting was an everyday thing, just to survive. I was determined to rise above that and make something of myself. Do you know what General Eisenhower once said? He said that what matters is not the size of the dog in a fight, but the size of the fight in the dog. Believe in yourself, Dolly, and you will achieve anything you want."

They resumed their walk through the woods, and when Christine realized that her father's mood was growing too serious, she began to feel a small coil of panic tighten in her breast; she had a premonition about what was coming.

Finally, Johnny said, "I have to go away again, Dolly. I'm sorry."

Christine was crushed, but she was not surprised. He had been vague and distracted all week, talking for hours on the phone, leaving the apartment at odd hours. He had that restlessness that always came over him when, as he put it, a deal was working.

She walked away from him, trying not to cry. She saw her immediate future once again, just like she always did, empty and bleak, with her all alone in that penthouse, lonely, craving the sound of her father's laughter, trying to eat Mrs. Longchamps's dietetic dinners. And mostly staying in her room.

"I'm sorry, Dolly," Johnny said, coming up and putting his arm around her. "I don't like it any more than you do, but the kind of deals I work, well, they have to be done where the money is and where the connections are. You'll understand someday." He took her face between his hands. "But I want you to know that I love you, Dolly, and I always will. You're the reason I go away so much—I want you to have the best life. Each other is all we've got."

She hugged him tight, forgiving him the business trips and the girl-friends and her loneliness. Everything was going to be all right, she knew, when she was no longer a child but a grown-up. Then they would be in business together, and he would take her wherever he went.

Christine was going to do her secret, forbidden thing again. She couldn't help it; she felt miserable.

Whenever Johnny was away, the housekeeper put Christine on a diet, but Christine's system wasn't used to digesting fresh vegetables and salad greens. They gave her an upset stomach, and she had tried to remedy it with her own cooking. Now she had a terrible stomachache.

Sitting miserably in the spacious penthouse living room, with its polished floor, deco art on the walls, and clock ticking in the entryway, making the place feel like a museum, Christine gazed morosely at her father's latest gift.

The day after he had left for New York, a hi-fi player had been delivered to the apartment, complete with all of Como's and Crosby's LPs; the bodyguards Hans and Will had set it up for her. It had been exciting at first—not even Martha Camp had a hi-fi yet! But after a while the excitement wore off. It was no fun having a hi-fi if there was nobody there to share it with her.

She had decided that there was only one thing that would make her feel better—she would do the forbidden thing.

She dressed hurriedly, and a few minutes later she was down on the foggy street. She hurried along California until she came to the cable-car stop, then she climbed on board and held on to a pole, even though there was room to sit inside, because riding the cable car through the fog was part of the excitement.

She got off at the end of the line and joined the evening pedestrians on Market Street, hurrying, looking over her shoulder now and then to be sure she hadn't been seen. Then, finally, she was there, bathed in the light of a thousand bright bulbs, feeling her excitement mount as people milled beneath the marquee, buying tickets, going into the theater lobby.

Already her spirits were rising, because her friends were here, inside, waiting for her. After purchasing a ticket from the woman in the booth, Christine went straight to the candy counter, where she bought a large box of buttered popcorn, which was what she and Johnny always had when they went to the movies.

Movietone News came on first, with a report about Senator Joseph McCarthy warning President Truman that there were communists in the State Department, followed by a brief fashion announcement on the new Christian Dior look: "This year's French chic will be narrow peg-top skirts with cummerbund or belt. And here's good news, ladies. Thanks to modern methods of ranch breeding, you can have that mink stole that every woman yearns for, at an affordable price and in a variety of colors." A Woody Woodpecker cartoon came next, which meant that the feature was about to start.

Christine sat in the darkness of the movie house, happy and solaced and feeling as if she belonged. She loved the smell of a movie theater and the shared anticipation that always rippled through an audience as the main film was about to begin—row upon row of escape seekers, like herself, bracing themselves for the adventure. This was Christine's most favorite place in the whole world, and when Johnny wasn't around, it was her world, it was her secret disobedience. Johnny Singleton didn't disapprove of movies themselves, it was simply that she could only go to them with him. Sometimes he was just too protective.

When the main feature came on, Christine felt her heart begin to race: *King Solomon's Mines.* She had already seen it six times.

Movies took away the loneliness, they made her forget Martha Camp's cruel words, and Charlene's Chubbies, and Mrs. Longchamps's vegetables. Movies were like enormous doorways, opening wide and beckoning to her to step inside and, for a little while, live another life in another world. The first time Christine had sneaked out to see a movie on her own was three years ago, when Johnny was away. Before he left, he had taken her to see *It's a Wonderful Life,* and they had cried together at the end, telling each other that, yes, there were such things as angels and miracles. When the pain of missing him got to be too great, she had gone back to recapture that closeness and intimacy. Although she had discovered that going by herself wasn't anywhere near as much fun as going with her father, she did derive a certain pleasure from it, and she had been surprised, two hours later, to realize that, for a short time, she had been happy.

After that, every time Johnny went away, Christine escaped into a movie. In the movies, no one made fun of her, or scolded her for being fat, or, like Johnny's blond girlfriend, looked at her almost in disgust. The characters in films accepted her as she was, they drew her in and welcomed her into their adventure, whether it was sailing the Spanish Main with Errol Flynn or solving mysteries with Basil Rathbone and Nigel Bruce. Christine might dance with Fred Astaire or Gene Kelly; she might be Maureen O'Hara being kissed by Cornel Wilde. Best of all was to be Valentina Cortese in *Thieves' Highway* or Susan Hayward in *House of Strangers,* because those were Richard Conte movies, and he looked so like Johnny.

Christine sat now in the darkness devouring buttery popcorn as she watched Allan Quartermain lead a safari through the African wilderness, and although she knew what was going to happen next, it was just as exciting as it had been the first time she saw it. She paused, her hand in the popcorn box, and held her breath.

When Deborah Kerr started to faint and Stewart Granger ripped her blouse open, Christine thought that she too was going to faint.

And then she realized that she really *was* feeling faint; there were alarming pains in her abdomen. Putting the popcorn box on the floor and gripping the arms of her seat, she hoped the discomfort would pass. But the cramps got worse until she finally jumped up and rushed to the ladies' room. She hurried into a cubicle, and just as she pulled up her skirt, she saw blood on her slip. Christine stared at it in dumb shock. Then she screamed.

An usherette came in and found a hysterical Christine, twisting this way and that in front of the mirror, trying to see where the blood was coming from. "I'm dying!" she wailed. "Oh God, help me!"

"Oh lordy," muttered the usherette, a woman in her fifties crammed into a tight uniform designed for someone much younger. "You're not dying, sugar. Here," she said, unrolling toilet paper and folding it into a thick pad. "Put this inside your panties and go back into the theater and tell your folks to take you home right away."

"I didn't come with my folks," Christine said miserably. "I came alone."

"At this hour of the night? Well, sugar, get yourself home as fast as possible. Your ma will take care of you."

Christine sniffed. "I don't have a mother," she said. She looked at the usherette through swollen eyes. "Are you sure I'm not dying?"

The woman sighed and said, "No, sugar, you ain't. It's something all girls get at your age. You'll live."

"But what is it?"

"You get a female relative to tell you that, an aunt or a cousin."

"But I don't have—"

The usherette steered Christine to the door and said, "You get home now."

Christine ran all the way back up California Street and banged on Mrs. Longchamps's bedroom door. The housekeeper was distressed, calling Christine a poor neglected thing. She tried to explain to the girl, through her Victorian embarrassment, what was happening. "It's a wonderful thing," the housekeeper kept saying, showing Christine how to use the clumsy pads. "It's God's miracle and our special woman's gift. It means we can have babies. It means we are women."

Mrs. Longchamps didn't sound terribly convincing, and Christine hadn't seen any particular happiness or pride on her face as she had talked. Yet Christine felt herself grow excited nonetheless, because if she was a woman now, if she was grown up, then that meant that soon her father would take her with him on business trips instead of leaving her at home.

She read and reread the postcard that had come from Johnny, telling her how much he loved her but that his business trip had to be extended. She lay back on her bed and pressed the postcard to her heart, hoping to draw her father's love out of it.

Suddenly she felt a presence nearby. She opened her eyes and saw Hans standing in the doorway, his flat, colorless gaze on her.

"I hear you're a big girl now," he said, coming in and looking down at her, his eyes seeming to linger on her breasts. "How would you like me to be your boyfriend? I know about you, Christine, about your sneaking off to the movies. Now, I wouldn't want to tell your daddy, and if you're nice to me, I won't."

She sat up on the bed and drew her knees up. "What?" she said.

"I told you. I won't tell your father as long as you're nice to me." He came into the room and closed the door. "It's the housekeeper's night off and I sent Will on an errand. You and me have the place to ourselves, little girl."

"I . . . I have some money," she said, confused. "Eight dollars. You can have—"

Hans laughed. "You don't have to pay me for it, girlie. I'll give it to you for free."

"What?"

He reached down and seized her wrist, and she cried out.

"Be quiet or I'll have to get rough," he said, pulling her up off the bed. "Christ, but you're heavy. Actually, I like 'em plump. So how old are you now? Twelve? I like 'em young, too."

Christine tried to twist away, but he grabbed her other wrist and pulled her up against him and held her fast around the waist. His face was inches from hers; she looked into his colorless eyes and saw no depth in them. "Please. Don't," she said.

"Now, your daddy," the bodyguard went on, pinning her arms behind her with one hand while he fumbled under her blouse with the other, "your daddy likes 'em skinny. Like that blond bitch. But I like a girl with meat on her bones. And baby," he said as he squeezed her breast, "you've got—"

It was then that she started to scream. He plastered his mouth over hers and ripped her blouse open, but Christine continued to struggle. She felt something hard pressing against her thigh. A gun! He was going to kill her!

Then suddenly she broke free and ran for the door. He caught her and swung her around, slapping her hard across the face. "I told you to be nice!" he shouted. "Now I'm going to have to get rough."

He thrust his hand up under her skirt, but Christine kicked and fought. They fell against the nightstand, knocking picture frames off and shattering the glass. She felt his cold fingers on her bare flesh as he tried to force her legs apart.

His strength began to overcome her. Pinned against the wall, she started to cry.

And then suddenly the bedroom door crashed open. Hans flew back away from her, and Christine saw Johnny fling the startled bodyguard around and then throw him out into the hall. "You bastard!" he cried. "You filthy bastard!"

Christine stumbled out of her room, clutching her torn blouse, and watched in horror as her father beat Hans unconscious, blood spattering the floor.

When Hans lay still, Johnny came back to Christine and took her into his arms. "Are you all right, baby?" he said. "Are you all right? Did he hurt you?"

She sobbed into his neck, still shaking with fear. "Daddy, w-what are you doing here?"

"Mrs. Longchamps telephoned me. She told me about . . . what had happened at the movies. I thought I should be with you. I wanted to surprise you."

Christine was startled to see tears running down his face. "I'm all right, Daddy," she said in alarm.

"I'm going to make it up to you, Dolly. I'm going to take care of you and protect you. No one is ever going to hurt you again."

As Christine sat glumly in the visitors' parlor of St. Bridget's Convent School for Girls in Tiburon, she realized that she had misinterpreted her father's words when he had said he was going to protect her. She had thought he was going to stay at home; she hadn't dreamed that he would send her away.

One of the sisters came in, a young woman in a long black habit with countless veils and a starched wimple and a collar that creaked. "Everything is in order, Mr. Singleton," she said in a soft voice. "Christine can stay with us starting immediately."

"Thank you, Sister," he said. "May we have a few moments alone?"

When the nun had left, Johnny turned to Christine. She thought that she had never seen him look so awful. His face was drawn and haggard, as if he had gotten old in just twenty-four hours. And Christine felt somehow that it was her fault.

"Now listen, Dolly," he said very gravely. "This is just for a short time. I realize now that I can't protect you like I want to. So you'll be safe here while I do some rearranging of my life."

"Do they know—" she began.

He gave her a quizzical look, then said, "Oh, no, Dolly, they don't. No one knows about what happened but you and me."

Christine could not put her feelings into words. She felt worthless and dirty. After knocking Hans out cold, Johnny had called a doctor, not for Hans, who was dragged away by Will, but for Christine, to make sure she was all right. It was the doctor's examination that had upset her the most, the man's cold, clinical inspection of her body, not being kind or gentle about it, but brusque. It had felt far more humiliating somehow than what Hans had done to her; it had left Christine feeling she had been violated twice.

When the doctor had left the room and murmured to Johnny, "Your daughter is still a virgin, Mr. Singleton," she had burned with shame.

"It's all my fault," she said. "I was bad."

He took her by the shoulders and said, "Don't you ever say that. You're a good girl, Dolly. You're a special person, and I'm proud of you, proud that you're my daughter. I always want you to hold your head up high, like you were a princess, because then people will know how special you are."

"I'll try," she said, crying.

"You'll be safe here, Dolly," he said, drawing her into his arms. "The sisters will take good care of you, and pretty soon you'll have forgotten everything that happened. We'll start over again, you and I."

She had held on to him and cried. "Please don't leave me here! Please take me with you!"

"Don't worry, Dolly," he said, gently wiping the tears from her cheeks. "It won't be for long. Just for a little while. We'll be together again real soon. And we'll never be apart again."

Perth, Western Australia

As she rode in silence to the airport, with Charmie next to her and Ricky sitting up front with the driver, Philippa took out the folder Ivan Hendricks had brought. She stared for a long time at the classified ad: "Anyone knowing the whereabouts of, or information leading to, Christine Singleton . . ."

Then she looked again at the photograph of Beverly Burgess, who appeared reluctant to have her picture taken, and she wondered, What does this woman know about Christine Singleton?

Philippa shivered in the car's air-conditioning.

Was it possible that Beverly Burgess knew *everything?*

·····································★

The phone rang four times before a sleepy voice answered, "Yes?"

The caller's voice came over a long-distance line: "It's about Philippa Roberts."

A parrot squawked irritably and was immediately silenced. "What about her?"

"She's leaving Perth. She's going back to California. She's planning a surprise visit to the Starlite corporate headquarters."

There was a pause, and then the sleepy voice wasn't sleepy anymore. "A surprise visit? That means she suspects something. What else?"

"After that, she goes to a Palm Springs resort called Star's. She thinks her sister might be there."

"Okay, find out where she stays in L.A., who she sees, her every movement, and then report back to me. But first, there's something I want you to do . . ."

··★

Frieda Goldman had always wanted to be rich. Not just wealthy, or moneyed, but outrageously, obscenely, filthily rich. She had also always wanted to be one of the hottest agents in Hollywood—Superagent, womankind's answer to Swifty Lazar. And now, at long last, it was about to come true.

When the tram finally docked near the top of the mountain, Frieda said a hasty good-bye to Carole Page and Dr. Isaacs, the two women with whom she had shared the limousine from Beverly Hills, and made her way as quickly as she could to the main building, a castlelike structure from which inviting lights beckoned. By the time she was flying up the front steps toward massive doors that looked like they belonged on Notre Dame cathedral in Paris, her teeth were chattering and she was shivering so badly she thought she would never be warm again. There was snow *everywhere*.

A bellman had met her at the tram, explaining that her cabin was some distance from the Castle and that therefore he would be driving her to it, and he had pointed at something that looked like a golf cart. But Frieda was in too much of a hurry to bother with her room. First things first. Get to a phone, find out where her client, Bunny Kowalski, was, and then get herself up to Bunny's room. She couldn't wait to see the look on the girl's face when she told her the news about the Syd Stern deal. That ought to snap Bunny out of whatever funk she'd dropped herself into.

The main hall of the Castle slowed her down for an instant. Frieda had never seen anything like it. Designed to resemble an enormous Gothic entry hall, with stone walls, tapestries, coats of arms, and suits of armor, Star's main lobby was brilliantly lit with Christmas decorations. Fires roared hotly in three of the largest fireplaces Frieda had ever seen. The chandeliers were massive upside-down-wedding-cake affairs blazing with thousands of lights that cast glittering reflections on large blown-up photographs of Marion Star hanging on the walls. Somewhere a violinist played something romantic, reminding Frieda of the Palm Court in the Plaza Hotel in New York. A large star-splashed sign near the coat check room announced the Christmas ball, four days away.

She found the telephones—French boudoir rococo types nestled in private booths lined in red velvet. Her hands shook as she dialed the operator; she trembled not from the cold but from excitement. She thought she was going to absolutely explode with her news.

A busy signal:

"Operator, would you try again, please?"

No luck. Bunny's line was still busy.

Well, at least it meant she was in her room, wherever that was. The switchboard wouldn't give Frieda the room number. "It's our privacy policy," the cheerful young thing at the other end explained. "But I'll be glad to put you through."

When a third attempt got the same busy signal, Frieda decided to try again in a few minutes. In the meantime, she looked around and saw a sign pointing discreetly to the exclusive boutiques—Laise Adzer, Cartier, Bijan for Men—and decided that the first thing she was going to have to do was get some warm clothing. The rayon blouse and linen pants weren't going to cut it.

Returning to the phones a short while later with a full-length mink over her arm, she found the four booths occupied. She waited some more, holding on to her overnight bag and attaché case, wondering if she should just go to her room and try calling from there. "A cabin," the bellman had said. Frieda pictured something made of logs with Sergeant Preston cooling his heels out front.

Delicious aromas were starting to fill the air as more and more guests in evening gowns and dinner jackets filed through the lobby and headed toward the dining rooms. Frieda detected roast duck and thick gravies, freshly baked bread and spiced walnuts, and had to fight her desire to sit down to a serious dinner. Her weight was up again and she was back on a liquid diet; she had remembered to pack several packets of powder into her overnight case. As she looked around the hall at the famous and should-be-famous, spotting Meryl Streep, who, all in white, looked as if she should be the angel on top of the Christmas tree, Frieda detected not an ounce of fat in the crowd. The industry was unforgiving on that score; it was almost impossible to be fat *and* successful in Hollywood. For a woman, at least.

Finally a telephone was free and Frieda maneuvered herself, her two cases, and the newly purchased coat into the cubicle. As she sat down, the price tag popped out of the sleeve—twelve thousand dollars. Just like that, she had laid out twelve thousand dollars for a coat she would wear for maybe one whole day. But it didn't matter, because as soon as Bunny signed those contracts, Frieda could have a coat for every day of the year if she wanted.

This time Bunny's line rang, and it was picked up after a minute with a sleepy, "Hello?"

"Bunny! It's Frieda! I'm here at Star's."

A pause. Then, "Frieda! Gosh, what are you doing here?"

"Are you all right, Bunny? You sound odd."

"I'm okay. I've had the flu and I'm just weak, that's all."

"The flu! That's what depression does to you. You haven't been taking care of yourself. Are you sure you're all right?"

"Frieda, what are you doing here at Star's?"

"I came to see you, Bunny," she said, trying to control herself. She wanted to blurt the news. "What's your room number? I'm coming right up."

"Oh . . . no, Frieda. Not now, not tonight. I . . . I really don't feel up to it. And I'm expecting the doctor any minute. The doctor that took care of me a few days ago has left Star's, and they said his replacement was due to arrive today. I'm waiting right now to see him."

"Her," Frieda said, suddenly annoyed. "The new doctor is a her. She rode with me in the car from Beverly Hills. Listen, I *have* to come up now. I have something very important to discuss with you."

"I'm really not up to company, but I'll be fine tomorrow. How about tomorrow night? I'm sure I'll be all better by then."

Frieda stared at the telephone in bafflement. She had only ever known Bunny to be up-front and honest; in fact, the girl seemed to have a neurotic horror of telling a lie. Frieda suspected that it had something to do with Bunny's fear of her powerful industrialist father. And yet at the moment she had the distinct feeling that Bunny was hiding something. Frieda wanted to say, What's going on? Why have you stayed here so long? But instead she said, and it killed her to say it, "Well, I guess tomorrow night will have to do. If that's the only way."

"Frieda, what's this all about?"

It's about ten million dollars and turning your name into a household word. "I don't want to tell you over the phone. Get some rest, and we'll talk tomorrow night."

"Let's make it for dinner then. I'm on the third floor in the east wing, in the most amazing room. Your eyes will pop out when you see it!"

After she hung up, Frieda tapped her expensive acrylic fingernails on the top of her overnight case, agitated and restless. This was not what she had expected; something was definitely odd here. Was Bunny *really* sick? There had been something odd in her voice. Frieda shook her head, the iron gray page boy staying perfectly hair-sprayed in place. Bunny was simply incapable of lying. Well, tomorrow she would know.

Now there was the problem of what to do until then. Of course, there were phone calls to be made and contracts to go over; Frieda had other clients she was working deals for. But the Syd Stern deal was foremost in her mind, and she knew it was going to be difficult to focus on anything else. She looked around the busy lobby, wondering what people did at a place like this.

There was probably the usual entertainment: dining and dancing, maybe a nightclub act with some famous Vegas performer. Frieda had noticed a sign in the lobby informing guests of the continuous showing of Marion Star's films in the forty-seat theater on the second floor. And judging by the numbers who crowded around glass display cases filled with Marion Star's personal effects, a lot of people came here to indulge their curiosity about the legendary actress. Although the murder had taken place nearly sixty years ago, interest in it was still keen, due mainly to the fact that it involved sex and Hollywood, two delicious ingredients in any mystery. But also because, to this day, the murder of Dexter Bryant Ramsey remained unsolved.

There were a lot of hot people here, Frieda noticed: award-winning stars, producers, and directors—the whole spectrum of Hollywood types seemed to be swirling by. She watched the way they made their entrances, the places where they chose to sit in the great stone room that looked like a set from *Robin Hood,* deferring to or steamrolling over one another, major stars cold-shouldering the minor stars, establishing just who was who. Frieda found a kind of irony in the way the sultry portraits of Marion Star, once known as the supreme sex goddess of the screen, gazed down through the decades at the new generation of Hollywood royalty with her sultry, sad, sexy eyes. Frieda wondered if the looming specter of a long dead and nearly forgotten star reminded these new gods and goddesses of their own mortality.

Hot people, all of them, she thought again. And now, dammit, Frieda Goldman was going to be just as hot as the hottest of them. Just as soon as she got to Bunny.

Looking at her watch as she continued to tap costly fingernails on the case she cradled in her lap, Frieda thought she was going to absolutely explode, knowing what she knew—the most sensational news since the last Oscars were announced. News, she was certain, that was going to snap Bunny out of it and send her down from this mountain hideout faster than you could say "producer's gross."

The Oscar ceremony had, in fact, been responsible for the emotional tailspin that had driven Bunny to hide herself away at Star's. In a surprise move that had startled Hollywood, Bunny Kowalski, a relatively unknown character actress in her twenties, had received a nomination for Best Supporting Actress for her small but notable role in *Children Again*. In the time between when the nominations were announced and the winners were revealed, Bunny had suddenly found herself the center of rather bewildering and unexpected attention. People went out to see the movie and agreed that, yes, small though her part was, she *made* the movie. And everyone started to ask who *was* this rather impish, not pretty little actress who could make you laugh or cry and see the pathos in life with just a look, a spoken word?

For a while, Bunny Kowalski had shone.

And then she didn't win the award. Afterward, despite the prestige of having been nominated and the notoriety it had brought to Bunny, further success remained elusive. There simply were no movie roles for her. She was too short, too elfin; no one took her seriously; she wouldn't look credible with most leading men. "Too character type," one casting director had said. Finally, depressed and thinking that her career was over before it had started, Bunny had accepted a gift from her wealthy industrialist father: an open-ended stay at the luxurious Star's, where she could hide, nurse her anxieties, and reconsider her future in Hollywood.

Frieda had spent the time since the awards trying to find parts, any part, for Bunny, and she too had been starting to despair when the jackpot had come along in the unexpected form of a scrawny young director named Syd Stern, Hollywood's newest wunderkind. A phone call to Frieda's office and the next day she was having lunch with Stern in the Polo Lounge.

Syd explained over salmon mousse and Stolichnaya martinis that he had noticed a new movie trend beginning to emerge from the film industry, movies made from Cinderella stories, like the box-office biggies *Working Girl* and *Pretty Woman*. Syd told Frieda how he had studied the demographics of those audiences and had found that the financial success of such movies was due to the overwhelming attendance of the over-twenty-five-year-old female audience. While other studios were still aiming for the kid and teen markets, he had said, or for the Rambo-type action films that drew men to the theaters, sharp-eyed Syd had woken up to the fact that women between twenty-five and fifty, with money to spend and fantasies in need of fulfillment, were a box-office gold mine waiting to be tapped.

Now here was where Frieda came in, he said, and the reason why he had called this meeting. He had a new idea—a series of adventure films involving the same heroine, loosely based on Indiana Jones—but in order for it to work, Syd said, he knew he was going to need someone special, someone fresh and different. He had been quietly looking around when he had seen Bunny Kowalski's performance in *Children Again*.

What he liked about Bunny were her impish looks. "Like Puck," he had said to Frieda, "in *Midsummer Night's Dream.*" Bunny had a lush, Kewpie-doll figure and a bewildered child's face that endeared her to female audiences. She wasn't someone they envied or hated, but someone to whom they could relate, thinking here is a woman who is awkward at love, or clumsy in aerobics, or freaked out by cellulite. She wasn't like the hundreds of slender, beautiful actresses who filled Hollywood and who all seemed to look alike, Syd had said with enthusiasm. Physically, Bunny was unique, and that was her big plus. He envisioned Bunny as a kind of new antiheroine, like the antiheroes of the sixties, the Gene Hackman and Al Pacino characters that the audiences had rooted for just because of their flaws or for being on the fringes of society. Bunny Kowalski came across like that, he had told a flabbergasted Frieda, who had not touched her steak tartare. Bunny was going to be box-office gold.

And so, two lunches and countless phone conversations later, the deal had been set.

But one thing was turning Frieda into a nervous wreck on this snowy winter evening just days before Christmas. This was such a big, juicy plum that as soon as word was out, there would be a stampede to Syd Stern's office. Already, word was leaking out about his proposed series and that he was looking for the right actress. Sure, Syd said he wanted Bunny, but until he had Bunny's signature on these contracts, there were no guarantees.

Frieda decided to call Bunny back and tell her the news right now, but when she rang, there was no answer.

And so Frieda reached again for the phone, this time to call home and tell them where they could reach her—she had left in such a hurry she hadn't had time to phone. Then a young man walked by, wearing a tuxedo with a red cummerbund. He was tall, well built, with shoulders out to here, olive skin, and blue-black hair done in an interesting way—crew cut on top, sides swept back over his ears to join long hair at the back. Frieda watched him, partly because he was incredibly watchable. She also thought how refreshing it was to see that there were still some young men who hadn't gone in for the dirty-hair look. Did they honestly think it was sexy, all those superstars at the Oscars who looked as if they hadn't bathed in a month? How would *they* like it if women decided to join the dirty-hair trend?

When he suddenly turned and smiled right at her, she glanced back over her shoulder to see whom he was looking at. When she realized it was her, she thought he had mistaken her for someone else. But when she saw how long he stood there, still smiling, and how one eyebrow arched in an unmistakable want-to-get-it-on? fashion, Frieda was shocked. She was certainly old enough to be his . . . well, aunt, and she knew she was no beauty, being a rather horsey-jawed woman in her fifties. He paused, giving her one last look, as if asking her a silent question, and then he moved on, blending into the beautiful crowd.

Frieda stared after him. What had *that* been about? she wondered as she picked up the phone and asked the operator for a number, area code 310: Beverly Hills.

While waiting for her call to go through, Frieda gazed at her reflection in the glass partition between the phone cubicles, and she thought, as she often did, My God, I look like an *agent*. Which to her meant slightly mannish, bossy, hard-nosed. Not that that was what female actors' agents looked like; in fact, the majority of women agents in Hollywood looked like actresses themselves, being careful cultivators of slender bodies, full lips, fuller hair. Frieda was a walking stereotype, and she knew it. In her thirty years in the business, no one had ever said to her, No kidding, *you're* an agent? when she had told them what she did.

As she heard someone answer the phone at the other end, she gave another quick look in the direction of tuxedo-with-a-smile, and she wondered, What had *he* seen when he had looked at her?

"Hello, sugar?" she said into the phone. "It's Mother."

"Mom!" came her daughter's voice; in the background were sounds of people splashing in a swimming pool. "Where *are* you? Your secretary called and said you had to go out of town all of a sudden!"

"I'm at Star's."

"That place in Palm Springs? What are you doing there?"

"I came up here to see Bunny."

"Oh, *Mother*." Followed by the sigh Frieda knew so well. "When are you going to start representing winners?"

And Frieda wondered how she and Jake had managed to raise such a snob.

"Isn't there snow up there now, Mother? You know how you can't stand the cold."

"I bought a fur coat. I'll be warm enough. What? Of course it's *real* fur, darling."

Frieda's daughter was a vehement environmentalist, crusading to save planet earth by using string bags at the supermarket, separating all glass, plastic, and aluminum, recycling all paper and cardboard, including used Post-its. And above all, boycotting such man-made products as plastics, Styrofoam, and fake fur. "Mom," she had said three months ago, when Frieda had been looking at faux ermine, "are you aware of the amount of pollutants and toxins that are poured into the environment when fake fur is manufactured? It's worse than Styrofoam. And, like Styrofoam, fake fur isn't biodegradable. When you throw away an old fake-fur coat, it goes into the land, poisoning the planet. Real fur, Mom, doesn't cause pollution when it's made, and it's biodegradable because it's organic, a natural part of the environment." But she did draw the line somewhere: only ranch-bred fur was allowed, nothing trapped.

"How long are you going to be there, Mom?"

As far as Frieda was concerned, her own private fur jury was still out, but she bought the real stuff to save the family peace, such as it was. "I'm not sure how long I'll be here, darling," Frieda said. "I might have to be here for another day or two. It depends." Frieda heard childish whining in the background. "How's Princess?" she asked, referring to her three-year-old granddaughter.

Princess was the child's real name; it was actually written on the birth certificate. Frieda had thought it a bit on the fringe until she had seen the roster of Princess's preschool class, in which there was a Beauty, a Countess, and a Precious.

"Mom, you're going to be proud of your granddaughter. Do you know what she wants to be when she grows up?"

Frieda braced herself. "What?"

"A neonatologist."

"Last week you said she wanted to train Viennese Lippizaner horses."

"I took her to St. John's to see Maureen's new baby in the nursery. Princess was very impressed with the neonatal monitors. She announced that she is going to design better ones. Isn't that marvelous?"

Frieda sighed. "She's only three years old."

"And very complex, Mom. You *will* be here for Christmas, won't you?"

And suddenly there he was again, the attractive young man in the tuxedo. He seemed to be looking for someone, not anyone in particular, just someone. And as he walked by he smiled at her again, giving her the same look he had given her a few minutes ago. It nonplussed Frieda, who was unused to male attention, especially from a male who looked as if he could have any woman in the place. And then she recalled what her friend had told her, about Star's special "escorts." Was he one of them?

She pushed him from her mind. Other women had sex with strangers, paid for it even, but not Frieda Goldman.

"It depends," Frieda said into the phone, following the young man with her eyes and wondering how the hotel handled payment for the special escort service. "I have business to take care of here."

"You're being very mysterious, Mom."

"I take after my granddaughter," she said, thinking, It's Bunny who's being mysterious. *Too* mysterious. "I'll call you when I know something."

She hung up and immediately dialed again, reading a number from a business card. "Hello," she said when she got an answer. "Mr. Bradshaw, please." Then, "Hi, Mr. Bradshaw, this is Frieda Goldman. Yes, fine, thank you. I was just wondering—that Lamborghini I ordered this morning"—the one with the two-hundred-thousand-dollar price tag—"does it come in any other colors besides red, white, and black?"

Dr. Judith Isaacs was getting acquainted with the small private clinic of Star's, which was located on the second floor of the west wing of the Castle, cut off from the rest of the mansion by a closed doorway marked PRIVATE. The medical suite consisted of a small operating room, a recovery room, a substerile room, and a supply room. She came upon a cupboard labeled Tits, and as she gazed at pale blue boxes, stacked upon one another on the shelves, she heard a voice behind her say, "Those are the breast implants."

Judith turned and saw a woman she judged to be around thirty, very thin, with pale brown hair, wearing a T-shirt and jeans. She came into the room with a smile on her face. "Cheeks are in here," she said, pulling out a drawer. "Chins and noses in this one; penises over there." She smiled broadly at Judith. "Hi, I'm Zoey Larson, the nurse. You must be the new doc."

Judith took the outstretched hand. "How do you do," she said.

"I suppose Simon Jung told you about me. I'm a registered nurse," Zoey said, "with experience on the floor and also in the operating room. I've been here since Star's first opened two years ago. The clinic's pretty quiet; mostly we see sports sprains, the occasional stomach upset, rashes, and minor infections. We also see a lot of sex-related problems, like bladder infections, vaginitis," she added with a laugh. "Something about this place makes people get romantic. We also see respiratory problems because the guests forget that they're eight thousand feet above sea level. We get only the beautiful people here at Star's, and if they aren't beautiful, we make 'em that way! Three plastic surgeons from Palm Springs schedule private patients up here," Zoey continued, reaching up to push a hank of brown hair out of her face. "They check in with us afterward and come up the mountain to do post-op care. The routine stuff is left to the resort doctor, which is now you," she said with a grin. "Welcome aboard."

"Thank you," Judith said, looking around and spotting, in the substerile room, an ashtray full of cigarette butts.

"If you have any questions," Zoey said, "I'll be glad to answer them. Have you ever worked at a resort like this?"

"No," she said, "I never have."

"It's not like a real hospital, I'll tell you! We see a lot of famous people, movie stars, like that. We get some real doozies, too, because we're so private." Zoey folded her arms and leaned against a cabinet. "Most of our patients are in the building, just down the hall. We currently have four. I'll let you in on a secret, Judith," Zoey added with a conspiratorial smile. "You've landed a cushy job."

When the nurse stepped away from the cabinet, Judith caught her own reflection in the glass door. She stared at herself for a moment, as she had found herself doing lately, as if she were looking at a stranger. Judith saw a woman in her late thirties, not bad looking perhaps, with thick waist-length mahogany hair worked in a long braid down her back. Judith had never had problems with her looks; it was her mind she had always focused on. Was it good enough? Was it up to par? Could she make it through medical school and four years of residency? It had always been important, for as far back as she could remember, that she face mental obstacles and overcome them. She wasn't into physical fitness; brain marathons interested her more. Judith had graduated at the top of her medical school class; she had excelled during her internship and residency in Michigan. And that was why, when she had had her practice at Green Pines, in northern California, she had received invitations from medical centers and medical schools around the country hoping to recruit her. She had been a young woman going places. Now, she was a not-exactly-young woman who was already at a place. A "cushy" place.

Zoey said, "You'll have things really easy here, Judy. I do most of the work running this clinic. Having a doctor in residence is to satisfy a legal requirement."

Judith looked at her. Zoey had a pleasant, open face, and she stood relaxed, with her arms crossed, as if she were entertaining in her own living room. Judith thought about the time she had once asked an operating room nurse—a woman who had automatically addressed her as Dr. Isaacs—why some nurses addressed female physicians by their first names, even when meeting them for the first time. The nurse had said, "I suppose it's to be friendly, to let them know they are part of a sisterhood." But Judith wasn't so sure. For some reason, female nurses accepted the authority and superior status of male physicians and would never think of addressing a male doctor, especially one they had just met, by his first name. But when they saw a female physician, it seemed that they saw just another woman.

As Zoey's last confidently spoken words continued to hang in the air, Judith thought about her employment interview for Star's. She had not been hired by the owner of Star's, Beverly Burgess, whom Judith had never seen and whom she had yet to meet, but by the very handsome and elegant Simon Jung, the general manager. They had met at the Ritz-Carlton in Palm Springs for dinner, and they had talked. "We're looking for a physician who doesn't mind isolation," he had said. "You will be expected to live at the resort, and it can get lonely. Dr. Mitgang, your predecessor, found the quiet life too boring, which is why we decided this time to look for someone who is happy with this sort of arrangement, and also a physician who is used to managing a small clinic. I understand, Dr. Isaacs, that you live in an alpine community right now. You must be used to skiing injuries, that sort of thing."

Simon Jung had then looked at her application. "You're not married, I see."

Judith thought of Mort, her husband, and their last afternoon together after fourteen years of marriage. Mort was watching college football, and his team, the team of his alma mater, wasn't doing well. With each unscored touchdown, his silence deepened. Judith had been about to put a casserole in the oven. Instead, she put it on top of the TV and said, "I'm leaving you."

He hadn't said anything and she had packed her bags. The Bruins lost and so did Mort and Judith.

"I'm divorced," she said to Simon Jung.

"Any children?"

She hesitated. "No," she said. "No children."

"This really is a great job," someone was saying to her. She looked at the thirtyish woman in the T-shirt and jeans. "Most employees live in the valley and come up every day on the early tram," Zoey continued. "But I'm on twenty-four-hour call. I don't mind it. The pay is great, and since I'm among the few employees who live up here on the mountain, I get to use the resort facilities—as long as I don't interfere with the guests, if you know what I mean."

Judith looked into the woman's broad smile.

Simon Jung had outlined the fringe benefits Judith would receive while working at Star's: an apartment in the Castle, meals in the dining room, where excellent cuisine was served, maid service, room service, a generous salary, and light duties.

When he had said, "Do you have any questions?" Judith had said, "Will I have to take care of any children?"

"Children? No. Children aren't allowed at Star's. No one under eighteen."

And that was what had sold her. The nearest kids were down in the valley, eight thousand feet below.

"Judy?" Zoey said. "Would you like to meet your patients?"

Judith said "yes," looking around again, avoiding her reflection in the glass of the surgical cupboard. Whoever that woman was, whoever she had been, she no longer existed. Judith Isaacs was no longer the *other* Judith Isaacs. She had come up here to bury herself in the snow and she was never going to leave. "I also want to make some changes around here. Starting with no more smoking," she said, indicating the overflowing ashtray. "And I would like that label removed," she added, pointing to the Tits cupboard. "By the way, do you own a uniform?"

"Sure. But it really isn't necessary here," Zoey said. "I mean, it's not as though we're a real clinic, is it? The patients all know who I am."

"I would like you to wear a uniform whenever you're on duty. And if you don't mind," Judith said, "I would appreciate it if you addressed me as Dr. Isaacs for now. Shall I call you Nurse or Ms. Larson?"

"Just Zoey is fine," she said, turning frosty. "Is there anything else?"

"I would like to see my patients now."

"Yes, Dr. Isaacs."

They left the clinic, which had once been guest bedrooms, and walked down a darkly paneled hall. As Judith followed Zoey, her medical bag in hand, she thought of the movie *Jane Eyre,* when Orson Welles as Mr. Rochester said to Joan Fontaine, "Do you faint at the sight of blood?"

"The first patient," Zoey said as she stopped before a door and handed Judith a chart, "came in for chest implants a week ago."

"You mean breast implants."

"No, *chest.* The patient is a man."

When Judith saw him, he was vaguely familiar to her, the star of a popular TV sitcom. His torso was wrapped mummylike with tight pressure bandages. Muscle-shaped silicone pads had been inserted under his chest to give him a body-builder look; it was a variation on the breast implant procedure, and it was becoming the latest thing for men to have done.

"Our next patient," Zoey said as she and Judith continued down the hall, "was admitted three days ago. Dr. Newton performed surgery on him day before yesterday, and he's been in a lot of pain all day. I've had Dr. Newton paged, but he hasn't answered yet."

Judith read the patient's chart as she walked along. "Mr. Smith," the chart said—not his real name. When she saw the real name she was momentarily taken aback. "Mr. Smith" was a screen legend, known mainly for playing romantic leads in swashbuckling and adventure films; Judith had grown up on his movies. Coming from a small community in northern California, she wasn't used to dealing with famous people.

"Does he have a fever?" she asked as they neared his room.

"Vital signs were normal an hour ago," Zoey said.

"Does he have any difficulty urinating?"

"No. I suspect his problem is with the incision, but he won't let me look at it."

Judith scanned the chart again. According to Dr. Newton's notes, Mr. Smith was sixty-nine years old, six feet one, 195 pounds, well nourished, and in good health. Treatment: abdominal liposuction.

Zoey knocked on the door and said, "Mr. Smith? The doctor's here."

As with the previous patient, Judith was startled when she entered the room. She had expected to find a gloomy setting with a monstrous four-poster bed draped in heavy velvet curtains. These rooms didn't look at all like they belonged in the Castle, nor did they look like hospital rooms, with pale peach wallpaper and airy curtains, white carpet, plush desert-tone furniture, and Southwest paintings on the walls. But the subtle hospital signs were there: the oxygen outlet in the wall near the bed, the hookups for monitors, the track in the ceiling for drawing a curtain around the bed, and of course the bed itself, which was a standard hospital bed.

And then she saw the man sitting up in that bed. With his silver hair, tanned good looks, and monogrammed silk pajamas, he added the final touch of elegance to the room.

Judith hesitated for a split second. There was a time when this man had been her screen idol.

"Who are *you?*" he asked in his famous cultured Scottish accent.

"I am Dr. Isaacs, the new resident physician."

"I'll wait for Dr. Newton," he said, waving her away.

Zoey said, "We're trying to locate Dr. Newton, Mr. Smith. But it'll take a while. He's down in Palm Springs."

Judith approached the bed and said, "Since your personal physician is unavailable at the moment, Mr. Smith, perhaps I can help." Closer up, she saw the fine dew of perspiration on his forehead, the shadow of pain around his eyes.

"But you're a woman," he said.

"Zoey tells me you're in pain."

"It can wait for Dr. Newton."

Aware of Zoey's eyes on her, Judith said, "It's important that we determine the source of your pain, Mr.—" She stopped herself before saying his real name. "If the pain is being caused by something that is interfering with your blood circulation, then there is danger of losing the affected area."

"Losing it?" he said, looking at her.

"Yes. A body part that isn't receiving blood will die." She held up her hand and squeezed the base of the little finger on her right hand. "Like what happens with frostbite."

He murmured, "Good God," then he said, "I suppose you know who I am?"

Yes, she did. She couldn't stop thinking of her favorite movie of his, when he had played a pirate and Rhonda Fleming was his unwilling captive, back in the forties. "You're my patient," she said. "And one," she added more gently, "who is in a great deal of pain. Now please, I'll just take a look and see what I can do."

"I don't feel right about a woman taking care of this," he said unhappily.

"Mr. Smith," Judith said, "for years women have gone to male gynecologists. Would you have been surprised if they had complained?"

"That's different."

"Why?"

He gave her a wary look. "Are you a real doctor?"

She smiled. "Of course I am. What a question."

"In my experience," he said, "which is considerable, real doctors don't work in places like this. Doctors on cruise ships, for instance. Aren't they doctors who can't make it in the real world?"

"Well," she said, "I'm the only doctor here at the moment, real or not." She paused and added, "I was also married for fourteen years. Does that help?"

Judith asked Zoey to leave the room, then she set her medical bag down and drew Mr. Smith's blanket down to just below his navel. While she inspected the pressure dressing that had been secured around his pelvis like a girdle, explaining that she was looking for subcutaneous bleeding and signs of infection, Smith kept his eyes on the window, where snowflakes gently fell. He saw the silhouette of alpine forest against the night sky. He willed himself far away from the pain, and the embarrassment. "I promise you," Dr. Newton had told him before the surgery, "that you will come out of this with the abdomen of a younger man."

"Such torture," he said now with a sigh. "All for the sake of vanity."

Judith gave him an encouraging smile. "Everything looks fine," she said as she drew the blanket back up. "I'll give you something for the pain. If you have any more discomfort be sure to call for the nurse at once." She smiled and touched his shoulder. "I know it's uncomfortable, and I'll do whatever I can to relieve it. Our main concerns are infection and bleeding. It is essential that the incision be kept clean and that this pressure dressing be kept in place."

"I'm aware of the seriousness, Doctor," he said. "It's my vanity that galls me. The fear that a paunch will destroy my reputation. Not that I really had a paunch, but I saw the signs. For the first time, exercise wasn't helping. May I ask your name, Doctor?"

"Dr. Isaacs," she said. And then added, "Judith Isaacs."

"And may I call you Judith?"

"If you wish."

"The nurse says you're just starting here, a new job. Now I'm curious. Where does an experienced and clearly competent physician suddenly materialize from? I mean, what have you left behind in order to serve the cream of humanity up here?"

She reached back to make sure her hair was still neatly braided—a nervous, self-conscious gesture. She didn't answer him.

"Do you mind if I ask you a personal question, Judith?"

"It depends," she said.

"What is a young, pretty woman like you doing in this isolated place? Why aren't you out in the world, getting involved with life?"

"I was involved with life, Mr. Smith. And now I want to try something else."

He gave her a searching look. "I sense something closed about you," he said.

She looked at him, remembering when she had been fourteen and had first seen him on late-night television, in an old black and white movie with Olivia de Havilland. Young Judith, adolescent and hormonal, had fallen desperately in love.

And now, thirty-eight-year-old Judith was stunned to experience the same swift sexual charge. "I'll check on you later," she said, starting for the door.

"I'm sorry if I've embarrassed you," he said. "I don't know why I suddenly got so nosy. I don't normally ask personal questions like that." He smiled charmingly, although a ripple of pain distorted it. "Especially on the first date."

She came back to the bed, amazed to feel how she was reacting to him, and afraid of it. "I won't be far," she said quietly. "I'll be having dinner with my new employer, so if you should have any more trouble, or if you"—*just want some company*—"need something to help you sleep, have the nurse come and get me. I'm on twenty-four-hour call."

St. Bridget's Convent School, Tiburon, California, 1950

Christine sat in the parlor amid the lemon-polished furniture and vases filled with fresh flowers, her only companion a white plaster statue of Saint Bridget, patroness of Ireland, standing in a holy niche with daffodils at her feet. The open windows admitted sunlight, bay breezes, and the sounds of girls enjoying an afternoon visit with friends and relatives. This was the seventh day in a row, since her arrival a week ago, that Christine had sat patiently and silently in the visitors' parlor, waiting for her father to come, the suitcase, as always, on the floor beside her, her coat laid neatly over it.

Christine looked again at the clock on the wall. The minutes were inching by at a phenomenally sluggish pace. Surely time had never been this slow in the past, not even when she had languished in the penthouse, waiting for her father to come home. She went to the window and looked out at the driveway entering the convent grounds, expecting to see a familiar black limousine coming through the gates, because she knew for sure that her father would come today, this being Saturday, the one day of the week when visitors were permitted on the grounds. He would arrive at any minute and say, "Okay, Dolly, everything is taken care of. I got us a house in the marina, and I've taken a job on Montgomery Street so we'll never be apart again."

Christine watched with envy the girls on the lawn and in the formal gardens, talking and laughing with parents and brothers and sisters, picnicking on the grass with their families, or sitting on white wrought-iron garden chairs, drinking tea, chatting with the nuns. She felt a pain radiate out from the center of her breast, a deep, lacerating pain that hadn't eased since the day her father had left her here, one week ago.

She didn't like St. Bridget's. Since she was only a temporary student and not permanently enrolled, she had not been put with the other girls, but instead had been given a room by herself in the wing where the novices lived, away from the students, away from the staff of religious sisters who ran the convent, as if she were a kind of pariah, contaminated in some way. The novices' wing was maddeningly quiet, the young women in simple gray habits moving down the halls whispering prayers, under strict rules neither to speak nor to look at someone unless it was absolutely necessary. Christine felt cut off from the world. She had cried herself to sleep every night, trying to understand what had happened, what she had done to cause this.

The incident with Hans, the way he had attacked her, the things he had said, his hands on her body . . . Had she somehow caused it? Was it her fault that he had done what he did? Christine thought about the time she had overheard Mrs. Longchamps gossiping with the doorman of their apartment building about a woman in the neighborhood who had been sexually attacked. "I'll tell you what I think," the housekeeper had said. "She was asking for it." How did a woman "ask for it," Christine wondered? Was *I* asking for it?

The bells in the tower chimed and Christine, startled, looked at the clock. It was already time for the visitors to leave! She watched the girls hug and kiss their guests good-bye, and she wanted to shout, No, don't go yet! My daddy is still coming!

A group of girls came into the parlor, led by a fourteen-year-old named Amber who had honey-colored hair, a large bosom, and a beautiful face. As the girls passed through, Amber pointed to Christine and whispered something to another girl, who giggled. Christine felt her cheeks burn. It was not the first time Amber had done such a thing, pointing rudely at her and whispering to another girl, who then laughed. Christine wondered what it was that Amber always whispered that others found so funny. She looked down at her old-fashioned dress, which she knew did not disguise the fact that she was fat. The other girls all looked smart in their school uniforms, Amber in particular, tall and slender and already womanly, giving the white blouse and pleated navy skirt a kind of fashionable style.

A nun finally came into the parlor, a long wooden rosary clacking among the folds of her voluminous black habit. When she saw Christine standing there all alone in the fading sunlight, the long shadows gathering around her, she said, "Dear oh dear! It's time to get ready for dinner, child. Come along now."

Christine gave one final forlorn look out the window, where she saw the last of the visitors' cars leaving and the gates closing—a scene of brutal finality, she thought, as though she were being locked inside a cage. Then she released a sigh that was almost a sob, picked up her suitcase and coat, and followed the nun back into the convent.

The dining room was a large hall with beam ceilings, tall stained-glass windows, and a stone floor. The resident girls sat at long tables running the length of the hall, while the staff sat on a raised dais at the head of the room, their tables facing out toward the girls. This was where Christine had been placed, at the end of the staff tables, next to an elderly nun who was almost deaf. While Mother Superior, in a white habit, led the students in grace, Christine peaked over her folded hands and saw Amber at the nearest table, watching her.

Dinner was served by the novices, young women who were learning discipline and sacrifice; they did most of the work at the convent and ate their meals in the kitchen after all the tables had been cleared. When a plate was set before Christine, she stared glumly at the honey-glazed ham and candied yams.

The food was one of the worst aspects of St. Bridget's. On her first morning there she had been expected to breakfast on hot chocolate and waffles in syrup. While everyone else had seemed to regard this as something of a treat, Christine had known that to eat it meant that she would feel shaky and light-headed by midmorning. So she had pushed the food around her plate, arousing the curiosity of the elderly nun at her side, who had muttered something about sulking children not appreciating the good Lord's bounty. By noon, having not touched the breakfast, Christine had been very hungry and had been devastated to see that lunch consisted of a fruit salad and juice. With the elderly nun giving her a sharp look, Christine had forced herself to eat it. By afternoon she had been so sick and light-headed that she had almost fainted in chapel.

It wouldn't be for much longer, she reassured herself. Her father would come soon and take her home.

As she tried to swallow the sweet ham, Christine looked around the noisy dining room and saw Amber staring at her, and she was surprised to see a trace of hostility in those unsettling gray eyes. Christine sensed that the girls resented her, and she supposed it was because, as a temporary guest at the school, Christine didn't have to abide by the strict school rules. She also didn't have to wear the school uniform but was allowed her own clothes, had a private room instead of sharing in the dormitory, didn't attend classes, and sat with the staff at meals. She was clearly too privileged for the girls' liking. As if to confirm her suspicion, she saw Amber say something to the girl next to her, who then shot Christine a look.

Please come for me, Daddy, she prayed silently. Take me away from here. I'll never be bad again, I promise.

At the end of dinner, after the prayer of thanks, a nun came up to Christine. It was Sister Gabriel, who had admitted Christine into the school a week earlier. Christine liked Sister Gabriel, who seemed kinder and more understanding than the other nuns. She was also very pretty, Christine thought, despite the starched wimple that pinched her face.

When she said, "Will you come to my office with me, please?" Christine's heart jumped. Daddy was here! He *had* come after all!

But to her disappointment, Sister Gabriel's office was empty.

"Please sit down," the nun said.

Sister Gabriel's voice was lilting and melodious and seemed to match her lovely looks. "I asked you here, Christine," the nun said, "because we have received instructions from your father regarding your stay here. He has sent us payment for half a year's room and board, and he has asked us to enroll you in the school."

Christine stared at her. "What do you mean?" she said.

"You are joining the school, Christine."

"Oh, I don't think so. That's not what my father told me."

"I have his instructions right here."

"It's a mistake. My father said I would only be here for a little while."

"I understand your confusion, Christine," Sister Gabriel said gently. "I know you weren't planning on staying with us for long. But here is his letter to us. And he sent a letter to you also," she added, handing her an envelope.

Christine looked at her name written on the white envelope—it was in her father's handwriting. Inside she found a letter, two photographs, and a hundred-dollar bill. Through stinging tears she read his words: " . . . sorry to have to do this, Dolly, but it's necessary right now . . . Always remember that you are special. Hold your head high like a princess . . ."

From far away she heard Sister Gabriel's voice saying, "You will be measured for a school uniform, and you will be assigned a room in the dormitory."

When Christine could no longer make out Johnny's writing through eyes swimming with tears, she looked at Sister Gabriel, unable to speak.

"I tell you what," the nun said as she came around the desk and placed a hand on Christine's shoulder. "We'll go straight to the dormitory and you can get settled in. The girls are at chapel, so this will give you a few moments to yourself. I'm sure you'll be happy here, Christine. I've decided to place you with one of the older girls, so that she can help you make the adjustment. Her name is Amber. Well, her name isn't really Amber, it's Alexandra Huntington, but a tradition was started in this school many years ago, a tradition started by the girls, of having everyone go by a nickname. I think it makes them feel more like sisters. I know you and Amber will get along just fine."

★ ★ ★

Christine had just finished unpacking her things and placing them in the small dresser at the foot of her bed when she heard the girls coming down the hall. She froze.

"Well!" came a voice from the doorway. "What have we here?"

She turned and saw the girls standing there, Amber towering over them because she was the tallest, her honey-colored hair framing an arrogant, pretty face. The girls clustered nervously around Amber, excited, as if ready to imitate her every move, follow her every command. And suddenly Christine was afraid.

"Who are you?" Amber said. "And what are you doing in *my* room?"

Before Christine could reply, the older girl walked in, grabbed a slip out of Christine's suitcase, held it up, inspected it, then dropped it on the floor. "Looks big enough for an elephant," she said, and the others giggled.

Amber faced Christine directly, hands on her hips, and said, "This is *my* room. I asked you what you're doing here."

Christine searched for her voice. She had never been surrounded by so many girls before; she had no idea how she was supposed to handle a group. Martha Camp was one thing, but six or seven pushy girls was another. "I—" she said. "I—, I—"

And Amber turned away, threw up her hands, and said, "Aye, aye aye aye aye." Her admirers burst into laughter.

The fourteen-year-old turned and leveled her gaze at Christine. "Look," she said, "I know you've been assigned to this room. So you have to learn our rules. You see how many beds are in here? Four. That one over there, by the window, is mine. I run this room, understand? And I run this hall. I make the rules. And the rules go like this: You keep your garbage on your bed, you don't get any floor space, you can't use the closet, and the radio is off-limits to you. If you want to put pictures on the wall, you ask my permission first, and then *I* say what you put up. And if you go running to Sister Gabriel like a tattletale, you'll be dealt with most severely."

Amber walked over to Christine's nightstand, moving with a swishy sashay that made her skirt swing, and she reached for the double photograph frame Christine had placed there. In one frame was her father's picture, in the other, her mother's.

Amber's gaze settled for a long time upon Johnny, then she said, "Who's this?"

"My father."

"Hmp," Amber said contemptuously, dropping the black plastic frame onto the nightstand with a clatter. "What does he do?" she said.

Christine gave her a baffled look. "What?"

"What does your father do? How much money does he make?"

"I . . . don't know."

Amber turned to the others, pulled a face, and mimicked, "I don't know." She turned back to Christine and said, "Let me tell you something, Chubby, I don't like peasants. My mother is a countess. She's in France right now, vacationing with the king and queen of England. We're very wealthy and very important, so I can't be bothered dealing with people beneath me. Do you understand?"

Christine didn't understand at all, but she said, "Yes."

"What's your name?"

"Christine Singleton."

"We don't go by real names here, Singleton. We have nicknames. Mine is Amber. You'll need one, too."

"Well," Christine started to say, "my father calls me Doll—"

Amber's eyes turned hard. "You don't choose your own nickname, idiot," she said, and the others snickered. "*I* choose your new name for you. When I have decided, I'll tell you. In the meantime, you don't have a name, is that understood?"

And again, although she didn't understand at all, Christine nodded.

"And one more thing," Amber said as the bells chimed and the girls began to disperse to their rooms, "you put your garbage where I tell you to." And she reached into the dresser, pulled out Christine's neatly folded things, and tossed them onto the floor.

Sister Gabriel handed out the last of the packages and letters in the parlor, and when she said, "That's all, girls," those who had not received mail drifted away silent and dejected. Christine was among them; she had been at St. Bridget's for one month, and she had not heard from her father.

Unable to bear the laughter and excited chatter of those who had gotten mail, she went outside, where sunshine spilled over beds of bright pink petunias and purple pansies. Every day she went to mail call in hope, and every day she left in disappointment. But she did have that first letter, the one she had received in Sister Gabriel's office, and she would console herself with it now, reading it in privacy, pretending that it had just come today.

She went to a small grotto that stood at the edge of the convent's perfect gardens; inside, a rose arbor enclosed a shrine to the Virgin. The white statue of Mary stood among moss and bougainvillea, and a trickling fountain created an atmosphere of serenity, repose, and forgiveness. Christine had come here often in the last three weeks, and she had always had the place to herself. But today she was startled to find someone else there, a girl she had seen in the halls and at meals, a short, chunky girl with freckles and a frizzy mass of hair that was such a deep red brown that it was almost the color of burgundy. She was sitting on the marble bench and she was crying.

"Are you all right?" Christine said.

The girl looked up. "Oh, yes," she said, running her hand under her nose. "I just got some bad news, that's all."

Christine sat next to her, offering a clean handkerchief.

"Thanks," the girl said.

"Gee," Christine said. "I'm sorry about . . . whatever it is." She noticed the crumpled, tear-stained letter in her lap—a short sheet of paper, torn out of a dime-store pad, with just a few lines written on it.

"It's from my mother," the girl said, drying her eyes and handing Christine's handkerchief back. "She says she isn't coming for my birthday after all."

"Oh."

"It's not my mother's fault, really. It's just that, well, after my father died she got married again, and her new husband, well, he thinks I'm in the way. That's why they sent me here. They live back east, and they don't come to visit much. I just get so blue sometimes, you know?" She managed a smile. "My name's Frizz, what's yours?"

"Christine. Is your name really Frizz?"

"No, that's just the name the girls call me here. You're new, I know. I've seen you around."

"I've seen you, too. You're the one who got into trouble for goofing off in Sister Immaculata's history class."

"Yeah," she said with a smile. "That was me. So why are you here? At St. Bridget's, I mean."

"My father travels a lot, and I don't have a mother, so he thought it would be best if I was here. Why do they call you Frizz?"

"Amber gave me that name because of my hair. She says it's ugly. She's right. I hate my hair."

"I think it's a very pretty color. Mine is so ordinary. I wish I had your color."

Frizz stared at her with swollen eyes, then said, "I don't have any friends here, do you?"

When Christine shook her head, Frizz said, "Well, why don't you and I be friends then?"

As they walked across the lawn toward the school, with the bells in the tower chiming the dinner hour, Frizz said with a sigh, "It's just as well that Mom isn't coming for my birthday, I suppose. She always depresses me when she visits, always talking about the fun things she and my stepfather are doing. I don't like him. He didn't even adopt me, so my last name isn't the same as theirs. He's such a jerk. And my mother's always criticizing me. I can't ever please her. I'm going to be thirteen next week. How old are you?"

"Twelve."

As they followed the hall toward the dining room, passing a group of girls who were squealing over a photograph one of them had just received—the picture of a male cousin, whom the others all declared was a real dream—Christine saw Amber up ahead.

"How did Amber get her nickname? Is it because of her hair?"

"I heard that she chose her own nickname when she got here," Frizz said as they took places in the dining hall. "It's because her mother is a countess, she said that she had the right to pick her own name."

"But why Amber?" Christine said, curious about the girl who was making her life miserable. Christine's existence, in just three short weeks, had been reduced to the single element of survival. She had quickly learned to avoid encounters with Amber. Fortunately, the two did not attend the same classes, and so confrontations during the day were rare, but evenings were dangerous, when the girls had free time while the nuns were at their prayers. That was when Christine had to be her most vigilant. She found on her first night in the dormitory that it was not wise to climb into bed without first drawing the covers all the way back and checking the sheets. That first lesson had involved a harmless garden snake, but she would never forget it. Mornings could be hazardous as well. Christine had learned to hang back and wait until Amber was finished and gone before she dared use the communal bathroom down the hall. It meant rushing to get dressed and then receiving a scolding by one of the sisters for always being late to breakfast, but after having gotten locked in one of the toilet cubicles one morning, and another time coming out of the shower to find her clothes and towel gone so that she had had to run wet and naked down the hall to her room, Christine had decided that a scolding was preferable.

"So why did she choose Amber for her nickname?" Christine asked.

Well," Frizz said in a conspiratorial tone as she pulled out a chair and sat down, her burgundy-colored hair falling over her shoulders and brushing the table. "She bragged about getting hold of a copy of *Forever Amber*. If the nuns had found out, Amber would have been expelled from the school. Anyway, she went about telling everyone how she had actually read it from cover to cover."

Christine was well acquainted with *Forever Amber*. She had not read the book, but she had seen the movie five times, and the image of Cornel Wilde, with his long hair and bare, muscular chest, suddenly flashed in her mind.

Frizz continued, "Amber claims that she's just like the Amber in the book. She likes to think she's fast."

"What you mean?"

Frizz leaned over and whispered, "You know, in the *bedroom.* Amber claims she's *done* it. Just like the real Amber, sleeping with all those men."

The sisters came into the dining room then, and the girls all fell silent. The grace prayer was recited, and when the novices served dinner, Christine received a shock. While Frizz and the girls around her were handed plates of spaghetti, with garlic toast and small side cups of grated Parmesan cheese, Christine had been given a plate of carrot sticks, cottage cheese, and peaches.

"Uh oh," Frizz murmured. "Looks like Mother Superior has put you on a diet."

Christine stared in horror at the celery and carrot, knowing that they were going to give her an upset stomach later. The cottage cheese was plain and unpalatable, and the peaches would never do, being sweet.

When she heard snickering, she looked up and saw Amber giving her a snide smile. Others giggled, and one of them softly chanted, "Fatty, fatty, two by four, can't get through the kitchen door . . ."

Christine continued to look at her plate. She couldn't bring herself to pick up her fork. The delicious aromas floated around her; she saw girls eating the pasta with relish. Tears stung her eyes. Daddy, she thought, where are you? Why haven't you written to me, or called me, or come to take me away? What did I do to deserve this? *What did I do?*

"Sister Gabriel," Christine said after she had knocked on the office door and was invited to come in. "May I please telephone my father? It won't be a long call. I know he's away on a trip and that it would be long-distance, but he hasn't written to me, not even a postcard, and I'm worried."

"I understand how you feel," Sister Gabriel said gently. "But your father told us he would be out of reach for a little while, and that just as soon as he has a number where we can contact him, he will give it to us. Be patient, my dear. It will just be a little while longer, I promise."

"But you know where he is, don't you? He must have given you an address where you could reach him in case of an emergency."

"Christine, believe me, you have not been abandoned here. You trust me, don't you? Put your faith in God and soon everything will be all right, you'll see."

She was thoughtful for a moment, then said, "May I ask you a question, Sister? I'm fat, I know I am. But why is it such a bad thing? Why does Sister Michael seem to be mad at me because I'm overweight? Why do the other girls ridicule me? I mean, supposing Jesus was fat. We don't know what he looked like. There are a lot of paintings of him, but there are no descriptions of him in the Bible. Maybe Jesus looked like Friar Tuck, fat and jolly. Sister Gabriel," Christine said earnestly, "why do people make fun of anyone who's fat? What if we can't help it? People wouldn't laugh at someone in a wheelchair, would they? Why does being slim make you so much better? Is thinness next to godliness?"

The young nun gave her a startled look. "Christine," she said, "God loves you just as you are. Trust in him, trust in the Lord and his Blessed Mother, and the burden of your pain will be lifted. They love you, I promise you. They love you."

When Christine returned to the dormitory, she found Amber holding her usual nightly court on her bed, the other girls lounging around in pajamas, rolling curlers in their hair and plastering cold cream on their faces, while the radio played "Ragg Mopp."

"Well, if it isn't Sister Gabriel's little pet," Amber said.

Christine tried to ignore her. When she went to get her nightgown, she saw that her parents' photographs were missing from the twin frames.

She confronted Amber, her heart pounding. "I know you took them. Where are they?"

"Why should you care? They never visit you. You've been here a month and you've had no visitors, no letters, not even a phone call. So why should you care where their pictures are?"

Something snapped inside Christine. "Tell me where they are or you'll be sorry."

"Why? What are you going to do? Run to Sister Gabriel? I suppose you've been whining to her that we're mean to you. You're pathetic."

"And what about you? You put on airs, Alexandra Huntington, but you don't get visitors either, and you also never get any mail or phone calls! I'll bet your mother isn't even really a countess!"

The girls fell into shocked silence as Amber leveled her gaze at Christine. She stood up slowly. Towering over Christine, she said, "You'll pay for that. You're going to be very, very sorry."

Hans slowly picked himself up from the floor, blood streaming down his face and staining his shirt. He staggered toward Christine, a gun in his hand, pointed directly at her. Johnny was hidden somewhere in the shadows nearby, saying, "I can't help you this time, Dolly. I have to go away. We'll never see each other again . . ." Hans fired the gun and Christine screamed.

She opened her eyes and looked around. As she adjusted to the blinding afternoon sunlight, she remembered that she was in her dormitory room, alone. It was Saturday and the other girls were with their visitors, even Amber, who, although she never had visitors of her own, was always invited to join the others. But Christine, unable to face another disappointing Saturday, had decided to lie on her bed and retreat into fantasy; instead, she had fallen asleep and retreated into nightmares.

Looking at the clock on her nightstand, she saw that it was time for mail call. She hurriedly washed her face and combed her hair and got to the parlor just as Sister Gabriel was calling out her name.

"Look, Frizz!" she said, showing it to her friend. "It came from *Italy!* Look at the stamps! My father is in Italy! And feel how thick the envelope is! He's written pages and *pages!*"

When they rushed off together to open it, neither Christine nor Frizz saw the sudden, dangerous look in Amber's eyes as she watched them go.

The letter was all about Johnny's travels, and Christine sat on her bed, reading it out loud to a rapt Frizz, who had gotten no mail. Johnny had included a bundle of postcards, pictures of Rome and Pisa and Florence; a wine label soaked off a bottle of Chianti; and a ticket stub from the Milan opera. Christine spread them all out on the bed while she and Frizz pored over them, sighing and thinking, *Italy!*

But as the afternoon stretched on and the dying sun sent long, melancholy beams of light across the scattered postcards, Christine began to feel a new sadness steal over her. She wanted to be there with him. She missed him so much . . .

By the time they went in to dinner, Christine's joy had settled down to a quiet, somber mood, and she had no appetite. Especially for the cottage cheese and carrot sticks that were placed before her. As she stared at her plate, she was unaware that she had suddenly become the center of a dangerous form of attention.

"Hey, psst, Christine!"

She looked up and saw one of Amber's friends, an athletic girl named Ginger, holding up something from her plate. Christine received a shock when she realized what it was.

"Want one of my pork chops?" Ginger whispered.

Christine didn't see Amber's sly look or hear the suppressed giggles of the others. She saw only the pork chop, thick and juicy, dangling from Ginger's delicate fingers. And suddenly she was back in the penthouse, at the long dining table, and Johnny was in the kitchen, dancing around in a tuxedo and apron.

"But . . . don't you want it, Ginger?" she said.

"I'm allergic to pork," the other girl said, casting a quick, mischievous look toward Amber. Christine saw nothing; her eyes were riveted to the chop.

"Well?" Ginger said, swinging it before Christine's face as if it were a hypnotist's pendulum.

"Yes," Christine heard herself say. "If you don't want it, that is."

"Good! Here," Ginger said, and she put it on Christine's plate.

A girl sitting on Christine's right leaned over and said, "Better not eat it here. If Mother Superior were to catch you . . ."

"Yes," Christine said, and she quickly hid the pork chop inside her napkin. As she wrapped it up and slipped it into her skirt pocket, she felt herself become excited. She would eat it later, after the lights were out and everyone was asleep. She would bring the pork chop out and eat it so slowly that it would take an hour, savoring each salty bite as she read Johnny's letter again and studied each precious postcard.

Amber spent the evening in another girl's room, listening to records, her usual entourage with her, and Christine, alone in their room, hoped that this was a sign that Amber was starting to lose interest in teasing her and would maybe leave her alone from now on. It was nearly time for lights-out. Christine went to the bathroom to wash her face and brush her teeth, in good spirits for the first time in two months. Her father had written to her, and she was going to snack on the cold pork chop when everyone else was asleep.

But when she returned to her room, she found all the girls there, and Amber, sitting on her bed, holding up the pork chop. "We came to watch you eat it," she said.

Christine suddenly got a sick feeling. "What?"

"You heard me. Come on, piggy. Oink oink."

"Please . . . don't do this."

"Well, do you want it or don't you? If not . . ." Amber started to throw the chop into the wastebasket.

"Wait," Christine said. "Don't do that."

"Do you want it?"

She stared at it, bewildered and confused. Amber was making fun of the pork chop, and somehow that was making fun of Johnny.

"You want it," Amber sneered. "I know you do. That's why you're so fat. All you do is eat, eat, eat." Amber held the chop up high and said, "If you want this, then you have to get down on your knees and beg for it like a dog. Come on, nice bow wow."

"Leave her alone!" shouted Frizz, who had appeared in the doorway.

"Shut up, you," Amber said, and two girls barred Frizz's way.

"Please, Amber," Christine said. "Why are you doing this to me?"

"Do what I say or I'll throw it away. On your knees! Come on," Amber said, "hold up your paws like a good little dog."

"Christine," Frizz cried, "don't do what she says."

Amber whispered to one of the girls standing next to her, who turned and whispered to another. In the next instant they seized Frizz and pulled her into the room, pinning her arms behind her.

Picking up a pair of scissors from her desk, Amber walked slowly over to Frizz, opening and closing the sharp scissors while waving the pork chop at Christine.

The air was suddenly charged with fear and excitement as the girls watched and waited to see what Amber was going to do. She snapped the scissors close to Frizz's face, then she said, "I think this girl has too much hair. I'm going to give her a haircut."

"Leave her alone," Christine said.

"Eat the pork chop like a good little doggie and I will. Otherwise . . ." Amber made vicious slices in the air with the scissors.

When Christine looked at the pork chop that Amber held out to her, Frizz said, "Don't do it, Christine. I don't mind. I hate my hair." But there was a sob in her voice.

Christine felt the eyes of the girls riveted to her; she heard the frightened thumping of her own heart as she looked from Amber's cold expression to Frizz's eyes, wide with terror. "No," she said at last, "I won't do what you say. And you aren't going to hurt Frizz, either."

To everyone's surprise, she pushed past Amber and pulled the other girls away from Frizz. Facing Amber again, Christine said, "And you're not going to hurt us ever again. You're mean and cruel, Amber, and I feel sorry for you. And anyone who follows you and does what you say can't feel very good about herself." She looked at the others, who wouldn't meet her eye. "You make fun of us because we're not perfect like you, but at least we have our pride. My father taught me to respect myself. And that's just what I'm going to do, Alexandra Huntington. I'm not going to let you bully me or Frizz ever again."

9

....★

"Don't worry, Dolly. It won't be for long. We'll be together again real soon."

As the voice echoed down from the past, Philippa laid her pen down and looked out the window of the Starlite private jet at the night and stars and black ocean below. After a refueling in Fiji, they were now headed for Southern California. The cabin was dimly lit. Charmie, sitting across from Philippa, was reading; Ricky was in the galley making coffee and heating up danishes for the flight crew. They were the only passengers on board.

When the sense of foreboding started to come over Philippa again, she picked up her pen and tried to concentrate on her work. She read the last line she'd written: "Two qualities are required to determine success: they are commitment and self-discipline." This was in the pep talk chapter of her book, *The 99-Point Starlite Weight Loss and Beauty Plan*, a chapter to which the reader was invited to turn again and again for inspiration. The writing contained nothing new; rather, it was a condensed collection of the philosophies and adages that had, over the years, become trademarks of Starlite: "Success is knowing what you want." "Winning is determination."

Philippa stared for a moment at the page that was only half-filled with writing and finally put her pen back in its case. She couldn't concentrate. A growing sense of impending loss was taking her mind away from the task at hand, back to a foggy night in San Francisco, forty-two years ago, when she had experienced her first traumatic loss, a night in which she had lost everything, including her innocence. There had been no forewarning, no premonition, no sign preparing her for the sudden, drastic turn her life was about to take. And it made her think of the two other catastrophic losses that had occurred in her life: the first, when she had gone to a dingy apartment behind Grauman's Chinese Theatre back in 1958, when the course of her life had been determined forever; and the second, when she had stood at Point Resolution and watched the *Philippa* go down.

Was another such turning point waiting for her at the end of this flight? she wondered. Philippa tried to analyze her fears; she didn't know which frightened her more, the possibility of losing her company or discovering that one of her friends had betrayed her. Please, she prayed silently to the black night beyond her window, if there is a traitor in the company, don't let it be one of us.

There was a low table between her and Charmie's seats, and on it were a tray of fresh fruit, a plate of biscuits, and a crystal pitcher of Perrier with lemon slices floating in it. Pouring herself a glass, Philippa tried to settle back in her seat. There was so much to think about.

Beverly Burgess in Palm Springs was on her mind. Ivan Hendricks had asked Philippa back in Perth, "Does the name Burgess sound at all familiar to you?" She had searched her memory, but had found no Burgess in her past. She pictured again the full-page ad for Star's that Hendricks had shown her, a splash of silver stars against a dark blue background. The interior of the Starlite corporate jet was decorated in shades of blue, with silver stars woven into the upholstery, and Philippa wondered again if it was true what she had heard about the coincidences that occurred in the lives of twins who had been raised separately. She recalled in particular an article she had read not too long ago about twin sisters, separated at birth, who had married similar-looking men, had the same hobbies, donated to the same charities, and had even given their children the same names. Were the names Starlite and Star's, and their disturbingly similar logos, proof that Beverly Burgess was her sister?

"Are you all right?" Charmie asked quietly, setting down her book and removing her reading glasses.

"I don't know," Philippa said. "I'm worried about what we're going to find at the other end. I can't stop thinking about the threat of a corporate raider taking Starlite, or the fact that it might involve someone within the company, someone very close to me. Are you sure no one knows I'm coming?"

"Believe me, they haven't a clue. They all think I'm in Ohio, as I usually am at this time of the year. When you walk through the doors of Starlite's offices, you'll shock everyone out of their socks."

That was precisely what Philippa wanted to do—observe their reactions to her sudden return. Something, surely, should show on the faces of the guilty ones.

"I wasn't prepared to leave Perth yet," she said as the plane suddenly shimmied and vibrated. The pilot had warned them that they might skirt a tropical storm. "I always felt that as long as I was there, and I kept alive the hope that he had somehow survived, that he *would* come back. But by leaving, I almost feel as though I'm robbing him of that chance. Does that sound crazy?"

"No, it doesn't." Charmie leaned over and put her hand on Philippa's. "But you have to let go eventually, Philippa. He would want you to. He would want you to think of the future, not the past."

"You're right, of course." Philippa smiled. "Esther is so excited that I'm coming home for the holidays. She's anxious for me to meet her boyfriend. So, in a way, Charmie, I'm glad you came and rescued me from Perth. If Esther's as serious about this boy as she sounds, we might be planning a wedding soon."

"And soon after that," Charmie said with a glint, "you might be a grandmother."

"Good heavens! Aren't I too young to be a grandmother?"

Charmie took a sip of her gin and tonic, the plastic bracelets on her wrist clacking together. "Age is a state of mind," she said, eyeing Ricky's rear end as he walked past her down the aisle with a cup of coffee and took a seat behind her.

Since Philippa had swiveled her chair so that she rode backward, she could see Ricky over Charmie's shoulder. He was watching her. She said to Charmie, "I think I'll go and freshen up a bit."

The lavatory at the back of the plane was slightly larger than the ones on commercial aircraft, with fresh towels, individually wrapped soaps, lotion dispensers, and a padded bench that folded down over the toilet so that the sink could be converted into a vanity. Quietly closing the door behind herself but not locking it, Philippa turned on the cold faucet and splashed water on her face. As she was patting it dry with one of the thick velour towels, she heard a discreet knock at the door.

And Ricky's voice, saying, "Are you all right, Miss Roberts?"

She said, "Yes," and waited.

He opened the door, gave her a questioning look, then came all the way in and closed the door behind himself. "Are you sure you're all right?" he said more quietly.

"I'm worried," she said. Philippa had filled Ricky in on the reason for the trip—the threatened corporate takeover, the possibility that Hendricks had found her sister. "And I'm a little scared."

"Everything will be all right," he said softly. Then he put his hands on her waist and drew her to him. Whenever they touched like this, chest to chest, pelvis to pelvis, Philippa was always amazed at how good he felt, how hard his young body was. She slipped her arms around him and buried her face in his neck. He held her gently at first, massaging the tense spot between her shoulder blades; then his embrace grew tighter. She drove her hands through his long hair; his mouth crushed hers, his tongue tasted sweetly of sugared coffee. Suddenly she wanted him, quickly, now.

She reached down for him; he moaned. He lifted her up onto the edge of the sink, pulled her panties off, pushed her skirt up around her waist, and entered her, so abruptly and with such force that it took her breath away. He reached up under her blouse and half lifted her, rocking her as she clung to him, their mouths pressed together.

When the plane shuddered, they weren't aware of it. And when they heard a knock on the bathroom door, Philippa barely got out a breathless "Yes?"

It was Charmie. "The captain suggests you take your seat. He says we're about to enter some turbulence."

And Philippa started to laugh, muffling it in Ricky's luscious hair.

Philippa's photo was taped to the mirror, and as Danny Mackay worked on his disguise, he fantasized about the different ways he could punish her.

Maybe he would string her up by a rope and let her dance like a hooked fish, the way *he* had in the county jail. He might even let her die, just as he actually had, and then revive her, the way he had had to be revived, because the jail doctor, who had been paid a fortune for his involvement with the faked suicide, had screwed up his timing and had had to perform CPR to bring Danny back and *then* declare him dead. It was a real high to imagine how she was going to cry and scream and beg him to let her go. Danny was going to savor it. And maybe, when he found her down in Western Australia, he wouldn't rush in to kill her right away. He might make friends with her, and it would be a real turn-on to have her being all nice and friendly with him without knowing what he planned to do to her. Hadn't she done the same thing to him, pretending to support his political campaign, donating money and everything, all the while plotting his humiliation and destruction?

As Danny finished gluing the small beard to his chin, he couldn't keep from smiling at the thought of facing Beverly—or Philippa, as she called herself now—and getting her to like him while he savored his secret plan.

He stepped back from the mirror and regarded his work with a critical eye. Since his face was known to millions of people—never mind from being TV's top evangelist, but from his presidential campaign as well—it was important that he disguise himself enough so that no one would recognize him and start putting two and two together.

Satisfied with the alteration in his appearance, Danny went methodically around Quinn's house and selected a few things to take with him: a press badge that might come in handy, a wallet containing seventy-three dollars in bills and change. Finally he took up the file labeled "Philippa

Roberts," peeled the photograph off the mirror, and slipped it in with the notes Quinn had made on her.

Danny looked around to see if there was anything else he might need, his eye skimming past a folder with the words "Burgess/Star's" written on it. Then he turned and looked out to sea, where a mother-of-pearl sunrise was bringing the Pacific out of a dark night into a misty dawn. He saw that the tide had come in, washing up onto the smooth sand, leaving it shiny and frothy and erasing all traces of the three graves Danny had dug there during the night.

As he left the house, feeling high on the morning and life and revenge, he thought of the secret hit list he had once had, a private roll call of the people who had crossed him one way or another in his life. He had systematically punished them, one by one. Danny decided that the best of them had been a kid back in Louisiana, a hotshot Cajun who claimed Danny and Bonner had raped his sister. He had reported them to the authorities, but the police had had to let young Danny and Bonner go, because the girl, it turned out, confessed to having spent the night with them willingly, as most women did after one of the boys' revival meetings. Danny and Bonner had left town laughing, but when their tent show brought them back through that part of the South a few months later, Danny had sneaked out in the middle of the night, rousted that hotshot from his bed at gunpoint, taken him out to the swamp, and buried him up to his neck in mud. By the time the search party found the boy, the alligators had already gotten to him.

No sirree, Danny thought as he started up Quinn's Toyota and watched the Pacific Coast Highway traffic for a break. No one crossed Danny Mackay and got away with it. And the revenge was never simple and clean; Danny liked to be creative, make it count.

As he whipped the Toyota onto the highway, zipping around a Porsche and cutting off a Maserati, feeling powerful and invincible—a man couldn't die twice, could he?—Danny thought of how there had been a time when the secret list had been long, containing the names of rich men as well as poor. But now the list was very short, because it had only one name on it: Philippa Roberts. And he planned to be very imaginative with her indeed.

★

10

"Hey! Look at this!"

Larry Wolfe came out of his bedroom and stood in the living room of the bungalow, holding up a bathrobe. "Look what they give us!" he called out.

Andrea Bachman, Wolfe's assistant, unpacking in her own room on the other side of the living room, glimpsed Larry through the half-open door. She had already seen the robes hanging in her bathroom—thick midnight blue terry with silver piping and silver stars embroidered over the breast pocket. "I don't think the hotel is giving them to us, Larry," she said. "We use them while we're here. We don't keep them."

"Sure we do. There's no sign saying otherwise."

She didn't argue. Andrea wanted to say, "Larry Wolfe, you're so stupid you make regular stupid look smart." Instead she just said, "Whatever," and went on with her own unpacking. Her days of worshiping every little word Larry uttered were over. Now he was starting to annoy her.

But he was right in one respect: the bathrobes were unexpected. Most hotels provided plain white ones, but Star's had class. As evidenced by the toiletries in the bathroom. Andrea had expected the usual little packets and bottles of some particular brand—most often Sassoon or Fabergé—but here she had been pleasantly surprised to find, on the pink marble Pullman, Nina Ricci designer soaps; Jovan Night Blooming Jasmine body mousse; Caswell-Massey almond oil bubble bath. Clearly, people came to Star's to be pampered.

Her bedroom had come as a delightful surprise as well. Forget the usual hotel-white sheets; Andrea's were a bright raspberry color, the spread was a Laura Ashley calico with matching shams instead of ordinary pillows. There was even a vase of fresh purple hyacinths—in December!

When she went into the living room, she found Larry already dressed for dinner and inspecting himself in the big gilt-framed mirror over the fireplace. It was still a new experience for Andrea not to feel the old sexual pang every time she looked at him. No longer did her heart stop when she saw him; she could now regard him with objective eyes. Larry Wolfe, forty-four years old, dark haired and chisel jawed, was handsome in a cookie-cutter way, right out of the master of ceremonies mold. Put him in a tux and stick a microphone in his hand, and there you have him. He was sharp and fine; most women breathed heavily when they saw him. What they didn't know was the shallow person those good looks hid. Further, not only did Larry Wolfe not have a deep end, he was a bore. Andrea had once overheard him talking to a friend about an affair he was having with a well-known actress. "She hates the word *fuck*," Larry had said. "When I say to her, 'Let's fuck,' she gets mad. She wants to call it making love, and she won't let me touch her unless I do. So one night I said, 'Let's make love,' and while we were in bed making love, when she wasn't looking, I fucked her."

Larry Wolfe.

"When did you say Yamato was meeting us?" he asked, talking to Andrea through the mirror.

"In four days," she said, reaching for her coat. Mr. Yamato was a wealthy Tokyo businessman who was eager to finance Larry's next picture—the Marion Star story. It would be Larry's first foray into producing. After receiving his Oscar last April, Larry had discovered that he was no longer satisfied with being just a screenwriter; now he wanted to produce. There was bigger prestige in being producer, more money, more power, more women.

"Okay, let's go," he said, heading toward the door without helping Andrea with her coat. "I need a drink." He opened the door and walked through, letting her trail behind. In fact, Andrea, forty-two and self-proclaimed plain, had followed Larry around like an afterthought for years. But that was going to end. As they got into the little electric cart that she had called for to take them to the Castle, Andrea gave Larry a smile that said he was the best thing since screw-top wine bottles. She had to be careful not to give herself away. Because she was biding her time.

To get even.

In the bungalow a few yards away, Carole Page was finishing the preparations for her first encounter with Larry Wolfe. And she was thinking, Some things can't be bought with money. Or with power, or influence. But only with sex. When you got down to it, she decided as she checked her makeup, sex was the ultimate currency. There was nothing it couldn't buy. And what Carole Page, movie star in trouble, was going to buy was a man. Specifically, Larry Wolfe.

She left her bedroom and went into the living room, where a young man with a wide smile and a tight butt had earlier lit a fire in the fireplace. On the hearth was a polished brass bucket filled with pinecones dipped in wax. When tossed into the fire, they crackled and gave off brightly colored sparks. It was only one of the beautiful touches Carole had found in her bungalow. When she had first arrived, she had noticed the fragrance of orange blossoms in the air. She had puzzled over its source until she had found a ring, filled with oil, on top of one of the light bulbs in her bedroom. It was very romantic. If only Sanford could be here to share it with her.

But of course he couldn't be, not with the seduction she planned. "I'm going for a rest," she had told her husband when the shooting of her latest film was done. "I'm absolutely exhausted." Carole was not so much exhausted in the body as in spirit. Anyone with eyes could see that *Challenge Girl,* the movie she had just finished starring in, was a bomb.

But she was going to see to it that her next film was not a bomb. When she had read about Larry Wolfe purchasing Marion Star's long-lost diary with the intention of making a big-budget film out of it, Carole had seen her opportunity. She did some research on the screenwriter and discovered that he was a jerk with an ego a mile wide. But he was a gorgeous jerk, and he apparently already had a lot of Japanese money backing him. She researched him a little further and learned what Larry liked in women: "I need to know that the conquest is mine," he had candidly confessed in a *People* magazine article. "Women who throw themselves at me, and there are a lot of them, don't get anywhere. But put an unreachable woman in my path and I'll go to any lengths to get her. The harder she is to get, the more I pursue her. That's the game, you see? Pursuit and conquest. There's no bigger high."

So Carole had her strategy. She was going to get Larry by making him think *he* got *her.*

When she had read in Liz Smith's column that Larry and his assistant, Andrea Bachman, were coming to Star's to claim the diary they had bid on and won and to scout the old mansion as a possible location for shooting, Carole had gotten on the phone and secured a reservation for the same dates. Larry was due to arrive today. Now all she had to do was find out where he was, contrive a casual encounter, and then appear uninterested.

As she reached for her Russian sable coat, she felt her lace bra strain against her breasts. "I'd swear they're getting bigger," Carole had complained to her plastic surgeon. "Liposuction permanently removes fat cells," he had said, "and when fat cells are removed, the body doesn't create new ones, it just finds a new place to store fat. In your case, Carole, you had your thighs suctioned, so your body is sending fat to the only other likely place—your breasts."

Which, of course, had made the implants a waste.

Closing her eyes, Carole tried to will her headache away. She had a mild hangover from all the champagne she had drunk during the drive earlier to Palm Springs. "Fear of the tramway," she had said to her limousine companions, Frieda Goldman and Dr. Isaacs. Had they believed her? She doubted it. She winced to think of how she had downed that entire bottle of Dom Pérignon. She should know better; alcohol always loosened her tongue. Carole was just thankful that she hadn't blurted out anything like, "I'm going to Star's to fuck Larry Wolfe, so he'll put me in his next movie." She had been sober enough to stop short of that.

As she slipped into her coat, a painful memory suddenly flashed in her mind: a magazine cover with Carole's picture on it and the headline "Is Carole Page's Career Over?"

After three film flops and saying good-bye to forty, Carole found herself staring into has-been limbo. And it scared her. She was also resentful. She was a good actress; everyone said so. But lately she had found herself acting in some pretty sorry vehicles. The number of roles for "older" woman rapidly diminished with each passing year. The Screen Actors Guild had recently uncovered some scary statistics: while 71 percent of all feature roles went to men, and only 29 percent went to women, the percentage of film and TV roles available to actresses over forty was a miserable 8.8 percent.

Only one thing could save her now, she knew, and that was a screenplay written by a man named Larry Wolfe, currently the hottest screenwriter in Hollywood. Last April's Oscar win had clinched that. And now he was going to produce his own movie as well as write it, which meant he had casting power. Larry was the reason for the sneaked condom in her purse: to seduce him into signing her. But she only had a few days in which to accomplish it. Sanford expected her back at their home in Beverly Hills for Christmas, back with her fears and wrinkles and desperate memories of better days.

And Sanford, her sexy, virile husband, making love to his "beautiful movie star." How much longer could she hold on to him?

As she went to the door, she caught her reflection in the mirror, a tall, striking blonde who looked like she could pass for thirty. But it wasn't fleeting glances that worried her, it was the close-ups. Would she be able to make love with Larry Wolfe, wondering if the little lies could be seen: the pucker where the liposuction tube had gone in; the dimples where she'd had her lower ribs removed; the hairline scar from the tummy tuck?

Carole thought of these marks as the signs of age, like counting the rings of a tree; the more cosmetic surgery scars, the older the woman. Soon, she knew, she was going to add tracks behind her ears for the jowl lift, a scalp seam for the forehead lift, and the little craters left after the removal of her back teeth. All designed to make her look not-forty. Would Larry Wolfe see these little lies and be turned off? Or worse, just laugh at her and say she was too old to play a twenty-five-year-old sex goddess? And then what? Were her days with Sanford numbered? Was she going to appear in one more flop, was she going to look too old for a part she was playing, were people going to start shaking their heads in pity—and send Sanford in search of a new beautiful movie star?

This was her biggest fear: not so much of a fizzled career, but of losing Sanford. Carole had been a big star when they met, and she knew that that was partly what had made him fall in love with her—her fame and stardom. He had told her often enough in their early days together, and he continued to remind her of it. Some men might resent being outshined by a wife's limelight; Sanford basked in it. But would he still want her if she was a has-been? "I want to keep you proud of me, darling Sanford," she whispered to her reflection. "I couldn't bear to have you watch me fade into obscurity, another aging actress who can't find any roles. I know that it would slowly erode our relationship, and ultimately I'd lose you. And if I can't live with you, my love, then I wouldn't want to live."

When Andrea Bachman saw the Castle, she was instantly reminded of the opening scene in the movie *Rebecca*—a mysterious house standing in moonlight, a woman's voice saying, "Last night I dreamt I went to Manderley again . . . secretive and silent Manderley . . ."

As the golf cart hummed along the concrete path that led from the bungalows to the main building, their young driver, bundled in a parka, giving them some wholesome facts about the place—"Health club is over there, indoor tennis courts down that way"—Andrea kept her eyes on the house. She thought it looked romantic, medieval, and sinister all at once. Kevin Costner's Robin Hood could scale those towers and turrets and battlements. No need to build a set for the Marion Star story; the real thing was going to make a helluva location.

Not that the story itself was shabby. The crime that had been committed here nearly sixty years ago, on July 4, 1932, had never been solved. Ramsey's murderer was never found, and neither was the young and beautiful Marion Star. They say that when she saw her lover's body, sprawled naked in what the newspapers dubbed the Obscene Bathroom, Marion had run out into the night, hysterical, and had somehow gotten lost in the snow. And then, after the spring thaw, when a search party made up of Riverside County sheriffs, forest rangers, and local police had scoured the area for miles around without recovering her remains, it was speculated that wild animals had devoured her.

There were other mysteries surrounding the murder as well, certain tantalizing facts that hadn't been reported in the papers but that had nonetheless made the rounds of the gossips—something about Ramsey's body having been mutilated in a symbolic way.

As they drew up in front of the mansion, where two doormen greeted arriving guests, Andrea thought again what an exciting screenplay Marion's story was going to make. She couldn't wait to get hold of the long-lost, recently discovered diary, which Larry had paid an enormous price for and which Andrea was going to start reading that very night.

One of the doormen came down the icy steps to assist Andrea onto the red carpet. "Good evening, madam," he said, and she saw that he was a good-looking young hunk in his twenties. She couldn't recall when they had stopped calling her "miss" and had started with the "madam." Although her fear of life past forty wasn't as acute as Carole Page's, all the same, when she had celebrated her forty-second birthday, Andrea had momentarily felt the chilling specter of time's passing.

"Excuse me, sir," said the young doorman, who was dressed in a heavy woolen overcoat with a Russian-style fur hat on his head—William Hurt in *Gorky Park*. "Aren't you Larry Wolfe, the screenwriter?"

Larry gave him a bored look and said, "Yes, I suppose I am."

"Gosh, this is a great honor, Mr. Wolfe. You really deserved the Oscar."

Larry walked past the doorman without a word.

The young man hurried up to the heavy doors that led into the Castle. As he drew them open, he said, "Would you have any tips for a struggling young screenwriter, Mr. Wolfe? I mean, I know I could never hope to be half as good as you, but—"

Larry said, "I'm on vacation," and waved him off.

"Don't take it personally," Andrea said gently to the crestfallen young man.

"I suppose *he* never struggled or needed a break."

"Please, don't let it bother you. Mr. Wolfe is cranky when he's hungry." She reached into her purse and brought out a twenty-dollar bill. "Perhaps another time," she said, pressing the bill into his gloved hand. "When he's in a better mood."

As she entered the brightly lit entry hall where young women in uniforms were relieving guests of their coats and scarves, Andrea watched her handsome employer smile graciously at a pretty young thing, showering her with the attention that the doorman could never get from him, attention of an entirely different kind. Larry Wolfe was the sort of man who attracted women with uncanny ease; they seemed to throw their souls at his feet. Women everywhere seemed to be in love with Larry. This had once been the cause of endless anxiety for Andrea, back when she had been a secret member of those ranks, when she had sometimes thought her lust for her boss could fill a stadium, before her eyes had been opened and she had realized what a true son of a bitch he was.

Back before she had decided to take revenge on him.

As she handed her coat to one of the maids, Andrea found her thoughts returning to a smoggy evening on the UCLA campus, seventeen years ago . . .

The night air had been hot and perfumed; the moon, big and orange. Couples were wrapped in lustful embraces, and twenty-five-year-old Andrea, trying not to look at them, was so engrossed in thoughts of sex and love that she did not see a young man suddenly step out into the path in front of her, causing her to jump and drop her books.

"I'm sorry," he said, bending down to retrieve her things. "I didn't mean to startle you."

Andrea realized that he took the evening screenwriting course with her. His name was Larry Wolfe, and she thought he was one of the most gorgeous males she had ever set eyes on.

"I'm sorry," he said again with a smile. "I thought you saw me." She noticed that a curl of black hair had fallen onto his forehead. "I'm Larry, I'm in the screenwriting class with you. I've been wanting to talk to you."

That floored her. Andrea harbored no illusions about herself; she knew she had unremarkable features and an equally unremarkable personality. Guys did not go out of their way to encounter Andrea Bachman. Especially handsome, muscle-bound jocks like Larry Wolfe.

"What about?" she said, wishing he would give her books back to her. She had nothing to hug to her chest, nothing to hide behind.

"Well, I've got a problem, and I thought you might be able to help me. If you wouldn't mind, that is."

Fifteen minutes later they were sitting in Ship's Coffee Shop on Wilshire Boulevard, sharing a plate of French fries and two coffees beneath garish bright lights. During the walk from UCLA, through crowded Westwood where couples strolled hand in hand, Larry had told her about himself. He was twenty-six, a Southern California native, worked as a waiter at the Spaghetti Factory in Venice, and his ambition was to get into the movie business. He had candidly confessed to Andrea that he didn't have the knack for acting; he didn't have the patience to learn technical stuff like editing and special effects; and he didn't want to take the time to get a degree in motion picture arts.

"Finally, I decided that writing a screenplay would be the easiest way to break into entertainment," he said. "That's why I signed up for the course. And when our instructor praised your screenplay tonight, I was impressed."

Andrea blushed. She hadn't thought Larry was paying attention at the time.

"I'm interested in this contest they're having," he said. "The best screenplay of the class will win five thousand dollars, plus it will be shown to important directors and producers. I need to win that competition, Alice."

"Andrea," she said. She knew all about the competition, because she was going to enter it herself. And she was planning on winning. It was vital that she won.

A shy young woman who lived with her parents in a plain stucco house in Santa Monica, Andrea Bachman had been what they called a "late in life" child, having been born in an era when it was unusual for a woman over forty to have a baby. All her life, Andrea had been made to feel that she had been living with elderly people; now that her mother was seventy-two and her father eighty-six, Andrea's few acquaintances thought she lived with her grandparents. She had an unfulfilling job as a secretary with an insurance company in Culver City, where she felt as if she faded into the bland walls and file cabinets and went unnoticed by everyone, including her boss.

Andrea had to escape; she was determined to excel in some way, to make herself distinctive. She had always wanted to be a writer; she had even sold a few short stories to magazines and had been told that she had promise. And so when she had seen the ad in the *L.A. Times* for the screenwriting course, which was limited to twenty students, she had thought that this might be her chance. Now, seven weeks of studying and writing later, the instructor had told Andrea, in front of everyone, that her screenplay showed incredible promise. Andrea had glowed. Just as she glowed now, under Larry Wolfe's attention.

"I mean," he said, popping a French fry into his mouth, "what a great profession to get into. I read that William Goldman got four hundred thousand dollars for his screenplay for *Butch Cassidy and the Sundance Kid.* How long do you suppose it took him to crank it out? A few weeks maybe?"

Larry stopped and stared at Andrea then, and she suddenly felt self-conscious. "So," she started. She coughed, said, "Excuse me," then asked, "So what is it you want me to do?"

"Nothing, really. I mean, I don't want to impose on you. A talented woman like yourself must be pretty busy . . ." He let the words drift away on the air-conditioning currents.

And Andrea fell in love.

Now, as she handed her coat to one of the maids in the Castle's medieval foyer, she put those memories aside and looked around at the riches exhibited in Star's main hall—display cases containing mementoes and Marion's personal effects; enormous blown-up photographs of Marion, her sad gaze fixed for eternity. What *did* happen that night? Why was the murder never solved?

Andrea had to hurry after Larry as he strode across the Castle's main hall toward the dining room, where the maître d' greeted him as if he were a long-lost brother. Men were as taken with Larry Wolfe as women were, but for different reasons.

When the maître d' explained apologetically that there would be a wait for a table, Larry instructed Andrea to send a note of complaint to the resort management, then he turned and headed for the cocktail lounge, with Andrea dutifully following, as she always did. She needed to keep up the masquerade for a few more days; she didn't want to arouse his suspicions.

Carole walked up the steps of the Castle's entrance nervously toying with the chain of her evening purse. She should turn away right now, she told herself, and go home, go back to Beverly Hills and her husband and her failed career.

"Good evening, Miss Page," the doorman said.

She summoned up her dazzling smile and saw on his shining young face that she still had what it took. Inside, as she slipped out of her Russian sable coat and handed it to an attendant, she looked around to see if Larry Wolfe was there yet.

There were quite a few guests milling around the lobby, standing in front of the massive fireplaces or sitting on brocaded sofas and chairs among potted palm trees, helping themselves from the trays of champagne and hors d'oeuvres brought around by cute waiters. She went to the cocktail lounge, where she paused to assess the crowd.

Who's minding Hollywood? she wondered as she recognized familiar industry faces.

The lounge was romantically dark, with stained glass behind the bar, medieval shields on the walls, and deep booths to hide in. Christmas lights twinkled along the wainscoting, and the pianist was playing something vaguely holiday sounding. Carole's heart jumped when she saw Larry Wolfe and his assistant, Andrea Bachman, in the far corner.

She wondered for a moment how to orchestrate a chance encounter, but she finally decided to just glide by, all glitter and white satin, pretend to just happen to recognize Larry, and then congratulate him on his Oscar win.

Larry did not see Carole coming, he was so consumed with his thoughts. For one thing, Marion Star's diary was going to be sensational, certain to earn him another Oscar, this time for Best Picture, because the producer always got that. For another, he was looking forward to meeting the owner of this resort, Beverly Burgess, who he had heard was something of an enigma. Nothing interested him more than a mysterious, unattainable woman; in fact, they were the only kind of women he could relate to or get sexually aroused by. He would single one out and commence to explore her, like a dark continent, thrilled with the chase and discovery. He could become so fascinated by a woman's mystique that it sometimes bordered on obsession; the more elusive she was, the more unattainable, the greater Larry's attraction. Which was why, when a director friend had told him about the owner of Star's, Larry's interest had been captured at once. "Beverly Burgess is quite a looker," the director had told him upon returning from a week at Star's during the summer. "I only caught a glimpse of her, she doesn't socialize much. But she's just how I like them, tall and thin and classy. And as near as I can determine, there isn't a man in her life."

Larry Wolfe was very much looking forward to taking a tour of the Castle with the elegant and unreachable Miss Burgess.

"Well, hello," a silky voice said. "You're Larry Wolfe, aren't you? Congratulations on your Oscar."

Larry looked up, startled. "Hello," he said, taking in the ash-blond hair, the glitter of diamonds, the deep plunge of her evening gown. His eyes settled upon the necklace of soft, fat pearls that lay between her breasts. "Miss Page, this *is* a pleasure. Won't you join us?" he said.

Carole hesitated. "Well, I'm really waiting for a table in the dining room." She looked around the lounge and was relieved to see that there were no vacant seats.

"Then join us until you're called," Larry said.

"Well," she said again, uncertainly. But finally she did sit down, sliding into the booth and saying, "This is my first time here. I have the most marvelous bungalow. It even has its own pool."

"What a coincidence," Larry said with a smile like an ad for dental implants. "I'm in the other bungalow. So I guess that makes us neighbors. How long will you be staying here?"

"Just a few days. I'm here for a rest. And you?"

Larry wasn't subtle about his inspection of her cleavage as he said, "You've heard of the murder that took place here, Dexter Bryant Ramsey, the movie director in the thirties? I'm going to make a movie about it. Write it and produce it."

"Really," Carole said, declining the macadamia nuts Larry offered to her. After seeing Marion's photos in the lobby and remembering that she had been twenty-six when she disappeared, a young sex goddess who had always worn slinky, clinging clothes with no bra or panties underneath, Carole realized that she was going to have to go on a starvation diet to get down to the right weight. She'd done it before. Any actress whose career depended on looks had to accept the torture that went along with achieving those looks. She could tell by the way Larry was assessing her tonight that he thought she looked sensational. He didn't know the suffering she had gone through: the tedious hair weaves, eyebrows painfully waxed, pores scraped, lips pumped up. It didn't seem fair. Larry was only two years older than she, and all he had had to do to look good tonight was comb his hair.

"How did *Challenge Girl* go?" he asked innocently, as if he hadn't already heard. "I understand there were production problems."

That disaster, she thought. Carole had been entirely wrong for the part. The movie would play only in the Midwest and then drift to the cable channels for a quiet death.

"I hear Syd Stern has something new that's shaking everybody up," Larry said. "A new character, similar to Indiana Jones, but female. They're saying it's going to be big for whoever lands it."

Andrea said, "I heard that Syd has already found someone but he isn't saying who."

Carole didn't really care. Syd Stern's new antiheroine was not a part she could play. But Marion Star, now *that* was a part for her.

She sighed, toyed with the bowl of nuts, and said, "I do wish Sanford could have come with me. This place is so romantic."

Larry laughed. "Then why would you want your husband here?"

Carole gave him a frosty look. "It is possible to be married and still be in love."

"You'll never convince me," he said. "So why didn't Sanford come with you?"

"He's just so busy these days, what with this latest mania to tear down beautiful old homes in Beverly Hills and replace them with fifty-thousand-square-foot monstrosities. I'm certainly glad that whoever bought this lovely old mansion decided to keep it the way it was."

Larry looked around the lounge, briefly wondering if the mysterious Beverly Burgess was somewhere in the crowd. Then he returned his attention to Carole. "So what are you going to do here all by yourself?"

She conjured up the look of an aloof, unattainable woman. "I'm here to rest and keep to myself. If I can't have Sanford, I don't want anyone."

And the spark of interest in Larry's eyes glittered a notch more brightly.

Andrea addressed herself to the margarita she had been nursing. She had watched this scene played hundreds of times: Larry's seduction of the uninterested female. But Carole Page was at least a cut above his usual bimbos; a large cut above, in fact. Andrea admired Carole's acting. She had heard *Challenge Girl* was a bomb, and she wondered if Carole was here because of depression.

A man came up to the table then, tall with dark hair silvering at the temples and wearing an expensively tailored suit. "Pardon me, Mr. Wolfe." he said. "I'm Simon Jung, the general manager of Star's. I was wondering if you would like to meet with Miss Burgess now."

Larry experienced an instant of indecision: to stay here and delve into Carole Page or meet the elusive Beverly Burgess. A cliché popped into his mind, the one about the bird in the bush. So he turned to Andrea and said, "Why don't you go with Mr. Jung and get things started while I stay here and keep Carole company?"

Paintings of nude men and women covered the walls in an endless variety of sexual embraces—kissing, fondling, making love. Andrea was spellbound.

As she looked around, taking in the amazing bathtub where Ramsey had been killed—it was made of hand-cut lead crystal, completely transparent and large enough to hold several people—Simon Jung was saying, "It really isn't obscene, but rather beautiful, in an erotic sort of way. The moral atmosphere of the thirties caused the press to label this room in such a way."

Andrea tried to trace his accent. French? He was incredibly polished; if he were an actor she would cast him in the role of a nobleman or a distinguished scientist. He could step right into parts played by Christopher Lee.

They finally left the bathroom—Andrea had somehow expected to see bloodstains in the tub—and walked down a long hall lined with suits of armor. "Mr. Jung," she said, "it has been rumored that something was done to Ramsey's body after he was dead. Was he mutilated in some way?"

"He was castrated," Jung said.

They arrived at an office where a gigantic model of Star's stood on display, and Andrea was introduced to Beverly Burgess, who, to Andrea's surprise, wore large sunglasses. "An eye condition," she explained. From what Andrea could see of her, Beverly was a good-looking woman, with brunette hair done in a stylish shag. As she gave Andrea the diary, an old leather-bound book, she said, "We came across it when we were doing some remodeling in the north wing."

Andrea hefted the book in her hands, amazed to think that in here she might find the mystery to that long-unsolved murder. "I would think the police would be interested in this."

"The case was closed long ago," Beverly said. "They decided that Marion had killed Ramsey and then perished somewhere in these mountains."

Andrea opened the diary to the first page, and read the thin, spidery handwriting: "I guess you'd say I lost my virginity twice. Or three times. Or four, or five, it depends. Both men had me that night; they took turns with me. It was the son I was in love with, but his father wanted me also. I can't say which of them first took my virginity. They got me drunk, undressed me, and kept me in the bedroom until they were satisfied, by which time I would say that I had lost my virginity several times over. I never saw either of them again. I was fourteen years old."

Andrea closed the book.

Seeing the look on her face, Beverly said, "It's rather frank. And brutal in some places."

"So I see," Andrea said thoughtfully. "Well, thank you, Miss Burgess. I won't keep you. And Mr. Wolfe is anxious to read this and get started on the screenplay." Which was a lie. Larry had no intention of reading the diary, nor of writing the script. But no one knew that. Not a soul in the world knew that the great Larry Wolfe was a fake, or that he and his "assistant" had been acting out a charade for seventeen years. How innocent Andrea had been back then, when she had offered to read his screenplay for the contest . . .

She had arranged to meet Larry at the student union on the UCLA campus. She had his screenplay with her. It was awful. It was worse than awful, it stunk. And she had to think of a gentle way of breaking it to him.

She couldn't be honest with him, she couldn't just tell him to give up writing, that he didn't have what it took, because Andrea had been brought up by the rules and ideals of an older era, highest among which was that a girl always protected a boy's ego. "Praise him," her elderly mother had said. "Make him feel like a king. Always defer to his judgment, even if you don't agree with it. Men have such delicate egos, it's up to us women to see that they always feel good about themselves. Look at your father," who had been sixty-nine years old back then. "I haven't always agreed with him, and some of his habits irritate me, but I keep my mouth shut. That's my place, and that will be your place, too, Andrea, when the time comes."

Which was why, as she had watched Larry approach her from across the busy cafeteria, pausing here and there to exchange words with friends even though he knew she was waiting for him, Andrea had gone over and over in her mind delicate ways in which to tell him his screenplay was a disaster.

"Hi, Alice," he had said, joining her at last. "So, what did you think of it?" He leaned forward so that biceps that bulged. When he looked at her, two invisible rays came out of his green eyes and zapped the logic center of her brain.

"Well," she said, removing the script from the manila envelope with shaking hands.

"Hey," he said with a smile. "Take it easy." And he placed his hand over hers.

Andrea flew around the universe a few times and then came back down to earth.

"So what did you think of it?" he asked.

She had planned to say, "It's a bit too masculine for my tastes; I don't understand war stories." Making the faults of the screenplay sound really like *her* faults, the way her mother had taught her. But instead she heard herself say, "It has promise."

"Great! Tell me what to do to make it better."

What to do? Burn it. But when she looked into his smile, realizing that if she told him the truth she'd never see him again, she said, "I think maybe what you could do is alter the main character a little. He comes across too . . . harshly. He's rather cruel to women. The opening is slow, you should start with some sort of action since it *is* an action film. And then . . ." The list was endless. "And, um, while the locale is exotic, I don't think Iceland is a likely setting for a couple of Vietnam vets to go off their heads. Manhattan on a crowded afternoon would create more tension."

"Hmm," he said with an attractive frown. "It sounds like a lot of work. And I just don't have the time, what with my schedule at the restaurant and all . . ." He tilted his head and smiled. "Do you think maybe you could see your way to helping me out a little on this? I'd be awfully grateful."

"All right," she said, while another part of her brain was saying, Are you out of your mind? And then suddenly a very strange and unexpected thought popped into her head: she was twenty-five years old and still a virgin.

What exactly that had to do with Larry Wolfe and his screenplay she had no idea, but she suddenly realized that she just *had* to help him, if for no other reason than just to see him again. When she said, "Okay, I'll help you," Larry had said, "Great! I tell you what, how about if I just leave the script with you and you do what you can with it? Get it to me in time for the next class meeting, and I'll take you out for a bite to eat at Ship's. How's that?"

Andrea had said yes, selling her soul for a hamburger.

When she returned to the cocktail lounge, she found Larry still trying to overwhelm Carole Page with his charm. Andrea stood there holding Marion Star's diary, thinking how much she had loved him back when they were students at UCLA, and how she had loved him in the years since. But it wasn't because of those days, or those years, that she was now plotting his downfall. It was because of something that had happened so recently that it still seemed to burn into her heart, a brand-new wound.

It was for that that Larry Wolfe was going to pay.

11

·····································★

St. Bridget's Convent School, 1954

" 'The young gentleman was about two and twenty, tall and well limbed. His body was finely formed and of a most vigorous make, square-shouldered, and broad-chested; a nose inclining to the Roman, eyes large, black and sparkling. His hair fell no lower than his neck, in short easy curls; and he had a few sprigs that garnished his chest in a style of strength and manliness. Then his grand movement, which seemed to rise out of a thicket of curling hair—' "

"His what?" one of the girls said.

"Shhh," said the others.

"Go on, Dee Dee," Christine said. "Keep reading."

" 'He had immediately, on stripping off his shirt, gently pushed her down on the couch, which stood conveniently to break her willing fall. Her skirt was up over her face, her thighs were spread out to their utmost extension, and between them the red-centered cleft of flesh—' "

The girls gasped.

" 'The young gentleman changed her posture from lying breadth- to length-wise on the couch; but her thighs were still spread, and the mark lay fair for him, who, now kneeling between them, displayed to us a side view of that fierce erect machine of his.' "

"Good heavens!" blurted Frizz.

"Shhh," hissed the others.

Dee Dee's voice continued quietly as her audience, their faces cast in the glow of flickering candlelight, listened with held breath. " 'He looked upon his weapon himself with some pleasure, and guiding it with his hand to the inviting slit, with ease sheathed it up to the hilt, at which Polly gave a cry. "Oh! Oh! I can't bear it. It is too much! I die!" were Polly's expressions of ecstasy.' "

"Wait!" someone whispered suddenly. "I thought I heard something."

Dee Dee quickly hid the book under a pillow while one of the girls near the door cracked it open a few inches and peered out into the dark hallway. It was nearly midnight; everyone at St. Bridget's was asleep except for the members of the secret Starlets club, who had met in Christine's room for a reading of a highly erotic book called *Fanny Hill.* Dee Dee had smuggled it in, and she read segments at each meeting.

"My mistake," the girl at the door said, closing it. "The coast is clear."

They all sighed with relief. Everyone knew that punishment would be severe if the nuns should find out about the secret club. On the nights that it met, the girls pretended to go to sleep, and then they waited until the light went out under Sister Gabriel's door, at which point they gathered in Christine's room for an hour or two of forbidden pleasure.

"Read some more, Dee Dee," a girl named Lanie Freeman said. Lanie's nickname was Mouse, because she was the smallest of the group and had tiny, mouselike features. "Read that part again where she twists her legs around his naked loins."

The others giggled.

"I think that's enough for tonight. The gentleman finally got Polly. We'll see who he gets next week."

"One thing I still don't understand," another girl said, "is what was that bit about his grand movement. What's that?"

"It's the same as his 'engine of love-assaults,' " Dee Dee said, and a few of the girls frowned. Only the oldest ones—Christine, Frizz, and Dee Dee—understood what *Fanny Hill* was really about, and even they were a bit vague on some points. But all the girls, down to the youngest, who was eleven, grasped the fact that it was about sex, and even though they couldn't quite picture what was going on, they were titillated all the same.

But the Starlets club wasn't just about reading dirty books. It was also about experimenting with makeup, discussing fashions, giving one another perms, and sharing secrets, fears, and dreams. The club had its early beginnings four years ago, shortly after the pork chop incident, when Amber's popularity had begun to dwindle as the girls had gravitated toward Christine and Frizz. They began to gather in Christine's room, now that she no longer shared with Amber but with Frizz, and talk for hours after lights-out.

On this rainy night, twelve girls were crowded into Christine's room, where the air was thick with the fragrances of cosmetics, perfume, nail polish, and Toni perm solution, all mingling with the pungency of burning candles. In an attempt to straighten Frizz's hair, Christine was rolling it onto huge brush curlers, using a hair straightener they had bought at Newberry's during one of the school outings to the city. While Frizz sat with a towel around her shoulders, munching from a giant box of Milk Duds, other girls were giving one another manicures and pedicures, inventing hairdos, and trying on sheer nylon stockings, wearing gloves to keep from snagging them. They consumed potato chips and candy bars and Coca-Colas, all prohibited by the sisters. The club rule was that only luxuries, only forbidden things were allowed at Starlets meetings; anything the sisters permitted, such as writing letters, ironing, or mending, was outlawed. And so as the girls applied Coty, Maybelline, and Hazel Bishop products to their faces, or tried on jewelry and lingerie, they talked, mostly about boys and sex.

Lately they had been getting most of their information from Dee Dee, who was seventeen, like Frizz, and very worldly. She was the newest member of the club, having arrived at St. Bridget's only a few weeks ago from Philadelphia, where there was a popular local TV show called "American Bandstand." The show sounded heavenly to the boy-starved girls of St. Bridget's who all wished they could go to a *real* school and dance the bunny hop on Friday nights with (gasp) boys.

Dee Dee was deliciously daring because she had stitched down the pleats of her school uniform so that she practically wore a straight skirt. She also had a boyfriend back in Philadelphia with whom she had gone "all the way." While Dee Dee had never divulged the actual details of her intimacy with Chuck, the girls all imagined it must have been like something out of *Fanny Hill,* Dee Dee with her skirt over her head, Chuck coming at her with his "weapon."

"What color is that?" one of the girls asked Mouse, who was putting on lipstick.

"It's called Raspberry Torte," Mouse said in her funny little voice. "Do you like it?" She had applied it too thickly and it went outside the lip line; she was so small, and had such tiny features, that the effect was more clownlike than flattering, but she smiled so eagerly that they assured her it made her look like a movie star. She giggled and proceeded to apply more.

What the girls liked best about these secret meetings was how good they always felt afterward. They came together to seek reassurance and approval from peers, to allay their adolescent fears and insecurities, to confirm to one another that they were *all right.* They all agreed that Christine Singleton, whom they affectionately called Choppie because of the pork chop incident when she had stood up to Amber, was the central force in Starlets. She had a way, the girls realized, of making them feel better about themselves. She wouldn't let any girl say "I'm dumb" or "I'm ugly." And if you really were dumb or ugly, she'd say, "Well, let's see if we can find a way to change that." Each new girl in the group would say that, after you got to know Christine, you forgot that she was so fat.

"There's still something I don't understand about *Fanny Hill*," said a fifteen-year-old girl who was tweezing her thick eyebrows in the hopes of looking like Audrey Hepburn. "Why is the man's thing referred to as a pistol or a battering ram? And just what *does* he do with it, anyway?"

While an animated discussion broke out, with all sorts of outrageous speculations put forth by the innocent girls of St. Bridget's, Frizz sighed, popped a Milk Dud in her mouth, and said, "I've never going to get involved with men. I'm going to have a career."

"Of course you are," Christine said as she squirted solution on a hank of Frizz's hair and rolled it around a curler. "I have every confidence in you."

Frizz raised the hand mirror to her face and frowned at the helmet of brush curlers on her head. "If I could just do something about this hair!"

"We'll figure something out. If this doesn't work, maybe something else will."

"I wish I were a blonde," Dee Dee said as she applied a fresh layer of polish to her toenails. "Like Marilyn Monroe. I tried dyeing my hair once and my mother nearly killed me."

"Put lemon on your hair and stand out in the sun," one girl offered. She had purchased some long, dangly earrings at Woolworth and was turning her head this way and that to see how they caught the candlelight.

"How about just bleach?" Mouse offered.

"Peroxide," said another.

"Marilyn Monroe's hair isn't naturally blond. How does *she* do it?"

"I would give *anything* to look like her," little Mouse said wistfully, shifting her attention away from her heavily rouged lips to her hair, which was, no denying it, a mousy brown.

Christine was reminded then of Amber, who had been naturally blond and the envy of the school. Christine recalled the night she had gotten out of bed to go to the bathroom and had found Amber bent over one of the toilets, vomiting. "Are you sick?" she had asked, and Amber had shot back, "Shut up and don't be so ignorant." And then she had done an astonishing thing. She had stuck her finger down her throat. "Why are you making yourself throw up?" Christine had asked, and Amber had said, "You don't expect me to be fat like you, do you?" And Christine had thought in shock, She would rather be sick than look like me.

She wondered now, as she rolled the last prickly curler into Frizz's hair, if Amber was happy. She had graduated a year ago. To everyone's surprise, her mother had come to the ceremony, a slender, elegant woman who had arrived in a Rolls-Royce with a crest on the door, and the nuns had addressed her as "Countess." So Amber hadn't been lying after all, and the girls' envy had increased, although Christine thought that Amber had looked unhappy as she rode away from the school.

Mouse said something funny, and all the girls laughed. When Christine saw how Mouse beamed at the attention, she thought how different the pixyish girl was at these secret meetings from the rest of the time. During the day, Mouse was so quiet you forgot she was there. Her self-esteem was so low that, at twelve, her shoulders were already curving inward toward her chest, like a little broken bird. Mouse was one of the many girls at the school who was an inconvenience to her parents and who had been put away here so they could get on with their lives.

It was Mouse who had given the club its name. When she joined a year ago, shortly after she came to St. Bridget's, it had taken her a long time before she got up the nerve to even talk. While the others freely expressed their secret desires and dreams, Mouse had sat huddled in a corner, like a dog that had been whipped. But finally, one night, with encouragement from the others, she had squeaked out her private dream: "To be a starlet." And so that's what they were called, from then on.

"Well?" Frizz said when the last curler was in.

"The instructions say we wait thirty minutes."

"This stuff stinks. Do you think it'll work?"

"You are going to look *dynamite.*"

Christine was trying to cheer her friend up because of what had happened that afternoon.

"I can't face her alone," Frizz had said that morning, referring to her mother, who was making one of her rare visits. "Please come with me and be my moral support. I know why she's here. It's because I graduate soon, and I just know what she's going to say. Please help me convince her to let me go to New York and study drama."

Christine had agreed to go because she had met Mrs. Randall several times before, and she knew the kind of effect the woman had on her daughter. And also because Christine believed strongly in Frizz's dream to go on the stage. She thought her best friend had natural talent; Frizz was uninhibited and liked to entertain, and St. Bridget's own drama instructor, a lay teacher from Marin who came in to teach twice a week, had said that Frizz had real potential and that she should pursue theatrical study. But Mrs. Randall wouldn't hear of it. People who worked in theater, she declared, were among the lowest of society's classes, and she wasn't going to see her daughter get involved with such riffraff. Unfortunately, Frizz's real father had died years ago, and Mrs. Randall had gotten married again to someone who distanced himself completely from anything involving the girl. So there was no one Frizz could appeal to.

As they had sat in the sunshine on the convent lawn, with the salty smell of the bay occasionally whispering through the trees, Christine could see where her friend had gotten her personality. Frizz's mother was a flamboyant woman who wore bright red lipstick, furs, diamonds, and who looked at her watch a lot. It struck Christine that Mrs. Randall seemed slightly embarrassed by her daughter, although she couldn't guess why. Frizz's Aunt Lois had also come, a quiet, plain woman who sat with her hands folded in her lap as if she were attending a church service.

"You can't come and live with us," Mrs. Randall had said. "Our apartment is just too small and your stepfather wouldn't like it. We have our social life to think of. You simply wouldn't fit in. I should think you would jump at your Aunt Lois's generous offer to take you in after you graduate."

"But Aunt Lois lives on a farm, Mama," the seventeen-year-old had said. "I don't *like* farms."

"Well, you're hardly in a position to choose, are you? You can't stay at St. Bridget's after you graduate. Where would you go?"

"I want to go to New York, Mama. I told you. I want to study the theater."

"And I've already told you that that is out of the question. And I must say that you're acting very ungrateful. Lois is being kind, and you don't seem to appreciate it."

"Please, Mama—"

"It's settled, my dear girl, and that's that."

As she watched Christine apply the last of the lotion to the curlers, Frizz said, "I visited my Aunt Lois once, when I was eleven. In her way, she is kind and gentle, but she's so God-awful quiet. She doesn't even have a radio in her house. She bakes all day long, or sews, or knits, and then sells the stuff at the local church bazaar. That's what she'll try to turn me into. Can you *see* it? I would die of boredom!"

"Your mother can't make you do it, can she?" Christine asked. "After all, you'll be eighteen by then."

"Oh, Choppie, I'm not strong like you. I can't stand up to her."

"Sure you can," Christine said with a smile. "You've just got to believe in yourself. You've always got to have hope."

Christine's own hope came from the letters her father sent regularly each month.

They arrived from exotic places, such as London and Stockholm, and they were always full of vivid descriptions, especially of the food: "I have discovered the delight of snails, Dolly. And frog legs, if you can imagine it! Loaded with garlic and swimming in butter. I'm collecting recipes, and someday I'll cook these marvelous dishes for you." Johnny always put postcards in with the letters, and once in a while a souvenir—a theater stub from London, a ticket to a museum in Rome. Christine had decorated the wall beside her bed with them, creating a colorful collage of foreign scenes and monuments.

She wrote faithfully back to him, addressing the letters to a post office box in nearby Marin, because he had given up the apartment in the city. She told him about her classes, her favorite subjects, the fun she and Frizz were having, about Starlets and all her friends.

The letters had helped the months drift into years, until before she knew it she was celebrating her sixteenth birthday under St. Bridget's roof. She had hoped her father would come then, but he had written from Holland, including a bag of tulip bulbs, which she had given to the convent gardener. Nonetheless, a bouquet of flowers and a box of candy did arrive at the school on the day of her birthday, from a florist in San Francisco, and a card, written by someone else, that said, "Happy sixteenth, Dolly, from your loving daddy." She wished he would telephone just one time, or that there was a number where he could be reached. In four years, she had not once heard the sound of his voice.

As she looked back over her time at St. Bridget's, she was surprised to see how comparatively easily, after those first troubled months, she had adjusted to convent life. When she wrote to her father that she had been put on a diet and that the carrot sticks were making her ill, Johnny had sent instructions to the school that his daughter was to eat the same food as everyone else. Solace in one form at least had returned to her life, and the best nights were when macaroni and cheese was served, or fried chicken, or mashed potatoes and gravy, because these brought comfort.

But mostly, Christine's adjustment to life at the school, and her happiness over the past four years, had been because of her friendship with Frizz.

"Okay," she said, stepping back and holding up a mirror. "All done."

Frizz regarded her reflection for a moment, then looked up at Christine. "I'll miss you, Choppie, when I go," she said. "If I hadn't had you for a friend while I was here, I don't know what I would have done. The thought of going on without you is more than I can bear. Hey!" she said suddenly. "I have a great idea! Why don't you come to New York with me? We can get an apartment together, and jobs, and we'll be like sisters."

"I'd like that, Frizz, but I'm going to live with my father when I get out of here. Why don't you study drama here, in San Francisco? You could live with us."

"Would that be all right? I mean, what would your father say?"

"He's traveling most of the time. I've written to him all about you. I'm sure he wouldn't mind having you with us."

"But he doesn't have a place. You said he gave up the apartment. You write to him at a post office box."

"Then we'll find a new place, one that's perfect for all three of us."

"Gosh, that would be swell! We'll both find jobs and we'll—"

A scream suddenly tore the air.

The girls fell silent and looked at one another.

"Where did that come from?" Christine said, jumping to her feet. She looked around the room. "Where's Mouse? Did anyone see her leave?"

"She said she had to go to the bathroom."

When they heard another scream, Christine ran down the hall to the bathroom and burst through the door.

"Help help help!" Mouse was screaming, her eyes screwed shut, her hair dripping wet. She was running blindly around the bathroom, clawing at her face, which was a terrifying red.

"Mouse!" Christine yelled, running to her. "What happened? Oh, Mouse!"

A shattered bottle lay on the floor, and toxic fumes filled the air.

As she got hold of the girl, Christine cried, "Frizz! Somebody! Get Sister Gabriel! *Hurry!*" Then she dragged Mouse into one of the shower stalls and turned the cold water on full force. "Open your eyes!" she said. "Mouse! Open your eyes!"

But Mouse was hysterical, flailing her arms and screaming. So Christine grasped her chin and turned her face into the spray, getting Raspberry Torte lipstick all over her hands.

The others stood in shocked silence as they watched Christine hold the screaming girl under the spray, trying to keep her face turned up to the water, while Mouse did a little dance on the tiles, flagging her arms up and down and howling in pain.

When Sister Gabriel arrived in her nightdress, carrying a first aid kit, she took one look at Mouse and said to Frizz, "Run to the kitchen and fetch the bottle of olive oil. Quickly! Dee Dee, run and wake up Mother Superior. Tell her to call an ambulance!"

As she set the kit on the floor and opened it, she said, "What happened?"

"She put that stuff—" Christine said, terrified. She was still holding on to the sobbing Mouse; they were both soaked through. "In that bottle. She put it on her head."

Sister Gabriel picked up a shard of glass and murmured, "Merciful heaven." The bottle had contained the cleaning fluid the novices used to scrub down the bathroom tiles.

The nun stepped into the shower, mindless of her nightdress or that her white cap was getting wet, and took Mouse from Christine. "There, there, my dear," she said. "Keep your face up to the water. We have to flush it out."

Mouse was quieter now, her thin little body shuddering with painful sobs, her faced smeared with garish lipstick. Sister Gabriel said, "Just a few more minutes, and then I'll put a dressing on your eyes." When she reached up to stroke the girl's head, a great handful of hair came out.

The girls gasped. Christine put her hand over her mouth, suddenly feeling sick.

When Frizz came back a minute later with the olive oil, the girls watched in frozen silence as Sister Gabriel brought Mouse out of the shower, wrapped a towel around her, and then poured a few drops of oil into each eye, after which she applied sterile gauze and then wrapped a bandage around the girl's head.

Christine stared in horror as more chunks of Mouse's hair came out.

Mother Superior was trembling with fury; even though she tried to control herself, Christine and Frizz saw how the scarf around her head quivered as she spoke. "Do you know what you girls have done?" she said, each word slicing the air like a knife. Spread out on her desk were cosmetics, nylons, bottles of permanent wave solution, all confiscated from Christine's room. Among them was the well-thumbed book, *Fanny Hill; or, Memoirs of a Woman of Pleasure.* Christine felt her cheeks burn with shame.

"This secret club was your idea, wasn't it, Christine?" Mother Superior said. Because she had been roused from bed, and the hour was late, she was wearing a plaid robe over her nightgown. Behind her, rain washed down the windows and bare tree branches tapped the windowpanes. The ambulance had taken Mouse away an hour ago; it was feared that she had been permanently blinded.

"You are a disgrace to this school, Christine Singleton," she went on, her fury barely contained. "You encouraged the other girls to do wrongful things, you encouraged poor little Lanie Freeman to try to change her hair color. You made her believe that her life would be better if she were blond. And so she poured cleaning fluid on her head, thinking it was ordinary bleach. Through your own vanity, Christine, you have caused a terrible thing to happen. If that poor girl is blinded for life, it is your fault. I hate to think of what your future is going to be like. You are vain and selfish. You think rules are only for other people. You are never going to amount to anything. I am ashamed of you. And you, too," she said to Frizz. "Well? What do you girls have to say for yourselves?"

"I'm sorry, Reverend Mother," Frizz whispered, her head bowed. The curlers had long since come out, and her hair looked kinkier than ever.

"I'm sorry, too, Reverend Mother," Christine said. "I'm sorry about Mouse, I really am. And if she's blind, then I'll never forgive myself. Only—just please don't tell my father about this."

"It's too late. He already knows."

Christine stared at her. The rain that was washing down the windows seemed to beat harder at the panes. "You *spoke* to my father?" Christine said. "You spoke to him tonight? You know where he is? Where is he, please tell me!"

"I'm afraid I can't do that, Christine. I'm sorry, I shouldn't have said what I said."

"What are you going to do?" Frizz asked as the two sat listening to the rain. Christine had not been able to get any more information out of Mother Superior regarding her father, only that he had somehow persuaded Reverend Mother to allow Christine to remain at the school.

"They know where he is," she said. "They have a telephone number for him, they've known it all along, and they won't tell it to me." It was midnight. She tossed a tennis ball back and forth between her hands while she stared at the rain-washed windows. "But I'm going to find it."

"How?"

"The records are in Mother Superior's office. The cabinet isn't locked. I saw her put my file away."

"Gosh, that's awfully dangerous, Christine. You could get caught, and then what will she do to you?"

"I hope she expels me."

"You don't want that, Choppie, because then your father would get mad."

Christine threw the ball so that it bounced against the dresser and rolled under Frizz's bed. "Maybe that's what I should have done long ago. Maybe I should have forced him to come and get me. Well, that's what I'm going to do now."

"I'll go with you."

Mother Superior's office wasn't locked, and the girls searched through the files with flashlights stolen from the kitchen. When Christine found her folder, the flashlight beam trembled on the page as she read: "Christine Singleton, born Hollywood, California, 1938. Father's occupation, Businessman. Mother, deceased." There was an emergency phone number for Johnny.

"I found it, Frizz!" Christine whispered, and she hastily wrote down the number. But she was puzzled—it was a local exchange.

"Is he in San Francisco then?" Frizz said, her face illuminated in the pale glow of her flashlight. She was searching through the files for her own folder, out of curiosity.

"I don't know," Christine said. "I don't understand. Mother Superior said she spoke to him tonight. If she called him at this number, then he must be in the city." She went through the rest of the file, most of which was concerned with childhood illnesses, vaccinations, reports written by her various private tutors. Until she came to a lined page that contained notes in Sister Gabriel's handwriting, information, according to the date, that she had written down the day Christine had been admitted to the school four years ago. One word leapt off the page.

Adopted.

"Formal adoption took place in Hollywood, California," Sister Gabriel had written, "when Christine was two weeks old. Mr. and Mrs. Singleton brought the baby back to San Francisco, where she has lived ever since."

She stared at the page. "I don't understand," she murmured.

"What's the matter?"

She looked at Frizz. "It says here that my father isn't my real father. That I'm adopted."

"Oh, there must be some mistake."

Suddenly, certain things became clear: the night Johnny's blond girl-friend had said, "Maybe her mother was overweight. Did you ever see her?" And on another occasion, during their picnic on Tiburon, when Christine had asked if she looked like her mother. "You're like her in spirit and heart, Dolly," he had said. Now Christine realized why there was no resemblance between her and the ethereal beauty in Sarah Singleton's picture—they were not related.

"No," she whispered, "it isn't true. I don't believe it."

"Maybe you were an orphan," Frizz said. "Maybe your father was protecting you from something awful."

"Yes, that must be it," Christine said, finding a glimmer of hope in that. If her real parents had died and Johnny had rescued her, well, that would somehow make it okay, wouldn't it?

She went through the file again, shaking so badly that she dropped the papers and had to gather them up. She found no birth certificate, no mention of who her real parents were. But there was a notation in the corner of her admissions sheet, written in Sister Gabriel's handwriting: "There is no communication between the natural parents and Mr. Single-ton."

The room suddenly swung around her.

No communication . . .

Could they still be alive? Her parents?

Frizz had been going through her own file, and she suddenly said, "Oh God, Choppie! My mother didn't give the school an emergency number! It says here that she didn't want them to contact her if anything happened to me! That they were to take care of it themselves!"

She reached out for Christine's arm. "My mother doesn't want me," she said. "She's never wanted me."

When Frizz's hand touched her arm, the room stopped moving, and

Christine stared at the damning word again: *adopted.* "My real mother didn't want me either, Frizz. She gave me away when I was two weeks old."

The two girls stood in the cold, dark office listening to the rain, the air around them heavy with betrayal. Christine tried to assimilate her new knowledge: that Johnny had lied to her from the day she was born, telling her he was her father, that the dead Sarah was her mother. And then later, putting her in St. Bridget's and promising that it wouldn't be for long, that he'd come back soon for her. Lies, all lies.

She looked at the rain and thought how cold and empty it seemed, like her own insides. "I'm leaving, Frizz," she said at last. "I won't stay here anymore. I'm leaving this place tonight."

"How can you?"

Christine had some money. An allowance of ten dollars had been doled out to her every month out of the money her father sent semiannually to the school, and she had put it away in a shoebox under the bed. It came to several hundred dollars.

"I'll go with you."

"I have to go alone, Frizz. I'm going to find my father." The only address was the postal box she already had. But now she had a telephone number.

"I want to go, too. We don't have to go the same way. We can part when we cross the Bay. I couldn't bear to stay here without you. I have some money saved. I'll go to New York. I have a cousin there who'll help me. She doesn't like my mother either!"

The two friends regarded each other in the thin glow of their flashlights, and suddenly they saw that they weren't girls anymore; their childhoods were over. "Yes," Christine said, "we'll both go."

Frizz said, "I hate my mother. I've never hated anyone as much as I hate her. I wish I didn't have anything to do with her. I wish I were someone else. I wish I could change my identity."

"Take my name if you like," Christine said. "After all, it isn't my real name anyway, is it?"

"And you can take mine. Here." Frizz pulled her birth certificate out of the file and handed it to Christine. "I was born in 1937, a year before you, but you could pass for seventeen. So from now on, I'll be you and you'll be me."

They took the first ferry at dawn. The rain had stopped. They were carrying raincoats and suitcases; both had changed into civilian clothes and left their uniforms behind. When the ferry docked at Fisherman's Wharf, the girls stood for a long moment in the biting morning air, breathing in the salt of the sea that mingled with the fish smell from the seafood stalls that were just opening for business.

"I'll never forget you, Choppie," Frizz said solemnly.

"Me neither," Christine said.

"You've got my cousin's address. Write to me."

"I will. Friends forever."

"Friends forever."

They embraced for a long minute, sniffing back their tears. Then Christine watched Frizz walk to the end of the cable car line that would take her into the city, her mass of untameable hair rising up in the mist in an explosion of burgundy-colored kinks.

Then Christine looked around for a phone booth.

When she found one, she wedged her suitcase inside and got a nickel out of her purse. The first phone call was to San Francisco General Hospital, where Mouse had been taken.

It was some minutes before she convinced them that she was a relative: "I'm her older sister. I'm away at college and I just heard the news. I won't be able to get there for a few days. Can't you please tell me how she's doing?"

Finally the nurse said, "She's lost most of her hair, and there's some scarring on her face, but we think her eyesight has been saved."

"Thank God. What? A message? Yes, please tell her that Christine called. And tell her, please, that . . . I'm sorry."

Then she took out the phone number she had copied from her file. She paused before dialing. What should she say to him? What would her first words be? Should she come right out and ask him why he had told her so many lies? Or should she just forgive him, right here and now, and pretend she didn't know the truth, just say to him, "Daddy, I'm coming home."

She dropped the nickel in and dialed. When a man's voice answered, "Department of Corrections," she was momentarily taken aback. "I'm sorry," she said, "I must have the wrong number." She got another nickel and dialed again, getting the same answer.

When she asked the man at the other end of the line if this was the number she was calling, and he said it was, she asked to speak to Johnny Singleton.

"Is he staff or inmate?"

"I beg your pardon?"

"Is he on the staff or is he an inmate?"

"What do you mean?"

"Does he work here?"

"Yes."

"Hold on . . . Sorry, I have no listing for a Johnny Singleton on staff. What is his job classification?"

Christine grew distraught. "I don't know. You have to have him listed. He's my father. This is the number he gave the school in case of an emergency. You have to know where he works."

"Just a moment, miss, I'll transfer you."

She clutched the phone as she listened to the minute of silence, and when the next male voice said, "Inmate Services," her fear grew.

"I'm trying to get hold of Johnny Singleton," she explained, "but the other person transferred me. What is this place? Where am I calling?"

"This is the Department of Corrections, miss."

"Yes, but where?"

The man at the other end paused, then said, "This is San Quentin State Prison."

She stared at her reflection in the glass.

The man said, "Did you say Johnny Singleton?" and there was a chilling familiarity in the way he said the name.

"Y-yes, he's my father. I have to talk to him. He must work there, the other man must have been mistaken when he said he wasn't on staff."

"Can you identify yourself in some way, miss?"

She started to cry. "No—" she said, and it came out in a squeak. "I . . . I'm sorry, I must have . . . the wrong number."

She hung up and stumbled out of the booth.

Her daddy, in prison. San Quentin. Maximum security. For the worst crimes. What had he done to put him in there? Maybe Martha Camp had been right all along—maybe Johnny *was* a gangster!

And what about all those letters from exotic places, when all this time he had been here, just across the bay in that horrible prison? He must have had someone mail those letters for him.

She went to the water's edge and took Johnny's picture out of her purse. Why didn't you tell me? she silently asked the smiling, handsome face. Why couldn't you trust me? Was it because of the incident with Hans? Did you kill him, is that why you're in prison? Why did you lie to me again—our whole life together has been based upon lies. And now there's nothing left to keep it together.

She tore up her mother's and father's pictures and tossed them onto the bay. As she watched the pieces float away on the tide, she heard Mother Superior's words again: "You are never going to amount to anything." And Christine thought, You're wrong. I'll show you, I'll show everybody. I'm going to be someone, just the way Johnny told me to be.

I'm going to fight for what I want, and someday I'm going to be some-body.

Finally, she took out Frizz's birth certificate and thought, I am no longer Christine Singleton. I have nothing to do with Johnny or his name. From now on I am going to be the person on this piece of paper. I am going to be Philippa Roberts. And I am going to *be* somebody.

DAY
TWO

·····································★

The telephone conversation took place in secret, to make certain that it wasn't overheard.

"I've been informed that Philippa Roberts is on her way to Los Angeles, where she will be visiting the Starlite headquarters. I'm afraid this calls for an immediate change of plans."

There was a moment of silence while the person on the other end spoke, disturbed only by the impatient squawk of a parrot.

Then: "I have someone watching her and reporting to me. We have to be cautious now. We must proceed very carefully. What? No, it's too late for that. She's already on her way. She'll be there in a few hours. Yes, I'm prepared. Let me emphasize this: she knows nothing so far. And she is never to know. Is that understood? Here is what I intend to do . . ."

13

··★

They looked like Martians, materializing suddenly out of nowhere, two slender unisex beings encased in bright pink and orange Day-Glo skins, joined together by wires that led from their heads to a yellow box between them. Their feet didn't touch the ground as they glided past the Starlite limousine, across the busy street, and up to a giant chocolate donut that was three stories tall.

Charmie watched the young pair sail up to the sugar shop on narrow blade skates and order something through the window at the bottom of the donut, their bodies constantly in motion as they moved to the music emanating from their shared Walkman. After they received their order, they glided off again, each cramming a donut into his/her face, the blade skates skimming the sidewalk as if it were air.

Charmie shook her head and said with a laugh, "Welcome back to Southern California, the land of fruits and nuts. See what you've been missing, Philippa?"

Charmie and Philippa and Ricky were riding in the limousine that had met them at the airport. The partition behind the driver was up, sealing the three passengers in a cell of plush, soundproofed comfort. There were soft drinks and a bucket of shaved ice, plus a tray of cold cuts and cocktail breads; from hidden speakers the gentle music of station KOST came like a breeze.

Charmie was creating a miniature pepperoni and cheddar cheese sandwich for herself, while Ricky stared through the smoked-glass window at California.

"Will we see any film stars, do you reckon?" he asked when he saw a sign that read HOLLYWOOD, 17 MILES.

As the limo moved through the heavy traffic, Charmie poured a diet

Coke, taking care not to spill on her emerald green rayon caftan. "You never know what you'll see in L.A.!" she said with a laugh.

Philippa was also looking out the window, thinking that there was no place on earth like Los Angeles in December: the surrounding mountains were all topped with snow; the smog-free air was as sharp as hand-cut crystal; and tonight, she knew, the basin was going to be a glorious blaze of glitzy, gaudy Christmas lights, with commercial buildings and private homes competing to out-holiday one another, while the streets were going to be crammed with impatient holiday traffic. Los Angeles in December, where every day was an orange grove kind of day.

She was suddenly glad to be home.

As the limousine swept past familiar sights and street signs with names that triggered a wave of nostalgia, Philippa found herself thinking of things she hadn't thought about in a long time. She had been born very near this place, in Hollywood; she had drawn her first breath in this city, and she hoped someday to draw her last here. She had lost her virginity not far from here, in a street behind Grauman's Chinese Theatre. And it was not far from here that Starlite had gotten its start, just over the Santa Monica Mountains, a quick dash through the Sepulveda Pass into a town with the impossible name of Tarzana. A memory flashed in her mind: paintings of Tarzan, long-haired and nearly naked, wrestling with lions and riding elephants through jungles. Paintings that had hung in the Tarzana post office many years ago. She wondered if they were still there.

When the car climbed an on-ramp and joined the traffic on the Santa Monica Freeway, Philippa stared out at the orderly palm-lined streets of Century City and Santa Monica; she could just glimpse in the distance the thin blue ribbon of Pacific Ocean that stood like a mother-of-pearl wall guarding California. Beyond that, thousands of miles away, lay Perth, and Point Resolution, and the place where the *Philippa* had gone down. She felt the invisible threads stretch away from herself and out over the many miles, connecting her with the man she would never stop loving.

Him, too, she had met not far from here, over those mountains through the Sepulveda Pass. This had once been his home, as it had been hers. And coming back now, Philippa was suddenly filled with a sense of pilgrimage, and of destiny.

"Do you want to check into the hotel first?" Charmie said as the car neared Century City. "I thought you might want to freshen up before facing the barracudas." Although Philippa still had a house in Beverly Hills, she had closed it up when she had gone to Australia to claim her inherited villa. It was simpler, for now, to check into a hotel. Later, after the mess with Starlite and Miranda International was cleared up, after she found out who Beverly Burgess was, she would consider what to do next: return to Perth or stay here.

"No, thank you, Charmie," she said now, her anxiety showing in her posture, the way she sat slightly forward in her seat, with her hand resting on the door handle as if ready to spring out. "I want to go straight to the office." She turned to Ricky. "After the car drops us off, you go on to the hotel and get us checked in. Make a lunch reservation for one o'clock."

"Yes, Miss Roberts," he said, and Philippa added more quietly, "Welcome to California, Ricky. I'm glad you came with us."

The building that housed the main offices of Starlite Industries rose an impressive forty storys above Wilshire Boulevard on land that was riddled with earthquake faults. Philippa never ceased to marvel at the optimism of Los Angelenos—their skyscrapers got taller as the day of the Big One drew nearer. It was almost as if they were saying to nature, "Come on, shake us down, we dare you."

"Well, Charmie," she said as they stepped out of the limousine in front of the glass and brick building, where a bronze fountain sprayed a giant hydrangea of water. Philippa squinted up to the top of the building and saw how the amber-glazed windows flashed back the sharp morning sun. "A moment of truth is about to be upon us. We'll go straight up, no announcement. Let's carefully watch everyone's reaction when they see me. If there is a corporate takeover in the works, and if it does involve someone inside Starlite, they're bound to give themselves away at my sudden appearance."

Starlite Industries occupied the upper floors of the building, with the executive offices being at the very top. Philippa and Charmie stepped out of the elevator into a quiet reception area that was decorated in subdued tones, with hidden lighting illuminating the Starlite logo, tall and imposing behind the receptionist's desk. There was a glass case displaying a collection of books, the various hardcover and paperback editions of Philippa's books: *The Starlite Diet and Beauty Program, The Starlite One-Hour Diet,* and the four Starlite cookbooks. They had all been international best-sellers, and a very scholarly, personal book by Philippa titled "Hyperinsulinemia: Its Causes, Detection, and Control Through Diet" had sold well.

The receptionist, who sat between a massive poinsettia plant and a mini Christmas tree, was a young woman who hadn't been with Starlite for long and had never met Philippa. "Ms. Charmer!" she said. "I was told you'd gone back east for the holidays." She reached for the intercom. "I'll let them know you're here—"

But Charmie said, "No, don't," and she and Philippa breezed past and through the double doors on the other side. It wasn't until after they had gone that the receptionist suddenly realized who the other woman was. Philippa's photograph was on the books in the glass case.

The plaque on the door read HANNAH SCADUDO, FASHION DESIGN. Philippa and Charmie walked into a large, sunny office where artists sat at computers and drafting tables in the noisy, busy workroom. People were hurrying this way and that, phones were ringing, papers lay scattered on the carpeted floor, bolts of fabric were stacked from floor to ceiling, and the thick smell of coffee and stale donuts filled the air. A seismic time wave hit Philippa. Fashion design had always been one of her favorite departments, ever since they had decided to start a clothing line catering to larger women, marketed through a chain of dress shops called The Perfect Size. Hannah's department was always exciting, with creativity flowing like electric currents. Being here again sent Philippa back to the early days when they had discussed Hannah's designs in a turquoise booth at a Cut-Cost Drugstore. That long-ago dream was now real; they had made it come true. Was it now in danger of being shattered?

Hannah's office looked as if it had been plucked out of a department store by a passing tornado and dropped here. Fabrics, patterns, half-sewn dresses, sketches, and tape measures lay everywhere, while Hannah's desk top could not be seen for the massive catalogs, stacks of delivery bills, letters, Styrofoam cups half-filled with tea, and gum wrappers in the hundreds.

When Philippa saw her friend in the corner, draping slinky material over a size-eighteen mannequin, a look of deep concentration on her face, words Hannah had spoken to her thirty years ago echoed in her mind: "You know, if you changed that round collar to a V neck, you'd take ten pounds off." Philippa experienced a sharp stab of love mingled with fear, and she thought, Please, Hannah, don't let it be you. Don't be the traitor among us.

Charmie said, "Hi, Hannah," and Hannah Scadudo turned, said, "Oh my God," and briefly caught hold of the mannequin as if to steady herself; then she hurried to Philippa, her hands extended, a smile on her face. "Philippa! My God! What a wonderful surprise!"

They embraced, but not before Philippa had noted the flicker of fear in her friend's eyes.

"Hello, Hannah," Philippa said, realizing that this woman whom she had known for so many years—Hannah whom nothing seemed to touch, who was somehow changeless—had altered during Philippa's absence. Her square face had high cheekbones, and her eyes had a slightly Asian cast to them. She always declared there must be American Indian somewhere in her ancestry and that it perhaps accounted for her being "so well preserved." But today, on this December morning with Los Angeles sunshine streaming through the floor to ceiling window, Hannah Scadudo suddenly looked every minute of her real age.

Philippa thought, Something is wrong here.

Tears rose in Hannah's eyes as she said, "I can't tell you how glad I am to see you! Oh Philippa, we've missed you!" The last time Hannah had seen Philippa was when she and her husband Alan had gone to Western Australia, six months ago, for a visit.

"I've missed you too," Philippa said quietly, wishing suddenly that she could be anywhere but here, doing anything but this.

"Charmie!" Hannah said. "We all thought you were in Ohio. Why didn't you tell us? We've never kept secrets before."

Philippa said, "Are we keeping secrets now, Hannah?"

Again, a small gallop of fear in Hannah's dark brown eyes. But she kept up the smile. "Philippa," she said, "whatever do you mean?"

"Where can a woman get a drink around here?" Charmie said suddenly.

They went down the hall to the executive lounge, which was deserted and which, when the door closed behind Philippa, was blessedly silent. A mirrored bar lined one wall, facing the windows that gave out onto a spectacular view of modern skyscrapers and palm trees. Charmie went straight to it, reaching for the bottle of Bombay Sapphire gin and a glass. "What are you ladies drinking?"

"Nothing for me," Hannah said. She held her shaking hands before her and added with a laugh, "Too much coffee!"

"I'll have a Perrier," Philippa said, and she sank into the embrace of a leather sofa. "Hannah, it is good to see you," she said. "How are the kids?" The "kids" being adults themselves with children of their own. Philippa was godmother to Hannah's second girl, whose middle name was Philippa.

While Hannah spoke breathlessly, bringing her friend up to date on her family's latest news—"Jackie is doing brilliantly in Santa Barbara, and we always thought she had no ambition"—Charmie poured the drinks.and brought them back to the sofa group. Handing Philippa the Perrier and tasting her own tangy gin, she settled down next to Hannah and said, "Esther's in love. Again."

"Yes, I know," Hannah said. "Jackie told me. She says Esther and her boyfriend go around the campus like Siamese twins." Hannah's daughter was the same age as Philippa's; the two had grown up together and now attended the same school. "It's your turn to be a grandmother, Philippa!" Hannah said.

As Philippa sipped her drink, she looked at her two friends through the broad mote-dusted sunbeam that spilled into the room. Hannah with her short brown hair, perpetually dressed in tones of beige and tan, seemed somehow sparrowlike next to the colorful Charmie, with her shimmering green caftan and outrageous bright yellow plastic jewelry, her flyaway blond hair barely captured by the scarf on top of her head. And Philippa felt a sudden pang of nostalgia for the old days, for the truckloads of memories the three of them shared.

"How does it feel to be back?" Hannah said with a quiet smile.

"I don't know yet really, I'm still jet-lagged."

"Tell Hannah the good news," Charmie said, plastic bangles clacking on her wrists.

"What good news is that, Philippa?"

Before Philippa could reply, Charmie said, "Ivan Hendricks thinks he's found Philippa's sister."

"For real?" Hannah said. "Is he sure this time?"

"No, we aren't sure. Ivan flew back before we did; he's looking into it further. She lives at a resort called Star's. Do you know it?"

"I've heard of it. You know Julianna Livingston, the socialite? I ran into her at Spago a week or so ago, and in the course of the conversation she told us that she had received an invitation to the Christmas ball at Star's. It's quite an honor, I understand."

"Why was she invited? Does she know the owner?"

"I don't think so. She said she had no idea why they'd asked her. But someone like Julianna is on every invitation list in town—at least the ones that count. So that's why you came back!" Hannah said with an audible trace of relief in her voice. "Because Ivan might have found your sister!"

Philippa suddenly felt very tired. She wanted to go back to the hotel and lie down. "I came back, Hannah," she said, "because we have a problem."

Hannah glanced at Charmie and then at Philippa. "What kind of problem?"

"I'm calling a special board meeting, Hannah. I want to meet with every one of my executives and I will expect individual department reports, and then I will examine the corporate accounts. Charmie has alerted me to an alarming discrepancy that has to be looked into."

Philippa kept her eyes on Hannah and thought she detected a slight change in the color of her face. "You haven't found any problems with *your* books, have you, Hannah?"

"No, not at all. I mean, what kind of problems?"

"Errors, discrepancies in the figures that can't be explained. Invoices, perhaps, from companies that don't exist?"

Hannah began to fiddle with the bracelet on her right wrist. "No, I haven't come across anything irregular. If I had, I would have reported it. Oh for goodness sake," she said with a laugh. "You've quite flustered me! What's this all about?"

"I'll explain at the board meeting, when I have more facts."

"Alan and I are having a Christmas party in a few days, and you simply must come. Maybe Esther and her new boyfriend can ride down with Jackie and her boyfriend. You, too, Charmie, if you don't go to Ohio."

"I can't promise," Philippa said. "I have no idea how my schedule is going to work out. But I do know that in four days I will be holding the board meeting, in Palm Springs."

"Palm Springs! Why not here?"

"Because Star's is in Palm Springs, and I don't know how long I'll be there. But Palm Springs is beautiful this time of the year." Philippa smiled. "I think a drive in the desert will be good for you. Take you away from this chaos."

The door opened and a man entered. "Hannah, there you are," he said. "I've been looking for you—"

He stared at Philippa, then he broke into a smile. "Philippa! How good to see you! What a wonderful surprise!"

Alan Scadudo was Hannah's husband and chief financial officer of Starlite Industries. The two had been with the company for as long as Philippa and Charmie had; they were among the founding members.

"Have you come back to us for good?" he said, drawing Philippa into a tight embrace. Alan was Philippa's height, five feet eight, which he supplemented by adding two inches with heel lifts. He had also had hair transplants, and when he was close to her, Philippa could see the little dots at his hairline.

"Philippa says there's a problem, Alan," Hannah said quickly. "She's calling an emergency board meeting."

"Yes, this disturbing business with Miranda International."

"What have you been able to find out, Alan?"

"Not much, I'm afraid. I spoke with the president of the company over the phone, a Gaspar Enriques, who assured me that their intentions are entirely friendly. But when I asked if they would sign a standstill agreement, he refused. Quite politely, of course."

"That doesn't sound friendly to me. Do you suspect a hostile takeover?"

"It certainly looks like one."

"Alan," Philippa said, "I want you to fly down to Rio right away and meet with Enriques in person. See what you can make of it, try to find out what interest Miranda has in our company. And get him to sign that agreement."

"Yes, certainly, Philippa. Whatever you say. I'll leave at once."

"And another thing, Alan, I'm calling a meeting of the board in four days. I want everyone to attend. Is there anyone who isn't available?"

"We're all here," Hannah said, "except for Ingrid." Ingrid Lind was the buyer for Starlite's fashion line; she worked directly under Hannah.

"She's in Singapore right now on a buying trip. Is Ingrid essential? I don't believe she's due back for another two weeks."

"I want to see everyone on the board, including Ingrid. Call her back. I want to see all the books, spreadsheets, and profit and loss reports for the past five years, plus invoices, payment vouchers. Get an internal audit started, Alan, and bring the results to the meeting."

"What's it about?" he asked.

"It's about a million dollars," she said, signaling to Charmie. "In the meantime, we're going back to the hotel to rest."

Hannah rose and said, "When do you go to Palm Springs?"

"Charmie and I will be checking in to the Marriott Desert Springs tomorrow night. That's where the board meeting will be held."

At which time, she thought unhappily, she would find out who were her friends, and who were the traitors.

14

Hollywood, California, 1958

Philippa looked up from her work and saw that he had come into the drugstore again—the man with the haunted look.

She didn't know what it was about him that caught her attention so; they had never exchanged words, she didn't know who he was, where he lived, or what he did. But his looks intrigued her. It wasn't so much the khaki trousers and baggy sweater and sandals, the unruly black hair, the very handsome face, all of which did make him look unreal, like something out of a movie. It was more the man himself that she was drawn to, the mouth that looked as if it had never smiled, the eyes that seemed to look into another, more disturbing world. He came into the Cut-Cost Drugstore on Hollywood Boulevard every Friday for the ninety-nine-cent lunch special, always alone, walking with indifference or standing in a slouch, smoking an endless chain of cigarettes as he sat hunched over a two-hour cup of coffee, peering into his cigarette smoke as if looking for answers or trying to forget them.

Philippa had first noticed him three months ago, when she had filled in temporarily at the lunch counter when the regular girl was sick, and she had watched him every Friday afternoon since, her curiosity growing. Now, as she stocked Toni home permanents on a shelf, she watched him and thought that there was something lonely about him; she sensed that something or someone had hurt him once and that he carried the pain around with him like an invisible load. She couldn't guess his age, but his face was lined, so she thought maybe around forty. And when she saw how he counted out the exact change for his bargain lunch, and how he accepted coffee refills until the waitress told him he would have to pay again, Philippa thought, He needs someone to heal him, someone to take care of him.

"Philippa? Miss Roberts!"

She spun around. "Yes, Mr. Reed?" Reed, the manager of the drugstore, the man who had hired Philippa four years ago, thought she was a good worker, dependable, cheerful, never called in sick. But she tended to be a bit of a daydreamer; he sometimes had to repeat her name before he got her attention.

Philippa was trying to break herself of that habit; she knew Mr. Reed and others thought she was either deaf or that her mind wandered. They didn't know that Philippa wasn't her real name. Once, when a woman had come into the store with a little girl, saying, "Now behave, Christine," Philippa had turned around, thinking the woman was talking to her.

"I need you to work the ice cream counter, Philippa," Mr. Reed said. "Dora had to go home, she said she wasn't feeling well."

Before leaving the cosmetics department, Philippa paused at the Revlon display and checked herself in the mirror. It hadn't bothered her before, but now she suddenly wished her face weren't so pudgy. But at least her hair was nice; thick and auburn, and drawn up into a ponytail that fell past her shoulders. And she wore a little lipstick, and sometimes nail polish, but she didn't allow herself anything extravagant beyond that. She was saving her money.

On the day she tore up her parents' photographs and tossed them into the bay, Philippa had left San Francisco. She had gone straight from Fisherman's Wharf to the Greyhound bus station, where she had purchased a one-way ticket to Hollywood. Her hopes and dreams had made the long journey with her, tucked safely away in an invisible trunk. Compartments of that unseen trunk had also transported her determination to make something of herself. "You are never going to amount to anything," Mother Superior had said. But Philippa was going to prove her, and everyone else, wrong.

When she arrived in Hollywood, she had walked up and down the streets looking for the glamor she had expected to find, the movie stars, the settings of her favorite films. Instead, she found tidy little motor courts and modest storefronts and palm trees—an endless march of palm trees. She came upon a quiet street behind Grauman's Chinese Theatre, where houses were set far back, with big lawns that sloped to the sidewalk. The houses all had deep verandas and steep roofs—Philippa learned later that these were called California bungalows and that they had been built just after the turn of the century. One of them had a Room for Rent sign in the front window.

The landlady's name was Mrs. Chadwick.

"There's four other boarders," she had explained as she puffed up the stairs, "two schoolteachers who work over to Hollywood High, a gal works a travel agency, and Mr. Romero, who says he's a scriptwriter for the studios, but I ain't never heard his typewriter going. Mr. Romero'll invite you into his room for a drink, but his feelings won't be hurt if you turn him down. He's harmless. You seventeen, you say?"

"Yes," sixteen-year-old Philippa said. "I have my birth certificate if—"

"Ain't necessary." At the top of the stairs Mrs. Chadwick looked the girl up and down. "You look like a big eater," she said. "Oh, don't worry, I don't mean it critical. I have an appetite myself, and I must say, I put out a good table. My boarders don't starve, I can tell you that. Well, here's the room. Five dollars a week, a month in advance. Bathroom's down the hall."

The room was small, but it was sunny and airy, with palm trees right outside the window. Philippa could see the big H-O-L-L-Y-W-O-O-D sign on the distant hills.

That same afternoon she had gone job hunting. The few restaurants she applied at turned her down flat. "The uniform won't fit," they said. But she was lucky at the Cut-Cost Drugstore on Hollywood Boulevard, because the employees wore large smocks so it didn't matter that she was overweight. Cut-Cost was one of those new modern drugstores that sold other things besides drugs, like underwear and percolators, and had lunch and ice cream counters. She was hired that day at seventy-five cents an hour to do everything from sweeping up to running the checkout. Or selling ice cream cones, which was where she went to work now while she kept an eye on the tormented man who was chain-smoking at the lunch counter.

The day she got the job at Cut-Cost, Philippa had gone down the street to Hollywood High School and registered for evening adult classes. Within a year she received the high school diploma she should have received from St. Bridget's. Now she was attending evening classes at a local junior college, with the hopes of eventually obtaining a bachelor's degree. When the other employees at Cut-Cost looked at Philippa, or when Mrs. Chadwick's boarders engaged her in conversation, they saw a determined young woman who was quiet, kept to herself, and worked hard. Sometimes Mrs. Chadwick would sit on the front porch of her California bungalow and hear the girl's typewriter clacking away upstairs as Philippa did homework assignments, and she would wonder what drove the child so.

A woman came up to the ice cream counter then and ordered a double scoop of vanilla, and when Philippa saw her wine red hair, she thought of Frizz and wondered if her old friend was still getting along in New York City. The two had exchanged letters frequently at first, and it had been strange to address an envelope to Christine Singleton and to open mail addressed to Philippa Roberts. Frizz had told her all about her life in Manhattan, how she shared an apartment with three other aspiring actresses while working at a deli to support herself, closing her letters with "I miss you more than I can say, Choppie. I hope we can be together again someday." But after a while the letters had started to get shorter and further apart until, to Philippa's dismay, Frizz stopped writing altogether. Her last letter, which came a year ago, had been little more than a brief note saying, "Don't know if I can make a go of it here. Maybe Mother was right." Philippa had written back, asking Frizz to come to Hollywood, but she had received no answer.

Rinsing off the ice cream scoop, she turned around and was startled to see him standing there, the stranger with the haunted face, reading the list of flavors behind her. He carried a spiral notebook, and a cigarette dangled from his lips. Philippa's heart jumped; she had never been this close to him before. He was so very handsome, in the dark, square-jawed way she liked.

She was just about to say, "May I help you?" when two teenage boys who were loitering at the magazine rack looked at Philippa. One of them said, "Look at the porker they've got serving the ice cream," and his friend said, "That's like having the mouse watch the cheese!"

Their laughter was cut off by a sudden word from the man, who turned to them and snapped, "That's bloody rude of you, don't you think?"

The boys gave him a startled look and began to say something when he cut them off with, "Why don't you go somewhere and immolate yourselves?"

They went away, saying "fuck you" over their shoulders. He turned back to Philippa and said, "Stupid kids." When he gazed at her she saw very dark eyes that looked right at her and, she felt, straight down into her soul.

She tried to think of something to say, a way to thank him, when he said with a half smile, "What the hell, one scoop of vanilla."

Philippa served it up neatly, giving him an extra-large scoop, and he took the cone and slapped a nickel on the glass counter. She thought she saw sparkles in the black eyes when he said, "Keep this up and you'll bankrupt the company."

She watched him go, confused by her sudden feelings. It was some minutes before she realized he had left his spiral notebook on the counter. She hurried outside, but when she looked up and down Hollywood Boulevard, he was nowhere in sight. She decided to keep it and return it to him the next time he came in.

A name was written on the cover: Rhys.

★ ★ ★

Philippa stared at herself in the bathroom mirror. "That's bloody rude," he had said. He had defended her. When the boys had insulted her, he had defended her. But there was more to it than that. It was the way his eyes had not only looked *at* her, but *into* her.

He was so tall, so good looking, so self-assured, it seemed. And yet. And yet . . .

Something is troubling him.

As Philippa went back into her room and tried to settle down to her studies—tonight, Psych 101—she had a hard time concentrating. She couldn't get him out of her mind. She looked at the spiral notebook he had left on the ice cream counter. She hadn't opened it, but now, overcome with curiosity, she finally did and read the first page. It appeared to be a poem of some sort:

> *Lavender shoe polish.*
> *Midgets on the moon.*
> *Singing peas.*
> *End the Resurrection just when you need it . . .*

She turned the pages. "Existence comes before essence," he had written. "We create ourselves after we are born. God was invented as an excuse, as a place to lay blame. Without God, *we* are responsible. And *we* have the Bomb."

Philippa suddenly felt sad. She pictured his handsome face, with its melancholy shadows, the neglected clothes, the black tousled hair and soulful black eyes. What pain did he carry inside? When had he lost hope?

She went to the window and looked out at the lights of Hollywood twinkling through the evening smog. She could hear the constant traffic on Hollywood Boulevard, where the sleepless, the cruisers, the sightseers thronged steadily up and down the street.

Philippa had not allowed herself to think of boys in the past four years—or men, now that she had turned twenty. From the minute she had run away from St. Bridget's, her path had been set, her goal clear and beckoning. To make something, *somebody*, of herself. She wasn't sure yet just who she was going to be, or what her exact purpose was, but she knew it would come to her and she would recognize it when it was there. And along the way, she was going to prepare herself. She had made the commitment to work hard and sacrifice; she filled her time with her job and school, leaving few idle hours. When she did have a free moment and her mind wandered into daydreams, she disciplined herself back to reality.

There were to be no lovers in her life, no men; they would only let her down.

Once in a while she thought of Johnny. Although she knew that the day would come when she would no longer be angry with him, when the feeling of betrayal would eventually subside, for now she could not forgive him for his deceits and for abandoning her.

When she heard the theme from *The Lucy-Desi Comedy Hour* come faintly up through the floor, she realized that Mrs. Chadwick had finished her kitchen chores and had settled down to watch TV. Philippa went back to her desk, where she had been been trying to study. She pushed her homework to one side and brought out a small book that was bound in floral cloth. She had bought it at the Hallmark store on the boulevard, and with it a small fake-gold pen. The first thing she had written in it was "Believe in yourself and you can achieve anything."

Philippa thought of the little book as her spiritual guide, her own self-written bible. In the many months since that first entry, she had written "Attitudes are more important than facts." "Think defeat and you will be defeated; think success and you will be successful." "They conquer who believe they can."

And she thought how different her own private notes were from those Rhys had written.

She was unpacking Easter baskets and chocolate bunnies wrapped in gold foil. Mr. Reed knew Philippa was the only one he could trust for the job, because everyone else on his staff would eat the stock before it made it to the shelves. Philippa, although overweight, never touched candy. It was Friday, and she kept her eye on the lunch counter as she arranged the baskets, taking care that no two colors stood side by side, making it a prettier display and giving the impression that the store had more of a variety than it really did.

And then she saw him.

She hurried down the aisle, her heart pounding. He had just sat down on his usual stool at the lunch counter when she came up, pulling the notebook out of the large pocket of her pink smock and saying, "Excuse me? Mr. Rice?"

When he didn't turn around, she put the notebook on the counter by his arm and said, "You left this here last week, Mr. Rice."

He turned and looked at her, black eyes once again shooting through her. "It's Reese," he said quietly.

"I beg your pardon?"

"The name, it's pronounced Reese."

"Oh—" She felt her face burn. "Mr. Rhys—"

"Not Mister," he said with a lifting of one corner of his mouth that might have indicated a smile. "Just Rhys."

"Yes, well, you left it here and I thought it might be important . . ."

"Important?" he said, looking at the notebook as though he had no idea what it was. "Words. Just words." He turned his dark eyes on her again; they lingered on her face for a moment, as if he were trying to read something there, and then again, that hint of a smile, and he turned back to his coffee.

It was one of those perfumed, balmy May evenings when Los Angeles seemed wrapped in warm velvet. Philippa had worked late because two girls had called in sick, and as she hurried home, her thoughts were on the assignment that was due tomorrow night in her art history class. When someone came out of the apartment building just up ahead, she wasn't really paying attention. But when he stepped beneath the glow of the porch light and she saw who it was, she stopped.

Rhys.

He walked down to the sidewalk at a casual pace, the notebook in his hand, a cigarette in his mouth. Philippa suddenly found herself following him, hanging back far enough so that he wouldn't see her. When he reached Hollywood Boulevard, he went to a well-lit bus stop and slouched there, squinting through his smoke at the garish neon signs along the street. Philippa stayed back in the protection of the Bank of America entrance, wondering where he was going at this late hour. There was traffic in the street, but there weren't many pedestrians, just a few tourists haunting the deserted forecourt of Grauman's Chinese. A bus came along a few minutes later, bound for Sunset Boulevard, and Rhys got on board and rode away.

Philippa went back to the apartment building he had come out of and read the names on the mailboxes.

There it was: number 10—Rhys.

She went out the next night, right after her art history class, and she got to Rhys's street just as he was coming out of his building. She followed him again and watched as he got on board the same bus. When she did this for the next three nights, which were not school nights, she wondered if he was going to a job, because it was always at the same time, always the same bus.

On the sixth night, she decided to skip her English literature class and follow him. Philippa got on the bus two stops before Rhys's and huddled down in the back so he wouldn't see her. As usual, he was waiting at Highland. As she watched him take a seat and slump against the window, she hoped it wouldn't be a long ride, or that there were transfers, because the hour was late, and the city, so late at night, frightened her.

When the bus stopped along the Sunset Strip, Rhys got off; Philippa saw him go through a plain doorway with a sign over it that said "Woody's."

For the next week, Philippa hurried home right after evening class and got on the bus before Rhys did, watching him get off at Woody's, until finally, on a night when she had no school, she worked up the courage to get off two stops past Woody's and walk back. She hesitated on the sidewalk before approaching the plain wooden door, wondering what could be on the other side, wondering, in fact, if she should knock or just go in.

Her dilemma was solved when a strange-looking couple came around the corner and went in, just pulling the door open and going inside. The man was wearing a sweatshirt, khaki pants, and sandals; the woman was dressed in a black leotard and a baggy sweater, her face a peculiar chalky white with heavy black mascara around the eyes. Philippa realized that they were beatniks; she had seen some on TV, but this was the first time she had ever seen any in person.

Afraid, but thinking of Rhys, she pulled the wooden door open and stepped inside. She had to wait until her eyes adjusted to the darkness, despite the fact that she had just come in from the night. While she waited, she heard peculiar sounds and smelled odors she wasn't familiar with. The sounds, she realized after a moment, were bongo drums, beating in an irregular rhythm; the smells were a pungent, sick-smelling smoke mingled with the thick aroma of coffee. When her eyes adjusted to the dim light, she saw a stairway leading down into a cavernous room crowded with tiny tables and chairs.

She made her way slowly down the stairs, afraid that someone might come up and tell her to leave. By the uncertain light of the many candles that flickered on the tables she saw that the walls of the coffeehouse were unpainted bare brick, and nothing was hung on them. The floor was wooden and littered with cigarette butts; the tables were small, and the chairs looked uncomfortable. The place was crowded with bearded men, and with women who wore no lipstick and too much eye shadow.

As Philippa made her way to a vacant table and squeezed behind it into the wobbly chair, she felt her excitement mount. She had entered a wondrous, forbidden world, an upside-down world where nothing was normal, as if all rules had to be broken. The flickering candlelight and bongo rhythm seemed to seep into her skin and invade her body, electrifying it with a sense of daring adventure. Philippa's head swam with the smell of smoke, which didn't smell like regular cigarettes; she saw that everyone was drinking coffee and talking while a man on a small stage beat bongo drums. She looked around, tense, excited, her pulse throbbing in cadence with the drum. She tried to spot Rhys in the crowd, but the room was too dark and smoky. She could only barely make out pale faces in the irregular candle glow, the faces of people who looked dissatisfied, lost somehow, as if they only came out at night while the real, the normal world slept. And then she saw Rhys walking up onto the stage and taking a seat on a tall stool. No one clapped or acknowledged him; they just continued to smoke and drink coffee.

Rhys began to talk. "No solution is possible, therefore action is impossible. Existence precedes essence. We are forlorn because we have lost God. Now we have the Bomb. We are nothing but bags of meat. We create ourselves, yes, but why? There is no purpose. Born, breathe, die. No design, only chaos. There is no point at all. We have the Bomb. There will be no tomorrow."

Philippa looked at the faces of the people around her, saw how intently they now watched Rhys, how drawn into his sadness they were. And she suddenly wanted to stand up and say, No, you're wrong.

When he was finished, people snapped their fingers instead of clapping. As he left the stage, Philippa wondered if he had seen her and maybe would come to her table. But Rhys disappeared. She drank an awful cup of thick coffee and listened to a very strange guitarist until finally she left, troubled by what she had seen and heard.

Philippa went to Woody's again after that, taking a later bus so Rhys wouldn't see her and sitting against the far wall to hear him recite his strange and sad philosophy. And that night he looked straight at her.

While he recited his melancholy poetry, he kept his eyes on her as though she were the only person in the crowded room, as if he were giving the message directly to her, his dark eyes seeming to say, See? Aren't I right?

Afterward, a beautiful woman went up on the stage and kissed him. Right on the mouth. They talked for a moment; Philippa could see him laughing. Then the woman went back to her table and Rhys threaded his way to where Philippa was sitting.

He didn't take a chair. He stood gazing down at her through the smoky darkness, then he said, "You shouldn't be here. This place isn't for you."

"I wanted to see what you do."

He laughed softly and sat down. He leaned forward on his elbows, and she saw two microscopic candle flames in his black eyes. It occurred to her that Rhys would have no trouble hypnotizing people. "You're young," he said. "Not in years. I don't know how old you are. But in soul and spirit. You're a very young spirit, very hurtable. You don't know anything yet, and maybe you shouldn't. Go away from this place. Go back to where you can be young."

"I wanted to talk to you."

He shook his head. "Let me have someone take you home," he said. "It's late, and there are predatory spirits on the streets. Joe, the bongo player, he'll take you home in his car. I don't want you to get hurt because you came to see me."

"Let me stay."

He reached out and found a tendril of hair that had escaped her ponytail. He drew it out and seemed to examine it by candlelight. Then he tucked it gently back behind her ear. "I'll go get Joe."

Philippa couldn't sleep. She had to see Rhys. She had to tell him how wrong he was, that there *was* hope, there *was* a future. She was also driven on a deeper, more instinctive level: the need to be with him, maybe to touch . . .

She waited until it was late, when she was sure he would be back from Woody's, then she hurried down the deserted street and ran up the stairs to number 10, her heart pounding. She listened outside his door.

She knocked.

There was no answer.

"Rhys?" she said.

She tried the doorknob. The door opened easily and swung away from her. "Rhys?" He wasn't there.

His apartment came as a shock. There were bare bookshelves, and yet books were stacked in towers all over the floor. The only furniture was a stained mattress on the floor with a single Madras spread and a small table with an old Remington typewriter on it. Clothes spilled from a duffel bag as if he had just moved in; ashtrays overflowed with cigarette butts and ash; empty whiskey bottles littered the floor. And strangely, there was nothing on the walls except a dime-store picture of Jesus in a plastic frame, underneath which someone had written "Fried shoes."

Philippa looked around at his things. At his records—Miles Davis and Thelonious Monk, Woody Guthrie, Depression ballads, and a record that turned out to be a long poem entitled "Tentative Description of a Dinner to Promote the Impeachment of President Eisenhower." And his books, which were all about Oriental philosophies, Zen Buddhism, and existentialism. For some reason, Rhys had four copies of *The Stranger* by Albert Camus. There was a *Life* magazine spread out on the floor, opened to a series of graphic pictures showing Soviet secret police being gunned down by Hungarian rebels. A page had been torn out—a picture of Marilyn Monroe in a wedding gown feeding a piece of wedding cake to her bridegroom, Arthur Miller.

Philippa went to the typewriter and saw that a roll of butcher paper was threaded through it; no separate pages, just a running stream of consciousness. She looked at the last thing Rhys had written: "In this papier-mâché town we have to sneer at the unGod ones who sneer at our own chase after the unique loneliness of unlife, the singularity of oneness with forever, the essence of the nonborn eternity cycle."

In the margin, he had written, "The young spirit came to the old papier-mâché town."

And then all of a sudden he was there, in the doorway. "So you came," he said softly, closing the door behind him. He offered her the cigarette he had been smoking. It didn't look like a Chesterfield or a Winston, but she recognized the smell from Woody's. "What is it?" she said.

"Boo," he said, putting it in an ashtray. "Pot."

She shook her head. "I want to talk to you," she said.

He looked at her. "So talk."

"Rhys. You're unhappy—"

"We're all unhappy. I think you are, too," he said quietly, coming close to her. "You're driven and determined because of something or someone. But you'll be hurt in the end. By me, I suppose." He reached up and touched her cheek. "You shouldn't have come here."

"Why do you believe the sad things you do?" she said, seeing her reflection in his dark eyes as if she were looking up from the bottom of two deep wells. His hand moved to her ear; she felt him tracing its outline. "Where do you come from, Rhys?" she said. "What has made you this way?"

"I haven't come from anywhere. I'm here, now, that's all. I invented myself."

"That doesn't make sense."

He smiled. "This is a world in which carpenters are resurrected, and you say I'm not making sense." His hand moved under her chin, slowly, gently. "We exist. That's all. After existence comes essence. We create ourselves, each second, each minute. And then we cease."

His touch was setting her on fire; she was having difficulty breathing. "You make it sound like there's no point to anything."

"There isn't. Life is pointless. *We* are pointless."

"Someone once told me that I was worthless," she said, tears shimmering in her eyes. "Mother Superior told me that I wouldn't amount to anything. But she was wrong. And you're wrong, Rhys. Your attitude is wrong."

He shook his head, his dark eyes sad. "Existence is all that is real," he said, trailing a fingertip down her throat and under her collar. "We exist. Period. And how or why we exist is meaningless. Humankind is an accident. We have no purpose. You and I have no purpose, together or apart. We just simply *are.*"

"That is so sad."

"No, not sad," he said with a sigh. His finger was now tracing the outline of her lips. "Just *there.* It simply *is.* We get born, we breathe, we die."

"And don't you believe in anything?"

"Belief is just a word."

"Why have you given up like this, Rhys? What made the fight go out of you? When I was a little girl and other kids made fun of me because I was fat, I would go running to my father. And do you know what he told me? My father told me that the winners stand up for themselves and the losers just lie down and take it. Don't be a loser, Rhys." Her voice caught. "Please, don't—"

He bent his head and put his mouth over hers. He drew her into his arms slowly, pressing her to him gently, as if to get her used to the feel of him, his hands exploring her hair, her shoulders, her back as he kissed her this way and that, and then with his tongue, just so tenderly that Philippa wanted to cry. How could he be so sad and yet so loving? She clung to him; she wanted to take him all the way inside her and keep him there until he was healed.

He reached up under her blouse and unhooked her bra. When he touched her breasts, she gasped.

"It's all right," he murmured.

He took her face between his hands and looked at her for a long time with the sweet-sad smile of someone who is saying good-bye. He unbuttoned her blouse and kissed her breasts, her nipples.

She wanted to say the proper words, but she didn't know them; she wanted to touch him, but she didn't know where. He took her hand and guided it down, and when she took hold of him, he made a sound deep in his throat.

"Rhys," she whispered.

He said, "We have all night. The first time must be the best time, because there can't ever be a first after this."

He took her to the bed and undressed her, slowly, kissing her in between, touching her all over, while she found the way to caress him, to meet his kisses with passion. He was teaching and she was learning, but she wouldn't be aware of that until much later.

★ ★ ★

Afterward, he smiled down at her. "So, there's a tigress in the papier-mâché town."

She moved her hands over his bare shoulders. She had been surprised to find him so muscular. "I love you, Rhys."

He kissed the tip of her nose. "Your world is another world from mine. Your purpose and my purpose aren't joined. You'll never understand—" He stopped. He kissed her, deeply. Then he said, "*I'll* never understand."

"What happened to you, Rhys?" she said. "Was it something long ago?"

"Long ago? When I was a little boy, something terrible happened to me. Something unspeakable. But it was supposed to happen. Or it never did. I don't know."

"Let me help you. Let me make everything better for you."

The corners of his eyes creased in the hint of a smile. "I want to write for a while," he said softly. "And you need to sleep. When you wake up, I'll take you home."

He covered her with the blanket. As Philippa drifted off to the sound of his typewriter, she thought, Through my love you'll be healed.

....★

15

Dr. Judith Isaacs couldn't shake the feeling that there was something strange about this case. On the surface, everything appeared normal: Carolyn Mason, age twenty-four, had come to the Star's clinic for a routine prenatal checkup.

"I came up here for a rest, Doctor," the young woman had explained at the beginning of Judith's examination. "My obstetrician told me to see a doctor while I was here, just to be sure."

Just to be sure of what? Judith wondered as she stripped off her gloves and turned away from the exam table. As far as Judith could determine, this was a healthy, straightforward pregnancy with no complications. Carolyn Mason was in her sixth month; amniocentesis at sixteen weeks had found no abnormalities in the fetus, which was a girl; and Carolyn herself had no complaints, no discomfort. She also didn't seem the slightest bit worried about her condition or the baby's. She had come into the clinic cheerful and confident, chatting about the beauty of Star's and how she wished she could stay for Christmas but that she had to go home in a few days. So what was it that was niggling at the back of Judith's mind, nudging her with a silent alarm that said that, evidence to the contrary, this was an unusual case?

As she eased Carolyn's legs down from the stirrups, she said, "You can get dressed now, Miss Mason."

"Is everything okay, Doctor?"

"Everything is just fine. You and the baby are doing well."

"Oh, I know," Carolyn said, smiling. "I feel fine. And this is such a special baby."

As Judith washed her hands at the sink, she scanned the brief medical chart she had written up on Carolyn. It contained very little data: the patient was a model who lived in North Hollywood, she was in excellent health, unmarried, this was her first child.

"I'm not gaining too much weight, am I, Doctor Isaacs?"

"No. Some weight gain is to be expected. But don't try any drastic dieting. You both need nourishment."

Carolyn pulled a cable-knit sweater over her head and said, "I joined Starlite, was that all right?"

"What did your obstetrician say?"

"She said it was okay to watch my weight, as long as I was careful and did it safely, like joining Starlite. They have a special weight management program for pregnant women, did you know that? It's driving me crazy, though! I'm an absolute hamburger freak! Royal Burgers. You know, the barbecue special? I heard on TV a while back that the woman who used to own the Royal Burger chain—what was her name, Beverly Highland— is still supposed to be alive. You know, like Elvis? Crazy. Why would a woman pretend to be dead? Especially when she had everything."

Judith said she didn't know, that she didn't pay much attention to tabloid gossip.

"You're so lucky to live here, Doctor!" Carolyn enthused as she laced up her snow boots. "Not that I don't like my job, I do! But to actually live all year round in such a beautiful setting. I'll bet you meet a lot of famous people."

Judith smiled and said, "Yes, I do," thinking of Mr. Smith in one of the private suites down the hall, whom she was due to see in a few minutes. She had not seen him since their first visit, last night.

"How long have you lived here, Doctor?" Carolyn said.

"Actually, I only arrived last night. Carolyn, may I ask you something? The father of the baby, is he here with you?"

"Oh yes. They wouldn't let me come alone. They don't let me go anywhere alone!"

"They?"

"The baby's father and his wife. We go everywhere together." Carolyn laughed. "It's not what you think, Doctor. I'm not having an affair with a married man, or involved in a threesome, or anything like that. I told you this is a very special baby. Well, the father is special, too. Not only is he married to someone else, he's also my brother."

Judith gave her a questioning look.

"It's a bit complicated," Carolyn said, "and goodness knows what's going to be made of it after the baby is born! My brother and I are very close, and there's nothing I wouldn't do for him. So when he and his wife tried for years to have a child, and finally, after three miscarriages, they were told that she would never be able to carry a baby to term, I volunteered to carry the baby for them." Carolyn paused. "The doctors did an in vitro fertilization—you know, what they call test tube fertilization—using my brother's sperm and his wife's egg. They implanted the embryo in me, and then I was given hormone shots to make the pregnancy take.

"Isn't it marvelous, Doctor?" Carolyn added, beaming. "I'm going to give birth to my own niece!"

After the girl left, Judith looked for Zoey, the nurse, wondering what was taking her so long. She had breezed through the clinic earlier, in a wrinkled uniform, saying something about having to do bedside care at one of the cottages. Her attitude had been so sullen that Judith knew they were in for a rocky time.

Judith paused to check herself in the bathroom mirror before going down the hall to visit Mr. Smith. As she straightened her hair, she suddenly froze. When was the last time she had done this before seeing a patient—practically primping? Judith realized with growing uneasiness that she was not reacting to Smith on a doctor-patient level, but on a more basic, male-female level. She also knew that there was no real professional reason for her to be seeing him; Dr. Newton, his own physician, had come up to Star's that morning and had spent nearly an hour with Smith. And as Dr. Newton left, he had informed Judith he would be back that evening to check again on his patient.

Still, she reminded herself as she made sure her white lab coat was spotless and wrinkle free, when Newton wasn't here, she was responsible for Mr. Smith.

She hadn't been able to stop thinking about him. It wasn't just that he was a famous movie idol; it was the man himself, those probing eyes, the resonant Scottish baritone, the way he had seemed so sincerely to want to know about her, where she came from, why she was here, even though it was apparent he was in pain. Judith recalled what Zoey had said last night when she welcomed Judith to Star's: "There's something about this place that makes people get romantic." Judith wondered if it was as simple as that—that the atmosphere of Star's somehow intoxicated people.

She had certainly seen guests who appeared to be happily in love when she had passed through the lobby last night. And then when she had finally dined with her new employer, Miss Beverly Burgess, and Simon Jung, Judith had sensed something between the two of them. It had been a pleasant two hours; Simon Jung had acted the perfect, gracious host who did most of the talking while Miss Burgess seemed content to listen. To Judith's surprise, Beverly had worn enormous sunglasses that hid nearly half her face. An eye ailment, she had said vaguely. Judith had come away from the dinner having learned nothing much about her new boss.

Except for one thing: that Simon Jung was obviously in love with Beverly, but that Beverly had, for whatever reasons, retreated from him.

★ ★ ★

"So, Doctor," Mr. Smith said when Judith finished taking his blood pressure, "how do you like it here so far? Are they keeping you busy?"

She closed her medical bag and sat down. Winter sunshine streamed through the windows, cutting almost blinding rectangles of light on the rose-colored carpet. Her patient, the legendary Mr. Smith, with his Scottish accent and monogrammed silk pajamas, was sitting up in bed giving her a questioning look. What could she tell him? That so far she had treated two sprained tennis wrists and a mild case of the flu. That, plus examining a young woman who was carrying the implanted fetus of her brother's wife and reassuring Frieda Goldman that her client, Bunny Kowalski, was well enough to have visitors. Frieda's agitation, and the way she had embraced her leather attaché case, had made Judith wonder if Ms. Goldman was here to make one of those astronomical movie deals one always read about.

"I'm kept busy enough," she said. "I'm certainly not bored."

"Are you treating any famous people? Besides me, I mean."

"You know I can't talk about my other patients. Or are you just testing me to see if I might tell other people your secret?"

"I admit it has me worried. Oh, not that *you'll* tell, but that the secret might get out. Tell me truthfully, Judith. What do you think of a man my age having this kind of operation? I mean, such vanity, for one thing, trying to turn back the clock. And it doesn't very well suit the image people have of me—*real* men don't resort to such devious measures as liposuction. Do they?"

"Why not?" she said. "If it helps you to feel better about yourself."

"Doctor," Smith said as he folded back the blanket, "will you assist me to the window, please? I'm afraid that because of this pressure bandage I have a devil of a time walking."

She slipped an arm around his waist and helped him across the room. Despite being nearly seventy, Smith was in excellent shape; Judith could feel a trim, athletic build beneath the silk pajamas. He also gave off a faint, expensive scent, the signature of a man who, despite being in pain and in a hospital, was meticulous about his grooming. Again she experienced a vague, unsettling stab of sexual desire. "Do you recognize any of these people, Doctor?" Smith said as they looked out the window and saw guests enjoying the morning in the pine forest. "Take that fellow down there, for instance, the one who's posturing. He's Larry Wolfe, the screenwriter. I met him once. He's an arrogant prick." He looked at Judith with a smile. "Does it startle you to hear me say that?"

"I have no idea who Larry Wolfe is."

"Good for you. If he knew that, it would kill him. I've heard that Larry

Wolfe is grooming himself to take God's place; he's talked to God about stepping down."

Smith continued to stare out at the snow-blanketed pine forest. "I remember the first time I saw snow," he said softly, a trace of nostalgia creeping into his voice. "It was many years ago, I was only a boy, and my father had taken me fishing in Liffey Valley. It rarely snowed there, but that winter I recall that it did." He smiled at Judith. "Liffey is in Tasmania, where I was born. I later grew up in Scotland, but Tassie is my real home. Tasmania was Errol Flynn's home, too, you know. We once starred in a picture together; Flynn was the good pirate, I was the bad one, but I was the better swordsman. It always astonishes me to find how many people don't know where in the world Tasmania is." He gave Judith a teasing look. "Do you know, Doctor?"

"Isn't it an island off the southern tip of Australia?"

"A million points for you, Doctor. And for that you win—" He suddenly winced.

"Pain?"

He reached for her. "It's nothing I . . . can't handle."

As she helped him to the chair, she said, "There's no need to play the pirate here."

He smiled through his pain, and in the brief instant before he sat, when he was holding on to Judith and her face was just inches from his, he said, "Do you know who you look like? Lovely Jennifer Jones when she played opposite Gregory Peck. You have the same coloring, the same vulnerable look."

Judith saw the fine dew of perspiration on his forehead, the lines of pain around his eyes. She eased him into the chair, then she went to her medical bag and opened it.

As he watched her draw up a syringe, Smith said, "Are you wondering why I had this operation secretly done here, at Star's, instead of in a Beverly Hills doctor's office and recuperating at home?" He paused and rolled up his sleeve so Judith could give him an injection.

"This will ease your discomfort," she said. "Please go on with what you were saying."

"It's because this operation must be kept a secret. Men with my kind of reputation aren't permitted to resort to cosmetic surgery. At least not for something like an abdomen that was starting to betray my age. I've always kept fit; I work out every day. But nature was beginning to mock me, and when I saw that no amount of dieting or sit-ups was going to help me this time, I decided to go for the desperate gesture. I only pray that I'm not found out."

"Would it be so bad? People are having liposuction done all the time now."

"I fear that it will affect my image. And also," he rolled his sleeve down, "frankly, the way women would relate to me afterward. I would be wondering if a woman with whom I wished to become involved might see me as less of a man for having stooped to such an unmacho tactic as cosmetic surgery."

"I think you're being too hard on yourself. Men have cosmetic surgery; women don't have a monopoly on it."

"Not for my generation, Doctor. This is entirely alien to me. And highly embarrassing."

At that moment, the door opened and a sullen Zoey came in carrying folded sheets. "I'm here to change your bed, Mr. Smith," she said, not looking at Judith.

The nurse worked in silence, filling the room with palpable hostility. Smith gave Judith a questioning look and said, "What a remarkable place for a hospital. Until a minute ago, I'd forgotten I was in a clinic, recovering from surgery. Look at this room, and that setting out there." He waved toward the window. "If only all hospitals could be like this."

He looked at Zoey, who snapped the sheets and attacked the corners with a ferocity that made him give Judith another quizzical look.

"Are you familiar with the legend of this place, Doctor?" he said, trying to dispel the tension in the air. "Despite my age, I wasn't here the night Dexter Bryant Ramsey was murdered. I was only ten years old at the time. But a lot of famous celebrities were there—Gary Cooper, Fairbanks, even Hearst was supposedly among the guests. There had been a big party that night, with a guest list that read like Hollywood royalty. But, curiously, by the time the police got up here the next day, everyone had cleared out and had established solid alibis elsewhere for the night Ramsey was killed. Those were the golden days of Hollywood."

He paused, looked reflectively at Judith, then said more quietly, "Marion Star was my first love, you know. I was fourteen years old and her movies had only just made it to Tasmania. *Queen of the Nile,* it was. One look at those darkly smudged woebegone eyes and I was lost. I have never since quite met a woman who could measure up to her."

His gaze followed Zoey as she moved about the room with an efficiency that verged upon caricature. She emptied wastebaskets, refilled the water carafe, and then disappeared into the bathroom with an armload of fresh white towels.

"Are you a movie fan, Judith?"

"I was when I was younger," she said, catching herself before she added, And I was madly in love with you. She was noticing how the morning sunlight streamed through the window and caught the silver highlights in his hair. "We don't have a movie theater in Green Pines."

"Films today frighten me," he said. "There are no rules, no limits.

There was a time when the industry was very closely policed. Ever hear of the Hays Office? Willie Hays told us what we could and could not do in movies. Remember how in the forties and fifties people slept in twin beds, even married couples? The rule was the beds had to be at least eighteen inches apart. If two people were shown on one bed, one of them had to be fully dressed—not just in pajamas, but in evening clothes or something. And the man always had to have one foot on the floor. It's amazing now, to think of it."

He paused and settled his dark blue eyes on her in a way that made Judith think he was trying to come up with a way to word something— something personal. It made her heart skip a beat. And then he said, "The Hays Office was responsible for society's morals. Did you know that the ending of Tennessee Williams's play *Streetcar* was changed? In the stage play, Stella goes back to Stanley, even though she knew he raped her sister," Smith said as Judith watched a red-tailed hawk perch on a pine bough outside his window. "But in the movie, Stella leaves him. Better for public morals, Hays said. Of course they couldn't say the word *rape* then. In the newspapers it was called criminal assault. In the fifties, a woman could be kicked and beaten and thrown down the stairs and the newspapers would say she had *not* been criminally assaulted. Did you know, Judith, that Marion Star was partly responsible for the creation of the Hays Office? The Legion of Decency, in fact, was established as a reaction to her films."

"Were they so bad?"

"They were wonderful. But the world was in a depression, and there were those who resented Marion's rather generous life-style. So they said she was immoral. Today her movies are classics—refreshing and fun, reminding us of a more genteel age in films. Now they're making—" he shuddered "—*Rambo.*"

Zoey came out of the bathroom, dumped the used towels and linens into a hamper, and left without a word. Smith said to Judith, "I sense, ah, discord between you and your nurse. Is there a problem?"

"I don't know. How are you feeling now? Is the medication taking effect?"

"As a matter of fact it is. Can you assist me back to bed, please?"

As Judith helped him walk, once again putting her arm around his trim waist, he said, "You told me you had been married for fourteen years. Are you still married?"

"We were divorced last year."

"I'm sorry to hear that. Are there any children?"

"I'd rather not talk about it."

He paused before getting into the bed and looked at her. "What is it?" he said. "What's wrong?"

"Nothing is wrong."

"Oh, you're a tough lady I suppose?" he said. "Hard on the outside to hide something vulnerable on the inside?"

As she helped him get settled and drew his covers up, she said, "Why does a woman have to be hard only on the outside? Can't I be tough all the way through? Bite into me and you'll find shoe leather all the way to my spine."

He shook his head. "You have a soft center. I can hear it between your words. It's sitting in the pupils of your eyes. Do you want to tell me about it?"

Judith sat on the edge of the bed. "I never know what to say when people ask me if I have children. You'd think by now that I'd have rehearsed an answer, but I haven't. I did have a child—a little girl. She died two years ago. But whenever I'm asked if I have children, I don't know how to respond. Do I say no, as though she never existed? Or do I say yes, except that she's dead, and then suffer through the questions and explanations?"

"I'm not asking you to explain."

"No, but you want to know, and I'm not going to tell you. Kimmie's dead and that's all there is to it."

"Is that why you're burying yourself up here, among snow and pine trees and movie stars?"

"Now you know my secret."

"You know something? I just realized—what I told you about my problem, about why I really had the operation here—I never even told Dr. Newton the real reason. I told him that I wanted to recuperate in peace and quiet, away from telephones and interruptions. I didn't tell him that I'm embarrassed by this and would hate for my secret to be found out. But I told you the real reason, Judith, and you're the only person in the world who knows it. Now isn't that something?"

"Nevertheless, I can't tell you about Kimmie," she said softly.

"And I'm not asking you to."

She met his eyes and was surprised to see a challenging look in them, one that didn't match the giving texture of his voice. He suddenly had an opponent's eyes, and they looked straight at her as if to say, Your move.

She turned away from that look, from the challenge in those eyes. She refused to accept the dare—the dare to be a woman. Since Kimmie's death and her subsequent divorce from Mort—a spiteful, blame-laying divorce—Judith had felt her heart slowly go hard, as if it were petrifying with time. She told herself that her capacity for loving had died with Kimmie and that Mort had killed all sexual desire within her. In the two years since, Judith had looked at every man she met, even the suave Simon Jung, with stunning indifference.

Until now.

"Do you have children?" she asked.

"I never got around to getting married and starting a family. But there is time yet."

"You know, Mr. Smith," she said, "it really isn't fair. Men can produce children nearly all their lives, they can put off having a family until they feel like it. But women are restricted to certain years."

"That makes up for the fact that only women can have babies," he said. "Was it Erica Jong who said something about men resenting women because they can go about their daily lives, working and playing, while creating new little humans inside their bodies?"

She gave him a surprised look. "Are you a *feminist*, Mr. Smith? Don't let anyone know it, it will spoil your reputation as a great lover."

"On the contrary. For a man to be a true lover, he must truly understand women, as the legendary lovers did—Casanova, Errol Flynn. I knew Flynn; he wasn't a cad. He was kind and generous and caring to women. He genuinely loved them."

"And you?" Judith realized with a start that she was flirting with him, but she couldn't seem to help herself. "It makes you sound feckless and faithless, Mr. Smith."

"No, not feckless or faithless. When I love a woman it is with devotion and passion. And when she is with me, she can be sure that she is the only person on my mind."

A picture suddenly formed in his mind: his hands untangling the thick mahogany braid that fell down her back, unbraiding it and bringing the lush hair forward, over her bare shoulders and bare breasts. It surprised him. When was the last time he had experienced this kind of desire for a woman?

And now that prim, doctorly braid maddened him, the way it rested so neatly against the chaste whiteness of her lab coat. He had noticed earlier that the braid was bound at the tip with a plain, no-nonsense rubber band, and it brushed the small of her back, pointing down to a tight, athletic derriere. In his mind, he saw himself touching her there, too.

"I've heard that it's common for patients to fall in love with their doctors," he said. "But does the reverse ever happen? Do doctors ever fall in love with their patients?"

Their eyes met again, and Judith suddenly found herself wondering what it would be like to be kissed by this man.

"Only the ones who fall for smooth talkers," she said, rising abruptly from the bed before he could see the sudden throb of pulse in her neck.

"Will you have dinner with me, Judith?"

"I never dine with patients, Mr. Smith. Besides, you'll be home before you know it. Dr. Newton is going to discharge you in a few days."

"I know. The day after the ball. Are you going to the Christmas ball, Judith? Perhaps you would do me the honor of going with me?"

"We'll see how you feel by then," she said. *How we both feel* . . .

"And dinner? Anything the dining room serves can be sent up. The Cornish game hen is excellent here, and so is the rack of lamb."

She suddenly saw it: a table for two set up by the fire, candles glowing, wine glittering in crystal. But she knew it wouldn't be about food or friendship, not for her at least. For Judith it would be the trap that would make her fall in love against her will. And that was something she was determined not to do again.

··★

16

When Danny Mackay slipped into the the vicuña sports jacket and turned to look at himself in the mirror, he received a shock. But it was only a split-second shock, and the salesman hadn't seen it. It happened every time Danny caught his reflection in a mirror or in one of the store windows along Rodeo Drive. He would look at himself and see the face of a stranger, with a closely cropped beard, black hair, horn-rimmed glasses.

It was a deception he had to remind himself of constantly—that he was no longer the Reverend Danny Mackay, worshiped by millions, one heartbeat away from the White House. Danny had almost given himself away that morning when he had unloaded Quinn's cheap Toyota and bought himself a brand-new Jaguar. It wasn't the cash sale that had nearly blown his cover—Beverly Hills car salesmen were used to extravagant cash transactions—it was when it came time to fill out the papers. But Danny had smoothed his brief fumble with a smile and had driven out of the showroom laughing.

From there he had made a stop at Vuitton to purchase a set of luggage; then a brief visit to pick up the fifteen-thousand-dollar Rolex watch he had promised himself; and now he was at Bragg on Rodeo, buying a whole new wardrobe, from silk briefs to cashmere overcoat. Using cash all the way.

As he removed the jacket—which had a price tag of forty thousand dollars—and handed it to the salesman, saying, "I'll take it," he looked at the stranger in the mirror and thought, I'm reborn again, a ghost who can get away with anything.

Slowly slipping into the leather jacket he had bought earlier, Danny moved his gaze to the young saleswoman who was pretending to straighten items on the scarf and glove counter behind him. She had been watching him for the past half hour. Danny knew he looked good, and he knew that she was thinking the same thing. He gave her one of his sexy, lazy smiles, and she blushed. But she didn't look away.

As he took in her large breasts, thinking that she was no innocent the way she had arranged that gold Christmas corsage on her sweater, he thought it too bad that he didn't have time to get to know her better, but he had a first-class ticket for an evening flight to Australia and he had to be heading over to the airport. Besides, he didn't want to waste his new power screwing a salesgirl. Danny had always known that his pleasure in sex was somehow connected with his passion for violence; the two seemed to him to go together. His wife—now his "widow"—could attest to that. Taking that salesgirl to bed right now might diminish his drive to punish Beverly Highland. Worse, taking that girl to bed might prompt him to kill her afterward, weakening his power all the more. And he was saving that power for when he found Beverly, or rather Philippa, as she was now calling herself.

He left the store and unlocked his car to allow the store clerk to put his purchases in the back. It had started to drizzle, giving the silver and white Christmas lights along Wilshire Boulevard a soft-focus look, and as Danny waited for his purchases to go into the trunk, he saw a young woman walking slowly along the sidewalk, looking in the windows. She had arched eyebrows and an arched nose, as if she were trying to lift herself up from the rest of the world. A black man in a chauffeur's uniform walked behind her; in one arm he carried packages, with his other hand he held an umbrella over her head, protecting her from the rain while he himself got wet.

Danny smiled. That was the way to live.

When everything was in the trunk and the clerk had gone away with a hundred-dollar tip, Danny slid behind the wheel of his expensive new car and felt new power surge through him. Money, he thought, the true aphrodisiac. He opened the glove compartment and took out the newspaper photograph of Philippa Roberts, under which Quinn had written "Is this Beverly Highland?" Although the face wasn't quite Beverly as he remembered her, he knew she would have had to alter her looks. The plastic surgeon's knife was no stranger to Beverly. She had used it before to deceive Danny and the world; she would do it again. He toyed now with the idea of not killing her after all, but of doing something far worse, like cutting up her face, giving her some scars that no amount of plastic surgery could ever erase. Maybe he would also fix it so that she never enjoyed sex again—now that was an amusing prospect. But first he had to find her.

After that, Danny was going to have the freedom and power to do anything he wanted. Because he wasn't going to stop with Philippa; since leaving Otis's beach house, Danny had added a few more names to his private hit list, the first of which was the bastard who had won the election that Danny was supposed to have won three years ago: the president of the United States. After he took care of him, Danny had plans for others who had deserted him when the scandals broke during the primary election, with headlines such as "MACKAY'S NAME LINKED TO BEVERLY HILLS BROTHEL," "MACKAY OWNER OF PORNO MAGAZINE," and photographs dredged up from the old days, of Danny and Bonner in an old backyard washtub with a Texas farm wife, of Danny with a can of beer in his hand, grabbing his crotch for the camera. All orchestrated by that bitch Beverly. She had spent years constructing an elaborate frame-up, all with the aim of getting Danny down on his knees before her, begging her to save him. The bitch had made him crawl to her, just because of some dumb abortion he had made her have so long ago he barely remembered it. And then, after he did beg her and she threw him to the wolves anyway, everyone deserted Danny—his wife, her father the big-mouthed senator . . . Well, the list was endless. Now, with his new invisibility, Danny could pass a death sentence on anyone.

Before guiding the Jaguar into the busy holiday traffic, Danny paused to regard the very address on Rodeo Drive that had caused his destruction three and a half years ago and had driven him to commit "suicide" in jail—Fanelli's Men's Shop, with the butterfly logo on the facade. Behind the second-story windows was the place where police claimed Danny had run a whorehouse—an establishment that Danny had known nothing about, because it had been run by Beverly Highland. The men's store was no longer called Fanelli's, the butterfly was gone, and a directory beside the entrance listed the businesses that now occupied offices that, less than four years ago, had been rooms designed for illicit sex. But erasing the evidence didn't lessen the crime. When he found her, he was going to remind her of this address and the butterfly with which she had mocked him.

Danny turned on the car radio and pulled out from the curb, causing a Cadillac to screech to a halt. Danny laughed as he tore out into traffic.

The San Diego Freeway had come to a complete stop as the rain came down harder and southern Californians tried unsuccessfully to deal with it. Sitting behind a truck, Danny felt his nerves draw tight; he drummed the steering wheel, his knee pumping up and down. He wished he could take out his gun and shoot every driver around him. And he might have done it if he had thought it would clear the lane for him.

He had to get to the airport; he had to get down to Australia and find Beverly. The need to punish her was building in him like volcanic lava; if he wasn't moving soon, Danny knew he would erupt.

When he saw other motorists getting off the freeway to take alternate routes, Danny decided to do the same, pulling out of his lane and riding the shoulder so that he could cut in front of the line of existing cars. He ignored the angry honks and whipped down the off-ramp, squealing onto Century Boulevard.

A red light caught him and he was stuck again, breathing other cars' exhaust fumes and wishing he could just rid the world of useless people. Danny was just beginning to entertain himself with the vision of a sparsely populated planet, having just enough people to serve him, when his attention was captured by something.

A sign on a tall building: Starlite Industries.

The headquarters of the company that Beverly owned under the name of Philippa Roberts.

When the light turned green, Danny whipped a sudden right turn, even though he was in the middle lane, roared down the street, and braked in the red zone in front. He couldn't believe his luck. And what a stroke of genius. Of course! Why waste time searching Western Australia for her when he could get her address right here?

Providence, my man, he told himself, as he entered the foyer. This was no accident; you were *brought* here.

He laughed softly as he rode up in the elevator, watching himself in the mirrored wall and thinking what a knock-out good-looking stud he was. From his silk boxers to his leather bomber jacket, he was pure *GQ*. Image made the man, he told himself. Look power, and you *are* power. Dress in eight thousand dollars and people give you respect. After all, Danny wasn't a nobody. Besides having come a blink away from the Oval Office, he had written that blockbuster best-seller back in the sixties, *Why God Took the Kennedys;* he'd gone to Vietnam Bob Hope style and dazzled the troops; he had lived in penthouses in Houston and Dallas; he had had any woman he wanted. Danny was often amazed to think how many miles and years he had come from the days when he was the ragged son of a poor West Texas sharecropper, when they had lived in shanties wallpapered with newsprint; he hadn't owned a pair of shoes until he was twelve. The alligator shoes he wore now probably cost more than his useless father had earned in his lifetime. And Danny had accomplished it all just by selling religion.

Looking at his image in the mirrored wall of the elevator, he smiled the languid, sexy-sly smile that had made him famous. "God can be bribed," he said softly, quoting the preacher who had set Danny on the road to fame and riches. "I'm in the protection racket," Billy Bob Magdalene had

said the night he had caught twenty-two-year-old Danny and Bonner
trying to rip off the till during a tent revival. He had caught them with
his shotgun, trying to sneak out; Bonner had peed his pants but Danny
had kept his cool. "Let me tell you two pudknockers about this religion
bidness," Billy Bob had said back in his trailer. "First, I remind folks that
God is so angry with them that He's got it on His calendar to squash them
soon's He can get around to it. Then I kind of hint that I got some special
in with the Lord, like I got His ear. Then I let it sort of slip that, for a
small sum, I might just whisper a few words in God's ear in their defense.
It never fails. They come into my tent as shit-scared sinners, and they
leave feeling fully insured."

That was the beginning moment of Danny's rise to power, when he and
Bonner had signed on with Billy Bob Magdalene's traveling tent revival.
Later, of course, they'd tossed the old preacher out into the desert near
Odessa, and changed the name of the show to Danny Mackay Brings
Jesus.

And hadn't the world loved him for it? Hadn't they flocked to Danny's
tents to hear his hellfire preaching? Hadn't they sent their dollars to him
in great rolling waves until the Good News Ministries was worth billions?
And hadn't that bitch Beverly spoiled it all by tricking him into owning
a whorehouse called Butterfly and then telling the police?

She was going to pay. She was going to pay.

When the elevator reached the top floor, Danny made an entrance into
the reception area as if he owned the place.

"Howdy," he said to the young woman behind the desk.

She looked up from the book she was reading, and when she saw Danny,
a look swept across her face that he had seen thousands of times before,
a reaction, he knew, that had its roots not in her brain but in her pelvis.
Quickly closing the book and flashing a beautiful smile, she said, "May
I help you, sir?"

"I'm looking for Miss Philippa Roberts."

"Miss Roberts isn't here, sir. May I take a message?"

He produced Otis's press pass and showed it to her. "I want to do an
article on Miss Roberts; I'd like to interview her. I wonder if you could
give me her address?"

"I'm sorry, but I'm not allowed to give out such information. But if you
like, I will give the message to Miss Roberts's secretary."

"That would be just fine, sugar," he said, turning on the Texas genteel.
He leaned against the desk, gave her a long appreciative look, then said,
"Anyone ever tell you you got the prettiest eyes? I interviewed Cher once,
you talk about pretty eyes. But you got hers beat cold. Did you know
that?"

"Oh . . . thank you," she said, flustered.

Danny grinned. He knew that the minute he left she was going to whip a mirror out of her purse and inspect her eyes. "You sure you can't tell me Miss Roberts's address? It would save me a heap of trouble. And I'd mention you in the article. Would you like to see your name in the paper? I'd tell the world about those beautiful eyes of yours."

"I could get into trouble . . ."

"You know, sugar, I understand. And the devil knock me dead for putting you on the spot like that. You just forget I even asked. Besides, I'm a whole lot more interested in you right now than Miss Roberts."

He did a slow turn, taking in the tasteful reception area, the glass case filled with books, the subdued lighting, and soft music coming from hidden speakers. One thing he had to hand to Beverly Highland; she had learned about real class.

His gaze came to rest on a box of Christmas candy beside the reception-ist's telephone. Danny smiled and said, "Isn't that kind of forbidden, considering this is a diet place and all?"

She reddened and said, "Well, I'm not on a diet."

He moved his eyes up and down her body, then said, "I'll say you're not, and don't you ever think of trying it. Mind if I help myself?"

"I beg your pardon?"

He picked up a small red and white striped candy cane. "May I have one?"

"Oh, yes, help yourself."

"You know, sugar," he said, moving the candy cane slowly between his lips, sucking on it, "I sure do like sweet things. I wonder if you'd do me the honor of going to dinner with me sometime."

She blushed bright red. "I'd love to."

"Unfortunately, I'm flying down to Australia tonight to interview Miss Roberts in Perth."

"Oh, but Miss Roberts isn't in Australia. She's here."

He stared at her. "She's here? You mean in Los Angeles?"

"Miss Roberts came back this morning. In fact, you just missed her. She went back to her hotel."

"Now ain't that a pleasant surprise . . . Where do you suppose I could find her?"

"Well, Miss Roberts checked into the Century Plaza Hotel, but you'll have to hurry, she's going to Palm Springs tomorrow."

"Palm Springs? Do you know where in Palm Springs?"

"I'm sorry, I don't."

"Thanks, sugar. You've been a big help." He winked. "I'll be in touch."

★ ★ ★

Danny had no luck with the desk clerks at the Century Plaza Hotel. "I cannot give you a guest's room number," the young man in the blazer said, "but if you would care to leave a message . . ."

Danny walked around the enormous lobby for a few moments, trying to decide what to do, when he saw the restaurant and realized it was lunchtime, and an idea came to him. On a hunch, he went up to the hostess, who said, "Yes sir, may I help you?"

"I sure do hope so, ma'am. I'm supposed to join some friends here for lunch, and my secretary got the times mixed up. So I don't know if the reservation is for one or two o'clock. I was wondering if you could tell me."

"Certainly. What is the party's name?"

He started to say Beverly Highland and then remembered that she was going by another name. "Roberts. Philippa Roberts."

The hostess scanned the reservation sheet, then said, "Ah yes. Miss Roberts's reservation is for one o'clock."

Danny took a seat on a pink-brocade chair, hidden behind a leafy ficus, and watched everyone who came to the restaurant.

When he saw her, a jolt went through him. It was her all right; she looked just like the news photo he had lifted from Quinn's beach house. Here she was, just feet away from him, Beverly Highland, the woman who had humiliated him, made him get down on his knees and beg, and then had destroyed him. For this woman, Danny had dangled at the end of a jail cell rope, died, and come back to life with half a brain. It was only his hatred of her, his burning passion to see her suffer, that had brought him through that ordeal at all.

How innocent she looked, he thought, how sweetly serene and refined, her shoulder-length hair all shiny brown, the simple business suit and briefcase. She didn't look like a black-widow spider. And there wasn't much resemblance to the woman who had sat in his hotel room on that last night, her platinum hair pulled severely back into a tight French twist, giving her an icy villainess look, all cold and passionless and deadly. Now, in her new guise, she looked soft and warm and harmless. But it was a facade that didn't fool Danny. She could try all she wanted to deceive people into thinking she was someone else, but Danny knew who she was—the woman who had killed him.

And now here she was, almost within reach . . .

But he held back. Not now, not yet. He wanted to savor it; he wanted to fantasize about the many ways he was going to punish her; he wanted to build himself up to the point where his pleasure at torturing her was going to be sublime.

As he watched her move toward the restaurant, Danny felt the sexual tension tighten within him. He realized he was going to have to let some steam off after all; if he didn't, he would't be able to keep going at this rate and maintain control.

He went back to the registration desk and got himself a room for the night. Then he joined the crowd in front of the hotel who huddled under umbrellas against the rain while waiting for their cars. When he got his Jaguar, Danny struck out into the rainy afternoon in the direction of Beverly Hills, charged with energy and power. He was thinking of the large-breasted salesgirl with the gold corsage back at Bragg on Rodeo. She didn't know it, but she was about to have the evening of her life. Perhaps the *last* evening of her life.

·······································★

17

Hollywood, California, 1958

Philippa threw up in the bathroom. This was the seventh morning in a row, and one of the other boarders had alerted the landlady to it. So when Philippa came out, Mrs. Chadwick was waiting for her.

"What's wrong, honey?" the woman said. "You didn't have a bite of breakfast—haven't for a week. So how come you're throwing up?"

"It must have been something I ate last night."

"Come here, honey, I want to talk to you." They went into Mrs. Chadwick's apartment, where blond Danish modern furniture stood on spindly wrought-iron legs and the kitchen contained the latest ultramodern turquoise appliances. The TV set, tuned to *Dragnet,* was the focal point of the living room and had a trio of sleek black panthers arranged on top of it.

"Can I ask you a personal question?" Mrs. Chadwick said. "When was your last period?"

Philippa was startled. Why would her landlady want to know that? "I can't remember. I guess I've skipped one. Maybe two."

Mrs. Chadwick sighed. "Honey, you're pregnant. Don't you know that?"

"Pregnant! Oh no, I can't be. I'm not married."

The landlady sighed again. This wasn't the first young female boarder she had had to illuminate on the facts of life. "You got any family? Folks somewhere maybe?"

Philippa thought of Johnny in San Quentin and shook her head.

"Mmm," Mrs. Chadwick said. She had wondered from time to time in the past four years about her quiet boarder, why the girl had no friends her own age, no family, never talked about where she came from. But Mrs.

Chadwick prided herself on being a landlady who wasn't nosy; as long as the rent came regularly and on time, and the lodger was clean and quiet, she kept out of their business. She liked Philippa Roberts; so sweet, so reliable. Even helping with the dishes at night, which she didn't have to do, and sometimes bringing things home from the drugstore, like opened candy boxes that couldn't be sold or leaky perfume bottles that had to be tossed out. Mrs. Chadwick liked these simple gifts, and the girl's occasional company when she didn't have night school. They would get together sometimes and watch *What's My Line?* and share a bowl of buttered popcorn. And Philippa was sensible, not crazy like some girls who were making fools of themselves over this Elvis person. So Mrs. Chadwick felt this was one time it would be all right to interfere.

"What about that boyfriend of yours?" she asked. "The one you been seeing?" Mrs. Chadwick had her doubts about this so-called boyfriend. He never telephoned, never came by; she might almost suspect that there was no boyfriend at all and that Philippa had made him up, except that the poor girl showed the obvious signs of being in love and she went out most evenings. And, of course, now this. So there was a boyfriend, but Mrs. Chadwick couldn't help thinking that there was something suspicious about the relationship, something that made her think that when he heard this news he wasn't exactly going to hand out cigars.

"Is it true?" Philippa asked Mrs. Chadwick. "Are you *sure?* I mean about my being pregnant?"

"Well, I'm no doctor, honey, but you've got the signs." Mrs. Chadwick put her hands on her wide hips and gave the girl a sympathetic look. Men. Mrs. Chadwick knew all about them, and she had had her fill. "I have to ask you another personal question. It's the only way to find out. Have you been sleeping with your boyfriend?"

Philippa felt her cheeks redden. "Yes," she said. "I have."

"Well then, honey, you're going to have a baby all right and you'd better tell that boyfriend of yours."

"Yes," Philippa said, experiencing a baffling mixture of fear and excitement all at the same time. A baby. *Rhys's* baby.

"I must tell him right away!" she said, and she started to leave.

But Mrs. Chadwick put her hand on Philippa's arm and said, "Listen, honey. Sometimes men . . . well, they don't react to this kind of news the way you'd expect them to. What I'm trying to say is . . ." *What I'm trying to say is that Mr. Chadwick married me because I was pregnant with his baby. He didn't like it, but he did it. I was lucky. We ended up having a decent marriage, until that heart attack got him.* "Just remember, honey, that it might come hard to him, this kind of news. If he reacts wrongly, just give him a few days, let it settle into him, let him get comfortable with it, like a new sofa. Everything will work out, you'll see."

"It will be all right, Mrs. Chadwick," Philippa said, her eyes shining. "You don't know Rhys. He's a very loving man. This baby might be just what he needs to change his life around."

As Philippa hurried out, the landlady watched her go and thought, I've heard *that* one before.

Philippa went first to her room, where she had only last night wrapped a present that she was going to give to Rhys. It was her little book bound in floral cloth, in which she wrote inspirational thoughts. In the two months that she had been seeing him, she had witnessed more of his sadness and fatalism; he was tender and loving in bed, he was a slow, considerate lover, he always made her feel special. But then he would return to his typewriter where the roll of butcher paper was cranked out each day, covered with defeatist philosophy. She had tried to get through to him, to make him see his worth, his value, but she made no impression. Perhaps this little book, which contained her philosophy—"Believe and succeed" and "Always remember that you are special"—would help him. That Rhys would regard such homilies as simplistic she had no doubt, but he needed to be reached, one way or another. She didn't yet know what unspeakable event had occurred in his childhood, but she knew that it was the root of his low self-esteem, his belief that he, and all people, were worthless and doomed.

She had tried so many times to talk to him after they made love, when they were lying on his mattress and he would toy with her hair. She would try to explain that there was worth in everyone, and hope, and the ability to make life better. But he would only laugh softly and stroke her, as if she were a child who had just uttered something compellingly naïve. She couldn't get him to take her seriously. But now there was going to be a baby. Part of her, part of him. Maybe this would make him realize that there was, after all, a future.

When she turned down his street, she realized that she was walking so quickly she was almost running. She couldn't wait to tell him the news. Perhaps Mrs. Chadwick was right and Rhys wouldn't take the news well, or maybe he would be ecstatic and ask Philippa to marry him. Whatever happened, it would turn his life around in one way or another. He would finish his book, send it to a publisher, and live for tomorrow, for the future of their child.

As she was hurrying up the steps of his apartment house she thought she heard a car backfiring. And when she entered the building, she saw Mr. Laszlo, the landlord, running up the stairs two at a time. By the time she reached Rhys's apartment, several other tenants were banging on the door and calling to him.

Philippa pushed through and used the key Rhys had given her. The first thing she was aware of when she opened the door was the pungent smell of smoke—but not the usual marijuana smell. Something else.

And then she saw him slumped over his typewriter, a curious berrylike stain on his temple.

She saw the gun on the floor, still smoking.

"Mein Gott!" cried Mr. Laszlo, and then the other tenants were suddenly animated. Someone shouted for the police, another for an ambulance, while Philippa walked slowly forward, staring at the closed eyes, the peaceful expression on Rhys's handsome face. She gently drew him back from the typewriter; his head flopped unnaturally. She looked at the last thing he had typed: "There are no more words."

The room seemed to tilt.

She saw men running in; they swam through the water of her tears. Numbness, like novocaine, crept up from her feet all through her body as she stood off to one side and watched men in uniforms take away the man she had loved—men in dark blue with badges; men in white with medical patches on their sleeves, unfolding a stretcher. Someone with a pad and pencil came up to her and asked her some questions. She noticed he had a pimple on his chin.

"That's the girlfriend," someone said, and Philippa recognized by the accent that it was Mr. Laszlo. "She come *after* the gunshot. Mr. Rhys, he kilt himself. *Mein Gott."*

As Rhys was carried out on a stretcher, a sheet over his face, his arm fell down and Philippa saw the strong square hand that had so many times explored her body, and that had written such sad words, and that had ultimately fired the gun.

People kept coming up to her and saying things, but she stayed where she was. After Rhys was gone, she heard Mr. Laszlo say, "He got a brother in Sacramento. I call him. Yes, he come get all this stuff."

Philippa walked over to the typewriter, picked up an end of the paper, and began unraveling it. The words made no sense, she couldn't read them. But finally she came to ". . . plump partridge in this papier-mâché town. Her face, with the sweet roundness of a cherub, she was like a pure, baby angel, when she opened her mouth to speak, light came out. Her soul is young. She has a long road to walk before wisdom will carve her up. She lay in my arms like a warm little quail . . ."

The next thing she knew rain was falling over her, and lights seemed to go runny around her, and she was vaguely aware of headlights and of other pedestrians and someone asking her something.

She went past Mrs. Chadwick's boardinghouse and kept walking. She saw a tour bus pull up in front of Grauman's Chinese and people get out. At Hollywood and Vine, couples sat in a coffee shop and ate butterscotch sundaes. The newsstand on Cahuenga was battened down for the night. Cherokee Books was dark. Palm trees drooped in the rain; where had the sunshine gone? A panhandler asked her for a dime. Runaway kids huddled under the awning of the Golden Cup, looking for someone to take care of them.

And then Philippa was back at Mrs. Chadwick's and she was walking up the front steps and then up the stairs to her room, barely aware of her drenched clothing, the squishing of her shoes, the little voice in her abdomen that kept saying, Why? Why? Why?

Philippa awoke to the sound of her teeth chattering. In fact, her whole body shook as if she were cold, and yet she realized she was burning up.

She looked around, discovered that she was in her own room, in her bed, in a nightgown, but she had no memory of getting there. She saw her clothes crumpled on the floor—the blouse and skirt she had worn to tell Rhys the good news—and the little floral cloth-bound book lying on her desk next to the history paper she had been working on for a midterm grade. It occurred to her that she might fail that class.

She wondered how long she had been in bed, and she shook some more, so badly that it alarmed her.

Memories of her long walk in the rain came back in patches, but not her memories of Rhys. What she had found when she unlocked his door and went into his apartment. No, she wouldn't think about that.

Now she was burning with fever. She felt terribly sick.

And then the cramps hit.

Mrs. Chadwick had made herself a tub of that new stuff called California Dip, the mainstay of every social gathering these days, and she helped herself generously to it with each potato chip that she plunged into the bowl. She was comfortably ensconced in her Relax-a-Sizer, her feet up in big fluffy slippers, and she was watching *I Love Lucy,* her favorite show. Lucy had just said, "Ricky, you're impossible," and Ricky had just said, "You're the one who's impossible, *I* happen to be quite possible," when she thought she heard a noise outside her door.

Mrs. Chadwick considered herself to be very modern—she had one of those fancy remote control devices that let you mute the TV set with the touch of a button. Which she did. And as she listened, hearing the rain that had been punishing Southern California for three days, she thought she also heard another sound. It was almost like someone knocking, but very softly.

"Who is it?" she said, annoyed at being disturbed. All of her tenants knew better than to disturb her during "Lucy," even if she *was* just watching reruns.

The tap-tap-tapping continued until she said, "Oh for goodness sake," and got up and went to see who it was.

Philippa was standing there, in her nightgown, looking as white as flour. "Mrs. Chadwick," she said in a faint voice, "I don't feel well."

And then she lifted up a hand and there was blood on it.

"Oh my God!" the landlady said. She caught Philippa as she was about to slump to the floor and brought her inside. As she helped the girl into the bedroom, she saw the blood on Philippa's nightgown and spotting the floor. "Jesus, child!" she said. "What happened?"

Philippa started to cry. "He's dead," she said. "He shot himself. If I had gotten there a minute sooner, I could have saved him. It's all my fault."

Having no idea what she was talking about, Mrs. Chadwick settled her on the bed, then lifted up the nightgown. When she saw the bleeding, she said, "I'm calling a doctor."

But Philippa, with startling strength, suddenly seized the landlady's wrist and said, "No. Don't do that. Doctors make reports."

"Honey, you're having a miscarriage!"

"Please. Don't call a doctor. I don't want a record . . . of . . . it."

Mrs. Chadwick hesitated and then reluctantly admitted that this might be one of those woman moments that forever must remain a secret. So she rolled up her sleeves and got to work. She sat with Philippa all through the night, during the whole painful process that was like a birth, with labor pains, blood, and everything. But she didn't call a doctor. Not yet. She respected Philippa's wish, for now. But if it got out of hand, there was the telephone, just in case.

But finally the ordeal seemed to run its course and Mrs. Chadwick put all the towels into a large plastic bag and twisted it tightly shut. Then she cleaned Philippa and put her into one of her own flannel nightgowns and let her sleep. And she thought for a moment about life, how it wasn't like it was on TV, then she went back into her living room and saw that the rising sun was spilling its beams over her furniture. She wondered for the first time in a long time how her marriage with Mr. Chadwick would have ended up if *their* baby had lived.

The next afternoon Philippa opened her eyes and the first thing she said was, "Was it a boy or a girl?"

"You couldn't tell, child," Mrs. Chadwick said gently, dipping buttered toast into a soft-boiled egg and offering it to Philippa. "It was just a little bit of a thing. Nowhere near a baby yet."

"Mrs. Chadwick," Philippa said, lucid for the first time in hours, "I wasn't able to help Rhys. He didn't take me seriously."

"Don't talk, honey, just eat."

She pushed Mrs. Chadwick's hand away. "No, I have to tell you. There was a girl at the school where I was, poor Mouse—she tried to change her looks and almost blinded herself. And then there was Frizz, who always hated the way she looked, believed other girls who told her she had ugly hair. Even Amber, who must have hated herself, to be so cruel, to force herself to throw up."

Mrs. Chadwick nodded, even though she had no idea what Philippa was talking about.

"And now Rhys," Philippa finally said. "He hated himself, too. I tried to make him see himself differently, to like himself, to accept himself as he was, but all he saw was death. He was doomed. I couldn't reach him."

"I'm sure you did what you could, honey."

"Help me up, please," Philippa said.

She made her way to the window and looked out at the brand-new sunshine washing over the Hollywood Hills. She wondered if she had been born not far from here; her school file had simply said "Hollywood." Maybe her real mother was still out there somewhere, not far away at this very moment, looking at the same rain-washed sunshine. "Rhys didn't take me seriously, partly because I'm fat," she said. "He called me a plump partridge, a quail, a child with a young soul. No one takes a fat girl seriously." She turned and looked at Mrs. Chadwick. "But I'm going to change that. I'm going to have to if I want to influence people and help them somehow. The Mouses and the Frizzes and the—" her voice caught "—Rhyses of the world. I'm going to become thin, someone people will listen to. Someone important. And I'll never be fat again."

....★

18

"I'm telling you, Sylvie, it was the best sex I've ever had."

Frieda Goldman's eyes snapped open. She was in one of the massage rooms of the Starlite salon at Star's health club, stretched out on a towel, trying to relax as Marcel, a real Frenchman, worked the essential oils of carnation, jasmine, lavender, and basil into her tense flesh. Marcel was a licensed *arôme-thérapiste* in France, where they took seriously the practice of treating stress and minor physical ailments with fragrances. Frieda had decided to avail herself of the service before her dinner appointment with Bunny; she was so excited that she hadn't slept well the night before, and although she had spent the morning on the phone busy with other deals and making contacts, work had not had its usual therapeutic effect on her.

Syd Stern had called. "Did you get her to sign?" he had said abruptly. "Tonight for sure," Frieda had promised, her mouth filled with the chalky residue of Mylanta tablets.

Since Frieda rarely drank before sundown and she had given up smoking long ago, she had decided to come to the health club to try to relax her fifty-three-year-old bones. As Marcel worked wonders with his miracle fingers—carnation oil into her neck, to ease those muscles, and lavender into her temples, for the headache—Frieda's peace was disturbed when two women walked by in the corridor beyond, talking about sex as they came to a halt outside her cubicle.

There was the sound of someone stepping up onto scales and moving weights along a balance beam. And then: "I'm serious, Sylvie. The *best* sex I've ever had."

Frieda tried to tune them out. She needed to think; her nerves had gotten to the point where she felt as if she were a gun about to go off.

"But how can you have sex with a perfect stranger?" Sylvie asked.

"It's a lousy job, Sylvie," the other woman said, "but someone's gotta do it." And they both laughed.

"But seriously, how is it handled? I mean, did you pay him or what?"

Again, someone stepped up on the scales, the weights were moved, the balance beam went *thunk,* and someone muttered, "Oy."

"Oh no, nothing so tacky as that. It's all done very discreetly. You just kind of let it be known to the management that you're here all alone and that you'd like some company for the evening. Next thing you know, they're calling you and telling you that you've got a dinner escort. So I go to the dining room and there's this gorgeous male, late twenties, waiting for me. And I mean gorgeous—black hair, shoulders out to here, and he treats me like I'm the Queen of Sheba. We have a pleasant dinner, a few drinks, some small talk, and then I ask him if he'd like to come to my room for a nightcap."

"And? And?" Sylvie said.

"And, so you can imagine the rest."

"But how do you *pay* for it?"

"It shows up on your bill when you check out. Under room service."

"Do you know how much it's going to be?"

"I have no idea. And I tell you what, Sylvie. I don't care. For sex like that—I mean *all night long,* my dear—I'd pay anything."

A few seconds of astonished silence. "But doesn't it make you feel guilty? I mean, what about Gary?"

"What about him? All he knows is that every time I come home from a week at Star's I'm cheerful and easy to get along with. There's nothing better to pump life into an old relationship!"

They laughed again and moved on, while Frieda lay beneath Marcel's massaging fingers, thinking about the young man in the tuxedo who had given her the eye the night before when she had arrived, and whom she had run into again that morning in the lobby at the Castle. One again, he had given her one of those sexy smiles, and to Frieda's astonishment she had gotten a feeling deep in her pelvis. Had *he* been Sylvie's friend's dinner companion? What *would* it be like to have sex with him? And all night long . . . she couldn't even imagine it.

Sex! Frieda thought, nearly laughing out loud. So when was the last time *she* had had sex?

They came back, Sylvie and her friend, from whatever they had done down the hall. Now Frieda heard the water fountain run as the two women continued to talk. "By the way, did you know that Larry Wolfe is here, the screenwriter? That man's a real hunk. I swear he belongs in *front* of the camera, not behind it."

"I heard he was here to write a screenplay of Marion Star's story. Mind you, I'm too young to remember, but her lover was murdered here, in the famous bathroom. Have you seen that room yet? *Very* naughty."

Frieda tried again to tune them out. Larry Wolfe's latest project didn't interest her—the Marion Star role wasn't something Bunny could play.

"Hey, you know who I ran into this morning? Jay Stonehocker—you know, that schlock director who makes millions churning out those awful karate action films? Anyway, we got to talking, and he told me that Syd Stern—you know him, sort of Spielberg-ish—is developing a new project, a series of adventure films starring one woman, a female Indiana Jones. He's looking for someone to play the part."

Frieda was suddenly alert.

"You know who would be good for it?" Sylvie said. "My niece. She's studying to be an actress. And my husband and Syd Stern are like *that;* they golf together, you know. He'll take a look at her if I ask him. In fact, I'm going to give him a call."

Frieda was up and out of there before Marcel could begin to rub the basil behind her knees.

"You're fine, Bunny," Judith Isaacs said as she closed her medical bag. "You're ready to face the world again."

"Thank goodness," Bunny said. "My agent is here, she called a few minutes ago, just before you arrived. She's frantic to see me. We were supposed to have dinner tonight, but she insists on coming over right away."

"Yes. I spoke with Mrs. Goldman this morning. She's very concerned about you, but I assured her that you're all right and that there was no reason you couldn't see her."

"I wonder why she's here," Bunny said as she tied the sash of her bathrobe and picked up her orange juice. "Frieda says she has something important to discuss with me. She normally isn't so secretive, so I'm guessing it's a movie deal—I'm *praying* it's a movie deal."

As she reached for the bottle of vitamins beside her bed, Bunny glanced at the photograph that stood among a clutter of Kleenex, cough syrups, throat lozenges, and sleeping pills. It was a picture of Bunny with her father, the wealthy industrialist who was paying for her extended stay at Star's. The photo had been taken four years ago when Mr. Kowalski had taken his daughter on a cruise around the world for her twenty-first birthday. They were standing on the deck of a cruise ship, smiling self-consciously at the camera, trying to look like a close and loving father and daughter. Bunny had been relatively thin then, because she had just come out of a three-month stint at an expensive fat farm, only one of many where she had spent her adolescence. But she had gained the weight all back, and then some, on the cruise.

And her father had been far from happy about that.

In fact, for as long as she could remember, Bunny's father had been displeased with her for one reason or another. Bernie Kowalski, the man she could never please, no matter what she did. Sometimes he would look at her with something in his face that said, How could someone like me, rich, sophisticated, powerful, produce such a nebbish? Her part in *Children Again,* though praised by critics and well received by the public, had embarrassed him. When Bunny hadn't received the award for Best Supporting actress, he had said it was a good thing, because now maybe she would come to her senses and give up this insane Hollywood dream.

Even when she was younger, she could never please him. He would look at her as if she had somehow let him down. But Bunny couldn't help how God had put her together. She had been called Gidget all through school, even though she wasn't really small; it was because her "lush" figure made her look shorter than she really was. She was the girl in the fifth grade class who had breasts before anyone else. But it was her Kewpie-doll look that had made her such a hit in that last movie, everyone said, and probably why she had earned an Oscar nomination. "Fine," her father had said when she had shown him the reviews. "So now you're going to make a career out of being chubby and awkward? And how many parts like that do you think come down the pike? No daughter of mine is going to degrade herself taking the freak roles that decent actresses turn their noses up at."

When she saw that Judith was preparing to leave, Bunny said, "It must be fun working here, Dr. Isaacs," stalling her, hoping to keep the doctor a few minutes longer. Bunny had had so little company in the past few months that the loneliness sometimes made her want to scream.

"I don't know if fun is the word," Judith said with a smile as she paused at the door with her hand on the knob. "But it is interesting."

"You must deal with a lot of superfamous people. Dr. Mitgang, the man who was the house doctor before you, told me a lot of biggies come here for secret plastic surgery. Do you ever see any of them? How does it make you feel?"

Judith thought of Mr. Smith. What could she say to Bunny? That for some strange reason a deep, physical part of her was reacting to him while her head was telling her to keep twenty feet away? "I'm afraid I can't discuss other patients."

"Oh sure, I understand. Heck, I wouldn't want you talking to other people about me." A supermarket tabloid lay on the coffee table, and Bunny pointed to it, saying, "I know, only people in checkout lines read them. But I like to keep up on industry gossip. I was in that particular tabloid once, you know," Bunny said, speaking rapidly to hide her fear. Frieda was coming soon. Was she going to be mad when she found out Bunny had been keeping a secret from her, had in fact been lying? And Bunny couldn't even think of how her father was going to react when he found out what she'd done. "They ran an article on me when I got the Oscar nomination. It was all about the crash diet I went on before I made the movie. I lost twenty pounds in five weeks. Not healthy, huh? Scads of women wrote to me asking for the secret. But all I did was starve. Literally. No food between my lips for thirty-five days. And I got sick afterward. The story of my life—starving and getting sick. I gained it all back after we finished shooting." Bunny paused, trying to think of something to add, something to prolong Judith's departure. She was so nervous. "Is there a specific diet you recommend, Doctor?"

"I think the Starlite program is good."

"Yeah, I eat their frozen dinners."

"If you have any more problems," Judith said, "just ask for me," and then she was gone.

Bunny closed the door and turned around, surveying the suite she had occupied for the past month. It was done in what was known as the grand touch style. In the bedroom, which was more like a boudoir, there was a four-poster bed with chintz drapes and matching chintz comforter, pillows, sheets, and shams, all a creamy ivory splashed with tiny pastel flowers. A little girl's room, Bunny thought. Very frilly and fussy, right down to the cutesy lamps and the bows on the pillows. The drapes over the windows were the same dusty pink as some of the flowers in the chintz; the carpet was a teal that also spattered the fabric. The sitting room was furnished with an arrangement of three pink-and-blue brocaded love seats around the fireplace, with a maple coffee table in the center, its ornately carved feet resting on a carpet so extravagantly floral that Marie Antoinette might have picked it out. Fat cherubs with lampshades on their heads and paintings of people in powdered wigs completed the awesome decor.

This was the fourth room Bunny had occupied since she had come to Star's. She had moved each time because of boredom, and she had discovered with each move that no two rooms at Star's were alike. A person could come here many times and never have the same experience twice.

It was time to get ready to face Frieda.

As she ran water in the tub that had gold swans instead of normal faucets, Bunny felt both excited and afraid. Frieda was sure to react well to Bunny's news. But her father, of whom she was terrified, was a different matter. And he had promised to come and get her in a few days, to take her home in time for Christmas. "Home" being an apartment in a complex that had gone condo in the seventies, four sterile rooms in Century

City, thirty flights up, where Bernie Kowalski hung his hat maybe ten days out of the year.

With the steam swirling around her, Bunny recalled the last time she had seen her father—a week before the Oscar ceremony, when she had pleaded with him to come to the Shrine Auditorium and sit in the audience. Bernie Kowalski would have none of it, believing that making movies wasn't honest, that actresses were whores. In a way, she was glad he hadn't come, because she hadn't gotten the Oscar after all; later, she was even happier that he hadn't attended the post-Oscar party with her, where people had fawned over the lithe, slender actresses but had ignored the impish Bunny. Of course, Bunny hadn't expected to compete with such luminous guests as Madonna and Michael Jackson, or any of the other faces that could have filled five years' worth of *National Enquirers*. And Bunny hadn't expected to be invited to the really special after-Oscar parties, such as the Kevin Costner bash that was rumored to be so exclusive that guests had to telephone after the show to find out its secret location. But, after all, she *had* received a nomination, and she *had* collected good reviews—thumbs up both from Siskel and Ebert—so she had thought a little veneration should come her way. But no, she had stood off to the side alone, stuffing Wolfgang Puck's designer hors d'oeuvres into her mouth without even tasting them and wishing she were anywhere else in the world—with her father, even—than there.

Frieda arrived while Bunny was in the bedroom putting on her makeup. "Come on in!" she called out. "It's open!"

Frieda walked in, stopped when she saw the aggressive decor, then, closing the door, said, "Are you all right?"

"Just finishing getting dressed. Make yourself at home."

"My home never looked like this! Hurry up, sweetheart, we are about to have a celebration. I've brought a bottle of your favorite—Mandarine Napoleon."

"Frieda, that stuff is expensive."

"And we are going to get expensively drunk!"

"So what's it all about?"

"I'll wait till you come out." Frieda frowned at a painting of two cherubs pouring water over a goddess in a pond. "I have a surprise for you."

"And *I* have a surprise for you!"

Frieda paced between a table skirted with heavy fabric that puddled on the floor and a tall marble pedestal with a Roman bust on it. This was decorating at its best.

"Okie-dokie," Bunny finally called from the bedroom. "Here I come!"

Bunny came out, and Frieda turned to stare.

"Well? What do you think?" Bunny said, twirling around. Dressed in a slinky white dress with spaghetti straps and plunging back, Bunny appeared to be tall; she had a small waist, medium-sized breasts, slender legs, long, full blond hair, upturned nose, sculptured chin, and full lips. It was Bunny, and yet it was not. The lushness was gone, all homeliness erased; she was a picture of breathtaking, sexy glamor. She looked, in fact, like a lot of other actresses in Hollywood. "What do you think?" she said excitedly, continuing her slow turn to give Frieda the full benefit of all these months of plastic surgery. "I've had *everything* done, more than Cher I'll bet! Liposuction, ribs removed, back teeth pulled—no one can call me fat and dumpy anymore. No more comic, Kewpie-doll roles for me! Well, what do you think, Frieda? Are you surprised?"

She turned around to see Frieda lying on the floor in a dead faint.

··★

19

The Corvette took the dangerous curves of the canyon road at high speed,
tires squealing on the asphalt, the electric blue body flashing in and out
of circles of light from the street lamps.

Hannah Scadudo gripped the steering wheel in desperation, her eyes
fixed on each hairpin turn ahead as the 'Vette flew over the center line
and back again, Hannah's body braced for the impact that might come
at any moment and crush the fragile fiberglass body of her car, herself with
it. She was racing against time, racing to catch up with it and pull it back
like a runaway horse, reining in the hours and days that were getting away
from her. Four days, Philippa had said. In four days there was going to
be a major board meeting with reports from all the members and a
thorough examination of company accounting.

What was Philippa expecting to find? Why had she really come back?
A discrepancy in accounting did not necessarily mean wrongdoing was
involved; it could simply mean calling for an audit and making an adjustment to fix the error. And this business about Miranda International, that
too could have been managed from Australia. And as for the so-called
sister in Palm Springs, Ivan had found "sisters" before and Philippa
hadn't gone rushing off to look at them. Certainly not from the other side
of the world. Philippa's unexpected and unannounced return could only
mean she suspected some kind of foul play within the company, that
someone inside was a traitor. Hannah's foot pressed down on the gas
pedal. Four days—was there enough time?

When the towering wrought-iron gates of her Bel Air estate suddenly
loomed in the headlights, she reached up to the visor and pressed the
button of the infrared opener, racing the sports car through the gates
before they had opened all the way, so that the passenger side of the car
was scraped. When she reached the top of the long driveway and entered

the paved circle in front of the house, she slammed on the brakes, sending the Corvette into a half spin. When the car jolted to a stop, she closed her eyes and rested her head on the steering wheel.

Feeling her heart galloping in her chest, Hannah remembered what Dr. Freeman had said after her last physical about taking it easy, reminding her that her mother, Jane Ryan, had died at age forty-eight of a heart attack, six years younger than Hannah was now. But Hannah couldn't take it easy now; there was no time.

Philippa, Philippa, cried her silent mind. Why did you have to come back just *now*?

Hannah raised her head and looked at the house, an elegant Mediterranean-style villa that had been built back in the forties. It had sixteen rooms, an indoor swimming pool, a bowling alley, and it was valued at eight million dollars. Tasteful Christmas lights glowed in the downstairs windows; silver lights twinkled in the trees and bushes framing the impressive arched entrance. It was a beautiful, inviting house, but Hannah couldn't bring herself to go inside. Not yet. She had to calm herself; she had to fabricate some semblance of normalcy, or else others might get suspicious.

Did Philippa suspect her? Was that why she had suddenly come back without telling anyone? Hannah felt betrayed. Charmie had had everyone believing she had gone to Ohio, as she usually did at this time of the year, to spend the holidays with her son and his family. Instead, she had sneaked off to Australia and brought Philippa back. The fact that Charmie hadn't told Hannah of her plans, hadn't confided in her after nearly thirty years of sharing everything and not keeping secrets, wounded Hannah deeply. It meant that Charmie and Philippa, her two closest friends, no longer trusted her.

As Hannah sat in her car, shivering more from dread than from the cold, she realized that what she feared most about Philippa discovering the truth was what it would do to their friendship.

Before getting out of the car, Hannah quickly checked her appearance in the rearview mirror. Her very short dark brown hair was neatly in place, the gray hairs disguised by a rinse; the tiny gold loop earrings caught reflections from the Christmas lights, making her look younger, she hoped, than her fifty-four years. But what Hannah was specifically looking for was the face of business-as-usual. The situation was too delicate now, too dangerous for her to risk giving everything away.

A maid greeted her at the front door, "Good evening, madam," holding her hands out to receive Hannah's purse and coat.

"Good evening, Rita. Is Mr. Scadudo home?"

"No, madam."

"Find Miss Ralston and tell her to see me in the library, please."

The library was a darkly paneled room with a Spanish tile floor, leather furniture, and a wrought-iron chandelier with real candles, which shed flickering light on Mexican handicrafts and pre-Columbian art. Hannah went straight to the bar and fixed herself a Bloody Mary, strong.

Miss Ralston came in, a capable-looking woman in her sixties who lived alone, had never been married. She had been Hannah's personal secretary for nearly ten years; she balanced the Scadudos' very full and busy social calendar, and she was compensated with a generous salary and a new car every other year.

"Good evening, Mrs. Scadudo," Miss Ralston said as she set a clipboard, yellow legal pad, and stack of mail on the bar. Hannah had tried long ago to get the two of them on a first name basis, but it was Miss Ralston's wish that they keep the relationship formal.

As Hannah brought the Bloody Mary to her lips, she realized that her hand was shaking. She wondered if the secretary had noticed.

"The party arrangements are coming along, Mrs. Scadudo," Miss Ralston reported, producing a pen and addressing the legal pad. "The caterer came by this morning, and after inspecting your kitchen, he said he will have no trouble with the special desserts you requested. There is more than enough room for his staff to work. I reconfirmed the order with the florist . . ."

While Miss Ralston reviewed the myriad details for the Scadudos' upcoming Christmas party, Hannah could barely keep still. She was anxious to get upstairs and be alone. And she had to make a phone call. An urgent, life and death phone call.

"Nearly everyone has RSVP'd," Miss Ralston went on in her crisp way. "Only three couples have said they can't make it. That brings the guest count to a hundred and seventy-five."

Hannah raised her drink again and was startled to find that the glass was empty. Fighting to keep her hands steady, she mixed another, a little heavier on the vodka this time, and tried not to gulp it down. She glanced at her watch.

Why was Philippa calling the meeting in Palm Springs? What was wrong with the Starlite offices, so near and convenient for everyone? Palm Springs was going to waste an entire day; it was at least a two-hour drive each way.

She wants to get us on neutral ground, Hannah thought. She wants to bring us out of the familiarity and security of our offices, out into the open where we will have no advantage. She wants to see if we can survive out of our comfortable corporate environment.

Hannah was shocked by her thoughts. They seemed so cynical, so uncharitable. But then wasn't that how Philippa's sudden return to Los Angeles appeared? As though everyone at Starlite—her friends—were criminals?

Oh God, Hannah thought as she clenched her glass. Let it just be the business with Miranda International that has brought her back. Don't let it be the other—not until I've taken care of it.

Miss Ralston was saying, "The special Christmas tree ornaments you ordered from Saks are ready, Mrs. Scadudo. And the twenty-foot Ponderosa pine has been reserved for the morning of the party."

Hannah paused with her drink, realizing that her secretary was staring at her, waiting for an answer to a question Hannah had not heard. There was so much to do—the Christmas party, her children and their families coming for the holidays, the special surprise she had planned for Alan . . .

She put her glass down abruptly and said, "Yes, it's all very good, Miss Ralston. Thank you. I'm going to go upstairs for a few minutes." She looked at her watch again. "Mr. Scadudo should be home soon." *And I must make that call before he gets here.* "So if you don't need me for a little while . . ."

Before Miss Ralston could say anything, Hannah left the library.

She climbed the great curving staircase and went down the hall to the master bedroom suite, where she took care to close the large double doors behind her.

She turned on the lights and leaned against the door, trying to calm herself. Was she really feeling pressure in her chest, or was it just her imagination? Hurrying across the plush carpet, she picked up the phone that stood on her ornate Louis XV correspondence desk and, with trembling hands, dialed. Realizing she had dialed the wrong number, she hung up and tried again. While she listened to the ringing at the other end, she was afraid she wouldn't be able to hear whoever answered, her heart was pounding so loudly in her ears.

And then the phone at the other end was picked up.

Talking softly so as not to be overheard, she said, "We need to make the transfer right away. Philippa suspects something. She's back in L.A. She's called a board meeting. She's going to go over *everything.* Please, we must do it as soon as possible, before she finds out."

She listened to the reply. Then the line went dead. Suppressing a sob, she hung up the phone and looked around the room.

It did not strike her as strange to suddenly think now, after all the years that had passed, of another bedroom, in another house, a bedroom that had been one-sixth the size of this, with a cramped double bed, threadbare chenille spread, braided rug on the floor, and a secondhand dresser that Alan had refinished. This bedroom in the Bel Air mansion had a large circular bed with a satin canopy spreading down from the ceiling like the kind one saw in fairy tales. The carpet was so thick it retained deep footprints; the furniture was all custom-made, imported. There was no comparison between that smaller, dismal bedroom of years ago and this suite that could house royalty. And yet it was the other one Hannah wished she were in now.

As tears stung her eyes, she thought that she had never felt so helpless, so trapped. In four days the board meeting was going to be called and the company records were going to be examined. And every member of the board, including Hannah and her husband, were going to have to be prepared to answer questions.

Panic swept over her again, sending her flying across the room to where a large Impressionist oil painting hung in a gilded frame. Pushing it aside and shedding light on the small wall safe that was hidden behind it, Hannah quickly worked the combination, fumbling with it several times before she got it right. When the safe was open, she drew out a locked metal box, a small leather case with brass buckles, packets of envelopes bound with ribbon, and finally, from the very back of the safe, a portfolio made of greenish black eelskin, polished to such a high shine that she could see her face reflected in it.

She went to the bed and emptied the contents onto the satin bed-spread. There was a pile of stock certificates of various colors, each denot-ing different face values. The most valuable ones—the silver certificates—were worth a thousand shares each. Hannah spread them out so that she could read her name on each one. They were all signed and dated, the earliest ones going back to over twenty years ago. All together they totaled a hundred thousand shares. Of Starlite Industries.

People didn't keep stock certificates anymore, of course, but Hannah cherished these certificates, which represented only a portion of her inter-est in the corporation, because they were special. They had been gifts over the years, given to her by her husband for birthdays and anniversaries; the thousand-share certificates had come from Philippa. Combined, they represented more than money or a chunk of a company that was worth hundreds of millions; for Hannah they symbolized an important part of her life, the most important part, perhaps. And now she was going to have to give them up.

She felt almost as if she were selling a child.

How had it come to this? she thought unhappily, thinking of that crude little bedroom in the San Fernando Valley where she and Alan had spent many rapturous nights making love. She wished they were back there again in the creaking secondhand bed, lying in each other's arms and wondering where the next mortgage payment was coming from. Hannah thought she would give anything—the house in Bel Air, her maids, even her precious Corvette—to be able to undo the mess she was in.

But she couldn't go back. The disaster that had been brewing was about to break, and she felt helpless to stop it.

When the phone rang, she jumped. She stared at it for a moment. Could it be . . . ?

She ran to answer it. "Hello?"

"Hi, Mom!" came a chirpy voice. Her youngest daughter, Jackie, calling from college.

Hannah forced herself to sound cheerful. "Jackie darling, how nice of you to call. Is everything all right?"

"Everything is wonderful, Mother! Vincent and I have decided to get married."

"Oh . . . how marvelous . . ." Hannah placed a hand on her chest. Her heart quivered for a moment, then resumed its normal rhythm.

"I want the wedding in June," Jackie said, "in the garden, and it must be absolutely the biggest wedding that the world has ever seen! Esther's going to be my maid of honor, and four of my sorority sisters are going to be bridesmaids, as well as Sue and Polly. And guess what! Vincent's parents are going to give us a trip to the south of France as a wedding present! They have a villa there, and Vincent and I thought we would . . ."

As she listened to Jackie's excited speech, Hannah's eyes strayed to the collection of photographs in many different frames standing on her writing desk, on the dresser, on her nightstand. They were mostly of her children—when they were babies, or starting school, wearing Halloween costumes, graduating from the sixth grade, high school, and finally college. But there were older photos, of a very young Hannah shyly holding hands with Alan, love shining in both of their eyes. On her nightstand there was a portrait of Alan taken just two years ago, with an inscription that read: "To Hannah My Love, Forever and Always." And finally, there was a black and white picture of three crazy young women making faces at the camera—Hannah, Charmie, and Philippa—in their twenties, desperate, penniless, and struggling, but hopeful. Hannah had always thought of Philippa as the glue that bound them together.

Continuing to listen to her daughter chatter over the phone, she looked at the photos and knew that she was going to fight to make everything right again. She had never believed in doing anything the easy way just to get it done; that was what had made her and Philippa and Charmie such fast friends from the start. They were all determined to overcome their handicaps and take on the world. But this fight now would be for more than to save her friendship with the other two. It would also be for Alan, and for her children, to keep them proud of her. Hannah had once overheard her daughter tell some friends, "My mom is the greatest fashion designer that ever lived. She was the first one to give large women permission to wear bright colors and bold prints. She liberated them from tents and dark colors." Hannah didn't want to destroy that.

She was suddenly startled when, as she gazed at the precious objects around the room, they began to disappear, one by one—a photograph from the dresser, the pen set from the desk, the amethyst-handled letter opener. Blink, and then gone. The artifacts of her life, the things that made Hannah Scadudo, vanished one after the other, as if she were trapped in a *Twilight Zone* episode. She rubbed her eyes and looked again. Everything was still there, as it had been; it was only her fear, her imagination that was sending these precious mementoes into the void. Her life, slowly slipping away until she too vanished and the world went on as if she had never existed.

"Well, I have to go, Mom!" Jackie said, reminding Hannah that she was standing there with a phone to her ear. "There's a *massive* barbecue down on the beach. And moonlight swimming, for those brave enough!" Jackie was a marine biology major at the University of California at Santa Barbara. "Bye. See you in a few days."

As Hannah hung up the phone, she tried to feel excited over her daughter's news. Jackie, the last of her children, finally getting married. It completed a perfect picture. And, yes, they would have the biggest, most sensational wedding the world—or at least Bel Air—had ever seen. Nothing must spoil it for Jackie. Nothing.

When Hannah heard a chime downstairs, the signal that a car had come through the main gates, she hurried to the window, parted the drapes, and held her breath as she watched the long driveway that wound up the hill from the street. After a moment, she saw the headlight beams emerge from behind the trees, illuminating the red bricks that paved the drive, and then she saw the shiny grille of Alan's Mercedes. She dashed back to the bed and frantically gathered up the stock certificates.

She ran to the safe, dropping half of them, scrambling to pick them up and stuff them in haphazardly. Alan mustn't know; *he mustn't know.* She heard the front door downstairs, muffled voices. "Good evening, Rita, has Mrs. Scadudo come home yet?" And then footsteps across the black and white tiles in the foyer.

She thrust the last of the stock certificates into the safe and then frantically shoved everything else back in. They didn't fit. She took it all out and tried again—the metal box, the leather case, the ribbon-bound envelopes.

She imagined Alan coming down the hall, approaching the doors to the master bedroom suite. She fumbled and dropped things. She looked over at the doors. She pictured his hand reaching for the gold knob. Finally, everything fit. She slammed the safe shut, twirled the lock, and swung the painting back into place.

The bedroom door opened. "There you are, dear," Alan said with a smile on his face.

She spun around. "Alan!"

"I'm sorry," he said, the smile turning into a frown. "I didn't mean to startle you. I thought you might have heard me coming up the drive."

"I—I was just about to get into the bath," she said, moving quickly away from the wall.

Alan's eyes flickered to the painting, which hung slightly askew. Then he looked at the bedspread, which was disheveled. "Is everything all right, Hannah?" he said, coming in and closing the door. "You look pale."

"I'm fine," she said, going to the bathroom and turning on the light. "It was just, well, such a shock to see Philippa today. I wasn't expecting her, were you?"

"No, I wasn't. But she was bound to come home some time. I knew she wouldn't stay buried in Australia forever. Darling, are you sure you're all right?"

She poked her head through the open doorway of the bathroom and gave him a winning smile. "Of course I'm all right. But we're running late. We've got to get you to the airport. I wish you didn't have to dash off to South America tonight. We have something to celebrate! Jackie telephoned with wonderful news!" Then she disappeared back into the bathroom.

"What about Jackie?" Alan called, but his voice was drowned out by the sound of water running into the tub.

He dropped his newspaper and briefcase onto the rumpled bed and went to the painting. He studied it for a moment, then reached up and straightened it. Hannah came up behind him suddenly and put her arms around him, resting her head on his back and saying, "I love you, Alan. I love you so very much."

"Hey," he said, laughing softly as the turned and took her into his arms. "What's all this?"

"I'm just so happy with you," she murmured against his neck. "We have such a good life together. I'll miss you while you're in Rio. Will you miss me?"

"You know I will."

"Do you love me, Alan, do you?"

"Of course I love you, darling."

She held tightly to him as she closed her eyes and thought, I mustn't lose Alan's love, I mustn't lose *him*. If I did, I wouldn't want to live. Not after all we've been through together, after all these years.

....★

20

San Fernando Valley, California, 1959

Hannah Ryan thought that the way the seat of Alan Scadudo's pants fit snugly over his rear end was positively obscene.

And she loved it.

She had just come in out of a torrential rain, soaked and dripping, with the day's lunch order from Baumgartner's Deli. She hadn't had far to go—on sunny days the trek from Halliwell and Katz to Baumgartner's on Ventura Boulevard usually took three minutes, but during one of southern California's rare storms it seemed to take forever. She had hurried down the aisle between the twelve brokers' desks, which were arranged facing the Dow Jones board up front, her shoes squishing inside her boots as she distributed the sandwiches. She had collected money as she went, running into a problem when she reached Mr. Driscoll. He had ordered a hot pastrami on rye, and he looked at it askance, commenting that it was cold. When he told her he was short of change and that he would "catch her later," she had remained standing there with her hand out, water from the sleeve of her raincoat dripping onto his *Wall Street Journal.* Finally he had dug into his pocket, counted out the exact change, and slapped it into her icy palm.

And now she was at Mr. Scadudo's desk, where he was standing with what twenty-one-year-old Hannah thought was a wonderful *man's* frown on his face, reading a printout just off the Teletype. She was secretly in love with Mr. Scadudo, who was studying to become a CPA. "Here you are," she said, handing him the tomato and onion and jack cheese on a Kaiser roll, extra mayo, wrapped in wax paper. "Forty-two cents, please."

"Thanks," he said without looking at her and not taking the sandwich. She placed it neatly on his messy desk, which was covered with margin calls and confirm notices. "Jesus," he said. "International Petrochemical has announced a two-for-one split. I knew it!"

He absently reached into his pocket, counted out change, and dropped it into her outstretched hand. When the money, still warm from where it had just been, fell into Hannah's palm, lust rose up to her ears and pounded there for a few seconds, then settled back down into her abdomen, where it throbbed like a steady little engine whenever she was around Mr. Scadudo. She could have stood there forever, inhaling his Old Spice, but she had other sandwiches to deliver.

As she finally headed back to the lounge, where she looked forward to getting warm and dry, she passed the cashier's cage and saw Mrs. Faulkner, the office supervisor, talking to a young woman who was saying, "It's all so exciting to me! I know exactly *zip* about the stock market!" Hannah thought, New account, since opening new accounts was one of Mrs. Faulkner's many duties.

Inside the lounge, Hannah shed her raincoat, boots, and shoes and brought a towel out of the ladies' room. As she dried her short brown hair, she could hardly contain her excitement. After work today, she had an appointment with a counselor at the Greer Art Academy in Glendale, a small but prestigious school that had a highly acclaimed fashion design department. The school was expensive, and neither Hannah nor her parents, with whom she still lived, could afford the tuition, but Hannah had applied for a scholarship that, if she received it, would cover half her expenses. The counselor had called the night before with the good news: the scholarship was hers. The appointment that afternoon was to fill out the admission forms and to work out a class schedule that would allow Hannah to work at Halliwell and Katz, because she still had to come up with the rest of the tuition, which was why she had insisted Mr. Driscoll pay her for his sandwich. Every penny she earned went into a carefully monitored savings account. Hannah hadn't slept all night, she was so excited. Ever since she was a little girl, she had dreamed of being a dress designer, but not just for any women. She wanted to design clothes for the overweight woman.

Hannah herself was overweight; she had been for as long as she could remember. While on her mother's side Hannah was French and possibly Indian, her father was pure Irish, and many of her relatives were immigrants who had come out right after the war with rationing in the old country a recent hungry memory. Here in the United States, where food was plentiful, if you didn't stuff yourself at big family gatherings you were considered ungrateful, and children were admonished to eat until they thought they might burst. Hannah couldn't ever remember being thin; her mother was fat, and so were her aunts and female cousins, and the one thing they all had in common was difficulty finding clothes. There was only Monica's Overweight Shop on Sherman Way, where the clothes were dowdy and there was a feeble selection.

But Hannah had a dream. There was a big need out there and she was going to fill it. Having learned to sew when she was still in grammar school and having taught herself about fabrics, discovering which draped well, which flattered, she made clothes for herself and her female relations, all of whom declared that Hannah had a gift. But she needed to go further— she needed more extensive training. And Greer offered it.

The only obstacle was money. While her family was not poor, they could only afford to pay for her brothers' college educations, and even with the Greer scholarship and her savings, it still wasn't enough. But Hannah's money problems were about to be over. And that was what she was going to inform the counselor that very afternoon, to make sure nothing stopped them from accepting her.

When her hair was dry, Hannah inspected herself in the mirror. As she regarded her vaguely Indian features and high cheekbones that people said would make her look pretty if she weren't so fat, Madeline came in to freshen her makeup.

Madeline was Mr. Katz's private secretary, holding the position that Hannah had applied for two years ago and that she hadn't gotten because they said she was too young and inexperienced, being just nineteen years old and only a year out of high school. However, when they had offered her a lesser job, to work in what they called the "cage" as a general office worker for two hundred dollars a month, with a chance to be promoted to secretary eventually, she had taken it. Since then the coveted honor of working for Mr. Katz had been held by four different women, Madeline being the latest, and each time Hannah had been passed over she had been told it was because Mr. Katz needed a more experienced secretary.

And now Madeline was leaving. Hannah didn't pretend to be sorry to see the pretty blonde go, because now the job would be hers; it would be her ticket to Greer.

The lounge door opened and, for an instant, the room was flooded with the noise of the clattering Teletype and an outburst from Mr. Driscoll: "Whoa, there goes Kodak again!" Mrs. Faulkner came in, and when she closed the door, the lounge was quiet once more.

"It's another heavy-volume day, ladies," she said as she slumped down onto one of the sofas and set her purse and lunch sack next to her. "I'm betting it'll be twenty million by the end of the day."

"Uh oh," Hannah said. "That'll mean overtime on the confirm notices."

Ardeth Faulkner opened her lunch sack, bringing out an enormous meat loaf sandwich, Fritos, and a Mars Bar, and said, "I saw the way you made Driscoll pay you for his sandwich. Good for you. He's always trying to stiff people. Lousy cheapskate."

"It was my money," Hannah said as she opened the fridge and took out the cottage cheese and a diet Fresca she had brought for lunch. "I can't afford to buy lunch for a man who earns ten times what I do."

"You sure do want to go to fashion school awful badly, don't you?"

"Oh," Hannah said excitedly, stirring fruit cocktail into the cottage cheese, "I can't think of anything I'd rather do! And I see my counselor this afternoon!"

The lounge door opened again, and Alan Scadudo, the margin clerk for whom Hannah burned with lust, came in. "Whew!" he said as he went to the coffeepot and filled a Styrofoam cup. "Heavy volume today. It'll be overtime for all of us."

"I don't mind," Hannah said, looking at him. "I can use the money."

As he stirred Coffee-mate into his cup, he turned around, a soft-spoken young man with thick hair and glasses, nice brown eyes, and the kind of personality that made you imagine he took in stray animals. He was short, but that didn't bother Hannah. "Yeah," he said, "well, *I* don't want to work late."

When he said that, Hannah's heart filled up and ached. He has a date, she thought. He's going out with someone.

Just before he left, he paused and looked Madeline up and down, and Hannah didn't miss it. It made her feel even worse. Take a dress off a hanger and put it on Madeline and it looked as if it were still on the hanger. Mr. Scadudo clearly liked skinny women.

After he left, Ardeth said to Hannah, "You really go for him, don't you?"

"Is it that obvious?"

"Only to me." When she saw Madeline staring at herself in the mirror, not saying anything, Ardeth looked over at Hannah. They exchanged a glance and then looked away, suddenly embarrassed with themselves, and for Madeline.

Mr. Katz's secretary was leaving Halliwell and Katz in disgrace. In fact, she had been fired. "She had you-know-what happen to her," Mrs. Faulkner had said, pulling Hannah to one side a few days ago. And when Hannah had said, no, she didn't know what, Ardeth had whispered, "Pregnant!" And Madeline wasn't married. "We're a respectable firm," sixty-year-old Ardeth Faulkner had added with a self-righteous sniff.

Madeline finally turned away from the mirror, looked first at Hannah and then at Mrs. Faulkner, paused as if she wanted to say something, then left quietly.

Hannah slowly ate her cottage cheese, taking sips of diet Fresca in between, then said, "By the way, when is Madeline's last day?" The college counselor would want to know when Hannah's improved financial status would go into effect.

Ardeth peeled her hard-boiled egg with care, keeping her eyes on the egg instead of on Hannah as she said, "Mr. Katz gave her a month's notice."

"Well," Hannah said, "I'm certainly ready!" calculating that in just three weeks her salary was going to double.

Hannah didn't notice at first that the other woman avoided looking at her. It was only when she seemed to pay unusually close attention to her meat loaf sandwich that Hannah sensed something was wrong. She waited, and finally Ardeth looked at her and said, "I'm sorry, Hannah, but you aren't going to get the job."

Hannah stared at her. "What do you mean?"

"I mean," Mrs. Faulkner said, salting her egg, "that I've already hired her replacement. You saw her. The young woman who was at my desk a while ago."

"You mean the one who said she knew nothing about the stock market? I thought she was a new account! How can you hire her over me? You certainly can't say she's more experienced than I am! Ardeth, that job is mine!"

"I know," the other woman said, looking unhappy. "It's just that Mr. Katz—"

"Ardeth, remember when I filled in for Madeline when she was out sick for two weeks and how Mr. Katz praised my efficiency? Remember when I discovered how sloppy Madeline kept her files, and that her letters were always full of mistakes? Ardeth, she can barely take shorthand! Mr. Katz was so impressed with me that he even told you about it. He surely must want me to take her place."

Ardeth stared at her sandwich as if it had suddenly gone bad, then abruptly wrapped it in the wax paper, shoved it back into the brown sack, and faced Hannah squarely. "Look, I want you to know that I have nothing to do with this. I know you're a good worker, I know you're being wasted in the back office. But the fact is, Mr. Katz told me that he doesn't want you for his secretary."

"Doesn't want me! But why?"

Ardeth tried to find the best way of saying it, but finally just said, "He said . . . he says you're too fat."

Hannah stared at her.

"I'm sorry," Ardeth said. "I really am. If it were up to me—"

"But didn't you tell him that my qualifications should mean more than how much I weigh? Didn't you tell him the job was *mine*? You mean I've done all the jobs around here that no one else would do, and studied the stock market, to be rewarded like *this*?"

"Hannah, this is just as painful for me to say as it is for you to hear—"

"No, it isn't! Ardeth, I need that money!"

"Listen to me. You didn't get the job two years ago because of your weight. That first girl, the one you competed against, didn't do anywhere near as well on the tests as you did, but Mr. Katz liked her looks. He said he didn't want a fat secretary."

Hannah sat back in shock. She pressed her lips together and fought the rising tears. "He said that?" she whispered. "Mr. Katz actually said *that*? Do they all think that, the brokers, everyone in the office? Do they all think of me as a fat girl?" she asked, suddenly looking back and realizing things she hadn't been aware of before: the interviews she had gone on, not getting one job offer; the interviewer who had asked her how much she weighed, penciling it in the corner of her application; Mr. Driscoll accusing her in a teasing way of eating the entire box of office donuts, even though Hannah hadn't touched even one; and finally, Mr. Reardon trying to talk a client into buying some stock, the man saying, "Is it a good investment?" and Reardon saying, "Do fat girls fuck?"

"Is that how the world sees me, Ardeth?" she asked in a tight voice. "They look at me and all they see is a fat girl? They don't see who I am, they don't see *me*?"

"Hannah," Ardeth said, trying to be reasonable. "Mr. Katz's secretary deals with important clients, she is the first person they see, she represents this firm to the public, it's important how she looks."

"What am I? Don't I iron my clothes? Do I smell? For heaven's sake, Ardeth, I take pride in my appearance, I'm always careful about how I look! I make all my own clothes. You yourself are always telling me how smartly dressed I am." Her chin trembled. She had never felt so ashamed. "Ardeth, you act as if you agree with him!"

"I don't, Hannah. I honestly don't. But if you could just lose some weight—"

"Lose weight! Have you ever been fat? How can you know what it's like? If you've never had to lose weight a day in your life, how can you *know*?"

Ardeth couldn't respond. It was true that she had always been slim and had never had to watch what she ate; she just assumed that people were fat because they ate too much.

"Ardeth, I've been fat ever since I was a child. My parents are overweight. I know for a fact that I don't eat as much as you do. Just compare your lunch with mine."

"I'm sorry, Hannah," Ardeth said, wishing Katz hadn't put her in this unpleasant position.

"Tell me, does everyone who looks at me think of me as a fat girl?" Oh God, Mr. Scadudo—"

"Let me give you some advice, Hannah," Ardeth said firmly and a little impatiently. "First of all, if you want to get ahead in this world, lose weight. That's a fact of life. And second, I've got to be honest with you, if you want to be a fashion designer, face it, no one is going to take a fat fashion designer seriously." She bit into her egg and said with a full mouth, "Well? Are they?"

The women sat in molded plastic chairs that looked too fragile to bear their weight, occupying themselves with magazines or needlepoint, trying not to look as if they were in the waiting room of the Tarzana Obesity Clinic. As Philippa checked in with the receptionist, she looked around at the patients, eight of them, who ranged in ages from their early twenties, like herself, to one who she guessed was around seventy. All were overweight, some severely so. And she wondered what each of them had tried before coming here, to this place of last resort.

In the year since Philippa had lost her baby and had decided to change her image, she had attempted many popular reducing diets. The first had come out of a magazine, "guaranteed if followed to the letter." It started off each day with half a grapefruit, a dish of strawberries, and a glass of skim milk. But by midmorning Philippa was shaking so badly and feeling faint, a film of perspiration covering her body, that she had eaten her lunch, which had consisted of cottage cheese and half a peach. But by noon she was shaky again and so weak that she could barely stand. Since her lunch was gone, she had been forced to eat, blowing the diet.

Then she had purchased the best-seller *Calories Don't Count*, by Herman Taller, M.D. The food required for the regimen was high in fat: steaks and ground round, bacon, sardines and tuna fish packed in oil, blocks of cheese, eggs and margarine to fry them in. In addition, she was supposed to drink two tablespoons of oil before each meal. The diet called for 65 percent of her intake to be fat, which meant eight ounces of meat for lunch and twelve ounces of meat for dinner, along with fried eggs and fried potatoes and the tablespoons of vegetable oil. The diet had made her nauseous; she gave it up. She had then tried the lemon juice gimmick, but had only ended up with a hyperacidic stomach. Laxatives were another currently popular solution, an experiment that lasted half a day. The egg-and-grapefruit-only diet had been so boring that she'd gone off it after a week. Then she'd simply restricted herself to five hundred calories a day and had nearly fainted at her job. Now, almost a year after Rhys's death and the loss of her baby, after months of trying to diet, she was five pounds heavier. In desperation she had finally taken Mrs. Chadwick's advice to seek professional help. Unfortunately, the only help available was from private physicians, who charged enormous fees.

As she took a seat and waited for her name to be called, Philippa looked around the waiting room and wondered about the other women there, what their stores were, what had motivated them to come to a place like this. The woman in the unfortunate purple pants and shell top, for instance—was she here because her husband was tired of her? The lady in the ill-fitting skirt and yellow blouse—was she facing a twenty-year class reunion? Philippa tried not to stare at them, but her curiosity drove her to study their faces surreptitiously while she pretended to read a magazine. And in all their expressions she saw one feature in common: the look of dejection that accompanies low self-esteem. What unhappiness with themselves, she wondered, had brought them here?

The scene had an almost surreal quality to it. Out in the real world, at the Cut-Cost Drugstore, for example, where she still worked, or at West Hollywood Junior College, where she was taking the final night classes that would earn her a degree, people came in such a wide range that they all kind of blended in. Her political science class, for instance, had some elderly people, a few young high school dropouts, Hispanics, some very fat people, some very thin ones, and a woman who was terribly short. But no one stood out. The mix somehow evened them all out—crowds, the great equalizer. But here, in a small room where eight women sat self-consciously as if they were waiting to audition for some movie fat-lady role, the effect was stunning, to say the least.

The air in the waiting room seemed to hang heavy with apology, eight women generating a single thought: Forgive me for the eyesore that I am. They seemed to sit with drooping eyes and downcast shoulders that said, I hate myself. It made Philippa think of Mouse, the little half-developed thing that had almost blinded herself in a desperate attempt to become normal. Mouse had given off this same signal, an apology for being what she was.

Philippa watched in fascination as one very large woman in an unflattering avocado-colored dress worked savagely at creating an enormous afghan right there in the waiting room, spinning out an orange and brown zigzag pattern with such nervous zeal that the blue crochet hook was but a blur. Another woman was polishing off the last of a very large 3 Musketeers bar, and when she opened her purse to stuff the wadded wrapper in, Philippa glimpsed more wads. Were they a week's worth, she wondered, or the result of a mere morning's work?

She was suddenly upset for all of them. She wanted to say something, to bring to a halt whatever inexorable process was under way in this little waiting room. But she had no idea what to say. And as it occurred to her that these women were in some way doomed, just as Rhys had been, hurtling themselves toward some subtle, grotesque form of self-destruction, her anxiety deepened.

At that moment, the door to the inner office opened and a young woman came out, nearly running. Her cheeks burned and her eyes were full of fire. When she slammed her purse down at the receptionist's window, everyone looked up, startled. A heated exchange passed between her and the receptionist. "That's not the price you quoted me over the phone!"

The receptionist, embarrassed, tried to say in a low voice, "There is an additional charge for the weekly menus."

"But the doctor didn't *do* anything! No examination—he didn't even take my blood pressure! He barely looked at my face, and he wouldn't answer any of my questions. For goodness sake, I was in there less than ten minutes!"

"I'm sorry, Miss Ryan, but—"

"And on top of that I have to pay for bus fare because I live in Woodland Hills. Both ways! I can't afford this!" As she fumbled for her wallet with shaking hands, her purse fell. Lipstick, eyebrow pencil, compact, a roll of Life Savers, and an unusual number of pennies went skittering everywhere. As Philippa, who was seated near the reception window, helped her gather up her things, she said, "If you wait for me, I'll be glad to give you a ride home."

"If it's not out of your way," Hannah said, eyes glistening with incipient tears. "I'd appreciate it."

Philippa was called in a minute later.

Dr. Hehr's was like no doctor's office she had ever seen. The walls were covered with photographs of women, fat and thin—before and after shots, Philippa realized when she looked more closely—accompanied by framed letters thanking Dr. Hehr. Clutter was everywhere; a stack of medical journals looked as if it was about to topple to the floor; plants and knick-knacks seemed to have been placed about by an absentminded decorator; and the venetian blinds that admitted sliced views of Ventura Boulevard were dusty. When Dr. Hehr finally walked into the office, he dominated the room with a jolly kind of largeness. He was huge, with bushy eyebrows, chubby cheeks, and a white lab coat that only barely buttoned over his stomach.

He took her hand into his big paw and, giving her a hearty handshake, boomed, "So, Philippa, you want to lose weight! Well, you've come to the right place. There is no better diet under the sun than the one I invented. Just look at these photos," he said, pointing to the pictures of fat-thin women on the walls. Many of them were inscribed "With my deepest gratitude" and "I couldn't have done it without you." Dr. Hehr said, "These are my girls. Aren't they wonderful?"

Some of the "girls," Philippa noticed, were many years older than he.

He opened her file and read the sheets that she had filled out in the waiting room. "I see here, Philippa," he said, "that you're five eight and weigh two ten." He looked at her. "That's sixty pounds overweight, according to the Metropolitan Insurance chart. How old are you?"

"Twenty-one."

He regarded her over the rims of his glasses. "It says here that you only eat dinner. Is that true?"

"Yes."

"And I'm not surprised!" he boomed, startling her. "You see, little girl, it's not necessarily overeating that causes obesity, it's *incorrect* eating. And all you girls are guilty of that. But don't worry, I have invented the perfect diet that is guaranteed to get you down to the weight you're supposed to be. It's no ordinary diet, I'll tell you that. It took me years to design and perfect. I'm sure you've been on dozens of diets before; all you girls have. It's a hobby with you. But the charm of my diet is that you don't count calories." He leaned forward and fixed his eyes on her. "But what you have to do is follow the diet *to the letter*. Is that understood?"

"Yes, Doctor."

"Now then, I am going to give you a menu each week that you must follow exactly—I mean to the letter."

"Yes, Doctor."

He paused and looked at her for a moment, then said, "You know, you're very pretty. It's too bad you're fat. But we'll take care of that. Just leave everything to me." He stood, indicating that the interview was over. "You'll do well on my diet, Philippa. I spent years devising this plan, I know it works. Well, just look at all my happy girls," he said, gesturing again to the pictures on the wall. "Just be sure you eat exactly what's printed here," he said, handing her a mimeographed sheet. "Don't try to make any changes. When you come back next week, you'll be weighed, and I'll give you the next menu. You see how easy it is? If you don't lose weight," he said, "it's because you're cheating. I can always tell."

As she walked out of Dr. Hehr's office, Philippa scanned the first sheet and saw that breakfast every day consisted of fruit and fruit juice. Mid-morning snack was an apple. In fact, she saw with rising dismay, the diet was loaded with fruit. She knew already that she was going to be plagued with shaking and light-headedness.

Before she left Dr. Hehr's office, he said, "One last thing, young lady. The first and hardest thing you are going to have to do while you are my patient is cut out sweets. Is that understood?"

"But I don't—" she started to say.

He held up a hand. "I know what you're going to say, it's what all you girls say," he laughed, "that one donut in the morning isn't going to hurt, or a small slice of pie after dinner. But you must avoid all sweets—cakes, cookies, candy, ice cream. It will be hard at first, oh I know! But if you just stick to that one piece of advice, you'll see the weight drop off. Now then, girlie," Dr. Hehr said as he placed an arm around Philippa's shoulders, "just stick to this diet and you'll see amazing results. Some of you gals lose as much as seven or eight pounds in the first week. But only if there are no changes, no substitutions, no rearranging the order of what you eat. Is that understood?"

Philippa was reading the lunch listing for day five—a broiled hamburger patty—and wondering how she was going to broil a hamburger on the hot plate in the employees' lounge at Cut-Cost.

But she said, "Yes, Doctor," and left.

The young woman who had dropped her purse was waiting for her, and instead of heading straight for Woodland Hills, they decided to go across the street to the Cut-Cost Drugstore and get something to eat at the lunch counter.

She said her name was Hannah Ryan, and as soon as they were settled into one of the turquoise booths at the back of the drugstore, just on the other side of a partition from lawn care products, she slammed her purse down again the way she had on the receptionist's counter and said, "They have no right to charge that much! I'm so mad! I thought they were going to *help* me! I was so *sure.* I've tried everything else, even that ghastly grapefruit-and-egg diet, but nothing works! I'm desperate, you know?" she said, presenting two probing eyes to Philippa.

"Yes, I know," Philippa said, and then she confessed her own dissatisfaction over the visit with Dr. Hehr.

"He kept calling me 'girlie,' " Hannah said. "I hate that. I'll bet if I went back in there right now he wouldn't know me from Mamie Eisenhower. So why should we go there? What do they have to offer us? This stupid diet looks like any ordinary low-calorie diet." She waved the mimeographed sheet that was an endless repetition of eggs, cottage cheese, string beans, and fruit. "So what are we paying such an exorbitant fee for?"

"The incentive," Philippa said. "We've hired ourselves a policeman. Dr. Hehr will make us stick to the diet. It's the weekly weighing-in, by someone other than ourselves, that we're paying for. The commitment, in a strange way, to someone else, because we can't seem to commit to ourselves, I guess. We'll dread getting a lecture from Dr. Hehr if we don't lose weight, and we'll be thrilled with his praise when we do. That's what we're paying for."

"I suppose you're right," Hannah said more quietly. "I am lousy dieting on my own, I always give up. I know I need policing, or encouragement, or whatever. And a weekly menu, too, I suppose. Oh shoot, it's just so expensive. But there is nothing else, is there? I tried going to a gym in Reseda, and they put me on this awful wheat germ and carrot juice and then made me do half an hour of calisthenics. And that was expensive, too, so I quit. I've got to be careful with my money if I'm going to go to Greer."

When the waitress came to take their order, wearing a faded turquoise uniform with a large starched handkerchief in the blouse pocket, Philippa thought of her own Cut-Cost Drugstore over the hill in Hollywood, where she still worked, after five years, as a stock clerk, because she couldn't be promoted to lunch counter waitress on account of the uniforms being only small sizes. Philippa and Hannah ordered the Cut-Cost chef's salad and two glasses of iced tea. When they were alone again, Hannah explained to Philippa about her ambition to become a fashion designer and her determination to go to Greer Art Academy.

"But I can't do it unless I lose forty pounds in five months. Yikes . . ."

She shook her head and Philippa noticed for the first time tiny gold earrings under the edges of Hannah's cap of short brown hair. She noticed with fascination that Hannah's ears were pierced; Philippa had never known anyone who did that. "I have so many strikes against me," Hannah said as she took a straw out of the plastic container on their table, picked off the end of the wrapper, and very slowly peeled the wrapper down. "Heredity, for one," she said. "All the women in my family are fat. My grandmothers and great-grandmothers were fat. Heck, I was a fat baby! That's why I don't see how Dr. Hehr's diet can work for everyone. I mean, I was expecting some sort of custom diet, you know, like where he analyzes each of us and comes up with a diet to suit? One of the women in the waiting room was telling me that she had been thin all her life until she had her two babies. She gained thirty pounds all at once and can't get it off. But isn't her chemistry different from mine? Won't she have an easier time of it? I knew a girl in high school—Maria Monokandilos, from Greece. She binged in the eleventh grade and got very fat, fatter even than me. In the twelfth grade she got a boyfriend, went back to normal eating, and the fat just melted off. So you see, our cases are all different. Yikes," she said again, pulling the wrapper back up the straw and slowly drawing it down again. "And what an awful name for the place. Tarzana Obesity Clinic. It's degrading, it sounds like a punishment. It should have a more encouraging name."

Philippa lined up her spoon, knife, and fork on the paper napkin, then said, "How about . . . Lovely Ladies Beauty Society?"

Hannah laughed. "Young Princesses of America!" She smiled. "I'm sorry. I've been doing all the talking. I just got so mad."

"That's all right. You're only saying all the same things that are on my mind."

"Are you married, Philippa?"

An image flashed in her mind, Rhys slumped over his typewriter as if he were asleep, the dark smudge on his temple looking like the smudge of ash one received on the forehead on Ash Wednesday—a final benediction. After she recovered from the miscarriage, she had gone back to Rhys's apartment, but there was no trace of him there. Mr. Laszlo had told her that the brother had come and cleared out all of Rhys's things. He'd even taken the body back to some hometown up north, so there wasn't even a grave she could visit to say good-bye. It was as though Rhys, and the baby, had never even existed.

"I'm single," she said, "and I live in a boardinghouse. That's one of my problems. My landlady is a terrific cook, and her feelings get hurt if you don't eat what she fixes. I haven't the heart to turn her food down, she's like a mother to me. The mother I never had, I guess."

At Hannah's questioning eyebrow, Philippa added, "I was adopted as a baby. I don't know who my real parents are."

"You don't have a family?"

"No. No brothers, no sisters, no relatives at all."

Hannah couldn't imagine what that would be like, her own family being so extensive that she sometimes thought she must be related to half the world's population. She could recognize a relation in an instant, her megafamily being divided between two sets of genes, the boys always inheriting the Ryan proclivity for adultery, the girls, the LaCross Indian eyes.

"When I was a kid, it was humiliating to be fat," Hannah said. "Kids choosing teams, and I was always left standing. And when the teacher assigned me to a team, they all groaned."

Philippa told her about St. Bridget's, about Amber throwing up.

"What do you suppose it's all about?" Hannah said when their salads and iced tea arrived. "I mean, does it all boil down to sex? Girls want to be thin to catch men, don't they?" she asked, thinking about Alan Scadudo and that tight fit of his pants across his buttocks. Sometimes, when she allowed herself to look, she noticed the snug fit across the front as well. "Do men really only want thin women? If only they could be fat-blind like they're sometimes color-blind!"

The both laughed and began to eat.

"I feel better," Hannah said after she added a lot of sugar to her tea and too much Thousand Island dressing to the lettuce. She attacked her food with the gusto she had been taught since childhood.

"You notice that Dr. Hehr is no slim chicken," she said between crunchy mouthfuls. "He doesn't have to be. He's a man. Men don't worry about the same things we do. I wonder if they worry about anything at all."

"I suppose they have their insecurities," Philippa said, picturing Rhys.

"I suppose you're right. They worry about being too short, I guess, or that they might lose their hair, or that they aren't supermen in bed." Mr. Scadudo popped into her mind again. "There's this man where I work. He's around my age, maybe twenty-two or -three. He's short, but it doesn't seem to bother him, and I like short men. He's very quiet and sweet. He's going to night school to study for the CPA exam. I fantasize about him all the time, but I don't think he's even aware that I'm alive. Do you suppose he'll notice me when I'm thin?"

Suddenly, the salad seemed too green. The colors weren't natural beneath the drugstore's bright fluorescent lights. Hannah pushed her bowl aside and reached for her iced tea, holding the glass before her with both hands like a bridal bouquet. "When I was a senior in high school and had yet to have anything even remotely resembling a boyfriend, my cousin took pity on me and set me up with a blind date. She and her boyfriend picked me up, and when we went to get Ernie at his house, he started to get into the car, saying hiya and all that, but when he saw me his face fell so hard you could practically hear it hit the curb. And I saw how he hesitated before he got in, like he was thinking all in a split second, I can get out of this if I run right now."

She fished into the glass for the wedge of lemon and toyed with it with her spoon. "He went through with the date. Brave boy. We went to the Reseda Drive-In to see this foreign film called *La Strada* that none of us could understand, and my cousin and her boyfriend had the audacity to make out right in front of us. Ernie never said a word to me, never looked at me; he pretended he was interested in the movie. When he and my cousin's boyfriend went off to the snack bar during intermission, I heard Ernie say, 'Jesus, Don, you didn't tell me your girlfriend's cousin was—' I didn't hear the last word, but I sure can guess what it was."

"How awful," Philippa said.

"What about you? Any luck with boys?"

"My luck is worse than yours. I never made it to a drive-in."

Hannah leaned forward and said in a low voice, "I'm twenty-one years old and still a virgin. Of course, I'm not married, but it still makes me feel somehow unaccomplished. Maybe there will be some cute guys at Greer." She sat back and said, "If I ever get there. God, I'm starting to hate myself. I'm starting to believe all those years of antifat propaganda. Maybe the rest of the world is right, maybe I am just fat and worthless."

"No you're not," Philippa said. "Don't say that."

"That was the way Dr. Hehr treated us. Making us feel guilty. How can those other women who sat there waiting to see him put up with that?"

"Hannah, when I was twelve I almost submitted to a humiliating act because I believed I deserved it, I thought I was worthless. But at the last minute, I stood up for myself. Those women just haven't learned to do that, they haven't found a way to believe in themselves. They're still convinced they're worthless and deserving of whatever rotten treatment they get."

"I can't go back to that ghastly clinic. I can't afford it. If I go there, I'll never be able to afford to go to school. But if I don't lose weight . . . Oh, what the heck!" Hannah said, looking over at the glass display above the counter, where a few weary-looking triangles of pie sat on white plates. "I'm going to splurge and have some cheesecake. That's what my mother always has when she's feeling low. How about you? I'll spring for it!"

"I can't eat cheesecake," Philippa said. "I can't eat anything sweet. I react funny to it. I don't know why."

"Maybe you have a metabolic disorder, you know, like diabetes. You see? That's why I think Dr. Hehr should have taken blood samples or something, to see what our individual needs are. What a jerk."

While they waited for her cheesecake and Philippa's coffee, Hannah said, "You know, if you changed that round collar to a V neck, you'd take ten pounds off."

When Philippa gave her a puzzled look, she said, "Sorry, I didn't mean that as an insult. Fashion design is my hobby. I've been doing it ever since I was a kid. A *fat* kid. I learned a long time ago how to make clothes help me to look thinner." She blushed a little. "I guess I don't look like a fashion designer, do I? I mean, fashion designers aren't fat. But do you know what Coco Chanel said? She said if you dress shabbily, people remember the clothes. But if you dress well, they remember the woman.

"You know what I think would work on you?" she said. "Because, actually, the dress itself is really very nice. It's just that round collars fatten the face. Here," she said, and she lifted over her head a thick gold chain with a heavy medallion at the end, a round piece with some kind of bird sculpture on it. She placed it over Philippa's head and straightened it on her chest. "There! It softens the curve of the collar, draws your lines down, makes you look thinner on top. Scarves and heavy necklaces are good for that."

Philippa turned and tried to see her reflection in the plastic wall of the partition. "You're right, it does make a difference. I'll have to remember that," she said, and she started to remove the necklace.

"Keep it," Hannah said. "It wasn't expensive. And it certainly isn't real gold!"

"But it's lovely. I really couldn't."

"Philippa, you've helped me to feel better by listening to me. There's no one I can talk to. My friends are all thin, and my family sees nothing wrong with being fat."

As she looked into Hannah's smile and felt the weight of the heavy medallion "draw down her lines," making her ten pounds thinner while she just sat there, Philippa suddenly experienced an old feeling, one that hadn't touched her since the night of her thirteenth birthday, when Frizz surprised her with a secret midnight birthday party in the dorm. Nine girls had come, bringing small presents, and clever Frizz, knowing Philippa's difficulty with sweets, had somehow managed to sneak down to the kitchen and fashion a birthday cake out of Spam. It had even had candles in it. Philippa knew that she and Hannah Ryan were going to be friends.

"Listen," she said. "Let's meet again, here, one week from today, at this same time. For the next seven days, we'll both follow Dr. Hehr's diet, we'll follow it religiously. If we think we're going to fall off it, we'll give each other a call. Next week we'll weigh ourselves on those scales there." She pointed to the drugstore entrance. "We'll give each other incentive. You won't go back to the clinic, but I'll go, and I'll get the new menu next week and pass it on to you. That way you'll save money. What do you think?"

"Oh, yes!" Hannah said, and two things popped into her mind: the lovely, oak-shaded campus of Greer Academy, and Alan Scadudo's wonderfully sculpted ass.

···★

"Okay, these are the facts surrounding the unsolved murder of Dexter Bryant Ramsey," Andrea said as she read to Beverly Burgess from her notes. "The victim was shot once through the head, although witnesses gave conflicting accounts of the number of gunshots they heard. Servants reported that at least thirty guests were in residence at the time, and yet none of those guests was still here when the police arrived. The police were not called to the scene until approximately fourteen hours after the murder was committed. The gun was never found. And"—she glanced up at Beverly Burgess—"Ramsey was castrated after he was dead. Do I have everything?"

Beverly was taking Andrea Bachman on a private tour of the one wing of the Castle that had been preserved just the way it had been left sixty years ago. Tours were offered to guests once a day, in the afternoons, and they were escorted by a guide who titillated them with outrageous tales as they peered into private apartments where screen legends once stayed. The air in the hallway was thick with the old, musty smell of pressed roses and stale perfume; the furniture was dark and heavy; oil paintings of people long dead lined the walls. It was an atmosphere conducive to unsolved mysteries and romantic tragedy.

"Yes," Beverly said, "I believe that's everything." Because this wing was not centrally heated, she and Andrea were warmly dressed: Andrea wore a cowl neck sweater, tweed skirt, and boots; Beverly wore a black fox bomber jacket and cashmere slacks. She also wore oversized sunglasses, despite the fact that they were indoors.

Andrea flipped through her notes. "And one of the upstairs maids reported seeing someone run out of the house right after the gunshots. She said she couldn't tell if it was a man or a woman." She looked at

Beverly. "The police believe it was Marion, but it could have been anyone, couldn't it? One of the guests maybe."

Beverly nodded. "And this was the wing," she said as they walked past closed doors, "where the guests were housed that night. They were all staying in these rooms. All had access to the bathroom where Ramsey was killed." She pushed on a door and it swung silently away, revealing a stunning Oriental room with black lacquered furniture, Japanese tatami mats, silk pillows, rice paper lamps, and a pair of magnificent silk Japanese kimonos framed in glass, hanging on the wall.

"Eerie!" Andrea said, speaking softly, as if afraid of disturbing the room's occupant—except that there were no occupants. No one had slept in this room since 1932, the night of Ramsey's murder.

"I wonder which one of Marion's famous guests slept in this bed," she said. "Clark Gable? Cary Grant? They were on the list, weren't they?"

She went to the window, parted flimsy gossamer drapes, and looked out at the wintry pine forest surrounding the Castle. Snow had fallen during the night, cloaking everything in a fresh, blinding whiteness, and the sunlight was so sharp and clear that Andrea could see Palm Springs and the other communities in the Coachella Valley below, stretching out in green and sandy patches to the vast desert beyond.

She turned to Beverly, who was inspecting a blue porcelain bowl. There were those huge sunglasses again, the ones she had worn last night when she and Andrea had met. "An eye condition," Beverly had said. So why did Andrea have the strange feeling that Beverly was hiding behind them?

In fact, it was clear to Andrea that Beverly Burgess was hiding in general; as the owner of this resort, she was conspicuously *not* in evidence. Which was why Andrea had been surprised that morning to receive a phone call from the reclusive Miss Burgess, offering to personally show Larry Wolfe and his assistant around Marion Star's private apartments. Larry, of course, had no interest, his first words over scrambled eggs and bacon being, "I'm going to see what the skiing is like here. Maybe take in some tennis. Use the pool." In other words, go in search of Carole Page, who had left him panting in the cocktail lounge the night before after making it quite clear she wanted to be left alone.

So Andrea had joined Miss Burgess in her office, where Beverly had been in the process of reviewing the day's menus with the head chef. Andrea had been struck by how comfortably authoritative Beverly was; clearly a woman used to giving orders. But who was she really? Where did she come from? What was her history? And how had she been able to afford a place like Star's Haven and then convert it into a luxury resort? It suddenly struck Andrea as ironic that Beverly Burgess, a woman of mystery, should take up residence in the home of another woman of mystery.

"Do you think there was a cover-up?" Andrea asked. "I mean, all those guests who were here that night for Marion's big party, really famous Hollywood celebrities, and yet they weren't here when the police arrived. And then the police not being called until fourteen hours after the murder was committed, long after other people had come here and gone—the head of Ramsey's studio, two big-shot producers, a studio lawyer, and Ramsey's brother, all of whom had been telephoned by someone in the early morning hours and who had made the long drive from Los Angeles and up the mountain road to take care of whatever needed taking care of before the authorities arrived." She paused. "Like removing the murder weapon or tampering with other evidence."

They left the Oriental bedroom and continued down the hall, following a plan of the house that Simon Jung had drawn up, showing the locations of the management offices, the ballroom, dining rooms, gift shops, forty-seat theater, medical clinic, and patient rooms. Another wing comprised the private suites where management and permanent staff lived and, on the third floor, the ultraluxury guest suites. Andrea stopped in the middle of the hall and frowned. She looked up at the ceiling.

"That's odd," she said.

Beverly looked at her. "What's odd?"

"The floor directly above us—it isn't shown on this plan. What's up there?"

"Just empty rooms," Beverly said. "We use them for storage. There was no need to include them in the plan."

Andrea gave her a look and was about to say something more when Beverly pushed open a pair of padded doors studded with copper and stepped into the opulence of outrageous art deco. Pale peach and sea-foam green were the dominant colors of the enormous bedroom, whose walls were covered in striking murals of racing cars, greyhound dogs, and lightning bolts, all giving the dizzying effect of speed. Marion's bed stood upon a raised platform, and four statues served as bedposts—slender Erté-like nudes with long hair streaming out behind them.

"It's amazing," Andrea said as she slowly looked around. "How could anyone get any sleep in a place like this?"

Beverly pushed a button by the door, and the parquet floor began to move.

Or so it seemed. Andrea instinctively grabbed for the bed draperies as the floor rolled away under her, leaving her suspended on a transparent glass plane. "Now this is something I don't care for!" she said with a laugh as she looked down into the room below, where there was a large swimming pool, filled with shimmering green water.

Andrea walked cautiously out to the center of the floor, finding the sensation both frightening and exhilarating, as if she were walking on air.

"Mr. Jung showed me this last night. Can you imagine it? People up here could look down on the swimmers below, and people below could look up and watch whatever was going on in this bedroom. It would make an incredible scene in the movie."

As they watched a few guests swimming back and forth along the length of the pool, unaware they were being observed, Beverly said, "May I ask you something, Miss Bachman?" She turned those dark sunglasses to her and Andrea saw twin reflections of herself looking back. "When Mr. Wolfe writes his screenplay about Marion Star . . . will he be fair to her?"

Andrea didn't know how to respond; the question was so unexpected. She certainly couldn't tell Miss Burgess what Larry's instructions had been that morning: "See what you can find out about Marion's porno collection. I've heard she had quite a stash of raunchy films and books. Also, get as much as you can on the orgies and opium parties she was rumored to have. And that story about the USC football team, when she entertained them in her bedroom, find out how she did it. I mean, was the whole team in the bedroom at once, watching each other fuck her, or did she call them in one at a time?"

"Is it important?" Andrea asked now.

Beverly walked over to the fireplace, which was taller than she, and ran a hand along the deco molding that included nude women, suns, and planets. From this distance, Beverly, so slender and carrying herself well, looked to Andrea like a woman in her thirties. It was only when you were close that you saw the fine lines around Beverly's mouth, the creases in her forehead, the silver strands highlighting her dark brown shag cut. Andrea placed Beverly in her late forties and wondered if she'd ever been married. A woman like that, of such obvious wealth and refinement, surely must have an interesting background. And yet, as far as Andrea could determine, Beverly Burgess seemed to have no background, no past at all.

"Is it important?" Beverly echoed. "Yes, it is. I would hate to see Marion's story sensationalized. I would hate to see her . . . her life exploited or trivialized. Will Mr. Wolfe do an honorable job?"

Andrea's perplexity deepened. Why should Beverly care? "I do contribute a certain amount of input on each of Mr. Wolfe's projects," she said. *In fact, I do all the work.* "I'll see what I can do."

She felt Beverly's eyes watching her from behind those sunglasses. It was almost as if they enabled her to look inside a person; Andrea had the unsettling feeling that Beverly was aware of her true relationship with Larry. But of course no one could really know about that because Andrea had worked hard to conceal the truth. It shamed her now to look back to seventeen years ago and see how gullible she had been, how eager for his attention, like a lap dog with no pride.

★ ★ ★

When Andrea heard that Larry Wolfe had won the screenplay competition, and the top grade in their screenwriting class, she was not surprised.
It was a good script; Andrea had personally made it so. What surprised
her was that he didn't call to tell her, but that she had had to learn about
it in the school newspaper.

Andrea felt awkward about calling a boy, even though she was twenty-
five years old. She hadn't had any experience at it, and her mother had
always taught her that it was something nice girls didn't do. But, as days
and weeks went by and she didn't hear from Larry, Andrea finally got up
the courage to dial his number. "Hey, Alice!" he said. "Wow, so you heard
my news. Isn't it great? I couldn't have done it without you. I've told
everybody that. I'm glad you called, I lost your number. I've been dying
to see you. What do you say we get together and celebrate?"

Andrea's heart was in her throat, her virginity lurking somewhere behind it. Even her feet were two little puffs of cloud that she knew would
never touch earth again. "Yes," she said. "I would love to. Where?"

"How about our usual place, Ship's? Are you free?"

Our usual place . . . Are you free . . . It was as if they already had a
relationship. This was how it was between people; this was what love felt
like. The excitement of it! The sudden, intense desire!

Larry arrived forty-five minutes late, but Andrea didn't mind. Love
meant forgiving, she decided, and sexual desire meant patience. I would
wait forever for you, she thought as she ran down to his car after hearing
the honk.

Instead of going straight to Ship's, they drove to Malibu, where they
sat in the car and watched the waves roll onto the moonlit beach. A green
luminescence floated on the water, making the inside curve of each wave
glow beautifully. The Chevrolet parked next to them had fogged-up
windows and was rocking.

They listened to KRLA on the car radio, and Larry told her all about
himself, while she paid rapt attention, trying to ignore the Chevrolet. As
Larry munched on a box of Jordon almonds and covered the complete
subject of Larry Wolfe, Andrea wondered wildly if he had brought her
here to neck. Was she about to be kissed for the first time? Were they
in fact going to go further, like the couple in the next car? A lot of girls
lost their virginity in cars, she knew; maybe one was being lost right now,
in that rocking Chevy. When Larry stretched his arm along the back of
the seat, her heart jumped. He was about to make his move!

"The reason I brought you here, Alice—"

"Andrea."

"Is to tell you my great news. I've sold the screenplay to a producer. He wants to make a movie out of it."

"Oh Larry, how wonderful!"

"Yes, well, unfortunately, they're asking for some rewrites."

"Rewrites? Which parts?"

He smiled sheepishly. "Well, to tell you the truth, I don't know because I didn't read it."

"You didn't read it? You mean you turned in that script without looking at what I had done to it?"

"Hey, I trusted you."

Andrea was nonplussed. She had worked so hard on that screenplay, staying up late, calling in sick, drinking gallons of coffee while she agonized over plot, characterization, pacing, wanting to do a good job, fantasizing about how grateful he was going to be, maybe even hugging her and telling her she was wonderful, working so hard on it and devoting so much of her time to his screenplay, because it needed so much work, that she hadn't had time to do a good job on her own, ultimately receiving a mediocre grade in the class. And now he was admitting that he had never even read it.

"Will you help me?" Larry said, and when she hesitated, he said, "Never mind, I understand. Hey, I still owe you dinner. Come on, let's celebrate."

They went to Ship's, which, it being Friday night, was crowded with college kids and movie patrons. Larry couldn't seem to sit still. He would take a bite of his burger and then jump up to hurry away and talk to someone who had just come in or was just leaving. Andrea sat in the noise and glare of the coffee shop, feeling the currents of life eddying around her as people pushed by, laughing and calling out to one another. She let her corned beef hash go cold as she watched her unbelievably handsome escort charm people at other tables. She put raisin bread in the toaster and accidentally burned it because she couldn't keep her eyes off Larry. His energy was infectious; she fell more and more in love with each whirlwind moment, not wanting the evening to end, not wanting this to be her last time with Larry. By the time he came back to their table to finish his burger, Andrea found herself saying that she would love to help him with the rewrites.

But Andrea had discovered that agreeing to help Larry didn't mean actually working *with* Larry, which was what she had hoped for, but rather her taking his screenplay and redoing it on her own. But she didn't mind. She was in love. There was a real man in her life at last, and the prospect of meeting with him again fueled her creativity at the typewriter.

They met again at Ship's, where the individual toasters at each table were a hit with the local college crowd. Andrea made sourdough toast for Larry while she explained what she had done with the screenplay.

He thanked her eloquently and promised to call.

He didn't. At least not until three months later when, once again out of the blue, Andrea's phone rang and she answered it and heard the voice from her sexual fantasies saying, "Hi, it's me," as if they'd sat in Ship's just the night before. "I'm really sorry I haven't called, but I've been so busy. I quit my job at the Spaghetti Factory and got myself an apartment in Hollywood on Fountain Avenue."

He told her the progress of the screenplay. "They expect the release date to be sometime next summer. But hey, guess what! They want me to write a sequel."

"Oh, Larry, that's wonderful."

"Boy, I just can't bear the thought of doing it without you, you know? It's like I've come to think of you and me as a team. What do you say we join up and become partners?"

Andrea couldn't believe what she had just heard—"team," "partners"—it was almost like a marriage proposal.

"Yes," she said so quickly that it knocked the breath out of her. "Yes, I'll be your partner."

"You see, Miss Bachman," Beverly said from behind those huge sunglasses, "Marion Star was betrayed. By Hollywood—by the men who used her. I would like Mr. Wolfe's movie to vindicate her."

Andrea, who knew all about betrayal, wondered why Beverly Burgess felt so passionate about it. Had Beverly been betrayed at some point in her life, by a man?

"I'll do what I can," Andrea said, baffled by Beverly Burgess's passionate defense of a woman she had never met.

"I grew up hearing sex sounds coming from my parents' bedroom," the words in faded ink read. "My father, Earl Winkler, had a voracious appetite; my mother's duty was simply to comply."

Andrea was reading Marion Star's diary in a small, quiet, librarylike room in the Castle called the Chinese Room, where Marion Star used to hold mah-jongg parties. She and her guests—Mary Pickford and Clara Bow had been regulars—would dress up in silk kimonos and play through the night. The room's special attraction was an eight-inch jade sculpture in a display case: it resembled an erect penis, and it was said to have been a gift to Marion from Alla Nazimova, exotic silent screen star. Guests at

Star's came to the Chinese Room to ogle at the exotic sex toy or to write letters at one of the several private writing desks. Or simply to read, as Andrea was doing, curled up in a leather wing chair, deeply engrossed in Marion's story.

"I can't recall what my mother looked like when she wasn't pregnant. Her body was always stretched and swollen, always hidden beneath baggy dresses. I wonder if she would have been slender; did she have nice curves, was she feminine? And I remember that she always limped and she was always tired so that I had to do most of the work around the house and see to my brothers and sisters, because Momma was so worn out. After Joey was born, I overheard Momma beg my father to leave her alone. He didn't, and she had three more babies after Joey. She was thirty-eight when she died of complications from a miscarriage. That was the year I ran away from home. I was fifteen and I knew all about sex. And its power.

"It was not until some years later that I learned that my mother's miscarriage had not been an accident of nature. She had caused it herself."

A couple came whispering into the Chinese Room, disturbing Andrea as they walked past, heading for the infamous jade gadget. The man murmured, "I heard that John Barrymore once . . ." He dropped his voice. Then said, "In this very room." And his female companion giggled. Andrea turned the page and continued reading.

"The day I met the famous movie director Dexter Bryant Ramsey, I was seventeen years old, it was ninety degrees in Los Angeles, and I was about to freeze to death, trapped in a huge block of ice.

"When I had first arrived in Hollywood, I got a room at the Salvation Army Hotel for Women on Gower Street. My roommate, Greta, was struggling to get into the movies; it was she who warned me about casting couches. 'Every man in this business is after just one thing,' she said. Greta worked at the Coconut Grove, and she got me a job there as a hat check girl. I didn't work the coat room for long, however, before I was promoted to working in the show. The Grove put on fabulous floor shows that consisted mainly of nearly naked girls on elaborate floats. They didn't dance or anything. The only talent required was to sit or stand in a seductive way.

"The night Ramsey saved my life, I was supposed to ride out on the float encased in a block of ice, completely naked. They assured me that I would be okay, since the hollow center was heated by a hidden electric coil. I didn't want to do it, I was afraid. But I was told that I shouldn't complain since I was going to be the star of the show. And I didn't like the nudity, either, even though the other girls weren't going to be wearing anything more than a few daisies.

"So I climbed a ladder and lowered myself into the ice. I was scared.

And it was so cold. Greta made me feel better when she said that even though the ice was transparent, you couldn't really see anything. The show started and the float was pushed out onto the floor. The audience went wild when they saw me. Men literally jumped out of their seats when they realized I wasn't wearing anything. The problem was, our float caused such an uproar that nobody noticed how badly I was shivering. The electric coil had failed and I was starting to freeze. My head was near the top of the hole I stood in, but when I tried calling out, no one could hear me because the orchestra was playing and the customers were all shouting and whistling.

"The float did a slow turn, and I became more and more frightened. My feet went numb, and my skin seemed to burn where it touched the ice. I started to scream. I tried to climb out, but there wasn't enough room to move my arms. There was the audience—I could see them through the ice—laughing and clapping and excited by the spectacle, and I realized in terror that I was going to freeze to death before the show was even over.

"And then suddenly a man was climbing onto the float, scattering the other girls and their daisies. He made his way to the top of the ice and reached in, grabbed me under my arms, and pulled me straight out, quickly wrapping me in the heavy topcoat he had been wearing. The crowd went wild. They must have thought it was part of the act. I remember that he rushed between the tables, carrying me, and then out a side entrance; then we were in the back of a limousine and I couldn't stop my teeth from chattering. But he gave me some brandy from a silver flask and kept saying, 'There, there, you're all right,' in this lovely, rich, deep voice. And then he took my face in his hands and seemed to study me. He said, 'Christ,' and I burst into tears.

"I didn't know at the time that my rescuer was one of the biggest men in Hollywood. I had seen his movies back in Fresno; Dexter Bryant Ramsey was known for making big-budget spectacles with lots of costumes and sets and thousands of extras. When I awoke the next morning in his Benedict Canyon home, in a big bed with satin monogrammed sheets, he brought me breakfast—caviar and champagne!—and assured me that I had slept alone, that he had spent the night in a guest bedroom. He sat on the edge of the bed and said, 'You're very beautiful, do you know that?' And then he said what I suppose every seventeen-year-old girl dreams of hearing: 'I'm going to make you a star.'

"Dexter took me everywhere with him after that: to a séance at the house of Rudolph Valentino whose spirit guide, Black Feather, spoke to us; to gambling ships anchored off Santa Monica, just beyond the three-mile limit; to Tuesday nights at the Trocadero and Sunday afternoons watching polo in the Brentwood wilderness. He introduced me to a world I had never dreamed possible, where a three-thousand-dollar hand-beaded evening gown lasted for the duration of one party and was then discarded; a world where cars were upholstered in the skins of rare snow leopards and toilet seats were made of solid gold.

"Ramsey made me over. He hired Hollywood's top makeup artist to create a 'look,' a man who had perfected his craft by preparing San Francisco's most expensive prostitutes for their high-paying clients. Between him and Ramsey they decided that I should be a sex symbol. Just as Mary Pickford strove to maintain her image of virginal innocence— offscreen as well as on—so was I made to cultivate an aura of raw sexuality and immorality. That was when Ramsey gave me my new name, Marion Star, because he said Gertrude Winkler did not sound like a sexpot. Everywhere we went—parties, restaurants, movie premieres—Ramsey observed men's reactions to me and took notes. Then we would come home and he would instruct me in how to walk, how to speak. Whenever I asked him when he was going to put me in one of his movies, he would say, 'Be patient.'

"But patience, when you're eighteen, is a foreign word. I wanted to be an actress, but even more, I wanted my handsome Dexter Bryant Ramsey to make love to me. In all this time, even though I lived with him, he never once touched me, so that I was beginning to wonder if he ever would."

Andrea closed the book. She had a sudden compulsion to see what the author of this extraordinary diary looked like. Remembering the small theater on the second floor, where Marion's movies ran continuously, she packed up her things and left.

Andrea was able to stomach exactly ten minutes of the classic silent film *Her Wicked Ways* before she had to leave the theater in disgust.

The scene that drove her out showed Marion, nineteen years old and naked, taking a bath in a transparent tub full of champagne. She was surrounded by men, all of whom were fully dressed. Her character was a supposedly "liberated" young woman who got her sexual kicks from teasing men. But when the camera panned in for close-ups, when Marion was clearly supposed to look coy and conniving, there was a glimmer of fear in her eyes.

Andrea took to the cold night in fury, following the narrow paved path from the Castle to her bungalow, bent forward into the cutting mountain wind as she thought about what she had learned today from Beverly Burgess, from Marion's diary, from the movie. Now she knew why Beverly was so passionate about Marion being treated decently in Larry's screenplay. She shuddered to think of *Her Wicked Ways*. Such exploitation! That poor girl, nineteen years old, used, manipulated, prostituted by the man she loved.

It was all Andrea could do to keep from going straight to Beverly and saying, "Listen, don't worry. Larry isn't the writer, I am. And I'll see to it we tell Marion's real story."

But she couldn't tell Beverly the truth just yet, not until she saw the culmination of her months of carefully orchestrating her revenge against Larry. Mr. Yamato was due to arrive from Tokyo in four days, bringing with him his generous financial backing for Larry's movie. They were to meet here at Star's; Andrea was to have a proposal ready. But what neither Mr. Yamato nor Larry were aware of was that they were both in for a surprise.

Because of what Larry finally did to her eight months ago.

A gust came up so powerfully then that Andrea had to turn her back to it. And as she briefly faced the Castle, seeing it through the increasingly heavy snowfall, she thought she saw, up on the floor that wasn't shown on the plan, a figure standing at one of the windows, watching her.

···★

This time the telephone was picked up after one ring; the call was expected. It rang on a special line, because it was a special number; only two people in the world had access to it.

"Philippa is staying at the Century Plaza Hotel," a voice said. "But tomorrow she leaves for Palm Springs. She's called an emergency meeting of the board. Everyone will be there."

"Is she aware of anything?"

"I don't think so . . . not really."

"Make sure it stays that way. Keep on her trail; don't lose her. And if you don't have a gun, get one."

DAY THREE

13

"I haven't had an orgasm in eight months," Shirley suddenly announced.

Knitting needles and flipped-through magazines went still as the other women in the waiting room all looked at her.

"I don't know if the problem is with my husband or me," Shirley went on, speaking with an urgency that made you think she was about to catch a bus and wanted to get everything said before it got there. Shirley weighted 290 pounds; she had been coming to the Tarzana Obesity Clinic for one month. "Dick and I used to have such a great sex life. I never had a hard time coming, but now—nothing."

Her companions stared at her. They had been talking comfortably for the past twenty minutes, ever since Philippa came into the waiting room and said, "Hi, is anyone having as much trouble on this diet as I am?" and they had all started to talk. But confessions so far had skimmed along a safe, nonthreatening plane: one woman said she wanted nicer clothes, another wanted to look good in photographs. Shirley's comment broke a scary rule, and no one knew what to say.

In fact, some of them weren't sure what she was talking about, like Mrs. Percy, who was seventy and had arthritis so bad that her hands looked like crabs. "I didn't know women had them," she said.

It seemed she had spoken for them all, because there were nods of agreement.

"Well, we do, honey," Shirley said, "and I'd give anything to know what's affecting me. I mean, Dick and I still have sex as often as we can, but after five kids, and putting on the pounds with each one, here I am a blimp and facing a baffling problem. I tried asking *him* about it," she said, thrusting her beehive hairdo in the direction of Dr. Hehr's office, "but he just said not to worry about it."

She thought a moment, staring at a poster on the wall that showed an obese woman about to put a big piece of cake into her mouth, with a caption underneath that said "Think First!" Then she said more quietly, "I think maybe it's me. I don't like the way I look, my body, I mean. When we get into bed, I feel myself kind of freezing up. I'm getting inhibited about my fat."

Cassie Marie spoke up next. "I get really bad cramps every month. They're so bad sometimes that I can't even get out of bed. My gynecologist suggested that they might ease up if I lose weight." Cassie Marie weighed 190 pounds; only five minutes ago she had said she wanted to lose weight so she'd look good in photographs.

"I work in a drugstore," Philippa said, and eight sympathetic expressions turned to her: Go on, honey, spill it all. "Mainly in the cosmetics department. Some girls were having trouble deciding what kind of powder to buy the other day, so I tried to give them some advice. After five years, I know cosmetics pretty well." She shrugged. "They just stared at me, and then they went away, giving each other amused looks."

"Sure!" Shirley said. "How could a fat girl possibly know anything about anything! Especially about looking beautiful!"

Murmurs of agreement rippled around the waiting room, and Philippa thought of how Rhys would pat her on the head whenever she had tried to tell him anything. Would he have listened to her if she had been thin? Would he be alive now if she hadn't had these sixty extra pounds?

The only one who hadn't spoken so far was Bobbie Ziegler, who worked at the Bank of America down the street. Now she said, "My mother died when she was forty-five. She weighed two hundred and fifty pounds. I'm forty-four and I weigh two hundred and thirty. I'm so scared."

"I guess we're all scared in one way or another," Cassie Marie said, and she attacked her orange and brown zigzag afghan with her crochet hook.

Philippa looked at her watch. It had been a week since her first visit to the Tarzana Obesity Clinic and she was dreading facing Dr. Hehr.

Exactly as she had predicted, her first week on his diet had been a nightmare of shaky hands, dizziness, and heavy perspiration. At times in the afternoons she had thought she might even faint, it got so bad. But she was determined to stick to Dr. Hehr's menu, determined to lose weight. When the stomach pains and diarrhea got to be too much, she thought of Hannah Ryan, her new friend, suffering through the same thing, and so she had faithfully eaten exactly what was written on the menu, and at the times prescribed. But at the end of the seven days, Philippa had lost only one pound.

Now she asked the others how they had done in *their* first week, and all claimed dramatic results. Millie Fink said she had had an astonishing eight-pound loss. Knowing that Dr. Hehr was going to accuse her of cheating, Philippa sat dreading her interview. She wondered if Hannah had had any success. They hadn't spoken since their lunch at Cut-Cost a week ago; they were to meet again in a little while, after Philippa's appointment, and weigh themselves on the drugstore scale.

Dr. Hehr fixed a stern eye on her, but it held a twinkle nonetheless, to show that he cared, like a father, and that he understood female weaknesses. "Little girl, you've been cheating."

"I have not," Philippa said. "I followed the diet exactly."

"Mmm," he said, "I doubt that. Your mind is on other things—boys, most likely. That's the trouble with you girls. You don't concentrate. You don't dedicate yourselves to anything. I said, Philippa, that you have been cheating on my diet."

"But I haven't!"

He laughed. "You can't fool me, little girl. The facts speak for themselves. You should have lost more than one pound this week. The average loss is six pounds. So, tell me," he said, leaning forward like an uncle she could confide in, "what did you do? Sneak some donuts? Stop by the ice cream store on the way home?"

"Dr. Hehr, I followed the menu exactly as it's written. As a matter of fact, I wanted to ask you why I feel so awful on it."

His bushy brows lowered and cast shadows over his eyes. "You shouldn't feel awful on my diet. You're supposed to feel *healthy*. Mmm," he said again. "What do you mean by 'awful'?" When she described her symptoms, he said, "Have you ever been tested for diabetes?"

"No. At least, I don't think so."

"It's a remote possibility, but that might be your problem. All that fruit—fructose, you know, is a form of sugar. All right, let's stay on the safe side for now. Here's the second week's menu. If the fruit bothers you, well, then, substitute with a vegetable. See how that works. On your way out, make an appointment with my nurse for a glucose tolerance test."

"I owe it all to you!" Hannah said as they settled into their booth and Philippa handed her the next week's diet menu. The surface of the table was sticky, but they could see the streaks where it had been wiped with a damp cloth. "I lost four pounds!" Hannah said. "I had no idea! Thanks to you, Philippa. I feel like celebrating." Her eyes squinted over at the cheesecake display, then she looked back at Philippa. "I guess I shouldn't, huh?"

Philippa smiled.

"You were right," Hannah said, nearly bouncing on her seat, the little gold earrings flashing with enthusiasm. "Dieting with a friend is so much easier! All week I was tempted to cheat, but I kept thinking of you, sitting at your landlady's sumptuous table, sticking to your cottage cheese and hamburger patty. I focused on today, too, on getting on that scale by the door. You know what? I didn't want to disappoint *you.* Isn't that weird? I didn't want you to think, Oh well, Hannah's a lost cause. So I stuck with it. Four pounds!"

Visions of Alan Scadudo danced in her head.

"But now we have to figure out what *your* problem is," she said, calming down. "I didn't feel shaky or light-headed even once; in fact, I've never felt better. What if you do have diabetes?"

"Then I'll take care of it. You had no problems at all?"

"Oh well, my mother's mad at me," Hannah said. "She takes my dieting as a personal insult because we have the same body, the same dumpy shape. She figures if I don't love my body, then I clearly don't love hers. I'm insulting her somehow."

She scanned Dr. Hehr's second-week menu and said, "Cabbage Tuesday and Thursday night again, I see. All you can eat. Big deal. We're allowed one slice of wheat bread a day now. That's good. Still a lot of fruit, though." She looked at Philippa. "What are you going to do about this?"

"Oh, I'll stay with it. Eat more vegetables and cut back on fruit. Maybe the blood test will turn something up."

That night Philippa took out her little cloth-bound book, the one she had wanted to give to Rhys in the hope that the wisdom it contained would save him, and she wrote, "No one is fat on purpose."

She then wrote about the other clinic members, whom she referred to as "sisters" in the little book. She started the list with Shirley and her sexual fears, and Mrs. Percy, who was hoping to ease her arthritis with weight loss, and Cassie Marie, who had debilitating cramps. She added Rhonda, a switchboard operator who wanted to look good for her daughter's wedding so she wouldn't embarrass her; Millie Fink, the pet shop owner, who at fifty had just gotten divorced and was anxious to date again; Thelma, who thought her husband was cheating on her; and the very morose Dottie, who, after much encouragement from the others, made the painful confession that her husband hadn't touched her in years.

As she sat back and contemplated the list, barely aware of the "Dragnet" theme coming up through the floor from Mrs. Chadwick's living room, Philippa realized that she was beginning to understand some of the hidden and more serious ramifications of being overweight. Within the four plain walls of Dr. Hehr's waiting room, she had felt the currents of anger, fear, unhappiness, depression, and, worst of all, defeat.

★ ★ ★

During the second week Philippa lost four pounds, and the unpleasant side effects, though still there, were greatly reduced. But when she went in the following Saturday and tried to explain this to Dr. Hehr, he said, "Your blood tests have come back normal. You don't have diabetes, no hypoglycemia, no blood problems whatsoever. I want you to go back to eating the full fruit allowance."

"But it makes me feel so awful, Doctor, I can hardly work. People at the drugstore have noticed."

"It's all in your mind, little girl. Trust me. Your body will make the adjustment, and then you'll thank me for having been firm with you."

But when Philippa stood on the scale in the waiting room the following Saturday, after a week of constant hunger, cravings, and feeling faint, she was crushed to see that she was only down a pound and a half.

She joined the now familiar faces and, taking a seat, said, "Hi!" trying to hide her acute disappointment. "Are any of you having difficulties with this diet? I can't seem to handle the fruit. And I'm not losing as much as the rest of you are."

"I'm sure having problems," Shirley said, casting a quick glance toward the nurse, who, at that moment, was weighing someone on the scale outside her window. "I can't eat grapefruit. It burns my stomach something awful. I told Dr. Hehr, but he said it was my imagination. So I eat it."

"My problem is the spinach," said Cassie Marie, her orange and brown afghan nearly completed, she crocheted so fast. "I just can't digest it. But I eat it because we have to, don't we?"

"You know what my real problem is," said a newcomer named Miriam, who weighed over three hundred pounds and who was needlepointing a canvas held on stretcher bars. She had been with the clinic for six weeks but had had to change her Thursday appointment to Saturdays. "I'm a nibbler. That's just the way I am. But we aren't allowed any snacks on this diet. Oh, I've lost twenty-nine pounds so far, and I'm thrilled with that. But it's so god-awful boring. And I do get hungry between meals."

"But there are good things about this diet," Mrs. Percy said with optimism, her crippled hands in her lap. "We don't count calories. I've always hated that. It's such a bother."

When Philippa met Hannah at Cut-Cost, her friend said she had lost another two pounds; she was ecstatic.

"It's you!" she said. "It's *all* because of you! Philippa, you were right about the need for a policeman. I just wish it was going better for you."

"It will," Philippa said, "just as soon as I figure out what my problem is."

"By the way, one of my cousins, who is heavier than I am, would like to join us next week. Would you mind?"

Philippa didn't mind at all. In fact, she was thinking of inviting two of her clinic "sisters" to the Cut-Cost get-together, Shirley and Cassie Marie. "I think they could do with a little outside help," she said with a smile.

Philippa realized with dismay that the diet had become the focus of her life. All she could think about was food. In the past, before the diet, she would go all day without eating, without feeling hungry until late in the afternoon, by which time she could look forward to dinner. But now, by starting off with juice and a slice of toast and a piece of fruit, she was ravenous by nine o'clock in the morning. She would spend the next three hours focused on the cottage cheese and hard-boiled egg that was waiting for her in the refrigerator in the employees' lounge. Dinner was the best meal on Dr. Hehr's diet, because he allowed six ounces of meat—he always specified what kind of meat, such as a lamb chop one day, hamburger the next—and unlimited amounts of vegetables. Philippa found herself taking advantage of those unlimited vegetables, stretching the meal out over the evening, nibbling on carrots and green beans while she studied and did homework.

Hannah brought her cousin to the next Cut-Cost lunch, and three of the obesity clinic patients came with Philippa. They had to take the biggest booth, and then it was a squeeze. They shared secrets and confidences and left declaring that they felt a lot better than whenever they left Dr. Hehr. By the following week, all eight of Philippa's clinic sisters wanted to follow her to Cut-Cost, and Hannah's cousin, who had started the diet and lost three encouraging pounds, brought two friends. They had to move the lunch meeting to Denny's down the street, where individual tables could be put together to accommodate the large group. Hannah volunteered to type up the menus for those who didn't go to the clinic, because she had access to a good electric typewriter at work.

During her fifth week, when she had lost only another one and a half pounds, Philippa noticed that even though Dr. Hehr supposedly put out a new menu each week, it was really all the same—an uninspired, unimaginative cycle of cottage cheese, vegetables, and fruit, with small amounts of bread and meat, but *always* wheat bread, and *always* hamburger or a lamb chop. And because the main problem the Saturday group shared was overwhelming cravings—"I'd rather be dead than live like this," one had said, threatening to quit until everyone talked her into staying—Philippa decided one evening to sit down and dissect the Tarzana Obesity Clinic diet.

And what it boiled down to was a standard twelve-hundred-calorie reducing diet.

What, therefore, was the magic to it? What made Dr. Hehr's menus so special, and so effective?

Breaking the diet down further, and discovering that all the food fell into five classifications—fruit, vegetable, dairy, meat, and bread—Philippa then analyzed it even more closely. Referring to a calorie counter she had bought, she found that even though portions of food within each group were of different sizes—such as the one-half cup of beets allowed for lunch one day and the single carrot allowed the next—the caloric values were the same.

"The calories are already counted for us," she told the group, which had grown to fourteen, the following Saturday. They took up one-half of the Denny's private dining room and lunched on salads and cottage cheese while Philippa enchanted them with a talk on her week of discoveries. "That's one of the reasons Dr. Hehr's diet is so easy. We don't have to count calories."

"But there are still problems with it," Hannah said; she continued to have difficulties with the cabbage requirement. She had had an embarrassing moment involving Mr. Scadudo and the Teletype machine; she prayed he had thought the machine was responsible for the rude sound.

"I know," Philippa said, "so I carried the formula one step further. I thought, What if you ate green beans for dinner instead of cabbage, so long as they were the same caloric equivalents? I mean, for example, what would happen if, instead of having the required half a grapefruit on day three, I ate an orange? And why couldn't the unlimited vegetables at dinner be spread throughout the day? It makes sense, doesn't it?"

So they decided to experiment.

The next day, Hannah arrived at Halliwell and Katz an hour early, when no one was there. Using the electric typewriter in the office of Mr. Katz's new secretary, she typed out the five food groups with those foods allowed on the diet listed underneath, with their specific portions. The bread list was the shortest, containing simply: "Wheat bread, one slice." The longest list was the unlimited vegetables, which contained twenty choices. Copying from Philippa's notes, Hannah then typed how much from each list was allowed per day, such as two slices of wheat bread, three fruits, two selections from the meat and fish list, and so on. After reading it over, she realized that Philippa was right: it was essentially still Dr. Hehr's diet, but it was flexible now, and more convenient. Plus it allowed for variety.

She took copies to the group the following Saturday, where sixteen women met at Cut-Cost for the weigh-in and then moved on to Denny's for what they now called the "luncheon meeting." They all agreed to try the modified diet and see what happened.

But there was still the problem with depression and discouragement. For some, the weight loss wasn't quick enough; for others, the results had not brought the happiness or solutions to their problems that they had expected. Many in the group operated on the philosophy of "If only I could lose weight, then . . . *I could get that job; get married; be rich; be happy.*" Others were encumbered with the burden of self-hatred. Miriam couldn't take that scale anymore, seeing the weight on the lower poise bar stick firmly at the three-hundred mark, so she took her needlepoint and went home. Thelma dropped out and said she was going to go to a marriage counselor. Mrs. Percy said she was too old and simply gave up.

As Philippa and Hannah browsed through underwear at Monica's Overweight Shop, dubiously eyeing girdles and bras, the only items Hannah couldn't sew herself, Philippa said, "Something is missing. A diet menu isn't enough. We need something more, something to help us keep going when we feel like giving up."

They paused at a rack displaying Playtex 18 Hour girdles, all white and thick and sensible looking. The new lacy lingerie that was starting to come out was going to be a long time getting to Monica's. "I've noticed something," Hannah said, wondering if she should spring for another girdle. She owned the national average, four, because all women, even the skinny ones, wouldn't dream of going out without a girdle on. "Whenever you give the group one of your pep talks, you know, about believing in yourself and all that, they always leave feeling jazzed, eager to accomplish anything. But by the next Saturday, they've fizzled. Why not write a few words of encouragement that we can carry with us, like we do the menu cards?"

So Philippa chose some inspiring words from her cloth-bound book and gave them to Hannah, who typed them onto three-by-five cards during her lunch hour. When Mr. Scadudo came by and tossed off a comment about "our industrious little Miss Ryan" with a smile, Hannah blushed and realized that he had just flirted with her for the first time.

At the Denny's luncheon meeting, where the waitress, used to the large crowd by now, patiently distributed the salads and diet plates, Hannah handed out menus to those who had not just come from the clinic, and Philippa passed out the three-by-five cards, on which three sentences had been typed:

"Believe in yourself."

"You are special."

"You can alter your life by altering your attitude."

Cassie Marie said, "I use my grapefruit allowance as a dessert. I sprinkle cinnamon on half a grapefruit and stick it under the broiler for a minute. It tastes *decadent.*"

Others then suddenly offered recipes they had been experimenting with, all perfectly within the bounds of the diet, but that they had been afraid to admit to. Hannah, thinking that this must be how the miracle of the loaves and fishes got started, wrote them all down to type them up and hand them out next week.

Philippa reduced her fruit intake to one apple every evening. She lost four pounds the first week, two and a half the next. She ate vegetables all day long.

As Ardeth Faulkner opened the file cabinet by Hannah's desk, she gave Hannah a wry look and said, "I've never seen you eat so much before. I thought you were trying to lose weight. You'll never lose weight if you eat constantly like that."

Hannah was snacking from a plastic container of carrot and celery sticks. She was near the end of the second week of their experimental diet, and she had already lost four more pounds. But she didn't say anything. She was staring at Mr. Scadudo, who was bent over his desk with the phone to his ear, talking excitedly about an over-the-counter stock that had just gone up two points. Apparently he owned shares in it. Ardeth was saying something about "constant eating makes you fat," and all Hannah could think about was the day that was going to come when Mr. Scadudo would finally notice her as a thin woman. He had nice lips, she thought. Although her experience in kissing was limited to an unfortunate eleventh-grade dance called Tropical Dream, which she had attended with a clammy cousin named Alvin, her imagination told her that it could be very pleasant with a man who knew what he was doing. So she ignored Ardeth and kept munching on her carrots, watching those tight pants over that tight butt.

At the next Saturday meeting, which had to be moved to Hannah's house because six members who were losing weight successfully had brought friends and Denny's could no longer accommodate them all, everyone agreed that the experimental diet, while effective, was still boring. Philippa got to work and injected more variety into it by adding strawberries (one-half cup), and pineapple (one-quarter of the whole fruit), and white bread, as a break from the monotony of wheat.

The following week, she had lost two more pounds, Hannah had lost another pound and a half, and the group, now numbering twenty-two, was so thrilled with the diet that it took Philippa five minutes to call the meeting to order.

Philippa finally told Dr. Hehr she was leaving. The fact that Dottie and Millie Fink and the others had already left didn't seem to ruffle him, because his waiting room was as full as ever with hopeful new patients.

"Well," he said congenially, "no hard feelings. You girls always think you can do these things on your own. What you don't realize is that you need someone to keep you in line, make sure you don't cheat."

"But I've been losing weight, Dr. Hehr. And I've improved the diet."

"Oh, I doubt that, little girl. Everyone's an expert these days."

When she tried to show him her own typed list, he waved it away good-naturedly and said, "You'll be back. I guarantee it, you'll be sitting in that chair again one day real soon."

It was late one November afternoon when the stock market was very active and the office of Halliwell and Katz on Ventura Boulevard was hectic that Ardeth Faulkner came by Hannah's desk and said, "You know, honey, you don't want to overdo this diet of yours. You look fine just as you are. You should stop now. You don't want to lose too much weight."

And then Renata, the switchboard operator, came by and said, "You're losing too much weight. You have to think of your health."

And Hannah had thought: Stop now? At one seventy-five?

She had twenty-five pounds yet to lose.

On the other side of the Santa Monica Mountains, Sheri, the lunch counter waitress who made twice as much money as Philippa because she could fit into the uniform, came up to her in Cold Remedies, where she was stacking aspirin boxes in neat rows, and said, "You been sick? You're getting awfully thin. You should see a doctor."

At the following Saturday meeting, where twenty-nine women of all ages, shapes, and sizes marched through Hannah's bewildered mother's kitchen to step up on the bathroom scale and shout out their week's success, Hannah and Philippa exchanged their strikingly similar stories. Shirley said, "They liked us fat because they had someone to look down on!" Shirley had lost twenty-one pounds and her sister-in-law had stopped speaking to her. But she was getting her orgasms back.

★ ★ ★

Hannah came to work one morning and, as she was hurrying down the aisle, Mr. Driscoll, who had once tried to stiff her for the price of a sandwich, grabbed her by the wrist and said, "You're looking good, kiddo."

By now, Philippa had expanded the bread list to include one-half a bagel and one-half a hot dog bun; to the dairy list she had added one ounce of cheddar cheese; the meat list now included a pork chop and a frankfurter. The variety made the diet easier to follow, and she had started calling these interchangeable portions "exchanges." No one in the group got bored anymore; there were no more problems with undigestible cabbage or fruit that made you shaky. And when they felt their spirits lag, they read Philippa's homey little aphorisms, such as, "As you think, so shall you be," and they kept losing weight.

As did Hannah. Rescuing her wrist from Mr. Driscoll, she continued on her way back to the cage, where she noticed, for the first time, that Mr. Scadudo was watching her.

When Philippa had lost fifty pounds, she approached Mr. Reed, her manager at Cut-Cost, for a promotion and a raise, saying that she had been there for nearly six years and had earned it and that the toffee-pink clerk's smock now swam on her. He said no and she quit, handing him the smock.

Hannah went to an employment agency and placed applications. She had lost forty-five pounds with fifteen to go. A week later she interviewed for a top secretarial position with McMasters and Sons on Sherman Way in Reseda. They offered her $450 a month if she could start in two weeks. It was more than Mr. Katz's secretary made. She hated to leave Mr. Scadudo, but she needed the money if she was going to go to Greer. She gave it a day's deliberation. Alan's rear end lost.

Hannah and Philippa decided to get an apartment together in the Valley, since all of the group members, who now numbered over thirty, lived in either Encino, Tarzana, or Woodland Hills. Philippa got a job as assistant manager at Fox's Drugstore on White Oak in Encino, and she finally had to tell Mrs. Chadwick that she was moving out.

Mrs. Chadwick, who had seen it coming after Philippa lost the first twenty pounds, gave her a hug and a stuffed pale blue poodle with a yellow bow around its neck and said, "You're going to go far, honey. Just don't forget me. I'd like a visit now and then."

The first Saturday meeting they held in their apartment on Collins

Street behind Ventura Boulevard consisted of thirty-four women, many of whom had been with them since the turquoise Cut-Cost booth months ago; the rest were friends and relatives who had joined since. All were considerably thinner, and happier.

It was a sultry Valley night, the air swimming with the perfume of orange blossoms. The women sat on chairs, the sofa, the floor, or stood along the walls; they had all already weighed in, Philippa had handed out the diet to the newcomers, Hannah had distributed recipes and the latest inspirational message ("Hold your head high and let people know how special you are") and the atmosphere was charged with eagerness, anticipation, and visions of stunning successes.

"We need a name," said Hannah's cousin. She had been with them from the start and had lost thirty-eight pounds and found herself a man. "We can't just go on calling ourselves 'the group.' "

Others spoke up then, crowding the already hot and perfumed air with suggestions. It was a minute or two before Philippa realized that the doorbell was ringing.

She went to answer it and she saw an overweight young woman standing there, with a baby on one hip and a huge canvas bag slung over her opposite shoulder. Her straw-colored hair formed a startled cloud around her head in the porch light, and the night breeze rustled a truly large tent dress of a blinding lemon yellow. Philippa thought she had come to join the group. But as she was about to invite the newcomer in, something made her stop and stare.

The woman on the threshold also stared. Then she said, "Choppie?"

"Frizz?"

In unison: "My God!" And they hugged each other as well as they could considering the baby and the oversized bag.

They laughed and cried and said things at once: "When—" "Where—" "I wrote—" "You stopped writing—"

"How did you find me?" Philippa asked.

Frizz said, "I still had your Hollywood address. So I went there and your landlady told me where you'd moved."

"Frizz, I can't *believe* it! Come on in!"

"No, you have company, and my husband is waiting—"

"Husband!"

"I got married. We have a baby. This is Nathan."

Frizz offered the gurgling baby and Philippa took him, stunned by the flood of emotion that rushed over her, making her suddenly feel tender and wobbly and dumb. She had once calculated that between the time Mrs. Chadwick told her she was pregnant and the miscarriage had been twelve hours. *I had a baby for twelve hours. I was a mother for half a day.*

"Are you just visiting California or what?" she said, afraid to hold Frizz's baby for too long.

"We've moved here! Ron, my husband, was transferred by his company. We live in Tarzana, on Avenida Hacienda. Oh, Choppie, isn't it wonderful? My God, you look fantastic!"

"And you. You're blond now! Look at your hair!"

"I found a way to straighten it and get rid of that awful color I used to have."

Philippa noticed that although Frizz had gained a lot of weight, she had a beautiful face. "You really do look good, Frizz," she said seriously.

"I learned makeup in drama school. I'm so good at it that I can even make an ugly like myself look presentable!"

"You were never ugly," Philippa said, noticing belatedly that, under her makeup, Frizz had a black eye. On her upper arm was a fading yellow-green bruise the size of a thumb. "What happened, Frizz?"

"Oh me, I'm such a klutz! Fell down some steps!"

Just then, a masculine voice from a battered Ford parked in the street called, "Hey, Fattie! Come on! I haven't got all night!"

"Who is that?" Philippa said.

Frizz forced a laugh, embarrassment on her face. "That's my husband, Ron. I was thin when I met him, but since the baby I've gained weight."

Philippa looked at her old friend. Fattie, her husband had called her.

"Oh well," Frizz said, reaching for the baby. "He's right. I am a cow."

"Frizz, please come in."

"No," Frizz said, but her face, when she looked past Philippa into the living room full of chatting, smiling women, took on an expression of someone wanting to be brought in out of the cold. "You have company," she said.

"It's my diet group."

"No kidding. A diet group? What a good idea. Does it work? I guess it does—look at you, beanpole."

"Why don't you join us?"

"I don't think so," Frizz said as she cast a quick, nervous glance toward the car at the curb.

"We were just trying to come up with a name," Philippa said.

"Hey, remember our old Starlets group? You were always good at names and at getting people together, getting them to talk. But you can't call this group Starlets, of course."

"We do need something nice sounding," Philippa said, wishing Frizz would stay, wishing she would bring her old funny self and this little bundled baby into the group.

"How about Star*light*," Frizz said with a laugh, humming a few bars of "Stella by Starlight."

"Hey, Fattie!" from the car. "I mean *now!*"

"I have to go. Here's my phone number," Frizz said as she pressed a piece of paper into Philippa's hand. "Call me. But wait until after Tuesday. Okay?"

"What happens Tuesday?"

"That's when Ron goes out of town."

"Oh, Frizz," Philippa said softly.

"You know what? I'd rather you didn't call me that anymore. I mean, Frizz isn't me, is it?"

"No," Philippa said. "I'm sorry." And then she wondered how they were going to work the names, since they had swapped names nearly six years ago. "Do you go by Christine Singleton now?"

"No. I did for a little while, but I stopped going by Christine when I got married and needed my birth certificate. I sent home for a copy of it. I guess my first name is still legally Philippa—isn't that strange?—but all my friends back in New York call me by a nickname that I kind of like. It's a play on my married name, which is Charmer. They call me Charmie."

···★

24

Because he was a VIP prisoner—he had practically been the president of the United States, for God's sake—Danny had been given a special cell all to himself and was allowed certain privileges, such as keeping his own clothes, including tie and belt. It was the tie and belt that he used now, tying them to the light fixture in the ceiling to create a makeshift noose. He got it good and tight around his neck, checked his watch for the precise time, and, when he heard footsteps coming down the hall, kicked the stool out from under him.

He was astonished at how quickly the noose cut off his air supply and squeezed the vital veins in his neck. A moment after his feet swung in empty space, when he was hanging only by his neck, Danny panicked. Oh Jesus, he hadn't known it was going to be like this! Even though he knew help was just outside his cell door, and that Dr. Fortunati was going to cut him down, a deeper, more primitive part of him took over. He fought and struggled at the end of the noose, legs kicking, hands clawing frantically at the tourniquet around his neck.

His breath was trapped in his lungs. No matter how hard he tried to suck air in, nothing came down his windpipe. My God, he thought. I'm killing myself! I'm actually going to die!

Danny sat up in bed, awakened by his own strangled cry.

Drenched with sweat, his sheets in a twisted jumble, he stared wildly around the room, trying to remember where he was, *who* he was.

It looked like a hotel room—an expensive hotel room. But what hotel? In what city? He got up and went to part the drapes; brilliant daylight stabbed his eyes.

Where the hell am I?

He tried to think. What day was it? What *year* was it?

He quickly stepped back from the drapes, afraid of being seen, although not knowing why he should be afraid. Where the hell was Bonner? Why wasn't he here to take care of him? Danny made his way back to the bed and fumbled with the clock on the nightstand. It was noon.

He realized with a shock that he was naked. He usually slept in shorts, sometimes a T-shirt, but never in the buff. His head pounded, as if he were hung over, except worse. And then he discovered that his penis was sore. How in hell had *that* happened?

Danny buried his face in his hands and tried to force the memories to come. He pressed his palms into his eyes until they too hurt, as if through pain he would remember.

And then suddenly, he did remember. It all came back to him. He was in a suite at the Century Plaza Hotel, and he was in L.A. because he was stalking Beverly Highland, who was going by the name of Philippa Roberts.

And he had just had a bad dream. A very realistic bad dream. Jesus . . . He had never known such terror in his life.

As he went to the wet bar in his suite and poured himself a Jack Daniel's, he recalled those last moments of icy terror, hanging by his belt, when he had realized his mistake: that the footsteps coming down the hall outside his cell hadn't belonged to Fortunati but to someone else and that their timing had somehow gotten screwed up. As Danny had danced at the end of his tie-belt noose and seen blackness rolling toward him from all sides, he had realized that he had moved too soon and that he was in fact about to kill himself.

And then Fortunati had arrived and revived him with CPR, pronounced him dead, and gotten his body out of the county jail. And Danny had been free.

A tremor shook him so badly that he spilled some of his drink. Reaching for a cocktail napkin, he saw the newspaper on the bar. He didn't remember buying it or reading it, and when he saw the date, he froze. It was tomorrow's date. Which meant that he had blacked out again, this time for almost twenty-four hours, of which he had no recollection.

Danny tried to call back those hours, to reconstruct his movements, but everything remained a blank. His last memories were of seeing Philippa Roberts go into the hotel restaurant for lunch, and then he had driven to Beverly Hills to ask the large-breasted salesgirl out to dinner. But what happened after that? Had she accepted? Did they go somewhere? And did he screw her, as he had planned? Had he then killed her? But where? What had he done with her body? Had he made sure there were no witnesses?

Danny had no idea. His mind was a blank. All because of that bumbled faked suicide. All because of Fortunati.

Well, Fortunati had paid spectacularly for his mistake. The newspapers reported that Dr. Fortunati and his wife and four children must have died from smoke inhalation before being burned almost beyond recognition by the fire that had mysteriously broken out in their Holmby Hills mansion during the night, completely destroying the house and the garage containing Fortunati's vintage-car collection. But they hadn't died of smoke inhalation; they had been burned alive, all six of them, right down to Fortunati's six-month-old baby. They had been tied up and made to watch as Bonner went from room to room setting the house on fire. That was right after Danny and Bonner had had their fun with Mrs. Fortunati and the twelve-year-old daughter, of course.

Bonner—Jesus. He suddenly remembered, Bonner was dead. But how? *I killed him. I killed my best friend.*

Danny started to cry wrenching sobs. He didn't want to be where he was, he wanted to go back, roll away the years like a worn carpet and find himself at the beginning again, before the wealth and power, before the tent preaching, before the skinny runaway, Rachel, who was now Philippa Roberts—even before she came into his life. He wanted to be barefoot and little again, at an age before he knew his rags were a disgrace, when he hadn't known shame for his illiterate, groveling-like-a-dog father, when the whole world, the sun, and the stars were all encompassed within one beautiful woman, his mother, whom he had called his Texas Rose.

"I'm sorry, Mama," he cried softly into his hands. "I didn't mean to let you down. I tried to be somebody. And I almost made it to the top. I almost had the power."

Suddenly, Danny was remembering the day he had first learned about power. He and Bonner had been nineteen years old and living the high life in San Antonio; the two had gotten drunk with a friend and decided to rob the poor box of a local church. Actually, it had been the third kid's idea, and Danny and Bonner had gone along. On their way out of the church, the three nineteen-year-olds had paused to pee on the steps, and the police had caught them. While the other boy went free, Danny and Bonner had received sentences. They were sent to a work farm while their friend beat the rap because he was the son of the chief of police.

Power. Danny had thought about power during those blistering days on the road gang, before he and Bonner managed to escape. That was what power did for you. You spoke and people danced. You lifted your finger and people moved. You controlled the strings, you called the shots. Power, real power. It was then, as he sweated under the unforgiving Texas sun and beneath the eye of one mean, ugly guard with a shotgun, that Danny made the decision that, someday, he was going to be the one with the power.

It was shortly after that, while homely little Rachel was busy spreading her legs at Hazel's place to keep Danny in money, that he had come across the book that had turned his life around. He had it still. He went to his suitcase and pulled it out, an old, thumbed volume that he had practically memorized. The important parts were underlined: *The man who would be prince must be unencumbered by morals and ethics; he must be part lion and part fox. A man who strives after goodness in all that he does will come to ruin; therefore a prince who will survive must learn to be other than good. The only sure way to possess a conquered city is to destroy it.* In the margin Danny had written, "This goes for people too!"

It was *The Prince,* by Machiavelli, and it was Danny's bible.

Reading the old familiar words somehow brought peace to Danny; they reminded him of who he was, his purpose in life.

To catch *her* and punish her like he'd never punished anyone in his life. What he had done to the Fortunatis, what he had done to the police chief's son, were church picnics compared to what he was going to do to Rachel/Beverly/Philippa.

Invigorated and emboldened again, and no longer worried about what had happened to the large-breasted salesgirl he had clearly spent the night with, Danny went to the phone and asked room service to bring him up a stack of hotcakes with plenty of butter and syrup, scrambled eggs, country-style sausage, and a pot of coffee. Nothing gave him an appetite like Machiavelli!

Then he called the front desk and asked to be connected to Philippa Roberts's room. He was told the line was busy.

She was still here. She hadn't left for Palm Springs yet.

Danny went to the bar and poured himself another drink. He laughed softly to himself. The terror of the night had subsided; he felt like his old son-of-a-bitch self again. He returned to the sliding-glass door that opened onto a balcony, and he looked out over Los Angeles, a kind of phony-looking city that might have been made up of movie props. Certainly not a place anyone could take seriously.

Danny laughed again. So what if he couldn't remember the last twenty-four hours? It just made him one day closer to his encounter with Philippa Roberts.

25

··· ★

San Fernando Valley, California, 1961

"To make a man notice you," Hannah wrote, "you have to be sexy, and being sexy means dressing right." She paused and looked through the window over her kitchen table to watch a few of the apartment house residents cavort in the pool. It was spring, the evening air as smooth as butter, and serious flirtations were under way as the singles who lived in the fifty-apartment complex gathered in the central courtyard with six-packs and portable radios. Hannah was trying to write her weekly fashion tip for Starlite, but she couldn't concentrate. It was springtime for her, too, and her lustful thoughts kept turning to Alan Scadudo.

It had been nearly a year since she had quit her job at Halliwell and Katz and gotten a better one with McMasters and Sons; eleven months, to be exact, since she had seen him. She was amazed at how much she still missed him, how intrusive her fantasies about him continued to be. She would be typing a business letter or cutting a dividend check and she would find herself picturing him making love to her, trying to imagine the feel of him inside her. Of course Hannah could only ever go as far as her imagination permitted, because although she was nearly twenty-three years old, she had yet to experience sexual intercourse with a man. She had no idea what it really felt like.

As much as sex was on her mind these days, there was no one she could talk to about it. Certainly not her mother, who had come to terms with Hannah's thinness but who was now experiencing heart trouble; nor could Hannah talk to her zillion female cousins, not one of whom could keep a secret to save her life. She sometimes wondered if she could talk to Philippa, who also didn't have a boyfriend. But Philippa didn't seem at all concerned about men; they never talked about their sex lives.

But there were some club members who did. In fact, very often that was all the Monday-night group wanted to talk about; she wondered if they were a particularly oversexed bunch. It was funny how that went, Hannah thought, how the characters of the Starlite groups varied, Monday being so man/sex oriented, Wednesday zeroing in on recipes, Friday night being particularly demanding of Charmie and her makeup demonstrations. And then there was the peculiar Thursday-night group, which was tiny because that was the night *The Untouchables* was on TV and all of female America couldn't be torn away from Robert Stack. Starlite had grown to the point that it had pushed out of its old Saturday-afternoon bounds and now consisted of eleven groups—one for each night of the week, three on Saturday, three on Sunday—with a total of 342 members. In just under a year.

It was word of mouth that had caused the growth, of course. A cousin or a friend, or even a stranger, would look at a member and say, "How did you lose all that weight?" And they would hear all about the diet that was simple and fun to follow, a diet that allowed you to nibble all day long if you wanted, or that you could alter to suit your own cravings and life-style. There was also the weekly meeting away from husbands and kids, with women in your same boat, talking and laughing, or just getting a load off their chests, while you picked up a few fashion and cosmetic hints, as well as a weekly letter that contained a little pep talk to keep you going through the week. When she heard all this, the cousin or friend or stranger would say, "How can I join?" and that was how it went.

In fact, there was a waiting list now, and Philippa and Hannah and Charmie—if Ron was out of town—were going to have to sit down and try to figure out where to go from here. Right now, Hannah took four groups, Philippa took four, and Charmie took three. But when Ron was in town, Hannah and Philippa had to divide up Charmie's groups. All of which was very demanding because there was also the time required to write the fashion tip and Philippa's letter, each calling for some research to keep the news updated and fresh, while at the same time they had to maintain their own full-time jobs at Fox's and McMasters and Sons. Which left little time for a personal life, such as men and sex.

Or Alan Scadudo.

Hannah tried to type another sentence, but it was no use. She hadn't seen him in a year, but her interest in him hadn't cooled one degree. The problem was, since she no longer worked at Halliwell and Katz, how was she going to arrange to run into him? She just had to see him . . .

Realizing how late it was—she and Philippa and Charmie were to meet an hour before the Saturday-night group—Hannah forced herself to address the issue of this week's fashion tip on "How to Catch a Man's Eye," reminding herself once again of her goal: to attend Greer Art Academy in Glendale.

Although Greer had given her scholarship and placement to someone else, Hannah maintained her determination to pursue a career in fashion design. And now that she had been working at an excellent-paying job for over a year, putting away a healthy part of her monthly check, she would soon be able to afford the entire tuition on her own. But there would be sacrifices. Once she started attending college she would have to curtail her involvement with Starlite, maybe even bow out altogether for a while. And if she wasn't going to have time for Starlite, how was she going to squeeze in a love life as well?

No, she told herself as she typed vigorously, pounding some sense into those little keys. Forget Alan Scadudo. You don't need him. Or his perfect rear end.

"Where *is* Charmie?" Philippa said, going to the door and looking out for the fifth time in the past hour. "She's late and she's supposed to be bringing the pamphlets."

She and Hannah were in the recreation room of their apartment complex, setting up chairs, putting out coffee and tea and diet soft drinks for the Saturday-night meeting.

"I guess I shouldn't have given this assignment to her," Philippa said as she set out copies of her latest inspirational message—"Believe in yourself and you can achieve anything"—which she had written in her little cloth-bound book years ago. She and Hannah both knew how unreliable Charmie could be.

It wasn't her fault, of course; it had something to do with her husband, although neither Philippa nor Hannah knew exactly what. Frizz, who insisted upon being called Charmie, couldn't be relied upon because she never knew when Ron was going to be out of town. He was a distributor for an auto-parts company, and he never knew from month to month what territory he was going to be assigned to. The orders would come in and his boss would call and Ron would pack a bag and go to San Diego, or Bakersfield, or even as far north as Portland, Oregon, and stay away for days, sometimes weeks at a time. Charmie would show up then at every meeting, lively and vivacious, contributing her flair for style and her knowledge of cosmetics, which she had gained during her two years studying theater in New York. "Project confidence," she would tell the insecure ladies, "and you will *be* confident!" She would hold makeup sessions, bringing her own very large personal supply of cosmetics, and give demonstrations on "how to slim down those baby cheeks and bring out those model's cheekbones." When she was there, Charmie was a hit. But she could only be there when Ron was out of town, because he hated the diet club; for some reason known only to himself, he did not want his wife to be a part of it.

Which was strange, Philippa and Hannah thought, considering that every chance he got, Ron Charmer would put his wife down in front of others, taking food out of her hand and saying, "You're too fat," or calling her Chubs and Fattie in public. Sometimes, Charmie had once confessed, he even went so far as to tell her that she disgusted him, she was so fat. But whenever she tried to go on a diet, he would get furious and make her stop.

On this luscious perfumey evening that just cried out for romance and sex, with sounds of laughter and splashing coming from the nearby pool and the heady sizzle of steaks on a barbecue driving them out of their minds, Philippa had entrusted her old friend with the responsibility of picking up the pamphlets they had gotten printed. Now it looked as if Charmie wasn't going to make it. Again.

Philippa had become so concerned that she had attempted to probe Charmie on the issue. That was six months ago, when Charmie had shown up at a meeting with her left arm in a cast, saying something about tripping over a curb: "Silly klutzy me." It had made Philippa think of other occasions, when Charmie would show up all of a sudden after several days' absence with a bandage on her forehead, confessing, "I tripped over a rug," or with an Ace wrap around her ankle: "Twisted it in the yard." But when Philippa had tried to ask her about it, Charmie had turned a face full of hard pride toward her, as if to say, Be my friend and don't make me tell you. Philippa hadn't pressed.

On this warm night, Charmie eventually arrived in time for the meeting, breezing in with a purple muumuu billowing about her to hide the weight she hadn't lost since becoming part of the group. And as usual, despite being flustered, with her butterscotch-colored hair flying out of a purple scarf, Charmie's makeup was perfect. It was a curious combination: the beautiful face and the out of proportion body. Charmie had taught Philippa and Hannah how to do makeup the same way, but they could never quite achieve the same effect. There was magic in Charmie's fingers when it came to shading cheeks and highlighting the forehead, a subtle cosmetic sculpting that had the stunning effect of actually slimming the face.

"Sorry I'm late!" she declared as she swept into the empty rec room. "Jesus, but traffic was a bitch! Here are the pamphlets, Philippa, and oh, they are marvelous. Hi, Hannah!"

They rushed forward to relieve her of the heavy cartons from the printer. "Where's the baby?" Philippa said. Charmie sometimes brought

Nathan to the meetings, where the two-year-old got fussed over by his many "aunties."

"He's with the sitter tonight," she said. "He was fussing. Oh Philippa, I've come up with the *greatest* idea! Listen to this: I'm going to make drawings of face types, you know, round faces, oval faces, like that. And then I'll hand them out and when I do makeup demonstrations the members can color them in according to their own needs. Isn't that a great idea?"

"I love it," Hannah said. "Can you do a practice demo on me? My face is so darned square."

"Oh sure, you with your cheekbones to die for. Fifty million women should be so lucky!" Charmie drew a thick folder from her oversized bag and dropped it onto the card table where the other handout sheets had been placed. "This week's cosmetic tip," she said. "I barely got it written, what with the baby having a fever and fussing so."

"But he is all right now?" Philippa asked, reading what Charmie had typed: "Today's Cosmetic Tip: If you use a face powder, use the loose, not the pressed kind, which contains wax (that's how they're pressed) and can build up on your face and look too thick."

"The baby's fine now," Charmie said. "I thought of making tonight's makeup demonstration on contouring the cheeks with blush, but I don't know if I have enough with me, and this group is the largest. Hannah, have you seen the pamphlets yet? They turned out a lot spiffier than I was expecting."

They opened the carton and pulled out the booklets, which Philippa had written and designed. The covers were blue with white stars, and inside there was such advice as "Expect the best and get it" and "Know what you want." It also contained Philippa's "Four-Step Plan to Success," which was:

1. Determine your goal
2. Establish your priorities
3. Decide what sacrifices you are willing to make
4. Get to work

"These pamphlets are *beautiful!*" Hannah said. "You know, now that I look at them, I don't think we should charge just fifty cents apiece. A dollar is certainly reasonable, considering what they're getting."

It had been necessary to start charging dues when the Saturday group had gotten so large it had had to be moved to the recreation room in their apartment complex. The manager charged a fee for the room, and since Philippa and Hannah provided coffee, tea, and diet soft drinks, along with incurring the expense of photocopying all the diet menus, Philippa's weekly letter, and Hannah's fashion tips, they realized they were running into debt. They settled upon a dollar per person per meeting. Now, not only were they covering their costs, at thirteen hundred dollars a month in dues, they were actually making a profit.

"We're getting more and more phone calls," Philippa said as she unfolded metal chairs and placed them at the card tables. Because the evening was warm, she wore shorts, the first she had owned in her life. She had bought them a year ago, on her twenty-second birthday, right off the rack at JC Penney, just like regular people. "Calls from all over. There's a group of twenty in Northridge who've heard of our diet club and want us to go out there and get them started."

"My cousin Nancy," said Hannah as she got the large coffeepot going, "who lost thirty-two pounds with us, says she's got all the teachers at her school interested, plus some Girl Scout moms and members of her ladies' club. But they're in Torrance. She says she can guarantee a showing of fifty people and she will provide the clubhouse."

"We can't handle it all," Philippa said.

"The groups are getting too big, too," Charmie added. "I can't possibly give a facial demonstration to forty women!"

A year ago, when it was still an informal Saturday get-together, the women had talked mostly about dieting and losing weight. But Philippa had steered them away from focusing too much on weight loss, asking Hannah to give a few words of advice on how to choose clothes that flattered ("Avoid gathered skirts") and Charmie on makeup ("Don't make one end of the eyebrow higher or lower than the other"). The purpose was to take the emphasis off weight and focus more on the total woman. The idea had caught on, but now they were running into logistics problems because the groups were getting too large and unmanageable.

"Maybe we should limit membership," Hannah said, wondering if forty Styrofoam cups were going to be enough for tonight. "You know, just put a lid on it right now and say, 'No more.' "

"That wouldn't be fair," Philippa said. After all, how could she deny to other desperate women the success and happiness she herself had found through the little Starlite club? How could she walk into an ordinary department store, browse through dresses on a rack, try one on without hating the sight of herself in the mirror, and revel in the freedom of such choice—there were *so* many fashions out there for slender women—how could she experience such freedom and say to others who were suffering the way she once had, No, you can't have this?

She thought of some of their graduates, such as Cassie Marie, who had recently gotten married in a size-eight wedding gown, or a girl named Juliett, who had weighed over three hundred pounds and been on the verge of suicide but who had slimmed down to a size fourteen and was now back in school. With each Starlite success Philippa would think of Rhys. Each time a member came up to her and said, "I used to hate myself, but look at me now," that sleeping handsome face would be there in her mind.

No, she thought, she would not close the doors to anyone.

"Oh God," Charmie said, "people are arriving already and it isn't even time yet. Will we have enough handouts, do you think?"

"We'll have enough," Philippa said. And she realized with a start that a vision was beginning to form in her mind. It hadn't been there a moment ago, but it was there now, coming into sharper focus with each breath she drew, like a television picture warming up.

While the room hummed with life as Hannah sat at the first card table to register the members, with Charmie next to her, taking their money and distributing the handouts, Philippa picked up the legal pad on which she had written a few notes for her opening talk, turned to a fresh page, and began to write quickly. As Cassie Marie set up the balance beam doctor's scale in a little anteroom that served as a bar when parties where held here, and she weighed each member in private, recording their gain or loss, Philippa sat at one of the card tables with a look of deep concentration on her face and wrote with furious energy, the pen flying across the page as the new vision in her mind became sharper, brighter, with spaces filling in and details popping up. She was suddenly so excited that the pen flew out of her hand and she had to catch it.

The rec room was soon filled with the dull roar of excited diet chatter: "lost four pounds . . ." "down to a size ten . . ." "I save my bread exchanges for dinner . . ." "frozen grapes take *hours* to eat . . ." "Charmie's right, blue eyeshadow should be outlawed . . ." Philippa only half heard it, part of her brain consumed with getting her new ideas down before they evaporated, the other part marveling at how far her little group had come in only eleven months.

She had tried to get Mrs. Chadwick to join, not so much for the weight loss as for the companionship. The television was all her former landlady had, and it made Philippa sad to think so, wishing to repay Mrs. Chadwick for everything she had done for her. But Mrs. Chadwick was happy where she was, serving heavy meals to her contented boarders and then retiring to sit before her TV set for an evening of *Armstrong Circle Theater*.

Dottie, who had once thought her husband was cheating on her but who had gotten him back after she lost forty pounds, came up to Philippa and said, "A lot of the members have brought guests! We don't have enough chairs for them all!"

Philippa stared at Dottie, then she looked down at the legal pad and was startled to see that she had filled four long pages with barely legible writing. And her hand was cramping.

"Have them sign in and stand along the walls," she said. "We'll pass around a sign-up sheet to form new groups."

"New groups!" Dottie said. "How will we manage that?"

Thinking of the exciting vision that had just been born, Philippa smiled and said, "We'll manage."

Finally she called the meeting to order. The last few to sign in and get weighed found their way to seats or places along the walls; the room buzzed for a few seconds, like a hive when the bees settled into it for the night, and then there was silence.

Philippa paused for a moment as she surveyed the faces all turned hopefully toward her, like flowers, she thought, following the sun. Her heart was racing. She wanted to blurt the news right now about the glimpse she had just been given of the future and how anxious she was to rush home and get started on making it happen. There wasn't a moment to lose! Her voice rang out as she introduced herself, her staff, and gave a brief explanation of what Starlite was all about. "It's time to cast off the myths and assumptions," she said, "that come with being fat. Society equates fat with dumb, and we are not dumb. We have to divest ourselves of our old image," she continued, this slender young woman who was the envy of the heavy ones in the crowd—she didn't look as if she had lost sixty pounds!—"and put a stop to people taking advantage of us, or putting us down, or making us feel worthless. Ralph Waldo Emerson once said, 'They conquer who believe they can.' Every woman in this room can accomplish anything she sets her heart to. Believe in yourself and you can achieve anything!"

When the applause subsided, one of the members raised her hand, stood, and said, "I really think we should begin each meeting with a prayer. I know a lot of us belong to Our Lady of Grace Church—"

"And a lot of us don't!" shouted Becky Baumgartner.

While everyone laughed, Philippa noticed a late arrival coming through the door—a man she had never met personally but whom she recognized with a start as Ron Charmer.

And a chill of fear went through her.

She looked around for Charmie, but her friend was in the back, getting her cosmetics ready for the demonstration.

Other members stood up to speak. "When I weighed two hundred and eighty pounds," said Rhonda, one of the obesity clinic originals, "the first thing I would do whenever I walked into a room full of people was to look around and see if anyone there was fatter than I was. If there wasn't anyone, if I was the fattest, then I knew I was going to have a terrible time. But if there was someone who was heavier than I, then I felt relieved. God help me, I even felt smug."

While everyone else voiced sympathy and said how brave Rhonda was to admit such a thing, Philippa kept her eye on Ron Charmer. She didn't like the feeling he gave her as he made his way quietly along the edge of the room, a skinny man in a tight T-shirt, with tattoos on both arms and a tautness to his face that sent alarms ringing in her head.

Another woman stood and said, "I just want to say that Starlite has enabled me to lead a normal life again. I used to be so fat that one time my husband and I went to a restaurant and we had to sit at a table because I couldn't fit into a booth." A murmur of understanding rippled through the group. "Everything was fine until it was time to leave. I stood up, and the chair came up with me. Everyone in the restaurant laughed. I wanted to die right then."

They all clapped when she sat down, but Philippa continued to watch Ron Charmer, who had slowly made his way up to the front.

When Charmie emerged from the back, wiping her hands on a towel, prepared to give her cosmetics demonstration, she smiled at Philippa, took a seat, and then looked around the room. When she saw her husband, she froze. "My God, it's Ron," she said, going white beneath her makeup.

He marched up to her and seized her by the arm, making her wince. The room fell silent except for the sound of the electric fans stirring the air.

"The baby-sitter told me where you were," he said in a low voice, but everybody heard.

"Please don't," Charmie said, trying to pull free.

Philippa saw how deeply his fingers dug into her flesh. And then she heard him say, ". . . this freak show," as he pulled Charmie to her feet, sending her chair over backward.

Hannah stood up and said, "Now just a minute—"

"It's okay," Charmie said. "He's right, I'd better go." She turned to Philippa with a look of intense shame and said, "The baby has a fever. I have to go. I'm sorry I caused—"

But Ron was already pulling her toward the door, Charmie tripping because one of her rubber thongs had slipped off her foot.

Hannah was naked. As Alan Scadudo gently eased her down onto satin sheets, she could see herself, her skin glowing and feverish, her body slender for the first time in her life. Alan knelt between her legs and gently spread them open. He, too, was naked, with fine muscular shoulders and a scattering of hair on his chest. He was stroking her large breasts and murmuring, "You're beautiful." Hannah reached up for him and drew him down onto her. She couldn't wait to reach around and clutch that exquisite ass . . .

She awoke with a start, finding herself in a tangle of damp bed sheets, her nightgown twisted up around her waist. That was the sixth erotic dream she'd had this month. No doubt about it, she was just going to have to work up the courage to go see him.

She telephoned Charmie and said, "Help!" Then she took two hours selecting just the right outfit. Even though Hannah was thin now, she still operated with a "fat" eye, making sure the sweater had raglan sleeves, a definite thinner, and a draped cowl neck; the skirt had stitched-down pleats and a subtle A-line; sling-back pumps with modest heels were de rigueur.

When Charmie arrived with her professional makeup kit, Hannah said, "I'm going after a man. Make me look like Elizabeth Taylor."

"You're prettier than she is. Calm down, you'll be gorgeous."

As Charmie did an artistic make-over, Hannah wanted to ask what had happened after Ron marched her out of the Starlite meeting the other night. But she and Philippa both knew not to bring up the touchy subject of Charmie's husband; they respected her desire for privacy.

When her friend looked breathtaking, Charmie said, "Go get him."

Hannah experienced a moment of hesitation, as twenty-three years of feeling inferior came back. But then she saw herself in the mirror—the trim waist, long legs, large breasts. Recalling Starlite's motto—"Believe in Yourself"—she gave Charmie a hug and hurried out.

It felt strange walking into Halliwell and Katz as a ex-employee; even stranger to walk up to the counter and wait to be noticed. Ardeth Faulkner bustled up with her phony smile and "May I help you?" but when she recognized Hannah, her face fell. Two reactions rippled across it, one chasing the other: first, pleasant surprise; then, remembered resentment. Hannah had left Ardeth with all the shit jobs she had done at H and K for three years.

"I'm here to see Mr. Scadudo," Hannah said coolly. "Is he around?"

"Alan left six months ago. He doesn't work here anymore."

Hannah hid her disappointment. She couldn't permit Ardeth to crush her twice in one lifetime. "He did? Where did he go?"

"He joined some accounting firm. He got his CPA and suddenly we weren't good enough for him anymore," Ardeth said, implying that a lot of people were walking around thinking Halliwell and Katz wasn't good enough for them anymore.

Hannah went back to her office at McMasters bewildered and disappointed. She had put it off too long, and now she had lost him! How on earth was she going to find him? What if he'd left the Valley? Or California, even?

She looked at her watch and felt a stab of panic. She had two hours to go before lunch, two long impossible hours in which Alan's trail could go cold before she had a chance even to start searching for him. Attacking her work with vigor to make the time pass quickly, Hannah mentally sketched out her plan of action. She was simply going to sit down with the Valley telephone directory and call every accounting firm listed. If that didn't produce Alan Scadudo, then she'd try the Los Angeles directory and all the other Southern California phone books she could lay her hands on. As a matter of fact, she decided as she glanced into her boss's office and saw that he hadn't come to work yet, why wait for lunch?

Pulling out the directory she kept beneath her desk, she flipped it open to the yellow pages and was looking for the accountants' section when the phone at her desk rang.

"Damn," she muttered, then answered it as cheerfully as she could, "Good morning, Mr. McMasters's office."

"Hi," came a voice that would have knocked her out of her chair if she hadn't been weighted down by the phone book. "Remember me? This is Alan Scadudo."

It wasn't possible. This was another dream, although it wasn't very erotic. She pinched herself. "Hello, Mr. Scadudo."

He explained how he had just telephoned his broker at Halliwell and Katz—Hannah could have smacked herself; of course, he had an account there, Mr. Driscoll would have known where to find him!—and that Driscoll had mentioned seeing her there at the cage just a while ago, talking to Ardeth. "So I thought, well, I wondered what you were up to these days so I called Ardeth and she said you'd been asking for me. I remembered that you had moved to McMasters."

Hannah mumbled something, for the rest of her life she would never remember what, and couldn't believe her ears when Alan asked her if she'd like to go out sometime, "You know, a movie, or dinner, or something. Are you free?"

Whenever Charmie lead a Starlite group, she left her little boy, Nathan, with Mrs. Muncie down the street, who also had two small children. As she was driving down Avenida Hacienda, feeling particularly uplifted by tonight's group—six more new members, and someone from the local paper doing an article—she did not at first notice, as she drove past her own house, the car in the driveway. But she stopped a few yards away, backed up, and saw that her husband was home.

Ron was supposed to be in Santa Barbara for two more days.

She suddenly had a bad feeling. When he had pulled her out of the meeting last Saturday night, Charmie had feared all through the silent drive home that she was going to be punished. But Ron had only said a few lousy things to her, gotten drunk, and fallen into bed. The next morning, he was gone and so was his sample case. The note on the kitchen table said, "Sorry about last night, honey. Didn't know what I was think-ing. Will be back Friday."

But his car, parked in the dark driveway, seemed suddenly threatening. Deciding to leave Nathan with the Muncies for a little while longer, she parked and went into the house.

He was in the kitchen, picking at the cold chicken carcass he had found in the fridge, drumstick in one hand, can of beer in the other. Charmie could tell by his posture that this was not his first beer.

"Hi," she said as breezily as she could, afraid to give herself away. Although he hadn't punished her on Saturday night, he had shouted at her that she was to stay away from that "fat freak show," and so she had promised not to go back to Starlite again. But he *never* returned early from a trip. "What happened? How come you're home?"

He lifted bleary eyes. "Where've you bin? How come the kid's not here?"

A shiver ran up her spine. In the old days, back in New York when he hadn't been drinking so much and they were dating, Ron had sent shivers up Charmie's spine—but shivers of a different sort. She had thought he was wildly exciting, being crass and outspoken and flicking the world away like lint off his sleeve. He had just gotten out of the army and was having a major blow-off to celebrate his freedom—the uniform and the saluting had definitely chaffed. They had laughed and made love and done crazy things in those first weeks, crawling into each other as a refuge against parental rejection: Ron's father had no more time for his son than Char-mie's mother had for her daughter. They were each other's balm. For a while. But then Charmie had gotten pregnant and Ron had changed. He'd had to get a job and had been quick to display his resentment. He didn't want the kid, and they'd had many fights revolving around the subject of abortion. How Charmie had managed to keep the baby she would never know, but a spark of hope had kept her going—hope that the baby would change Ron and make him see that not all families were as abusive as his.

The first time he had hit her was the day she came home from the hospital with the baby.

"Well?" he said, rising from the kitchen table, slamming beer and drumstick down. "I asked you a question. Where've you bin?"

"Ron, you're drunk—"

He slapped her hard across the face. "You've bin with those fat cows again, haven't you? *Haven't you!*"

"Please, don't—"

Even though Charmie outweighed him, he was stronger. Grabbing her painfully by the arm, he said, "It's time you were taught a lesson."

"Ron, you're—"

"Go on!" he bellowed. "Move!" And he shoved her through the door.

He pushed her down the hall, shouting, "Get in there! I'm going to show you who's boss in this house! Christ, how I ever came to be married to a sow like you!"

She started to cry. He pushed her again and she fell against the wall, gouging her shoulder on a bare picture hook. "Please!" she cried. "I'm sorry."

"Get in there!" he said, delivering a kick into her thigh that made her stumble into the bedroom, terrified of what was going to happen next. He had done this to her once before, in a motel on Route 66, when they had driven across the country. She hadn't given the doctor in the nearby town her real name.

"Come on," he growled, tugging at her pink and lavender muumuu. "Get this rag off."

"Please," she said, "can't we just—"

Another slap across the face silenced her.

She tried to undress slowly, to buy time, to see if the alcohol would finally hit some sensitive part of his brain and knock him unconscious. She had been saved before that way. But he just stood there swaying, glaring at her with red, hate-filled eyes.

When she had all her clothes off, she tried to cover herself. They had been naked together many times; in the early days they had showered together. But now, as she stood there shivering and he made no move to undress, she felt shame burn through her until she thought she could die of it.

"On the bed," he said.

"No, Ron, *please*. I promise I won't—"

He knocked her down, sending her sprawling on the bedspread. "God, you're fat!" he shouted as he started to unbuckle his belt.

"Ron! No!" She tried to scramble away from him, but he strode around to the head of the bed, grabbed her wrists and pulled them up over her head. As she sobbed and begged him to stop, he strapped them together with the belt, then tied the belt over the rail of the brass headboard.

She was crying so hard that tears were running down the back of her throat, making her cough. She didn't see what Ron did next, but she heard the sound of his zipper and felt the bed dip as he got between her legs.

Screwing her eyes shut tight and curling her hands into fists, she waited for the painful assault. And when it came, with brute force, she clenched her teeth to keep from crying out. As he slammed into her, covering her with beer breath and grunts, Charmie felt such an intense wave of nausea that she was suddenly afraid she was going to be sick. She turned her head to the side.

It didn't last as long this time as it had on Route 66. When he finally stopped and pulled away from her, she prayed that this was it, that he would go back to his beer and leave her alone.

But he was far from finished. In terror she watched as he untied her wrists; there was a look on his face that she had never seen before. She thought, This time he's going to kill me.

Taking her by the hair, he dragged her off the bed and wordlessly pulled her out of the bedroom and down the hall. Yanking open a closet, he threw her in, sending her sprawling among old boots and junk. When she fell against a broken tennis racket, she felt a sharp pain in her ribs and heard a faint crack.

"Wait—" she said as the door closed. "No, please. Don't leave me here!"

But the door slammed shut and she heard the key turn in the lock.

"Ron!" she screamed. "Don't leave me here!"

The light bulb in the closet had burned out long ago, but even if it had worked, she couldn't have reached it. He had crammed her in with so much clutter that there was no room to move. And there was the alarming stab of pain in her chest each time she took a breath. But it wasn't worse than the pain between her legs. Down there, it wasn't so much a physical pain as a laceration of the soul.

"Ron," she whimpered, "please. I'm sick. I'm dying. Don't leave me here . . ."

And then she heard the front door slam and the sound of a car motor start up and go off down the street.

Alan took Hannah to Pacific Ocean Park, an amusement park built out on a pier, where they mingled with the crowd enjoying the sultry evening, bright lights, salty sea air, and wild, uninhibited fun. Their date started out shyly; they didn't touch as they walked along the midway, listening to the spiels of the barkers, watching boyfriends go by lugging the enormous stuffed animals they had won for adoring girlfriends. Romance surrounded them like a sweet, throbbing fog. They talked a little about themselves.

"You know, Hannah, I've always liked you," Alan confessed as they ate corn dogs on sticks, smothered in mustard. "But I could never get up the courage to talk to you. When Mrs. Faulkner told me you had been asking for me, I was flabbergasted. It gave me the confidence to call you. Otherwise, I never would have." He gave her hand a promising squeeze and then let it go.

Hannah had always known that Alan Scadudo was short, but she hadn't realized until now that he was actually shorter than she. But she didn't care; beneath the tight madras shirt and equally tight chinos, there were insinuations of a great physique.

They sucked on their corn dog sticks, then bought snow cones, one cherry, one lime. When those got too sloppy to eat and the paper cones collapsed, they tossed them away and bought cotton candy. Neither was really hungry; their appetite was for something else. But both were too shy to make the first move, and so food was the substitute.

They decided to take the Skyway ride from one end of the pier to the other, but as they rode in the little bucket suspended high over the ocean on a cable wire, Hannah got tense, and Alan put his arm around her. She let him leave it there. They went next on the roller coaster, and as their car plunged straight down toward the black, churning Pacific, Hannah screamed and held on to Alan, and he let his hand slip to her breast, where it remained for the rest of the ride. On the Octopus he got a little braver with his exploration as the buckets swung perilously up into the air and then down again. When Hannah didn't protest, he ventured a foray up under her sweater, fingers probing at the elastic of her bra. But it was on the Tilt-A-Whirl that he managed to slide his hand all the way under her bra, cupping a large, firm breast. As their car spun and went up and down, the rapidly changing centrifugal force pressed them together first this way and then that. With Hannah holding on tight to Alan, and he holding on tight to her breast, they got busy kissing. When she reached down and squeezed his erection, he thought he was going to explode right there in the Tilt-A-Whirl.

When the ride came to a halt, they stumbled off, dizzy more with sexual skyrockets than from having been thrown around. Alan kept his arm tightly around Hannah's waist as they walked numbly through the crowd, oblivious to the lights, the calliope music, the smell of hot dogs and generator fumes. They reached the seal compound, where people were tossing fish into foul-smelling water, and Hannah managed to peel herself away from Alan with a murmured, "I'll be right back."

He watched her disappear into a gray stone bunker with a little LADIES light over the door. When she emerged a moment later, he saw at once that she had removed her bra, and when he saw how those luscious breasts moved beneath the sweater, he thought the top of his head was going to blow off.

"Oh God," he said thickly, taking her hand. "Come on!"

The entrance to the fun house was sexually inviting, a great gaping red curtained doorway with a dark hole in the center. Alan managed to find a dollar bill for their tickets, and then he and Hannah slipped inside, still hanging onto each other as they had on the Tilt-A-Whirl, like twins who had been joined at birth.

They paused for a moment to adjust their eyes to the darkness. The noise inside was almost deafening; it was hard to tell if they were hearing a recording of music, laughter, or gunfire. As they followed the green luminous footsteps painted on the floor, they passed a couple entwined in the shadows, madly making out.

There were silly things in the fun house, more laughable than scary, but Hannah clung to Alan all the same, and he valiantly protected her from swinging skeletons, disembodied heads, and a floor made slippery from dropped soft drinks. They came to the trick mirrors and laughed at how funny they looked, all wobbled out of shape, changing as they moved. But when Alan saw how tall one of the mirrors made him seem, taller even than Hannah, he couldn't stand it any longer.

He flung his arms around her and began kissing the breath out of her. Hannah did not resist. They staggered and fell against a wall, the entrance to the hall of mirrors. Kissing greedily and madly groping for each other, they fell inside and sort of bounced off one glass wall and then another, ricocheting into the maze as he squeezed this and she grabbed that, unaware of the hundreds of images they created of themselves, while overhead a crazy strobe light made them look like actors in an old silent movie.

They fell against a transparent wall; Alan hiked up her skirt. She helped him frantically pull her panties down, while people nearby, half-blinded and confused by the strobes, fumbled like moles through the glass maze. He got his zipper down and was inside her between two flashes of the strobe; Hannah curled one leg around him as they bumped against the wall, and Alan managed to get her sweater up over her breasts. To passersby on the other side of the transparency, who laughed as they banged their noses against glass they didn't know was there, Alan and Hannah just looked like another entwined couple madly making out.

It was all over in a couple of minutes. Alan gave a violent shudder, and Hannah cried out. Then she was quickly smoothing down her skirt and drawing her sweater down before anyone could see, and he was zipping himself up. They hung onto each other, about to collapse.

"God!" he said, laughing. "That's why they call this the fun house!" He looked at her and kissed her again, long and deeply. "Hannah," he said, "let's get married."

She could hardly breathe. She felt a warm stickiness running down her legs; nothing had ever felt so good. "Isn't this awfully sudden?" she said breathlessly.

"We've been after each other for three years. I'd consider that a long enough engagement."

A dozen thoughts raced through her mind with the speed of a Tilt-A-Whirl: Greer Academy, her own fashion design business, her growing involvement with Starlite, her desire for independence. But all she could think of was Alan. "Yes," she said. "Yes, let's get married."

"Tell me," he said a few minutes later as they hurried out of the fun house, eager to go somewhere private. "What was the thing about me that attracted you the most?"

Her hand slid down his back and cupped a perfect buttock. "Your smile," she said.

Philippa was exhausted, but she was so energized, so excited, that she couldn't sit still. The clock on the kitchen stove told her she had worked nearly all through the night. Dawn would be breaking soon; she supposed she should go to bed and get some rest, because now that old Mr. Fox was turning over much of the drugstore's management to her, Philippa had to be fresh and alert for work. But she couldn't sleep.

She surveyed the mess she had made in the apartment and laughed at herself. There were notes and diagrams and pictures cut out of magazines strewn all over the place. Having borrowed the pastels and sketch pad Hannah used for designing her fashions, she had worn every shade of blue down to a nub, leaving colorful smudgy illustrations scattered about the apartment like stylish throw pillows. And she had run through nearly half a roll of adding-machine tape, the column of figures curling out of the machine and down onto the floor. The Valley section of the *Los Angeles Times* classifieds was folded neatly next to the telephone, little red circles indicating where Philippa had marked stores for rent. The first thing in the morning she would start making her calls. Because after her crazy night's work, moving figures about and adding up this and that and getting onto paper, in aggressive colors, the images that had plagued her for days, she knew now that her scheme was going to work.

She was going to make Starlite into a real business!

Going to the fridge and taking out a Tupperware container of cottage cheese and peaches, Philippa looked at the clock again. Hannah still hadn't come home from her date with Alan. She smiled. Apparently her roommate had found true love at last.

The phone rang, startling her, and she ran to answer it. At this hour, a phone call was likely to be an emergency.

"Philippa!" came Hannah's breathless voice. "Guess what! I'm married!"

"*What?*"

"Alan and I. We drove to Las Vegas! Oh, Philippa. We got *married!*" Philippa couldn't believe it.

"I haven't told Mom yet," Hannah said. "Oh God, she wanted me to have a big wedding. But Alan and I just couldn't *wait*. Oh, Philippa! I'm *so* happy! We'll be home in a few days. Oh God, you won't believe it!"

After she hung up, Philippa felt giddier and more energized than ever before. A Las Vegas wedding! How delicious, how unconventional!

And then: Charmie! She had to tell Charmie!

The phone rang and rang at the Charmer household with no answer; which was strange; Philippa knew that Ron was on a trip and that Charmie had taken tonight's Wednesday group. But she should have been home by now. It was so late that it was nearly dawn. Where could she be?

Dialing again and still getting no answer, Philippa felt a sudden chill of fear. It wasn't like Charmie, who was a light sleeper, not to pick up the phone. If she wasn't home, then where was she? And where was the baby?

Throwing a jacket on, Philippa grabbed her car keys and hurried out.

"Charmie?" Philippa called out as she rang the doorbell. "Charmie?"

She listened but could hear nothing from inside the house. Avenida Hacienda was quiet except for the periodic slap of newspapers on porches as the newsboy pedaled by. Dawn was just breaking over the tops of the ancient oaks that lined the street. Philippa looked at the driveway. Charmie's car was there; Ron's wasn't.

She rang the bell again, then she knocked. "Charmie?" She pounded. "Frizz, can you hear me?"

Finally she tried the doorknob and found it unlocked. As the door swung away from her, she called, "Frizz? Are you home? Frizz?"

She went inside, then she saw a smashed vase and a chair on its side; her alarm grew. "Frizz! Charmie! Are you all right?"

She listened. Thinking she heard a sound, she made her way toward the hall, pausing to listen. Yes, there it was, a faint thumping sound.

"Charmie?" she called again, more softly. "Where are you?"

The master bedroom was empty; she saw the crumpled sheets, the belt tied to the brass headboard. She followed the sound to a closet. She listened, heard something scuffling inside. She tried the knob and found it locked, but she noticed an old-fashioned skeleton key on a table nearby.

When she opened the door and found Charmie, naked and crumpled and surrounded by a heap of junk, she said, "Oh my God," and reached down for her.

"Philippa?" Charmie said weakly. "Help . . . me up . . . please."

She cried out when Philippa tried to get an arm around her. Charmie took shallow breaths, held her rib cage; Philippa ran to the bathroom and came back with a robe, helping Charmie into it. "I'm calling a doctor," she said.

But Charmie said no, holding on to Philippa, steadying herself. Her face was swollen, her eyes were black and blue, and her upper lip was cut. "No doctor. Please, just . . . help me into the kitchen . . . water . . ."

Philippa started to protest, and then, remembering the plea she herself had once made to Mrs. Chadwick not to involve a doctor, helped her friend into the kitchen.

"My God," Philippa said as she settled Charmie into a chair. "What happened?"

"Ron. He caught me coming home from a meeting," she said, taking the glass of water from Philippa. After she gulped it down, she said, "Jesus, I hurt. I must have been in that closet for hours. What time is it? Why did you come here?"

Philippa filled a towel with ice from the freezer and gave it to Charmie to hold against her face. Then, putting the kettle on the stove and pulling out cups and tea bags, her hands shaking she was so furious, she said as calmly as she could so as not to upset Charmie, "Hannah called. She and Alan Scadudo ran off to Las Vegas and got married. I tried calling you but didn't get an answer."

"Las Vegas! Jesus—" She winced. "Oh God, Philippa, I feel awful."

Philippa found some aspirin in the bathroom, along with a bottle of iodine and some Band-Aids, and did what she could to fix the cuts on Charmie's face. When the tea was ready, she set the cups on the table and took a seat opposite her friend. "Do you want tell me about it?" she said.

"No."

"All right," Philippa said, although with difficulty, because she wanted to help.

"It's just that—" Charmie started to say. "Oh God, what a mess. How do these things happen?"

At the sound of the front door opening, they both froze, and then Ron stumbled into the kitchen. He looked terrible, and he reeked of whiskey. "Oh honey," he said when he saw his wife's swollen face. "Oh God, I'm so sorry. What have I done?"

He fell to his knees and buried his face in her lap, sobbing like a baby. "I'm so sorry! I didn't know what I was doing! Forgive me. Please forgive me. I promise I won't ever do it again. How could I hurt you? I love you."

When he raised his tear-streaked face, Charmie stroked his head.

"I'll make it up to you, I swear. How 'bout we go somewhere nice? How 'bout I take you and the kid to Disneyland? You know how much he loves Mickey Mouse. Can we do that?"

"Yeah, sure."

"Listen, I mean it this time. I'm going to quit drinking. I'll go to AA, I'll do anything. We belong together, baby, don't we?"

"It's all right," Charmie said. "Go on now. Get some sleep. We'll talk later."

He stumbled off to bed, never even acknowledging Philippa.

"Charmie, you can't let him keep doing this to you," she said.

"Stay out of this, Philippa, please," Charmie said wearily, switching the ice pack to her other cheek. "You wouldn't understand."

"But why do you let him keep hurting you like this?"

"You don't know, Philippa," she said, taking small breaths because of the stabbing rib. "You've never had a man. You've never been in love."

"Is this what being in love means? Being locked in a closet?"

"Let me tell you something. The first time Ron did something like this to me, I went home to my mother. Do you know what she said? She said she couldn't let me in because it wasn't convenient. That's all I ever was to her, an inconvenience. I'm sure if abortion had been legal in 1937, I wouldn't be here now."

"But that's no reason to stay with an abusive husband."

"Philippa, I'm not an inconvenience to Ron. He loves me. He *needs* me."

"Charmie, listen," Philippa said quickly, filled with fear. "I've been working on this wonderful idea for Starlite. It's going to be big and sensational. But I need your help. I can't do it alone. There is so much we can accomplish together—"

"I'm not coming back, Philippa."

"You can't mean that!"

"I don't need Starlite. I'm not obsessed with being thin like you or Hannah. My husband likes me just the way I am."

"But he calls you Fattie! He humiliates you in restaurants, in front of your friends! Charmie, don't you see? He's using fat as a weapon against you! He keeps you subordinated by keeping you fat. He makes you feel worthless so you think you deserve his abuse."

"I deserved what I got!"

Philippa stared at her in shock.

"Ron forbade me to go back to Starlite," Charmie said, looking away, "but I went ahead behind his back. I deserved what I got."

"Charmie, that's not true! No one deserves to be treated this way."

Charmie suddenly stood up, bracing her ribs and wincing with pain. "I don't want to talk about this anymore. It's our private affair and none of your concern."

"Maybe not, Charmie, but I'm your best friend. Remember how we once stood up to Amber—"

"Oh for God's sake, stop living in the past!"

"But it's important to remember the past. How you and I both were once—"

"I said stop it!"

Philippa tried to maintain control. "Please, come with me right now. I'll help you. We'll go get the baby and you can stay with Hannah and me. I have such big plans for Starlite and I need your help."

"You don't need my help, Philippa. You've never needed anyone's help. Hannah and I follow you around like a couple of faithful dogs while you spout your self-righteous bullshit. 'As you believe so shall you be.' Jesus! Do you really think anyone swallows that?"

Philippa stared at her. She began to shake. *I'm losing Frizz. Just like I lost Rhys.* "Please, Frizz, I know you're hurting—"

"Don't condescend to me! And stop calling me that! Just get your skinny body out of here and leave me to live my life *my* way. Okay?"

"Charmie—"

"Get out," she said wearily, leaving the kitchen and heading for the bedroom, where Ron's snores came through the closed door. "And do me a favor, Philippa. Okay? Don't call me anymore. And don't come back."

26

Judith picked up the phone after the first ring and said, "Dr. Isaacs." When she heard the voice at the other end, she suddenly went cold.

Glancing over her shoulder at Zoey, who was cleaning the operating room where Judith had just performed minor surgery, she lowered her voice and said, "How did you find me?"

As she listened to the chillingly familiar voice on the other end, she stared at the freshly washed surgical instruments draining beside the sink and tried to collect herself. Judith had come to Star's to hide, to run away. And now, on only her third day here, he had found her.

"It's useless," she said, keeping her eye on Zoey, trying to make sure the nurse couldn't hear. "We don't have anything more to say to each other."

Was there never going to be any escape from the past? Was she doomed to drag it along wherever she went, like Jacob Marley's ghost and its chains? Judith wondered now if she had made a mistake coming to Star's; perhaps the mountain remoteness wasn't going to protect her after all. The anonymity of a big city hospital might have been better—Massachusetts General, or Cedars-Sinai in Los Angeles . . .

"Yes, I'm still here," she said. "You shouldn't have called me—"

A light flashed on the panel over the door of the substerile room. Each of the five bulbs indicated a patient room, and the one flashing now belonged to Mr. Smith. Judith hadn't been in to see him yet this morning.

Zoey saw the blinking light, and Judith waited until she left the clinic suite before saying into the phone, "I don't want you calling me here again. I have nothing to say to you now, or ever." She heard the tremor in her voice. "Please," she said, "don't do this to me. I'm trying to start a new life. I've put the past behind me."

She paused to listen, her hand tightening on the receiver. "What do you want from me?" she said. "No, you mustn't come here! Please, leave me alone!"

She looked up and was startled to see Zoey standing in the doorway. "Mr. Smith is asking for you," the nurse said coolly.

"Yes, thank you, Zoey. I'm sorry," she said to her caller, turning on her professional voice. "But I don't have time to talk right now." She hung up, realizing too late that she hadn't said good-bye, making the call appear suspicious.

"I'll be in with Mr. Smith if you need me," she said to Zoey as she picked up her medical bag.

"What if you get a phone call, Doctor?"

Judith wondered, Had Zoey overheard part of the conversation? Her relationship with the younger woman had worsened since her arrival. Judith had found more problems in the clinic—sterile supplies that had gone past their expiration dates, dusty shelves, a sloppily kept narcotics book—and tension between doctor and nurse had mounted. Judith wondered now if she could even trust Zoey. "If there is an emergency," she said, "come and get me."

As she went down the hall, trying not to think about the phone call and how badly it had unsettled her, she concentrated on Mr. Smith, wondering why he wanted to see her. She had visited briefly with him again last night and had left when the visit had seemed to go on dangerously longer than was necessary. He had asked her if she liked to ski, and when she had said yes, he had told her of the wonderful skiing spots in Europe, saying, "You would love it there, Judith," making it sound almost, but not quite, like an invitation. And this morning, Smith had been seen by Dr. Newton, who had spent ten minutes with him and had then reported to Judith that the wound was healing well. So why was he asking for her?

When she knocked on his door, a young man opened it, and Judith received a shock. The room was crammed with flowers and balloons, stuffed animals, baskets of fruit, boxes of candy. Seated on the sofa and chairs grouped around the fireplace were three men going through what appeared to be an enormous sack of mail.

"Come in!" Smith called to Judith from his bed, which was strewn with letters and cards. "I've been found!"

"So it would appear. But I thought you didn't want visitors," she said, eyeing the men at the fireplace and noticing the plates of sandwiches and cups of coffee on the table between them. She wondered why Zoey hadn't told her about any of this.

"Those aren't visitors, Doctor," Smith said, pushing himself up in bed so that cards and envelopes cascaded to the floor. "They are my staff." The three men—Smith's publicist, secretary, and valet—were introduced to Judith; they briefly said hello and went back to the task of sorting through the mail.

"What *is* all this?" she said, setting her medical bag down and sniffing a bouquet of red carnations. The flower arrangements varied from a single rose in a crystal vase to elaborate sprays that stood on the floor in wicker baskets. Judith could read some of the names on the gift tags: the Paul Newmans, Gerald and Betty Ford, Bob Mackie. An enormous stuffed panda bear wore a big pink bow covered with signatures. There were baskets filled with oranges, pears, and mangoes; stylish crates containing gourmet foods and bottles of wine; and several distinctive gold foil boxes of Godiva chocolates.

Smith reached for something on his nightstand and handed it to Judith. "Word is out," he said in a tone she hadn't heard him use before—the voice of a man trying to control his anger.

She realized with a start that he had handed her a popular supermarket tabloid. The major headline read SCREEN LEGEND HAS SECRET BELOW-THE-WAIST SURGERY.

"Oh my God," she said.

"And I only had the operation five days ago," he said grimly.

Judith turned to the story inside and scanned it with rising dismay. Accompanying the article were several photographs of Smith when he was younger and more vigorous, in scenes from movies when he had played pirates and Robin Hood and dashing heroes. The only present-day picture was an unflattering one that made him look haggard, an unfortunate trick of bad lighting.

"Even though the article explains that I had minor liposuction done on my abdomen," he said, "the headline is clearly supposed to lead people to believe that my surgery was of a more intimate nature. People will see this and ask themselves what is it a man could have done that involves sex? I was worried about my vanity, but this is far worse! How do you imagine it leaked out, Doctor?"

"I have no idea," she said, realizing that beneath his controlled exterior burned fury. "Star's has a policy of protecting the privacy of its guests, and the staff is sworn to secrecy, especially regarding guests who come in for medical reasons. In your case, only the top management—Beverly Burgess and Simon Jung—know who you really are. The desk people don't know who Mr. Smith is."

"Well, the operator is reporting an average of twenty incoming calls an hour for me."

Judith looked at him. "Then *she* knows who you are."

"Yes, and I have already spoken to my attorney about it. We are going to sue this despicable rag of a newspaper. After all the years of battling to keep my personal life private, from my first days in films back in the early forties, this should happen! You know, Doctor," he said, "this might sound odd, coming from a screen legend, but I am at heart an intensely private person. It is something I have struggled with all my life—my desire to be an actor versus my need for privacy. It has not always been an easy balance. Every love affair I ever had was dogged by newspaper reporters. But this goes beyond common decency and good taste."

"I don't know what to say. I feel terrible about this."

"It's not your fault," Smith said, throwing the tabloid to the floor in disgust. "I suppose stories like mine are bound to break." He waved his arm toward the room. "And look what it brought me! I had no idea so many people cared."

"Of course they care," she said, feeling her anger mount. How *had* the story leaked out? "And if I were out there in the real world," she said, "and had heard of your hospitalization, I would have sent you a get well card, too. Is this why you wanted to see me?"

"I thought you should know."

She studied his face and saw lines of worry deepen in his forehead and around his mouth. "Would you mind if I asked your staff to leave the room for a few minutes?"

"Why? My own physician has already seen to me today."

"I know, but when he's not here you are under my care, and you do seem to be upset."

"Wouldn't you be, if your secret were published in a rag like this? Especially with a headline that is full of tawdry insinuation?" He waved the others out. After they had left, taking the large mail sack with them to continue sorting, Judith took hold of Smith's wrist and looked at her watch.

He began to calm down. "All this doesn't dazzle you, does it?" he said as she counted his pulse. "The flowers, the gifts."

"On the contrary, Mr. Smith, I'm impressed."

"No, I mean the show business aspect of it. All this doesn't want to make you swoon."

"I've seen flowers in hospital rooms before," she said. "Here, take this," and she slipped a thermometer beneath his tongue.

"Doctor," he said, taking it out, "you're overwhelmed by me, admit it. You're head over heels in love with me, have been ever since you were twelve."

"Fourteen. Now please keep this in your mouth. Infection is our most immediate concern here, so I need to monitor your temperature closely." She sat on the edge of his bed, rolled up his sleeve, and wrapped a blood pressure cuff around a surprisingly well-developed bicep.

Seeing that his pressure was normal, she removed the cuff and read the thermometer, making a notation on the chart as she said, "Everything is fine."

"Very professional, aren't we?"

"Well, after all, I *am* a doctor." When she started to rise, he took her hand and said, "Stay a moment, please."

And she was startled by the jolt that went through her when he touched her. She felt her defenses against him, her cautiously maintained professional facade, start to crumble. She was afraid to stay. Afraid she would weaken and he would guess how she was starting to feel about him.

"All right," she said, "if you wish. I'll stay a few minutes."

"Have a drink with me. I haven't had a painkiller in hours."

"Help yourself. But, I'm still on duty."

Reaching for the maroon silk dressing gown that lay across the foot of his bed, Smith managed to get into it and then onto his feet. But Judith saw that he winced with pain and that when he stood, he went pale. She reached out and steadied him. "I'll be all right," he said, putting his hand on his abdomen. "I had no idea this would be so bloody painful. Just steer me over to the bar and I'll be fine."

After he poured himself a snifter of Napoleon brandy, Smith sat in one of the chairs vacated by his staff and indicated for Judith to join him. "I want your opinion on something," he said. "They're asking me to do a television series. What do you think? Should I do it?"

"Why are you asking me?" She shook her head when he offered her a plate of very crumbly, buttery cookies.

"Scottish shortbread," he said, biting into one. "My biggest weakness. I'm asking you because I value your opinion. You're not like any woman I've ever met, and I know you'll be honest with me."

When she gave him a skeptical look, he said, "It's not a line, Judith, it's the truth. You see, you're the first woman doctor I've ever seen professionally. In the outside world, I would never have gone to a female physician, but here I had no choice, I was at your mercy. This makes you a unique woman in my experience."

"I'm not sure I understand."

"I have known many women intimately, Judith, but no matter how intimate we became, I always kept my secrets, my mystique. It was part of my charm." He smiled, and Judith noticed that he blushed a little, adding to that charm. "But, from you, Doctor, I have no secrets. At least, concerning the nature of why I am here. Also, you are the only woman who has ever seen me vulnerable. Except for my mother, and that was many years ago, I have never allowed a woman to see me in pain. No woman has ever had that power over me."

"I don't feel as if I have power over you, Mr. Smith."

"I know . . ." He gave her a searching look. "And that makes you all the more remarkable. You aren't here to manipulate me, but to see to my comfort. You have my interests at heart, not your own ulterior motives. Which makes you one very special woman."

She didn't want to hear this. And she did want to hear it. "Mr. Smith," she said, "you should have gone to women doctors in the past, and then you would know that I am not unique at all."

"I doubt that," he said. "So, should I do it?"

"Do what?"

"The television series."

"I'm afraid I couldn't say. I watch very little TV."

"What do you do for entertainment?"

"I read books, mostly. I lead an appallingly quiet and boring life."

"What are you running from, Judith?"

She looked away. "We were talking about you."

"I saw by the look on your face when you first came in that something had upset you. What was it?"

"I received a disturbing phone call, but I don't want to talk about it."

"Then tell me about your daughter."

"No."

"I wish I had had children, you know. But when I was younger, the thought of having a family just somehow never occurred to me, it never seemed to suit my life-style. And I did have my playboy image to maintain." He smiled. "Marriage was never a consideration."

"But you're thinking of getting married now."

He gave her a startled look. She hadn't asked a question, she had made a statement. "Yes," he said. "As a matter of fact, I am. How did you know?"

"I didn't. It was just a guess. Something from one of our conversations, I suppose. So who is the lucky bride?"

"I haven't decided yet. How about you? Would you marry me, Judith?"

"If I'm not busy that day."

"I'm very rich. I have homes in Beverly Hills, Palm Beach, Manhattan, and Rome. I have my health, as you can see for yourself, and I'm reasonably presentable. And now very fit," he added, touching his flat abdomen. "It could be a fun life—"

She laughed, then she grew serious. "I'm never going to marry again, Mr. Smith. I won't have any more children."

"You mean you can't."

"I mean I won't."

"Well then," he said, falling silent and staring at her.

Judith looked around the cluttered room, at the cards and letters, the baskets of fruit, the floral sprays with red ribbons that wished him well in gold glitter letters. There must be a thousand people represented here, she thought. More, she realized, when she saw a letter signed "All Our Prayers and Wishes, From the Town of Escondido."

Judith tried to imagine Smith's life—the homes he had just mentioned, how elegant they must be. A man who had made fifty-four successful films and won two Oscars must be very rich and must have legions of fans and friends. What a glamorous existence, Judith thought, suddenly viewing her own life in a small, thin spotlight: the childhood in San Jose, followed by college and medical school, and then settling into a calm marriage to Mort in a small mountain community where the only famous person Judith had ever met was Miss Northern California Logging of 1979.

"I've upset you," he said quietly.

She looked at Smith. How many women's bedrooms, or desks, or lockers, she wondered, did his handsome features grace? How many female hearts had he stirred up, was he still capable of stirring up? A lot of the get well letters, she noticed, were written on feminine stationery. "No, you haven't upset me," she said. "I just have something on my mind."

"You can tell me about it if you like. I'm an excellent listener."

She looked into his deep blue eyes, which had the crinkles of age and wisdom around them, and then at his shoulders, which were still broad, his hands, which were firm and strong. Judith suddenly wished she weren't his physician, but a woman who had the freedom to surrender to him. She wanted to be swept away by his dash, held and made love to in those inviting, masculine arms, and hear that capable Scottish baritone tell her that everything was going to be all right, that he would keep her safe, and that he loved her.

Startled by her thoughts, and by the sudden realization that her cheeks felt unusually warm, she stood and said, "I must be going, I have other patients to see."

He stood with her, with less effort than before, less evidence of pain. "Please have dinner with me tonight, Judith," he said.

God, but she loved the way he said her name, bringing it up out of the ordinary and giving it an aristocratic luster, and sounding somehow also as if he liked saying it. She marveled at how straight backed he was, how tall. She thought of her ex-husband, Mort, who at forty-six was already showing signs of giving in to age and gravity—the paunch, the beginnings of shoulder stoop. Mort was the kind of semi-antisocial artist who populates alpine towns; he spent his days in his damp studio, hunched over lumps of raw clay or blocks of wood, creating marvelous sculptures that were going to endure and remain unchanged for eternity, while their creator grew stouter, shorter, smaller. Mr. Smith, on the other hand, was the embodiment of a lifetime of athletic accomplishment. Judith recalled seeing a photo of him in the *Los Angeles Times* two years ago, when he was sixty-seven, playing polo at a charity benefit.

She would have loved more than anything to have dinner with him. But he was leaving Star's in three days. She would never see him again. Whatever attraction was growing between them could not be allowed to develop into something more. He had his glamorous life, his four homes, and plans to get married and father a child. There was no place in that sparkling picture for an ordinary, small-town doctor.

"I'm not asking you out of loneliness, Judith," he said, standing close to her. "I would like you to have dinner with me because I enjoy your company. More than that, I want to reach inside you and draw out your sadness. Maybe heal you, in a way, the way you're helping to heal me. Please give me a chance."

She was about to say yes when the phone rang, startling them both.

"Pardon me," he said. It was his attorney, and as Smith started discussing the tabloid article over the phone, the terms of the lawsuit, Judith prepared to leave.

Smith said, "Wait," and put the phone down.

He removed a flame-colored rosebud from a Erté vase and came up to her. "So you'll think about me," he said quietly, slipping it into the lapel of her lab coat.

27

Ingrid Lind had watched the Tiger God dance, and then she had brought him back to her hotel room where he made love to her. It had become Ingrid's tradition, at the end of every buying trip, to reward herself lavishly in Singapore, with food (remnants of a tandoori curry feast littered the tables of her suite); with jewelry (a buying spree had added rare black jade to her already vast collection); and finally, she rewarded herself with sex. The last time Ingrid was in Singapore, she had attended the festival of the Monkey God's birthday, and she had gone to bed with one of those celebrants, too—a wiry, copper-fleshed young Malaysian who had astonished her with his sexual gymnastics. The Tiger God, although not as creative in bed, had more endurance so that now, as the equatorial sun broke through her window, flooding her hotel room with stimulating light, Ingrid felt more contented and refreshed than she had in a long time.

And that was why when the telephone rang, she decided not to answer it. She wanted to lounge in the rumpled sheets and relive some of the finer moments she had spent with the Tiger God, who was deeply asleep at her side, his long black hair streaming across the pillow and almost down to the floor. Male dancers were by far the best lays in the world she decided.

Finally, unable to ignore the persistently ringing telephone, she picked it up. "Yes?" she said, brushing blond hair away from her face and fumbling on the nightstand for a pack of cigarettes.

"Ingrid," came the voice on the other end. "It's me, Alan."

"Oh . . . hello, Alan." Wedging the earpiece into her neck, she pulled out a Gauloise, lit it with her gold-initialed Dunhill lighter, and blew smoke into the sunbeams that crossed her bed.

Ingrid was staying at Raffles, one of the most luxurious and history-rich hotels in the world. One of the benefits of being a buyer for such a wealthy corporation as Starlite Industries, and one of the reasons Ingrid so liked her job, was the travel, which took her all over the globe as she searched for fabrics and fashions for Starlite's Perfect Size dress shops, from North Africa, where she picked up Moroccan turbans and headbands, to Egypt for cotton and linen, Pakistan for batik, and India for silk, until she ended here in Singapore, the import and export crossroads of Southeast Asia, where she rounded out the latest Perfect Size International line with such exotic accessories as reptile skin handbags, cloisonné jewelry, and human hair wigs.

"What's up, Alan?" she asked, lying back into the pillows and blowing smoke up to the lazily turning ceiling fan. The morning was already warm. It was always warm in Singapore, where the temperature rarely fell below seventy, even at night, all year round.

"I'm calling from Rio."

"Oh," she said, "the Miranda International thing. I heard."

"Listen, Philippa's back."

"Yes, I know."

"You know? How?"

"So what's the problem?"

"She's called an emergency board meeting three days from now, and she wants everyone there."

"Sorry, I won't be back in time."

"Well, I suggest you get back."

"What's it all about?"

"She's found a discrepancy in the accounting. A serious one."

Ingrid frowned. "In my department?"

"No. In foods. But get back here anyway. Pronto."

She closed her eyes and silently said, Screw you.

The Tiger stirred at her side, inhaling deeply, stretching his long arms. Ingrid rolled over and, reaching down, took hold of him. He moaned softly.

"Ingrid?" came Alan's impatient voice. "Is someone there with you?"

"Yeah, a silk merchant! G'bye," she said with a laugh. As soon as she hung up she was suddenly engulfed in the Tiger God's arms.

But, a minute later, Ingrid was telling her handsome god to go home. As much as she tried not to let Alan's phone call unsettle her, it had.

When the Malaysian dancer had gone, Ingrid went into the bathroom and stood for a long time under the cool shower, washing away the effects of last night's carousing on Arab Street in the Malay Quarter, where, with a group of Americans, she had watched a dazzling procession celebrating the virility of the Tiger God. The rowdy group had eaten vegetables on banana leaves and drunk authentic Singapore slings, and then Ingrid had brought the chief dancer back to her room at Raffles.

Turning off the shower and wrapping her naturally blond hair in a plush towel, she slipped into a Malaysian sarong, which had been tailored for her from expensive hand-painted batik. Most of Ingrid's clothes were custom-made, because Ingrid Lind was a large woman—not fat, but statuesque, reaching a height of six feet one inch and weighing 180 pounds. Having had difficulties finding clothes to fit for most of her thirty-six years, Ingrid had developed an eye and a sharp sense for what looked good and felt comfortable on the larger woman, which was why she had been recruited by Hannah Scadudo seven years ago to work for the fashion division of Starlite Industries. Ingrid had been twenty-nine then, single, ambitious, and possessing many appetites, her three most voracious being for food, gemstones, and sex. Ingrid had looked over The Perfect Size stock and had declared that what was needed was more variety, something with an exotic flavor to distinguish Starlite fashion shops from the other larger-size clothing stores that were sprouting up all over. And so, with Ingrid's creative input, Hannah Scadudo had created a new, more expensive line and called it Perfect Size International; it had turned out to be a hit. Bedouin-style caftans and Egyptian galabeyahs, accented with bulky jewelry, appealed to larger women who found the loose, flowing garments flattering and comfortable, as well as distinctive and rich looking. Ingrid's new costly fashions had been snapped up at once, making Perfect Size International a highly profitable line, and making Ingrid, after just a short time with Starlite, indispensable. Her fluency in several languages and her Scandinavian beauty had furthered her success, since Ingrid's travels took her mostly to dark-haired countries where blondes were unique and valued, especially among businessmen who were always eager to work deals with Ingrid. In Cairo, a wealthy Egyptian exporter named Ahmed Rasheed had once plucked a strand of her golden hair and paid her a hundred pounds for it.

That was before she had invited him up to her suite at the Nile Hilton, where they had made love all through the night.

Ingrid called room service and ordered oolong tea and a plate of fresh fruit, then she went to the window and parted the gauze curtains. Morning was breaking over Singapore Harbor, soft and opalescent, making the sky look like the underside of an oyster shell. Ingrid lit another cigarette and leaned against the window frame to survey the palm trees and exotic gardens that embraced the famous hundred-year-old hotel. When she saw a flash of red and green as a parrot flew by, she realized that she didn't want to leave this beautiful, peaceful place. She especially didn't want to give up Singapore's greatest gifts: the richest cuisine in the world; gold and silver and rubies and emeralds enough to appease even her; and finally, small, dark, sexually artistic men who appreciated statuesque blondes.

But Alan's voice kept running through her mind like a corny song. She didn't like him ordering her around; he wasn't her boss. Only Philippa and Hannah had authority over Ingrid, and they, Ingrid thought smugly, could be handled.

A hotel guest suddenly dived into the pool below, cleaving the blue-green water smoothly, his body skimming beneath the sparkling surface. Ingrid wished she could join him; she would have, if it hadn't been for Alan's phone call. Now that the working part of her trip was over and the new fabrics were on their way to the U.S., Ingrid had looked forward to spending some time enjoying this Asian paradise. She had promised a wealthy Englishman, a banker, that she would fly to Kuala Lumpur with him today and explore the Batu Caves. And then there was Mr. Chang, owner of the famous Jade House, with whom she had planned an excursion to Brunei. He claimed to be a friend of the sultan. But now it seemed she had to change her plans. *All* of her plans, including the secret financial arrangements she was working on with the banker and Mr. Chang.

All put on hold, because of Philippa . . .

When she felt a small thrill of fear go through her, Ingrid quickly suppressed it. There was nothing to worry about—yet. But still, it nettled her to think how smoothly things had been going at last, how close she was to independent wealth and to being able to leave Starlite, only to have her plans disrupted by the untimely and unexpected return of the company's chief executive officer. Ingrid had hoped Philippa would stay buried in Western Australia forever, waiting for her lover to come back from the dead. How had this fire gotten started under Philippa all of a sudden? Even more important, could she be stopped in time?

Quickly putting out her cigarette, Ingrid picked up the phone, dialed, and heard the telephone ringing in the next room. When her assistant answered, she said, "Something's come up, we have to get back to the U.S. right away. Cancel the rest of my social engagements here in Singapore with the usual apologies and get us booked on the first flight back to L.A. Let the hotel know we'll be checking out early. Oh—and have a bottle of Glenlivet sent to Mr. Chang, with my compliments. And Steve, whoever is in your room there with you, get rid of him."

It took Philippa a moment before she realized she was looking at a freak.

Spread out on her desk was a magazine advertisement composed of a headline saying "I Became a Size Ten in Only Twenty-nine Weeks!" with two before and after photographs, one showing a Mrs. D. of Des Moines, Iowa, when she weighed 300 pounds, and a current one, showing her at 125 pounds. It was not the 300-pound image that Philippa thought freakish, but the slender one; how, she wondered, could a woman reasonably lose 175 pounds in twenty-nine weeks? That meant a weight lost of

6 pounds per week, which was not only hard to believe, but extremely dangerous as well. Could the ad be a lie?

"This is one of our toughest competitors," Hannah Scadudo said as she handed Philippa a fact sheet about the diet center. "People find such rapid weight loss very appealing. And you see here, they advertise proudly that no exercise is involved, no meetings that have to be attended, no listening to lectures. In other words," Hannah said, "they're implying they they are *not* Starlite."

"But this diet is deadly, Hannah," Philippa said. "At that rate of loss, this woman couldn't possibly have just lost body fat; she must also have lost lean muscle, which means not just skeletal muscle but heart muscle as well. How do they do it? How can this company get away with such an outrageous claim?" Philippa scanned the information sheet and found her answer. "My God, they inject their customers with a pregnancy hormone. So you lose a lot of water, a lot of glycogen and heart muscle, but still retain your fat."

"Yes, but you look thin in the end."

Philippa's dismay had been deepening all morning, ever since Hannah had arrived at the office with an armload of files on Starlite's competitors. In the short time Philippa had been in Australia, there had been a boom in the U.S. diet industry, with storefront weight loss centers mushrooming in every town, over-the-counter pills and powders being sold by the millions, more and more physicians advertising help for eating disorders, supermarkets stocking thousands of "lite" products.

"Here's another stiff competitor," Hannah said, opening a file and handing Philippa copies of ads, outlines of the program, cost breakdowns, and demographics. "You'll notice that this company bases its success on making dieting easy. The client checks in once a week at the center and buys all of his or her food there; it's all prepackaged or frozen, which eliminates weighing and measuring portions. Great for people who don't have a lot of time or who don't want to bother much in the kitchen."

"Another covert jab at Starlite," Philippa murmured. As she surveyed the overwhelming amount of literature spread on her desk describing the vast range of diet programs—from fasting on liquids to groups based on Overeaters Anonymous—she realized that Starlite's competition was far greater than she had suspected. And when she thought of the hundreds of diet books she had seen in a local bookstore that morning, the public's growing demand for quicker, more streamlined weight loss, she began to fear that Starlite was in danger of becoming a cliché or, worse, a dinosaur.

The intercom buzzed. It was the receptionist informing Hannah that she had an important call.

"I'll take it in my office," she said, rising quickly.

But Philippa said, "You can take it here," and she picked up the phone and handed it to her.

Hannah hesitated, then took the phone. "This is Hannah Scadudo," she said cautiously. To her relief, she heard a voice say, "Hello, Mrs. Scadudo. This is the Emerson Gallery." For a moment she had been afraid that it was the people returning the panicked call she had made the night before. She had asked to meet with them as soon as possible, and they had not yet called back. She was going to try calling again tonight, to try once more to speed things up. The board meeting was only three days away; surely they would be reasonable . . .

"I hope you have good news for me," she said into the phone, hoping Philippa wouldn't detect her nervousness.

"As a matter of fact, we do, Mrs. Scadudo. We have found a seller who will agree to your price."

"You have? That's wonderful. When may I expect delivery? This is to be a surprise for my husband, you see, and—"

She listened, then said, "Yes, of course, that will be perfect. I will arrange with my bank to have the funds transferred at once. Thank you. Yes, Merry Christmas to you, too."

Hannah hung up the phone and walked over to the credenza where she picked up her purse. "That was the gallery I've had searching for the Freundlich sculpture I told you about in my last letter," she explained to Philippa as she opened her purse, took out a bottle of pills, put one in her mouth, and swallowed it without water.

When Philippa gave her a questioning look, Hannah smiled and said, "I have a headache." Then she buried the pills deep in her purse so no one could read the label. They had been prescribed by Dr. Freeman, who had instructed her to take one every time her heart bounced around, as it was doing now, jumping in every direction as if it were trying to get out of her rib cage. Every so often, Hannah's heart would plunge into a terrifying trill, quivering instead of beating, and Hannah would freeze, wondering if maybe this time it wouldn't start up again. Her mother had experienced the same symptoms before she had died of a heart attack at age forty-eight. She hadn't gone to a doctor about the problem, and so she hadn't had the benefit of medication. "It's your imagination," Hannah's father would say every time her mother complained of discomfort in her chest. "You women, always moaning about something." And so Mrs. Ryan had eventually learned to keep silent about her discomfort, until finally she was silent for eternity.

"And they found it?" Philippa said. "What did you say the piece was called?"

"*Phoenix.* It's an exquisite monument bronze by Helmut Freundlich, one of Alan's favorite artists. I was afraid I wasn't going to be able to get it, but the gallery found a seller." She placed her hand on her chest and said breathlessly, "For sixty-five thousand dollars! I hope Alan likes it!"

While Hannah remained by the credenza, waiting for the medication to take effect, for her heart to calm down, she inspected herself in the mirror, pretending to straighten her hair. She was wearing one of Ingrid Lind's imports—a handsome rust brown Tunisian caftan with a rope belt and copper jewelry that went well with her high cheekbones and Indian eyes. Although Hannah no longer had a weight problem, it was her policy never to design anything for other women that she wouldn't wear herself. And so she wore The Perfect Size fashions, although in a scaled-down version.

Hannah studied the heavy copper necklace that lay in the deep V of the caftan's neckline. She thought she could see it jump slightly with each struggling flinch of her heart. I mustn't follow my mother, she thought in desperation, too well aware that she was already six years past the age when her mother had died. I have so much to live for—Jackie's wedding, my children and grandchildren, retirement with Alan when we finally take that cruise around the world . . .

She thought about how she and Alan had made love last night, before he left to catch his plane to Rio. Had it been her imagination, or had his lovemaking been more thoughtful, more passionate than it had been in the last few years? It had been almost as if they were young lovers again instead of a married couple facing their thirty-fifth wedding anniversary. Alan had been so tender and gentle that her fears that he might suspect something were at least a little allayed. Surely she must have been quick enough last night to put the stock certificates back in the safe before Alan had seen. Because if he found out what she was up to, it would destroy everything between them.

Ricky came in then with a tray bearing tea service, Melba toast, and sliced peaches. He had also brought a copy of the latest issue of *The Wall Street Journal*, which he placed in front of Philippa.

Hannah watched the good-looking young man in the mirror, appreciating the tailored cut of his slacks and shirt, the smart tie and cuff links, the way his blond ponytail fell between his shoulder blades. When she caught the special look flashed between him and Philippa, she wondered again if there was more to their relationship than the purely professional.

"Mr. Hendricks telephoned, Miss Roberts," he said. "He's in Palm Springs and has started doing some more research on Beverly Burgess. He says he'll have a report for you tomorrow, at the Marriott Desert Springs."

So much to think about! Starlite's declining membership, the threat of a corporate takeover, the embezzlement of a million dollars, and the possibility that Ivan Hendricks might, after years of looking, have finally found her sister.

"Thank you, Ricky," Philippa said as she scanned the article he had brought. "Oh lord," she said a moment later. "Miranda International has bought another two percent of Starlite stock. They're getting closer to securing controlling interest of the company. I just pray that Alan is able to open dialogue between us and Miranda. I want to know who they are and why they are after my company. And most of all, I want to know their weakness so I can find a way to stop them from taking over."

"But Philippa," Hannah said, "even if they buy up all the public stock, they still can't touch us. We'll still own controlling interest."

"It's not the public shares I'm worried about," Philippa said, looking at her friend. "If Miranda got to one of *us*, that's all it would take."

Hannah shifted uncomfortably. "By 'us' you mean me and Alan and you and Charmie. We own the controlling interest. And which of us do you think Miranda could touch?"

"And Ingrid," Philippa said. "Don't forget her five percent."

Despite the enormous success Starlite had had with Ingrid's international fashions, the vivacious Miss Lind was still a sore point among Starlite's executive officers. When Hannah had wanted to bring the young woman into the company seven years ago, Alan had been so opposed to it that Ingrid had been the cause of the worst fight of their married lives. But Philippa had intervened; Hannah and Ingrid had prevailed. Nonetheless, Alan continued to make public his dislike of Hannah's chief buyer; he had even subtly planted this kernel of suspicion in Philippa's mind.

"I trust Ingrid," Hannah said. "I trust all of us not to sell," she added, trying to sound convincing despite the image of her own stock certificates spread out on the bed, waiting to be transferred to new owners.

"I'm leaving now," Philippa said as she stood and collected her purse and briefcase. "Ricky, if you would please, take a cab back to the hotel and get us checked out. I'm going to take a little drive first, before we get started for Palm Springs. There's something I need to see."

As the glass door whispered closed behind Philippa, blocking out the sounds of traffic on the busy Beverly Hills street, a young woman at the salon's reception desk said, "Hello, welcome to Starlite."

Philippa had rehearsed what she was going to say. "Thank you. I'm not a member, but I was thinking of joining. Would it be all right if I looked around?"

The receptionist was in her twenties, slender, nicely dressed, and she wore a name badge that said Mandy. "Certainly. While I show you our salon I can explain the various aspects of the Starlite program to you."

Philippa was taken into the main part of the salon, a large room with comfortable chairs arranged in an intimate grouping. The room was decorated in gentle blue tones, with easy-listening music piped in at an unobtrusive decibel level. Adjacent to the meeting room were the exercise rooms, private massage rooms, a spa and steam room, and hair and cosmetic salons, all decorated in peaceful shades of blue, with potted plants and subdued lighting. It was all very quiet, very private. A place to come and relax and be pampered.

"We have three groups a day at convenient hours," Mandy explained as she took Philippa around, "which include the diet meetings and classes in beauty and fashion. We also offer additional aerobics classes and personal beauty treatments such as facials, manicures and pedicures, and waxings."

As the receptionist went into more detail about how the diet worked, how the groups were attended, Philippa was struck by the silence in the place. There were only a few women in the spa; just one of the massage rooms was in use; and an aerobics instructor was waiting for her class to arrive. And the fact that only three diet groups a day were offered—one in the morning, one in the afternoon, and one in the evening—did not strike Philippa as convenient. What about women for whom only the hour before work was free, or lunch hour, or perhaps later at night? Even more disturbing was the news that there were vacancies in all three groups, every day except Saturday, which was full.

This Starlite salon on Roxbury Drive in Beverly Hills was the embodiment of Philippa's vision of years ago; it had been hailed as revolutionary back then, a place of beauty and elegance where women could enjoy a few moments of peace from the stresses of daily life, where they could find friendship and sympathy among others who had the same problems, where they could learn how to improve themselves and to like themselves and to gain self-esteem. Revolutionary, and so in demand in its growing years that new salons couldn't be opened fast enough. So why did this salon seem empty? Had the needs of women changed?

She recalled what Charmie had told her: "People are in a hurry these days, they want instant results. They aren't interested in putting time and energy into an involved program like ours. It worked years ago because housewives had the time. But now we've got to attract the professional woman who very often is a single mother as well. They need flexibility, plus the opportunity to be spontaneous."

As she listened to Mandy's enthusiastic sales pitch for joining Starlite, trying to convince her off-the-street prospective customer that "you're worth the time and effort it takes to get the results out of a program like ours," Philippa began to recognize the problem and also the way to resolve it. Starlite had to be brought up with the times.

As she thanked the receptionist and left with a glossy brochure, Philippa was already visualizing the changes that were going to take place. She felt her old excitement start to return, the thrill of meeting a challenge.

But there were obstacles. Philippa had to find out who was stealing from the company, and soon. And then the hostile takeover by Miranda International had to be stopped. Because once Miranda had control, then all those years, all their dreams and visions and hard work, might be lost.

Philippa hurried back to the limousine, gave the driver instructions to return her to Starlite headquarters, then picked up the phone and dialed Hannah's private line. As the car pulled away from the curb and joined the traffic on Wilshire, neither Philippa nor her driver were aware of the sleek black Jaguar that was following them.

28

Tarzana, California, 1963

"You know what you need, Philippa? You need a man. I mean, you're a healthy twenty-five-year-old woman. Don't you ever get, you know . . ." —he wiggled his eyebrows at her—"horny?"

She smiled and shook her head at Hannah's cousin. "Max, I'm not getting into that with you again. Especially not this morning and in front of all these people."

A small crowd had assembled on the sidewalk outside a storefront in Canoga Park. It was a bracing November morning, with the sun doing battle with gray clouds. For the moment, the sun was winning. Max was not.

"I mean it, Phil," he said, following her as she walked over to where Hannah and Alan were standing. Alan was holding the baby; Hannah was managing her eight-month abdomen, being pregnant already with their second child. "Don't you want to sit down?" Philippa said.

"I'm fine," Hannah said, shifting a little as she placed her hand on her lower back. "The ceremony's about to start, isn't it?"

"Yes." Philippa looked over her shoulder. "Isn't it exciting? Our thirtieth salon!" The fruits of her vision of two years ago, the night Hannah got married. The night Charmie left Starlite.

Hannah gave Philippa a quick hug. "Uh oh," she said. "Here comes Max again. And he's got his demented look on. Do you want me to call him off?"

Philippa laughed. "I can handle Max!"

"My family," Hannah said with a sigh. Approximately half the crowd there that morning to cheer the opening of the thirtieth Starlite salon were from Hannah's vast clan.

The only guest from Philippa's "family" was Mrs. Chadwick, wearing her Sunday dress and a new hat with silk carnations on it, alternately crying and telling people how she knew Philippa when she was just a clerk in a drugstore. "I've known all along she was going to be a big success."

And Philippa's success today consisted of owning thirty Starlite salons, each operating at a full capacity of eight hundred members, for a total of twenty-four thousand women. "Where else," a news columnist had written, "can women get away from the stress of families or jobs and enjoy an hour and a half of self-improvement among friends, losing weight on a diet that is both interesting and successful, learning about fashion and makeup techniques, receiving sympathy, and gaining inspiration through pep talks? This writer can give you the answer from personal experience: only within the privacy and safe, nonthreatening environment of Starlite's pleasant, chic little salons! Do yourselves a favor, girls, and check it out."

Among the crowd gathered today for the ceremony of cutting the blue ribbon to open this thirtieth salon were the six counselors who would work at this location; among them was Cassie Marie, whose nervous energies had once gone into eating Snickers bars and aggressively crocheting afghans. A Starlite counselor had to be a graduate of the diet program; before they went to work they attended an intensive six-week training course. Salaries were based on length of time with the company and the number of groups conducted, plus there were incentives such as profit sharing and the opportunity to move up within the ranks, all the way to the top position of area coordinator, which paid the most and offered the most prestige. So far, the thirty salons were scattered over southern California, but Philippa was working on plans to expand Starlite statewide, and then, as soon as possible, nationwide.

If only Charmie were part of all this, Philippa thought as two more florist's vans pulled up to the curb and men in coveralls began bringing out large floral sprays with ribbons that said SUCCESS and CONGRATULATIONS. But since the night two years ago when Philippa had found her friend in the closet, battered and bruised, they had not spoken to or seen each other.

Philippa had tried several times to mend the break. She had sent notes, made phone calls, and even once went by Charmie's house, only to have her knock go unheeded, even though she had felt the presence of someone inside. Finally, she had sent a bouquet of flowers—carnations, Charmie's favorite—with a note saying, "Please, let's be friends." But Charmie had not responded. That had been a year ago.

Thinking now of her best friend and wishing she were here, Philippa was reminded once again of her loneliness. Which was what annoyed her about Max and his insistence that she needed someone: he was right.

She pushed that negative thought from her mind. After all, how *could* she be lonely? With a brand-new house up in the Enrico hills, which commanded a view of the Valley, and the new Starlite office in Encino to occupy her mind and energies, there wasn't time to think of loneliness. Philippa was busy from morning till night, scouting out locations for new stores and converting them into salons, hiring and training counselors, purchasing new equipment, and making sure everything ran smoothly. She was constantly on the go, from Thousand Oaks to Escondido. When she wasn't on the road or checking up on the twenty-nine salons, she was working at a furious pace in her office, with the help of her staff, fielding hundreds of phone calls from members with questions: Was okra allowed as a vegetable since it wasn't on the list? What about Metracal and Sego? Could honey be used as a white sugar substitute? Or with suggestions: a recipe for faux lasagna made from eggplant and cottage cheese, or a delicious vegetable dip using nonfat yogurt and clam juice. All of which had to be researched, tested, and then incorporated into Starlite's massive data files ultimately to be passed on to members in the weekly handout sheets. Then there were the more personal letters that poured into the Starlite office from women who just had to say thanks and describe how Starlite had turned their lives around. Words such as "outcast," "unloved," and "freak" jumped off those pages and were followed by "popular," "in love," "job promotion." They were letters of praise. And whenever Philippa addressed a group, the members would clap and cheer, letting her know that she had many friends.

There were men in her life, too. When she could manage the time, she went out on dates.

Was *this*, she asked herself, the profile of a lonely woman?

And when sometimes she felt so lonely that she considered telephoning Johnny at San Quentin or writing to him, she would remind herself how busy she was and how many friends she had and how her success was growing, and she would tell herself that she didn't need Johnny, that she didn't need anyone. Her life was very full and she was happier than most people seemed to be.

Occasionally she would allow herself to think of Rhys. It had taken her a long while to get up the courage to read his book, *Searches*.

When Rhys's brother had taken Rhys's body back to northern California, he had also taken the butcher roll with all the words typed on it and had submitted it to a publisher. Last year it had zoomed to the top of the best-seller lists and been hailed as the "last great novel of the Beat Generation." And when Philippa was finally able to read it, she read the words she had read the night she found him dead: "Her face, with the sweet roundness of a cherub, she was like a pure, baby angel, when she opened her mouth to speak, light came out . . . She lay in my arms like a warm little quail . . ."

As she now approached the blue ribbon that fluttered in the morning breeze, waiting for the attention of the gathered company, Philippa saw her own reflection in the window—a tall, slender young woman in a wool skirt and smart little jacket with oversize buttons, her auburn hair taken up in a fashionable French twist and capped with a Jackie Kennedy pillbox hat. She smiled, because she was pleased with what she saw. This was not the fat, unhappy Christine Singleton who had had to buy her clothes at Charlene's Chubbies on Powell. This was no longer Rhys's round-faced cherub, his plump little quail. She was a woman in control now; a woman on her way to even greater successes. A woman who was definitely not lonely.

She cut the ribbon, flashbulbs went off, and everyone traipsed inside, where tables of food awaited—nothing fattening. All the dishes were made according to official Starlite recipes: hard-boiled eggs in tomato aspic; a salad of marinated cucumbers, mushrooms, and asparagus; sandwiches of cold chicken breast on rye bread; vegetables and yogurt dip. The drinks were diet sodas, coffee, tea, and skim milk flavored with nutmeg. The one concession to sinful indulgence was champagne, which the entire company seemed to head for all at once.

As everyone was congratulating Philippa, a red-faced Max suddenly came rushing in, shouting, "Jesus! The president's been shot!"

The salon had a twenty-one-inch television set, and Max rushed to turn it on while the crowd gathered around.

The television screen flared to life, displaying the words NEWS BULLE-TIN, and a voice was saying, "We interrupt this program—"

"Oh God, oh God," Max said as switched the channels. Every station had a similar news bulletin; finally he found one that showed a reporter standing on the lawn of what looked like a hospital, and he was saying in a grave voice, "We have received no word yet on the condition of President Kennedy, who was brought to Parkland Hospital here in Dallas immediately after being shot while riding in a motorcade through the city."

The room fell silent as everyone stared at the screen, dumbstruck.

"As you can see behind me," the reporter went on, his voice breaking, "a crowd is gathering outside the hospital . . ."

The camera slowly panned the scene. People were clustered on the lawn in front of the thirteen-story building. They stood or knelt in silence; many were weeping. A voice was coming from somewhere offscreen, addressing the crowd in a powerful, preacherlike voice. The camera continued to move, as if searching for the source of that voice, until it stopped on an old bus with a sign on the side that read "Danny Mackay Brings Jesus." A young man was standing on the dented hood of the bus, his arms outspread, calling his "brothers and sisters in Christ to join me in prayer for our beloved president."

Philippa saw how the crowd turned toward him, their faces bewildered and hopeful, like children waiting to be led. When he spoke, she felt the power of his spirit come through the television set. "I do not know what is going on inside that there building, my brothers and sisters," the young preacher cried. "We have to lift our voices up to God and let Him know that we don't want Him to take John Fitzgerald Kennedy to His bosom today. We know who the world's going to blame for what happened here today!" Danny Mackay shouted. "They're going to blame Texas! But Texas didn't shoot our beloved president. The devil did it!"

As some of the guests left the salon, a few slumped into chairs in shock, or, like Hannah, began to cry softly. Philippa continued to listen to the compelling voice of the young tent preacher.

He had a beautiful voice. It commanded. It persuaded. Just as he himself was beautiful and commanding. Tears streamed down his handsome face while he called upon the world to "show the Lord how much we love that man lying in this here hospital." Philippa began to feel his strength reach out and seize her. Danny Mackay said, "Let us offer ourselves up in the place of our fallen president," and the crowd shouted, "Amen." Philippa felt herself begin to tremble. Danny said, "Let us promise to return to the path of righteousness—for John Kennedy's sake!" and her eyes filled with tears. Danny stood with the sun behind him, his arms outstretched, his slender body shuddering with passion and magnetism, and he cried, "Make peace with the Lord right here and now, my brothers and sisters! Whatever is evil or dark or without love dwelling in your hearts—cast it out in the name of our beloved president!" He spoke to a crowd, but Philippa heard him speaking directly to her. "Promise the Lord right here and now," he said, "that you will cleanse your souls and embrace love and forgiveness and that you will walk a new path from this moment forward."

The prayer continued, coming spontaneously from an ambitious young man who just happened to be in the right place at the right time in history. While young Danny Mackay on his dented old bus was laying the foundation for his eventual rise to fame and wealth, Philippa no longer listened. He had touched her. He had opened up one of those dark places and shed light into it. And she suddenly saw what she had to do.

She must find her father. She must make peace with Johnny Singleton.

"Johnny Singleton," she said into the phone for the third time, impatiently. Since dialing the number, Philippa had been transferred twice, and now this person was no more help than the first two had been. "He's an inmate," she repeated. "I'm his daughter."

"I'm sorry, miss," the young man at the other end said. "But we don't have a Johnny Singleton here. What was the date of his incarceration?"

She could give him the year, but not the month or date. As she was put on hold for a third time, Philippa began to wonder if Johnny had been released. After all, it had been nine years since she had called San Quentin prison from Fisherman's Wharf.

Finally, the man came back on. "Who did you say you were?"

Philippa's heart jumped; his tone alarmed her. "I'm his daughter. Why?"

"If you're a close family member, miss, you would have been informed."

"Informed? Informed of what?"

A pause, and then, "Just—informed."

"I don't understand. Was he released?"

"I'm sorry, miss, but I'm afraid we can't give out any information without verification of ID. If you will contact us by mail, with a request in writing—"

"Please tell me where he is!"

But she got no further. When she hung up, she had a dark, sick feeling.

"Craziest thing about Kennedy's assassination," the private investigator said as he scribbled on the pad in front of him. His belly was so large that he had to stretch his arms straight out in order to reach his desk top. There was a faded green stain on his tie, and Philippa wondered how long it had been there. "It's made people suddenly want to look up old friends, old flames," he said. "To apologize, I guess, to make amends, set things right. His death made people see how quickly we can go—just like that." He snapped his fingers. "If Kennedy can die so suddenly, then what does that say for us mortals? My phone's been ringing off the hook for a week, folks looking for folks." He paused and gave her a leering look that she didn't like. She had found Mr. Dixon in the yellow pages. "So, you're lookin' for your daddy, are you? Awright, let me tell you what it's going to run you."

Philippa watched as Dixon jotted down some figures and dollar signs. After her futile conversation with the prison officials, Philippa had tried to think of where to turn, how to find Johnny. She was fighting a nameless fear growing inside her—that Johnny hadn't been released, that he had left San Quentin by another route. That he was dead.

"What was he in for?" Dixon had asked her at the beginning of the interview.

"I don't know," she had said. "Is that important?"

"It might be. After all, San Quentin is maximum security—death row, gas chamber. If the officials were as close mouthed as you say . . ." He had shrugged significantly, leaving the implication hanging in the air.

"I could write to the prison authorities," Dixon said now, stubbing out his cigar and releasing a loud belch that briefly wafted past Philippa with hints of onion and mustard. "But that would take time—bureaucratic red tape and all. I've got a friend down at the *Times.* I'll see him first thing in the morning, go back through the archives, see what I can dig up. I should have something for you by tomorrow afternoon. Here's my fee," he said as he shoved the notepad across the desk. "That'll be up front," he added.

Dixon delivered the next day, as promised. Philippa went to his dingy office overlooking Colorado Boulevard in Pasadena, where he boasted he held an orgy every New Year's Eve so that the next morning they could watch the Rose Parade "from this very window, best view in town."

She didn't open the thick manila envelope in his presence, but instead drove to Reseda Park. Despite its being Saturday, few people sat on the grass or visited the pond. An eerie kind of withdrawal seemed to have settled over the San Fernando Valley in the eight days since Kennedy's death. Traffic on the streets seemed lighter, crowds in the stores were thinner, and now the park, which was usually full of picnickers, was strangely deserted. The swings and slides stood empty; there were no rowboats out on the pond. One elderly man was feeding the ducks, but his movements appeared desultory, as if he really saw no point in it.

Philippa chose a bench beneath a very large old tree whose roots, poking up through the grass, were themselves as thick as tree trunks. She sat for a long moment staring at the envelope Dixon had given her.

He hadn't said anything about what it contained, just, "Here," shoving the envelope at her as if he didn't want anything more to do with it.

It occurred to her that she held Johnny's life in her lap, as he had once held hers many years ago. Philippa slowly opened the envelope.

The news clippings were photocopies held together with a paper clip, in chronological order, starting with 1950. They covered a sensational murder the paper called the Nob Hill Slayings, and she saw with a start that the murders had taken place just days after Johnny had taken her to St. Bridget's.

She read the clippings one by one: about the police investigation of the slayings, the anonymous tip received by the district attorney, Johnny's subsequent arrest, his trial, the guilty verdict—how all of it had been taking place while Philippa was at St. Bridget's, waiting for her father to come for her, her days of hope slowly turning to days of fear and anger, until that first letter from Italy had arrived. When she thought now of what it must have been like for him—hunted down and caged like an animal, protesting his innocence with no one believing him, her handsome Johnny all alone and unloved . . .

Tears fell onto the pages, smearing the ink. When the wind rushed through the park, she could feel November shifting to December, first hot, now cold, as if the wind were trying to find its footing. Only five pages remained, and she was suddenly afraid to read on.

She looked at the first and read what she had known was coming but what she had not wanted to see confirmed—that Johnny had been sentenced to the gas chamber. The next page contained several small items clipped from the *Times* on different days, all chronicling the legal complexities that delayed his execution. These were from the years that she was growing up in St. Bridget's, having fun with Frizz, not knowing that Johnny was on death row, not knowing that, despite his private anguish, he had somehow managed to have those letters sent to her from various places around the world, always cheerful, always speaking of better days to come.

She turned to the first of the last three pages, which was dated just one month after the day she had run away from St. Bridget's. When she read the headline—"Johnny Singleton, Convicted Murderer in Grisly Nob Hill Slayings, Dies Tonight in Gas Chamber," she let the folder and remaining two pages slip from her lap. She couldn't bring herself to read them; she knew they would contain a detailed account of Johnny's execution. The wind swept them up and carried them away.

Philippa remained on the bench until darkness stole softly through the park, kicking up dead leaves as it went, engulfing her until she could no longer see. And then she got up mechanically and somehow found her way to her car. There was only one place she wanted to be right now. She drove off, leaving Johnny behind.

As the park lamps came on, spilling pools of light over the brittle grass and murky pond, one of the photocopied pages fluttered out over the water and settled down faceup so that, briefly, the print could be read: "Johnny Singleton received a last minute stay of execution pending investigation of new evidence that has come up in the Nob Hill Slayings." A duck swam up and, thinking he had found supper, pecked at the paper until it sank beneath the surface, the ink obliterated.

The last page of Dixon's report was carried by the wind until it slammed against a tree trunk, where it was wrapped for a moment, lamplight shining on words that read, "Real Murderer in Nob Hill Slayings Confesses; Johnny Singleton Receives Full Pardon, Is Released Today from San Quentin." And then the wind snatched it away and carried it off for good.

As Philippa rang the doorbell at 325 Avenida Hacienda, she mentally practiced how she was going to open the conversation, what she would say to get Charmie to listen to her before she slammed the door in her face. *This is important, Charmie. I need to talk to you. Please, before you send me away, hear me out!*

When she was about to ring the bell a second time the door suddenly opened and a little boy of about four or five stood there, sounds of television cartoons blaring behind him. He was skinny and funny looking, and he was clutching a sandwich; there was a great greasy smear around his mouth. "Nathan?" she said, bending over to smile at him. "Do you remember me?"

He regarded her with big eyes, then he turned and ran into the house shouting, "Mommie! There's a lady at the door! She's wearing a red dress!"

When she heard Charmie's voice call back, "I'm coming," Philippa felt a lump gather in her throat. *Please, Charmie, just hear me out. You're the only one I can talk to about Johnny. Just give me a couple of minutes and then I won't bother you again. I'm just so sad . . .*

The door opened wider and Charmie, wiping her flour-dusted hands on a towel, her cheeks bright from the oven, said, "Yes?"

But before Philippa could say anything, Charmie cried, "Choppie!" and engulfed Philippa in an embrace that smelled of cinnamon and gingerbread. "My God, it's you! Oh Philippa . . ."

"Charmie, I'm so sorry—"

"Shut up. It was my fault. I was just so confused. You were only trying to help me. I'm *so* glad you're here."

"Johnny's dead, Charmie. My father. He was *executed.*"

"Oh, Philippa," Charmie said as she put an arm around her shoulders and led Philippa over to the couch.

"Why does life sometimes seem so hard?" Philippa said.

"Tell me about your father."

"I was stubborn, and I guess in a way I wanted to punish him for abandoning me at St. Bridget's, for not telling me I was adopted. But look where that stubbornness got me. I suppose a part of me kept thinking that I would see him again someday. But time ran out and I lost my chance."

"Don't blame yourself. You didn't know."

They talked about Johnny for a while, then about the past, recalling that last night in Mother Superior's office when they had read their files.

They sat surrounded by warm baking smells in Charmie's messy living room, while Porky Pig and Daffy Duck cartoons made Nathan laugh on the other side of the thin wall. Gradually Philippa and Charmie inched their way into the deeper waters of what had happened between them two years earlier.

"I'm really sorry about the way I treated you," Charmie said. "I know you were trying to be my friend. But things are better now, honestly they are. Ron isn't drinking as much these days. He hardly hits me anymore. We're okay. We're going to make it."

"Can you come back to Starlite, Charmie? I meant it when I said we need you. I'm having problems that only you can fix."

"You know, I've been tempted many times to go into one of those salons. I have a friend who joined a year ago. She couldn't stop talking about her damned group. She lost fifty pounds and learned how to dress well. I envied her. And you and Hannah. Sure, I'll come back. I'd love to. But only when Ron is away."

The cartoons ended and the little boy came running in. When he said, "Are you my Auntie Philippa?" she ruffled the orange hair on his head and said softly, "Charmie, I've decided to look for my real family. I want to find out who my parents were. Maybe I have brothers or sisters. It's something I should have done long ago."

29

The private phone rang, interrupting an important meeting. The call was taken in a secluded office, out of the hearing of others.

"Philippa has reservations at the Marriott in Palm Springs," came the report. "She's on her way there right now."

"I see. Then we're almost out of time." An exotic red and green parrot with a bright yellow face skittered on its perch and let out a piercing squawk. When the bird was silenced: "Were you able to make the arrangements?"

"Don't worry, the special arrangements have been made. Everything is in place."

"Did you get the gun?"

"Yes."

"Good, I'm on my way."

....★

30

"I'll *kill* you!" Carole screamed as she ran after Larry.

The fight drew the attention of several onlookers trudging through the snow on their way to the ski lift. One of them, a gossip columnist who was at Star's for the Christmas holiday, made a mental note that Larry Wolfe, the Academy Award–winning screenwriter, seemed to be having a secret hideaway fling with Carole Page, a still-beautiful over-forty actress whose career was rumored to be in trouble.

Carole stopped chasing Larry long enough to bend down, scoop up some snow, and form it into a ball. She was out of breath from laughing. Larry had started the snowball fight. Carole had been taking a walk away from the main buildings of Star's, where snowplows regularly kept the grounds and pathways clear, and was heading toward the pine forest when a well-aimed snowball had hit her squarely between the shoulders. Let it be Larry, she had thought, and upon turning, and seeing that it was indeed the man she was hoping to seduce into seducing her, she had taken off after him in mock anger.

She was wearing an ankle-length Canadian lynx coat and a white sable cossack hat—what she thought of as her Julie Christie in *Dr. Zhivago* effect. She was aware that the style had gone out with the sixties, but on her she knew that it still worked, complementing her ash-blond hair and blue eyes. And when she saw how Larry's eyes moved up and down her body, she knew her seduction plan was working.

She compacted the snow in her hands, leaned back, and let it fly. Larry ducked and ran after her, plodding through the snow, laughing, trying to catch his breath in the thin mountain atmosphere. Carole turned and tried to run, but she didn't try too hard. He grabbed her and they fell breathlessly into the snow. As they struggled, they laughed, Larry pinning Carole's hands over her head. Then he was suddenly serious.

"Let me come to your room tonight," he said.

Carole felt her heart do something funny in her chest. "No—"

"Yes," he said, and then he was fully on top of her, heedless of the stragglers on their way to the ski lift who tried not to gawk at the famous personalities cavorting in the snow.

"People are watching us!" she said.

"I don't care. Tell me I can come to your room tonight." Larry couldn't remember when he had been this sexually excited. Last night, when they had had dinner together while Andrea was off reading Marion Star's diary, he had thought Carole was interested. But then he had walked her back to her bungalow and suggested he come in for a nightcap, and she had left him standing out there in the snow, making it quite clear that the only man she was interested in, in *that* way, was her husband.

"Let me come to your bungalow," he said as he held her down in the snow, wishing he could do it to her right here and now. "I'll be discreet, I promise. No one will know."

He felt her start to relent, her body softening beneath his. The necklace of big pinkish pearls she always wore had fallen back and was lying at her throat, nestled in the collar of her white angora sweater. Why hadn't he noticed her before now? he wondered, feeling his arousal becoming intense. And then he knew: it was because he assumed she played around and was therefore available to anybody.

"Please," she said, pushing him away and sitting up and brushing off the snow. "I didn't come here to cheat on my husband. I told you last night that I always go away for a rest when I finish a picture, so I'm here for a rest, that's all."

Larry sat back, his mirrored Ray-Bans reflecting the whiteness of the snow. With the mountain wind stirring his thick black hair, and his square jaw framing a disarming smile, and the fur on the hood of his Alaskan parka sparkling with snowflakes, he looked, Carole thought, like a dashing Arctic explorer. She had felt his strength as they had briefly wrestled; she could imagine the muscled body that was hidden beneath the fur, and she understood why he had so many conquests to his credit. But he didn't turn her on. He wasn't Sanford, her sexual dynamo, her virile husband who made marathons of their lovemaking sessions. Carole knew that there was no way any man could compare to Sanford, not even sexy Larry Wolfe. Which was what made her situation so ironic: that she was here to force herself into having sex with a man whom she knew wouldn't be as good as her husband, in order to keep her husband. God, it almost gave her a headache.

"Are you sure you don't want me to come to your room?" he said. "I'll give you pleasure like you've never known."

"Please," she said again, with a show of less conviction. She didn't want to discourage him totally. "I just can't."

He stood up suddenly, showering snow on her, and said, "Well then I'm for a swim. The pool's heated. Care to join me?"

She shook her head, and he strode away.

As she watched him disappear into the pine trees, Carole smiled to herself. She almost had him hooked. Now all she had to do was reel him in, and the Marion Star role was hers.

"My coming-out party, so to speak," Andrea read in Marion's diary, "was held at Eden, Dexter's ranch out in the Valley. It was an unbelievable affair; all of Hollywood royalty attended—Cecil B. deMille, Gloria Swanson, the Douglas Fairbankses, Chaplin. Dexter spared no expense: when we sat down to dine, the women found alongside their place settings bottles of perfume made from flowers grown at the ranch. When the guests unfolded their napkins, they discovered hundred-dollar bills in them. A valet brought around a tray of expensive jewelry and perfumes for the ladies' perusal, and after dinner they rolled dice to determine in which order they could choose from the tray. Sly Dexter had slipped an uncut emerald among the jewelry and was amused to see that none of the ladies chose it.

"This was the night he introduced me as Marion Star. Dexter had spent two years creating me. The image was important, he said. Harlow had her platinum hair, Clara Bow's was red—she even had her two chow dogs dyed to match it—so he decided that I should be dark. He wanted me to smoulder. The idea was to make men think they would go up in flames if they were to make love to me.

"It was on this night that Dexter also announced that he was going to star me in his next picture, *Her Wicked Ways*. This came as much of a surprise to me as it did to the gathered company. I cried to realize that one of my two dreams was about to come true.

"As for my second dream, to have the great Dexter Bryant Ramsey make love to me . . .

"Since my image now was one of a licentious sexpot with a voracious appetite, even though I was only nineteen years old, Dexter insisted that I start going out with as many men as I could. I was not allowed to have a steady lover; it was important that the public think I was the character I was soon to play in *Wicked Ways*—in other words, a woman who needs many men to satisfy her sexual hunger. I hated this, but I trusted Ramsey. He was my father's age, very handsome and distinguished, and so I did whatever he told me to do. Which included going to bed with men I didn't care for. Some I even hated. It also included undergoing three abortions by a surgeon who was in Ramsey's debt.

"Dexter had buried my Fresno past and told the world that I was the only child of rich British tea plantation owners in Ceylon. I had run away, he told the gossip columnists, because I was being forced to marry an old maharaja. Whether anyone believed this or not, it didn't matter. My sexual escapades became daily material for the movie magazines. The public devoured it. What I could never understand was how Dexter was able to let me go off with strange men. Not only let me, he orchestrated many of my 'dates.' For two years, he had been my mentor, my protector, my friend, my idol—even my father, in a way. And now that he should not only allow me, but push me to go with these men, frightened me in a way. But whenever I cried or told him that I felt bad about it all, he would hold me and comfort me and tell me that it was all for my career, and that someday I was going to be the biggest star in Hollywood.

"When my movie, *Her Wicked Ways,* came out, it damn near caused a riot. The year was 1925, the film was silent, but they didn't need sound to know what I was up to on that screen. I followed it immediately with *Scheherazade,* playing opposite Valentino, the sexiest screen lover of the day, and together we set the world on fire. One half of the population condemned us, the other half wanted to be like us. Women wanted to be me, men wanted to go to bed with me. Within four months of the release of *Scheherazade,* the studio reported that I was receiving more fan mail per week than Mary Pickford.

"It had been nearly three years since my rescue from the block of ice by Dexter Bryant Ramsey; I was now *the* biggest female star in Hollywood; I could have anything I wanted. But all I wanted was Dex. But he, strangely, did not seem to want me."

Until eight months ago, Larry Wolfe had thought that there was one major turn-on in life: winning an Oscar. But now that he had the coveted statuette, he decided that the real turn-on was getting a woman who didn't want him. As he swam vigorous laps in the private heated pool in the walled garden of the bungalow he shared with Andrea, without swim trunks and therefore finding the sensation arousing, he thought about Carole Page and their romp in the snow earlier. Once again, she had made it clear that she wasn't interested in getting it on with him. It only excited him all the more.

Completing his final lap, he pulled himself out of the pool and realized that he had an erection. No surprise, considering he had been thinking about the elusive Carole Page. How was he going to get her into his bed?

The three bungalows at Star's had been designed for ultimate privacy.

Each had two large bedrooms on either side of a living room, where there was a wet bar, kitchenette, and fireplace. The pool, though small, was heated and enclosed within high walls. Snow frosted the tops of those walls, and stars splashed the black sky overhead, while the mountain air cut like glass. But Larry, although nude, was warm enough because of the outdoor heating lamps and the steam rising from the lime-green pool. As he reached for his towel, he saw movement through the sliding glass doors that led into the living room. A maid was inside, cleaning up what was left of the lobster dinner that room service had delivered earlier.

Larry thought she was decent looking and would no doubt be transfixed if he should even say a word to her. One quick crook of his finger and she would be in his bed, willing and ready. A total turn-off. Larry could spot them miles away, women ready for him. Even poor Andrea, he thought as he wrapped the towel around his narrow waist. He knew she had been in love with him for seventeen years. He saw that puppy look in her eyes all too often. But she didn't stand a chance. Not with him, or with anyone. In the movie industry, even if you were behind the scenes, looks meant a lot. And Larry often thought that Andrea must have been standing behind a door when *those* had been handed out.

As he pulled the sliding-glass door open, and then closed it behind himself as he stepped inside, the young maid glanced at him, turned bright red, and nearly dropped her tray. Larry gave her a suffering smile and gestured toward the door, indicating that she should leave as quickly as possible. Which she did. Then he went into the bathroom off his spacious bedroom and got onto the electronic stair-climber.

Through the open doorway to the living room, he could see Andrea's books scattered on the large glass-topped coffee table: *The Dexter Bryant Ramsey Murder; Marion Star: Hollywood Tragedy;* and *The Orgy Age.* He had to hand it to her—she was diligent when it came to researching a story. He vaguely wondered what she was finding out in the diary he had paid an astronomical sum for. It had better be dynamite; Mr. Yamato was flying all the way from Tokyo with his checkbook because of it.

Larry couldn't believe his luck. Shortly after the Academy Award ceremony, Andrea had mentioned to him that she had read about this Japanese businessman who had a thing for Marion Star—he collected all her movies and had hundreds of photographs of her around his house. Coincidentally, a diary had been found at Star's Haven, and the owner, Beverly Burgess, was putting it up for auction. "I think we should bid for it," Andrea had said, "and then let Mr. Yamato know that we're going to do the movie. I'll bet you he would be eager to finance it." That was when Larry had gotten the idea of producing the film as well as writing it.

And why not? he thought now as he pumped away on the stair-climber, feeling his buttocks and calves tighten and power surge through his body.

Just as he had once thought any schmuck could write a screenplay, the same seemed to be true of producing. Once again, poor Andrea had come through, and she didn't even know it. But Larry's conscience wasn't troubled. He figured that the world was divided into two camps, the givers and the takers. Andrea was definitely a giver, which in her case was the same thing as a loser.

As the sweat began to pour off his body and he felt his heart start to pound, Larry dismissed all thoughts of Yamato and Marion Star. His body was calling to him now with visions of Carole Page. What he was most in the mood for now was sex. With one specific woman. And he had to figure out how he was going to get her.

Outside, on the dimly lit path that was becoming littered with snow, Andrea picked her way carefully to the bungalow. She entered on her own side, coming in through the bedroom. Putting her things down and shrugging out of her coat, she went into the living room, where a fire roared in the flagstone fireplace. She listened for Larry and recognized the familiar sound of a workout on the stair-climber. She walked quietly to the open door and watched him unobserved.

This wasn't the first time she had seen his body. Many times they worked on the beach in Malibu, with Larry swimming and sunbathing while Andrea, all wrapped up, typed away on a manual machine. And she was reminded again of how stupidly in love with him she had been, so blinded by lust.

She was momentarily taken back to a magical summer eleven years ago, when she and Larry had been on location in New Mexico for the shooting of their latest screenplay. The director, Andrea recalled, had been very fussy and high-strung, demanding last-minute rewrites, so that Andrea had spent most of her time in a steaming trailer, perspiring over a type-writer. It would have been a dismal memory if it hadn't been for the director's assistant, a young man with a prematurely receding hairline, thickly lensed glasses, and a nonstop sense of humor. Santa Fe's answer to Woody Allen. His name was Chad McCormick.

As Andrea remembered it, Larry had gotten involved with one of the extras, a starlet who had spoken three lines badly; the two had spent the whole time taking junkets to Chaca Canyon, Albuquerque, and even down to Yuma, buying Indian pottery, eating chili and tacos, and making love while Andrea toughed out the script changes. She had been about to call it quits when Chad McCormick had come knocking at her door.

Chad had not been Hollywood, he had not even been "industry," which impressed Andrea. To be an aspiring director in a shark-infested town meant one had to join the sharks. But Chad was a gentle man, soft-spoken, considerate, and most amazing of all, honest. After their first margarita together in the cantina, they spent many nights under the southwestern moon, talking about whatever came into their heads. The first time Chad kissed her, when Andrea was thirty-one years old, she had thought the entire desert had thundered with the sound of skyrockets.

It had also been the first time in six years that she might have asked, Larry who?

And one night, after a lot of kissing but nothing more, Chad confessed that he loved her and that he wanted to marry her.

When shooting was done, Andrea and Chad returned to Los Angeles by way of the Grand Canyon, where they spent five nights in the Yavapai Lodge, making love beneath Indian blankets, Andrea not confessing to Chad that he was in fact taking her virginity. She recalled floating home from there, her head swimming with such girlish games as thinking of how her new name was going to sound—Andrea McCormick—and what they were going to name their children. But the dream was squashed when she came home to a moody, silent Larry who sulked for a week before telling her what was wrong.

"You're breaking up our team," he had said.

And although Andrea had reassured him that they would still work together after she and Chad were married, Larry's petulance deepened until she heard the unspoken ultimatum: get married and we're quits.

Unfortunately, her addiction to Larry had been greater than her need for Chad. They parted eventually, and Larry was restored to his cheerful self.

But he wasn't going to be cheerful for much longer, she thought now, turning away from the Michaelangelo David on the stair-climber. Not after what he did to her eight months ago.

It had happened the night of the Academy Awards. Larry had been nominated for Best Original Screenplay; they were up against some pretty stiff competition, but they thought they stood a good chance of winning. Somewhere during their seventeen years together, Andrea had sacrificed her identity because of blind Larry worship. His was the only name that went onto screen credits, so that the Oscar nomination was solely for Larry Wolfe. But Andrea didn't mind; his win was her win. Besides, he said he was going to tell the world in his acceptance speech how he couldn't have done it without Andrea Bachman. She had fantasized that he might even call her up to join him on the stage. Had anyone ever done that at the Oscars, she wondered, as they had sat in their second-row seats at the Shrine Auditorium, right behind Kevin Costner and Jeremy Irons. Andrea had boldly reached for Larry's hand and given it a squeeze. Their seventeen-year road had brought them to this place. If they won . . . If they won . . .

And Larry won. His name was read out and the audience clapped and the theme from the winning movie was played as he went up on the stage to accept the Oscar. And no one was clapping harder than Andrea; she even had tears in her eyes. And then he gave his acceptance speech.

And thanked everyone in the world.

Except her.

Andrea had sat there stunned. Larry had even thanked the barber who cut his hair—and the audience had laughed at that—then he had held his statuette high and marched off triumphant with the curvaceous young star who had given him the award.

And Andrea had sat there.

He had not mentioned her.

He had not even mentioned her.

And that was the moment her eyes had suddenly been opened.

It was also the moment when she realized she was no longer in love with Larry Wolfe. Nor had been, really, for some time.

And that was when she had begun to form a plan to get revenge.

In a big way.

31

San Fernando Valley, California, 1966

Charmie had only gone twenty feet into the freezing arctic of Cut-Cost Drugstore when she saw him. A man with a cart full of Laura Scudder's Potato Chips, party-size bags. He must have had a dozen of them, and a six-pack of diet Tab. But it wasn't his nutritional eccentricity that got her attention, it was the man himself. He was so . . . *man.*

She must have been staring because he gave her an embarrassed smile and said, "For my kid's birthday party," pointing to the monster bags of chips.

Charmie murmured, "Congratulations," as he walked by, and in less than a second a whole bunch of pleasant observations registered: that he was tall, broad, large, strong, and stunningly male. And young, maybe her own age, twenty-nine or so. Like an idiot she stood watching him push the cart toward the checkout, vaguely trying to calculate how many kids it took to eat ten pounds of potato chips, and then she caught herself, reminding herself that, yes, he was an eyeful, but he clearly had a family, and *she* was a married woman. *And* pregnant.

Which reminded her of her mission here at Cut-Cost, where the air-conditioning was kept at the approximate temperature necessary to freeze mercury. As she made her way through Feminine Hygiene and Foot Care, Charmie hoped there wasn't going to be a wait at the pharmacy; maybe if she got her pills and paid in a hurry, she could get back in time to catch one last glimpse of Mr. Hunk before he walked out of her life forever.

She was in luck. The only pharmacy customers were two adolescent boys who were taking turns pushing each other toward the window, whispering, "*I* ain't gonna buy 'em, *you* buy 'em." Charmie got her prescription filled and had to resist the impulse, when paying for it, to say, "And a packet of condoms for my friends here."

When she left the store, summer's blast furnace of heat hit her like a wall. She felt her body suddenly expand with the heat, the way it had suddenly contracted with the cold when she had gone into the drugstore. She paused to dig around for her sunglasses in the oversize purse she carried.

The bag, made of canvas, had been custom-made to match her tailored caftan. No more muumuus for Charmie; she now wore fashions that came from Hannah's nimble needle. After all, she was something of an executive these days, making top dollar as Starlite's cosmetics consultant; it was important that she dress the part. The caftan was made of imported Egyptian cotton dyed a luscious boysenberry, with honey-colored trim around the square neck and voluminous sleeves. The matching scarf that bound up her flyaway blond hair was meant to suggest the currently popular gypsy look, and the long earrings made of gold beads and some sort of giant seedpods threw in an added ethnic flair, so that the resulting look was a marriage between Africa and Carnaby Street. The outfit could have commanded a fat price tag in one of L.A.'s better stores, but Hannah limited her creativity to clothing friends and relatives. She didn't have enough time, she told everyone, to try to do serious fashion design; her three babies, and another on the way, saw to that.

As Charmie slipped the large sunglasses onto her nose, she gazed across the street at the new Starlite offices. The company was growing so rapidly that this was the fourth move in three years. Already, after just a few months in the building that had been designed, for some mysterious reason, to look like a Swiss chalet, Philippa was saying they were crowded again.

Charmie had to fight the temptation to go across and tell her friends the good news—pregnant, after seven years! It was such a heavenly surprise! But she couldn't risk it. Although Charmie had been careful to work at Starlite only when Ron was gone on trips farther away than Santa Barbara, and never worked the day after he left or the day before he was scheduled to return, still, the risk was always there. She had managed to keep the peace in her marriage so far, with only a few flare-ups now and then, like the time he was sober long enough to notice all the expensive clothes in her closet and he had beaten her up until she had confessed that she had bought them at a warehouse fire sale for real cheap and that it wouldn't happen again. Ron had thrown the clothes out and Charmie had limped for a month, but she was thankful that he hadn't found the hidden bank book for the secret account into which she deposited all of her earnings from Starlite. That money was for little Nathan, for college. However, despite such incidents, there had been enough harmony between them that they had actually spent some nice times together at the beach, at Disneyland, and up in the mountains, like a normal family. And also, of course, to get a new baby started. So, despite the good news she was practically bursting with, Charmie decided to wait just another few days, at which time Ron would be heading off to Fresno, where he would be for the next three weeks.

As she searched the parking lot, trying to remember where she had parked her car, Charmie wondered if Philippa had had any luck in finding a new private investigator. In the three years she had been searching for her real parents, Philippa had had bad luck with detectives. "Defectives," Charmie called them, men who all seemed to have dropped out of the same mold. They took her money, made a lot of promises, and in the end said, "No can do," and kept the money. Charmie wondered if they had even tried to find Philippa's family. It *was* a challenging case, she knew; Philippa had so little information to go on: born in Hollywood, 1938. Exact location, unknown. Mother's name, also unknown. Still, for the money she had paid out, something should have cropped up. But the last time Charmie and Philippa had talked, a month ago, Philippa had said she was going to dismiss the latest loser and look for someone new. Charmie wondered if she had found one, but she couldn't risk even a phone call to Philippa. As far as Ron knew, his wife hadn't had any communications with Starlite or her old friends in three years.

As she walked across the baking asphalt, feeling her leather sandals stick a little with each step, Charmie did not at first see the man sitting in the blue Mustang convertible, top down, his forehead beaded with sweat as he devoured potato chips. She was only three parked cars away when she realized that it was *him*, from the drugstore; she smiled, and he smiled back, shamefaced, and then he said something that she didn't catch.

"I beg your pardon?" she said, coming up to him and seeing that the passenger seat of the Mustang was packed with the monster potato chip bags. "I didn't hear what you said."

"I said, I guess you found out my secret."

Charmie saw a scattering of crumbs down the front of his tight T-shirt, where bulging pectorals beckoned promisingly. Her fingers itched to reach over and just brush those crumbs off. "What secret is that?"

He held up the bag and smiled sheepishly. "I don't really have any kids. I got these for myself."

"What's wrong with that? So you enjoy potato chips."

"Well, I have a problem. Compulsive eating, I guess they call it."

He wore his hair in a crisp military crew cut that emphasized the football-player-ness of his neck and shoulders. He looked air force, Charmie thought. Or maybe a body builder. From what she had seen in the drugstore and what she could see here—good God, the way the jeans stretched over his thighs!—he looked like he was in excellent shape. "You don't look like a compulsive eater," she said.

"Yeah, well, I work it off, I guess." Dimples appeared in his cheeks when he smiled. Charmie wanted to stand there forever, but, realizing that they had pretty much exhausted the potato chip subject, she said, "Well, good luck," and started to walk away.

"I try to diet," he said, "but nothing ever works. Diets are so boring, you know?"

Charmie suddenly thought, Uh oh. He had given her an opening, and now came the tricky part. She always carried Starlite booklets with her, ready to hand out should anyone express interest; the booklets listed the main office phone numbers, plus the addresses of the forty-eight salon locations throughout California. The only problem was, whenever she explained that she worked for the company, there was always that little flicker in the eyes that said, *You?* Charmie was the first to admit that she wasn't exactly a walking advertisement for the Starlite diet; in the six years since she had shown up on Philippa's doorstep when that little meeting was going on in her living room, Charmie had shed not a single ounce. But she usually rode it out with aplomb; let them think what they want, Starlite's program spoke for itself.

But now the thought that such a look might flicker in this man's eyes filled her with such dread that she almost didn't produce one of the booklets. But she didn't want to walk away just yet either, and there was nothing more to say to keep her there hanging around his Mustang as if she were sixteen instead of twenty-nine and married, the mother of one and, soon, two. But then he wasn't exactly giving her the brush-off. After all, she had been about to walk away when he had picked up the conversational thread. Doing a quick wedding-band scan of his hands and not finding any ring, she said, "Maybe this is what you're looking for," and she dug into her big bag and brought out a booklet. They were over fifty pages long now and came with glossy covers.

"Yeah, Starlite," he said, taking it from her. She saw how big his knuckles were; his fingernails were trimmed and clean. Definitely military. "I've heard of it."

"Oh? Does your"—she couldn't believe she was saying this—"wife belong?"

He laughed. "I'm not married. So you think this will help? I need to lose about twenty pounds."

Where from, your toes? "It will definitely help." She braced herself. "I guarantee it."

But when he looked from the booklet back to her, Charmie didn't see the usual *Oh yeah? Then why aren't you thin?* in his eyes. Instead those dimples deepened with an ingenuous smile as he said, "I might give it a try. What do I have to do?"

"Well, right now the salons are only for women, but we're starting to form men's groups in gyms. Victor's on Sherman Way, for example—"

"I'm familiar with it."

Her eyes flickered to his biceps. *Wow.* "They have Saturday groups. That's to make it convenient for men who work Monday through Friday." God, was she really sounding this obvious? Just come right out and ask the guy for a minute by minute rundown of his life.

He shrugged those Atlas shoulders. "Doesn't make any difference to me, I'm self-employed. I make my own hours."

"Oh?" *Doing what, training marines all day and wrestling Dobermans in your spare time?*

He gave that little laugh again that didn't go with such a large guy. "I'm a private investigator."

She nearly dropped her purse. "You're a *what?*"

"Please," he held up a defensive hand. "I'm no Peter Gunn. Whenever I tell people what I do, they get these crazy visions—"

"No, wait," she said. "I have a friend who's looking for a private detective. I mean, do you search for missing people and all that?"

"It's a big part of my business. Who's your friend looking for?"

"She was adopted, and she wants to find her real parents. But there are no records that she knows of."

"Can be a challenge," he said. "But I like challenges. I'll be glad to talk to her if you like."

Charmie couldn't believe this. There was Philippa, sitting in her office across the street, discouraged because the men she had so far found in the yellow pages had turned out to be less than honest and a bit slippery, and here, out of the blue, was a guy who not only wasn't seedy or sleazy, but had a John Glenn haircut and a GI Joe build. All-American and squeaky clean. Surely Philippa could trust *this* one.

"If you have a minute," Charmie heard herself saying. "She's right over there, in that Swiss-looking building."

"Sure," he said. "I didn't have any plans for the next hour except to eat these potato chips. Why don't I follow you over there? Which car is yours?"

And two minutes later she was driving out of the Cut-Cost parking lot, right across Ventura Boulevard and into the Starlite parking lot, without for a second remembering that Ron was at home, watching wrestling and baby-sitting Nathan.

★ ★ ★

There was a big fight going on at Starlite.

"Damn it, Alan," Philippa said as she walked into his office and threw a memo down onto his desk. "I asked you not to bring this up again. I will *not* hire outside people to work as Starlite counselors, and that's all there is to it."

He scowled at the memo. This was the third time in the past year she had discarded his idea, and he wasn't going to give up. "I'm telling you, Philippa, you're missing a great opportunity to raise profits. With trained therapists, women who have college degrees for God's sake, we can charge three or four times as much for membership as we do now."

"Alan," she said evenly, "my counselors have to go through the program. They have to know what it's like to be overweight and struggle to lose it. My members will not want to tell their troubles to some skinny person they feel can't possibly understand."

"Therapists are trained to understand!" he shouted back.

"I agree with Alan," said Hannah, who was sitting in the corner of his cluttered office, sorting through bolts of fabric. Although Hannah had an office of her own, where she wrote her weekly fashion tip, she liked to work in Alan's office whenever she could. "I think it's a good idea to hire professionals. Profits would go through the roof."

"Oh, Hannah," Philippa said in exasperation. "Have you forgotten your persecution so soon? Remember Ardeth Faulkner who'd been thin all her life and who said, 'Why don't you just go on a diet?' Remember how we didn't like talking to Dr. Hehr's skinny nurse? If we hired people who had never been through what we've been through, membership would *drop*, it wouldn't go up. Don't you see that?"

"Listen, Philippa," Alan said, getting up and coming around his desk. He had started wearing lifts in his shoes, so that now he was taller than his wife. But he wasn't taller than Philippa. "When you invited me to take over Starlite's accounting division, you also said you would welcome any financial advice I had to offer. I'm telling you, this is a wise move."

"Well we're not doing it. Not only for the sake of the members, but also for the sake of the counselors. Many of the women we employ would not otherwise be able to find jobs. And one of the important things they have to offer is their sympathy, because they were once fat like the rest of us, and that's something you can't get through a college course. Are *you* willing to tell the nearly four hundred counselors we currently employ that they're no longer wanted?"

Alan backed down. Again.

Philippa marched out of his office, nearly knocking Molly, her secretary, out of the way. It galled her how blithely, for the sake of profits, Alan was willing to forget the main purpose of Starlite, its origins, how it had started. And Hannah! If Alan said the sky was green, she'd agree with him!

"Are you all right, Miss Roberts?"

She forced herself to calm down. "Yes, I'm fine, Molly. Is that today's mail? Let's go through it as quickly as we can. I have an appointment this afternoon."

Molly cast a puzzled look at her employer before hurrying into the office. She had never known her boss to be so irritable. Everyone had heard the argument between Philippa and Mr. Scadudo—so unlike Miss Roberts. Molly wondered what was wrong.

What was wrong, and what nobody knew, was that Philippa had a serious problem, and worrying about it was affecting her mood.

"These are all requests for Starlite to open salons in other states, Miss Roberts," the efficient young Molly said as she placed a neatly gathered pile of letters in front of Philippa. Molly had decided some time ago that she had landed a plum job. Her boss, though demanding, was generous with praise and she appreciated good work, and the offices were attractive, with comfortable furniture and air-conditioning that never fritzed. "And these," Molly said, placing another stack next to the first, "are questions regarding the diet."

Pulling herself out of her preoccupation, Philippa read a letter on the first stack: "When is Starlite coming to Orlando, Florida?" she read, and a second: "I hate to cook and I'm no good at it. Are there any frozen dinners allowed on the diet?"

As she stared at this letter, her mind went back to her own problem: for some mysterious reason, she was gaining weight.

She set the letter aside and picked up another one, which, she saw, contained a recipe for a rich carrot cake that was by no means allowable on the Starlite diet. She set it down.

Why was she gaining weight? She should in fact have lost weight over the past week because she had had a bad cold and had eaten less than she normally did, subsisting mainly on fruit juices and tea with lemon and honey. When she did her weekly check on the scales, she had expected to see a loss, not a gain.

She was just looking at her watch—she had a doctor's appointment in a few hours—when Charmie made a theatrical entrance into the office, unannounced. "Philippa!" she declared in her usual breathless way. "I've brought someone to meet you!"

"Charmie! I didn't think I'd see you until next week. What—"

"You won't believe what I've found." Charmie looked at Molly, who stiffened, then said, "If you don't need me right now, Miss Roberts," ending it like a question.

Philippa said, "Thanks, Molly, we'll pick this up later. Would you please bring Mrs. Charmer and me a couple of diet sodas?"

"Make that *three* sodas!" Charmie said, then she turned to Philippa and said, "You are not going to believe this! I was just at Cut-Cost across the street and I met this man." Throwing down her oversize bag, Charmie pulled the office door open and said, "Come on in!"

A large, well-developed young man stepped a little self-consciously into the office, seeming to fill it up with his bulk and masculinity. As Philippa said, "How do you do," he held out a beefy hand. "I'm Ivan Hendricks, private investigator."

Philippa shot a surprised look at Charmie, who smiled and said, "What did I tell you?"

They got right down to it. Mr. Hendricks brought out a notepad and pen and asked personal questions in an impersonal, professional way. He nodded and wrote as Philippa told her story, while Charmie sat sipping her soda with her eyes riveted on Hendricks as if he were a piece of cake.

"What do you think, Mr. Hendricks?" Philippa finally said when she had finished telling him everything.

"I'd like to take a look at the file you've collected," he said. "But this looks like a fairly straightforward case."

"Will you take it on?"

Charmie shifted to the edge of her seat until he said, "Sure, I'd love to." Good, she was going to see him again.

"Now, I'm not making any promises, Miss Roberts," Ivan Hendricks explained. As he went on to outline his methods of investigation and his fees, Charmie got up and paced a little. She paused at the window to look out over Ventura Boulevard where palm trees wilted and the blacktop looked as if it were going to melt into tar pits and trap the cars like dinosaurs. She was listening to Ivan Hendricks's voice, which was as strong as his physique, when she saw a familiar car slow down at the red light and then take off again as soon as it changed to green.

Ron. It had been Ron. Right out in front of Starlite.

What was he doing out on the streets?

She realized he must have been on a beer run.

Had he seen her car?

Pressing her forehead against the window, she tried to see if her Volvo was visible from the street.

It was.

"Philippa," she said suddenly. "Excuse me, Mr. Hendricks. Philippa, I just remembered an appointment." She picked up her purse. "I have to go."

★ ★ ★

Philippa kicked off her shoes and walked on the cool linoleum; it felt good beneath her burning feet. It had been a hot, hectic day, starting with Ivan Hendricks, the private investigator, and ending with her doctor's appointment. As she opened her fridge and took out the makings for a salad, she assessed the two verdicts she had received that afternoon. From Hendricks: "I don't see why I should have any problems locating your parents." From Dr. Stahl: "It's a mystery to me why you're gaining weight."

Rotating her shoulders to get the stiffness and tension out of them, she went out onto the patio where the setting sun spilled ribbons of red, orange, and yellow across her seldom-used swimming pool, and she laughed softly to herself. She decided that if she were to sum up her life in just two words, she would say, Family and fat. When, she wondered wearily, had she not been motivated by one or the other?

She heard the phone ringing inside the house and went in to answer it. It was Hannah saying that Charmie was in the hospital, in bad shape. No, Hannah didn't know what had happened. Mrs. Muncie, Charmie's baby-sitter, had come to the house and found Charmie beaten up, actually in serious condition. Ron was nowhere to be found.

A few minutes later, as Philippa nosed her new Lincoln through the thick evening traffic on Van Nuys Boulevard, she pieced together what must have happened. First, Charmie showing up when they weren't expecting her, and then, standing at the window and suddenly announcing that she had to leave, rushing out in a fluster.

Philippa parked outside the hospital, hurried inside, and was directed to Charmie's room. To her surprise, it was a private room, which Philippa knew the insurance did not cover. And she thought, Ron must already be feeling guilty for what he had done.

"God, Frizz," she said, sitting down at the bedside and trying not to cry when she saw the IVs, the bandages. "You'll do anything for attention, won't you? And here I've been planning this outrageous bash for your thirtieth birthday, complete with dancing boys and everything. Remember Jamie, the cute parking lot attendant at Monty's Steak House? He's going to pop out of a cake. You've got to be in good shape for that—" Her voice broke.

"Did they tell you?" Charmie whispered through swollen lips. "I lost the baby."

Philippa stared at her. "Baby?"

"I . . . was saving it as a surprise. I was pregnant . . . Philippa, I feel like I'm dying . . ."

Philippa leaned close and pressed her hand on her friend's arm. "You won't die. Everything's going to be all right, you'll see. You'll get through this, you have to. We need you, Charmie. Starlite needs you. The mem-

bers love you, you know that. When you give your makeup demonstrations—shit."

Charmie's eyes shifted to Philippa and her cheeks seemed to move. It
looked like an effort to smile, but it came out as a grimace. "I can't believe
you . . . you said the 'S' word."

"Don't let us down, Charmie. Please. Don't let *yourself* down."

As Charmie's eyes rested on Philippa's face, they went flat, emotionless.

"You know what low self-esteem can do to people," Philippa said
quietly. "I suffered from it myself once, remember? And do you remember
poor little Mouse, who thought she was so homely—"

Charmie raised a weak hand to silence her.

"Yes, okay, you remember Mouse. And I'm lecturing you again, giving
you my cheery Pollyanna pep talk. But I'm torn up inside, Charmie. I
don't know how to help you, how to reach you. Listen, you mustn't dwell
on the baby you lost, you have to think about the baby you *have.* Nathan,
he's seven, he knows what's going on. I know what you're thinking, that
I don't know what it's like. But I want to tell you something that I've
never told anyone. I had a baby once, Frizz, in Hollywood. I lost it when
I had a miscarriage. You once said to me that I don't know what it's like
to love a man. But I do."

Charmie's eyes remained on Philippa's face, shuttered, hiding whatever
was going on behind them, but she listened.

Philippa spoke haltingly at first about Rhys, speaking his name for the
first time in eight years. Her story flowed a little more easily after a while,
until Rhys took form and shape in that hospital room, and she could see
him standing there, all handsome and brooding and dark, smiling ironi-
cally at her as if to say, I don't mind, go ahead and use me as a bad
example.

"He thought so little of himself that he ended his life. And that's what
you're doing, Charmie. You're slowly killing yourself. One of these days,
Ron will do it for you."

Charmie just stared at her, saying nothing.

"Listen to me, okay? Just this once. And don't be Charmie listening.
Be Frizz. Let's dream together the way we once did. Let's make plans for
the future. Starlite can be so fabulous, you know that. You also know how
much Starlite needs you. Frizz, you've got ideas, you've got energy. Just
think what we could accomplish if you joined us full-time. Remember
your ambition to be in the theater? Well, Starlite is your theater. I've seen
the way you perform for the members. Get well and come and join us for
real, Frizz."

Charmie stirred beneath the white sheets. Pain rippled across her face.
She opened her mouth and Philippa saw in shock that two teeth were
missing.

"Remember?" Philippa said. "When you got into trouble for goofing off in Sister Immaculata's class?"

But Charmie didn't smile. Her cheeks didn't even quiver.

"I'm going to let you sleep now." Philippa bent and kissed Charmie on the forehead. "I'll be back tomorrow."

As she rose from the bed she heard a whisper.

"What? What did you say?"

"Don't come."

"Charmie, I'm not going to let you drive me away this time."

"Please . . . if you love me . . ." She drew in a painful breath. "Let me rest. Let me heal. I need . . . to be alone. Don't visit me here. And don't let Hannah come . . ."

"I won't leave you."

"Yes . . . you will because I'm asking you to. I have to . . . think . . ." Charmie's hand moved across the blanket and found Philippa's. She gave it a feeble squeeze, popping up the vein where the IV needle went in. "Please," she whispered. "Let me do this my way."

A distant voice said, "Visiting hours are over in ten minutes." Charmie opened her eyes and looked around. Light from a full moon was slanting through the venetian blinds of her hospital room with the brightness of morning. Her mind was foggy. She wasn't sure how long she'd been there, or how many days ago it was that Philippa had visited. When she lifted her head and looked around she saw that the room was filled with flowers and stuffed animals from her friends at Starlite. She had one sharp memory, of Ron visiting, kneeling beside her bed and sobbing, begging her to forgive him. And of herself stroking his head and saying, "Shhh," as though he were the one who needed consoling.

Charmie searched inside her body to see if the wounds had healed. She felt no pain, only deadness, as if her own life had slipped out with the unborn baby—a double miscarriage.

She thought of poor little Nathan, seven years old. He had been taken to Hannah's after Mrs. Muncie found . . .

Charmie closed her eyes. What Ron had done to her this time.

She started to cry softly. Nothing had changed after all. The evil was still in him. And this time the little boy had witnessed it; poor little Nathan, screaming the whole time Ron was doing what he did to her.

Finally her mind began to clear. She remembered that her baby was safe with Hannah now because Ron had had to go on the trip to Fresno. Charmie vowed that Nathan was never going to go back to that house on Avenida Hacienda. And neither was she.

Weak, but with IVs no longer in her veins, she got out of bed and laboriously got dressed. As she kept alert for sounds outside her door, carefully applying some makeup, another memory flashed in her mind: Ivan Hendricks, the man whom she had encountered at Cut-Cost—how many days ago? Had Philippa told her he was working on the case? Charmie couldn't remember. It didn't matter. Nothing mattered anymore.

Peering out into the hall and seeing that the nurses at the station were involved with visitors, Charmie picked up one of the vases of flowers someone had sent her, slung her purse over her arm, and walked down the hall as brashly and confidently as she could, despite her weakness, as if she were a visitor on her way to see a patient.

Valley Memorial was a busy place, being so near the freeway, where lots of accidents brought customers. There were a couple of taxicabs parked in the great circular drive out front.

When she got in and told the driver her destination, he gave her a puzzled look. "You sure? Okay, lady," he said with a shrug.

As the cab sped down Sunset Boulevard, with the lights of Hollywood flashing by, she thought, No, she was never going back to Ron, back to that dingy house. It was over. Everything was over.

The cab eventually followed a winding mountain road, passing a few cars on the way. "You sure about this, lady?" the cabbie said again, giving his passenger a dubious look in the rearview mirror. Sure, he'd brought people here before, mostly tourists, but never anyone from a hospital.

"I'm sure," she said.

And finally they were there. She saw the domed buildings up ahead, the greenish rooftops illuminated by electric lighting and also by the light of the full moon. The parking lot to the Griffith Park Observatory was full; everyone was here to see the latest show in the planetarium, *Next Stop: Mars.* A chill wind blew, but she didn't feel the cold. She didn't feel anything.

She got out of the cab, leaving the vase of flowers behind, walked across the asphalt, and slowly climbed the steps at the side of the main building, which led up to one of the rooftop telescopes. Up she went, slowly, weak from having spent so long in a hospital bed, all the way up to the top where the telescope was pointed toward the stars. She was thankful that the roof was deserted. Sometimes there were lovers up here, making out as if their lives depended on it. But, for the moment, with the show going on, she had the roof all to herself.

She stood there looking out over the city, the wind whipping her blond hair and exposing wine-colored roots. She grasped the waist-high stone wall, tensed, took a deep breath, and leaning forward to look down at the long plunge to the concrete below. She finally stood back and shouted as loud as she could: "Ron Charmer, wherever you are—*Fuck you!*"

Five minutes later she was getting back into the cab, having asked the driver to wait; forty minutes after that she was standing on Philippa's doorstep saying, "All right. Let's make Starlite sensational."

························★

32

Frieda Goldman was depressed. Depressed, frustrated, and just plain mad.

Sitting in the living room of her cabin, which looked like some millionaire's hunting lodge, she gazed morosely at the beautiful late-afternoon sun shining through the pine trees, and she thought, Snow! She hated it. She had gone for a walk that morning to give the maids a chance to clean her room, and when she had returned, she had found the windows open. It had reminded her of what Jake, her husband, who had come from the East, used to say. "Californians! In the summer they close their windows, in the winter they open them!" Jake had loved the snow. He would have loved Star's.

Frieda would have loved Star's too, if her deal with Syd Stern hadn't fallen through. How could Bunny have *done* that!

Frieda couldn't really fault the poor girl. Not after losing the Oscar and then the shoddy treatment afterward—one casting director had actually said, "Her last movie was a fluke. She won't get parts. She'd be better off joining a circus." Well, Bunny wouldn't be joining any circuses now, not with her fabulous new looks. It had taken a lot of courage, Frieda knew, to make the decision to undergo such a total change and to suffer so many surgical procedures. Liposuction alone, of the abdomen and thighs, was painful and debilitating. Poor Bunny, going through months of torture—having her back teeth pulled, even, perfectly healthy teeth, so that her cheeks would fall in—only to discover it hadn't been necessary. Not only not necessary, but all that agony and loneliness had cost her one of the plummiest deals in recent movie history. And on top of that, since Frieda's reaction to Bunny's astonishing change was to fall to the floor in a dead faint, Bunny was now eating herself up with fear of how her father was going to react: Bernie Kowalski, so big, so important, and such a shit to his daughter.

Frieda got up, went to the bar, and poured herself an orange juice with a generous splash of vodka.

What a wretched morning it had been. First, having to call Syd and tell him about Bunny's metamorphosis, and Syd saying, "Well, that's very nice, Frieda, I'm glad she's gorgeous, but I can't use her. Sorry." And then next having to call the Lamborghini dealer and cancel her order for the two-hundred-thousand-dollar Diablo. And then going to the Castle with the intention of returning the twelve-thousand-dollar mink coat.

Frieda had wimped out on that one. She was going to keep the coat.

She was also going to keep the cabin, just a day or two longer. She had in fact intended to check out that morning and get back to her office in L.A., throw herself back into the business of working deals. But, as she had walked around the magnificent entry hall that made her think of Sleeping Beauty's castle and looked at some of Marion Star's personal things and heard the Christmas music and seen the lights and felt the heat from those monstrous fireplaces—and seen her handsome tux-with-a-smile go by—Frieda had realized that there was something compelling about the place.

It was funny; Star's was both quiet and noisy at the same time. She couldn't quite figure it out; there were a lot of guests milling about, browsing in the boutiques, speculating on who killed Ramsey, or sipping hot drinks beside the fire, but the atmosphere was subdued: the quiet hustle and bustle of the genteel rich. It made her think of the one time she and Jake had stayed at the Plaza in New York. The Palm Court was like this—crowded, busy, but strangely muted. And here at Star's there was a kind of magic in the atmosphere, something vaguely seductive, so that Frieda had found herself enquiring if she could keep the cabin a little longer when she had had no intention of staying another day. So now here she was—sitting in a thirties hunting lodge with antlers over the fireplace and sheepskin rugs on the floor and real log walls that were polished smooth and shiny, a lodge that Marion Star had built for her more outdoorsy guests, and where it was said Douglas Fairbanks had once stayed—and Frieda was depressed.

It had broken her heart to see Bunny's newly beautiful face go from joy, to shock, and finally to tears as Frieda had explained the purpose of her visit. Bunny had carried on so, she had looked at one point as if she wanted to rip all that new beauty out and make herself unappealing again. Frieda had tried to console her, but what could she say? That now that Bunny looked like dozens of other young women in the movies she was no longer unique; that now she was *really* going to have a hard time getting parts, because her competition had just multiplied by thousands?

Going to the window and looking out again, Frieda wondered if she should pay Bunny a visit. But there was nothing left to say. Bunny was miserable because her surprise for Frieda hadn't panned out and because she had botched the juicy deal with Syd Stern. But also because her father was coming in two days to take her home, and she was terrified about what his reaction to her new look was going to be.

"Frieda," she had cried, "all my life I've never been able to please him, he's always looked at me with such disappointment. I thought that by being beautiful he would finally appreciate me! But what if he looks at me the same way *you* do and thinks that I look just like every other actress in Hollywood!"

Frieda hadn't known how to answer that. Because it was true; Bunny was now a Hollywood clone.

When she saw how shadows were starting to stretch over the ground as the day died, Frieda's thoughts shifted to the coming evening. What was she going to do for dinner? Call room service? The thought of eating alone in this cabin didn't appeal to her. She could try Bunny, but Bunny had insisted she wanted to be alone. There were, of course, the three dining rooms in the Castle . . .

The Castle. Where beautiful people seemed to glide beneath the sparkle of the chandeliers, and among them . . .

Good heavens. Where had *that* thought come from!

Frieda pictured him again, the young olive-skinned man in the tuxedo, and the way he had smiled at her that morning, the same way he had smiled at her twice before. When she thought of him now, recalling those big brown eyes like chocolates, she got that squirmy, high school feeling deep down inside again. It made her laugh. Fifty-three-year-old lantern-jawed, hard-nosed female agents did not delude themselves into thinking they could possibly get it on with twenty-five-year-old sinfully handsome males who looked like South America's answer to George Raft.

Unless, of course, the young man was paid to do it.

Her heart skipped a beat and suddenly she was nervous. Because suddenly she realized what she was going to do.

"I don't believe this," she murmured as she picked up the phone and dialed the main dining room, the one with the forest green carpet and deep booths and a pianist who played only Chopin and Mozart. The dining room where there were no prices on the menu.

"Hello?" she said. "This is Frieda Goldman. I'm staying in room—"

"Yes, madam," came the cultured man's voice. "I have your room number. How may I be of service to you?"

How did they do that, know a caller's room number? "I would like to make a dinner reservation for myself for tonight, eight o'clock?"

"Certainly, madam."

"But I . . . uh, have a slight problem." She couldn't believe it. She was actually going to do it. "I don't like to dine alone. I was wondering if possibly . . ."

"Certainly, madam. I will see if there is another guest who also—"

"Actually," she said, squeezing the phone so tightly that she felt her pulse throb in her fingertips. This was ridiculous. The whole thing about escorts—it wasn't true. "I didn't want to dine with another guest." She took a breath. "Oh well, never mind . . ."

"I understand, madam. The hotel can provide a dinner companion for you, if you would like."

She held her breath. My God. "Yes, okay . . . um, that would be fine."

"Would madam prefer a gentleman?"

She frowned. As opposed to what? A slob? And then she realized he was referring to gender. "A gentleman will be fine," she said, and she quickly hung up, thinking, Frieda Goldman, you *can't* be serious!

Judith Isaacs delivered herself into the warmth of the lobby where the doormen and coat-check girls greeted her with the familiarity of fellow employees, even though this was only her third evening here. As she passed the glittering sign announcing the Christmas ball, which was being held the day after tomorrow—after which Mr. Smith was leaving Star's— she saw Simon Jung beside one of the large fireplaces, deep in conversation with Robert De Niro. How long was it going to take, Judith wondered, before she got used to the sight of celebrities?

When she arrived at the clinic on the second floor, shedding her down jacket and shaking out her long braid, she overheard Zoey on the phone in the substerile room. "Yes, Miss Kowalski," the nurse was saying. "I'll be there right away. Don't worry."

Seeing Judith suddenly appear in the doorway, Zoey's smile evaporated and she hung up.

"Did anything come up while I was out?" Judith asked, feeling daggers of resentment fly from the nurse's eyes. Earlier, Judith had asked Zoey if she knew anything about the tabloid story of Mr. Smith and his secret operation. "I know gossip sheets like that pay a lot of money for sensational stories about movie stars," she had said, watching Zoey's reaction.

The nurse had gotten defensive. "What are you asking me for?"

"Because very few people in the hotel know he's here. And even fewer know what he's here for."

"The leak could have come from Dr. Newton's office," Zoey said, pushing a lock of hair out of her face.

But Judith had already thought of that and had gotten hold of Dr. Newton in Palm Springs. He had been in a rage, having just seen the tabloid himself, shouting at Judith that neither he nor his staff had leaked the story. In twenty-nine years of treating celebrities, this was the first time anything like this had happened. "It came from *your* end, Doctor," he had said, almost implying Judith's involvement, even though she hadn't been employed at Star's at the time the tabloid received the story.

The subject had been dropped, but the glacial atmosphere had worsened between Judith and her nurse. They hadn't spoken all afternoon, even while splinting a fractured ankle and wrapping it in a plaster cast. Now Zoey said, "You had a phone call," and nothing more.

Judith was suddenly alert. Had *he* called again? "Who was it?"

She shrugged. "He didn't leave his name," Zoey said, watching Judith's face.

"I'm sure whoever it was will try again," Judith said, sounding as unconcerned as she could, and she started to leave. But when she saw Zoey open the medication cupboard and remove a bottle of Valium, she said, "What are you doing with those?"

"Bunny Kowalski called. She's very upset about something. She can't sleep. She wants something to calm her down, so I'm going to take her a few of these."

"I don't recall there being any orders in her chart for Valium."

"There aren't."

Judith stared at Zoey. She noticed that the collar of her nursing uniform bore a brown iron-shaped scorch mark. "Are you telling me," she said slowly, "that you prescribe meds to patients?"

"Hell," Zoey shrugged, "it's only Valium."

"Since when have you been licensed to prescribe drugs?"

Zoey looked up at the ceiling, as if she were dealing with a three-year-old. "Dr. Isaacs," she said with a show of forced patience, "I have been handing meds out for two years. I'm really more than a nurse here, I'm more like a physician's assistant. I mean, the doctor can't always be here, can he?" She challenged Judith with a blunt stare. "I mean, *she.*"

"You are a registered nurse, Miss Larson. You dispense medication upon a physician's orders. You are not legally permitted to prescribe them."

"I told you, I've been doing it for two years. Dr. Mitgang—"

"I don't care what Dr. Mitgang did." Judith held out her hand.

Zoey's look turned volatile as she slapped the bottle into Judith's hand and stormed out.

"By the way," Judith said, and Zoey paused in the doorway. "Mr. Smith's lawyer is putting together a very good case against that tabloid. And he is going to demand a large sum in damages. I have an idea they're going to cooperate and divulge the source of their story."

Zoey remained there for a moment, and then she left.

As Judith picked up Bunny's chart and dialed the room number, Zoey had to stop in the tiny corridor outside the substerile room to collect herself.

What right had that bitch to talk to her that way? This clinic was hers; Zoey had set it up before Simon Jung had even hired a doctor, and she had run it for two years with no complaints from anyone. And no one, not even a doctor—especially a doctor from some mountain town who was running away from something—was going to tell Zoey what to do. In fact, she was going to be sorry she had tried.

Frieda entered the dining room as if it were a combat zone, looking this way and that, ready to dodge bullets. Did absolutely every single person in this room know what she was up to? The maître d' approached and said, "May I help you, madam?"

"Frieda Goldman," she said, looking around at the glittering chandeliers and intimate booths, thinking she hadn't been this nervous since her first dance at Sequoia Junior High School when she had hoped Marvin Pormorsky would ask her to dance.

The maître d' led her to a corner booth, where a young man in a tuxedo immediately stood up. Frieda couldn't believe it. It was him, from the lobby.

They engaged in small talk. His name was Raoul, he said. No last name.

"You have an accent," Frieda said, wondering what to do with her hands. It had been—how many years?—since she had had a date. After all, this was no business meal, no Let's take a meeting, no Let's do lunch. She was here for one reason only. And so was he.

"I'm from Cuba." He flashed her a very white smile. "But I'm one of the good Cubans."

God, but he was gorgeous.

Frieda was starting to feel something she hadn't felt in years. And she also thought the dining room was warmer than it needed to be. And hadn't the noise level just gone up? No, she realized. It was her. All of her senses were suddenly heightened: the lights seemed too bright, the pianist played a polonaise too loudly, and the smell of food . . .

The people in the next booth had ordered chateaubriand, which was being prepared for them table side, with three waiters serving: one to carve the pink, tender meat; another to arrange creamy mashed potatoes in an artful circle around each plate; the third stirring an aromatic sauce over a little blue flame. The waiters worked as if they had been choreographed, depositing crispy thin cheese bread and silver bowls of steaming buttered vegetables on the table with a flourish, as if their act were half the deliciousness of the banquet.

Frieda looked away. While Raoul was telling her a little of the history of Star's—"It stood unoccupied for over fifty years, completely furnished"—Frieda found herself thinking of people back at home: Sandy, her housekeeper, begrudgingly taking care of Frieda's three fussy little American Eskimo dogs; her secretary, Ethel with the adenoids, constantly sniffing as if in perpetual disapproval; Frieda's daughter, the environmentalist snob; and three-year-old Princess, the biological phenomenon of the age. And suddenly she imagined them all standing in the doorway of the dining room, staring at her and Raoul, their mouths frozen into shocked little "Ohs."

"I'm sorry," she said abruptly, reaching for her purse. "I just realized that I'm not hungry after all. I don't know what I'm doing here."

"Is there something wrong?"

"I . . . I've received some very disappointing news today, and I don't really know why I stayed on at Star's. I should have checked out and just gone home. I'm sorry to have taken up your time, but I just don't want to . . . this isn't a good . . ." She stood up. "I'll just go back to my cabin if you don't mind."

"I understand," he said, also rising. "Perhaps you would like me to walk you back? The pathways can get very icy at night, very slippery."

She stared at him. He had misread her signals.

Her astonishment grew. No, he had correctly read her signals. She just hadn't known she was sending them. "Thank you," she said. "I would appreciate an escort."

He took care of everything, explaining to the maître d' that they had changed their mind about dinner, retrieving her mink coat and helping her into it, supporting her elbow as they went down the icy steps. Frieda had forgotten what it was like to have such male attention, to be so taken care of, to be made to feel so womanly.

Raoul had put on a long black overcoat that made him look so thoroughly elegant that other women stared at him, and it gave Frieda a greedy feeling. She wanted to say, He's mine.

They walked through the cold night in silence.

When they passed Larry Wolfe, who didn't acknowledge them but seemed intent on his destination, Raoul said, "He is the famous screenwriter. I read somewhere that he is going to produce a movie about Marion Star. It should be very exciting."

Frieda murmured a vague, "Yes." She couldn't have been less interested in the Wolfe-Star project.

When they arrived at her cabin, Raoul stepped politely back as Frieda searched her purse for the key. "Thank you for the escort," she said. "I'm sure I would have gotten lost!"

"I'll wait until you are safely inside."

"God, I'm cold," she said, wondering why she had said that, and then knowing exactly why she had said it.

"These cabins have fireplaces," Raoul responded right on cue. "A good hot fire is perfect on a night like this."

"Yes," she said, bringing out her key and looking right at him, knowing what was happening. "Providing one knows how to start a fire. *I* don't."

"I would be glad to do it for you, if you like."

"Thank you," she said, noticing how big and dark his eyes were and just getting lost in them and thinking, Why not? "I would appreciate that." And she handed him the key so he could open her door.

Inside, she shed her coat and watched him build a fire. He still wore the black overcoat, as if he intended to leave as soon as the fire was going. As he worked, he kept up a light banter.

Frieda poured herself a drink and said nothing.

When he was done and flames were struggling up through the logs, Raoul stood, brushed off his hands, and said, "There. Now you'll be warm all night."

Frieda thought, *Who wrote this dialogue?*

"It's a good hot fire," he said suggestively. "It will burn all night long for you and never go out."

All night long. Where had she heard that before? "Thank you . . ."

But instead of going to the door and saying good-night, as she had expected, he just stood there, smiling, watching her with big, sexy Cuban eyes.

And then she realized: it was her move.

A couple of odd thoughts went through her mind at that moment. She thought of Jake, who had died sixteen years ago of prostate cancer. "Marry again, Frieda," he had said when he was in Cedars-Sinai. "Or at least enjoy yourself after I'm gone." And then her daughter, who seemed to harbor some strange notion that widows, or women over fifty, belonged in nursing homes. More immediately, she thought of Bunny, looking so pitifully crestfallen upon hearing about the Syd Stern deal she had blown with her multiple surgeries.

"Would you like a drink?" Frieda said quietly, almost afraid of his answer—that he would say no, that he would say yes.

"That would be very nice, thank you," he said, and he removed the long black coat.

They sat on the sofa facing the fire. There was space between them, but not much.

"You're a very nice lady," he said, his face illuminated in the flames.

Frieda said, "Why do you say that?"

"A lot of people, when I say I'm Cuban, they think I'm a communist. You just told me I had a nice accent. I appreciate that."

"Tell me about Cuba," she said, and he did. While he talked, Frieda began to go soft. She stared into the flames and listened to him, and suddenly she was very glad she had made that dinner reservation.

When his hand lightly touched her shoulder, she didn't stiffen, she didn't even think. She just turned to him and smiled. He was so young, so very beautiful . . .

And when he kissed her, it was with such tenderness that Frieda was startled. She had expected a macho assault.

He took the glass out of her hand and drew her into his arms. She felt awkward at first, unused to the feel of a man after so many years. But instincts came back, and an enormous flood of desire. Raoul kissed so sweetly, not pushy or aggressively, but lightly and almost lovingly. He took his time, as if he had nothing to prove, no need to demonstrate how male he was. As if, in fact, he understood her fears and uncertainties and sensed that any sudden foray into other parts of her body too soon would put her on the alert. It was some time before his fingers moved through her hair, then down her cheek, her throat, along the collar of her blouse.

When the first button came undone, she drew in a sharp breath. His hand paused, but he kept kissing her, and Frieda melted against him. He went on with the rest of the buttons until she felt a hand that was both hard and soft at the same time insinuate itself under her bra and cup her breast.

The slow gentleness became urgency then, as she ventured an attempt at exploration, finding a hard chest, a hard stomach, and . . . a very hard erection.

Raoul murmured something in Spanish, slipped her blouse off her shoulders, and unhooked her bra. His hand slid up under her skirt and he began to kiss her where she hadn't been kissed in years.

It felt so good.

He drew away, smiling, and he stood up, starting to undress. But Frieda reached up, doing it for him, sliding the jacket and tuxedo shirt off his magnificent olive-skinned torso and then drawing down the trousers.

He reached for her and brought her to her feet. They kissed standing up for a long time, both of them naked, with his hardness pressing against her thigh.

"Hurry," she finally whispered.

He smiled again and led her to the sheepskin rug at the hearth, laid her down. He whispered, kissing her gently, "Let us enjoy it . . ."

And then he was inside her, hard, vigorous, youthful. Frieda gasped. *Was* it like this? Oh yes yes yes yes . . .

He took forever. Just when she thought they were coming to the end of it, he would suddenly slow down and then gently speed up again until once more she thought they must nearly be there. And then he'd go slowly again.

The last clear-thinking spot in her brain thought, Surely he can't go on like this forever. No man can.

But he did, until finally she dug her fingernails into his back and whispered, "Now!"

When she felt a tremor begin her toes and undulate up her legs, Frieda screwed her eyes tightly shut and thought, Oh God.

When the wave crashed over her—

An image—

Of Larry Wolfe.

"Oh God!" she cried out.

She fell back, gasping. He didn't roll off her, but stayed there, to be sure. And when she started to laugh, and then say, "*Oh my God,*" he gave her a quizzical look.

"Raoul," Frieda said. "Oh oh oh." She hurriedly moved out from under him and made her way to the phone by the sofa.

She dialed quickly, and after a moment said, "Lisa, honey! Yes, Frieda here. Get yourself up to Star's tomorrow morning, first thing. Yes, *Star's.* Palm Springs. Off the one-eleven just before you get to the Racquet Club. Lisa, bring everything you've got!"

She hung up and dialed again. "Sam, Frieda. Listen, I need you to come to Star's right away. First thing in the morning, leave before dawn. What? I don't care. Cancel it. You owe me, Sam, remember? Yes, Star's. I'll tell you when you get here. Oh and Sam, bring Jeanine."

As Frieda made other calls, dialing frantically, barking orders to people at the other end, Raoul watched in bewilderment. When she started on the fifth call, he reached for his shirt to get dressed, but she touched his hard, damp shoulder and whispered, "Can you stay?"

"For as long as you want," he said in puzzlement.

She winked and dialed another number. "Bunny! Frieda again! You sound like you've been crying. Listen— What? Dr. Isaacs brought you some Valium? Don't take it! I want you to be alert. Bunny, listen, I have to ask you—has anyone else seen your new looks? I mean, who knows that you had plastic— Only the doctors? Good! Bunny, put down the Valium and fasten your safety belt," Frieda said excitedly, smiling at Raoul. "Wait until you hear the idea that just came to me!"

And as she began to tell Bunny the scheme that had come to her, but omitting *how* it had come, Frieda kept her eye on Raoul, who lay there naked and young and handsome, and hard, on her sheepskin rug—a toppled Greek statue.

And suddenly she knew why she had stayed at Star's.

33

Danny Mackay sat drumming his fingers on the steering wheel of his brand-new Jaguar as he waited outside the Wilshire high-rise where the Starlite offices were housed. He had followed Philippa Roberts and her two companions here after they had checked out of the Century Plaza Hotel. They should reappear soon; the receptionist had told him that Miss Roberts would be leaving for Palm Springs today.

It was getting dark, and the Christmas lights festooning busy Wilshire Boulevard were starting to come on in white-and-silver twinkles. From somewhere nearby, Danny could just make out the melody of "We Three Kings," while shoppers and professional people hurried along the sidewalks, their arms loaded with packages, determined looks on their faces. Danny hated Christmas; it made him nervous. Memories of his mother, who had been so beautiful and who had died so young, always came back at this time of the year with knifelike pain.

Finally, his impatience was rewarded as the familiar white stretch limousine emerged from the cave of the underground parking lot. One of the passenger windows was down a few inches; he could see her profile. It looked like Beverly. It was Beverly.

As he followed the limousine onto the 10 Freeway heading east toward Palm Springs, Danny gripped the steering wheel in delicious anticipation of what he was going to do to her. It would be soon now—very soon.

"Operator," Alan Scadudo said impatiently into the phone, "what happened to my call to Los Angeles?"

When the answer came in a language he didn't understand, he said, nearly shouting, *"Não falo português.* I don't speak Portuguese."

"Desculpe-me, senhor. I am still trying. All the circuits are busy."

"Please keep trying, this is urgent."

"Yes, *senhor.* I will ring you as soon as I have your party."

Alan hung up and swore under his breath. It was vital that he talk to Philippa right away. He had a bad feeling about this visit to Rio and his meeting with the president of Miranda International. Something wasn't right here; Gaspar Enriques wasn't right. The old man had been too cheerful, Alan thought, too cooperative, and too quick to promise that he was going to stop buying Starlite now that he owned 8 percent of the stock, while pleasantly refusing to sign the standstill agreement Alan had brought with him.

He looked at his watch. His important visitor should be knocking on his hotel room door at any moment.

Christ, what a day it's been, Alan thought as he went to the window and looked out at the warm Brazilian night. The day had been hot, sizzling the city at just a hundred degrees, and now it had settled down to a humid seventy-two. Alan loosened his tie and thanked God the hotel was air-conditioned. He was staying at the Caesar Park on the Avenida Vieira Souto, where security guards stationed on the roof patrolled nearby Ipanema beach with binoculars to protect hotel guests from being victims of "beach rats," kids who stole anything they could get their hands on. It was on that very beach that Alan had earlier met with Gaspar Enriques.

Enriques had turned out to be one of those aristocratic old gentlemen frequently seen on Brazilian beaches who like to prove their virility by challenging the ocean. Alan was made to wait on the beach while the Brazilian septuagenarian dipped into the pounding waves, after which he jogged in place on the sand for half an hour, the gray hairs on his skinny chest sprinkling sea salt with every jolt as he and Alan tried to carry on a business conversation amid the crowds, the noise, and the insects. Alan had not come prepared for the beach; he had worn dark blue wool slacks and a very expensive silk Armani shirt, feeling ludicrous in socks with his cuffs rolled up, and carrying a briefcase. But he had discovered during the course of the meeting that this was not uncommon at Ipanema; he had seen other executive types meeting with client types on the beach, all in swimsuits, all carrying briefcases.

The real problem with meeting at such a place, for Alan, was that he couldn't wear his shoes with the special lifts inside, so he was reduced to his actual five feet six inches. Another problem was the wind—it blew back his carefully combed thinning hair, exposing the transplant dots to the whole world.

Even so, the women had eyed him with interest—those aristocratic, olive-skinned, full-breasted creatures whose legs seemed to go all the way up to their armpits. They were naked except for the tanga—the string bikini that had originated in Rio and that might as well not have been there at all. These beauties had a way of looking at a man, a kind of sliding, sideways glance that made him melt right into the sand—especially fifty-five-year-old Alan Scadudo, who hadn't been looked at like that since, well, since never. More than once he had had to say to Enriques, "I beg your pardon, what did you say?"

After an entire afternoon spent on the beach with the old man, eating ricotta cheese sandwiches, Enriques chatting happily away in perfect English, telling Alan every detail about Miranda International and its throbbing nut export operation, all Alan had come away with at the end of it was an enormous headache and a sunburn. Remarkably little had been accomplished. Now that he looked back over the encounter, he began to see it as some sort of charade, as though he and old Gaspar had simply been acting out a pantomime, dancing at the end of somebody else's strings, as it were, with nothing being really said or done. And now, as his watch ticked off the midnight hour and he waited anxiously for his important visitor, Alan's misgivings grew. Miranda International was definitely not to be trusted. Philippa had to be alerted at once.

When there was a knock at his door, he hurried to open it, only to see a waiter with a room service cart. Alan stepped aside while the man wheeled the food in and, with flourishes, set the table, remarking as he did so about the heat, the humidity, the latest soccer scores. When the waiter noticed a small hand-carved doll sitting beside the telephone, he grinned and said, "Ah, you believe in the luck of Iemanja, goddess of the sea? She's very powerful, *senhor,* a very, very lucky goddess."

Alan had purchased the tiny statue on his way back from the beach; it was a trinket for Hannah, and it had cost, after haggling, less then one American dollar. But he didn't say anything; he was anxious for the man to leave.

When he was alone again, he surveyed the feast that had been sent up—a fish and shrimp combination called *vatapa,* heavily spiced with paprika and peppers, with french fries and beans on the side, accompanied by a sweet egg custard and black coffee heavily laced with rum and sugar. As he listened anxiously for the arrival of his midnight caller, Alan wondered what had possessed him to order a traditional Brazilian dish when a hamburger would have suited him just fine. He draped a napkin over the revoltingly exotic food and pushed the cart away.

He was just checking his watch again when the phone rang. The operator had made his connection to Los Angeles.

"Hannah? Is that you, darling? Thank God. I thought this damn phone would never work."

"Alan? Are you all right? How is it going with Miranda?" she asked over a crackling line. "Were you able to work things out with Mr. Enriques?"

"I'm fine, darling. But Hannah, something funny is going on here,"

Alan said. "I met with Enriques and now I need to talk to Philippa. Right away."

"She left a little while ago. She's on her way to Palm Springs."

Alan chewed his lip. "Is she in the company car? Patch me through on a conference line. I need to talk to her immediately."

As Hannah put him on hold and hurriedly looked through her address book for the phone number of the limousine, she felt her anxiety mount. She had been sitting in her bedroom all afternoon and into the evening, waiting for a certain phone call. When the boudoir phone had rung on her Louis XV desk, she had literally jumped off the bed.

They were supposed to call and set up a meeting at which she would hand over her stock certificates in exchange for cash. The transaction had to take place before the board meeting in Palm Springs, which was only two days away. Time was running out.

Dialing the number of the limousine, Hannah spied her handbag across the room. Her pills were in it, and she suddenly needed them; her heart was starting to tap dance behind her sternum.

"Ricky," she said when the car phone was picked up, "it's Hannah here. I've got Alan on the other line. He's calling from Rio, and he wants to talk to Philippa."

Hannah listened while Alan spoke, his voice fading in and out as if it were being carried on ocean waves. "Something's not right down here, Philippa," he said, sounding uncharacteristically agitated. "Miranda is a small outfit. They deal in *nuts,* for Chrissake. And I know for a fact that they can't possibly afford the money they're paying out to buy Starlite stock."

"What did you learn from Enriques?" Philippa asked, her voice fading slightly as the limousine drove through Banning Pass.

"He was pleasant and polite, but very unenlightening. He didn't tell me much, just that he admires the Starlite corporation and would like to own some shares in it. He insists that there is no takeover planned, but he won't sign a standstill agreement. And another thing, Philippa—the man cannot make a decision on his own, and yet he's the president and owner of the goddamn company. I'd swear he's a front for somebody else."

"Why do you say that?" Hannah asked, cutting in. Her eyes flickered nervously to the wall safe, where the stock certificates were waiting.

"Because when I asked him if he'd consider coming to L.A. for a meeting, he said he'd get back to me on it. Well, he just contacted me here at the hotel a short while ago, saying he'd be glad to come. I asked him if he had had to consult with anyone before making that decision, and he had said no, he had just wanted to think about it. But I'd swear, Philippa, that he talked to someone else first, someone who wishes to remain behind the scenes. And I think that person is the one who is orchestrating a takeover. They're funneling funds through Miranda, and I think they plan to take us by surprise."

Philippa had been afraid of that. She was also prepared for it. "All right, Alan. I need to think about this. Come back right away. And bring Enriques with you. I'm most anxious to talk to him."

Philippa hung up, leaving Alan and his wife alone on the line. "When will you be home, darling?" Hannah asked.

"As soon as Enriques can leave."

"Alan, I'm worried."

"Don't be, honey. Everything will work out, I'm sure."

"Will you be back in time for our party? I thought we'd announce Jackie's engagement then."

"Sure, don't worry. Hey, I'm bringing you something," he said. "A special surprise. And it has nothing to do with Christmas."

"Just bring yourself home. I love you."

"I love you, too."

Alan was just hanging up when he heard a knock on the door. His visitor, at last.

The man was tall with a smoothly shaved head that reflected the ceiling lights in the hall. He wore a white linen suit, highly polished eelskin shoes, and gold rings on nearly every finger. Gaspar Enriques had sent him as a special favor to Alan. Alan had commented during their meeting on the beach that he was hoping to purchase a special gift for a special lady, something unique, not found in ordinary shops. "I know just the man," Enriques had said.

Alan offered his visitor a drink, but the man preferred to get right to business. The item he had brought with him was an exquisite antique crucifix at the end of a gold chain. The cross and figure of Christ were made of gold and were encrusted with Brazilian aquamarine, topaz, amethyst, and garnet. "But what makes this necklace so priceless, Senhor Scadudo," said the visitor, who had not given his name, "is that Princesa Isabel wore it when she signed the Lei Auréa, our emancipation proclamation of 1888, when she freed our slaves. When you purchase this necklace, Senhor Scadudo, you buy not only the gold and precious gemstones, but a piece of Brazil's history as well."

Alan held it up to the light. It was exquisite; so delicate, so finely wrought. He thought he could almost feel the passion of history in it. He felt a thrill go through him as he imagined her reaction to it; she certainly wasn't expecting such a gift.

When the man told him the price, Alan hesitated for a moment. He hadn't expected to pay so much. But he relented, because she was worth it. And it was going to make up for them having to be apart.

★ ★ ★

Hannah hung up the phone and wrung her hands. There was so much to think about. Getting the stock certificates out, overseeing arrangements for her Christmas party, Jackie coming home with her fiancé, the board meeting in Palm Springs, and of course the surprise she had for Alan. She prayed the Freundlich sculpture would arrive in time.

She looked out the bedroom window, from where she could see the terraced gardens behind the house already being prepared for the big Christmas party. Hannah prayed that everything went smoothly, for her and Alan, for Jackie and Vincent.

Feeling her heart do somersaults in her chest, Hannah hurried across the room to where she had left her pills. Not even Alan knew she was taking them; she didn't want to cause him alarm. Now all she had to do was wait for the phone to ring.

As Philippa hung up the car phone, she recapped Alan's end of the conversation to Charmie, who rode in the seat that faced backward, sitting sideways, her legs stretched along the seat, her back propped against the TV/VCR console, her lemon yellow silk caftan pooling on the floor of the limousine. "What are you going to do?" she asked, laying aside the book she had been reading.

"Something I hate having to do, and that I never thought I would have to. Charmie, it's time for the poison pill." Philippa picked up the phone again and tapped out a number. After a moment, she said, "Ralph? It's Philippa. I just spoke to Alan in Rio . . ." After she recounted the conversation to him, she said, "Meet me in Palm Springs in the morning. I'll be at the Marriott Desert Springs. I want you to do two things: first, lower our anti-takeover trigger from twenty percent to ten percent. Then draft a provision allowing Starlite shareholders to buy stock at less than market value. As soon as Miranda hits ten percent, the second provision will go into effect. That at least will slow them down and make a takeover more difficult and certainly more expensive. Do we have a white knight we can bring in, just in case? Good. See you then."

Charmie sighed, thinking of the old days when she and Philippa had run Starlite from a living room and the only legal thing involved had been a long yellow pad on which they had recorded the members' names. "I wish there was some way we could find out who's behind Enriques," she said, "and why they're trying to take your company away from you."

Philippa was thinking of Ivan Hendricks, who was at that moment snooping around Palm Springs for information on Beverly Burgess.

"When we see Ivan tomorrow, I'm going to ask him to do some looking into Miranda for us."

It excited Charmie that Ivan was back in their lives again, especially when she recalled their one stunning sexual encounter; she would swear that his hard, powerful body had left a permanent imprint on hers. "With luck," she said, wondering if she was ever going to have a second chance with him, "Ivan will have some information for us on Caanan Corp. And if there's a connection between the dummy Caanan and Miranda International, he might tell us who's behind all this."

Philippa looked out the car window but saw only blackness. The sun had set two hours ago; she and her companions had entered barren desert, where only an occasional dwelling or billboard glowed in the dark. The headlights of traffic coming from the other direction seemed to float by on the freeway like disembodied spirits. The moment felt strangely otherworldly to Philippa; she and Charmie and Ricky seemed to glide through the night in a silent space-age capsule. They couldn't hear the car's engine or the whine of the tires on the asphalt. The bar was stocked with food and drinks; the heater staved off the freezing desert night; the moonroof was rolled back to give a breathtaking view of the stars. Philippa felt curiously safe, insulated from the world and its dangers.

She was unaware of the black Jaguar that had followed them from L.A. and was behind them now.

Picking up her pen, she tried returning to the work she had been doing to make use of the time during the drive from Los Angeles to Palm Springs when Alan's call had interrupted her. She was writing on her Moroccan leather lap desk, tooled in antique gold, a birthday present from her daughter, Esther, who had bought it with money earned when she had worked a summer at Sequoia National Park. The ride in the Lincoln Town Car was so smooth that Philippa's handwriting was clear and legible: "Point Fifty-two: Eat only when hungry. Point Fifty-three: Exercise for one half hour three times a week."

She was still thinking about what she had discovered when she had visited the Starlite salon that afternoon. We haven't kept up with the times, she thought; we haven't kept our eyes and ears open to the needs of our members. We're stuck in a time warp, while other companies sprout up around us and fill the needs that we seem to be ignoring.

Turning to a fresh page, she wrote: "Popcorn. Tortilla chips. Salsa (all you can eat?). A glass of wine a day. Need to get caloric and nutritional values. Must observe latest eating trends and design a new menu for the nineties. Note: Possible national spokesperson? Celebrity? Why don't we come out with our own exercise video? One with some kind of sex appeal, gorgeous males doing aerobics, so that women will enjoy watching it."

She looked at Ricky then, who was asleep with his head against the window. As she studied the strong, young profile, the way his silky blond hair lay across his cheek, Philippa thought of the day of the Melbourne Cup race, when she and Ricky had watched it on TV together, and her horse, Beautiful Dolly, had won, and how she had impulsively hugged Ricky, and how he had held her tightly, a little longer than necessary, his hard body and hot kisses suddenly awakening in her all the desires that she had thought had gone down with the *Philippa*. For that, she was grateful to him. Ricky had brought her back to life.

But where did they go from here? If she decided to stay in Los Angeles, would he stay also, or would he want to return to Australia? And if he stayed, how was Esther going to respond to her mother having a lover who was only five years older than her own daughter?

Philippa pressed a button and her window whispered down, immediately letting in a gust of cold, slicing air. It felt good. The desert felt good. The stars were so three-dimensional, like magical Disney animation. The craggy peaks of the mountains could just barely be made out against the stars; the silence was unearthly. When she saw a shooting star streak across the black sky, disappearing into the blackness that she guessed was the craggy summit of Mount San Jacinto, she thought of Star's and wondered what she was going to find up there. Would she find a woman with her face? Would she look at Beverly Burgess and have the feeling she was looking into a mirror? Philippa felt the desert wind cut through her hair as she thought, Do my sister and I share subconscious fetal memories? Did we cuddle in our mother's womb, or did we compete for space? What embryo secrets did we whisper to each other? Were we fraternal or identical twins? Fraternal would mean that we each evolved from our own egg, but identical would mean that we came from the same egg, an egg that had been intended to be one person. So we would be like two halves of one person.

"Hello?" Charmie said suddenly, looking up from her book. "Why are we slowing down?"

Philippa pressed the button to lower the partition and see what was ahead. "Oh my God!" she said.

Charmie turned around and stared at a solid wall that seemed to stand across the freeway. There was nothing beyond it—no stars, no mountains, no taillights. And it was rapidly swallowing up the cars in front of them.

The limousine slowed sharply, then shimmied and swerved. Charmie cried out; Philippa put out a hand to steady herself, and Ricky, who was suddenly awake, reached for her as she fell into his arms.

In the Jaguar, Danny's mind was like a clenched fist, tight and ready to punch; he was getting high on thinking of all the things he was going to do to Philippa. It was important to keep thoughts like that alive; they put blood in a man's veins and gave him the strength to do what he had to do. He had once held the world in his palm, and then everything had been taken away from him—by *her,* by the bitch in the limousine up ahead.

Beverly Highland. The world thought she was dead. And she thought *he* was dead. Danny felt a thrill go through him. It was such a high—she didn't know he was alive. She had no idea what lay in store for her. She thought she was safe, that she had gotten away with it. But she was going to pay. Oh yes. Danny liked to imagine the look on her face when he caught up with her. He was going to give her a taste of what he had been through—make her hang by a leather belt, kicking and fighting for air, feeling her wet herself, the panic and terror . . .

Danny reached up and adjusted the rearview mirror so that he could see himself. He smiled the sly, lazy smile that had charmed millions. He knew he was still handsome, still had power over people from his looks alone. Danny had worked hard to cultivate that look, as Niccolò Machiavelli had advised over 450 years ago: *"The mob is always impressed by appearances, and the world is made up of mobs."* When Beverly saw this face again, a face that had once, years ago, made her crawl to Danny and beg him not to leave her, she would be crawling again, this time begging for her life. It gave Danny a hard-on to think of it.

When he returned his gaze to the windshield, he saw her limousine suddenly vanish through a solid wall that stood across the freeway.

"Jesus!" he shouted, and he slammed his foot on the brakes, sending the Jaguar into a spin.

DAY FOUR

34

This time, the phone call wasn't conducted long-distance, nor did it take place on a special line. Still, the conversation was a cautious one, conducted in private, and without the interruption of a squawking parrot.

"You're here," the caller said.

"It wasn't easy. How long do we have?"

"Not long."

"Let's get started then. By the way—"

"Yes?"

"Make sure you bring it."

35

San Fernando Valley, California, 1970

Philippa's young secretary, Molly, was the first to spot the black Mercedes-Benz with the darkly tinted windows as it pulled up in front of Starlite's Swiss-chalet offices. She looked out the window and said, "Holy smokes! It looks like we have an important visitor!"

Kitty, the switchboard operator, looked up from her board. "Who is it?"

"I don't know. It's some bigwig, though," Molly said excitedly. "A movie star I'll bet!" Ever since Philippa had appeared on *The Tonight Show,* Molly had anticipated a celebrity parade through Starlite. "Come and see!"

Philippa was in Charmie's office, discussing a plan for bringing out a special line of Starlite cosmetics, when they heard someone running down the hall. "What's going on?" Philippa said, opening the door and looking out to see a knot of women gathered around the window in the reception area, including Kitty, who had abandoned her post at the ever-ringing switchboard.

Molly broke away from the group and came up, saying, "A mysterious visitor has just arrived, Miss Roberts! There's a big black car out front with a chauffeur and everything!"

"We can't see who it is," Colleen, Hannah's assistant, called over her shoulder. "*I* think it's a gangster!"

Philippa and Charmie got to the window just as Mildred said, "The car's driving off! Shoot, they're leaving! They aren't coming in here after all!"

The knot dissolved in disappointment and everyone returned to work.

When Philippa reached her office, after making her way down a hall jumbled with file cabinets and storage boxes, she was thinking she wasn't in the mood to go out on a date tonight, even though it was to see a revival of films noirs from the forties. She wondered how Keith would take another cancellation.

He was the man she had been seeing for the past six months, a forty-three-year-old engineer who worked for McDonnell Douglas. Keith's list of qualities was as long and impeccable as a freshly done laundry list. He was clean, polite, nice, considerate, decent looking, laughed easily, and made good money. He drove a late-model Cadillac, sent flowers to his mother every year on her birthday, and was naïve enough to admit to having voted for Nixon. He shared with Philippa an interest in old movies, which was what their dates mainly consisted of.

Keith always held doors open for her, he knew how to dress, how to order wine, and Philippa was comfortable with him. But there was no spark in their relationship. She had even gone to bed with him, to see if that would set off the fireworks she longed for, but Keith had turned out to be just as polite and proper in bed as he was in real life. All through their lovemaking he had kept saying, "Is everything all right? Are you sure this is what you want?" He had sounded like a waiter.

If Philippa had to sum him up in one word, it would be *punctual.* Keith was the most precise, on-time man she had ever met, even in his lovemaking. She felt it always took him a prescribed number of thrusts within a prescribed number of minutes and then he was done, his hands moving over her body as if it were one of his engineering blueprints, executing maneuvers precisely, predictably, and on schedule.

Philippa hadn't been particularly burning to go to bed with him. It had just evolved, from saying good-night, to a chaste kiss on her doorstep, to hand-holding in the movies, and so on until they were between his sheets, which smelled of Oxydol. Both Keith and society had seemed to look at her askance, as if to say, What are you saving it for? It seemed to Philippa that the rules had been switched when she wasn't looking; the old days of girls guarding their virtue had turned into new days of girls proving their liberation by handing it out to anyone who asked.

One thing Keith had taught her about sex, though—and it was a big lesson—was that the way it was between men and women was *not* the way it had been between her and Rhys. Because the moody beatnik had been her first and only lover, Philippa had assumed that heavenly, maddening, earth-moving sex was the norm, that it was what everyone experienced. Keith had opened her eyes to the real world. Ten minutes after they got into bed, it was over. With Rhys it had taken all night, and Philippa had never doubted for a minute that he had been making love to *her*. With Keith, she had the odd notion that if she were to slip out for a quick donut and coffee and come back in time for the climax, he would never know she had been gone.

Keith had asked her to marry him. The scary part was, she was considering it.

She went into her office and closed the door, eyeing the overwhelming stacks of mail that awaited her. Her desk was also cluttered with remnants from the surprise party everyone had thrown for her thirty-second birthday. There was a birthday card from Mrs. Chadwick, the handwriting shaky, reminding Philippa that her former landlady was getting on in years. Finally, there was the most recent report she had received from Ivan Hendricks. He had been following all leads on babies born in Hollywood in 1938 on Philippa's birthday. He was checking county records, hospital records, and speaking with lawyers who handled adoptions. "But you might have been born at home," he had written, "and the adoption was handled strictly cash, no paperwork. Don't worry, Miss Roberts, something will turn up." And she thought: If only Johnny were still alive, he could fill in so much missing information.

"It's back, Miss Roberts!" Molly said, bursting in. "The black car is back and this time the driver is *getting out!*"

Philippa went to the window, and moving the curtain aside, saw a shiny black Mercedes-Benz, the windows tinted to hide the passengers from view. And the driver, sure enough, was coming up the walk to Starlite's front door.

He was a large man with a completely bald head that connected right to his shoulders without bothering with a neck, so that his earlobes settled on his stiff shirt collar—a James Bond nemesis, Philippa thought when he came through her office door. He was impeccably dressed in a gray suit, although she thought the jacket was suspiciously baggy, and he spoke mechanically, as if he had memorized what he had to say.

"My employer would like to join your program."

"Yes, of course," she said, signaling to a gaping Molly to bring a new member packet. "I can provide you with a list of locations so that your employer can choose the salon that is most convenient—"

"No salon," he said. "It will be done privately."

"I'm sorry, but the Starlite program isn't set up for that. Your employer will have to join a group."

"That's not possible."

Philippa glanced through the lace curtain over her office window at the darkly tinted windows of the Mercedes. She felt someone watching her from behind them. Who was it? Someone famous? Or someone who just didn't want to be seen; national security, perhaps?

She turned back to the driver who, she noticed now, had rather pretty eyes for such a hulking guy: a springtime green with a thick fringe of black lashes. "All right," she said. "This is irregular, but I don't see why we can't be accommodating."

When Molly returned with the glossy folder and brochures that went to new members, Philippa filled out the registration form, explaining, "The way the program works, members weigh in once a week, and then they discuss whatever problems or questions they might have with the group and with the counselor. At the end of the meeting, handouts are distributed and new menus are offered to those who have achieved certain levels of weight loss. For example—"

"My employer understands all that." He was abrupt, but pleasant about it.

"Very well. The sign-up fee is thirty dollars, and it's twenty dollars a month after that. If your employer wishes, she can send the payment to this office."

To her surprise, he took two bills out of his pocket, a ten and a twenty, and handed them to her.

"Please tell your employer that I cannot guarantee how the diet will work on its own," she said, writing out a receipt. "Starlite is based upon group support. It's not just a matter of counting calories, but much more."

"My employer understands that."

"It is also necessary that she weigh herself once a week, on a day of her own choosing, preferably in the morning. Normally, the group counselor would record a gain or a loss in this booklet, but in this case—"

"We understand." His mouth snapped up in a smile, and Philippa had the sudden notion that if she were to open his shirt she would find buttons embedded in his chest, labeled WALK, TALK, SMILE, ACT AMIABLE BUT TOUGH . . .

As she gathered the papers together, she said, "I'll need to know if this is for a man or a woman. The diet is different for each."

"We'll take both."

She gave him a smile. "Covering all bases, aren't you? All right, here you are."

Both she and Molly watched him go, and both were wondering, for different reasons, if he would be back.

"Insulin," Dr. Steinberg said. "That's your problem."

He was the fourth specialist Philippa had seen in as many years, and she hadn't expected any results. They always drew blood, ran tests, took an extensive history on her past and eating habits, and in the end, they shrugged, at a loss for an answer. So when Dr. Steinberg made his one-word pronouncement, she said, "I beg your pardon?"

"You have a rare condition called hyperinsulinemia, Miss Roberts, which means you have too much insulin in your bloodstream. You have, in fact, the very opposite problem that diabetics have, who can't manufacture insulin at all. The symptoms mimic hypoglycemia, but your problem isn't low blood sugar, it's high blood insulin. That's why you get the shakes so soon after eating something sweet. You ingest sugar, your body produces too much insulin, resulting in shakiness, light-headedness, and sweats."

He waited for her to assimilate this new information, then continued. "People with hyperinsulinemia are frequently overweight because of the two main actions of insulin." He enumerated them on his right hand. "First, insulin speeds up the conversion of sugars into stored fat; second, insulin *slows* the breakdown of stored fat into energy. So you see, insulin is in fact fattening. I even have a diabetic patient who refuses to take her insulin because she says it makes her put on weight."

All of a sudden, Philippa understood things that had once made no sense. Not being able to eat desserts; the sweet breakfasts at St. Bridget's that always made her feel faint by midmorning; Dr. Hehr's fruit-heavy diet that she could not tolerate, and on which she hadn't lost weight as fast as others did. And now, even something Dr. Hehr had once said to her came straight home: "It's not necessarily overeating that causes obesity, it's *incorrect* eating."

"When you had that cold," Dr. Steinberg said, "you said you drank a lot of fruit juice and tea with honey. Fruit is high in sugar. Oh, I know it's so-called natural sugar, and not the refined white stuff, but fructose has the same effect on the pancreas. And as for the honey in the tea, people don't understand about honey. It's almost as bad for you as white sugar is, because in a way it's refined—by the bees—but all the same it's pure sugar. Which your body doesn't need."

Philippa was suddenly excited. Here was the answer to a lifelong mystery. "What can I do, Doctor?"

"Keep your insulin levels low by eating protein and complex carbohydrates, which take longer to digest that simple carbohydrates." He smiled. "But of course you know all of this. From our discussions I can see that you've done a lot of research in human nutrition. Also, when you feel shaky, don't eat something sweet. A diabetic who is having an insulin reaction can do that because the sugar will stabilize the insulin that he has injected. But for you, it will only stimulate your pancreas to produce more insulin. When you feel shaky, eat protein—an egg or a piece of chicken."

He came around the desk and, putting a fatherly arm around her shoulders, escorted her to the door. "Another thing you can do," he said, "is avoid eating large meals. You'd be surprised how many overweight people say they only eat one meal a day. Usually it's a doozy. But let's say you're on only fifteen hundred calories and you save them all up for one meal. A big meal triggers massive insulin output from the pancreas. Small meals don't. Take those fifteen hundred calories and spread them out— you'll actually produce *less* insulin during the day.

"You'll keep your weight down," he said with a wink, "and you'll feel great. Trust me. I know what I'm talking about."

Molly said, "It's here again, the mystery car!" And the other girls in the office clustered at the front window hoping for a glimpse of fame.

"I'll bet it's Elizabeth Taylor," Mildred said. "I read where she put on a whole bunch of weight for her role in *Who's Afraid of Virginia Woolf* and now she's having a hard time getting it off."

Philippa looked up from the *Los Angeles Times.* She had been trying to put together a small book tentatively titled *Hyperinsulinemia and How to Control It,* certain that there must be other people like herself who suffered from the condition but who had no idea what it was or how to handle it. But she had been unable to stick with it because the front page of the newspaper had distracted her with horror stories from Vietnam and photographs of children crying over dead parents. A massive antiwar rally was going to be held at Century City the coming weekend; she had asked Keith to go with her, but he had declined, saying that there was a one-day Bogart festival in Santa Barbara that he couldn't miss. So she and Charmie were going to go and add their voices to the protest.

When she saw the dark silhouette of an automobile on the other side of her lace curtain, she folded her newspaper and set it aside. After a moment the driver came in. Exactly one week later to the minute. It occurred to her that such punctuality would impress Keith. The driver didn't sit down. He unfolded a sheet of paper and said, "We have some questions. The following items are not listed under any of the diet exchanges. We would like to know how they might be incorporated into the diet, if at all."

Philippa read the typed sheet: quail, pâté de fois gras, caviar, brandy, various breads. Not the groceries of a typical Starlite member.

She wrote her answers on the sheet: "Quail may be roasted, boiled, or broiled *without the skin.* Avoid caviar—salt content too high. Same for the pâté. The bread allowance is increased by one exchange in week four, providing the initial weight-loss requirement has been met. If fruits are not available, or cannot be tolerated, each fruit exchange may be substituted with *two* vegetable exchanges. No alcohol permitted at all."

She gave him the weekly letter, which was headed with "Believe in Yourself," the Starlite motto, and, in case the client was a woman, fashion and makeup tip sheets.

After he left, Molly and the others crowded at the window trying to figure out who it was, not a few of them wondering if the driver was single.

The Mercedes showed up with stupendous regularity after that—every Monday morning at exactly ten o'clock, always parking right out front, the driver always coming in with a typed list of unusual questions.

On the fifth morning, Philippa said, "May I enquire how your employer is doing?"

"The diet is having some success," was the limited reply.

By the end of the second month, Charmie had started managing to be coincidentally in Philippa's office, mainly to scope out the hunky driver. She had gotten nowhere with Ivan Hendricks. After a few unsubtle flirtations—"I admire a man who appreciates a good potato chip"—she stopped trying. He revealed nothing of his private life, but he didn't nibble her bait, so she concluded he had a woman somewhere. But there had been times when she had caught him looking at her in a certain way, and he'd seemed about to say something . . .

Although she was no longer married, having divorced Ron, she had kept her married name, liking the sound of Charmie Charmer—"Like an exotic dancer," she told people. She wondered what the no-neck driver with the pretty eyes did for kicks.

When she read the latest list of questions, she said, "Long Island duck! Kiwifruit!" She looked at Philippa. "What the hell is kiwifruit?"

"I think our secret client has expensive tastes." They both looked at the driver, but he wasn't telling.

At the end of four months, the driver announced that goal weight had been successfully achieved. So Philippa handed him the maintenance diet and wished his employer good luck.

"Do you suppose that's it?" said Charmie, a little disappointed. "Now we'll probably never know who it was."

But when an MG sports car pulled up in front two weeks later and Charmie saw who was getting out, she came into Philippa's office and said breathlessly, "Philippa! You'll never guess who's here! Paul Marquette! *Senator* Paul Marquette! *That's* who our mystery member is! I saw him in person once. God, Philippa, you should see him! The man's a hot fudge sundae. I could eat him with a *spoon!*"

"What makes you think he was our mystery member?"

"Oh, come now. For sixteen weeks in a row a black Mercedes driven by Tobor the Great pulls up, gets a diet, and drives away. Then Tobor announces that the diet was a success, and now this, out of the blue? Senator Marquette, Philippa! A *United States* senator!"

"But as far as I can recall, Senator Marquette wasn't overweight."
Philippa tried to remember when she had last seen his picture in the news.
He had been involved in a tragedy some time back—a son dying mysteri-
ously, causing Marquette to drop out of a senatorial race.

"Maybe his wife was fat," Charmie said, glancing out into the hall.
"Here he comes!"

A flustered Molly escorted the senator into Philippa's office.

Philippa rose to greet him.

He took her hand in a warm clasp and said, "I can't tell you how happy
I am to meet you, Miss Roberts."

Charmie had likened him to a hot fudge sundae. She was wrong. Paul
Marquette didn't have the perfection of a sundae. Philippa realized now,
seeing him in person, that he wasn't the perfectly handsome man the press
photos showed. In real life, the perfection was flawed, the features not
quite regular. The senator was more attractive than handsome, Philippa
decided, Cary Grant's first cousin. She shook his hand and said, "This is
an honor, Senator. And I must say, quite a surprise."

He wore white slacks and a white V-neck sweater over a blue shirt; his
hair was tousled from driving the convertible, and he was carrying a bottle
of wine. "The honor is all mine, Miss Roberts, I assure you," he said in
a rich, cultured voice that sounded as if he belonged on the stage. "I hope
I haven't come at an inconvenient time. I wanted to give you this, from
our special reserve."

She accepted the bottle and read the label: "Chardonnay, Château
Marquette, 1953." A gold-embossed sticker had been added. "Winner:
Prix d'Or, Paris, France, 1960."

"I hardly know what to say, Senator," Philippa said. "Would this have
something to with a certain mysterious car that has been visiting us?"

His smile broadened. "Yes. Those weekly visits were arranged by me.
I wonder, might I have a word alone with you, Miss Roberts?"

Charmie said, "I have to get going. Please excuse me," and she left,
giving Philippa a significant look on her way out.

As Paul Marquette took a seat, Philippa thought that he looked and
acted every inch the polished politician, despite his casual attire. His black
hair was silvering at the temples, and she recalled reading that he was in
his early forties.

"I hadn't realized that you were connected with the Marquette Wineries," Philippa said.

"That's where my fortune comes from," he said with a smile. "That,
and a mile of Wilshire Boulevard that my grandfather bought in exchange
for a wagon and a mule." He laughed. "The typical L.A. story! How many
times have you heard people say that their grandfather had the chance

to buy the corner of Wilshire and Crenshaw for two dollars but passed it up? Well, *my* grandfather did it."

He fell silent and seemed to assess her. His eyes were dark like Rhys's, she noticed, but not futureless like his had been; rather, Marquette's were full of warmth and life as if yearning to embrace that future. She wanted to know about the weekly visits of the Mercedes. Who had the Starlite diet been for? Not for himself; he was as tall and slender as he had appeared in the news.

"Marquettes have always been doers," he said quietly. "Which was what your weekly letter reminded me of. That I am a man of action. But . . . I had forgotten that."

He paused, as if he had rehearsed a difficult speech. "I don't know how much you know about me, Miss Roberts. During my last political campaign my son died. He was my only child, and I was too grief-stricken to go on, so I bowed out of the race."

"Yes," she said, "I remember," wanting to add, I was going to vote for you.

He continued: "I went into seclusion in which I consoled myself with alcohol and food. I ballooned up forty pounds. When I decided last year to go back into politics, I discovered that I couldn't get the weight off. I tried everything." He looked at her.

And through her. No one had done that since Rhys.

"I suppose you hear that a lot," he said. "I went to the best specialists, I had a gym built at the house, I even spent some time at a fat farm in Florida. Nothing worked. And then one night I saw you on television. You made me realize that I wasn't addressing the real problem—the fact that I was blaming myself for Todd's death. You see, Miss Roberts, what the media kept secret was that my son didn't die in an accident. He committed suicide."

He held his words for a few minutes, during which Philippa saw the glint of a gold band on his left hand, and she recalled that he was married to a beautiful Washington socialite.

"I was quite moved," Marquette said, "by how frankly you told Johnny Carson about your friend's suicide, how you blamed yourself, how you felt responsible for not having saved him. I knew at once that you understood exactly what I was going through. So I decided to try your program, and that was when I found the road back."

He stood up and thrust his hands into his pockets—a man unused to personal confessions. "It wasn't so much the diet," he said, "as it was those weekly letters of inspiration. 'Think defeat and you will be defeated; think success and you will be successful.' Words that a politician could live by, or anyone who wanted to get ahead in the world. I started to take your advice to heart." He smiled. "Do you know my favorite? 'It's not the size of the dog in the fight, but the size of the fight in the dog.' "

"I'm afraid it's not original with me. President Eisenhower said it first, and I learned it from my father."

"It got so that I couldn't wait for the week to pass in order to get the next letter. I had the feeling that you were speaking directly to me."

"A lot of Starlite members have told me that, Senator."

"I like the brochure you include with the new member information. You talk about yourself. It's hard to belive you once weighted sixty pounds more than you do now. But you know, it helped me to know that. For me, to be forty pounds overweight—I felt like a freak. But I couldn't help it. I was so torn up by Todd's death that I retreated into scotch and pasta. I canceled my social life, I didn't take calls from friends. I retreated to my house and drank and ate. As if that would bring Todd back."

While he went on to describe his descent into freakishness, describing how he had wallowed in guilt and self-pity, Philippa looked at that not handsome but definitely attractive face and thought, This is not a man who wallows. A man like Paul Marquette suffers silently, gallantly, nobly. He turns a firm jaw to the world while his heart quivers and wilts away. Philippa couldn't picture him with the scotch bottle; he was not Ray Milland trudging from pawnshop to pawnshop in *Lost Weekend*, pounding on their closed doors only to discover it was a Jewish holiday and they couldn't give him money for booze. As for the food binge? Philippa pictured Paul Marquette at Dodger Stadium, his shirtsleeves rolled up, ready to throw in that first ball, laughingly accepting a mustard-slathered Dodger Dog from a freckle-faced kid. Paul Marquette ate healthily, patriotically. He did not drown himself in self-pity and gnocchi with pesto sauce.

"I've shocked you," he said.

"Nothing about people and food shocks me, Senator. I've heard all the stories. I've even lived a few of them myself. I once almost got on my knees to beg for a pork chop."

"That's what makes you special," he said. "It's what makes Starlite special. The sympathy and compassion of people who have gone through the same hell. That was what gave me the strength to stay with your program. Because first you took away my shame, and then you gave me something to believe in again—myself."

A silence settled between them then, charged with connection and, to Philippa's surprise, sexual attraction. She walked into Paul's dark eyes and felt her knees give way.

"Then I have done my job," she said. "What you achieved was exactly what I set out to do twelve years ago. When I was growing up, I felt like an outcast because of my looks, and I know other girls were similarly unhappy. I didn't want Starlite to be just another diet program, because there is more to finding happiness and self-respect than being thin. My best friend Charmie never did lose weight, but she believes so strongly in herself that you don't notice her size."

"Yes," he said thoughtfully.

Philippa waited for him to say something further, and when he didn't, and she suddenly felt self-conscious beneath his probing gaze, she said, "I shall save this wine for a very special occasion, Senator."

"Please. Call me Paul. And you must come out and visit the winery. I'll give you a tour of it myself."

"Will I be expected to take off my shoes and stomp grapes?"

He laughed—the deep, rich laugh of a Shakespearean actor. "It's all very scientific these days, I'm afraid, with men in white lab coats and clipboards doing the work. Very boring. The history is interesting, though. The winery was founded in 1882 by my grandfather, François Marquette, which makes Marquette one of the oldest wineries in California. We not only survived Prohibition, we made our greatest profits then. Not making wine, you understand, but by shipping grapes to the East Coast, where people were making wine in their bathtubs. My grandfather was very wily. He sold casks of concentrated grape juice with warnings printed on them that said 'Do not add yeast or contents will ferment.' "

Philippa laughed.

Marquette regarded her for another thoughtful moment, then he stood and said, "But I've taken up enough of your time. I came by to thank you for what you did for me. You saved my life. And my political career. My confidence is back, I'm going to run for the Senate in the next election. Thanks to you."

Her eyes met his and were held, as he added, "It was a pleasure meeting you. And I do hope you will accept my offer to let me show you around the winery—soon."

··★

36

"Are you Christine Singleton?"

"Yes! How did you know?"

"I'm your sister, Beverly Burgess. My name used to be Beverly Highland, but before that I was Rachel Dwyer. Your last name is Dwyer, too. We're twins. I've been searching for you for so long, I can't believe I've found you at last."

"I've been looking for you, too. Isn't this wonderful? We're together again, after all these years."

"But there is danger."

"Danger? From what?"

"I don't know, but I sense it . . . nearby. I was once involved with a terrible man, Christine, a man named Danny Mackay. He's dead, but his memory still haunts me. I have been safe, but I fear now that my past is going to meet up with me again somehow. And it will destroy both of us. You must get away, Christine. You must go far away from me and never come back."

"No! We've only just found each other—"

Beverly awoke with a start.

As she lay in bed, listening to the silence of the Castle, she wondered why she should dream about her sister now, after all these years. Long ago, when she had still had hopes of finding her twin, Beverly had dreamed nearly every night about their reunion. But then, when the hope had faded, the dreams had gone away. Until now. Beverly was startled by the content of the dream, the realism, the intensity of its emotion.

She got up, wrapped herself in a robe, and went to the window, from where she could just make out the snow-laden pine trees and granite boulders embracing the house; far below, dawn was breaking over the desert.

What did it mean, the nightmare she had just had? Why should she dream about her sister now? And why, now that she was awake, did the awful feeling of dread that had gripped her in the dream continue to chill her? Knowing that she would not be able to get back to sleep, she picked up the phone, asked for room service, and ordered tea and toast to be sent up.

As she nudged her feet into slippers and went from the bedroom into the adjoining sitting room, where she turned on lamps to chase away the nightmare's lingering gloom, Beverly briefly considered ringing Simon Jung's apartment to see if he was awake and would perhaps join her for breakfast. But she didn't, reminding herself once again that she couldn't get involved with her general manager. She didn't want to risk losing his friendship. How could she possibly tell him what she was afraid of without revealing her past? And if she did tell him, what would his reaction be? She owed him so much. She couldn't have made Star's what it was without Simon's special touch; many of the original and innovative ideas had been his, such as offering chilled towels at the swimming pool during the summer. But Simon meant more to her than that; he was more than just the man who ran her hotel.

While she waited for breakfast to be brought up, Beverly paced the small sitting room that she had furnished comfortably with deeply but-toned upholstery and thick velvet pillows; on the walls hung tranquil country scenes. There had been a time, not long ago, when her walls had been covered with letters from famous people and framed awards and certificates, back when she had been a Beverly Hills socialite involved in charities and fund-raising. But now her wall displays pertained to Beverly Burgess, who had been born only three and a half years ago. There wasn't much, but her most cherished memento was a framed menu from Amanha, a popular restaurant on the Rua Barão da Tôrre in Rio de Janeiro, where she had first met Simon Jung. Those few weeks in Brazil, when they had strolled along Ipanema and Copacabana beaches in the moonlight, discussing plans for her new resort, were among Beverly's most treasured memories.

Next to the menu was a photograph of her and Simon on top of Sugar Loaf, with a breathtaking view of Rio in the background. They were smiling and relaxed, but they stood with an obvious space between them, a self-conscious posture.

Beverly had lied to Simon. She had offered him an invented past, phony reasons for her wealth, excuses for why she had never married. But she feared now that Simon was going to find out who she really was. Otis Quinn, the tabloid journalist, was coming to Star's—tomorrow. Was he going to expose those lies? Was that going to mark the end of her relationship with Simon? Would Simon judge her before she had a chance to explain about the place called Butterfly, where women had paid for sex, and a man named Danny Mackay, whom she had driven to suicide?

Beverly went into her private bathroom, a chamber done in black marble with gold fixtures. As she let the water run in the tub, she slipped out of the satin robe, glimpsing herself in one of the mirrors. She was still in good shape; she worked at it, being careful with exercise and what she ate. But there was a flaw: a tiny scar on the inside of her right thigh, just below her pubic hair, the only evidence of a tattoo she had had removed— the tattoo of a butterfly.

As the steaming water filled the tub, Beverly thought again about Simon.

Was he interested in a particular woman? She could only speculate, their private lives being something they had never discussed during their two and a half years together. Whom Simon entertained in his apartment, or whose room he visited, was none of Beverly's concern. But she had seen the way some of the female guests looked at Simon and the attention he had paid to some of them in return.

As she dipped a tentative toe into the hot water, Beverly felt herself begin to relax. Dawn was washing over the mountain, chasing away the shadows of her nightmare. If she was threatened—if Star's was threatened—she would fight. And perhaps, she thought as she glimpsed the brand-new day outside her window, the unexpected dream about her sister was in some way a good omen. A sign that there was always a reason for hope.

Philippa stood out on the balcony of her suite at the Marriott Desert Springs and watched the new day creep slowly across the desert. Moments ago, she had witnessed an astonishing phenomenon: just as the sun had broken behind her, Mount San Jacinto, which rose directly before her, had flared suddenly bright red, as if its slopes were on fire. It had blazed angrily for about thirty seconds, in an almost blinding crimson; in the next instant the fire had gone out and it was an ordinary snow-covered mountain again.

The desert air was biting and cold but so transparent that it made one think that this was what the moon's atmosphere would be like, if the moon had air. Philippa felt increasingly alive with each breath she took, as if pure oxygen, refrigerated by the snowy mountains encircling the desert, were filling her lungs. Starlite might be threatened, she told herself, but she was going to face the challenge with energy and determination. Whatever strategy her unknown adversary was using—the mystery person behind Gaspar Enriques—Philippa had been developing a few secret strategies of her own.

The first was a tactic known as a poison pill, a motion designed to render Starlite less desirable for anyone contemplating a hostile takeover. Her second course of strategy, should it come to that, was to call in a white knight, someone friendly to Starlite who would buy a large block of shares, thus preventing Miranda from obtaining controlling interest. Ralph Murdock, Starlite's attorney, had three such companies lined up, just in case. Whoever was behind Enriques and Miranda was not going to get Starlite without one hell of a fight.

She shivered inside her robe. The morning was cold, but she shivered more from the lingering effects of the strange dream she had had than from the winter temperature.

She couldn't remember what the dream had been about, only that it had frightened her. She had awakened abruptly, her heart pounding. Her impulse had been to leave her spacious king-sized bed and go to the other side of the suite, where Ricky slept in an identical bedroom, separated from her by a large living room, and curl up against his warmth and strength. But then she had looked over at Charmie, who was sleeping in the other king-sized bed, and she knew that it wouldn't be right. She and Ricky were no longer alone in the privacy of her Perth villa.

Ricky came out onto the balcony then, carrying papers and a cup of coffee from the room service cart. He wore a faded T-shirt, a souvenir from when he had crewed on a replica of a seventeenth-century square-rigger; on the front was a picture of the ship, *Sea Hawk,* and on the back it said "Yard Work Doesn't Always Mean Gardening."

"I've taken care of most of these, Philippa," he said, handing the papers to her. "But I've marked a couple that you might want to look at." He had spent the evening drive going through the faxes he had picked up from the office before they had left L.A. Mostly they were letters from people who had heard that Philippa was back in the U.S. and who had sent charity appeals, invitations to fund-raisers, requests to give speeches. The majority of the correspondence Ricky was able to handle himself. The special ones, such as the request from Oprah Winfrey for Philippa to appear on her show with Jenny Craig and Richard Simmons, Ricky marked especially for Philippa's personal consideration.

She took the letters and handed him the notebook she always kept at her nightstand; it contained a few notes she had jotted down for *The 99-Point Starlite Weight Loss and Beauty Plan.*

Their fingers touched as he took them; his eyes met hers.

And then he went back inside, reading the notes: "Point Sixty: Fixin's make you fat. Point Sixty-one: Take a breath between bites. Point Sixty-two: Wait twenty minutes before seconds. Point Sixty-three: Pee before you weigh yourself."

Ricky looked back at Philippa and wondered, Did she follow these rules herself in order to maintain that fantastic figure? He saw that she was still watching him. God, but he wanted her—the way her satin bathrobe fluttered open at the knee, revealing a smooth, tan calf; the way the collar flowed between her breasts, almost daring him to come and part the material and slip his hand inside; the disarray of her auburn hair, the early morning sleepiness around her eyes . . .

Realizing that he was becoming aroused, he put such thoughts from his mind and got to work.

As Philippa watched Ricky set up his electronic typewriter on the dining room table, she noticed that he hadn't shaved, so that a light stubble covered his jaw. Although his long hair was combed neatly back into a ponytail, she was aware of a sexy kind of casual messiness about him—the patched jeans, the T-shirt that had seen many summers.

Could it only be barely a month since she had first felt his lips on hers, those young, strong arms around her? It amazed her to recall how suddenly uninhibited she had been. After months of a rather formal relationship with Ricky, his one impulsive kiss had stripped away her reserve. To think of the way he had made love to her in the summer sunshine that spilled across her living room—his hands, hard and calloused from years of sailing, so gently exploring her body, his tongue caressing her, and finally, the powerful way he had entered her, lifting her hips off the floor with each thrust as she squeezed him deeper into herself. As Philippa watched him now at the typewriter, seeing how the sleeves of his T-shirt hugged thick biceps, a rush of hot desire shot through her. Moments after they had made passionate, impulsive love on her carpet, they had lain in each other's arms, exhausted, dazzled, and she had felt him grow hard inside her again. The second time had been even more stunning than the first.

Philippa allowed herself to watch him a moment longer—wishing, *wishing*—then she forced herself to draw in a bracing deep breath, filling her lungs with desert clarity, and remind herself of her purpose here. Later, when her work here was done, she would explore her startling new relationship with Ricky, but right now there was too much to be done to waste time indulging herself in fantasies. Ivan Hendricks was due any minute with his report on Beverly Burgess.

By coincidence, Charmie was also thinking about Ivan. Wearing a Ruth Norman caftan of red, gold, and black paisley-print rayon, and matching red, gold, and black bracelets, Charmie was trying to brush out her hair, which kept collecting, because of the dry air, in a blond cloud around her shoulders, flying up and crackling with each brush stroke. She wanted to look good for Ivan. And he was going to be here any minute!

The thought of it had robbed her of sleep; Ivan had visited her in erotic dreams, waking her in a fever. She had thought she was over him; it had been such a long time since she had last seen him. The man she had been dating for the past year, a wealthy Pacific Palisades stockbroker, was so attractive and so exciting—their trip last summer to southern Spain had been Sam's idea—that she had given little thought to Ivan Hendricks.

And then, to see him in Perth! When Ivan had walked into Philippa's living room just four days ago, Charmie had thought her heart would stop. He shook her hand and she felt something zing through her, and a memory had come back in such living detail that it had taken her breath away—the memory of one incredible morning, when she had been baking butterscotch brownies and had received the surprise of her life.

Charmie had just put a batch of brownies in the oven and was licking the batter off the spatula when she had heard a car in the drive.

Going to the kitchen window and looking out, she had been astonished to see Ivan getting out of his car, carrying a large, flat parcel. He had never been to her house before; she hadn't thought he even knew where she lived. He walked up the drive, looking right and left, and placed the package on her doorstep; he had been about to walk away when Charmie had opened the door, startling him.

"Miss Charmer!" he said. "I didn't think you were home! I called and got your answering machine. The recording said you were out."

"I always turn the machine on when I'm baking," she said with a smile, holding up her flour-dusted hands, flustered by his unexpected visit. "Saves getting batter on the phone," she said, laughing. "The benefits of modern technology. Please," she said, "come in."

He hesitated. "I'm interrupting you," he said.

"Please. Come in."

He brought the package inside. "This is for you," he said self-consciously.

As Charmie broke the string and tore away the brown wrapper, careful not to get flour on whatever was inside, she was aware of Ivan standing there, watching her. It was a hot summer day, and he was wearing a Hawaiian shirt tucked inside white slacks. The top buttons of the shirt were open, and she had a glimpse of dark chest hairs.

When the wrapping fell away, Charmie gasped. She held up the framed lithograph and looked at Ivan. "How did you know?" she said.

He blushed to the roots of his military crew cut. "I heard you telling Miss Roberts that you liked this artist, that you were collecting him because his style goes with your new house. You mentioned this particular print. So, when I saw it, I decided to get it for you."

"I don't know what to say. It's . . . it's beautiful! Thank you," she said softly.

They stared at each other.

"Well, I'd better be going."

"Please, stay and have some coffee," Charmie said, hurrying away into the kitchen so that he had no chance to refuse. "The brownies went into the oven a little while ago," she called over her shoulder. "They should be ready in about ten minutes."

"So," Ivan asked, coming into the kitchen, "how is your son?" looking around, as if to say, *Where* is your son?

Charmie turned and wanted to say, What about you, Ivan? Do *you* have sons—or a wife? Instead, she said, "Nathan is visiting his father for the summer. Ron might have been a lousy husband to me, but he's a good father to our son. After the divorce, Ron quit his job and went up to Oregon, where he opened a bait stand on the Rogue River. Every summer, he and Nathan spend a few weeks together, fishing. It's good. For them both."

Ivan nodded, as if he knew all about that. But he didn't say anything more—didn't let on if he knew about sons and ex-wives.

"The brownies smell heavenly," he said after a moment as he accepted a cup of coffee and stirred cream into it. Even though she had invited him to sit, he remained standing.

"Yes!" she said, opening the oven to check on the brownies. "Hardly allowed on the Starlite program! I never could stick to a diet. Doomed to be fat forever, I guess."

She felt him come close to her. "Please don't say that. You're a beautiful woman. You're perfect just the way you are."

"Well!" she said, nervously wiping her hands on the apron she wore over her caftan. It was one of Hannah's Moroccan imports—made of a loose-weave cotton dyed beige and wine red. Instead of buttons up the front, there were wooden pegs and loops. "I'm afraid you've really taken me by surprise. You're the very last person I ever thought I'd find in my kitchen!"

He was standing close enough for her to detect a cologne that mingled seductively with the aromas of butterscotch and chocolate. The kitchen had suddenly become very warm.

"I'm glad you were home," he said quietly. "I was just going to leave the painting and go." He paused, and the way he looked at her, his eyes traveling over her caftan, it almost felt as if his hands were doing the exploration. "I guess you and I have never been alone before."

That hasn't been my doing, she thought. "You're always so business-like," she said, leaning against the kitchen table because her legs were starting to feel funny. "You show up promptly on time, deliver your report to Philippa, and then disappear." She smiled. "Like the Lone Ranger."

He stepped closer. She saw confusion in his eyes, as though he were struggling with a decision. "The brownies smell wonderful."

"They're my own recipe," she said, barely able to find her voice. "I add butterscotch . . ."

"May I taste the batter?"

She looked at him. "Yes," she said, "of course—" But as she started to reach for the mixing bowl, Ivan suddenly took her by the shoulders and licked the corner of her mouth.

Charmie froze. There had been a smear of batter there; she hadn't known it.

It was most exciting thing a man had ever done to her.

And then he was kissing her on the mouth.

Her arms went up around his neck; he pulled her hard against him. "My God," he said, trying to kiss her everywhere at once, driving his hands into her hair. "I've wanted you for so long."

"Oh, Ivan," she breathed. He felt so good, so right. His mouth was perfect, he kissed hungrily and sensually, just the way she had imagined he would. She ran her hands over his body, feasting on muscles she had for so long wanted to touch.

He explored her breasts, fumbling with the wooden pegs in loops, finally ripping them open and plunging his hand into her bra. Charmie cried out. He stifled her cry with his mouth.

She hurriedly unbuttoned his shirt and spread it open, pulling it out of his belt. She moved her lips over his chest and down onto his hard, flat stomach.

When he reached back under her dress and unhooked her bra, she moaned, reached down for him, and gasped. She couldn't get her hand all the way around, he was so large.

Ivan lifted her breasts out of their lace cups and pressed them to his bare chest. There was an open jar of butterscotch topping on the table. Dipping his fingers in, he smeared some onto her nipple and licked it off.

They stumbled against the table, scattering crockery, their passion mounting, their movements growing frantic as they kissed and groped, trying to discover each other all at once. And they were so self-involved that, as Ivan hurriedly pulled her caftan up over her thighs and she frantically worked at his belt, they weren't aware that the phone was ringing.

But when a voice suddenly came loudly from the answering machine— "Hi, Charmie! It's Sam. I just wanted to say, you were *fantastic* last night!" She said, "Oh my God!" pulled away from Ivan, and dashed into the hall.

Before Charmie could hit the *mute* button, Sam managed to say, "How about you and I fly to Frisco next weekend? We'll get a room at the St.

Francis, and we'll never leave it. We'll just spend the whole weekend—"

She came back into the kitchen and looked at Ivan, who was buttoning his shirt and tucking it in.

"The drawbacks to modern technology," she said, modestly closing her caftan over her breasts. "Oh, Ivan . . . I'm so sorry."

He looked as if he had just received the worst news of his life. Then he came up and took her face in his hands. "This wasn't why I came here," he said softly. "I truly thought you weren't home. This can't be for us. I can't tell you why, and I won't come here again. But believe me when I tell you that you are a beautiful woman and that I've wanted you since the first time we met. You are a *real* woman, Charmie, who embraces life. I've never liked thin women; they always seem so breakable, making me hold back. I don't like to feel ribs or hipbones or collarbones when I'm making love. When I hold a woman, I don't want to hold a skeleton, I want to feel flesh, substance. I want *you.*" He smiled and touched her hair. "And I promise you, I will always remember this," and he kissed this corner of her mouth where the batter had been.

Charmie had just finishing brushing her hair when Ivan arrived at their suite.

"Make yourself comfortable," Philippa said. "Would you like a cup of coffee? You take it with cream, right?"

"Thank you." He looked at Charmie. "Hello," he said quietly.

He, too, was thinking of that morning in her kitchen; he had thought of little else since seeing her again in Perth.

"I'm sorry, Miss Roberts," he said when Philippa handed him a cup of coffee. "I wasn't able to get any new information on Beverly Burgess. No one knows a thing about her, and when I tried to get to see her, that watchdog of hers, Simon Jung, ran interference. Beverly Burgess is a more closely kept secret than Zsa Zsa's age."

"Did you go up to Star's again?"

"I had dinner there last night. Very elegant, but it's a good thing I have an expense account. Darned near froze my earlobes off, too. I did some casual asking around but didn't get anything much. And even though I hung around until the last tram down the mountain, Miss Burgess never appeared."

Philippa thought a moment, then said, "I had hoped to get a look at her before approaching her about the ad. If she isn't my sister, I think I would be able to sense it. I hate to just call and say, 'Hi, I'm Christine Singleton. Your ad says you're looking for me.' At least, not until I know who she is and why she's interested in me."

"Well," Ivan said, "there's going to be a big Christmas ball there tomorrow night. I figure this Burgess woman is bound to show up at it, since she's the hostess. Maybe you'll get a chance to look her over then."

Philippa went to the sliding-glass door and looked out at the day that was brightening; there were even a few breakfasters around the pool. "Ivan," she said, "where exactly is Star's?"

He went onto the balcony with her, the desert wind cutting through their hair and clothes. "There," he said pointing straight ahead. "That highest peak is San Jacinto. Do you see the two smaller peaks just below it? And the saddle in between? That's where Star's is. Nestled in that saddle."

Philippa stared at the spot, where a band of white lay cozily between two craggy peaks. There was no evidence of a fabulous resort there; all she could see was snow. "To think," she said, "that I might be looking at my sister right now . . ."

When Ivan heard the hopeful tone in her voice, he had to give himself a mental kick in the pants. At times like this, he always came perilously close to telling her what he really knew—the truth. But he had promised to be silent, and Ivan Hendricks kept his promises.

"And about Caanan Corporation," Ivan said, returning to the room and glancing at Charmie before helping himself to slice of pineapple from the room service cart. "The address is a drop all right, nothing but a vacant store. I've got a man watching it, but I doubt our friend will show. Most likely whoever is behind the bogus Caanan knows we're on to him. When are you holding the board meeting?"

"Day after tomorrow."

"You'll probably get your answers then."

Answers, Philippa thought, that she was dreading to hear. "Ivan," she said, "I need to find out some information about a company based in Brazil. Could you do that for me? It's very important."

"You want me to go to South America," he said.

"Can you?"

"You don't ask for much, do you, Miss Roberts?" he said, but smiling as he said it. He shrugged. "Okay. What's the name of the company?"

"Miranda International. They're trying to take over Starlite. I have to find a way to stop them."

"Brazil, huh?" he said, looking at Charmie, even though she hadn't spoken. "Sure, I'll go. When do you want me to leave?"

As Hannah hurried into her office, she thought her purse felt heavier than usual. But of course she knew this was her imagination—the added weight of a tiny safe deposit box key couldn't possibly make a difference.

Still, she felt it there all the same, tugging at her arm like a fretful child, as if telling her to forget her mad folly, go back to the bank, get those stock certificates out of there and safely back into the wall safe in her bedroom where they belonged. But Hannah knew there was no turning back. By this time tomorrow she would no longer own 5 percent of Starlite stock. Her portion was going to belong to the party whose telephone call had finally come, someone who had agreed to her offer and who would collect the shares at the arranged meeting place.

And after that, what? Philippa will have to be told the truth, she decided as she entered her office. I'll tell Philippa what I've done, and then I'll resign.

"Mrs. Scadudo," her secretary said. "Miss Roberts's secretary just telephoned from Palm Springs. The board meeting has been moved to a place called Star's."

Hannah looked at the slip of paper. The meeting was day after tomorrow, but the stock certificates would be transferred in time, and she would have received the nearly one million in cash for them. What she prayed for now was that when Alan returned from Rio, he wouldn't go to the wall safe for something and find the certificates gone.

"And Miss Lind is back from Singapore," the secretary added before hurrying away.

Ingrid came in from the designing room, fabulously dressed in a navy blue suit, white silk blouse, and low-heeled shoes. Her blond hair was carefully swept back into a small bun at the nape of her neck, where a large navy blue bow framed the sharp lines of her neck and jaw.

"Welcome home!" Hannah said, receiving her friend in an embrace. "How was your trip?"

"Exhausting and invigorating!" Ingrid said with a laugh. She towered over Hannah; she towered over everyone. "Here, I've brought you this. It's not your Christmas present, just a souvenir from Singapore."

Hannah gasped when she opened the gift box and saw that it contained an exquisite gold rope chain with a jade clasp. "Ingrid, you shouldn't have!"

"Believe me, that's what I was thinking when I bought it," Ingrid said as she drew a pack of Gauloises out of her purse and proceeded to light one. "I purchased it at Poh Heng, where the prices are calculated by abacus and based on the weight of the necklace and the prevailing price of gold. After which came the requisite haggling. It took me an hour just to pay for it!"

Hannah gave her another quick hug and said, "It really was sweet of you. Thank you."

"What did you think of the Kashmiri silk I sent this time?" Ingrid asked as they walked into the noisy designing room, where people worked at drafting tables and dressmaker's dummies.

"I've never seen such colors," Hannah said, linking her arm through Ingrid's. "The sea green is stunning! I have everyone working on it already. We have something summery in mind—bathing suit cover-ups, wraps for cocktail parties, that sort of thing." Hannah spoke energetically to hide her distress. In less than forty-eight hours she would no longer be working with Ingrid. And most likely they would no longer be friends.

Ingrid blew rancid smoke into the air, receiving a few covert looks from the designers. "Tell me about this emergency board meeting I was called back to attend. Alan sounded annoyed on the phone."

"He was annoyed because Philippa sent him to Rio and he didn't want to go."

"I don't see what he's complaining about. Rio is where you find the best seafood on the South American continent, and nothing surpasses Brazil for amethysts." Ingrid didn't mention the men, in which Rio also excelled.

"I'm afraid Alan doesn't see it the way you do!" Hannah wished Alan and Ingrid weren't so antagonistic toward each other. Their instant, mutual dislike when Ingrid was first brought in seven years ago had not softened. Hannah went on to explain about the threatened takeover by Miranda International and added that Philippa had called for an internal audit of all departments.

"An internal audit! What for?"

Hannah looked away. "Apparently she's found some discrepancies in the figures."

"Oh," Ingrid said as she paused to look over an artist's shoulder, where an illustration for evening wear was laid out on the drawing board. "Palm Springs, you say? That suits me just fine. The desert's a great place to find good silver jewelry, turquoise, and semiprecious stones."

"I don't know that it's in the desert exactly. We're meeting up in the mountains, at a place called Star's."

Ingrid's face lit up. "Star's! Well, well. It looks as if my aborted vacation in Singapore won't be a total loss after all." She was suddenly intrigued by the prospect of what Star's had to offer in the way of food. And men. "I think," she said after a moment, "that it is going to be a very interesting meeting indeed."

....★

37

Bunny's sitting room was a mess, with suitcases flung open, their contents strewn about, and canvas duffel bags lying limp and empty among bolts of fabric, wig boxes, scattered shoes, even a dressmaker's dummy. Frieda and her weary-eyed companions had just a little over twenty-four hours left in which to perform a miracle.

"This!" Frieda said at last, pulling out a bolt of dark chocolate velvet. "This is it! It's perfect!"

Jeanine, a gray-haired woman with small eyes behind wire-rimmed glasses, groaned and said, "I was afraid you'd pick that."

"You can do it, sweetheart," Frieda said. "I've seen you work miracles."

"Yeah, yeah," Jeanine said as she took the bolt from Frieda and draped it over the dressmaker's dummy, giving it a dubious look. But, plucking some pins out of the little cushion she wore on her wrist, she soon began to work magic, like Cinderella's little animal friends. Within minutes a gown began to take shape.

Even though Frieda's hastily gathered crew complained about the task they had been called upon to perform, none had refused the assignment. In fact, they had all agreed that this was a stroke of genius on Frieda's part and were happy to be on the team; happy also with the payment, for three of them, and the chance to work off owed favors for the other two. When they had asked her how she had come up with the idea, Frieda had just smiled. She couldn't very well tell them about her marathon sex with Raoul, which had ended just before dawn, a few hours ago. They would get visions of Faye Dunaway and William Holden in *Network*—Dunaway having sex with Holden, he on the bottom, she on top, while she talked excitedly about television ratings strategies.

It hadn't been like that with her and Raoul. When they got down to the business of making love, that was what they did: make love. That was after the brilliant idea had come to her when she had experienced the most stunning orgasm of her life and the face of Larry Wolfe had popped into her mind.

Raoul. Frieda hadn't felt so refreshed in years.

Now that the fabric had been chosen, Frieda addressed herself to the pastel sketches Sam was executing on a pad. She thumbed through them, discarded most, and said, "This one comes closest, but not close enough."

"You gotta understand," am said, "I ain't seen Bunny in her new metamorphosis," he said, pronouncing it meta-mor-*pho*-sis. "So I'm working blind. Where is she, anyway?"

"I sent her downstairs, to the theater."

"Did she get cheek implants?" he asked, a piece of chalk poised over his most recent sketch. Sam was the roundest man Frieda had ever seen, with an enormous round middle, big round head, and pudgy hands and feet. He reminded her of the tire man on Michelin guides. He was also the most talented artist she had ever known; all the studios used Sam, and so did various southern California police departments. "No," she said. "No cheeks."

"Chin? As I recall, Bunny had a chin like Andy Gump's."

"I think her chin might have been augmented," Frieda said.

Helen came out of the bathroom with a wig on a dummy's head. "What do you think, Frieda?"

She frowned. "Nowhere near. It has to be . . . I don't know, vampier or something. It's too nineties. And the color isn't right."

"You want black, don't you?"

"I don't know. She never made a color picture. Dark. Just dark."

The sitting room door opened and Bunny came in, red eyed from having been up all night, ever since Frieda's mind-blowing phone call. When Frieda told her the new idea, Bunny had immediately snapped out of her depression and begun making plans. She had thought Frieda would come up to her room right away, to discuss strategy. It was funny, though; Frieda had said, "I'll be there in a while," but had in fact shown up hours later. If Bunny didn't know better, she would have sworn there had been someone there in the cabin with her.

"Sweetheart!" Frieda said, jumping up. "What did you see?"

"*Robin Hood* and *Her Wicked Ways*. Frieda, I'm going blind from staring at that screen!"

"Show us something."

They all sat down and waited while Bunny got into character, Helen and Sam and Jeanine staring at her, hardly believing the transformation. When Frieda had said Bunny had had some plastic surgery, they hadn't expected *this*. She was a beauty; Sam couldn't wait to get to his sketch pad, Helen to her wigs, and Jeanine to the dress form. Now they knew what they were working with. When Bunny walked across the room and did the famous head toss, her small audience clapped and cheered enthusiastically.

"All right, come on!" Frieda said, retrieving her purse and taking Bunny by the arm. There wasn't a minute to lose; the Christmas ball was tomorrow night.

"Where are we going?" Bunny said.

"Back to the movies!"

Bunny laughed wearily. Where on earth had Frieda suddenly gotten such energy? It didn't matter; it was the result that counted. And when Bunny reminded herself of the secret plot she and her six companions were hatching, when she imagined the sensation she was going to cause at the ball tomorrow night, her weariness vanished and she went hurrying off with Frieda to fill her head with another few hours of Marion Star.

Queen Cleopatra was luxuriating in an enormous marble bathtub filled with goat's milk that just barely covered her breasts. As she ran a sea sponge over her body, the milk undulated, occasionally exposing her nipples. She invited her two handmaidens to undress and join her. As they did, the camera zooming in on their lower legs to show garments falling to the marble floor and then delicate feet walking down the bathtub steps, the music became erotic and sensual, intimating what was going on in the tub between the Egyptian queen and her maidservants.

Andrea had seen enough, as had been the case with *Her Wicked Ways,* which she had walked out on yesterday. She collected her things and left the small theater, stepping over the legs of Frieda Goldman and Bunny Kowalski as she went. Since it was one of Marion's talkies, she had gone hoping to see a more dignified film, but she had quickly realized that it was only another exploitation movie designed to titillate the public's prurient curiosity.

Andrea made her way back to the Chinese Room and took a seat in the leather wing chair. She had brought Marion's diary with her.

"Talkies arrived," Marion had written, "and Hollywood was thrown into a panic. The unspoken question everywhere was, Who is going to make it, and who is not? Many of us had bad voices, many of us simply could not act. So many big-time actors and actresses were big-time solely because they looked good on film, not because they could act. My darling Dexter kept telling me not to worry, that I would do fine in talking pictures. He told me he was developing a special feature, just for me, with sound and talking and everything. It frightened me. I was twenty-two years old and still not sure of myself.

"But I survived, I did make it into talkies. Not all of us did. Poor John

Gilbert—I do wonder if he was the victim of sabotage, as some claim. And my sweet Rudy. Valentino would never have survived talking pictures; his Italian accent was too thick, no one could understand him. I mourned with the world when he died. He had been such a dear friend, and a polished lover. After his death, Rudy was branded by men who called him a 'pink powder puff.' But it was their own insecurities and jealousies speaking, because they couldn't have been more wrong. Darling Rudy was a consummate sensualist, and he knew—oh, he *knew*—how to please a woman.

"But I made it into talking pictures. In fact, the public went wild for my voice. *Variety* said that it reminded one of mink. In 1929 Ramsey produced and directed the biggest-budget movie of all time, *Queen of the Nile,* and I was the star. It was for this movie that he made me perfect the head toss that was to become my signature. When *Queen of the Nile* came out, it caused a sensation.

"It also made me the highest-paid actress in the world and such a phenomenon in Hollywood that Ramsey calculated it was time for us to become lovers.

"There was no romantic buildup, no getting into the mood, none of the atmospheric devices he used in his films. We had just finished dinner one night and he said, 'Let's go to bed.' Looking back, I wonder if he had been building me up so that I would be worthy of him. A man like Dexter Bryant Ramsey didn't go to bed with just any woman. He had romanced ladies of title and distinction. Gertrude Winkler, the daughter of a Fresno shoe salesman, did not match up to Ramsey's high standards. But now I was Marion Star; now I could grace his bed.

"How strange to think that, after all the men I had been with, that I should be nervous that first time with Dex. I was bashful, like a bride, and almost reluctant to remove my nightgown. So Dexter did it for me. Actually, he ripped it off my body. Literally. It startled me and frightened me a little. And when we made love—could one call what we did making love?—it was more like an assault. I was too young and, despite my bedroom experiences, too naïve to understand at the time that, after having such Svengali-like power over me for five years, Ramsey still needed to exert his dominance.

"We became the king and queen of Hollywood after that. Everyone worshiped us, there was nothing we could not have. We ruled the world from our love retreat on Mount San Jacinto, and we held parties to which only the very specially chosen could come.

"It was there, at Star's Haven, that I bore our love child. Dexter had made me abort my other pregnancies, but since this one was his, he let me keep it. I named her Lavinia, for the character in *Wicked Ways.*

Andrea closed the book; it was the last page of the diary. She stared at the blown-up photograph that dominated the room: Marion's face, dark and smouldering, smoky eyes that swam with sensuality and sadness.

And suddenly Andrea wondered: Marion Star had disappeared in 1932. *Was it possible she was still alive?*

"How is your project coming?" Carole asked as she watched Larry dive into the pool. They were not swimming in one of their private bungalow pools but in the giant indoor pool at the Castle, where guests sat on marble islands out in the water or walked across the romantic bridge that was a replica of the Bridge of Sighs in Venice.

"What project?" Larry said when he surfaced, flipping glistening black hair out of his eyes.

She laughed. She thought he was joking. "The Marion Star project!"

"Oh, that." He pulled himself out of the pool. This was his fifth dive; he was doing it not for his own pleasure, but to show off his muscles to Carole, as if to say, Can you just imagine what this body can do in bed? He climbed out and sat next to her, reached out and touched her throat. "Do you wear these *all* the time?" he asked, meaning the pearl necklace Sanford had given to her before she had left for Star's. She was wearing a bikini, hardly a pearl necklace outfit.

"All the time," she said.

He grinned. "Even in bed?"

"Come on, Larry, about your new screenplay. Who are you thinking of casting in the role of Marion?"

"Why? Are you interested?"

As she ran her hands through her ash-blond hair, she saw his eyes flicker to her breasts. "It could be a challenging role," she said.

"For a twenty-five-year-old."

"Well," she said, "with the right lighting, makeup . . ."

"And George Lucas on the special effects."

She stood, gathered up her towel and lotions, and walked to one of the private changing rooms; she shut the door but didn't lock it.

"Hey!" Larry said, running after her. "I was only joking!" He knocked. "Come on, Carole. Lighten up."

"Go away!"

He forced his way in and pressed up against her. "Is it that important to you? Do you really want the part?"

She put her hands on his chest and gave him a shove. "Get out!"

"Listen," he said, reaching for her. The cubicle barely had room for two people; he had no trouble getting an arm around her. "I said I was sorry. I thought you could take a joke."

"I was serious, Larry," she said, trying to twist away from him. "I could do that part."

"Okay," he said, "so you were serious." He pinned her against the wall and began to kiss her.

She pushed him away again, but halfheartedly.

He pulled at her bikini top and it fell away. "All right. Let's talk about it," he said thickly.

Carole knew she had him then, but this was not the place. She had to get something in writing, a signature . . .

"Not here," she said breathlessly.

"Yes—"

"Larry, I'll have to scream."

He laughed. "What do you want? Champagne and roses?"

I want my husband. "Why not? If I'm going to have my first affair, don't I have the right to want it to be perfect?"

He gave her a long look, his hand squeezing her breast. "Okay," he said. "We could make a night of it. Just you and me."

"Tomorrow night," she said. "After the Christmas ball, come to my bungalow . . ."

Andrea had the bungalow to herself, since Larry, she assumed, was off somewhere trying to seduce Carole Page. She was at her typewriter, working up the proposal she and Larry were going to show to Mr. Yamato when he arrived day after tomorrow—a story line that Andrea was making so delicious that she knew Mr. Yamato would love it.

The deal with the Tokyo businessman had been her idea, even though Larry thought it had been his. After the humiliation of the awards ceremony, in which Larry had not acknowledged Andrea's contribution to his work—hell, her entire responsibility for his supposed work—her first impulse had been to march backstage, tell him off in front of everyone, and then walk out. But as she had watched Larry preen for the cameras and frankly tell everyone that, yes, he *was* a gifted writer, Andrea had decided to hold off and bide her time.

She pretended everything was as usual while she searched for just the right way to take her revenge. It came to her a few weeks later, when she read about Mr. Yamato, listed as the fourth-richest man in Japan, who had a thing for Marion Star. He was an avid collector and often amazed guests at parties by reciting all the dialogue from one of her movies, straight through without making an error. When Andrea recalled hearing that Marion Star's diary had been found during some remodeling at Star's Haven, her plan for revenge was born. That was when she began her campaign to get Larry interested in the Marion Star story, planting in his mind the suggestion that he might want to write that screenplay and get Yamato to back the movie. After engineering a meeting between the two men, which again Larry had somehow thought was his own doing, she then convinced Larry that, since it was sure to be such a box office hit, he would be wise to put some of his own money into the project.

She wasn't aiming for simple public humiliation; she wanted Larry's financial ruin as well.

Andrea went to the bar and poured herself a drink. It went down as deliciously as her anticipation of the look on Larry's face tomorrow night, when she gave him his Christmas "present" at the ball. Everything was in place, her plan was set in motion.

In just over twenty-four hours she was going to be a free woman, on her own for the first time in seventeen years. She knew exactly what she was going to do with that freedom. The first thing was to explore whether Marion Star might still be alive, and also find out what became of Lavinia, her love child.

And then she was thinking of seeing if she could find Chad McCormick, whom she hadn't seen since their brief but magical affair in New Mexico eleven years ago. She had heard that he was living in L.A. now and that he wasn't married . . .

38

Beverly Hills, California, 1975

The mansion on the hill was so audaciously illuminated that it looked like the Parthenon ready for tourists. A stream of cars entered the massive wrought-iron gates; at the front door, maids greeted the arriving guests, taking coats and wraps and giving the ladies small corsages of winter roses. The party was being held in the terraced garden at the rear of Philippa's new house where, under a striped awning, a band was playing. As newly arrived guests emerged onto the flagstone terrace and into the cool evening air, they saw a breathtaking view as the hillside sloped away from the house down into the canyon. Fairy lights twinkled in the trees; spotlights hidden in the grass cast upward beams on statues and bushes; the enormous swimming pool glowed with shimmering pale blue water. Under a magnificent canopy a feast had been set out: long tables with hams and roast beefs, each with a white-coated chef in attendance, carving knife ready; crystal bowls of artistically arranged salads; and chafing dishes of steaming delicacies. Young men in red jackets and tight black pants circulated through the crowd with platters of hors d'oeuvres.

Everyone ate and drank without reserve, because this was not exactly a "free" party—it was an event to raise money for Philippa's personal charity, Vietnamese war orphans. People were willing to write large checks for the opportunity to dance under the stars and hobnob with celebrities on an extravagant terrace that was said to have been patterned after the one at Versailles.

Philippa moved among her guests, wearing a simple long pale yellow gown with a white fur wrap because of the chilly evening, stopping to talk with people she knew and to be introduced to those she didn't—movie people who lived in estates nearby, politicians, bigwigs from universities and medical centers, the heads of corporations, doctors, lawyers, artists, and writers. A mix, but a wealthy mix. Being the president of such a large corporation as Starlite Industries, which was now traded on the New York Stock Exchange, Philippa enjoyed at last holding an A-list party.

As she stood with the mayor and his wife beside the pool, where fountains splashed at both ends, her gaze moved up to the third floor of her Tudor mansion, where a light glowed in one of the bedroom windows. She was filled with an almost unbearable yearning. That was where she wanted to be—up there, where her heart had already gone.

Philippa had learned, during her gradual rise in success and wealth, the art of appearing interested while her mind was really on other things. Smiling at the mayor and his wife, she drew her gaze from the bedroom window and took another quick look at the French doors opening onto the terrace, where guests were coming and going; she searched for the face she most wanted to see tonight. He hadn't arrived yet. He had promised he would come, but he wasn't here yet.

When she returned her attention to the mayor's wife, who was praising her, Philippa experienced one of the strange flashes she had been having lately. It wasn't a physical phenomenon, but a mental one, in which, quite out of the blue, she was suddenly ripped out of herself and taken to the edge of the crowd, where she observed the scene with an objective eye. And it would amaze her, in that split second before her self came flying back into her body again, to think that all this—the mansion, the guests, the waiters—was all hers. She had fulfilled her vow that someday she was going to be somebody. What would Johnny Singleton think of his little Dolly now?

Philippa was rich now because her company was rich. There were nearly six hundred salons around the nation, and plans to expand into Europe. Starlite also owned subsidiaries, such as Starlite Natural Beauty Products, a cosmetics division run by Charmie; Starlite Foods, which offered frozen dinners, low-calorie desserts, diet margarine, and high-fiber bread, all packaged in a familiar blue wrapper with a star logo in the corner; and the latest addition, The Perfect Size dress shops, a chain of stores across the country that offered fashions created by Hannah Scadudo.

"I want full-figured models," Hannah had instructed the advertising agency when the new line was launched. "Our customers want to see what the clothes are going to look like on themselves, not on a twig." Using larger-sized models in her advertising and also in the Perfect Size mail order catalogs was a revolutionary idea; Hannah believed that other manufacturers of larger-size clothing offended their clientele by modeling their fashions on skinny women, as if to say that those were the only women the clothes really looked good on. And she was right. Perfect Size fashions were catching on and starting to outstrip the established competition.

But the biggest boost to Starlite's success was the book that Philippa had come out with four years ago. *The Starlite Diet and Beauty Program* was now in its twelfth printing and still on the paperback best-seller lists. Opening with a brief history of the program followed by the personal testimonials of a few successful graduates, the book offered the diet plan in a simple, easy-to-follow format, along with Philippa's positive thinking philosophy and a chapter each written by Hannah and Charmie: "Dressing Thin" and "The Cosmetic Connection."

Philippa had also published a smaller book, *Hyperinsulinemia: Its Causes, Detection, and Control Through Diet,* which, while not a best-seller, continued to sell steadily to a select audience.

And when the Starlite offices had moved to their new glass tower on Wilshire, Philippa had decided to move from her house in Encino to this mansion in Beverly Hills.

As she left the mayor and moved on to other guests, she was joined by a breathless Charmie, who had a glass of wine in one hand and a chocolate truffle in the other. Her dazzling gold lamé caftan, with Belgian hand beading around the neckline and sleeves—one of Hannah's more breathtaking creations—shot diamondlike reflections over the flowering oleander bushes embracing this end of the pool. "The party's a big success, Philippa!" she said. "I knew you could do it!"

Eating the truffle and then dropping the napkin onto a tray held by a passing waiter, she touched the back of her hair, which had been gathered up in a gold lamé scarf, and eyed the waiter's rear end. She was thinking of Ivan Hendricks. They had invited him to the party and he had politely refused.

"Would you look at that child of mine!" she said, spotting Nathan, now a gawky fourteen-year-old appearing ill at ease in a tuxedo that looked as if four men had had to hold him down to get him into it; he was browsing through the buffet, eating everything in his path. Charmie had feared that his childhood had left permanent scars—the brutality he had witnessed, his father's alcoholism. But Nathan was turning into a nice, intelligent boy who had recently announced his decision to be a genetic researcher when he grew up. Not a day went by in which Charmie didn't get a scare, recalling how she had rescued him, and herself, just in time.

When she caught Philippa looking up at the third-floor bedroom window, she said, "Why don't you go up?"

"I can't leave my guests."

"Speaking of which, when does the star arrive?" Charmie was referring to Senator Paul Marquette.

"Soon," she said. "He'll be here soon."

After his visit to her office four and a half years ago, Philippa and Paul had become friends. Whenever he was in L.A., he made a point of seeing her, setting aside some of his time to have dinner and to talk. When he had reentered the senatorial race and won, he had said in his victory speech before fifty million television viewers that he owed his comeback to Starlite, specifically to Philippa Roberts.

"Hannah said you heard from Mrs. Chadwick today," Charmie said as they climbed the stone steps toward the upper terrace, where more guests were still arriving. "How is the old girl? Has she settled in?"

"She has her eye on every eligible male at Leisure World!"

Mrs. Chadwick, who was in her seventies, had finally confessed to Philippa, "I'm thinking of selling the house. People don't want to live in boardinghouses anymore, they want apartments. I'd like to live near my sister and her family in Arizona." Philippa had helped her sell the old house in Hollywood and buy a new condominium in an active retirement community outside of Phoenix.

Philippa recalled now how she had stood on the front steps of the old house and watched the blond furniture with wiry metal legs go into the back of the Salvation Army truck. She had had a sense that time was flowing past her, like a river. There goes 1957, she thought. And when the dilapidated aquamarine sofa had come out, Philippa had recalled how she had sat on that sofa and told Mrs. Chadwick all about Rhys.

It was a lifetime ago. And she had thought: My baby would be seventeen years old now.

"Well!" Charmie said when they reached the terrace. "Look who's finally arrived!"

When Philippa saw Paul, her heart rose. The sudden sight of him never failed to trigger yearning. At forty-seven, Paul Marquette seemed to be at the peak of his attractiveness. He and Francine made an entrance onto the terrace as if they were French aristocrats at the court of Louis XV, acknowledging the homage from those around them. Francine, Philippa noticed, had brought her usual icy smile.

Philippa had finally met Mrs. Marquette when she had visited the winery at Paul's invitation. They lived in a rambling Spanish hacienda, and Francine had received Philippa with practiced warmth and charm-school grace. When Francine had said, "You've done so much for my husband, Miss Roberts, none of the rest of us were able to help," Philippa had heard the distinct undercurrent of rivalry. She had wondered how the slender Francine had handled *her* grief over Todd's death. There seemed to have been no alcohol and pasta opiate for her.

"Welcome to my home," Philippa said now, shaking their hands.

"We're happy to be here," Paul said, while his wife smiled and nodded to others on the terrace. Francine Marquette had the unique talent of making it seem that she was the hostess, the one in charge, wherever she went, even when she was a guest at someone else's party.

"Paul," Philippa said, "there is something I'd like to show you." She smiled graciously at Francine. "Both of you."

"You go, Paul," Francine said, "there are some old friends here I haven't seen in a long time." Her manner was one of a woman determined to prove to those around her that she could let her husband go off with any woman and not feel threatened. She gave Philippa a brief condescending look and sailed away into the crowd.

Once again Philippa had to struggle with a pang of jealousy. Francine was, after all, Paul's wife. While she was just a friend. A good friend, who was occasionally seen with the senator at charity benefits or gallery openings. Philippa and Paul enjoyed an aboveboard, on-the-up-and-up relationship; not even the supermarket tabloids could point a finger. She had longed to ask, during one of their light dinner conversations, what he saw in Francine. His Gallic warmth and her aristocratic coolness seemed mismatched, but perhaps Francine was warm in private.

As they entered the house, where guests were scattered around the living room talking, Paul said, "It's good to see you again, Philippa. What a beautiful house."

"I still can't believe it's mine!" She had her arm through his, her hand resting in the crook of his elbow. "How have you been, Paul?" she said lightly, wishing she could say something more.

Philippa knew a lot of superficial things about Paul: where he had gone to school (UCLA, Stanford Law), what his interests were (sailing, classical music, Florentine art), his favorite books, movies, food, and colors. But she knew nothing deeper, nothing about the secret parts of him. Whenever they attended a public event together or dined at a restaurant, Philippa would keep the conversation light and charming, while the senator entertained her with tales from Capitol Hill. They would discuss diets, the latest breakthroughs in nutrition—"What do you think of Pritikin?"—or world events, or even just a movie.

Philippa had told Paul almost everything about herself, including her affair with the nihilistic Rhys. The only two facts she protected him from were the illegitimate miscarried baby of long ago and her gangster father who had ended up in the gas chamber. Philippa suspected that Paul had cultivated something of a rosy, fresh-scrubbed image of her, the all-American girl who had made good, from Catholic boarding school to corporate headquarters. She knew that her interlude with Rhys didn't tarnish her image; in fact, it added just the right dimension to make her even more interesting, but she was careful to protect Paul from the more depressing points of her life, not for her sake, but for his.

Philippa wished that she could tell him she was in love with him.

But Paul Marquette had a high-profile marriage to a high-profile socialite, and he was climbing the political ladder. Paul's way to the presidency,

Philippa knew, was going to be paved with Francine's charm, elegance, and connections. Francine Marquette would bring Camelot back to America.

So Philippa's romantic feelings for Paul had to stay safely tucked away.

As they started up the massive stairway, he said, "Have you heard anything new from your private investigator?"

"As a matter of fact, I received the most amazing news last week."

Ivan Hendricks had exhausted all the leads he had been following for the past few years. He had checked into nearly every female birth in Hollywood on or around Philippa's birthday in 1938. "Thirty-seven years ago," he said. "A lot of memories are shot, and a lot of people from that time aren't around anymore."

When he was ultimately left with three leads that he had not followed up on, he had gone back and done some tracing. After finding the first two—one woman was married and living in Bakersfield, the other had relocated to Alaska—Ivan had struck gold with the third.

This was one of the rare reports he made in person. Coming to the house and sitting out on the terrace, appearing a little discomfited by the richness of it all, Ivan had shifted his muscular bulk in the delicate white wrought-iron garden chair and said, "I was able to find out at Hollywood Presbyterian Hospital that a young woman named Naomi Dwyer gave birth to twins. It took some digging, but I finally got the name of the lawyer who handled the adoption of one of the twins. He wasn't easy to locate. Anyway, I finally located Hyman Levi and got him to tell me about it. Said the Dwyer woman kept one of the babies—didn't know where they went after that—but that one of the babies went to a couple named Singleton for a thousand dollars."

Philippa had been stunned. Johnny had bought her for a thousand dollars. Back in 1938 that had been a lot of money. And then: "I have a sister?"

"A twin sister, Miss Roberts. And providing she's still alive, I think I can find her."

As she mounted the stairway with Paul, Philippa said, "Ivan is in New Mexico right now, following up on a lead someone had given him about the Dwyers having lived there in a trailer park. Can you imagine it, Paul? A sister! A twin! And maybe my parents are still there. Maybe in a few days or a few weeks I'll be attending a family reunion in Albuquerque!"

They turned down a carpeted hall where old paintings of hunting scenes and grapes in goblets were spaced above the Tudor wainscoting. Philippa had bought the house furnished, and it contained many curious antiques. She paused before a door and knocked before entering a bedroom that was furnished with a frilly canopied bed and white furniture with floral decals. The wallpaper featured Winnie the Pooh and his friends; the thick canary yellow carpet had toys scattered over it. A young woman in a nanny's uniform was sitting at a tiny table laying out cups and saucers and teapots. A little girl sat with her, wearing a cotton-candy pink dress and frowning over the miniature tea set. They both turned when Philippa and Paul entered.

"Here she is, Paul," Philippa said with a smile. "This is Esther, my daughter."

The nanny got up, a little awkwardly because her chair was so small, and took the five-year-old by the hand. "Esther," she said with a British accent, "say hello to your mummy and her guest."

"How do you do, Esther," Paul said. "You're a very pretty little girl."

Two large almond eyes watched him without blinking. Black hair framed a round face and long-lashed dark eyes.

"Doesn't she smile?" he asked.

"No, but she will."

"Do you know anything about her?"

Philippa shook her head. "She was rescued by an American doctor during the fall of Saigon. He found her crying over the body of a woman— her mother, we presume. He couldn't get her to talk, so he named her for Esther in the Bible, who was also an orphan."

"Does she speak any English?"

"Not yet. But it has been explained to her that this is her home now and that I am her new mother. It will be difficult for both of us at first, but we'll work it out." She smiled at the little girl. "Won't we, Esther?"

Philippa looked at Paul. "I'm going to give her all the love that I can and make her as happy as I am able. I have such beautiful memories of my adoptive father. Johnny was so good to me, so kind and loving. I'm going to do that for Esther."

They left, quietly closing the bedroom door behind them, and Philippa said, "I'm still not sure about the nanny. I thought at first I should hire a Vietnamese to take care of Esther, because of the language barrier. But then I wondered if perhaps that might slow down her assimilation into her new life. It's not an easy decision to make."

"No decisions about children ever are," he said.

She wanted to ask about Todd, his son. She knew he had committed suicide, but how he did it, or why, Paul had never said, and Philippa would never ask.

"I can't thank you enough for using your influence in Washington to help me," she said. "It's so hard for single people to adopt children, even the desperately needy children, war orphans like Esther. I couldn't have done it without you."

"In a way, then," he said, "she's ours, isn't she?"

Philippa stared at him.

"I'm sorry," he said. "I shouldn't have said that."

They continued down the hall, which somehow seemed longer than when they had come that way a few minutes before. Sounds of the party drifted up from the terrace.

"I'm sorry," Paul said again. He stopped and faced her. "Philippa," he said, standing so close to her that she could see tiny black flecks floating in his blue eyes, "I want to hold you, make love to you. God," he said with passion, "I want to kiss you."

Philippa suddenly knew that he was serious and that the instant he touched her they would both be lost. Quickly she conjured two vivid images in her mind—of Francine, and of the child in the bedroom—and she said, "No, Paul. We can't."

"Why not?"

"Because this isn't for us. We have friendship, but whatever more we want, it wasn't meant to be. You have your life with Francine and your political dream, and I have Esther now, who's going to require all my love and attention."

He looked anguished, but his voice was calm, measured. "Are you angry?"

"No."

"Will you at least tell me how you feel about me?"

She hesitated. "No."

"Can we still be friends?"

"Oh yes," she said with relief. She was about to thread her arm through his, but she stopped herself. They mustn't touch again.

"Paul, one last thing before we join the party. I was strong just now. But I won't be again. Next time—"

"There won't be a next time, Philippa. I promise."

And she knew it was a promise he would keep.

39

As Danny pulled out of the driveway of the Rainbow Springs Lodge and turned south on Palm Canyon Drive, he felt his fury and frustration mount. This was one more place he could cross off his list of possible hotels where Philippa might be staying.

He had had her—last night, driving from L.A. to Palm Springs, Danny had actually had the bitch in sight, just up ahead on the freeway, skimming along in her nice safe limousine with him following close behind, entertaining himself with scenarios of the various things he was going to do to her, when all of a sudden a wall had materialized across the road, swallowing up her limousine and every other vehicle that drove through it. Danny had slammed on his brakes and only barely missed colliding with other cars before coming to rest on the shoulder of the highway, where he had stared in amazement at the sandstorm up ahead.

After composing himself, he had started up the Jaguar and, like the other motorists, gingerly entered the sandstorm, because there was no other way to go. It was like driving into hell—the car jerking and rattling as it was buffeted by the powerful wind, the sickening sound of grit scraping along the sleek body, sandblasting the polish right off the paint. Danny had crept along like a mole, unable to see taillights up ahead or headlights in his rearview mirror. He had been encased in a blinding, terrifying sand cloud that had howled around him as if it carried the tormented spirits of souls who had perished in the desert.

He had thought it would never end, that the entire world was being consumed by sand, when all of a sudden the Jaguar emerged into a crystal-clear night, where stars twinkled mockingly and motorists had pulled over to survey the damage done to their cars. But Danny didn't care about the Jaguar. He pressed his foot on the gas and took off down the highway, hoping to catch up with the white limousine.

But she had gotten away.

And so now he was going methodically around all the Palm Springs hotels, searching for Philippa Roberts, his fury rising with each no at each registration desk.

There were hundreds of hotels, motels, lodges, and motor courts, and so far Danny, posing as a friendly, howdy-ma'am journalist, with his dyed hair, fake beard, horn-rimmed glasses, and press credentials, had eliminated only a fraction of them. He was going about it systematically, figuring that a woman of Beverly's wealth, tooting around in a chauffeured limousine, would only stay in three stars or above. But he also figured, knowing what a dislike she had always had for the flashy and the popular, that she would gravitate toward small, tasteful, and elegant.

Rainbow Springs Lodge had been a perfect example, typically rich and discreet, with no hotel obviousness about it, no signs pointing to anything anywhere, just an ornate Spanish fountain burbling in the center of antique paving stones, lush foliage, and expensively kept parrots, as if it were a private residence. The sort of place where you had to be born knowing where the registration desk was, and, once you found it, where you didn't see any postcard racks or cheerful young things in hotel blazers. An assistant manager with a long nose and tall eyebrows had delivered Danny's thirty-sixth no of the day.

Now he drove along Palm Canyon Drive, pounding his fist on the steering wheel. The bitch was somewhere in this rich desert sprawl, somewhere among these damn date palms and fountains and golf courses. But where? *Where?*

When his stomach growled, he realized it was getting late and that he hadn't eaten all day. Pulling into the first restaurant he saw—Rosarita's, a Mexican place that had the usual Spanish tile floor and uninspired cacti in large pots—Danny took a seat on the patio, where patrons were continually sprayed with a fine mist from overhead misters. There was a drought on in California, water was being rationed from Eureka to San Diego, but Palm Springs was air-conditioning its outdoors with water.

When he ordered cheese enchiladas with a beef taco, refried beans, rice, and a beer, the waitress said, "You know, you look familiar. Do you come in here a lot?"

Danny treated her to one of his slow, lazy smiles to hide the sudden jolt she had given him. This was the one thing he was afraid of—that, despite the glasses and the beard, his face was still too recognizable. After all, it had beamed out of forty million TV sets and graced campaign posters and political buttons. Heck, this cute young thing in the frilly uniform could have been one of his Danny Girls, an army of energetic female youth that had marched across the country, knocking on doors and handing out "Danny Mackay for President" pamphlets.

"No," he said, looking her up and down. She wasn't bad looking, twenty or so, and she wore one of those dumb waitress uniforms that had an elasticized peasant top with a cinched-in waist and flaring skirt standing out on a dozen petticoats. "I've never been in here before, miss."

"You have a southern accent," she said, reacting to his smile and the way he looked at her. "Where are you from?"

"Oh, around."

"I know I know you from somewhere," she said in a cutesy way. "Don't worry, it'll come to me."

But Danny was worried, all through the enchiladas and taco and beans. And when she brought him a second, and then a third beer, and he saw how she studied his face, frowning in concentration as though thinking wasn't one of her usual habits, his caution grew. What if she were to recognize him? What if she were to suddenly say, "Hey, you're Danny Mackay"? What if she didn't read newspapers or watch television news and didn't know that the man she had been going to vote for three years ago but who had dropped out of the race because of scandal was supposed to have died in jail?

Jesus—it could be a mess. She could talk.

And ruin his plans.

So when she came back and asked him what he'd like for dessert, he turned on charm he usually reserved for only the classiest of women and said, "Well now, what are you offerin'?"

She met him one hour later, when she got off work. He swung by in his Jaguar and she climbed in, stiff petticoats rustling, tip money jingling in her tote bag. "Wow, what a snazzy car!" she said.

"Where shall we go, sugar?" he asked.

She looked at him for a minute, then cocked her head to one side, coyly. "You know, the more I look at you, the more I'm sure I know you from somewhere. It's driving me crazy!"

"Well, why don't we go for a little ride and maybe I can jog your memory?"

They decided to watch the sunset and headed up into the deserted foothills of the Santa Rosa Mountains, up along a dirt track, away from lights, buildings, and other people. He knew the car was turning her on, he could feel her getting all sexed up next to him. Danny had had years of experience in learning to know when a woman was ready.

He pulled the Jaguar to a stop and they looked out over the valley below, where a few lights were starting to come on in the dusk. "Guess what I brought," she said, pulling two bottles of beer out of her tote bag.

"Whoa, darlin'," he said when she started to open them. "Not in here! This is expensive upholstery. And it's not even four days old." He smiled and winked. "Let's get out and take in some of that fresh air."

A strong smell of sage was carried on the breeze; when the wind changed, they could hear a family of coyotes yip-yipping in the distance. The desert below was starting to change colors; it was going to be another breathtaking sunset. Danny and the girl leaned against the warm hood of the car as they drank their beers and talked about how hard it was to get ahead in the world these days. She was twenty and starting to get disillusioned. He told her he'd been here and there, done this and that, had a bit of luck with investments, which was how come he could afford the car.

The sex started casually, with the tentative kissing of two strangers who are new to each other's ways. But once the heat was on, they began to work together, both being old hands at what they were up to. Danny pulled down the peasant-girl top and poured beer over her breasts and licked it off. She giggled and squirmed and thrust her hand down his pants. Danny did it to her quickly after that, because he was in a hurry. Beverly was down in that valley somewhere, and he had to find her. But this little sidetrack had been necessary. The girl was eventually going to realize who he was and tell. It wouldn't do to have people start wondering if Danny Mackay was alive after all.

When he was done, leaving her panting across the hood of the Jaguar, her petticoats standing straight up to the sky, Danny opened the passenger door and got something out of the glove compartment.

"Wow!" she said breathlessly, getting to her feet and looking around for her panties. "That was something!"

She had her back to him as she searched the sand and sagebrush. "I sure wish I could remember who you remind me of—" She suddenly snapped her fingers and said, "I remember!" And just as she turned, saying, "You're just like my cousin Al in Oklahoma," she felt a sharp pain in her kidney.

She looked down at the knife embedded in the cinched waist of her uniform. Then Danny jerked it up; she gave a cry and slumped to the ground.

As Danny cleaned the blade on her skirt, he said, "Well, don't that beat all? Here I thought you were going to give me away, and it was only ol' Cousin Al all along. Just goes to show," he said as he got behind the wheel and started up the car, "even I can make a mistake now and then!"

He drove off into the sunset, the rear tires raining sand and gravel over her body.

··★

40

"Zoey Larson has been with us for over two years, Dr. Isaacs," Simon Jung said. "In fact, it was she who set up our clinic. Miss Larson came highly recommended from a plastic surgeon in Santa Monica. She helped him set up a new office and was his scrub nurse for six years."

"It is not Zoey's nursing skills I am questioning, Mr. Jung," Judith said. "It is her ethics. I simply don't trust her."

They were sitting in Mr. Smith's room. Night had fallen, casting gloomy shadows into the corners where the lamps had not yet been turned on, and a silver service of coffee sat growing cold on the coffee table. So far, Smith had not spoken.

"You have no proof," Jung said, "that Miss Larson gave the story to the tabloid." Despite the tension in the room, and Judith's obvious anger, Star's general manager remained politely unperturbed. This meeting was his idea; he had come to Mr. Smith's room like an ambassador arriving to inform King Fahd that Saudi Arabia would get all the jets it needed. He brought his expensively dressed self into the room, along with his refined Swiss accent and smooth assurances to Dr. Isaacs and Mr. Smith that he had the situation about the tabloid article well in hand. But as far as Judith could see, Jung had nothing in hand except for some well-rehearsed words of diplomacy.

"No, I have no proof," she said. "But I know she did it!"

"Dr. Isaacs, Miss Burgess and I are distressed about this whole matter and are as anxious as you to get to the bottom of it, but I have spoken with Miss Larson, and she insists she had nothing to do with it. If you could possibly offer something a little more substantial . . . ?" His voice trailed off in a question mark.

"I have no proof, it's just a feeling I have," Judith said, annoyed at how flimsy her words sounded. What was going on behind those acute Swiss eyes? she wondered. Was Jung thinking he had two squabbling females on his hands, that this whole thing was just about some petty power play between an upstart doctor and a resentful nurse? She glanced at Smith, who was sitting on the third loveseat that formed a grouping at the hearth. He had dressed for the occasion in slacks and a sweater, with a maroon silk ascot at his throat. Judith thought it made quite a change from pajamas; he no longer looked like a patient, a man who had undergone recent surgery and who had been confined to bed, but a man of wealth and power, a man in complete control. She wondered what *he* thought about her accusations. "Mr. Jung," she said, "when it occurred to me that the tabloid had to have gotten the story *before* the operation took place, since that edition was printed two days before Mr. Smith even came here, I checked the clinic log book and saw that Dr. Newton had scheduled the surgery over a month ago. Zoey had known four weeks ago that it was going to take place."

"And so did Dr. Newton's office staff. And so, in fact," he said, turning to Smith, "did your people."

Smith didn't reply.

"Dr. Isaacs," Jung said, "Miss Burgess is most anxious to be fair about this. We understand your concerns, but at the same time—"

"You don't want to fire Zoey on just my word."

"After all, Dr. Mitgang never had any complaints, and no other stories were leaked before this. But please be assured that if it was a Star's employee, we will take full responsibility. But for now, we have no solid proof that Miss Larson was involved."

"Then investigate her! Find out if she made a large deposit into her bank account recently. Or—"

"Dr. Isaacs," Jung said slowly, checking the time in a very smooth, artful way—he reached out to straighten the corner of a pillow, extending his wrist just far enough beyond his perfectly starched French cuff to offer him a quick view of his watch. It was done very discreetly, the perfected skill of a man who knows his time is valuable. "Might I suggest that you seem to be becoming rather personally involved in this matter?"

"My concern is not personal, Mr. Jung," she said in exasperation, "it is professional. The rights of one of my patients have been violated, and that makes me very involved. I am furious about what happened, and I believe my nurse is responsible. It's as simple as that."

When Simon Jung started to respond, Smith suddenly said, "This is getting us nowhere. I suggest we wait and see what my attorney uncovers. He flew to Chicago this morning to meet with the tabloid's lawyers. Perhaps they will cooperate and provide us with the source of their story. Until then, arguing isn't going to solve anything."

Jung stood up, smoothly and elegantly, as if he were the one terminating the audience. "I quite agree," he said. "That is, if Dr. Isaacs has no objections? In the meantime, Miss Burgess and I would be honored if the two of you dined with us tonight."

Smith waved a hand. "I'm not up to company yet, but thank Miss Burgess for me. Judith?" She also declined.

After the general manager left, Judith moved closer to Smith, a look of concern on her face. "Are you feeling all right? Can I do anything for you?"

"Step out of that sterile white lab coat and have dinner with me. As a friend, not as my doctor."

"I thought you didn't want company."

"You are not company, Judith. You are pure delight."

She turned away, feeling her heart start up its usual gallop whenever she was near him. "I would be happy to have dinner with you. Let me check in first and see if anyone needs me."

As she dialed the clinic, Judith felt her exasperation rise. Was Simon Jung correct in implying that she was jumping to conclusions? Were her feelings for Mr. Smith clouding her judgment? After all, just because a woman was sullen and sloppy in her habits didn't mean she wasn't to be trusted.

But as soon as Zoey answered, "Clinic," and Judith heard gum crack, her doubts fled. It *had* to have been Zoey. A nurse who was careless about sterile instruments and who handed out drugs to anyone who asked for them was not beyond selling secret patient information if the price was right.

"This is Dr. Isaacs. Has anyone asked for me?"

"No, but you got another one of *those* calls, Doctor. No message, like usual."

Thinking she detected a trace of gloating in the nurse's voice, Judith said, "Thank you. I will be with Mr. Smith should anyone need me."

"Oh? Mr. Smith?"

Judith hung up, shaking with rage. This was an intolerable situation. Zoey had to go.

"I'm so damn mad," she said. "Every time I see that awful article, I want to scream."

"You know, Judith, I believe you are slaying dragons for me. Now this *is* a switch. A damsel coming to *my* rescue."

"Why couldn't they have left you alone? What business is it of anyone's that you had surgery?"

"There is a paradox here that might cheer you up," he said, pointing to a thick stack of envelopes on his bedside table. "Letters from men asking me about the procedure I had done, what the results were, who was the surgeon, how much did it cost. In other words, Doctor, I've become something of a national spokesman for abdominal liposuction for men!" He laughed incredulously. "By being forced to come out of the closet, so to speak, I've opened the way for others to talk about it and to admit that they would like to have the same operation done. They're thinking that if a man famous for physical fitness, like myself, deems it okay to resort to cosmetic surgery to correct certain flaws, then surely it's okay for the ordinary man. In a way, that tabloid article has done some good."

"Do you know what I think? I think you're trying to cheer me up."

They regarded each other across the room.

"I'll call room service," he said, "and order for the two of us."

When Judith removed her lab coat and draped it over a chair, she experienced the curious sensation of feeling naked, even though she wore a blouse and wool slacks. It was the shedding of her protective covering, her professional shield against intimacy with Mr. Smith. Now she was vulnerable; she wasn't a doctor, she was a woman—a woman who had already loved and lost two people in her life and who could not bear to lose a third.

"Where will you go after you're discharged?" she asked, going to the window to watch evening settle over the desert below. As she saw the lights of Palm Springs and Cathedral City starting to wink on, she wondered how many love affairs were being consummated down there at that moment, how many illicit rendezvous were taking place, what powerful passions were coming to life as the sun died away.

"To my home in Florida," he said, "to complete my recovery. I'm scheduled to start filming a movie in Rome in a few months. After that, who knows? Maybe I shall consider the television series I spoke of."

A home in Florida . . . filming in Rome . . . It was a life she couldn't even begin to imagine. "Are you going to the ball tomorrow night?" she asked.

He went to the bar and poured two brandies. Handing one to her, he said, "It depends."

"On what?"

"On whether I can find a lady who will accompany me."

"May I ask you something?" she said, looking into her brandy, seeing how the liquid trembled. "I must know. Who do you believe, me or Zoey?"

He put his hands on her shoulders, turned her to face him, and looked right into her eyes. "You, of course. Did you doubt that? For one thing, you are so certain about what you say. But also because I know that my own personal staff did not leak the story, and I believe in the integrity of Dr. Newton and the people in his office. After all, treating celebrities secretly is their livelihood; they stand to lose a great deal over one foolish transgression. But after what you've told me about that nurse of yours—"

"She's not mine," Judith said, barely finding the breath to speak, he stood so close.

"It's funny about first impressions. I met her the morning I arrived here. Miss Larson got me settled into this room. And I recall thinking even then how glad I was that Newton was bringing his own nurse with him for the surgery. Now isn't that interesting? I don't know what it was about Miss Larson, but I didn't like the idea of her assisting at the operation."

Their eyes locked for a moment, and she felt the heat from his hands through her blouse. As he started to incline his head toward her, they were interrupted by a quiet knock at the door. Smith reluctantly withdrew his hands and went to answer it.

A waiter came in pushing a cart covered in a white tablecloth, with a vase containing white narcissi and a bottle of Cristal champagne chilling in a silver bucket. "What's this?" Smith said. He read the accompanying card: "Compliments of Simon Jung."

"What do you think, Judith?" he said, joining her at the window after the waiter left. "Shall we accept his peace offering?"

"I seem to be more upset over this whole thing than you do."

"You might be," he said, standing beside her so close that their shoulders touched as they watched the way night crept among the pine trees. "I've had many more years of experience with the press; I've learned to take sensational news with a certain aplomb. Or possibly I'm just as upset as you, except that I show it differently." He turned to look at her and was taken by a rather fetching little mole beneath her left earlobe. "Your approach is more direct. You rant and rave while I quietly hire a lawyer."

She looked at him and wondered why those dark blue eyes never quite came across on the screen. He was charismatic on film, but in *real* life . . .

She stepped away from the window and said, "I'd cultivate an ulcer if I didn't rant and rave."

Dinner arrived then, with two smiling waiters who came in murmuring, "Good evening, madame, monsieur." While one set up the table and served, the other went around the room turning on lights, drawing the drapes, and building a fire from logs that were placed in the brass hod each morning.

After they left, Smith poured the champagne, then held Judith's seat out for her, saying, "Madame."

They ate in the comforting warmth of the fire, the crystal, silver, and sparkling china, with Smith taking the elegance and gourmet food in stride, while Judith, who had always regarded a plain filet mignon steak as the height of cuisine, marveled at the banquet he had ordered: grilled swordfish with mint butter; a red radicchio lettuce salad sprinkled with goat cheese; paper-thin slices of bread that had been roasted with herbs and butter and grated Parmesan so that they were crisp and crunchy; and cold strawberry soup in silver bowls.

Not knowing where to begin, she followed Smith's lead by taking a little of the black caviar and spreading it thinly on a toast point. This was only the second time in her life she had tasted caviar, and she still wasn't sure she liked it.

"You know, Judith," he said, "the first time I was introduced to the really finest Beluga caviar was when we were shooting *The Golden Horde* in Iran. The shah invited the entire film company to his palace . . ."

Judith listened in fascination. He was talking of a world and a time that she had no place in; she had not, in fact, been born yet when *The Golden Horde* was made.

"Why do you wear your hair like that?" Smith said all of a sudden, interrupting himself.

She was startled. She had worn it in a braid since medical school. No one had ever commented on it, not even Mort.

"I was just wondering how it would look"—he waved his hands seductively—"loose."

She found herself thinking of the shah's palace and Beluga caviar and of all the glamorous love affairs Smith had had all over the world, with contessas and movie queens and wealthy socialites. He had once come close to marrying, she recalled now, an heiress who was believed to have been the richest woman in the United States. How could Judith, a family practice doctor from Green Pines, compete with a past like that?

And suddenly she realized that she *wanted* to compete—she wanted to be the unique woman in his life, the one woman whom he had allowed to witness his vulnerability.

She looked across the table and saw something dance in his eyes—the challenge of romance, of adventure.

Suddenly, she was very excited.

"Judith—" he began.

And then the telephone rang.

It was for her, a medical emergency. "I'm sorry," she said, hanging up and reaching for her white coat. "I have to go. An injury at the health club."

He stopped her at the door. "Will you come back?"

She looked into his eyes and smiled. "Yes, if it's not too late. I'll come back."

....★

41

Danny left his Jaguar with a hotel parking attendant and entered the exotic lobby of the Marriott. He had tried fourteen more hotels since he had had to kill the little waitress who thought he looked like her cousin Al. His urgency was mounting.

Where in all this damn desert *was* the bitch?

He went up to the front desk, flashed his press credentials, and said, "Howdy. I have an appointment with Philippa Roberts. Would you please let her know I'm here?" Danny had found that this ploy got him quicker results than just asking if she was registered. Don't inquire; just act as though you know she's there.

"One moment, please."

He stood there, tense, drumming his fingers while two parrots on perches over the lagoon tried to out-squawk each other.

Finally the young woman came back and said, "You may take the call on that house phone over there."

He stared at her.

Bingo.

He went to the white telephone, and when he said, "Miss Roberts?" he found himself speaking to a young man with an Australian accent. No doubt the jock he had seen with Philippa. Danny wondered if he had been one of the boys who had worked her brothel, Butterfly. For which he, Danny, had been arrested, humiliated, destroyed. "May I ask what this is about?" the jock asked. "I'm afraid Miss Roberts isn't aware of having an appointment with you."

Danny turned on the self-effacing charm that usually opened doors for him. "Well, ha ha, that was just a ploy. You see, I'm a journalist, and I would like very much to interview Miss Roberts for an article I'm doing. I was wondering if she could spare me some time?"

"I'm sorry, Miss Roberts is busy."

"How about tomorrow then?"

"I'm sorry, you'll have to make arrangements for an interview through her office in Los Angeles."

"Well, I've got a deadline to make. It won't take long, I promise."

"Sorry," the Aussie said, and hung up.

As Danny also hung up, thinking, You'll get yours, you little prick, he considered what he should do next.

It probably wouldn't be too difficult to find out which room she was in, but then what? Just march up there right now and give Beverly the surprise of her life? But that would take a lot of the pleasure out of it. Besides, the commando approach was for jerks; Danny Mackay had style, class. When he finally got Beverly, he wanted to do it with a certain flair, take his time with it, savor it.

Returning to the porte cochere, where young men in white shirts and Bermuda shorts were assisting guests with their luggage, Danny paused and squinted out at the December night. He was wondering what his next move should be when he happened to notice a white limousine parked in the temporary visitors' lot, adjacent to the underground parking garage. And a man in a chauffeur's uniform was standing there with his hands on his hips, eyeing the damaged paint.

It was her car.

Danny sidled over and said, "Howdy. Looks like you got caught in the same sandstorm I did. Nearly stripped off all my paint."

"Yeah," the driver said, scratching his head. "The desert is hard on cars. I hate to drive it looking like it this. Bad for the company image."

"Company?"

"Starlite," the man said, pointing to the license plate that read STRLT2.

Danny brought out a pack of cigarettes and offered it.

"Thanks," the driver said, lighting his cigarette from Danny's gold lighter. "I'd like to get it back to L.A. as soon as I can. Looks awful, doesn't it? Sure hate to drive it like this."

"So why not take it right back to L.A. then?"

"Can't. My boss needs the car tomorrow." He looked at Danny through their mingling smoke. "You wouldn't happen to know of a place around here that does good work, do you? I'm going to be stuck here in Palm Springs for a few days."

"I thought you said your boss needed the car."

The man ran his hand gingerly over the ruined shine, wincing as if it hurt him. "Only for tomorrow. She'll be up at Star's for a few days. That'll give me time to get this worked on."

Star's?

Why did that sound familiar?

"Sorry," Danny said. "I'm afraid I don't know this area well. Anyway, good luck."

Quickly claiming his car, he squealed down the drive and back onto Country Club and headed to a stretch of road where the desert rose in pure white dunes just feet from lush green grass. He parked and went through Quinn's wallet, finding among the bills a note Quinn had written to himself: "Room reservation, Star's morning tram." And it had tomorrow's date.

Danny couldn't believe his luck. So poor old Otis had been planning on going up to Star's, had he? And *she* was going up there, too. Talk about coincidence.

But no, Danny realized. Not a coincidence at all. Quinn must have known she was going up there; maybe he had decided to confront her at Star's and surprise her with what he knew.

Well, perhaps Quinn wasn't going to be able to pull off his surprise after all. But Beverly was going to be surprised all the same.

DAY FIVE

·· ★

42

The gun seemed to weigh more up here in the snowy mountains than it had down in the desert below. Tucked deep into his coat pocket, the weapon seemed to draw the arctic air into itself and become even harder, if that was possible, as if it were turning into ice. As he trudged through the snow, his collar turned up to hide his face, he wondered briefly if, removing his glove and touching the gun with his bare hand, his skin would stick to it like Krazy Glue.

When he saw someone up ahead among the pine trees, he stopped suddenly and watched. It was only a resort employee, one of those generic young muscular jocks, clearing snow from the wooden path that wound through the forest.

The man with the gun waited. He looked around, hoping to see his contact heading for the meeting point. He was anxious to get out of the cold and back into his warm cabin. Maybe call room service and order one of those lavish breakfasts Star's was famous for.

Finally, the jock, who wore a dark blue down jacket with the silver star logo emblazoned on it, picked up his tools and moved on. A moment later, another figure emerged through the trees, bundled up so that only the eyes were exposed; even those were hidden behind reflective aviator glasses.

The two walked together in silence until they reached the lookout platform, from where they could observe the morning sun slowly breaking over the desert eight thousand feet below.

"It was seventy degrees down there today," the first one said as he thrust his hands into his pockets and felt the cold gun. He thought it might even freeze to his skin right through his gloves. "Up here it barely hit thirty."

His companion didn't say anything for a moment. Then: "Are you sure Philippa arrives today?"

"I double-checked my sources. She's scheduled on the morning tram."

"Did you get a gun as I instructed?"

"Yes."

"Do you know how to use it?"

"Christ . . . yes."

"I'm counting on you. We haven't much time."

They parted at the lookout platform and went their separate ways. A little while later, after a light snowfall had obliterated their tracks, it was as though they hadn't been there at all.

43

···★

London, England, 1985

"My dearest Esther," Philippa wrote, "It is cold and raining here in London, and I miss you very much. I wish now that I had given in to you and brought you along, but I didn't want you to miss an entire month of school, despite what Mr. Berringer said about how well you are doing in the tenth grade. I promise you that I will be home for our birthday . . ."

No records had ever been found on the Vietnamese orphan christened Esther by the American doctor who had brought her out of Vietnam. Being at a loss for her date of birth, Philippa had told the child she could choose her own birthday, and Esther had chosen Philippa's. Every year they celebrated together; this year mother was going to turn forty-seven and daughter fifteen or so.

Philippa was in the sitting room of her suite at the Hilton, which had a view that looked out over Hyde Park, writing letters and listening to the rain against the windows. "By the way, Esther, Uncle Paul is coming to England to visit me," she continued. "Although he was very mysterious over the phone, I have a pretty good idea of what he's going to tell me: that he's decided to run for the presidency. He's been a likely candidate for a long time, and he's very popular with the people. How would you like that, Esther, having an uncle in the White House?"

Esther knew, of course, that Paul Marquette wasn't really her uncle, just a good friend of her mother's who would show up in their lives occasionally. He would arrive at the house in the black car with the giant of a driver who never talked, bringing a gift for Esther and then whisking her mother away without even taking off his coat or sitting down for a drink, the way her mother's other friends did.

Esther had startled Philippa one morning after one of Paul's visits by suddenly asking, "Are you in love with Uncle Paul?" The girl had just turned fourteen, a budding Asian beauty who was very popular at school and who had recently, with a teenage vengeance, discovered *boys.*

"Uncle Paul and I are old friends," Philippa had said. "We've known each other a long time."

A skeptical look had crept into those almond eyes, and Esther's round cheeks had creased into teasing dimples. "I think he's cute," Esther had said. "And you do, too. I can tell by the way you look at him."

Philippa paused to watch the rain beyond her window, and she pondered again the turnaround her life had undergone since Esther entered it. The early days had been difficult, as Philippa had predicted, because of the language barrier and because of the horrors the child had witnessed. Esther would awaken at night, screaming from nightmares. She would frown uncertainly at her American food; she didn't trust anyone and she would shrink from Philippa's touch. In those first months, Philippa would tiptoe into Esther's bedroom and marvel at the little girl curled up on the bed like a shrimp, her forehead moist, black bangs matted down. Philippa would sit with her through the night, the way Johnny had sometimes done for her, and she would be astonished at the overwhelming flood of love she felt for the child.

Glancing at the little traveling clock she had set out on the desk, she was startled to see how late it was. Paul had said he would arrive at her hotel at eight, which was only an hour from now. Leaving the letter for later, she went into the bedroom to get ready. They were going to have dinner at the Café au Lait, just a block from the hotel, where Philippa had made reservations.

There was no question, of course, of dining in her suite. The few times Paul had visited Philippa when she was staying at a hotel, such as the time she was in D.C. for a health and fitness conference, and the year before, when she was in San Francisco for a convention of businesswomen, he never came up to her room; they always met in the lobby, went out from there, and Paul later said good-night at the elevator. While they dined, they kept the mood light, friendly, on the surface. If the conversation threatened to turn dangerous, or if a silence stretched too long, they hurried in to amend it. Ten years ago, when they had stood in the hallway at her home and Paul had almost kissed her, he had made a promise. And he had kept it. They had not been alone since that night; they protected themselves with crowded restaurants, chauffeured limousines, brightly lit places; not a word about secret feelings and desires was ever uttered.

The phone rang with the curious, insistent double ring that British telephones have, and Philippa rushed to answer it. Don't let it be Paul, she thought, canceling at the last minute.

It was Paul, but he wasn't canceling. "I'm here, in the lobby. May I come up?"

Philippa was startled. He was an hour early. And he had never come up to her room before.

Because she hesitated, he said quickly, "It's important, Philippa. I promise I will be the soul of propriety. Five minutes, that's all I ask. I have something to tell you that I can't risk having overheard. And then we'll go on to dinner. Okay?"

"Of course you can come up, Paul," she said.

She hurried into the bedroom, her heart pounding. It was about the presidential campaign; she had known it all along. News of this magnitude could not very well be announced in public. Not yet.

When she heard the knock at the door, she pressed her hand to her chest to calm her racing heart, took a deep breath, and went to answer it.

"Paul, what a pleasant—"

He swept her into his arms and kissed her hard. "I love you, Philippa," he said, pulling her so tightly to him that she gasped. "My God, I love you so much."

Fifteen years of cautious restraint and repressed sexual hunger exploded in that one moment as they sank to the floor, mouths working against each other, tongues hot and probing. Philippa was unaware of the coarse carpet beneath her as she drew Paul down onto her. His kisses seemed to burn; his mouth never left hers as it moved this way and that, his hands entwined in her hair, imprisoning her head as his body pinned her down. Clothes only partially came off, rapidly, with buttons flying, a rushed zipper, panties nearly ripped away. And then he was inside her; she clamped her legs around his buttocks to bring him in closer, deeper. She ran her hands up under his shirt and dug her fingers into tight muscles.

Suddenly, in midthrust, he stopped and looked at her; he ran his fingers through her hair, spreading it out in an auburn fan around her head. Kissing her again, more tenderly, he sought out her breasts in a more gentle, mindful exploration. "My God," he whispered. "You're beautiful."

He sat back on his heels and drew her up with him. They kissed for a long moment, then he moved to the side and, scooping her up into his arms, carried her into the bedroom. He laid her down, parting her legs and kneeling between them. Finally removing his shirt and the tie that hung askew on his chest, he stretched out on top of her again, but languidly now, moving his body over hers, aligning them together as he kissed her mouth, her neck, her breasts.

A gust of wind brought rain against the windows. She felt Paul enter her again, but slowly this time, so that she felt every inch of him. When he was deep inside he began a gentle rhythm, and when they were finally moving together, he pressed her hands over her head and into the pillow, looking deeply into her eyes . . .

They were lying naked in bed, hot and damp among the twisted sheets, becoming intimate with the bodies they had lusted for for so long. Finally, Philippa laughed and sat up. "I'm hungry!" She reached for the phone, dialed room service, and when she ordered a cheese and fruit platter, water biscuits, and Perrier, Paul grabbed the phone from her and said into it, "Cancel that. We want two T-bone steaks, extra thick, rare. Fried eggs, runny, and french fries. And a bottle of Glenlivet."

He gave her a sneaky smile. "We'll burn off the calories. So, is this a successful trip?"

"So far. I leave for Paris in a few days, and then Munich. Starlite is popular with European women, except that they aren't so much interested in the diet as the beauty treatments—you know, the steam baths, facials, massages."

Philippa realized she was doing all the talking. She wasn't sure about what had just happened between them. There had been no questions, no preamble, no May I? He had asserted himself and she had acquiesced. Just as she had always known she would if he should ever touch her. But she wanted to know why now? Why tonight?

"There are some troubles back home, however," she said. "Hannah wants to introduce a new line called Perfect Size International, and she has hired a special buyer named Ingrid Lind. Hannah is wild about Ingrid, claiming she comes with excellent foreign contacts and an eye for exotic fashions and accessories. But the problem is, Alan has taken an intense dislike to Ingrid. It's the first time I've ever seen Hannah and Alan disagree on anything." Philippa didn't mention the other worry that was on her mind. Hannah had secretly started seeing a cardiac specialist and was taking pills. Philippa had found out by accident one day, when she had overheard Hannah on the phone with the doctor.

"Ah!" Paul said when he heard a discreet knock on the outer door. "Dinner has arrived."

Throwing on the terry bathrobe that had been placed in the bathroom for the guest's convenience while staying at the hotel, he went into the living room and opened the door to a smiling waiter pushing a service cart.

After the table was set up and the waiter left, they sat down to eat. "Wait," Paul said. He leaned across the table and opened Philippa's bathrobe, baring her breasts. "That's better." He reached for a roll and started to butter it.

Philippa took a knife and fork to her steak, which was still sizzling and running with juices. She watched Paul out of the corner of her eye, the way his robe gaped whenever he reached for something, exposing hard pectorals and a rippling stomach.

He gave her a grand smile as he raised his glass. "Steak and scotch! The perfect American meal!" But as he started to take a sip, some of the Glenlivet spilled from the glass and splashed into his lap. "Wow! That's cold!" he said.

As he reached for his napkin, Philippa said, "Let me," rising from the table, letting her robe fall all the way open.

She knelt beside him. He moaned and drove his fingers into her hair. The steaks and fries went untouched.

Afterward, as they lay entwined on the sofa, his hand casually cupping her naked breast, Paul said, "Philippa, I have something to tell you."

Philippa murmured a sleepy, "Yes?" Her head was nestled in his shoulder as she gently stroked his hard belly. They had made love for such a long time that she was exhausted and feeling very fine.

"Francine is leaving me."

Suddenly, Philippa's hand lay still on his abdomen. When she didn't speak, he went on. "Don't you want to know why?"

"Oh, Paul," she said, "of course. Goodness." She sat up.

"I've decided not to make a bid for the presidency. Politics was never me, it was really Francine. The ambition was hers, and for a long time I let her be ambitious for us both. But after our son died . . . our relationship died. She never said it, but I think she secretly blamed me for his death. He was on drugs, seeing a therapist. I wasn't around enough. I don't know. But she and I grew apart. In public we looked like a perfect couple, but in private we had become strangers. She became hard and focused on only one ambition—to see her husband in the White House. So when I said I didn't want to run for the presidential office, she served the papers."

"Oh, Paul!"

"Well, the divorce is overdue, really, and there are other candidates who will win the public's heart. It's being said that the Reverend Danny Mackay is going to run. He's the TV preacher, adored by millions, and I know the party will get behind him. But what about you, Philippa? What about us? I'm going to be free now."

Suddenly, she didn't know what to say. For fifteen years she had ached for him, dreamed about him, imagined what he would be like in bed. But she had never considered the possibility that her dreams might become reality. "What will you do?" she asked, prolonging her own answer. "Run the winery?"

"My brother can run the winery. I want to be a sailor. Philippa," he said, becoming excited, "I've had my eye on a villa in Western Australia. Come and share it with me. Be my wife and spend the rest of your life with me."

All of a sudden, Philippa realized she had been afraid of this. From the moment he walked in and took her into his arms, a small alarm had been sounding at the back of her head that there was more happening here on this rainy night than a sexual encounter that had been destined to take place. She got up from the sofa and put on her robe.

"It's not so easy for me, Paul," she said, turning away from him, suddenly self-conscious about her nakedness. "There's Esther to consider. I can't just pull her out of school, away from everyone she knows, all her friends. And I can't leave Starlite."

"Esther's only fifteen. Teenagers are adaptable. And you can still run Starlite from Australia. Anyway," he said, reaching for her, "I'm determined to change your mind."

But she drew away. "It's not that simple, Paul."

"It is if you love me. Do you?"

She looked at him, this wonderful man with the beautiful body who had made such exquisite love to her. "Of course I love you, Paul."

"And I love you. That's all there is to it."

He drew her into his arms again, and she knew he was right: they were in love, that was all there was to it.

"Yes, I'll marry you," she said, kissing him. "But give me a little time, there are things to work out."

"Of course, darling. I'll be flying down to Australia in a few days. I'll wait there for you. In the meantime, however . . ." He scooped her up and carried her back into the bedroom.

The Paris sky was cold and gray; it hung low over the spires of Notre Dame cathedral and the Seine as if prayers were the only thing keeping it from collapsing entirely onto the city. But Philippa was warm behind the glass wall of the sidewalk café, where she was enjoying a leisurely hour over croissants and *café américain*. She had made a date to meet Ivan Hendricks here, and as she waited for him, she went through her mail.

She read first the letters from Esther ("Mike is ancient history, Mom. That was before I met Jason!") and Charmie ("Nathan's company is transferring him to Ohio"). She saved Paul's letter for last. It was full of vivid descriptions of the Greek-style villa he had bought on the Swan River; he had sent along a photograph of himself at the helm of a seventeen-meter racing yacht, sun and wind in his face, the spark of victory in his eyes.

Philippa looked up to see a familiar figure coming across the cobble-stoned street, dodging Citroëns whose drivers honked impatiently. In eighteen years, Ivan Hendricks had hardly changed. Philippa could understand Charmie's attraction to him. He was a tempting physical specimen—she could picture him on the bridge of an aircraft carrier, binoculars hanging from his neck. Ivan had an easygoing personality and a subtle sense of humor, and he was very thorough in his investigative work. Like Charmie, Philippa often wondered about Ivan's private life.

"Bonjour, Madame Roberts!" he boomed in an atrocious accent as he pulled out a wiry little chair that actually squeaked when he sat on it.

"Hello, Ivan," she said, pleased to see him, but sad also. This was going to be his last report to her. The family reunion she had imagined taking place in Albuquerque, ten years ago, never materialized. The Dwyers, Philippa's real parents, seemed to have moved like Gypsies, making their trail hard to follow. Four years ago, Ivan learned that Mrs. Dwyer had disappeared after her husband was killed, apparently by her, according to the authorities. There was a child who ran away. She had been around fourteen years old.

Now Ivan said, "I finally found evidence of a girl named Rachel Dwyer working at an establishment in San Antonio, Texas, in the early fifties."

"An establishment?"

He cleared his throat. "A, um, bordello, Miss Roberts. A whorehouse. But she disappeared after that and I haven't been able to pick up her trail. She's vanished. I'm sorry, Miss Roberts, but I don't think we're ever going to find her."

Before he left, Ivan said, "But I won't give it up, Miss Roberts. I'll take on other clients and expand my agency, but I'll never stamp your case closed. Who knows? Maybe someday something will show up unexpectedly, something that will lead us right to your sister."

Philippa walked for a long time afterward, following the sometimes wide, sometimes narrow streets of Paris, involved in her thoughts. When she came to the Tuileries, the large, formal gardens facing the Louvre, she strolled among leafless trees and fountains that had been turned off for the winter. A lone ice cream vendor sat engrossed in *Le Figaro,* not even bothering to look up at the sound of Philippa's footsteps on the gravel. An elderly couple struggled by on canes, supporting each other, both in long black coats and berets. Philippa couldn't tell if they were male or female or both. And a young girl with long braids, wearing a school uniform, was kneeling in front of a crying child, looking at his mittened hand and saying, *"T'as bobo à la papatte?"*

Philippa looked at the barren trees standing against a gunmetal sky, and she felt a stab of disappointment run through her like a sword. Something had suddenly vanished from her life. The hope of finding her family, even though it had been a small hope, was gone. And Ivan's final report had been such a sad, despairing one: Philippa's father killed by her mother; her twin sister working in a Texas whorehouse. Would that have been her fate, too, if the Singletons hadn't adopted her for a thousand dollars? Johnny had given her a good life, the best he knew how. And Philippa had been sheltered in a convent, while her sister . . .

Where was she now, the woman who was Philippa's same age and who no doubt bore a strong resemblance to her? Was she still alive even, or had she come to some tragic end?

Philippa finally accepted the fact that she would probably never learn the truth, and that perhaps she had never been fated to know. It was time to stop searching, time to stop mourning the past and look toward the future.

Suddenly she saw her life rushing by, and she realized that she was wasting precious time. Hurrying back to her hotel suite, she said to her startled secretary, "Cancel Munich and Rome. There's been a change of plans!" Philippa picked up the phone and asked the operator to get her Perth, Australia. She couldn't wait to hear the joy in his voice when she told him she was coming to join him, *now*.

But as she was about to give the operator the number, she stopped. No, she thought, hanging up. *I'll go there instead.*

Paul was down there, sailing his new yacht, the *Philippa*, practicing for the Sydney-Hobart race.

I won't let him know I'm coming, she thought in excitement. I'll just show up. And he'll be so surprised.

··★

44

As the tram car bumped and swayed over the first support tower, the passengers laughed nervously and tried not to look ahead, where appallingly thin wires looped up to the top of the mountain, swinging perilously over deep canyons and ravines, seeming to just miss the ragged granite slopes and gnarled pine trees. The passengers also tried to keep from looking back to where the desert, flat and safe, slowly dropped away from them. They fixed their eyes instead on one another as they talked and smiled, many still clutching champagne glasses from the boarding lounge, most of them sitting, but a few brave ones standing and watching the mountain walls appear to draw nearer as the tram crept slowly up the narrow ravine.

Philippa sat in a wool coat, with a sweater underneath, but she felt the arctic alpine air nip at her ankles, where there was a small gap between the cuffs of her wool slacks and the tops of her boots. Charmie sat opposite, holding tight to a gin and tonic as she found the carpeted floor of the car immensely interesting. Ricky was one of the standees, one of the few who looked up at the towering mountain with something close to eager anticipation. He wore a dark blue ski outfit, purchased at the Marriott, and he looked, Philippa thought, very striking; she did not fail to catch the admiring glances he received from other female passengers.

She did not, however, notice that one of the passengers was staring at her—a man with dark hair, horn-rimmed glasses, and a closely cropped beard. His knee was going up and down like a jackhammer as he watched her. If she had been aware of him, she would not have known that when his hand went down to feel for something in his boot, as if to reassure himself that it was there, that he was touching a knife that only the night before had taken the life of a young waitress.

She was embroiled in thoughts fixed between two points: Beverly Burgess and tomorrow's board meeting. On the one side, she might be going to Star's to find her sister; on the other, to find a traitor.

A memory came to her from many years ago: Johnny, dancing around the kitchen in his tuxedo, saying to a young Christine, "Friends, Dolly! Always remember that friends are what count in this life. Family, relatives are fine, but you can't choose them. Friends you can choose."

She wondered now if, in a way, Johnny had been referring to himself, because he had not been her real blood father, but in fact her best friend. Had it been his way of preparing her for the truth he must someday tell her about himself—a day that ultimately never came? She would never know. But as she thought now of the deep love she and Johnny had had for each other, the trust and caring and respect that had marked their relationship, she understood what he had meant about friends. And it brought her some measure of comfort to think that, if Beverly Burgess did not turn out to be her sister after all, she still had her friends, about whom she cared a great deal and whom she loved dearly.

Charmie, Alan and Hannah, and now Ricky—these were her family. These were the ones she could count on and trust. Thank God, she thought, for Charmie and Hannah.

"Dear Philippa," Hannah wrote, "I write this letter because I cannot face you and tell you in person what I have done. By the time you receive this, the missing money will be restored to Starlite and the accounts will balance and I will be gone. I regret that I cannot offer you an explanation; believe me, it is easier on all of us if I don't. I also regret having to tell you that in order to replace the missing money, I had to sell my shares in Starlite, which, as you know, total nearly 5 percent. If, by this action, I have weakened your fight against the Miranda takeover, I am truly sorry. There was no other course of action open to me. I have valued your friendship more than I can say, and I will carry fond memories of our years together with me always."

She signed it simply "Hannah," folded the sheet once, and slipped it into an envelope, which she placed next to her purse on the bed. She would send it by messenger to Philippa at Star's after she had exchanged her stock certificates for cash.

Hannah dressed with unusual care as she got ready for her special meeting, which was due to take place at noon, on the northeast corner of La Cienega and Wilshire. When they had finally contacted her, agreeing on a price for her Starlite stock, the person at the other end of the line had specified the time and place where the exchange was to take place. Hannah had had no voice in it; she was their pawn. She selected a beige linen suit with heavy copper jewelry; then she combed out her short brown hair, dashed a hint of blush on her high cheekbones, and drew a soft brown line around her Indian eyes.

When she went downstairs she was surprised to find people traipsing through the entry with tables, chairs, and awnings. And then she remembered: her Christmas party. It would have to be canceled.

"There are going to be some changes concerning the party," she told her personal secretary, Miss Ralston. "I'll explain when I return." Realizing that she would also be telling Miss Ralston that her services would no longer be required, Hannah began to understand just how many lives were going to be affected by what she was about to do.

As she went through the front door, she saw an unmarked van pull into the driveway. A young man in T-shirt and jeans came up the steps carrying a clipboard; he was from the Emerson Gallery and had a delivery to make.

The sculpture—Alan's Christmas surprise! How could she have forgotten?

"Bring it inside, please," she said, standing back out of the way. A florist's truck had also just arrived, and men were unloading massive Christmas sprays of red and white carnations for the party. Hannah felt her anxiety grow. How on earth was she going to send all this back?

When the man from the gallery came in with a large box, he said, "Want me to open it for you? It's kind of heavy."

Hannah wrung her hands. It was getting late; if she wasn't at the meeting place exactly on time, the deal was off. "All right," she said uncertainly, feeling the familiar change in her heart's rhythm, a sudden uneven gallop that made her run back upstairs for her pills. She swallowed one dry, then put the bottle in her purse. By the time she was back downstairs, the sculpture was out of its packing.

"Wow," said the deliveryman, whistling. "This is really something."

Miss Ralston, who had been overseeing the distribution of flowers and tables, came over and said, "Oh my goodness, Mrs. Scadudo. What a stunning piece!"

Titled *Phoenix,* the sculpture was of an eagle made out of clear polyester resin, being born out of a darker eagle cast in bronze. It stood fourteen inches high and it had cost Hannah sixty-five thousand dollars. Alan had been trying for months to get it.

"Where shall we put it?" Miss Ralston asked, unable to take her eyes off it.

Hannah suddenly had an idea. Alan was due back from Rio today, and since there was a chance he would go straight to the office before coming home, Hannah would take the sculpture there now, as a surprise for him, to help soften the bad news she would tell him later. Hannah hoped to persuade Alan to go away with her—to sell everything they had and start over somewhere else.

As she guided the electric blue Corvette down the winding drive, aware that this was one of the very last times she would follow this route, Hannah had to fight back the tears in order to see where she was going.

Alan marched through the busy fashion department, where designers and cutters said, "Welcome back, Mr. Scadudo," and into Hannah's office. "Where is my wife?" he said to her secretary, abruptly and irritably; he was tired and jet-lagged and would have appreciated someone meeting him and Gaspar Enriques at the airport. He had been forced to take a cab and see to it himself that Enriques was checked into the Beverly Hills Hotel, whereupon the Brazilian gentleman had immediately changed into a swimsuit and taken off for the pool.

"I'm sorry, Mr. Scadudo," the young woman said. "She hasn't come in today. I don't know where—"

He turned and walked out. The next office down the hall was Ingrid's. He paused and listened at the closed door, wondering if Hannah was in there. Then, having heard nothing, he knocked and entered at the same time.

Ingrid was on the other side of the room, going through bolts of fabric with one of the head designers. "Alan!" she said. "What a surprise! They said your flight was due in at nine o'clock tonight."

"Christ, so that's why no one was there to meet us. We came in at nine o'clock this *morning.*" He ignored the person who was with Ingrid and, without being invited to do so, crossed over to the bar, poured himself a quick bourbon, and said, "Have you seen my wife?"

"Do you mean lately, or in general?"

"I'm in no mood for games, Ingrid."

"And I'm in no mood to be snapped at, Mr. Scadudo."

He glared at her. Then, glancing at the designer, who did not make any move to leave, he said, "Come into my office, please, Ingrid. There is something I'd like to discuss with you."

She followed him in, closing the door behind herself. "Yes, Mr. Scadudo? What did you wish to see me about?"

He looked at her, the tall, arrogant blonde who had said "Mr. Scadudo" with a certain disdain. "I'm not sure I care for your attitude," he said.

She smiled.

And then they flew into each other's arms, nearly knocking themselves off their feet.

"Oh God," he said, reaching down between her legs so that Ingrid cried out. "God how I've missed you."

She bit his neck, his ear, his lips. When she tore his shirt open, buttons went flying. They stumbled across the room, kissing, gasping, devouring.

He pushed her back across the desk, sending blotter, pens, and Hannah's picture flying.

"Do it!" she cried. *"Do it!"*

Hannah fought her way through the congested holiday traffic, careful of her Corvette's delicate body and expensive paint job, trying not to scrape it again—she would be needing to sell it soon. She had stopped at the bank, and now the million dollars' worth of stock certificates lay in a thick, scary packet on the seat next to her. She looked at her watch. She had forty-five minutes to get to the meeting place, which was only two streets away. There was time to stop by Starlite and leave Alan's sculpture in his office.

She hoped that it would soften the blow of what she had to tell him: that she knew he had embezzled nearly a million dollars from the company and that she had sold her shares to raise the cash to repay it. She wasn't going to be judgmental or make accusations or demand to know what he had done with the money. She planned only to tell him how she had found out, that she had suspected something for a while, and that, adding up certain things she had overheard during phone conversations and doing a quiet inspection of the company's accounts, she had put it all together. As far as she was concerned, the subject was closed; she and Alan would go away, sever their connections with Starlite, and try to establish a new life for themselves. She loved him, that was all that mattered.

But at no small sacrifice. Hannah knew that this would spell the end of her friendship with Philippa, and possibly imperil Starlite—would these shares give Miranda controlling interest?—but Hannah couldn't let that interfere with her determination to save Alan. Once the funds were replaced, she hoped that Philippa would drop the matter and not follow through with prosecution. Hannah was counting on their years together, and the fact that Philippa would want Hannah's children spared from finding out the truth about their father.

No matter what lies ahead, Hannah thought as she nosed the Corvette into her reserved parking space, Alan and I will meet it and we will survive, just as long as we have each other. The big house, the cars, corporate offices on the top floor—none of these matter if we don't have each other. It will be just like it was in the old days, when our love was all we needed.

"Well!" Alan said as he pulled a new shirt out of his suitcase and put it on. He laughed. "Look at these teeth marks! I look like I was attacked by piranhas! What will Hannah think?"

Ingrid retrieved her panties and held them up. Torn beyond repair. "Tell her you went swimming in the Amazon."

"She might get suspicious when she sees these bruises."

"She won't get suspicious, the silly cow. She hasn't been smart enough to catch on to what we've been up to all these years—she won't start now."

"Poor Hannah," Alan said as she picked up his jacket and removed something from the inside pocket. "Poor dumb Hannah. So blindly trusting. And now she's madly rushing around trying to raise cash so she can pay back the money we took. She thinks I don't know."

"How will she get it?"

He shrugged. "I imagine she's going to sell her Starlite stock. She's been spending an awful lot of time at the safe in our bedroom. If I know her, she'll be stupid enough to sell it to Miranda—just hand controlling interest over to them on a silver platter. Not that it's going to make any difference to us," he said with a grin as he came up behind Ingrid and put his arms around her. "By the time the shit hits the fan, you and I will be long gone and living the good life in Singapore. Is everything arranged with Mr. Chang and your banker friend?"

She reached down for him, playfully, and Alan was immediately aroused again. "I've taken care of everything. I even have the tickets," she said, biting his ear. "We leave tonight on Singapore Airlines, first class, one way. What's this?" she asked when she saw the package he was holding.

"It's a present. For you."

"For me? You generous bastard." When she opened it and the gem-stones encrusting the gold crucifix glittered beneath the overhead lights, the pupils in her blue eyes flared darkly, like a cat's. "Oh, Alan," she breathed. "It's beautiful!"

She lifted up her hair, and Alan tried to fasten the necklace for her, explaining its history. "Princess Somebody-or-Another wore it when she freed Brazil's slaves. Oh shit." The clasp wouldn't work; it was too old. "I hadn't noticed this before," he said. "I'll take it to a jeweler and get a new clasp put on it."

She turned around and gave him a long, lingering kiss on the mouth, rubbing her body against his. "Didn't you get anything for your wife?"

He went back to his jacket and fished out the little voodoo doll, hand carved from jacaranda wood, that had cost him less than a dollar. "She'll be thrilled with this. Hannah's always happy with cheap, crappy junk."

As Ingrid laughed and tossed the sea goddess into the air, and as Alan held the crucifix up to the morning sunlight, admiring his purchase, Hannah was, at that moment, standing on the other side of the door, holding her purse and the *Phoenix* sculpture. She had arrived in time to hear the sounds of lovemaking; she had heard every word of their conversation.

When her heart did something wild inside her chest, she was momentarily dizzy, and she had to reach out to steady herself. It was too soon to take another pill, so she closed her eyes and held her breath, trying mentally to will her heart back into a steady rhythm. And when, in the next instant, it did exactly that, she slowly exhaled, squared her shoulders, and opened the door.

They turned, startled. Hannah made a quick survey of the scene—the desk items scattered all over the floor, Ingrid's disheveled hair, Alan's zipper still down.

She gave him a long, hard look, then she turned and walked out.

Alan ran after her, catching her by the arm. "Let me explain."

"You know, Alan," she said in a tight voice, "the strangest thought came into my head when I saw you two. I was suddenly thinking of the night our first child was born—the plans you and I made, the promises we made, to our children and to each other. I was going to cover for you because—" She struggled for control. "Because I thought I wanted to protect you. I don't care what happens to you now."

"Hannah, listen to me. About Ingrid. It's not what you think."

"Alan, I heard everything. And now I understand a lot of things that puzzled me in the past—sudden business trips, unreturned phone calls, unexplained charges on our credit cards. You're right, I was stupid. Right from the beginning."

"What are you going to do?"

"I don't know." She twisted the handle of her purse. She still had the eagle sculpture under her arm, carefully protected in plastic bubble wrap. She realized she was about to cry. "I was willing to forgive everything, Alan, even your stealing from Starlite, which is like stealing from your own family. I would have forgiven anything—" Her voice caught. "As long as you still loved me."

"I do, Hannah. Believe me. Here." He showed her Princess Isabel's necklace, which he had been clutching as if it were a lifeline. "I bought this for you."

She looked at the necklace, and then at him. Ingrid's wild lovemaking had messed up his hair so that the transplant plugs showed. "Keep it. Sell it. You're going to need money for a good lawyer."

"You're not going to tell them about the million dollars, are you?"

"Philippa would have found out soon enough anyway."

"Hannah, don't do this to me—"

Ingrid suddenly emerged from his office, all tidied up, her hair perfectly combed, purse slung over her shoulder. She quietly closed the door as if she were leaving after a normal business day and walked in a dignified way down the hall, without looking at Hannah or Alan, until she disappeared around the corner where the elevators were.

"You'd better go after her," Hannah said. "From what I overheard, if she gets away you'll be left with nothing. And you'll never find her."

He hesitated, a torn look on his face, then: "Shit! Ingrid!" He ran down the hall. "Ingrid, wait!"

The first thing Hannah did was to stop at the bank, where she replaced the stocks in the safe deposit box. As she joined the crosstown traffic on La Cienega, passing the very spot where a man was waiting for her to arrive with stock certificates, Hannah thought about Alan and Ingrid, the sounds she had heard, the conversation on the other side of the closed door, and she felt herself grow curiously empowered by it. Alan had betrayed her, but in an ironic way, she had betrayed herself. Hannah thought back over the years, recalling things for the first time, and she saw how Alan hadn't even looked at her when she was a fat gofer at Halliwell and Katz. But once she was thin, he had taken her on the Tilt-A-Whirl. Thirty years ago, she realized, he had taken her for a carnival ride, and he had been taking her for one ever since.

And then Hannah thought about the waiting room at the Tarzana Obesity Clinic, where she had first met Philippa so long ago; she thought of the day Philippa adopted Esther, who was Jackie's age, and how the two kids became best friends; and finally Hannah thought of her other children, all of whom were coming home for Christmas, bringing grand-children with them. And suddenly Alan just didn't seem as important to her as he once had.

When she got home, a lot of thinking had been done, a lot of decisions made and conclusions reached. The first thing Hannah did was to tear up her letter to Philippa. Then she went downstairs and handed the sixty-five-thousand-dollar eagle sculpture to a startled Miss Ralston, saying, "This is for you. I saw how much you were admiring it."

Then she looked at all the flowers and decorations and things that had to be done for her big Christmas party, and she said to her secretary, "Well, shall we get to work?"

···★

45

As Judith made her way along the path from one of the cottages, where
she had been called to treat a bad case of frostbite on someone who had
thought it would be fun to ski in a bikini, she removed her down parka
and draped it over her arm. The sun was high, the sky clear, and the day
growing warm. Judith was feeling good—the best, in fact, that she had
felt in a long time. The day had dawned clear and bright, almost spring-
like, and Mr. Smith had telephoned to say he was sorry their dinner had
been interrupted the night before and he would be most pleased if she
joined him for lunch today. Judith had accepted and was looking forward
to it.

Two electric carts trundled by on the path, taking guests to bungalows,
cottages, or cabins—new arrivals, in time for the Christmas ball tonight.
Judith recognized one of them as Philippa Roberts, founder of Starlite.
When Judith had been pregnant with Kimmie she had gained twenty
pounds and had joined Starlite to take them off. There was only one
passenger in the second cart, a man in horn-rimmed glasses and a short
black beard. She only saw him for an instant, but Judith thought he looked
familiar somehow.

Otherwise, not many guests were out on the grounds today, despite that
it was a lovely warm morning; most, she knew, had already begun their
elaborate ritual of getting ready for the ball tonight. Although it wasn't
a costume ball, it might as well be for the personal preparations that were
going into it. But then, she reminded herself, these were people who were
used to being seen and being judged, often harshly. Like poor Bunny
Kowalski, whom she hadn't seen since the night before last, when she had
visited Bunny in her suite. The young actress had requested Valium but
in the end hadn't taken it. While she and Judith had been talking, Frieda
Goldman, Bunny's agent, had called, announcing some exciting news that

had immediately snapped the girl out of her depression. Judith assumed that Bunny was all right, since she hadn't called the clinic again.

But other people *had* called. Namely Mort. Her ex-husband was getting insistent upon coming up to Star's to see her—"I want to give us another try," he had said. Since his first call two days ago, when it had upset Judith that he had found out where she was, Mort had tried an impressive sixteen times to wear down her resistance and get her to invite him up. But what was there to talk about? After all the shitty things they had said to each other, there was nothing left.

As she turned down the path that led to the health club, Judith was startled to see a strange figure cavorting in the snow up ahead. She stopped and stared. The person was small, bundled up in a parka and woolens, but gangly, she could see, with long sandy hair streaming out behind. A child, she realized. Up here at Star's? It ran straight toward Judith with arms imitating a windmill, and suddenly Judith heard her own voice, two years ago, saying, "Be careful, spider monkey."

Kimmie!

Seeing a flash of mischievous blue eyes and cheeks like two red apples, Judith rushed forward. But when she got close the image vanished and she was alone again.

She hugged herself tightly. Don't come apart; not now, it's been two whole years . . .

She resumed walking, at a faster pace, eager to leave the apparition far behind. And when she reached the Castle she hurried through the lobby, slipped into one of the thickly carpeted vestibules that resembled a nave in a medieval church, and inserted her key into the elevator lock. Her apartment was in one of the four Sleeping Beauty–like towers, each of which was accessed only by private key-operated elevator.

"It's your mind's way of not letting go," Dr. Aldrich, a psychiatrist, had explained when she had told him about the visions of Kimmie that were cropping up with disturbing regularity. It could happen anytime, anywhere, and the hallucination, though brief, always left her frightened and nervous.

"But I don't *want* to keep seeing her, doctor," Judith had argued. "I'm a physician. I am reality based. I know my daughter is dead and gone."

"Intellectually, yes, but emotionally?"

Judith quit going to him after that. Twelve months of therapy hadn't helped; Aldrich had had the irritating habit, like Mr. Smith, of constantly probing her about Kimmie. The best way to break free from the past, Judith had decided, was not to talk about it or think about it, but to let it go. Which was why she had ultimately left Green Pines.

As she hurried inside her apartment and quickly closed the door, thankful she hadn't encountered anyone who wanted to talk, she went to the phone to see if she had any messages.

Her hand froze on the telephone.

Someone had been in her apartment.

She looked around. Her predecessor, Dr. Mitgang, had had the suite done in a monochromatic hybrid of deco and classic contemporary, and Judith had liked it enough to leave it. She appreciated the clean lines, the lack of clutter, the simplicity and neatness of the decor. But now she saw the signs of disruption: the classic Wassily chairs not perfectly aligned around the glass-brick coffee table, the way Judith always left them; the mirrored placemats on her Lucite dining room table smudged and askew; the enormous floor-to-ceiling abstract painting behind the sofa slightly tilted.

Leaving the phone, she went cautiously into the bedroom. It wasn't a ransacked mess; in fact, to the unaccustomed eye it looked painstakingly neat, like a showcase. But Judith saw the slight disarray of her burgundy and gray bedspread, and the single orchid plant on the gray storage headboard had been moved. But the final sign was the black and red Calder mobile lying on the floor, as if someone had accidentally knocked it off and hadn't bothered to replace it.

She quickly dialed hotel security, and a few minutes later a man in a navy blue blazer with a walkie-talkie attached to his belt arrived. He glanced around with a puzzled look on his face. "What makes you think someone has been in here, Doctor?"

"Because I didn't go out this morning until after housekeeping had been in, and I always neaten up after the maids have left." When he gave her an odd look, she said, "I like things to be just so. Someone came in here while I was gone and moved things around. Maybe they were searching for something. They certainly left enough fingerprints."

When he bent down to examine the chrome tubular frame of a Wassily chair to satisfy himself that there were indeed fingerprints there, Judith said, "I like my furniture to shine. I'm very particular about that."

"Was anything stolen, Doctor?"

"Nothing that I can see." Her jewelry was all there, and a wallet containing sixty dollars in cash. Nothing taken, but everything certainly had been gone through.

She clasped her arms around herself; she was starting to shake. She felt as if she had been violated.

The security guard made a discreet phone call, and Simon Jung arrived moments later, saying, "This is most distressing, Doctor." He sounded sincere. "Do you have any idea what they might have been after? Drugs, perhaps?"

She turned to him. "Do you smell cigarettes?"

He sniffed the air. "Yes, only faintly, I think."

"Well I don't smoke, Mr. Jung," she said, "but I know someone who does."

She found Zoey in the substerile room, languidly unpacking a shipment of sutures that had just arrived. Noticing that Zoey was placing the new sutures in front of the old ones, not rotating the surgical stock the way it was supposed to be, Judith said, "Miss Larson, I'd like a word with you."

Zoey gave her a slow, lazy look. "You got another one of those calls again, Doctor," she said, a smile playing at her lips. "I told him I was giving him your messages. I told him that maybe you just didn't want to talk to him."

"Miss Larson, I want you to pack your things and leave."

Zoey straightened up. "Huh?"

"You're fired. Pack your things and take the next tram down the mountain."

"What are you talking about!"

"My room was searched while I was out."

"So?"

"I believe you did it."

Zoey rested on one hip and folded her arms. She was not wearing her uniform, Judith noticed, even though the clinic was open and anyone could walk in. "Why would I want to search your room?"

"I don't know, maybe you were hoping to find out something about me, something you could blackmail me with."

"You're crazy. Why are you always trying to pin everything on me?"

"There was the smell of cigarettes in my room."

"Oh sure, and you think I'd be dumb enough to smoke while I'm searching someone's room."

"I can smell cigarettes right now, Miss Larson, and you're not smoking."

Zoey's flat brown eyes flickered. Then she said, "Sure, like I'm the only person in the world who smokes."

"The intruder also left a trail of fingerprints on my nice polished glass and chrome. That was very stupid of you. Now please leave."

"You can't fire me. Only Mr. Jung—"

"I run this clinic, Miss Larson, and that includes hiring and firing the nurse. And you are one sorry excuse for a nurse. You violated one of your profession's most sacred ethics—a patient's right to privacy. You searched my room and you gave Mr. Smith's story to that tabloid."

"I told you that story was not my doing!"

"I believe we are going to discover otherwise. Either way, I don't want you working here anymore. Pack your things. I've already alerted personnel. They will have your final paycheck ready."

Zoey's insolence dissolved into panic. "Listen," she said, "I'll pay you whatever you want. I got thirty thousand bucks for Mr. Smith's story— you can have half of it. *All* of it. Just don't make me go."

"Why? What's so special about this job? Is it the autonomy, being your own boss for most of the time? Is it drugs?" Judith flipped open the narcotics cupboard, which, by state law, should have been locked. "Or is it the movie stars maybe, you like being around celebrities?"

"I . . . I just like working here, that's all." Zoey began to wring her hands, and Judith saw perspiration on her upper lip. "This is the best job I've ever had."

"What about the surgeon you used to work for in Santa Monica? The one who recommended you so highly. No, wait," Judith held up a hand. "I don't think I want to hear it. He either fired you and gave you a good recommendation just to get rid of you or you held something over him— the sort of nasty secret information you were hoping to find in my room. Whatever you're hiding from, Zoey, I can't help you."

When Zoey tried to speak, Judith turned away and said, "I don't want to hear it. Just be out as soon as possible. And Zoey, you can count on me to write a letter to the state licensing board."

Mr. Smith was dictating into a machine when he opened his door. "Come in!" he said, turning the recorder off. "You're an hour early, what a pleasant surprise!"

He was dressed in dark brown slacks and a pale blue silk shirt with his initials on the pocket. His coloring was healthy; everything about him seemed to shine. This was not the ashen-faced man lying in pain she had met five days ago.

"Can I offer you a drink, Judith, or are you still on duty?"

She accepted a glass of white wine but didn't touch it as she told him about Zoey. "I guess she had been hoping to find out something about me, something sordid that she could hold over me. But all I was hiding was a poor dead child."

He waited, not pressing her.

The words came freely, on their own. "You see, Kimmie often faked illnesses, to get attention. Not that she didn't get any from either Mort or me—I think we were good parents. But there was a certain amount of jealousy about the sick kids, I guess. If I was called out to treat a child with measles, for example, I would come home and find that Kimmie had painted dots on herself and she would complain that she was sick. It was harmless really. She was only eight years old, I assumed she would grow out of it." Judith went to the window. Sunlight streamed over her like a golden shawl. "A medical conference came up, in San Diego. Kimmie didn't want me to go, because I would be gone for five days. But I wanted to go. For one thing, I was looking forward to a small vacation. I hadn't been out of Green Pines in a long time. For another, my paper on the management of wilderness emergencies was the keynote talk. And finally, some old medical school chums were going to be there. I explained all of this to Kimmie, promising to bring her a present from Sea World."

Judith looked at the wineglass in her hand, as if wondering how it got there. Then she said, "The night before I was due to leave, I was called away from dinner to treat a child who had fallen and cut his head. And so when Kimmie told me the next morning that she had a headache, I thought she was faking. I told her we'd have a wonderful time when we got back, that I'd take her to Playland, you know, all the things you say to mollify a child.

"The drive to San Diego took nine hours, and as soon as I checked into the hotel I called home. Kimmie was in the hospital. Mort said she had blacked out shortly after I left, and the physician who was taking care of her said she hadn't regained consciousness yet. He suspected intracranial bleeding. I left my car at the hotel and flew back to Sacramento, where I got a rental car and drove the rest of the way. It took me only four hours to get home instead of nine. But I was too late. Kimmie was dead."

A memory flashed in her mind, one that she hadn't thought of, hadn't allowed herself to think of, in a long time: Judith and Kimmie arguing over what Kimmie was going to go trick-or-treating as—a bride, or a rock star like Madonna. In the end, Kimmie had won, and she went as a bride.

"What was it?" Smith said. "What did she die of?"

"My daughter had a congenital cerebral aneurysm. A weak blood vessel in the brain that had been waiting for eight years to burst. It chose the moment I left for San Diego."

"And you haven't been able to forgive yourself for not being there. Judith, tell me: did Kimmie get sick because you went to that conference?"

"No."

"Would she have died from it anyway, even if you had been there?"

"Yes."

"Then it wasn't your fault. You're blameless."

"No. What I'm guilty of was not being there with her in her last moments of life. She might not have regained consciousness, but it was possible that she could hear, and mine wasn't the last voice she heard." Judith pictured Kimmie's hospital room, so stark, devoid of flowers and cards and balloons because she hadn't been in it long enough—making it look like no one cared. And Kimmie beneath the sheets, just a small wrinkle in them, her little chest no longer rising and falling.

"Do you have a picture of her?"

Judith carried one with her all the time, in a locket around her neck. When she showed it to him, he said, "Hmm. Funny looking."

"Yes, she was." She started to cry, and he took her into his arms.

"Judith," he said as he held her, "I have decided to cause a sensation and attend the ball tonight. Will you do me the honor of accompanying me?"

46

The day that Beverly Burgess had been dreading arrived at last: Otis Quinn, the author of *Butterfly Exposed,* was due to arrive at Star's.

It was time, she decided, to stop kidding herself. He had to be coming here because he suspected she was the Beverly Highland who had destroyed Danny Mackay; there could be no other reason. She saw the scenario already: he would accuse her of being Highland, then challenge her to prove that she wasn't. Either way, he would win. He would sell his story to the tabloids and she would have no defense. Look what had happened to Mr. Smith.

After all those years, nearly her entire life, spent in taking revenge on Danny Mackay, her careful planning, her patience, the complex traps she laid for him—orchestrating her own death and getting her reward in the end when Danny hanged himself in jail—all threatened to be exposed, sensationalized, possibly also trivialized. Her life's work about to be brought down to supermarket tabloid level.

She turned away from the window and looked at Simon Jung. He had asked her a question and was awaiting the answer. What a wonderful man, she thought. So polished and refined, yet sensitive and kind, without a trace of arrogance. Why couldn't she have met him years ago, in another, safer lifetime? Beverly had sometimes dared to let herself hope that, as time went on, perhaps she and Simon could have an intimate relationship. She longed to be in love again—and loved.

But Otis Quinn was going to put an end to that dream; she could feel it, she sensed the storm that was coming. He had come up on the morning tram and had been taken to his cottage. That was why Simon was here in Beverly's office—he had brought the latest list of newly arrived guests. There was the Philippa Roberts party from Australia, who had taken the bungalow left vacant when the Nobel Prize–winning author, Ricardo

Cadiz, had canceled; then there was the usual collection of famous Holly-wood names; and finally, Otis Quinn, freelance journalist. It was only a matter of time now before he would be pressing her for an interview.

How much did he already know about her past? No doubt everything: Hazel's whorehouse in San Antonio, where Beverly had worked when she was fourteen; the abortion Danny Mackay had forced her to undergo when she was sixteen; the pornographic magazines she had tricked the Reverend Danny Mackay into owning, as well as the ladies' bordello on Rodeo Drive. Even if Beverly didn't confirm any of this, or even if she denied it all, Quinn would no doubt sell the story anyway.

And she would lose her chances with Simon forever.

"Are you all right, Beverly?" he asked quietly, coming up to her so that she caught the faint scent of Bijan cologne. "Is there anything wrong?"

She sensed that Simon felt the same way about her as she did about him, but now she would never know. Perhaps if she had told him the truth when they first met two and a half years ago, they might have had a chance. But now it was too late.

Before she could reply, her secretary came in and said, "Miss Burgess, Andrea Bachman is asking to see you. She doesn't have an appointment."

"That's all right, Marie," she said, reaching for her sunglasses, thinking that they were probably no longer going to be necessary after tonight. After Quinn exposed to the world who she really was. "Please show her in."

"I'll be in the ballroom if you need me," Jung said, pausing for an instant, as if about to say something else. But he turned and left. Andrea passed him in the doorway.

"Hello, Miss Bachman," Beverly said, turning around just as she was putting on her sunglasses. "I've been expecting you."

"Yes, of course," Andrea said, "you knew I would figure out that Marion was still alive."

"I thought you might. What gave it away?"

"The way the diary is written. It doesn't read as if the events described in it were written shortly after they took place, but rather years later, with the hindsight of age, perhaps."

"Very astute," Beverly said, smiling. "But then, you are a writer, aren't you?"

"Where is Marion now? And what happened to her daughter?"

"She's here. Waiting to meet you."

"Which one, Marion or Lavinia?"

"She'll tell you herself."

Andrea knew exactly what to expect: an eighty-six-year-old woman living in the past, like Norma Desmond, wearing flapper dresses with tarnished sequins, surrounded by mementoes and faded scrapbooks, with heavy velvet drapes drawn closed over the sunshine, while she waited for Cecil B. deMille to direct her comeback.

So she was surprised to be shown into a delightfully sunny living room done in cheerful spring colors. And the elderly woman walking with the aid of a cane, dressed in a basic but perfectly tailored wool dress with a scarf pinned with a brooch at her shoulder, was no aging jazz baby trying to hold onto a long-gone past, but what Andrea thought of as a grande dame, walking as erectly as her age allowed, her pure white hair drawn back with tortoiseshell combs. When they shook hands, Andrea felt cool, smooth skin with arthritic knobs underneath.

"I've been looking forward to meeting you," the woman said. "I am Marion Star."

Andrea was momentarily speechless. To have spent the last four days reading this woman's diary, the private and intimate details of her life— what did one say? "I've seen you in the lobby, Miss Star!" she said in amazement. "You always sit in that curious chair at the foot of the staircase."

Marion laughed and escorted her visitors to the hearth, where a silver tea service had been set on a brass steamer trunk that served as a coffee table. Sunlight from the tall windows spilled over the setting, giving it, Andrea thought, a summer feel. "Yes, that chair!" Marion said. "It was from my movie *Robin Hood*. The sheriff of Nottingham dispensed his evil justice from it! I like to sit in the main hall and watch the guests in my house. I like doing it anonymously, and no one notices an old woman." Her eyes twinkled. "But you did, clever girl. Please, sit down. I hope you like herb tea. My doctor has forbidden me caffeine."

Andrea was spellbound as she watched Marion effortlessly pour from the silver teapot; her hands, though only four years from ninety, appeared strong enough, and capable. "And that staircase," Marion added as she handed cups to Andrea and Beverly, "I'll never forget the night John Barrymore got drunk and decided to slide down that enormous banister. He landed in my lap at the foot of the stairs and we both went sprawling!"

She turned dark and lively eyes to Andrea. "So you've read my book. And you guessed that I didn't write it back in 1932."

Sitting next to her on the sofa, and in such healthy daylight, Andrea saw that Marion wore very little makeup. There wasn't much resemblance to the sultry vamp in the photographs hanging in the main hall downstairs, but Marion's eyes were still sensual.

Andrea looked around the room and was surprised to find absolutely no trace of that era in evidence. The antique armoire displayed country crockery and wooden folk art. The walls were decorated with framed silhouettes and twig wreaths. There were vases of fresh flowers on nearly every available surface; a small willow table supported a collection of antique toy soldiers. But there were no photographs of Marion herself, or of Ramsey, or anyone from that era; no movie posters for *Her Wicked Ways*, no memorabilia from *Queen of the Nile*.

"I'm not what you expected, am I?" Marion said with an amused smile. "Perhaps you're even asking yourself if I really am Marion Star?"

It hadn't occurred to Andrea, but now that she thought about it, what proof was there?

"My real name is Gertrude Winkler," Marion said, "which was what it was before I met Ramsey. He gave me that ridiculous Star name. Nearly all of us changed our names in those days. Theda Bara was really Theodosia Goodman. And poor Rudy, his full name was Rodolfo Alfonzo Raffaele Guglielmi. Quite a mouthful. How I adored that man," she added wistfully. "But I adored Dexter Bryant Ramsey more."

Marion offered a plate of tiny buttered sandwiches to Beverly and Andrea. "Yes, I was Marion Star," she continued. "And I do have proof, should anyone ever care to challenge me. But who would? And besides, I have no desire to go public, as they say these days. I'm content to be Gertrude Winkler, and to allow this house to remain as a monument to a vanished woman." She smiled at Andrea and settled back with her tea. "Now, I imagine you have a thousand questions to ask me, Miss Bachman!"

"I hardly know where to begin."

"Surely the first thing you want to know is if I killed Dexter as the police said. Yes, I did. I murdered my beloved Dexter. I found him in bed that night with another woman. In *our* bed, with our baby in the next room. Do you know how he reacted when I caught them? He laughed. Right in my face. I kept a gun in my night table, for security. When I brought it out, the girl, whoever she was, ran out of the room. But Dexter kept laughing, daring me to pull the trigger. He was always such a showman. He actually got out of bed and walked away from me. I remember his last words: 'You don't mind if I take a pee before you kill me?' So I followed him into the bathroom and I shot him."

She paused. Then added, "You should have seen the surprised look on his face."

Andrea glanced at Beverly, then back at Marion. She tried to think how to word the next question, but Marion anticipated her again. "You want to know about the castration. I didn't do that. When I saw what I had done, that I had killed Dexter, I dropped the gun, ran into the nursery, bundled up Lavinia, and ran out into the night. Somehow, I got into one of the cars—I don't know whose—and drove down the mountain. I don't remember doing it or driving straight through to Fresno, to my sister's. I learned much later, of course, that the gun had disappeared and that someone had taken a knife to Dexter, but I had nothing to do with that.

Maybe someone thought they were protecting me by taking the gun. And maybe someone else decided to take their own form of revenge on him when they found the body. Dexter had many enemies. I suppose that whatever occurred in that bathroom after I ran out will always remain a mystery."

"What happened after you got to your sister's?"

"I went insane—literally. My sister took care of me and of my baby. She got rid of the car, and when the police came by to ask if she'd seen me or heard from me, she said she had no idea where I was. But I was very ill, and eventually I became too much for her to handle. Apparently I raved a lot, not making much sense. I tried on two occasions to kill myself, and it terrified her. So she decided to put me into an institution. I was committed under a false name and spent the next several years in two living hells—the one in which I had nightmares of killing Dexter over and over, the other in which I was brutalized by the inmates and staff, raped many times, and subjected to months of insulin shock treatment that almost killed me. When my sister found out what was happening, she took me out and brought me home, hiring a strong nurse to take care of me."

Marion paused to drink her tea. When she put the cup down, it rattled slightly in its saucer.

"One morning I woke up," she said quietly, her gaze focused on the silver sugar bowl, "and I saw a sparrow sitting on a branch outside my window. Spring sunshine filled the room and I was very hungry—for waffles, I recall. I had been ill for eight years, there was a war on in Europe, and the world had forgotten Marion Star. But I was healed."

"What happened to Lavinia?"

"She died in 1943, of polio. She was a beautiful child."

"And afterward?"

"It took me a while to regain my strength, but while I was convalescing I made several important decisions. The first was to let Marion Star remain vanished. The second was never to return to Hollywood. The movies had changed anyway; everything had changed. The third decision was to leave this house as it was, intact. I didn't know if I would come back and claim it someday. Legally, my sister had inherited it, so she had someone come and close it up; we had it watched, to make sure there was no vandalism. And finally, my fourth decision was to go into business.

"When I was making my millions in the movies, I had sent money regularly to my sister, who banked every penny. When I was well again, we had enough capital to go into business—real estate mostly. And as time went on and my emotional wounds healed, Gertrude Winkler became quite successful, and rich. My sister died several years ago on a golf course in Florida. She had had sex the night before with a man half her age."

"And that was when you put Star's Haven up for sale?"

"Yes, I decided it was time to let it go. But I wouldn't sell it to just anyone. Miss Burgess and I had many long talks before we agreed on the sale." She smiled at Beverly. "Now then," Marion said, livening up. "Tell me about this Japanese fellow who is so mad for me and wants to invest in a film about me."

As Andrea told Marion about Mr. Yamato, who was due to arrive tomorrow, an idea began to form in her mind that was suddenly so exciting she could barely sit still. She was going write *two* screenplays. The one for Yamato would be about the young screen goddess Marion Star, but the second one would open with her flight from the house the night of the murder, and it would chronicle her battle with insanity and her eventual recovery and ultimate victory over years of abuse and exploitation.

Both were going to be sensational films, and Andrea couldn't wait to get started.

47

"It was here, in this very spot," the good-looking young man in the blue blazer said, "that the body of Dexter Bryant Ramsey was found. To this day, no one knows who murdered him."

While the rest of the tour group murmured interested comments to one another and things like, "Well, I heard . . ." Danny Mackay was staring at the transparent crystal bathtub.

What a hot vision it created: Beverly's naked body sprawled here, just like the hapless Ramsey sixty years ago.

He had arrived at Star's on the morning tram, sitting in a seat not far from Beverly. It was the closest he had been to her since their last face-to-face, three and a half years ago, when she had made him beg for his life. She had changed; clearly some plastic surgeon had been paid a wad to alter her looks. She might fool other people, he thought, but she didn't fool him. It was Beverly all right, despite the fact that her two companions kept calling her Philippa.

It had briefly entered his head to take care of her right then and there, six thousand feet in the air, maybe dangle her over the side of the tram car and let her scream with terror for a few minutes before dropping her. But that would have meant getting himself arrested, and Danny didn't have jail on his appointment calender. After his work at Star's was done, he was going to head east, to Washington, D.C., where he was going to pay a little visit on his old friend, the bastard who had won the presidency that was rightfully Danny's.

After being taken to his cottage, Danny had walked around the resort, feeling himself fill up with power again; he had discharged some of it the night before on the little waitress. The whole place was buzzing about the Christmas ball tonight. That would be the perfect time for him to have his private meeting with Philippa, while everyone else was distracted. He would do what he had to do, then slip away.

And now he not only had the time slotted in, but the place as well. Here, in the Obscene Bathroom. It couldn't be more perfect. He nearly laughed out loud and had to stop himself. But he smirked; it was just too delicious. Because tonight Cinderella was going to meet her Prince Charming, but instead of a glass slipper, she was going to get a glass coffin.

....★

48

They met again, at the same lookout point where they had met that morning. It was night now, and cold, and the gun in his pocket still felt like a block of ice.

"Where is Philippa now?"

"In the third bungalow."

"Has she contacted Beverly Burgess yet?"

"She tried, but Burgess has been busy with preparations for tonight's ball."

"You know what to do then?"

"Yes. One question: what if Philippa doesn't go to the ball? What if she changes her mind and stays in?"

"Then we change our plans, too."

"She's got two people with her."

"I know. They're no problem. It's almost time. Get going."

The man with the gun walked away, leaving his companion to remain at the lookout, a silhouette against the stars.

"Jackie," Philippa said into the phone, "if you know where Esther is, please tell me. I've been calling her apartment all day and there's no answer."

Philippa was in one of the bedrooms of her bungalow at Star's, and she had interrupted getting ready for the ball to try to reach her daughter one more time. "I must have called ten times today," she said to Jackie Scadudo, who was Esther's best friend; they were both attending school at the University of California in Santa Barbara. "That's why I decided to try you. I thought she might be at your place."

"Gosh, Aunt Philippa, I really shouldn't tell you, it's supposed to be a surprise."

"Surprise? What is it? Where is she?"

"Esther's on her way to see you. When you told her last night that you were going to be at Star's for a few days, she decided to drive down and surprise you. She left around noon. She should be there by now."

Philippa sighed with relief but almost immediately was concerned again. "Is she driving alone? It's almost two hundred miles."

"No, her boyfriend is with her. Don't worry. Esther is a big girl now. Hey, you're seeing Mom tomorrow, aren't you? Give her my love. Bye, gotta go."

"Esther's on her way here, to surprise me," Philippa said to Charmie after she hung up. "Except that she doesn't know you can't get up this mountain without a reservation or an invitation."

Charmie paused in the final application of her makeup—copper eye shadow to complement the apricot caftan she was going to wear to the ball—and pointed at a large leather book on the bed, the directory of resort services. "It explains it in there," she said. "If you want to have visitors, you can leave their name with the desk in the boarding lounge at the bottom of the mountain."

"You know something, Charmie?" Philippa said as she picked up the phone and dialed. "I'm glad she's coming. Who knows how long the board meeting will take—possibly days. And then meeting Beverly Burgess—it could be a while before I can get up to Santa Barbara. It's been nearly a year since I've seen her and I do miss her."

Charmie regarded her friend in the vanity mirror. Philippa was wearing only a lace bra and bikini panties; her dress for the ball, a dove gray hand-beaded Isaac Mizrahi design, was laid out on the bed. Charmie suspected Philippa was going to ask Ricky to zip her into it.

In fact, when they had arrived at the bungalow and inspected the two bedrooms, each with two king-sized beds, a floor plan similar to the one they had had at the Marriott, Charmie had once again offered to take one bedroom by herself, leaving the other for Philippa and Ricky. But again, Philippa's old-fashioned sense of propriety and decorum had surfaced, and she had insisted that she and Charmie share one room, Ricky take the other. Very decorous, Charmie decided. But for how long?

Which led her to think about Ivan Hendricks. He would be in Brazil by now, sleuthing after Miranda International and Gaspar Enriques. Charmie wished he could have come to Star's with them, wished he could be attending the ball. She would have plied Ivan with the twelve-year-old scotch he was so fond of and then taught him a few dance steps he might not know.

When Philippa picked up her toiletries and went into the bathroom, closing the door behind her, Charmie returned to her own reflection in the mirror.

Ivan had been on her mind so much these past few days that she had given thought to little else—not even to tomorrow's board meeting or the threatened takeover by Miranda. He so completely monopolized her thoughts that she dreamed about him, intensely erotic dreams that had brought her nearly to the brink of orgasm. Despite the sexual skill of men she had been with, and Sam, who she was currently seeing and who was dynamite in bed, Charmie realized now that no man would ever satisfy her as she was certain Ivan could. Their one time together, in her kitchen, had been cut short, but she just knew that, given the opportunity, he would make love to her in a way no man ever had.

The sheer size of him! And that delicious military fitness, which made her feel small, more feminine. He was so generously endowed; Charmie craved to feel every inch of him inside her.

When she heard the sound of running water in the bathroom, she closed her eyes and slipped her hand inside her bra, trying to recreate Ivan's touch, recalling how he had licked butterscotch off her nipples.

What if she never had another chance with him? What if he reported from Brazil by telephone and then vanished to wherever it was he always vanished to, this time never to reappear? If Beverly Burgess was Philippa's sister, then that search was over. And once Miranda was stopped and the embezzler within Starlite found, Ivan's services would no longer be needed.

She sighed restlessly, thinking about how he had pulled her caftan open and lifted her breasts out of their lace cups. And then what she had discovered when she had reached down for him . . .

Charmie opened her eyes and gave herself a long, serious look in the mirror. No, she decided. She wasn't going to let him get away. Whatever it was that kept them apart, she didn't care. They had to be together; they *belonged* together, she just knew it. Somehow, she wasn't sure how, she was going to have her chance with Ivan.

Philippa came out of the bathroom then and tossed her toiletries bag onto the bed.

Charmie said, "Are you going to try to approach Beverly Burgess before the ball?"

"No. I'll just watch her tonight, try to see if I can *tell.*"

"And if she *is* your sister?"

"Then Esther is going to have a surprise of her own when she gets here!" Philippa had not gone into detail with her daughter about the unscheduled return to L.A., simply that it had to do with business. She didn't want to get Esther's hopes up and then disappoint her. The issue of family was a deeply sensitive one with them both; it was their special bond beyond the normal mother-daughter love—the fact that they were both adopted orphans.

"Speaking of surprises," Charmie said, "what do you suppose Hannah's cryptic phone call was all about?" They had received a message from Hannah saying that tomorrow's board meeting was going to prove unnecessary. "Do you suppose she's found something out?"

I pray so, Philippa thought. I pray that Hannah isn't planning on making a confession.

"Well, we can worry about business tomorrow," Charmie said as she rose from the vanity table, which, in the short time she had been there, she had managed to cover completely with bottles and brushes and compacts and shadows. It was a lot of junk and a lot of work, but Charmie's face was gorgeous; her shimmering apricot caftan, a vision. "Right now it's—" She shivered suddenly.

"What's wrong?"

"I just got the oddest feeling! What's that old saying? As though someone just walked across my grave?" She shrugged. "Must be jet lag. Anyway, as I was saying, it's time to go to the ball, Cinderella!"

"Almost ready," Philippa said, reaching for her pearl drop earrings. "I just have to slip into my dress."

Charmie said, "Uh-huh," and swept out of the bedroom, leaving a swirl of Passion fragrance in the air.

A moment later Ricky knocked on the door and looked in. "Miss Charmer said you needed me."

Philippa was momentarily speechless—she had never before seen Ricky in a tuxedo, and it made him look sophisticated, so worldly. Older, too. With his hair combed loosely over his shoulders, he looked as if he had just stepped out of a Christian Dior ad. "Would you mind zipping me up, please?" she asked.

He came up behind her and, placing his hands on her shoulders, kissed her neck.

"I've missed our being together," he said quietly. "It's been driving me crazy to be close to you all the time and not be able to touch you. I want you so badly, Philippa." He slipped his hands under her dress and pulled her against him.

She leaned into him, closing her eyes and succumbing to hands that caressed her stomach, her breasts. She felt his erection; she suddenly wanted to make love with him.

She turned around and they began to kiss, gently and exploringly at first, as if having to get to know each other all over again, and then with increasing passion. When Philippa started to reach down for him, he took her hand and said, "No. Let me do everything. I want to take care of you,

Philippa. I'm not rich, and I don't have important connections. All I have is my love for you. This is the one thing I can give you that no other man can."

He slowly drew her dress down, and then her panties. Easing her back onto the bed, he lifted her knees and spread them apart. She felt his smooth cheeks, his silky hair touch the insides of her thighs, his kisses warm and lingering. With his fingers he gently explored and opened her; he kissed her there, and she felt his tongue, firm and probing.

When she reached down and touched his hair, he grasped her hands and pinned them down to the bedspread, immobilizing her. Philippa squirmed as his mouth continued to drive her crazy. She tried to free her hands; she wanted him on top of her; she wanted to guide him inside her.

When he lifted her knees and pressed them toward her chest, opening her even wider, she cried out.

And then suddenly she gave up the struggle—she surrendered to the sheer pleasure of Ricky's loving skill. She felt her body melt and all tension run sweetly out of her until the entire universe, it seemed, was just one sublime sensation. His tongue probed deeply and then came out to flick her clitoris. He did this over and over until she began to feel the beginning swell of such exquisite pleasure that she delivered herself up onto it and let it carry her in wave after wave of shattering orgasm.

Afterward, she lay still, too exhausted to move. Ricky lowered her legs and came to sit on the edge of the bed, smiling down at her, stroking her hair. She smiled back at him and reached up to touch his cheek.

But when he said, "I love you, Philippa," it was the wrong thing to say. It was too soon, Paul Marquette still had her heart. She sat up and kissed him lightly on the lips. "Please don't say that. It's unlucky to be in love with me."

As soon as she said it she realized it was true. She hadn't thought of it before now, but the three men she had loved in her life—Johnny, Rhys, Paul—were all dead.

As if reading her thoughts, he touched her cheek and said with a smile, "Don't worry. Nothing's going to happen to me."

In his cottage camouflaged by pine trees, Danny Mackay was at that moment testing the sharpness of his knife and thinking that the first thing he was going to do was take out Beverly's Aussie toy-boy. No one gave Danny Mackay the brush-off, especially no snotty kid. And this knife, which had accomplished other missions for Danny, was going to do the job.

Danny had never liked killing with guns; they were too impersonal, placed too much distance between him and his victim. And guns were too quick. Well, he conceded as he slipped the knife into the leather sheath tucked under his belt, he might make it quick with the blond jock. But with Beverly, he was going to take his sweet time.

Checking the hour and seeing that it was time to get started, he inspected himself in the mirror once more to be sure the knife didn't show. Or the nylon cord. Or the gun. He wasn't going to kill with it; the gun had other uses. Danny had put on a tuxedo for the ball, but he wouldn't be wearing it for long; soon he would be changing into another outfit, one more suited to the occasion. And as for what Beverly was wearing to the ball tonight, she wouldn't have it on for long either. She was also going to be changing into another outfit: a pair of handcuffs and a homemade noose.

He couldn't wait to see the look on her face when she realized who he was.

Beverly had to try several times before she finally managed to slip the pearl drop earrings into her pierced ears. She was so worried about Otis Quinn that she couldn't keep her hands from shaking. Where *was* he? Quinn had arrived on the morning tram, and now it was evening. She had expected him to contact her by now. The waiting was turning her into a nervous wreck.

Which was why she jumped when she heard a knock at her door. Quinn?

But it was Simon: he had not yet changed into his white dinner jacket and black tie. He came into her living room and closed her door. "I received your message, Beverly," he said, a look of concern on his face. "You said you are not going to attend the ball tonight. Are you unwell? Shall I summon Dr. Isaacs?"

"No," she said. "I just—have a headache." Beverly had had every intention of attending tonight's event, having decided some time ago that it was going to be her "coming out," her first time in public without the sunglasses. The decision had been based on the fact that it was three and a half years since anyone had seen Beverly Highland's face on television screens and in newspapers; surely, she told herself, people's memories were fading. And then *Butterfly Exposed* had come out, by Otis Quinn, and it was filled with photographs of her, from the days when she had been a socialite philanthropist, raising money for various causes, specifically for Danny Mackay's presidential campaign fund. Now she could no longer take the chance. Someone in the ballroom was bound to recognize her.

"I hate for you to miss the ball, Beverly," Simon said, coming so close to her that she took a step back.

"I'll still be part of it, but up here, in private." She pointed to the large-screen TV built into one wall. It received transmissions from various ceiling-mounted cameras located throughout the Castle and the grounds, a system that enabled Beverly to observe what was going on around her resort without having to leave the safety and anonymity of her apartment.

"It's not the same as being there," he said.

"I don't mind," she said, turning away from him in case he could see the lie in her eyes. She turned the television on, and the screen was suddenly filled with a dazzling silver and white image: the ballroom, with its forty-foot Christmas tree, which had been flocked white and decorated with silver stars. The entire ballroom, in fact, was done in white: the drapes, the garlands, and the wreaths—a winter wonderland. A few guests had already arrived and were starting to help themselves from the massive buffet.

"Please, Simon," she said. "You go down and be the wonderful host that you always are for our guests."

"I had hoped for one dance with you, Beverly," he said.

They regarded each other across the room. Simon and Beverly had never danced together.

"It's what I want," she said softly. "Please."

He came up and put a hand on her cheek. "Let me help you, Beverly. Let me come between you and whatever it is that's frightening you."

She looked into his eyes and, for an instant, almost blurted it all out. But she held back, made herself be strong for just a moment longer, made herself hold on and keep the secrets inside. Until finally he said, "Very well, whatever you wish. I'll go and get ready for the ball now. If you change your mind . . ."

After he left, she tried to settle down and watch the monitor. But she soon discovered that she was in the grip of a strange restlessness. The scent of Simon's cologne lingered in the room; she could still feel his fingertips on her cheek.

Oh God, what was she going to do? Stay here? A prisoner in her own home, caged like an animal, while waiting for Otis Quinn to expose her? All her life she had been a fighter, but now Beverly saw herself acting cowardly.

She thought again of Simon. For as long as she could remember, she had been alone, shutting out men and love, relying solely upon herself with no shoulder to lean on. Simon said he wanted to share her burden, to be a shield against what was frightening her. Couldn't she now, at last, allow herself to draw upon someone else's strength? Wasn't it all right, finally, to let him in, let him help her?

After tomorrow, I might not have a chance with Simon again. After tomorrow, the world might be a very different place.

She went to her door and looked down the hall. Simon was already in his apartment, getting ready for the ball. Quietly closing the door behind her, her heart pounding, Beverly walked down to the end, where she paused and listened. She heard the shower going.

She tried his door. It was unlocked.

Beverly had been in Simon's apartment before; it was a curious reflection of another side to a man she both knew well and didn't know at all—Simon Jung, so neat and meticulous in his bearing, enjoyed a vaguely messy life-style. Books, magazines, and videotapes were lying about; a desk was covered with papers; a maroon silk tie was draped over the back of a chair.

She walked toward the bathroom, where steam was pouring through the half-open door. She could hear Simon in the shower, his feet squeaking on the tiles, a bar of soap falling with a thud. She looked in. A vague form was visible through the plastic curtain.

The bathrooms in the Castle were antique and oversized; the showers huge, with built-in marble benches and several shower heads arranged at different heights. The shower in Simon's bathroom could be converted into a steamroom or a large sunken bathtub with pulsating jets.

As Beverly slowly removed her clothes, keeping her eye on the figure behind the curtain, she inhaled the pungent scent of Irish Spring.

When she was completely undressed, she stepped to the other end of the shower and pushed the curtain aside. Simon had his back to her, soaping his chest and arms, his face held up to the spray. She eyed his firm rear end, the shapely legs. He had a swimmer's shoulders, and yet, she realized as she started to step in, she had never seen Simon in the pool.

He turned suddenly, startled.

"Beverly!" he said. And she moved smoothly into his arms, meeting his lips as if she had done it hundreds of times. Warm soap ran over her breasts and down her belly as she pressed up against him. He was instantly hard.

She felt his hands moving on her back, slippery from the soap, and then down to grasp her buttocks. She took his erection and guided it between her thighs, squeezing her legs tight together.

His tongue explored her mouth, and then he drew away and kissed her breasts, his tongue making her nipples grow firm. Reaching for a bottle of amber-colored shampoo, he squeezed the golden stuff all over her, working it into her skin with his hands, massaging her breasts, her lower back, and then up between her legs, his fingers gently probing, slipping inside.

As the warm water cascaded over them, soap making skin glide smoothly over skin, Simon turned on the other jets so that more hot water pulsated out at different angles, hard and vigorous. Beverly went slowly to her knees and took him into her mouth. He closed his eyes and moaned.

Suddenly he reached down for her, lifted her up and laid her back onto the marble bench, opening her legs wide and sliding into her, clasping her hard against him as he rocked her with deep, steady thrusts. She bit his lip and sucked his tongue as hot, perfumed water splashed over them, making their perspiring bodies ride smoothly together. Beverly drew her knees higher and curled her legs around his waist, bringing him deeper inside her. With an arm around her, clutching her tightly to him, his mouth working hers, Simon reached down and stroked her in time with his thrusts. When she started to come, she dug her fingers into his back, calling out his name, and she felt him empty into her at the same, staggering moment.

Carole, in her bungalow, tried not to think of her precious Sanford as she slipped into her Russian sable coat. She was desperately wishing that he could be with her tonight, that it was her sex-dynamo husband, the man who knew how to wrap a pearl necklace, whom she could look forward to being in bed with tonight. Instead, she was going to have to go through with her seduction of Larry Wolfe.

If she wanted the Marion Star role. Which she did. Because it would bolster her sagging career and make her Sanford's "beautiful movie star" for a while longer.

Coincidentally, Larry Wolfe, in the next bungalow, while adding a splash of Paul Stuart cologne to his admittedly chiseled jaw, was thinking of the same thing. Except that he was going to be making love to Carole Page for a different reason. Another notch on his gun handle, as it were. Of course, he didn't delude himself into thinking that it was him she was after, but it didn't matter. The result was the same. And this again was proof of the power that producers had in Hollywood. No one fucked the writer for a part in a picture, but the producer, now that was a different story. Carole Page was going to be just the beginning of a whole new bedroom career for Larry. And to top that off, like chocolate sprinkles on the whipped cream, he was meeting with Mr. Yamato tomorrow to seal their movie deal by handing over the proposal that good old reliable little Andrea had been working up for the past five days.

As he took a final look at himself in the mirror, realizing that he was going to knock every female dead tonight, Larry decided he was going to be magnanimous and give Andrea one dance. Just to let her know what she was missing.

At that same moment, in the bedroom on the other side of Larry's living room, Andrea was getting into her pin-striped suit with miniskirt, also thinking about tonight's ball. But for different reasons. She was looking forward to that special moment, during the ball, when she was going to give Larry his "present" and say, Merry Christmas. Jerk.

In the Castle, Judith Isaacs zipped up the conservative black cocktail dress that had served her well at many medical conferences. She was nervously anticipating the coming evening with Mr. Smith and experiencing also sadness and regret: she would dance with him and be swept away, and tomorrow he would leave Star's. A bottle of Cristal champagne had arrived at her apartment a little while ago, along with a white orchid corsage—from Mr. Smith. She now affixed the corsage to her dress, but she left the bottle unopened. Since Zoey had gone down the mountain, Judith was now the only health-care employee at the resort. She would need to stay sober; she considered herself to be on call.

And when she heard a knock at her door, she knew it was Smith—he had insisted on calling for her and escorting her to the ball, very gentlemanly, very old-fashioned, and very wonderful—and her anxiety heightened. Please don't let me fall in love tonight, she thought.

But as she was about to answer his knock, she called out, "Just a minute," went back to the bedroom, hurriedly untwined her long braid, brushed her hair out thick and wavy and long, and then went back to the door.

She said, "Hello," and he, seeing her hair, said, "Well now . . ."

In the third-floor tower apartment where cherubs wore lampshades on their curly heads and chintz was threatening to take over the world, Bunny Kowalski, all alone now with her agent—the fairy-godmother team having left a couple of hours ago—regarded herself, her astonishingly stunning self, in a full-length mirror and said, "When? When?"

And Frieda, so damned smug that she wished Syd Stern were here so she could say, Tough luck, Charlie, to him, said, "Soon, soon."

The big surprise of the evening, she knew, required perfect timing.

It was nine o'clock and the glittering event was under way. Simon Jung greeted the arriving guests in the main hall, which had been turned into a reception area for the spillover from the ballroom. Although Simon had tried to persuade Beverly to attend, she had declined. So he smiled now at one of the ceiling-mounted cameras, knowing that she was watching him on her private monitor. She had asked him to come to her apartment after the ball; there was something she wanted to tell him.

Carole Page arrived and moved among the celebrities, smiling and nodding to people she knew. The last time she had seen such a showing of famous faces was at the post-Oscar party at Spago. She was just starting to enjoy herself when Larry breezed past her with a martini in his hand. He gave her a smarmy wink that made her stomach lurch. And when he murmured, in passing, "At midnight," she said, "Yes," with a sick feeling.

In this crowd where the gowns had names as famous as the women wearing them, Danny Mackay, in a tuxedo and blending in, moved about unnoticed. He went up to a security guard in a Star's blue blazer, the bulge of a walkie-talkie on his hip, and said urgently, "There's something outside that I think you should see."

The guard followed him out, and what he saw, behind a massively leafy oleander bush, was the flash of a knife and the sudden crimson stain on his shirt. He gave Danny a startled look before sinking to the snow, dead.

Danny hurriedly changed into the man's blazer and slacks, made sure the body was well hidden, and went back inside, this time to mingle as a respected and trusted security guard.

Andrea came nudging up to Larry, who was trying to flatter the panties off some vacant blonde. "Can I have a word with you?" she asked.

"Not now, Andrea."

When she said, "Yes, *now*," in a way that got his attention, he told the blonde that he would be right back and followed Andrea to a relatively quiet spot beneath one of the humongous portraits of Marion Star, so that they were partially hidden behind potted palm trees. "Well?" he said impatiently. "What is it that can't wait?"

"Me, Larry," she said. "I can't wait."

"Huh? Can't wait for what?"

"Your public apology. For the snub at the Oscars. Followed up by your public confession that *I* am the writer and you are not. Do it here, tonight."

He stared at her as if she had just said Martians had landed. "What the hell are you talking about?"

Andrea couldn't believe how much she was enjoying herself. Champagne was fizzling in her veins, and she had called Chad McCormick earlier and he had been so excited to hear from her that he had said he was coming up to Star's right away to see her. It was amazing how, when things started to go right for you, they went right with a vengeance.

"I am talking," she said, "about the fact that I have written all the screenplays that you have taken credit for. And I am finished. I want what's coming to me."

"And just what the hell is that?"

"Credit, Larry. You got the Oscar that rightfully belongs to me."

"You mean you're in a wad over a fucking statue?"

"No, it isn't just the Oscar. It's the way you've treated me for all these years. When you told me not to marry Chad McCormick, you said it would break us up as a team. But that wasn't it, was it? We could still have been a team. You were just afraid that Chad would find out the truth. So you made me give up Chad for you."

When he saw that she was serious, he laughed and said, "This is rich! Entertain me some more. Just how do you intend to force me into making such an admission? You have no proof. You and I are the only ones who know the truth, and who will believe you over me?"

"You're right. So I guess this is where we part company."

"What?"

"I'm resigning from the team. As of now. Good luck with Mr. Yamato tomorrow. And with writing the screenplay."

"Hey, wait a minute. You can't walk out on me like that."

"Sure I can. Watch."

He blinked. He suddenly felt moist under the collar. "Okay, fine. Go. But just remember, you can't do the Marion Star story because I own the rights to it."

"You own the rights to your version," she said. "But anyone can come up with their own version, can't they? So long, Larry."

He grabbed her arm. "You walk out on me and I'll sue."

"Oh please do! Because then it will all come out at the trial. *I* can prove I'm a writer—can you?"

He stared at her, suddenly introduced to fear. But he kept his voice in a couldn't-care-less mode as he said, "So tell me what it is you want."

On the other side of the main hall, Carole happened to look their way and see Andrea and Larry in an intense conversation. She wondered what it was about. Again the thought of going to bed with him made her skin crawl, but she wasn't going to turn him away when he came to her bungalow tonight. She *had* to have that role.

As she continued to circulate in the main hall, she spotted a short, fat, balding man helping himself from one of the champagne punch bowls. His suit wasn't a perfect fit, his tie didn't go at all with the color of his jacket, and his socks, she noticed, were two different shades of gray. And when he turned her way, she saw that he had spilled a bit of champagne on his shirt. The sort of man people say, when they see him, Who let *him* in? Or they don't see him at all.

"Sanford!" she cried.

He looked up. "Carole! My darling!"

She rushed to him and into his arms. Kissing the top of his shiny head, since he was shorter than she, she said, "What are you doing here!"

His face was red, he beamed so. "I came to surprise you, my beautiful movie star! When you left me five days ago, I had a feeling that something was wrong. It bothered me all week. I couldn't work. And this is an eight-million-dollar account I've got!"

"Oh, Sanford," she said, filling her eyes with the sight of him. A small man, perhaps even an insignificant-looking man, but the marvel of the age when it came to the bedroom. "I'm *so* happy to see you!"

"It was bothering me all week, what might be upsetting you, and then I decided to have a talk with your agent. He said the new picture was a dog. Is that true?"

When she hesitated, he said, "My poor baby. You wanted to spare me from it. Do you think I don't know what's going on? Do you think I don't have eyes? You think I don't love you more than life itself?" He rose up on his toes and kissed her full lips.

"I thought you would leave me if I was a failure."

"Leave you? The best thing that ever happened to me? My sweet baby, you could dig ditches and I would still worship you."

"Oh, Sanford . . ." Her eyes filled with tears.

"But as it turned out, I've come with some good news for you. The biggest miniseries since 'Winds of War.' And you have the lead."

"What? Sanford! *Miniseries?* Tell me about it!"

"Financed by your very own husband, my dear. But I'll tell you in private," he said with a grin. "Where's your room?"

They headed for the front door, where Sanford retrieved his wife's fur coat, and they went out into the night to celebrate Christmas, and Carole's new contract, in their own private way.

Andrea was saying to Larry, "Just make an announcement to everyone here, tonight, that the Oscar was rightfully mine. That the idea was mine, and so was the screenplay—"

"You must be out of your mind."

"If you agree to do it, then I will continue to work with you and no one need ever know that all your previous screenplays were ghostwritten."

"You can't be serious! Hand over an Oscar to someone else? It's ludicrous!"

"Is it? Remember Milli Vanilli? They gave their Grammy back, didn't they? For lip-syncing their songs. Well, let's just consider this a case of write-sync. Give me the Oscar, acknowledge me as the winner, and I'll leave it at that. Otherwise, I walk."

"Fine, go ahead, bitch. See if I give a fuck. I'll survive."

She turned back to him. "You know, Larry, seventeen years ago you told me that William Goldman got four hundred thousand dollars for 'cranking out' *Butch Cassidy.* Well, let's see you *crank* one out."

Larry watched Andrea go. When he saw Carole go out with a man he recognized as her husband, it occurred to him that maybe this was not his night after all.

★ ★ ★

In the security blazer and carrying a walkie-talkie, pretending to talk into it, Danny made his way through the crowd unimpeded; celebrities like these were used to such men. When he saw Philippa, he stopped and watched her for a moment. She was standing with a group of people, her watchdog Aussie boy at her side. Danny did some quick thinking.

Up in her apartment, Beverly monitored the progress of the ball, switching from one camera to another. She saw Carole Page leave with a rather short man and Andrea Bachman walk away from Larry Wolfe, who seemed to have a dejected look on his face. Beverly was pleased to see her security guards in profusion, but not obtrusive. At gatherings such as these, it was important that the guests were well protected.

Beverly switched on the mezzanine camera just as Frieda was stepping out of an elevator with—

Beverly gasped.

She couldn't believe her eyes.

"Why are we getting off here?" Bunny said. She had thought they would ride the elevator all the way to the ground floor.

"It's more dramatic this way, sweetheart. We'll wait a few minutes before you make your entrance. To get the full effect and all."

When Danny saw the blond boy leave Philippa for a moment to fetch a drink, he decided to make his move.

"Excuse me, sir?" he said to Ricky. "May I have a word with you? It's very important. It concerns Miss Roberts."

Ricky looked over at Philippa.

"It's best not to alarm the lady, sir," Danny said. "I think we can work this out without upsetting her."

Ricky followed him out the front door and down the red-carpeted steps. "It's just around the corner here," Danny said, bringing Ricky to the place where the security guard's body was hidden.

When Ricky saw the body, he dropped down to one knee. "I don't understand," he said, feeling the man's cold neck for a pulse. "What happened? What does he have to do with Miss R—"

Danny's quick, sharp knife did the rest. A bright red track went from ear to ear, and Ricky's white tuxedo shirt was soon spreading crimson.

Danny went back inside and joined the crowd, wishing he could whistle, he felt so good.

Frieda and Bunny waited at the top of the grand staircase, away from the light, hidden in the recess of a closed door. A few people stared at them as they walked past. "When?" Bunny said for the thousandth time, she was so excited and nervous. And Frieda, just as excited and nervous, said, "When I say so. We want to be sure everyone is here."

Judith and Smith were walking through the snow and enjoying the stars overhead, neither of them inclined as yet to join the stars inside. She had her arm through his, and she was talking. "Mort was an artist. A free spirit. He created beautiful things out of dirty clay. But he had a problem with the fact that he worked at home while I went out every day to my office or the hospital. Someone called him a house husband once and he greatly resented it. When Kimmie died, Mort blamed me for not being there. I was the mother, he said. I was supposed to be around when the kid was sick. Looking back now, I think he was just venting all his bitterness at the inequality in our two stations. There were times when our mail came addressed to Dr. and Mrs. Isaacs."

"And so you came up here to bury yourself."

"In a way, yes."

"Well, I'm afraid I cannot allow that."

"What do you mean?"

"I intend to rescue you. Unless you have any objections to marrying a man so much older than yourself?"

"You have the dialogue backward," she said with a smile. "You're supposed to tell me you're too old for me, that I'm a young woman with my whole life ahead of me and shouldn't want to be saddled with an old—"

He stopped and took her by the shoulders. "You don't think I'm serious about this, do you? I mean to have you, Judith Isaacs. I'm going to court you and woo you in every way I know how, until you say yes."

"But—"

He put a finger to her lips. "Please say my name—my real name. I want to hear you say it."

She did, and then he was kissing her, and she was kissing him back, and as they held tightly to each other, she knew she was going to say yes.

★ ★ ★

Danny sidled up to Philippa and said, "Miss Roberts? I don't wish to alarm you, but will you come with me, please? A friend of yours is hurt."

She looked around. Where was Ricky?

"Oh my God," she said. "What happened?"

"We don't wish to alarm anyone. Just come with me, please. The general manager will explain."

He led her to an elevator that required a key, but Danny had it—he had a ring of master keys on his belt. As they rode up, she gave him a curious look. He didn't look like the other security guards she had seen around the resort. For one thing, none of them wore glasses or had a beard. For another, he seemed older than the rest.

The elevator doors opened, and he stood aside for her to go first. They walked down a long, chilly hall, where suits of armor stood in rigid silence and an old, musty smell pervaded the air. She had no idea where they were going.

"Can't you tell me what happened?"

"The general manager would prefer to explain it to you himself, ma'am. I was just sent to get you."

They entered an enormous bedroom that was done in classic pink and green deco, and Philippa recognized it as Marion Star's bedroom—she had seen the photos.

"Just in through there, ma'am," he said, and Philippa went ahead of him, to find herself, to her great astonishment, in an equally enormous bathroom with erotic murals of nude men and women on the walls. When she realized that he had brought her to the famous Obscene Bathroom, and also that there was no one else there, she turned around and said, "Now just what is—"

She saw the gun, pointing straight at her.

Danny smiled. "Don't worry, ma'am," he said, "I have no intention of using this on you. I'm not going to shoot you. Heck, the noise would draw attention. Although if you listen real good, you can tell that the party is far away from here, and very loud."

She went cold with terror. "What do you want?"

"First I want you to get out of that dress, nice and easy and slow. I want to watch you do it."

She started to tremble. "Who *are* you? What do you want?"

"Come on, Beverly, let's stop pretending. You must recognize me by now."

"My name isn't Beverly!"

"I said get out of that dress now!"

She reached behind with shaking hands and drew the zipper down. "I don't know why you're doing this to me."

He removed his glasses and pulled off the beard. *"Now* do you know?"

"But I don't know who you are!"

"Knock it off, Beverly, and kick the dress over here to me. That's right. Now take off the bra and panties."

Frieda decided it was time. She had been watching for Larry Wolfe—this whole performance was for him. Finally he was in the right spot, near the center of the main hall, not too far from the staircase, and looking toward them as he talked with some blonde. "Okay," she said to Bunny. "Let's go."

Frieda studied the lighting on the staircase, then she said, "Walk slowly down to the twelfth step and then stop there. Stay there. Don't move, no matter what."

"Wish me luck," Bunny said.

And Frieda kissed her cheek, saying, "You've got all the luck in the world, sweetheart. Go down there and knock 'em dead."

Bunny began her slow descent, and when she saw that no one had noticed her, she went even more slowly, stopping on each step and pausing, her hand on the banister. When a couple of people looked her way and stopped what they were doing to stare, she moved down another step. A few more guests fell silent, and then a few more. When she reached the twelfth step and found that she stood in a pool of light, she stopped and stayed there, not moving, barely breathing.

More and more people turned her way until the rest of the crowd, realizing that something was up, looked toward the staircase and fell silent. The silence was broken by whispers and gasps, and Bunny heard the name "Marion Star" run through the main hall like ripples from a rock dropped into a pond.

Bunny was slouching in a sultry way against the banister in a dark brown velvet gown that was so clingy she looked as if she had been dipped in chocolate. The black wig hugged her face in a bedroom way, and her darkly shadowed eyes smouldered.

The several hundred guests looked from her to the photographs of Marion Star, back to her. Their stunned expressions told her that Frieda's brainstorm had worked. Bunny wasn't just an actress dressed up—she *was* Marion Star.

While everyone stared at the apparition on the staircase, Smith came through the front doors and made his way through the transfixed crowd to Simon Jung. They engaged in a brief, urgent exchange, and then they left together.

★ ★ ★

Up in her apartment, Beverly was watching the spectacle on the staircase with the same awe as the guests. Bunny Kowalski was the *image* of Marion Star. It was unbelievable.

People started to clap. Slowly at first, and then with rising momentum, until soon the main hall was crammed with the most appreciative audience that any actress could hope for. And behind Bunny, wearing a modest black suit that she had purchased earlier at Armani, and hidden away from her client's spotlight, Frieda Goldman zeroed in on Larry Wolfe's too-astonished-to-be-true expression.

Syd Stern, eat your heart out.

In the Obscene Bathroom, Danny said, "Something good must be goin' on downstairs, darlin'. Hear them clappin'?"

Philippa was handcuffed. She still wore her bra and panties. When she had refused to remove her underwear, Danny had said, "That's all right, darlin'. Ah'm a gentleman," exaggerating his Texas accent. Then he had bound her wrists behind her and made her sit on the edge of the crystal tub. Now he was sitting on the solid-gold toilet seat watching her. He had put away the gun—she wasn't going anywhere—and had brought out the knife.

"I cut your blond lover boy with this," he said, fingering the blade.

"Please," she whispered. "What do you want? Let me go."

"Sure," he said with a smile. "Like you let me go three and a half years ago. Remember how I begged you?"

"For the love of God, I don't know what you're talking about."

"Jesus Christ, Beverly!" he boomed. "Stop pretending! Just admit what you did and maybe I'll go easy on you. Now don't keep tellin' me you don't know who I am!"

"I don't know . . . you're familiar, I guess . . ."

"Come on, Beverly."

"Why do you keep calling me that? My name isn't Beverly!"

"Oh, I suppose you want me to call you Rachel, like you did the night you made me crawl to you. Well, I played your game then, but it's *my* game now, and you're going to play by *my* rules!" He got up and walked to her, brandishing the knife close to her face. "And for starters, this is one of my rules . . ."

While Beverly was watching Bunny Kowalski's stunning entrance on the large TV screen, she reached for her tea on the desk and accidentally knocked the newspaper off; it hit the floor with a thud, falling open. Because today was the day of the ball, she hadn't had a chance to get to her mail or the paper, but now, as she picked it up to put it back on her desk, she saw the small headline for the first time: "Three Bodies Found Buried at Malibu Beach." She wouldn't have paid any attention to it except that when she replaced the paper on her desk, she caught sight of a name in the article, a familiar name: Bonner Purvis.

Danny Mackay's right-hand man and best friend.

Then she saw the second name: Otis Quinn.

Both brutally murdered. Both buried in the sand.

She froze.

But Quinn had checked in this morning!

She stood up. Her heart stopped.

Not Quinn.

Danny.

He was still alive.

She ran out of her apartment, down the hall, and stopped at the landing of the massive stairway, across from where Bunny Kowalski was still posing as Marion Star. She looked down at the hundreds of people below, all clapping and hooting, and she thought, He's here, disguised, and somewhere in this crowd.

She searched for Simon, but he was nowhere to be seen.

And then she felt . . .

She sensed something. Wrong.

"Crawl to me, bitch," Danny said, "or I'm going to string you up from that light fixture and let you dance the way I did in jail."

"Please," Philippa said. "You have the wrong person. I don't know who you are or what you're talking about."

"I've had it!" he shouted. He pulled a long cord out of his pocket, one end of which was tied in a noose, and he thrust it over her head, flinging the free end over the light fixture. "You'll change your tune when you realize I mean business."

"No!" she cried. "Oh God, no!"

"You don't think I'll do it? Well, I did it to your boyfriend. Your blond jock?"

She stared at him. "Ricky?" she whispered.

"Dead as a doornail."

"No!" she screamed. "Oh God! *Ricky!"*

"Stupid name for a kid," Danny said as he tightened the noose around her neck. It was then that he realized she was still wearing her bra and panties. "Got to get rid of these," he said, raising the knife.

"Danny," came a voice from behind him. A calm voice.

He looked over his shoulder to see a woman standing there, wearing a sweater and slacks, with brunette hair cut in a shag. She didn't seem upset, she just stood there, looking at him. "Danny," she repeated.

And then he looked at her again.

"Let her go, Danny," the woman said.

He narrowed his eyes. "Who the hell . . . ?"

"You know who I am," she said, coming into the bathroom. "Let her go, Danny. Whatever is going on here, it's between you and me."

His frown deepened.

In the next instant, someone else appeared in the doorway. "Beverly," Simon Jung said, "someone said they saw you come up this way . . ." His voice trailed off when he saw Philippa, and Danny with the knife.

"What's going on here!" Danny demanded, looking at Philippa and then at Beverly.

"You were wrong again, Danny," Beverly said, coming closer, holding her hand out. "I'm Beverly. Give me the knife."

"Stay where you are!" he shouted. Twisting around behind Philippa, he raised the knife to her throat. "One more step and I kill her!"

"You want *me*, Danny, remember?" Beverly said. "I'm Beverly. This is between you and me."

"No! Quinn said *she's* Beverly!" And the knife dug into Philippa's neck.

"But Quinn was wrong. I'm Beverly, Danny."

He licked his lips. Perspiration appeared on his forehead. "Prove it."

She appeared calm, but her voice betrayed her fear, shaking slightly as she said, "You found me in El Paso when I was fourteen. I was running away. My name was Rachel Dwyer."

Philippa stared at her. Dwyer! The name Hendricks had said was the name of her real parents.

"That's still no proof," Danny said, but with some uncertainty now. He shifted nervously. What the hell was going on here? What kind of game was this?

"All right," the other woman said. "I'll give you proof," and to his astonishment she unzipped her slacks and slowly drew them down. Stepping out of them, she came closer and said, "Look, Danny. Do you see this scar?" She pointed to the inside of her thigh, just below the panty line. "You had a butterfly tattooed here, remember? I was fourteen and we went over the border to get it done."

He stared at the scar. The knife began to tremble against Philippa's neck, and a drop of blood appeared.

"Let her go," Beverly said, her voice tight but firm.

Danny slowly removed his hand from Philippa's arm, still keeping the other one around her shoulders, the knife to her throat. And in a move that caught the others unaware, he dropped the knife and whipped out a gun. Philippa fell to the floor and scrambled away from him, the nylon cord trailing after her.

As Simon Jung quickly removed his jacket and put it around her, Danny smiled and said, "Now ain't that touchin'? Such a gentleman. You always did have good taste in men, Beverly." This last he said to the real Beverly. "So I made a mistake. Now how on earth could that happen?" Thinking of the waitress last night, he laughed. Two mistakes in a row.

"Well I won't be making any mistakes now, because I'm killing me three birds with one stone." He looked at Beverly. "Unless, of course, you want to beg me to spare you."

"Danny, listen—"

"I wonder if these fine folks are aware of what a bitch you are, Beverly. Why don't you tell them about the way you tried to destroy me? Tell them about the whorehouse in Beverly Hills that you tricked me into buying, making me think it was a legitimate business and then leaking the story to the press just when I was winning the presidential primary."

"Danny." She took another step closer.

He shouted, "Stay right there! Aw shit, I'm tired of this!" He raised the gun, took aim right between Beverly's eyes.

A loud bang thundered in the marble bathroom; Philippa screamed, and Danny went flying backward.

He landed in the tub, his head hitting the gold faucets with a sickening crack.

The three stood frozen for a moment, then Beverly rushed forward and knelt on the edge of the tub. "He's dead," she said in disbelief. She turned and looked back. Where had the shot come from?

Simon ran into the bedroom, but there was no one there.

Except for Marion Star, who was coming toward him, hobbling on her cane. "I heard a noise," she said.

"Did you see anyone, Miss Star?" Jung asked. "Did anyone run past you?"

"Nobody that I saw."

He left the bathroom and hurried down the hall to a telephone.

Marion walked into the bathroom, and when she saw Danny sprawled in the tub, a shot through his chest, she shook her head and said, "This bathroom always was bad luck."

Beverly went through Danny's pockets and, finding the key to the handcuffs, went to Philippa, who was leaning against the wall, huddled in Simon Jung's dinner jacket, shaking. "Are you all right?" Beverly said as she freed her wrists and lifted the noose over her head.

Philippa looked at her. "Where do you know Christine Singleton from?"

Beverly gave her a startled look. "She was my sister, my twin. We were separated when we were babies. A family named Singleton adopted her. Why?"

"I'm Christine Singleton."

They stared at each other while faint sounds from the ball filtered up to them. No one had heard the shot; the party hadn't been disrupted.

"You're Christine?" Beverly said, studying Philippa's face. "I don't understand. I thought you were Philippa Roberts."

"I ran away when I was sixteen and changed my name."

Beverly's astonishment grew. "So did I. But . . . how did you find me?"

"The ad you placed in the *Times.*"

Beverly said, "But I placed no ad," just as Simon Jung returned, saying, "Security is on the way up. And so is Dr. Isaacs."

Simon looked at Beverly. "*I* placed the ad," he said.

"You!"

"I knew you had given up looking for her. That photograph in your office of a young woman with two babies—I've seen you stare at it many times. And I recalled you telling me once about hoping to find your sister. We were still in Brazil. You had said her name was Christine Singleton."

He turned to Philippa. "Are you all right?" he asked, bringing out a crisp white handkerchief and putting it to her neck where the knife had nicked her.

"Yes, thank you," she whispered.

He returned to Beverly. "I wanted to help you," he said.

"Did you know . . ." She looked at Danny, lying in the crystal tub. "Did you know about that, too?"

"When I saw how that book, *Butterfly Exposed,* upset you, I read it. So I knew that you were Beverly Highland, that you had changed your identity. And that you didn't want me to know."

Beverly looked at Simon for a moment, recalling their recent lovemaking in the shower and thinking of their future together. Then she turned to Philippa. "Then . . . you really are my sister?"

"Yes," Philippa said in amazement. "And so I suppose you're mine."

They said, "Oh," together, just as the head of security barged in with a team behind him. "Rogers is dead, sir," he said to Jung. "We found him in the bushes. The Palm Springs police have been notified." He went over to the bathtub and looked at Danny. Then he looked at the others gathered in the Obscene Bathroom. "Who shot him?" he asked.

But no one knew.

THE
MORNING
AFTER

....★

49

Philippa had been sitting at the bedside nearly all night; she was beginning to nod in the chair. A suspended IV bottle caught the first slanting rays of morning light as the day broke through the window of the recovery room in Star's private clinic. Although there was room to accommodate three postoperative patients, only one bed was occupied.

And as new light began to spread through the small surgical suite, the occupant in the bed struggled for a moment to open his eyes. He stared at the ceiling, then, with great difficulty, rolled his head to the side and gazed at Philippa. He tried to speak; he couldn't. So his hand sought hers.

When she felt his touch, she was startled awake. "Ricky," she said, smiling gently, "how are you? How do you feel?"

"Hell of a . . ." he whispered. The bandages around his neck moved slightly as he swallowed. "Hell of a . . ." he tried again in a hoarse whisper, ". . . sore throat."

Philippa leaned over the bedside rail and brushed the hair back from his forehead. "My God, we've been so worried."

He smiled weakly. He was pale; he had lost a lot of blood, but Judith Isaacs had said he was going to live. When she and Smith had first come across Ricky in the snow, a great crimson puddle around him, she had not been so sure. But when she had rushed him back to the clinic for emergency surgery, recruiting the help of two physicians who had been attending the ball, she had discovered that although the young man's throat was cut nearly from ear to ear, the major neck vessels had been spared. The wound, it turned out, was only superficial, with a slight laceration in the trachea, which she had been able to suture.

"I told you," he croaked, "that nothing . . . was going to happen . . . to me. What—" Again he swallowed with difficulty. "What happened?"

"I'll tell you all about it later. Oh, Ricky, I'm so glad you're going to be all right! You could have been killed."

"Naw," he said in his Aussie drawl. "When whoever it was got me . . ." he drew in a painful breath, "and I saw the knife, I remembered something I . . . had read . . . once, about bending your neck and the arteries go in or something . . ."

"Shh," she said, her eyes glistening. "Don't try to talk. Dr. Isaacs explained it to us. The man who attacked you didn't cut deep enough—" Her voice broke. "Oh, Ricky, I'm so sorry."

He reached up and touched her hair. "Philippa, I have to tell you something."

"No, don't talk. Go back to sleep. Save your strength."

"I have to say it. I should have said it . . . long time ago. I lied to you. I didn't have a mate on the *Philippa*. I made that up so you'd . . . give me a job."

"I know," she said, stroking his hair.

"How did you know?"

"Because Paul told me he had an all-American crew."

"You knew? Then . . . why did you hire me?"

She smiled. "Let's just say I admire resourcefulness."

Judith Isaacs came in then, wearing a blouse and slacks under a white lab coat, a stethoscope around her neck. Her hair was no longer loose about her shoulders but plaited into a braid down her back. She had never made it to the ball. "Miss Roberts," she said, "you wanted me to let you know when the morning tram arrived. It's almost here. How is our patient doing?"

Philippa leaned over and kissed Ricky on the lips, murmuring, "I'll be back as soon as I can." Then she turned to Judith and said, "Thank you for saving his life, Doctor."

There weren't many people milling around the tramway platform at this early hour. Most of the guests were in their rooms or cottages, sleeping off the effects of champagne, or, if they were awake, talking about the murder that had taken place right over their heads. The police had questioned everyone. No suspects were found. And no gun.

When the Palm Springs detective had discovered Quinn's ID on Danny, he had said, "I think this is the man we've been looking for. We believe he's responsible for killing at least five people, maybe more. Do you have any idea who he was?"

Before either Beverly or Philippa could reply, Simon Jung had said, "No, we don't know who he was." He looked at Beverly. "He was a stranger, we don't know why he did it."

The police left just before dawn, taking Danny Mackay's body with them. "Whoever shot him was defending you and Miss Roberts," the detective said. "My guess is we'll probably never find out who it was."

Now, at the boarding area, several guests were waiting for the regular morning tram to arrive—some were leaving, such as Carole Page and her husband; others were there to greet arrivals, such as Philippa, who was expecting Hannah and Esther.

Marion Star was there, bundled up in a stylish wool coat, telling Bunny Kowalski that she could wear her gowns in "their" movie. Bunny was there because her father was due on the morning tram, and she was going to tell him that not only was she going to stay in Hollywood, but that he just might as well start getting used to the idea that his daughter was an actress.

Frieda, at the same time, was busy working a deal with Andrea for Bunny to play young Marion; they stood under a snow-laden pine tree discussing terms, while Larry Wolfe sulked off to the side.

And Beverly was there, with Simon Jung, saying good-bye to their guests.

Philippa thought her sister looked beautiful in the morning sun, despite the fact that the two of them had sat up all night, talking, mostly at Ricky's bedside, where Beverly had joined Philippa in her vigil. They had covered so much through the dark hours, filling in their separate pasts, and they still had so much more yet to go. After today's board meeting, whatever the outcome, Philippa was going to stay for a while at Star's.

Charmie came up the path then. "How is Ricky?" she asked. Charmie was warm inside a bulky cable-knit sweater with a bright pink watchman's cap pulled over her hair. Her nose and chin, bitten with cold, matched the color of the cap.

"He's going to be all right," Philippa said. "Thank God. Dr. Isaacs has sent for a private nurse to come and take care of him."

Charmie searched Philippa's face, and then, looking over at Beverly, who was smiling and dispensing farewells as though last night had been an ordinary night of the week, she said, "Well, at least there's one mystery solved. Ivan found your sister after all."

But that still left the question of the embezzled million dollars, and why Miranda International was trying to buy out Starlite.

But the biggest mystery was, Who had saved Philippa's life? Who shot Danny Mackay?

"The tram must be almost here," Charmie said, noticing how the small crowd began to converge on the boarding platform. She saw Bunny and Frieda and Andrea madly shaking hands, and Carole Page hanging on to her husband as if they were a honeymoon couple, and Larry Wolfe looking like he hadn't slept in months—

Charmie's mouth dropped open. "Philippa!" she said. "Why—there's Ivan!"

"*What?*" Philippa turned around, and there he was, Ivan Hendricks, looking like a member of the Soviet police in a heavy overcoat and big fur hat.

When he saw them looking at him, he came over and gave them a sheepish, "Hi."

"Ivan!" Charmie said. "You're supposed to be in Rio!"

"Yes, well," he dug his boot into the snow, "I know . . ."

"What are you doing here?"

"It's kind of complicated. Miss Roberts," he said, "do you see that man over there?"

She looked to where he was pointing and saw a man in a long black overcoat, with a black muffler around his neck but wearing no hat, so that she saw perfectly combed white hair stirring lightly in the morning breeze. He was in his seventies, handsome and distinguished, bearing a remarkable resemblance to Richard Conte, the actor.

Her eyes widened.

It couldn't be . . .

When the man turned and saw her, he hesitated, then he walked up to her, the hint of a smile on his lips.

"Daddy?" Philippa whispered.

"Hi, Dolly," Johnny said.

"Oh my God, it *is* you!" She threw her arms around him. "Oh, Daddy, Daddy!"

"Dolly," he said, burying his face in her hair. They held each other tightly.

She drew away, tears in her eyes. "I don't understand! I thought you were dead!"

"I know you did, Dolly," Johnny said softly. "I received a pardon. I had been wrongfully convicted."

"But . . . why didn't you let me know you were alive!"

"I didn't know how you'd take it. And also because it would have complicated your life. By the time I got out of prison and could track you down, you were on your own and doing well." He paused to reach out and touch a tear on her cheek, love and tenderness shining in his eyes. "I knew you were mad at me for leaving you in the convent. I spoke to the nuns, they told me how unhappy you had been. But that wasn't what I had intended to happen. I really had meant to leave you there for only a few days, until I got us another place. And then a murder rap was pinned on me, and I was never able to come and get you. I had a friend send letters from Europe."

"Daddy," she said, not knowing whether to laugh or cry, "I forgave you a long time ago!" She wiped the tears off her cheeks. And then she frowned. "But . . . how do you know Ivan?"

Ivan spoke up, a sheepish expression on his face. "I work for your father, Miss Roberts. I've worked for him for years."

"Then you knew all along that my father was alive!"

"He made me promise to keep quiet. I'm sorry, Miss Roberts. It was hard, I'll tell you." He turned to Charmie and said, "You and I didn't meet by accident that day in the drugstore. I'd been watching you and Miss Roberts for some time. Mr. Singleton had hired me to. He wanted me to get personally involved so that I could report to him. You have no idea how many potato chips I had to eat before you noticed me!"

Charmie stared at him, wondering if the thin mountain air was making her hallucinate. "All is forgiven," she heard herself say.

Johnny turned to Philippa and said, "Can we go for a walk, Dolly? There are some things I'd like to tell you."

They headed away from the others, walking over crunchy snow, feeling the warm sun on their shoulders as they breathed in the frosty mountain air.

Charmie, still in a daze, watched them walk away, and then she felt a hand on her arm. When she turned, Ivan drew her into his arms and kissed her hard.

"Ivan!" she said. "Oh, Ivan . . ."

"You don't know difficult it's been for me," he said. "That morning in your kitchen—I thought I'd go out of my mind. You don't know what it took to stop myself, I wanted you so badly—and still do. But I'm out of a job now. I'm free." He grinned. "And I'm craving butterscotch brownies in the worst way!" Then he added more quietly, "And you . . ." And he kissed her again.

Philippa put her arm through Johnny's, and he laid his hand over hers. "When I got out of prison," he said, "and the nuns told me you'd run away, I nearly went crazy searching for you. But when I did find you, you had started your own company, and you seemed so happy, I decided to let you think I was dead. You see, Dolly, even though I didn't do it—the murders, I mean, that I was sent up for—and I received a full pardon, I was still connected to the mob. I wouldn't have been good for you. I was proud to see you doing so well on your own. And I've been watching out for you ever since."

"So when Ivan told you I was coming to Star's you decided to come too?"

"Well, it's not exactly like that, Dolly. Yes, I knew you were coming to Star's—Ivan told me he thought he might have found your sister. In fact, I'm responsible for the fact that you got accommodations on such late notice. Ricardo Cadiz, the novelist, is a friend of mine. I knew he was coming to Star's for Christmas. I asked him to cancel his reservation. He owed me a favor. From the minute you left Perth, I've been in constant phone contact with Ivan, who kept me apprised of your movements. But I didn't come here to be reunited with you, Dolly. I had hoped to come and then leave without you ever knowing I had been here."

"I don't understand. Why did you come then?"

"To make sure the board meeting was a success for you."

She stared at him. "You know about the embezzlement?"

"Yes. And I was afraid for your safety. You were going to expose a criminal within your organization."

"You know who it is!"

"Alan Scadudo."

"My God," she murmured. "Alan."

"I was afraid he might harm you. That was why I asked Ivan to carry a gun. He doesn't normally."

She suddenly pictured Danny Mackay, lying dead in the bathtub.

As if reading her thoughts, Johnny said, "I guess it's a good thing I asked Ivan to carry the gun. When he didn't see you in the ballroom last night and then saw Beverly go upstairs, looking as if something was wrong, Ivan decided to investigate. He did us all a favor, shooting Mackay."

"Oh, Daddy," Philippa said as they walked among snow-covered pine trees, reminding her of their walks in Tiburon, long ago. The arm that supported hers felt as strong now as it had then. "What else do you know?" she asked. "Do you know about Miranda International?"

He nodded.

She searched his tan, lined face, still handsome after all these years. "Are *you* Miranda International?"

"I'm behind it, and a lot of other ventures as well."

"Then why are you trying to buy us out?"

He laughed. "I'm not. I did it to alert you to the embezzling that was going on within your company. When Ivan told me that you had gone to Australia and were staying there, I became concerned. I was afraid that, because of your grief over Paul Marquette, you were going to drop out of life, letting go of everything you had worked for. I didn't want you to make the same mistakes I did—to run from the truth, from reality.

"I couldn't warn you directly, because then I would have had to show myself. I wanted you to find it on your own. I knew a threatened takeover would make you go through your books to see what Miranda could possibly want. I was counting on the fact that you would find the million-dollar discrepancy."

"Then there is no takeover?"

He smiled. "Starlite is safe, Dolly."

She started to cry. He took her into his arms and held her. "It's all right, Dolly," he said. "We're together again."

"Daddy," Philippa said. "I want you to meet my sister." She took Johnny by the hand and led him to where Beverly was talking to Simon Jung at the arrival platform. When Philippa introduced Johnny to her, he took Beverly's hand between his and said in a voice filled with wonder, "You and I have already met. You were the other baby."

He shook his head, his eyes glistening, as the memory of that highly emotional day, years ago, came flooding back. "My wife and I couldn't have children, Beverly, so we found a lawyer who made arrangements for an adoption. I remember the morning we went to the hospital. Your poor mother was so upset to have to give one of you up for adoption. She didn't want to let either of her babies go, but your parents were poor, they desperately needed the money. I promised her I would take good care of her child. My wife and I had so much to give." Johnny's eyes filled with love as he looked at Beverly. "It could have been you," he said quietly. "I had my choice. You were both such tiny, perfect dolls. I could just as easily have chosen you."

Philippa and Beverly looked at each other then, amazed at the strange turns of fate, both realizing that, if Johnny had chosen differently, each would have lived the other's life.

Johnny grew serious then as he said to Beverly, "I know now what you went through, how you suffered at the hands of Danny Mackay. I wish I had watched over you the way I watched over Christine. I could have spared you so much pain. But I just didn't know."

"And now look at you," Johnny added, his smile returning, "two beautiful women."

Beverly laughed. "But I was very homely as a child."

"And *I* was fat," Philippa said.

Simon Jung came up then and said, "The tram is here."

Philippa became alarmed. "You're not leaving, Daddy, are you? I won't let you!"

Johnny laughed and patted her hand. "Don't worry, I'm not leaving."

As they walked toward the boarding platform, they passed Smith, who was saying to Marion Star, "Do you know, dear lady, that you were my first love?"

"And I have admired your talent for so many years," she said in reply. "I have always wanted to meet you. And I've always wondered, why didn't a handsome rogue like you ever get married?"

"By coincidence, my dear Miss Star, I *am* getting married. To my own doctor, in fact."

As the tram came clanging into the docking bay and young men in parkas rushed out to steady it for the disembarking passengers, Philippa watched for Esther, who had called last night to say she and her boyfriend would be on this tram; then, thinking of Ricky, who was going to be all right, and of Beverly, who stood on one side of her, and Johnny, who stood on the other, Philippa smiled.

She had her family at last.

ABOUT THE AUTHOR

KATHRYN HARVEY is the pseudonym of a major author. She is currently at work on her next novel.